The men

WOMEN'S RITES

BARBIE KORMAN
Her beauty is her ticket to the future, but her greatest gift is her attraction to a reality larger than life. . . .

MARIA TRAPETTI
Drawn to the church by a force she can't explain, she must fight to find an identity not created for her by her vows or her family. . . .

JOE DIANNI
A Catholic priest trying desperately to shed the taint of his origins and come to terms with his secular passions . . .

HANK ROLLES
An archeologist who learns that honor can corrupt as thoroughly as money . . .

PHILOCLES WILLIAMS
A wealthy lawyer whose strange personal creed is the product of a devastating secret . . . .

TOM SHORE
A talented writer who wants more than critical acclaim . . .

WOMEN'S RITES

BEVERLY BYRNE

FAWCETT GOLD MEDAL • NEW YORK

A Fawcett Gold Medal Book
Published by Ballantine Books
Copyright © 1985 by Beverly Byrne

Library of Congress Catalog Card Number: 84-40486

ISBN 0-449-12903-9

This edition published by arrangement with Villard Books

Manufactured in the United States of America

First Ballantine Books Edition: July 1986

Author's Note

This is a tale of three women and the men whom they loved and hated, who sometimes betrayed them. One is separated from the other two by six hundred years, but she is nonetheless part of the same story. None of these characters are real people; I made them up. Making things up is a novelist's stock in trade.

Nonetheless, there are some who will recognize in these pages a world once shared. *Pace,* friends. It's only a story, only the shape and taste and feel of a memory. Barbie and Maria are neither me nor you. They are fragments of our yesterdays, seen through the prism of now. To those who find a part of their past herein I offer with love a glimpse of how it was, and a storyteller's version of how it might have worked out.

Beverly Byrne
Lanzarote
1984

... And these are the sons of Noah:
Shem, Ham, and Japeth;
and to them were sons born after the flood. ...
Each of them became separate nations,
distinct in speech and in blood. ...

—GENESIS

PROLOGUE

THE LADY

THE STATUE WAS OF A WOMAN BARELY SIX INCHES HIGH, small enough to fit comfortably in the palm of the Jesuit's hand. On the terrible occasion when first he saw her he'd looked at the tiny lady with pain; not until later did his archaeologist's eye become that of a lover. Now the brief time of his stewardship was ended and the lady stood on an ebony table in surroundings dedicated to the buying and selling of beauty, and she was not diminished. The Jesuit found some solace in that.

The other man in the room spoke, breaking the respectful hush. "A unique treasure, Father Rolles. Fifteenth century, you claim, from Lanzarote in the Canary Islands? Perhaps. Anyway, she's incredibly lovely. Fetch a good price if she's genuine." The dealer in rarities and discretion smiled. He had that diffident sort of English politeness the priest instinctively distrusted.

"She's genuine." Rolles' American inflections sounded strangled as well as alien. As if the damp tendrils of London fog had insinuated themselves through the window into the back of his throat, choking him. As guilt was choking him.

The priest wore a battered pullover and faded jeans. They were a contrast to the elegant atmosphere, and probably a mistake. He should have worn a black silk suit and a dog collar, but his only such outfit reeked of mothballs. He cleared his throat. "I'll say it again: the statue is genuine."

The other man tapped one manicured finger on the ebony table and leaned forward. "I don't know. With due respect for your professional reputation, Father, it seems impossible. The original people of the Canaries were primitives. Before the European conquest they didn't have metal tools. How could they have carved that face? Look at it."

Both men looked. The black lava-stone statue was of a woman in a full-length robe. That much was explainable—the imposition of simple craft on a naturally occurring shape. But the olivine changed everything.

Olivine, gemstone of the ancients, ordained by God for inclusion in Aaron's priestly breastplate; a dark green magnesium deposit found in volcanic rock $(MgFe)_2SiO_4$, also known as chrysolite or peridot. The lady was kissed with it in an inch-wide seam from the top of her head to the hem of her gown. Like the shape, this too was a fortuitous accident of nature. Not, however, the delicately carved face; that was neither accident nor simple craft. The face was art—pure, soaring, and awesome, a benediction on humankind.

The features were exquisite, perfect in each minute detail. In a space as big as a man's thumbnail, exactly as big as Father Hank Rolles' thumbnail, was portrayed everywoman. Joy tinged with sorrow, beauty an infinity beyond prettiness, a hint of laughter around the mouth, a suggestion of compassion about the eyes. And as frame, the black lava stone, like a nun's veil. Ultimate desirability linked to perfect chastity, each man's secret dream.

"Maybe the face was carved later," the dealer said.

"Not a chance." Rolles stretched his legs. They were long and hard-muscled in their sheath of denim. He noted that the carpet was the same shade of faded blue as the cloth, and toyed with the pipe in his pocket, stalling for time. There seemed to be no ashtrays. He left the pipe where it was. Disgust rose acid in his gorge. He forced himself to ignore it, remember that he was here to make a deal. The only life he found tolerable depended on it. "Look, I'll tell you again. No work was done on it later. I know where and when the piece was discovered."

"On the island of Lanzarote?"

"Yes. Just as I said." Rolles' mouth tasted of ashes.

"Perhaps," the dealer murmured again. He leaned back, and a subtle change in his manner announced that they'd passed the first stage of the negotiations. "Religious artifacts

2

pose special problems, you realize. Your Church can be difficult about such things."

"I never said she was a religious object," Rolles said softly. "No suggestion that she's miraculous. No cures, no liquifying blood, no tears on some feast day." The dealer allowed himself a smirk. The Jesuit stared him down. "The Church has nothing to do with this. All I'm saying is that the statue was made on Lanzarote, sometime previous to the fourteenth century." All. Shit, that was a genuine miracle. More real than most.

"Very well, Father. But you do claim that the present owners are a convent of nuns." The dealer paused and waited.

Rolles nodded. The overuse of his title was beginning to annoy him, and he regretted saying anything about the nuns. A mistake, but he was a novice in these matters, with no talent for deception. The silence grew uncomfortable. "Can you sell her?" he asked bluntly. "There are other ways . . ." He let the threat hang free.

A flicker of something like avarice lit the hooded eyes of the dealer, then it was gone. His tone was cool and assured. "Yes, I can sell her. Buyers of beauty abound in my world. There's the matter of price, of course, and security. I guarantee my clients discretion and freedom from repercussions. But you know that; it's why you came to me."

"There will be no repercussions," Rolles promised.

"I'll have to determine that for myself."

"I don't understand." The Jesuit felt his palms dampen with sweat.

"It's not important that you do. All you have to do is leave the statue here for a few days. I'll make some inquiries." He waved away the priest's gesture of dissent. "Don't worry, you can be assured of the same discretion I'm discussing."

Rolles didn't like it, but he had no choice. It had been difficult to learn this man's name and whereabouts. An archaeologist asking such things inevitably raised eyebrows. "Very well. How much?"

"When we sell the lady, you mean? As an estimate, I'd guess about fifteen thousand pounds. Clear to you after my commission. Sorry, I mean to the nuns."

Rolles figured that to be about thirty-six thousand dollars. He was selling cheap. It wasn't much to pay for a man's honor. He stood up. "Okay. When do I come back?"

"Surely that won't be necessary. I can phone you."

"No. I'll return whenever you say."

The dealer smiled. "As you wish. The day after tomorrow, then. At five."

Rolles started to go, and briefly wondered if he should ask for a receipt. Absurd. Like everything else about this transaction. The Englishman accompanied him to the door, opened it, then closed it swiftly behind him. They didn't say good-bye.

Outside, the fog was thick, trapped by the narrow mews into which the flat opened. It lent an air of the macabre to the activities of the afternoon. Self-loathing crawled up Rolles' spine and lodged at the base of his brain. He suspected it would become his constant companion.

The alley debouched into a broad avenue. The fog was less dense here. He stood for a moment, trying to get his bearings, to stop trembling. On the other side of the street a redheaded woman waited for the lights to change. Rolles stared at her, a surge of hatred tightening the muscles of his belly. The traffic halted noiselessly, muffled by the fog, and the woman came toward him. It wasn't she. He could tell as soon as she was a few feet from the curb. This one was ordinary-looking, not beautiful, and probably not Jewish.

Rolles turned his face away when she approached. He thought of all the stupid anti-Semitic remarks he'd parroted in childhood and he wanted to weep. The ghosts of old sins had come to keep company with the new.

There was a telephone kiosk on the corner. He toyed with the idea of calling the convent, and rejected it. Maybe Maria would be an antidote to the poison of the redhead, but he didn't want to talk to her. Didn't want to because he wanted to so much.

Suddenly, irrationally, he started to run. For long minutes his anguish pounded through the soles of his shoes onto the hard, unyielding pavement. Finally his breath came short and painful and he had to stop and lean against a wall. A few passersby looked at him oddly, then hurried on.

The Jesuit started to laugh and knew he was on the edge of hysteria. A man pursued by his own history and that of two women. "Fuck history," he said aloud, and walked on alone.

SOME MILES AWAY THE REDHEAD WAS ALSO ALONE. SHE WAS wrapped in silence; it surrounded her, caressed her, sustained her. Every muscle of her perfect body was fluid and relaxed. Her eyes were closed and her breathing so slow it was hardly breathing at all. The presence for which she waited came slowly, remained with her for an interlude that was outside of time, then departed. She opened her eyes, stretched languidly, and finally stood up. A gown of pure beige silk lay across the foot of her bed and she touched it gently, her awareness of the tactile pleasure heightened by the perception of reality that had gone before.

In the deepening twilight, she began to dress for the ceremony.

THE DEALER LOOKED FOR A LONG TIME AT THE EXQUISITE statue. A clock chimed the hour, and sighing reluctantly, he took her to a safe in another room and locked her away. Someone knocked on the front door and he went to answer it. In the dark, the lady smiled and smiled.

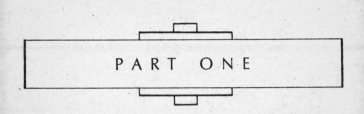

PART ONE

THE
SMALL
TOWN

I N 1955, WHEN SHE WAS THIRTEEN, MARIA TRAPETTI resolved to enter the convent. She reached this decision one Saturday afternoon in summer, in Saint Anthony's church on Revere Street in Revere.

Maria knew nothing of her Sicilian ancestors and little of the city of her birth, a town once described as a festering boil erupting from the north side of Boston. She was familiar only with this small section, awash in tomatoes and cheese and olive oil and wine. On Revere Street such English as was spoken had a rising inflection on the end of each word, and was accompanied by much movement of the hands. Reality for Maria was that, and the faint smell of incense and candle wax in Saint Anthony's. On this particular day it was also the vision of herself wearing a veil and a saintly smile.

The girl agreed to this sudden image of her future as soon as it crossed her mind. "Yes," she whispered in the silent church. "Yes, I will be a nun." This declaration she made to the figure of the crucified Christ hanging in vivid, multicolored agony on the wall above her head. It was possible to count the drops of red blood on the face of the savior. There were thirteen of them. And thirteen gold thorns piercing his pink forehead. Maria had ascertained the numbers years before.

Behind her the rustling of women and children waiting their turn in the confessional ceased. Maria looked around. Only one figure shared with her the cavernous interior of the church, an old lady dressed entirely in black. Maria believed there was a law that said grown-up women must always dress in black; she was not startled by the somber and bent form kneeling at the shrine of Our Lady of the Miraculous Medal. Maria passed the praying figure on the way to the velvet-draped box at the rear, and recognized her in the glow of the candles flickering at Our Lady's beige plaster feet. It was Mrs. Ciolino, who lived above the bakery. The smell of bread seemed to hover around Mrs. Ciolino. It overcame even the incense.

Maria hesitated, not because she was interested, only because the old woman made her think of Nonni, her grandmother. The mother of Maria's mother lived with them; she shadowed the lives of her daughter and her grandchildren. Maria knew what Nonni would say when she heard of this intention to be a nun. The girl shuddered at the thought of the explosions that would rock the little house. She flinched as if she already felt the blows of broom and folded dish towel that would fall on her head.

Mrs. Ciolino stared at the child who was staring at her. Sweat beaded the old woman's upper lip and accentuated a moustache of sparse black hair. Maria believed that growing a moustache and hairs on one's chin was also something every woman must do after she got married and had children. Maybe entering a convent would save her from that. Mrs. Ciolino moved aside on the kneeler, so Maria too could pray to Our Lady of the Miraculous Medal. The girl shook her head. They looked at each other for a few seconds more. Then, with neither warning nor cause, Mrs. Ciolino began to weep. She made no sound, but huge tears ran down her creviced cheeks and fell from her pointed chin.

The tears terrified Maria far more than did any of Nonni's outbursts. She began to shiver. "Why are you crying?" She whispered the words because they were in church, but they echoed as if she had shouted them.

"Because you are a girl and you must be a woman someday," the old woman said softly.

Maria knew herself to be already a woman. She had been having periods for over a year. But she could not say that with Our Lady looking on. "It's all right," she blurted out. "I'm going to be a nun instead."

Mrs. Ciolino wailed aloud, as if some new and terrible affliction had been added to those she already bore, and Maria fled to the confessional.

In the years that followed, Maria's determination did not waver, despite the fact that she entered Revere High School and her horizons broadened somewhat.

THE PACKARD STARTED WITH RELUCTANCE AND MADE ODD shuddering noises. Ann Jessup, teacher of typing, shorthand, and business correspondence, looked around the parking lot of Revere High School. There was no one to ask for help because it was late August of 1959, and the term hadn't yet begun.

The car survived as far as the junction of Broadway and Beach Street, then stopped. Ann was a coping sort of person, born of coping stock. She managed to glide close to the curb before the motor died. The thin line of grass, laid or left there by some functionary with notions of civic beauty, was burned brown, and thick with summer's dust. The sun accentuated its inadequacy. In the middle of the intersection was a broad circle of equally starved grass, bisected with streetcar rails, and on the far side a huge sign proclaimed BELL OLDSMOBILE. Would they know about Packards? No, she decided. There was a small service station to her right. She locked the car doors and walked to the station.

The mechanic was unavailable, he wouldn't be in until the next day. They would push the car into the garage, and phone when they had diagnosed the problem. Ann Jessup unlocked the doors once more, retrieved the books and papers she had gone to the school to collect, and began walking.

At this end Beach Street was wide and impersonal; it didn't threaten. She could take a fairly safe route home if she chose, but it was longer, and she was hot. Her navy linen dress felt damp under the arms and her blue-and-white spectator pumps chafed at the heels. She turned down Shirley Avenue and felt at once the shock of the alien and impure.

There was a terrible noise and a noxious smell. Both came from a slaughterhouse for chickens. The letters over the door were in Hebrew and she didn't know what they said. What could they say? How did one advertise the ritual killing of chickens that they might be—what was the word—kosher? Yes, that was it. If the chicken had its neck slit by a filthy old man with a beard and dirty fingernails, it was fit to be eaten by one of the Chosen People. She knew the thought to be petty and anti-Semitic in the most mindless sort of way, and she was ashamed.

In the bohemian world Ann had inhabited so briefly long

11

ago, and mourned ever since with a secret and terrible ache of privation, all this would have been called "local color" and "divine." Why couldn't she see it like that? Perhaps because it was too close to home. The litter of the gutters, the strange smells, the clusters of men, women, and children in bathing suits that exposed fat and trembling flesh while folded beach chairs hung from their hands like fitted appendages, all were an invasion. Theirs was an occupation begun before she was born, but Ann Jessup was heir to the Yankee dismay it had aroused. Liberalism was a cloak donned much later, after the attitudes perceived in childhood were graven deep.

Guilt and resentment combined to make her greeting more than usually affable when a girl said, "Oh, hello, Mrs. Jessup," with a rising note of question and surprise.

Ann squinted into the sun and felt the momentary panic of a teacher confronted by a student whose name she could not recall out of the classroom. But there was no mistaking this one. True, the girl had grown even taller over the summer; she was more willowy and nubile. But the dark red hair drawn back into a pony tail was the same, so too the unexpected amber eyes. "Hello, Barbara. How are you?"

"Hot." The girl wore a green bathing suit partially covered by a man's white shirt with the sleeves rolled up and the shirt-tails tied tightly at her waist. Her long legs were brown; they glistened with sweat and crystals of salt. "As soon as you get half a block from the beach it's unbearable," she said. "I didn't know you lived around here. I mean . . ." She stammered with sudden embarrassment. That one's teachers lived anywhere at all was not to be discussed. They were sexless, ageless creatures born each morning in the corridors outside their classrooms.

Ann understood the girl's awkwardness. She remembered when her own teachers had worshipped with her family in the Congregational Church across from the high school. The gap that now separated her from Barbara Korman had not existed back then. "Not far," she said. "On Campbell Avenue. I was driving home and my car gave out at Bell Circle." She added the information as a kind of peace offering. To end what war she could not have specified.

"Oh." Barbie too seemed to feel pressure to say more. "Are those scripts, by any chance?" She nodded toward the stack of papers in the older woman's arms.

Ann smiled. "No, I'm afraid not. Work schedules, plans for

my classes, things like that. The scripts are for fun. I do them when all this stuff is out of the way." Then, because it still didn't seem possible to walk on without being rude, "Have you had a good summer?"

"All right, I guess. I worked at Filene's parttime. My dad's a salesman there, he got me the job. But it was hot traveling back and forth to Boston on the streetcar."

"Yes, I'm sure. I have to go, I'm afraid. I'll just pop in here first and pick up some groceries." The older woman turned to the market door because it provided a means of escape. That proved to be an illusion; Barbara followed her inside.

Ann felt sudden panic. Once, many years ago, she had ventured into one of these stores on Shirley Avenue, and it had been filthy and utterly confusing. It was full of foods she didn't recognize, and the labels were printed in a foreign alphabet. This one was different, thank God. It was clean and bright and obviously new. She grabbed a box of Royal Chocolate Pudding off the nearest shelf, relieved by the familiarity.

"Have you been in Arthur's Creamery since it was remodeled?" Barbie asked. Having seen that Mrs. Jessup bought chocolate pudding like everybody else, she was emboldened.

"No, I'm afraid I've never been here before at all. I shop on Broadway usually." Why didn't the child go, take her elegant body and her tawny alien flesh to wherever it belonged.

"They just reopened last week. I cut the ribbon. My uncle owns it," Barbie added with pride.

Ann looked around and could see the dead remains of a floral tribute. GRAND OPENING AUGUST TWENTIETH, NINETEEN FIFTY-NINE was written in gold sparkles on a dusty streamer. "How nice," she said.

They moved together to the glass-enclosed counter displaying cold meats. She and Barbara had become a kind of enforced tandem, and Ann's head was beginning to ache.

"You first, Mrs. Jessup," the girl said politely.

"No, that's all right. I'm not sure what I want." She'd almost asked for sliced ham before catching herself. "I'll look for a minute."

"Okay. A pound of pastrami, Sam. Sliced thin."

The man behind the counter was grizzled and wore thick glasses. His fingernails however, were clean. "Not pastrami," he told the girl. "Cornbeef."

"But my mother said to get pastrami. You've got some right there." Barbara pointed an accusatory finger, tipped in bright red, to a corner of the display.

"I know I got some. You think I need a *pisher* like you to tell me what I got?" He made a mocking gesture as if to strike her. Barbie blushed at the language he'd used in front of Mrs. Jessup. Sam didn't notice. "I'll tell you why cornbeef, Miss Smarty Pants. Because your mother called up and said so. 'Not pastrami, cornbeef. Be sure and tell Barbie.' So I figure your Uncle Harry must be there for supper. Because the auxie meets tonight and Harry Slotnick can't stand he shouldn't get his two cents in. Even if he has to come all the way from Chelsea to do it. And he's the only *mishuganer* I know doesn't like pastrami."

Barbie giggled. "Okay. Cornbeef."

Sam wrestled a great hunk of meat into a machine and dropped red slices edged with white fat onto a piece of paper. "A little over. I'll put it on your mother's bill." He spindled a note of the cost, then turned to the strange woman. "What can I get you, lady?"

"That smoked salmon, how much is half a pound of that, please?"

The man turned and looked at the cans behind his head. "Salmon I got, pink and red and three brands. But smoked salmon I don't know."

"Mrs. Jessup means the lox, Sam," Barbie said with embarrassment.

"Oh! So why didn't she say lox? Hey! Mrs. Jessup from the high school? You had my Hymie. Remember? I met you that night when he had the lead in your play. Something about corn."

"*The Corn Is Green.* In fifty-six. I remember. How is Hyman?"

"Fine, thanks. Very good. He's at Harvard, you know. Next year he graduates. Then law school."

"That's wonderful." She tried to remember him, but only conjured up a short, dark boy with severe acne. She'd gotten a creditable performance out of him nonetheless. She also remembered that he was very bright. So many of them were. It was yet one more offense.

"The lox is eighty-five cents a half pound," Sam said.

"Oh. Too expensive, then."

"So I'll give you a quarter." He had the fish on the counter before she could protest. He didn't put it in the machine, but wielded an enormous knife with competence. "You like it sliced thick or thin?"

"Thin, please."

Sam winked at Barbara. Thin-sliced lox was something only a *goy* would prefer. Or a *mishuganer* maybe, like Harry Slotnick. He cut and wrapped the fish and slapped it on the scale. It registered over a half pound, but he wrote forty-two cents on the package. The paper was already stained with the oil of the contents. Mrs. Jessup removed her white glove before she took it.

"Thank you."

"You're welcome. A little cream cheese, maybe?"

"No, that's all. Good-bye. Remember me to your son, please." She turned to locate the checkout counter, and wondered why he had suggested cream cheese from all the myriad things in the display case that she hadn't bought. No one was behind the cash register, but Barbara was still beside her.

"Uncle Arthur," the girl called. "Mrs. Jessup wants to pay. Shall I take the money?"

Ann felt that everyone in the store must be staring at her. Apparently no one paid cash. They charged. She had wandered into some private temple and intruded on an arcane ritual. A man appeared from the rear.

"I'll take her money. It's my store, somebody wants to give money it goes to me. How are you, darling? Still slaying all the boys?" He pinched Barbie's buttocks as he walked by. She blushed because Mrs. Jessup saw.

Finally they were back on the street. The woman wondered if they must yet make inane conversation. No, she decided. She had proved her liberalism. "Good-bye," she said. "See you next week when school starts."

"Yes. Good-bye."

Then, because Ann was embarrassed and felt inadequate, and understood neither emotion, "Maybe you and Maria will come to tea with me sometime soon. We can talk about this year's production."

Barbie grinned. "Maria doesn't drink tea, just coffee. But I do. I'll tell her."

Ann watched the girl stride off, carrying her beauty and her near nakedness unconcernedly down the hot womblike street, then she turned and walked in the opposite direction.

In ten minutes she reached Campbell Avenue. It was a bastion that had somehow held when the Jews came. More, it was an oasis. The big old houses stood secure and dignified behind lush lawns regularly mown and watered. On all of Shirley Avenue, Ann realized, there wasn't one touch of green. It must be true about Jews being non-agrarian.

"BARBIE? YOU GOT THE CORNBEEF? COME IN HERE AND SAY hello to your uncle Harry."

"I got it. It's in the kitchen." Barbie went into the living room, dutifully kissed her mother and her uncle, then walked back to the hall. "You mind if I close the door? I've got to make a phone call."

"Close it if you want," Sophie Korman said. Then, to her brother, "Teenage girls. Nothing but secrets."

"Jake Ruben told me last week that his wife got their daughter a phone of her own. Put it in her room. Told Jake if she didn't she'd go crazy. No one could ever call her because the kid was always on the line."

"So Jake can afford. Good for him." She didn't say any more. Harry was needling her because Moe didn't make enough money to buy them a house in Marblehead like Jake Ruben. They had all grown up together in Boston's West End, the Rubens, the Slotnicks, and the Kormans. Jake Ruben had even proposed to her. Sophie turned him down for Moe Korman, but selling used cars turned out to be more profitable than selling shoes at Filene's. So the Rubens had a new ranchhouse in Marblehead, and the Kormans lived in a four-room flat on the third floor of a house off Shirley Avenue.

Sophie didn't mind. Jake's daughter didn't look anything like her Barbie. Nobody had a girl more gorgeous than hers. Barbie had always been a pretty child, but when a few years ago her baby fat melted away, it revealed the extraordinary. Her cheekbones were pronounced and broad, and accentuated enormous amber eyes flecked with gold and set aslant. Her nose was short and straight, and her full mouth trembled over a chin that could have been modeled by a Renaissance sculptor. Above these perfections was heavy bronze hair. A swash of shimmering color, as if an artist beset by enchantment had signed his creation with a flourish. At eighteen Barbie was lovely; when she reached her prime, she would be breathtaking.

Sophie could hear Barbie's voice droning in the hall, interspersed with high-pitched giggles. She must be talking to Maria. Who else? Some of Sophie's friends thought she was crazy to allow her daughter to be best friends with a *shiksa,* an Italian girl from Revere Street. But Sophie Korman faced them down. She was modern; she'd been born in this country and didn't speak with an accent. She was raising Barbie in the American way.

"She still running around with the *shiksa?*" Harry asked.

"For God's sake, Harry, they're girlfriends! They're not getting married. Besides, Maria's a fine girl. I like her." Sophie rose and opened the door to the hall. "If that's Maria, invite her to supper Tuesday night. It's Daddy's birthday. I'm making *kugel.*"

"Yeah, Ma, sure." Then, into the black mouthpiece once more, "So Mrs. Jessup said maybe we could come for a cup of tea. I told her you only drink coffee, but I guess that doesn't matter. Did you know she lives on Campbell Avenue? It's right near here. You're going to get the lead this year, Maria. I know you are. Why else would she ask us over?"

"JUST FOR THE DOG TRACK," SOPHIE SAID. "IT'S ONLY FIVE weeks."

"You're crazy." Moe shook his head; it was bald and made a round shadow dance across the wall by the bed. "We talked about it, we agreed. It's too risky. I make enough, we don't need—"

"Barbie needs. It's her senior year. There's the prom, all the other things. She needs."

"I get a discount at the store. She always looks beautiful."

"You don't get a discount in the basement. Even with, I can't buy anything but *shmattas* upstairs. The good stuff is too expensive. In the basement I get dresses from Neiman-Marcus, from Saks Fifth Avenue even. With the labels still in."

This was Sophie's passion and her voice betrayed the depth of her commitment. She was a woman gifted with an eye for color and line and texture; in another time and place she would have been an artist, or at least a designer. Instead, she dressed her daughter in beauty. She and Moe wore what was cheap and serviceable, but Barbie was always arrayed like a princess.

"You've been listening to Harry," Moe said.

"Harry's *mishuge,* I don't listen to him. I make up my own mind. You know that. Harry thought I should marry Jake Ruben."

"That's what this is all about. Jake Ruben's new house in Marblehead. We had it for supper even. Cornbeef and potato salad and Jake Ruben's house."

17

"That's silly. It's about the dog track. Moe, they pay twenty dollars a week. Just to have a couple of phones and to look from the back porch."

"It's risky. What about the police?"

"They pay off the police, you know that. Besides, they're all *goyishe kops.*"

The weight of her certitude oppressed him. "Go to sleep, Sophie. We'll talk about it tomorrow."

"YOU'RE SO SMART, MARIA. YOU OUGHT TO GO TO COLLEGE. Why don't you at least apply for a scholarship?"

"My family wouldn't let me. Besides . . ." She stopped speaking. Not even to Barbie had she confided her secret about entering the convent. The endless battle at home was enough; she didn't want to fight with Barbie too.

"Besides what?" the other girl insisted. "You should go to college and become an English teacher. Everyone says so. Maybe Mr. Marcus would talk to your folks."

"It wouldn't make any difference. Anyway, literature and French are the only things I'm smart about." She could see that Barbie was going to continue the discussion. To forestall that, she whispered with sudden urgency, "Who are those men? What are they doing?"

"What men?" Barbie looked around. "Oh, you mean Nat and Sid? They're bookies. They're using the pantry as an office."

Maria's black eyes widened. "Bookmakers? Racketeers?"

Barbie giggled. "You make them sound like crooks. They're not. Just ordinary bookies. They pay to work here because if you use binoculars you can see the tote board at the dog track from the back porch. My mother's putting all the money away. She opened a special account in the post office. It's for my prom gown and things like that." She bit her lip and was sorry she'd said the last part. Maria's father probably wouldn't let her go to the prom.

"We'd better get some more of this done." Maria bent her head over the notebook. "It's almost four-thirty. I'll have to go soon."

They worked in silence, interrupted only by the ringing of the telephone in the pantry, and enveloped in the waves of cigar smoke that issued from its dim interior. Once in a while Maria would hear a terse comment such as "The little guy wants two on Lady Fancy in the fourth. Yes or no?"

Two what, Maria wondered? Not two dollars, certainly. Two hundred, maybe. Two thousand, even. She didn't hear the response, so she couldn't know whether or not the bet had been accepted. It bothered her, distracted her from the problem of Laertes' motivation. "How did they get all those phones?" she asked suddenly. Mrs. Giotti had been waiting almost a year for a telephone. She came regularly and wailed her discontent to Maria's mother.

"I don't know," Barbie said idly, still staring at her book. "Paid off somebody in the phone company, I guess. Like they do the police."

Barbie's casual acceptance of such things frightened Maria. She didn't like to think of her friend going to hell. Long ago she'd made up her mind that it wasn't true that because they'd killed Christ all Jews went there anyway. But this was different. A year ago, before Father DiAnni came and began preaching his sermons on justice, she might not have recognized that. Now she understood that God disapproved of the oppression of the poor. So He wouldn't like it that Mrs. Giotti, who was old and sick and alone, had no telephone, while the bookmakers in the Korman flat had three. It was New England Telephone's sin, of course, but Barbie seemed implicated.

Mrs. Korman came in and interrupted these uncomfortable musings. "So the brainchildren are still at it," she said, beaming over the tops of her shopping bags. She had lately taken to carrying home the groceries rather than having them delivered. It meant thirty cents more to put in Barbie's account for clothes. Besides, it was good exercise.

Barbie rose and began helping to put away the food. They had moved everything out of the pantry when Nat and Sid took over. Now the cans were stacked on a table beside the sink. There was a pyramid of B & M Baked Beans and Chicken of the Sea tuna. Barbie placed the cans carefully, arranging the labels so they made a pattern. "Don't waste time," her mother said.

"It looks nicer."

Maria closed her notebook and unloaded the second bag of food. There were two boxes of Prince's Spaghetti. "I'll get my mother to make you some homemade pasta sometime," she told Mrs. Korman. "It's a lot better than this."

Sophie smiled. "I'm sure. Homemade is always better. I'd love to taste it." She was very fond of Maria. She'd never admit to anyone that she worried every time Barbie ate at the Trapetti house. She was sure Italians were dirty. Not that Maria didn't always look nice and clean.

"I've got to go," the girl said now. "I promised I'd be home by five."

"Why go?" Sophie said. "Stay for supper. I'll ask my Mendy to give you a ride home later." The Kormans didn't have a car, but Sophie's nephew Mendy did. He lived just around the corner.

"Thanks, but I can't. I have to baby-sit tonight. My mother goes to the Altar and Rosary Society." Carlo Trapetti might be home, but he would not be responsible for the care of the six children younger than Maria.

"I'll walk to the streetcar with you." Barbie checked her hair in the mirror in the hall that divided the kitchen and the living room on one side from the two bedrooms on the other. Much better, Sophie claimed, than flats where all the rooms opened into each other. A compensation for being three flights up. "Have we got any shampoo?" Barbie called to her mother. "I have to wash my hair later."

"Of course we have shampoo."

Satisfied, she accompanied Maria into the street.

Revere was a dense and patternless maze hugging a curve of sandy beach that stretched for nearly five miles. The boulevard was devoted to stands where you could "pitch till you win," or buy fried clams, or ride an unsafe roller coaster; behind the shorefront was a jumble of shops and tenements sprung from the earth without benefit of architect or urban planner.

The inhabitants, however, had created their own version of residential zoning. It was very simple. An imaginary line stretched from midway on the beach to the border with Everett, the adjacent inland town. On one side of this line lived the Jews; on the other, the Italians.

Transportation was largely a matter of streetcars and a few buses. The handful of Yankees and Irish wedged into isolated corners of the blintz and ravioli sprawl used the buses to travel to the far end of Ocean Avenue, where people named O'Toole or Kelly were found. Ocean Avenue was close to Lynn, where others of that species lived. Neither Barbie nor Maria knew much about the section, though Maria had a special interest in Lynn of late. The two girls were part of the ruling majorities. Their world was bound and demarcated by the streetcars that ran along Beach Street and Broadway.

Barbie accompanied Maria as far as the stop near Bell Circle and waited with her. "Did you see *Seventeen* this month?" she asked.

"No." Maria didn't admit, even to her best friend, that she wasn't allowed to buy the magazine.

"There's a picture of a girl who looks just like you," Barbie said. "Her hair's cut very short. You'd look great with that hairdo."

"My father doesn't want me to cut it." Maria's dark chestnut hair was thick and very curly and it didn't suit the ponytail she wore in emulation of Barbie's, but in Carlo Trapetti's mind short hair was the mark of a fast girl. Maria didn't try to explain. It wasn't important anyway. Soon she would have it all cut off.

The streetcar arrived and she boarded and put her dime in the cash box, saying, "Revere Street," so the driver would know why she didn't pay fifteen cents. He handed her a green paper ticket that enabled her to change at Broadway without paying an extra fare. When she sat down beside the window, she could see Barbie's tall figure moving away. Fog was drifting in, and Maria thought her friend looked very romantic enveloped in the mist.

THE STREETCAR LEFT MARIA OFF AT THE CORNER IN FRONT OF St. Anthony's. She wondered if she had time to pay a visit, then decided she'd better not. The way home led past the rectory. Young Father DiAnni was outside pruning the roses.

"Hello, Maria. How are you?"

"Fine, Father. How are you?"

He smiled and said he was very well. Then he cut off the last bloom of autumn and handed it to her. It was pale yellow and fragrant, and when she took it the priest suddenly realized that someday she would be lovely. Maria's face was a perfect oval covered by flawless skin. The delicate bone structure reminded him of a picture of a painting he had once seen. Father DiAnni looked away.

"I've got to go," Maria said after she thanked him for the rose. Then she turned back. Her black eyes were clouded with pain and worry. "Can I ask you something?"

"Of course. Anything." He was full of love for her, not as a pretty young girl, but as a member of his flock who looked to him for guidance and truth.

"Is it a sin to rent part of your house to bookmakers?"

The curate didn't know what to say. "I don't think I understand. There are no bookmakers in your house, are there?"

"I don't mean me. It's not important who. Is it a sin, that's all?"

21

Father DiAnni prayed for guidance. It was among the more difficult questions he'd been asked since he was ordained last year. "I think it usually is. Always, in fact. On the face of it because it's illegal. But in an individual case, one would have to know the circumstances, the motives . . . A lot of things," he added lamely. He knew he sounded like a professor of moral theology, and he hated himself for it.

Maria didn't hate him, but he'd confused her even more. "Okay," she said. "Thanks."

After that Father DiAnni watched her carefully whenever she came to his Mass, or he saw her on her way home from school. He always made it a point to greet Maria warmly, but she never responded with any further confidences. He also tried to inquire discreetly into the incidence of bookies on Revere Street. Except for the identity of a newspaper man who took bets on the numbers, he discovered nothing.

MARIA WAS NOT UNAWARE OF THE SPECIAL INTEREST THE curate took in her. Like all the girls in the parish, she had giggled and made silly remarks when Father DiAnni was posted to St. Anthony's. He was so young and handsome. Like a movie star, with black curly hair and broad shoulders. But the comments were utterly innocent. For all of them Joseph DiAnni's Roman collar was as much a wall of separation as steel and barbed wire. It was absolutely unbreachable, and none of the virginal children who yearned over his good looks considered him any more a three-dimensional, living man than they did the celluloid images they watched in the Revere Street Theater.

Maria didn't go to the movies much. She had to help her mother with the younger children, she had to study, and she had, after all, been given the lead in the dramatic club play to be produced in March. Were it not for the dramatic club she might even have seen less of Barbie. Nonni was ill and there was more than the usual amount of work at home. But the play, *The Taming of the Shrew*, was important to both girls and their friendship didn't starve for lack of communication, as it might otherwise have done.

The dramatic club was presenting Shakespeare in modern dress. It was a daring innovation thought up by Ann Jessup, who had real talent as a producer and director and no place to vent it but the unlikely ground of Revere High School. Everyone knew that once Ann Jessup had dreamed of being an actress and had gone to New York. Then the war had come and she returned to her parents' house and got married and became a teacher in the high school from which she herself had been graduated. Only the most perceptive recognized that the annual production of the dramatic club was Ann's link with all that might have been. That was why she drove the students to unheard of, almost professional, efforts. They, in turn, responded because the annual play had become famous, and the passport to trips to distant cities where the dramatic club competed against those of other high schools, and almost always won.

Barbie didn't act. For all her beauty, she had no talent on stage. She did backstage work. This year she was in charge of costumes as well as sets. It delighted her to imagine Maria, who was playing Katherine, in the lovely clothes she and Mrs. Jessup were borrowing. "You're going to look gorgeous," she told her friend repeatedly.

"My father better not come," Maria said, thinking about the strapless red gown she was to wear in the last act.

"It's a play at school. He won't get mad about that, will he?"

Maria shrugged. Carlo Trapetti was unaware of any of this and he certainly wouldn't expect to attend the performance. "It doesn't matter," Maria said. "He has to work all three nights." It was a lie; later she would have to confess it. Never mind, it was worth it. Better than trying to explain or, worse, having yet one more thing to fight with her father and mother about.

The rehearsals temporarily ended on the twenty-second of December, the day before the Christmas holiday began. As they left the auditorium Barbie said wistfully, "I suppose I won't see you till school starts again. I mean, with your grandmother so sick and everything."

Maria felt a pang of guilt. She hadn't invited Barbie to her house in ages because she was ashamed of the fights and worried that one of her brothers or sisters might say something about her wanting to be a nun. "Why don't you come over," she said quickly. "Come Christmas Eve." The house would be full of people then, and her father would be full of wine. There wouldn't be any arguments on Christmas Eve.

Barbie hesitated. Was it all right for a Jew to go to an Italian house on Christmas Eve? It wasn't sin she was worried about. That concept was outside her world; Barbie's parents weren't religious. She questioned only the matter of loyalty. It seemed

23

unthreatened by the invitation. "I'll see if I can. Call you to-morrow."

For Catholics, Christmas Eve was a day of abstinence; meat was forbidden on the vigil of the nativity. In practice, on Revere Street the fast had become a feast without violating canon law. There was indeed no meat. Instead there was cala-mari, and baccala, and a mountain of ravioli stuffed with spinach and cheese, and numberless deep square pans of la-sagna, and jugs of homemade wine. The living room of the Trapetti house was floating in tomato sauce and redolent with garlic and with dozens of people. Their human smell mingled with that of the food to produce an aroma Barbie found slightly frightening. It was strange and exotic and disconcert-ing.

"Eat," a little round woman dressed in black told her re-peatedly.

She didn't know who the woman was, but each time an-other plate of food was thrust into her hand Barbie smiled and said thank you and did as she was told, because she didn't know how to refuse. After two hours her stomach was rebel-ling at the onslaught of strange ingredients, and her head was spinning from two glasses of wine. Maria was busy in the kitchen, so her friend was left alone much of the time. Barbie sat in a corner and continued to eat.

Finally there was a movement of the crowd toward the front bedroom where coats had been piled. Maria appeared at Bar-bie's side. "You're coming to church?" she asked.

"I don't know. I didn't plan on it."

"Come," Maria said. "It's beautiful. Afterwards my cousin Sal will drive you home."

Barbie looked at the clock in the hall. It was almost mid-night. "My folks will worry."

"Call them. They'll be waiting up for you anyway."

She dialed the number and her mother answered on the first ring. "I just didn't want you to worry," she told Sophie. "Maria's cousin Sal is going to drive me home in a while."

"She's a good driver, this Sal?"

"Not she. Salvatore. A boy."

"Just you and him? In the middle of the night?"

"No, of course not," Barbie lied quickly. "A lot of people. It's a big party, Ma. A family party. Don't worry. I'm fine."

"Okay. Have a good time. Tell Maria I said hello."

The guests left the house in small groups, spilling out of the

24

door in a wave of talk and laughter and smells. They coalesced with other groups from other doors. The street was as full of people as if it were midday. Barbie and Maria walked together, a little apart from the rest. "I've never been to a church," Barbie confided.

"You'll like midnight Mass," Maria said. "It's beautiful."

St. Anthony's was dark when they entered. Barbie was surprised at the silence. People stopped talking as soon as they crossed the threshold. They knelt or sat as if alone, despite the overflowing crowd. Latecomers had no place to sit. Apparently Catholics didn't issue tickets for the holy days the way they did in the synagogue on Nahant Avenue. Moe Korman always bought three. Mr. Trapetti didn't have to worry about tickets. Everybody just made their funny one-legged bow and stood wherever they could find room. Another strangeness struck Barbie. At Rosh Hashanah or Yom Kippur, the only times she went to the synagogue, the noise of talk was overwhelming. Here she was deafened by silence.

It was all something like the movies. Up front the "stage" was waiting. She was startled when the lights started to go on, rather than become yet more dim. She'd expected a kind of spotlighted performance; instead, the whole church blazed with light. There were flowers and greens everywhere. Each statue had its vase or plant. The altar was a solid bank of pine branches, and to one side was a life-size nativity scene, also surrounded by flowers. Barbara felt the ravioli and the calamari churn in her stomach. She would have enjoyed the spectacle more if she had not eaten so much.

Suddenly everyone stood up. Still in silence. Then the organ thundered a triumphant chord and a procession of costumed men and boys came into view. On either side of her people made the sign of the cross, and Barbie pressed her hands to her sides in fierce, embarrassed loyalty to Shirley Avenue.

She could see better than most because of her height, and because when the others knelt she sat rigidly on the hard wooden bench. At one point there was a particularly solemn hush, broken only by the clamor of a bell rung by a small boy on the altar. Everyone seemed to shrink further onto their knees, to contract themselves in some act of deepened concentration. Barbie sat very still, not wishing to offend, not daring to suggest by even the merest tilt of her head that she was worshipping their God. Behind her a man muttered. "Might as well not come if you're going to do that." His finger poked into her spine. She didn't move or indicate that she heard or

25

felt his rebuke. Maria's face was buried in her hands; she was unaware of the incident.

Finally it was over. They went out and found Sal's car, an old Ford, and Maria rode with them to keep Sal company on the way back. There was a light on in the front window of the Korman flat, but it was the only light on the street. "Don't Jews celebrate Christmas?" Sal asked in surprise.

"No," Barbie said.

"Of course they don't," Maria added. "They believe the messiah hasn't come yet. Otherwise they'd be Christians."

Sal nodded and said no more. When Barbie went to bed, she thought about Maria's explanation. It had never occurred to her that she was waiting for the messiah. Now she tried to imagine the shape of that expectation, and found it nonexistent.

It was the following month when Barbie saw the statue. She'd gone for a walk. Something she'd taken to doing more and more frequently of late. It was a practice that worried Sophie. She never knew anyone who went for walks by themselves, the way her Barbie did. Still, how could you tell a girl she shouldn't go out in broad daylight? So Barbie walked.

On this day she headed along the boulevard, deserted in winter, toward East Boston. Not by design, just because the wind was at her back if she went in that direction. Eventually she came to the foot of a steep hill where she'd never before been. Atop it was a statue of a woman. The statue was as tall as a three-story house, and Barbie had only to walk a little nearer to see it clearly. The bronze lady had a beautiful face. The eyes seemed to look right into her own. Also beautiful feet, bare except for sandals, with each toe distinct and lifelike. There was a billboard nearby. "The Madonna of the Universe," it proclaimed in large letters. Underneath was a plea for funds to erect a pedestal for the statue, so that it would be seen for miles around. Barbie wondered who the Madonna of the Universe was supposed to be, and resolved to ask Maria since the thing was obviously Catholic. She forgot about it, however, and the two girls never discussed the subject.

Maria always went to confession, not to young Father DiAnni but to Father Pasco. Not only did she prefer telling the older man her sins, but he was party to her secret plan and had become an ally. Moreover, he was her pastor, so his recommendation would be necessary if she was to be accepted into the convent.

On the third Saturday in February, he surprised her by saying, "Perhaps you should postpone the idea of being a nun. Your grandmother is very ill, you're the eldest child, your mother will need help at home."

Maria made no response, but left the confessional in tears. An hour later, when the church was empty, she was still kneeling at the side altar of Christ Crucified and crying. Someone knelt next to her and took her hand. It was Father DiAnni. "It's not as bad as all that, is it?"

She blew her nose and said nothing.

"Come outside and we'll talk," the priest whispered.

Outside was an enormous parking lot. It was covered in snow and the wind was bitter and penetrating. "Come around to the side." Father DiAnni led her to the sacristy porch. It was out of the wind and out of sight. "What's wrong, Maria? Can I help?"

"No. Thank you, but no."

"You're sure? Try me. I've got a good ear." Dear Lord, he thought, what do I say if she's pregnant?

"I want to enter the convent," Maria blurted out.

He stared at her. Somehow he hadn't associated piety with Maria Trapetti. She was a good Catholic girl, but her parents, like most of those in this parish, refused to pay for a parochial school. So how come she had this attraction to religious life? Instantly DiAnni felt guilty about questioning the mysterious ways of God. "That's a wonderful ambition," he said. "It's pleasing to Our Lord. Why cry about it?"

"My parents don't want me to go. Now Father Pasco says my mother needs me at home and maybe I shouldn't go." Maria turned crimson as soon as the words were out of her mouth. It was a mortal sin to repeat what one heard in the confessional. "I shouldn't have said that," she added quickly. "What he said in confession, I know it's a sin to talk about it."

"Not for you," Father DiAnni said gently. "The seal of the confessional only binds the priest, not the penitent. You can say anything you want."

She sighed with relief. "I didn't know that."

DiAnni felt a surge of anger. "There's a lot you don't know. There hasn't been much in the way of teaching the faith in this parish. Tell me, Maria, why you want to be a nun?"

She tried to answer but couldn't. Her words came out jumbled and unintelligible.

27

"Look," the priest said, "why don't you come to see me in the rectory. Wednesday nights, after the Legion of Mary meeting."

"I don't belong," she said.

"That doesn't matter. Come at eight-thirty. After the meeting. If you want, I'll tell your mother and father I want to see you."

"It's okay. You don't have to do that."

"But you'll come? We'll talk about it, Maria. Your wanting to be a nun, and why. If you still want to do it after we've talked, I'll help you."

"I'll come," she said.

THE MEETINGS BETWEEN MARIA AND FATHER DiANNI WENT on for six weeks before they were interrupted by the production of *The Taming of the Shrew.* "I can't come next week," she told him. "I'm in the high school play."

"Are you? I didn't know you were even in the dramatic club. It's very good, isn't it?"

"Yes. I've been a member since I was in ninth grade. It's the best club in the school."

"What part do you have in the play?"

She told him and he smiled. It wasn't hard to imagine her having the lead. She was such an attractive child. Not a child, either. He looked at her for a long moment, then looked away. "I'd like to see the play," he said.

"I have a ticket for you," Maria answered shyly. "I want you to have one of the two free tickets I get as part of the cast."

"But they must be for your parents."

"It's all right. My father never goes to things like that. And this year my mother is afraid to leave Nonni."

"I'll be there," he said, smiling.

He went on the last night. Afterwards Maria and some of the others from St. Anthony's parish invited him to the cast party in the typing room across from the auditorium. He noted that the Italian kids were greatly outnumbered by the Jews, but that Maria was in a class by herself. She wasn't the prettiest. Her friend Barbie was clearly that. But there was something about her, particularly now when she was flushed with triumph. She'd been wonderful as Katherine. Everyone knew it, and so did Maria.

Later he drove four of them home to Revere Street. He dropped Maria off last. She lived closest to the rectory. Before they reached her house he pulled off his clerical collar and opened the button of his shirt. Maria didn't say anything, but when she turned to thank him for the ride and for coming to the play, she could see that he had curly black hair on his chest, and that it showed once he'd removed his badge of office.

"You'll come next Wednesday night?" he asked as she was getting out of the car.

"Yes." Then she paused with one foot out the door and said, "When will you tell me if you'll talk to my parents about my being a nun?"

"Next week," he promised. "We'll talk about that next week."

PREVIOUSLY THEY HAD DISCUSSED ONLY THE GENERAL teachings of the Church. The priest wanted to be sure that she understood her religion. He was appalled at the ignorance of so many of his flock. It had been objective discussion, having nothing to do with her personally, or the question of her vocation. Now he said, "Are you still sure? After everything we've talked about?" He leaned forward and put his hand over hers where it lay on the desk.

"I'm sure," Maria said. She could feel the flesh of his palm and her heart was beating, but she didn't waver. "I've been sure since I was thirteen years old."

DiAnni felt an unreasoning anger. "We don't have to stick to what we thought when we were thirteen. Part of growing up is being able to admit when you've made a mistake."

Maria pulled her hand away and sat primly in the hard-backed chair. "I haven't made a mistake," she said.

"Okay," he sighed. "I'll talk to your folks."

"What about Father Pasco?"

"I'll talk to him too."

IT WAS MIDSUMMER, AFTER THE PLAY AND THE GRADUATION ceremonies that marked the end of her high school career were fading memories, when the letter from the Servants of Bethlehem arrived. Maria was accepted as a postulant. She was to enter the convent in Lynn on September 15, Feast of the Holy Cross.

She went to Father DiAnni's office to share the news. He wasn't there, but when she left the rectory she met him in the street. "They've accepted me," she said simply.

"That's wonderful. Let's take a walk and talk about it."

They headed away from the beach and its crowds to the de-

29

serted fields where the old narrow-gauge railroad used to run. No one else was in sight. Maria gave him the letter to read.

"It's a beautiful feast to start out on," he commented.

"Yes. What feast was it when you entered the seminary?"

"I don't remember," he admitted wryly. "I think nuns do that kind of thing best. Better than priests do."

"Maybe because they're women."

Father DiAnni laid his hand on her shoulder. It was almost bare beneath her sleeveless blouse. He could feel the ridge of her bra strap. The image of her breasts clouded his vision; and he ignored it. Temptations like that were an ever-present part of his priesthood. He didn't worry about them anymore. Only about giving in to them. "Don't think you have to be less than a woman when you're a nun," he told her. "It should be the same thing."

Maria nodded. She turned away so his hand would no longer touch her flesh. She had recurrent dreams about Father DiAnni and she was making a novena to the Little Flower to protect her from impure thoughts. "I'll remember," she said.

"Good."

The time came to say good-bye. Maria spent her penultimate night "in the world" with Barbie. On graduation day Maria had told her best friend that she intended to be a nun. Barbie had now had a number of weeks to become accustomed to the strange idea, but she still felt terrible about the coming separation. On this, their last time together, the girls took a walk, then went to a drugstore for a soda. They didn't talk about serious things, but they hugged each other hard when they parted. "I'll pray for you always," Maria promised.

"I'll never forget you," Barbie said.

Both girls were crying. It was as if Maria were stepping off the edge of the planet. It didn't occur to either of them that they might see each other again. Revere and the convent in Lynn were separated by infinity.

The next night Maria spent with her family. Aunts and uncles and cousins gathered as if at a wake. Once more the impending departure was not discussed. Everyone ate a lot instead.

Maria wanted to go see Father DiAnni, but she had promised the Little Flower she wouldn't do it. She had waved to him last Sunday after Mass. That was her farewell. Finally, on the morning of the last day, she wrote him a note promising he would always be in her prayers.

THE NEXT DAY MARIA TRAPETTI TOOK HER PLACE AMID THE eleven other girls soon to be postulants in the Congregation of the Servants of Bethlehem of Dublin, Inc. Her place was exactly in the middle because she was five feet four inches tall and the shorter girls were in front, the taller behind.

A nun called Mother Bridget walked up and down the row, straightening a white collar here, tugging at a black skirt there. That the girls were bareheaded always bothered Mother Bridget. Each year when she went through this ritual with the new entrants the same thing disturbed her sense of order. It was offensive that the postulants processed into the church with their different-colored hair showing. Not until they wore short black veils would they please her sense of symmetry.

Nonetheless, she was novice mistress and she knew her duty. "You look fine, children," she told them. "God bless. It's time now." With one look at the hopelessly bulging breasts of the tallest girl, Mother Bridget flung open the door of the chapel. The organist, who had been awaiting this signal, trumpeted the refrain of the Lourdes hymn.

"Immaculate Mary, our souls are on fire . . ." the assembled sisters sang with vigor. The would-be postulants began to process. They moved slowly, with measured step paced by the organ and the acolyte. Someone had said he was Mother Bridget's nephew. When the chorus came, the sound swelled. Most of the guests knew this part as well as the nuns. "Ave, Ave, Ave Maria," they intoned. "Ave Maria."

Maria had a sudden unbidden vision. She had died and become a saint and they were singing to her. Then her cheeks flamed with the wickedness and audacity of the notion. "You come here to serve," Mother Rose, the Provincial Superior, had told them that afternoon when they assembled in the front room of the convent. "Not to get, but to give. If you are worthy, you will be brides of Christ. No woman can aspire to a greater honor." But here was she aspiring to sainthood, despite what she knew of herself and her sins.

The procession neared the front of the chapel and the line of *prie-dieux* reserved for them. Maria longed to sink to her knees. She saw her mother standing on the aisle and looked away. Her mother wore black because Nonni had died two months ago. Maria knew now that all women didn't necessarily do that. At least not once one left Revere Street.

Her father wore black too. Not in mourning—he had

loathed his mother-in-law and never disguised it—but because his only suit was of that color. To see one's daughter enter the convent a suit was required. Carlo Trapetti considered his suit a fitting garment to memorialize the years of battles and the hysteria of women confronted with the insanity of a child who would not be beaten into submission. It had not seemed to him very important what the eldest of his seven children did, as long as she did not shame him by becoming a whore or making a baby. But the four years of turmoil in his house was another matter. Now it was over. Maria and Father Pasco had gotten their way. Carlo had donned his only suit in acknowledgment of their victory. Still, the day was a kind of celebration for him. With both Maria and Nonni out of the house, he would have peace.

His wife, however, was sobbing. He wanted to comfort her but dared not do so among all these strangers and nuns. Most of the other women were sobbing too. Perhaps they enjoyed it. He turned his attention to the altar.

The Mass was already far along. The fat priest with the pale Irish skin and the red-veined, bulbous nose was about to read the gospel. Carlo rose with the rest. From behind he couldn't tell which of the girls was Maria. He started to ask his wife, but she elbowed him in the ribs to indicate that he must be quiet.

". . . if you would be perfect, then go, sell what you have and give to the poor, and come follow Me." Father Boyle looked at the assembly and smiled with satisfaction. They sat down and he waited until the fidgeting and jockeying for space had ended before beginning to preach. He found his eyes continually straying to the thrusting bosom of the postulant at the end of the row, and he disciplined himself to look only at the crucifix on the wall at the rear.

"Forty years ago," he began, "Mother Mary Columkill came from Dublin to Boston with three sisters. They wanted to serve Christ's poor and needy in America. This is the measure of their accomplishment and their courage." He waved an expansive hand to include this brick and glass chapel, built three years earlier, and the other buildings of the complex; he nodded his head to indicate the crop of future servants kneeling before him. "I do not need to tell you parents what happiness is yours today, or what a noble gift you have given. After all, you have known these sisters in your schools and in your homes."

The Trapettis had no such familiarity. Irish nuns from Lynn

didn't venture into their neighborhood in Revere. Besides, Italian children went to the public schools where education was free and the Church couldn't steal an extra fifty dollars a year from the pittance a man earned swinging a pickax or kneading endless mountains of dough. Still, Carlo nodded his head dutifully.

"I can see in your faces the joy and the pride you feel," Father Boyle said. "And I can see the sadness. It is no easy thing to give up your daughters, your precious jewels, to the Church. But you know how great will be your reward." He continued in this vein for another five minutes. When he realized that the temptation to stare at the blonde's enormous breasts was getting the better of him, he ended abruptly. "God bless you," he said, and returned to the altar.

Maria wondered why he had said nothing to them. She wanted comfort and inspiration. She wanted to be told that she was making a magnificent and noble sacrifice, not that her parents were. She recognized this thought as being sinful, like her earlier dreams of sanctity, and quickly said another Hail Mary in penance.

Then she followed the other girls to the altar, and the priest clumsily tied on her short black veil, assisted by Mother Bridget, who caught a strand of Maria's thick brown hair in the knot and pulled the strings so tight they pressed against her scalp. When she returned to her place, Maria resisted the urge to adjust the headdress. She would suffer this pain in reparation for her sins.

Afterwards they all went to the big front parlor for tea and dry cakes studded with hard, tasteless raisins. Maria's mother looked at the table and sniffed. "You'll starve here," she whispered to her daughter. "This is what they serve to company?"

"It's just a snack, Mama," Maria said. She already felt the pangs of hunger beginning in her stomach, but the habit of defending the convent had been fortified during the four years of struggle to realize her dream.

"I bet you the Ortoni nuns do better than this," Mrs. Trapetti insisted. In the last year, when she had recognized that Maria could not be dissuaded from her insanity, she had waged a campaign to make her daughter enter the convent of some Italian nuns in East Boston, not these Irish women who didn't even know how to feed guests.

"I want to teach, Mama," Maria said wearily. She had been saying that for months, supported by Father Pasco, who, influenced by Father DiAnni, agreed that Maria should not join an order whose chief work was housekeeping in seminaries.

Mrs. Trapetti sniffed again. She had gone to a Christmas bazaar at the Ortoni convent and dragged Maria along. The Italian nuns served an assortment of cannolis and *pizza dolce*, there was even a platter of ravioli in case anybody was really hungry. "You'll starve," she repeated. "What did they give you for lunch?"

"I had lunch at home," Maria said. "With you, don't you remember?" She could still taste the lasagna that had been her last food at her mother's table.

Mrs. Trapetti turned away as if this memory was too painful to contemplate. She spied her husband standing alone in the corner and immediately went to bring him another of the dry, uninteresting cakes. Maria stood alone and listened to the waves of conversation eddying in the square, ugly room.

Like the chapel, it was newly built of brick and glass, and the angular chairs were all of pale wood with green vinyl covers. The unyielding shiny surfaces bounced and magnified all sound, and voices echoed and re-echoed around Maria's head. The words sounded like a foreign tongue, hard and sharp, with none of the melody of Revere Street. It was language uncushioned by ricotta cheese and tomato sauce and red wine.

She reached up a tentative hand to loosen the knot of the veil, then remembered her promise to endure the discomfort in penance. Mother Bridget appeared at her side. "It's time, child," she said. She had yet to address Maria by name. "Go say good-bye to your parents."

Later they were ushered to the dining room, called the refectory, and shown their places. "This table is for you," Mother Bridget explained. It was near the door to the kitchen. "Tomorrow I will explain about serving and clearing. The postulants do that job at all meals before they eat. Not tonight, though." Instead she showed them their individual drawers with the white linen napkins they were to tie round their necks, and the single spoon with which they ate all their food.

First, however, they knelt behind their seats for the long grace in Latin. Then they waited until the fifty or so nuns had been served by two young sisters wearing white veils. Novices, Maria realized. The progression from postulant to novice to vowed nun had been explained to her before she came. Mother Rose, the Provincial, had given her a little booklet telling about the way of life of the Servants of Bethlehem. Maria thought about it while she waited for her supper. Finally the meal arrived. It consisted of a bowl of thin soup in which floated bits of corn and potato, accompanied by a slice of Wonder bread without butter.

She thought of what her mother had said, and what the booklet had avoided mentioning.

2

DURING THE SUMMER THAT FOLLOWED GRADUATION, Barbie saved money. She had a job at the Boulevard Theater. It paid eighty cents an hour, and Barbie worked as many hours as she could get. Most weeks her take-home pay was around twenty-four dollars. Invariably she put twenty in the post office savings account, and kept the rest for pocket money. The day her passbook showed two hundred dollars she felt rich.

The previous September, at the start of her senior year, there'd been talk of her trying to get into the general studies program at Boston University. "You'll need all A's and B's this year," Mr. Marcus had told her, "and a good score on the college boards. I think you can do it." Barbie wasn't a good student, Mr. Marcus knew it and so did she; only her looks were extraordinary. Still, Mr. Marcus was so encouraging that Barbie screwed up her nerve and applied.

Sophie and Moe thought it was a splendid idea. Sophie visualized her daughter as a cheerleader. Moe saw her in the role of a happy-go-lucky coed, like Jeanne Crain or June Allyson in the movies. The money for a college education was the major worry. "I'll talk to Harry and Arthur," Moe said. Barbie had two uncles in the auxie, that should count for something.

They still called it the auxie, even though it had become a credit union years before. The purpose of the organization, however, remained the same. It existed to loan money to *landsmen* who were unlikely to be deemed creditworthy at banks run by *goyim*. Any bank would have envied their collection rate. Bad debts were almost nonexistent because the loan committee knew its applicants with an intimacy no bank could match, and the pressure to pay back was applied by your cousin, your brother-in-law, and maybe your brother. People didn't welsh on the credit union.

"Arthur says it'll be okay," Moe announced a week later. "They'll make the loan in our name, but we'll only pay the interest. They'll refinance it periodically, and Barbie can pay back the principal after she graduates."

"Harry says maybe we'll only have to pay half the interest," Sophie said. Having proved that her brother was better than Moe's, she retired from the world of high finance.

The college boards were administered in the high school auditorium over a two-day period. Results came back in a matter of weeks. Barbie's scores were very low. "I was so nervous," she told Mr. Marcus. "I just couldn't think straight."

"It's okay, honey." He saw her huge amber eyes fill with tears. "So you won't be a college girl. With that face and that *tuchas,* you should worry." He wondered what his colleagues would think if they heard him. Screw them. That's what was wrong with the system, that's why he was here.

Ben Marcus got his doctorate in English Literature when he was twenty-four. Brandeis offered him an associate professorship, but he turned it down, married the girl he'd loved since they were both nine years old, and took a job teaching English in his old high school. There were times during his school years when he'd dreamed of blazing new trails in literary criticism, but in the end Marcus had faced his own limitations and decided he'd rather be a big fish in a small pond. And he delighted in the notion of lording it over the Wasp faculty who'd made their anti-Semitism so apparent when he was a kid.

He was one of the first Jews on the faculty of Revere High, and the only Ph.D. in its history. Marcus loved rubbing their noses in that. He also worked hard to get a couple of Italian boys teaching jobs. "The damn Yankees in that place don't know fuck-all about these kids," he repeatedly told his wife.

"They didn't do so bad by us," she reminded him. "I had a look at our yearbook the other day. Do you realize that something like eight percent of our class went to Harvard?"

Marcus grinned. "Yeah. That's part of it, the bastards never could stand it that we're so smart."

"Survival of the fittest," she said. Marilyn Marcus had a degree in sociology from Northeastern. "We've had all the losers bred out of us for a couple of thousand years."

"So tell me how lucky we are," her husband said bitterly.

Now, looking at Barbie, Marcus thought of his wife. Barbie was never going to be like Marilyn, she didn't have the same toughness. "It's okay, honey," he repeated, pushing a box of Kleenex across the desk. "It doesn't matter. You want me to tell your folks?"

She blew her nose loudly. "No, I'll do it."

That show of character pleased Marcus.

SOPHIE AND MOE WEREN'T ALL THAT DISAPPOINTED. THE interest payments would have been tough to meet, and four years was a long time. "So what'll it be instead?" Moe asked his daughter. "Filene's has good employee benefits, and you like clothes. Maybe you can get into their buyer training program."

"No," Barbie said. "I want to go to secretarial school. I sent for some catalogs." She went to her room and returned with three brochures extolling the virtues of learning shorthand and typing and the excitement of becoming a "gal Friday" to a high-powered boss.

"Looks good," Moe said. "Which one? I heard a lot about this Katharine Gibbs."

"I think I'd prefer a smaller place," Barbie said. She selected the catalog of the school she found least threatening and passed it to her mother. "The tuition is less, too."

The following week she made an application and went for an interview. By the time she was graduated and discovered that her best friend was to be a nun, Barbie also knew what she'd be doing the following year.

THE AUXIE ADVANCED THE MONEY TO PAY THE SECRETARIAL school. They made the same deal they'd originally offered, and Moe didn't worry because the sum was considerably less and the size and duration of the payments smaller. Barbie was to continue working at the movie house on Friday evenings and during Saturday and Sunday matinees. What she earned would take care of her carfare and lunch money. "The money you got saved, darling," Sophie said. "It's all for clothes. You're going to that place looking like a million bucks."

All during August mother and daughter pored over copies of *Seventeen* and *Glamour* and *Mademoiselle*. Tawny colors were in, and Sophie chortled because they were the best for

Barbie's vivid coloring. "I never put you in pastels," she said. "Not since you were an infant. Your hair and your eyes show up best in neutrals, or maybe full colors. Or a little black sometimes. For contrast." Barbie nodded in agreement. Sophie Korman had more fashion sense than all the buyers in Filene's, and her talents as a shopper were formidable. "We won't start until late," she said. "Just a couple of things right away, to get by with the first few weeks. But the main wardrobe we buy in October, after the good stores are already trying to get rid of their fall lines."

Four days before school began, they went to Boston. Sophie insisted that they leave the house by seven-thirty. Barbie's eyes were barely open when they walked down Shirley Avenue to the subway station across from the beach. "It's a blessing we got this now," Sophie said. "At least in the winter you can stand inside and wait for the train. Not like it used to be on that Beach Street."

The M.T.A. had recently added an aboveground extension to its Boston subway system. It went as far as Wonderland Dog Track, so people from Revere no longer had to take a streetcar to Maverick and change. You could ride what they called the Orient Heights line and be in town in less than twelve minutes. Sometimes Barbie took the old route anyway; the stop was closer to the house. But Sophie always rode the subway.

It let them off practically in Filene's. They were there by eight-fifteen, which meant they had forty-five minutes to wait until the store opened. "Maybe we can get a cup of coffee," Barbie said.

"Are you crazy? The line will be a mile long in a few minutes." Sophie dragged her daughter to the basement entrance she favored. The black janitor sweeping the stairs recognized her and grinned a greeting.

"Mama," Barbie said, "you ought to start a business. Some kind of personal shopping service."

"You're my business," Sophie said grimly. "What do I need with buying clothes for *meiskeiten* when I got you?" Her small, overweight form was held stiff and ready for battle. When the door was unlocked, she was the first one in, pulling Barbie behind her.

Four hours later they emerged exhausted but triumphant, their arms loaded with bundles. They'd spent only forty-two dollars of Barbie's money, but she had four outfits that would see her through the early autumn. "In a few weeks we'll get

39

the rest," Sophie announced. "You're going to knock 'em dead, you'll see. You want to go upstairs and look for a scarf to go with the beige dress? We can use Daddy's discount."

"Mama, I'm starving!" Barbie wailed.

Sophie gave in; she didn't need her daughter with her to get the scarf, she'd do it some other time. They went across the street to Woolworth's cafeteria and had hot dogs and coffee, and lemon meringue pie for dessert.

BARBIE HAD BEEN ATTENDING THE SECRETARIAL SCHOOL FOR three weeks when the man approached her. The school occupied one floor of a building on Tremont Street. Just below it was something called the Wentworth Agency. Barbie had noticed the name on the list of tenants beside the elevator, but she didn't know what it signified.

On this particular morning she was early because she wanted to practice typing before her first speed test. No one was in the tiny self-service elevator except herself and a middle-aged man she barely noticed.

"I want to talk to you," he said suddenly.

Startled, Barbie looked at him. He was about her father's age, with thin, sandy-colored hair, and prominent red veins on his cheeks and nose. "I beg your pardon? Do you mean me?"

"There's nobody else here, is there?" He grinned, and when the elevator stopped at his floor, he wedged his body against the door so it wouldn't close. "I'm Frank Wentworth. From the modeling agency. Frankly, I've been watching you all week."

Barbie's amber eyes opened wide, the gold flecks sparkled. "You have?"

"Yes. Look, don't be frightened, I'm a respectable married man and I just want to talk to you. Come have a cup of coffee. Your classes don't start for half an hour."

She didn't intend to agree, but he'd taken hold of her arm and was tugging her out of the elevator. Barbie didn't know what to do except go along. Anyway, it was broad daylight and this was a public building.

Wentworth used his key to open a door with gold lettering on its glass upper half. The room was dark until he switched on the lights. Barbie wondered why he didn't open the drapes at the window, but she didn't say anything. There was an electric percolator on a table by the door, and Wentworth busied himself making coffee. "What's your name?" he asked.

"Barbie Korman."

"Where are you from?"

"Revere."

"Hello, Barbie Korman from Revere." He poured two cups of coffee and handed one to her. It hadn't finished perking and it was the color of pale straw. "Help yourself to milk and sugar." He indicated a carton and a sugar bowl and waited while she diluted her drink. Then he swallowed his and put the empty cup down. "I suppose you know you're gorgeous," he said.

Barbie turned bright red and didn't know what to say. She was wearing a box-pleated buff twill skirt with a black blouse. The blouse had a small peter pan collar and long sleeves with cuffs in the same material as the skirt. The close-fitting garment seemed to suffocate her. "It's awfully warm in here," she said.

"Yeah. Why don't you unbutton your collar."

She did, then realized she shouldn't have. The man was trying to peer down the front of her blouse. She began to feel afraid. "I have to go, Mr. Wentworth. I've got a test this morning."

"Don't you want to know why I asked you in here?"

She was afraid she already knew. "I'm sorry, I've got to go." She picked up her black patent leather handbag and moved toward the door.

Wentworth got there first and barred her exit. "Don't rush off. Nobody that looks like you should be studying typing and shorthand. You ought to be a model. Believe me, I'm in the business and I know."

"I don't think my folks would like me to do that." She had a vision of posing nude for artists, and her blush deepened.

Wentworth put his hands on her shoulders and stared into her eyes. He was a head taller than she and very broad. His bulk blocked the door. "Don't be nervous, kid," he whispered. "Frank Wentworth puts his money where his mouth is. You could be big-time if you listen to me."

"Mr. Wentworth, please—"

"Look," he said. "I'm a professional, see. Like a doctor. Bodies are my business. And faces. There's nothing personal in it." He dropped his hands, and suddenly he was cupping her breasts. Barbie was frozen by surprise. A few of the boys she'd dated in Revere had tried to feel her up, but she never let them get away with it.

"Good," Wentworth said. "I was afraid you might wear a padded bra. You don't."

41

"Leave me alone!" His exploring touch shocked her into speech. "You let me out of here!" She pulled away.

Wentworth made another grab for her, but to do so he had to step away from the door. It was lucky for him he did. It swung open with a force that would have knocked him over if he'd still been leaning against it.

"Good morning, lover boy," a cool voice said. "What have we here, jail bait before breakfast?"

Barbie stared at the tall gray-eyed blonde who entered the office. Actually, she'd noticed the woman a couple of times in the lobby. Her clothes were always fantastic. This morning the woman was wearing a gray flannel suit with a straight skirt and a tunic top. When she walked to the window and pulled open the drapes, the skirt exhibited a slit that went above her knee and showed long, shapely legs sheathed in very sheer stockings. "Was he promising to make your fortune, kid?" she asked quietly.

"I've got to go," Barbie whispered. She felt dizzy and sick to her stomach. She knew she was going to be terrible at the typing test.

"The door's open," the blonde said.

Barbie started for it, tottering slightly on the high heels to which she was still unaccustomed. But the woman's voice stopped her. "Wait a minute. You're the redhead. Don't rush off. I've been meaning to talk to you."

"That's what he said." Barbie looked with loathing at the man standing silently in the corner. He was lighting a cigarette and pointedly ignoring both women. She turned back to the blonde. Sunlight streamed into the room. Barbie felt herself washed in its penetrating light. She was conscious of the Neiman-Marcus labels in her blouse and skirt, and grateful for them.

The older woman studied her as if she were a specimen under a microscope. Keeping her eyes on Barbie, she spoke to the man. "Get out of here, Frank. Go down to the Combat Zone and stare at the strippers and jerk off."

Barbie heard him mutter "Bitch" under his breath as he left.

"I'm Helene Wentworth," the blonde said. "I apologize for my husband. But if he said you ought to be a model, he was right. He says it to anything in a skirt, I'll grant you that. But in your case it's the truth." She unbuttoned her tunic while she spoke and shrugged it off. Underneath she wore a white silk blouse that fitted her body like a second skin. It was an exceptional body.

Helene Wentworth walked closer to Barbie, then circled her. The girl was thoroughly confused. She stood where she was and didn't say anything. Helene put her hand under Barbie's chin and tipped her face back. "You do anything to your hair, or is it natural?"

"I don't do anything." Her voice was a tremulous whisper.

"Don't know much about makeup either," Helene said. "Great clothes, though; you've got excellent taste."

"My mother buys all my clothes."

Helene smiled. "Then she's got excellent taste. Filene's basement, right?" Barbie nodded. "And you're from, let's see . . . Chelsea maybe, or Revere."

"Revere," Barbie acknowledged.

"What's your name?"

Barbie told her. Helene had her thoroughly mesmerized. She knew she ought to go up to class immediately, but she couldn't break away from the older woman's intense gaze.

"I don't suppose you spell it with a C, do you?"

Barbie spelled her name.

"Funny," Helene said, "you don't look Jewish." She laughed at herself and added, "It's true, you don't. You could use Cole for business purposes."

"I'm not ashamed of my name," Barbie said stiffly.

Helene sighed. "Don't be stupid. Listen to me, kid, I've been around this business a long time. Longer than I'll admit. I was your age when I started and I'm not going to tell you when that was. I've got a hell of a body now and I had an even better one back then, but tits and asses are a dime a dozen. Yours are good. Maybe great. I won't know for sure till I see you stripped. But they're not what makes you special. It's your coloring and your bones that are dynamite. Besides, big boobs are an asset for a showroom model like I was, but I don't think that's your scene." She reached over and turned the girl toward the light pouring in the window. "Jesus! You're a frigging miracle."

Barbie stared at her, dumbfounded. She'd never heard a woman use such language and she didn't know what to make of Helene Wentworth.

Helene smiled and released her grip on Barbie. "Okay, I can see you've had enough shocks for today. I'll give you just one more. If you do what I say, you could be making thirty thousand a year twelve months from now. Maybe more, but certainly no less. Now, this is Friday. Go upstairs and study like you're supposed to. Monday lunchtime come see me here and we'll talk some more. I promise you my creep of a husband won't be around."

Barbie couldn't figure out a way to tell her parents what had happened. At the supper table she tried a dozen times, but the words wouldn't come. Because it was Friday night two candles burned in tall brass holders, polished to mirror brightness. The Kormans weren't religious. Sophie hadn't kept kosher since her mother died, but she always lit the *shabbat* candles. The candlesticks and the matching fruit bowl had come steerage from Russia, like the family. To Sophie they were a symbol of her Jewishness, something like being circumcised. Whether or not you were Orthodox, some things you didn't give up.

Across the flickering light of the candles, Moe studied his daughter. "So how did the test go today?" he asked.

"Okay, I guess." It hadn't, it had been terrible because she was upset by what preceded it. The teacher had shaken her blue-rinsed head and said, "You'll have to do better, Miss Korman, or we won't be able to keep you."

"How many words a minute?" Moe persisted. He was always interested in details.

"I don't remember," Barbie said lamely.

"Leave her alone, Moe. She's been studying all week and she's got to be at work in half an hour. Eat your soup, darling."

Barbie finished the soup and started on the roast chicken and stuffing. She had eaten the same thing once a week all her life. Maria could never stay for supper on Friday nights because of it. Sophie had balked at the idea of serving anybody fish on *shabbat,* even Maria. Barbie thought about her friend and had to swallow hard not to cry. If Maria were still here, she would have someone with whom to discuss the extraordinary events of the morning. Thirty thousand dollars. She wasn't sure there was that much money in the world.

Finally she escaped to the theater and was busy selling tickets for a while. Then she relieved the girl at the popcorn stand, and eventually it was ten-thirty and time to go home. She walked across Ocean Avenue and started up the hill. The lights were still on in Izzy's Drugstore and she considered stopping for a hot chocolate, but decided against it. She needed to save her money for carfares and lunches. If you earned thirty thousand dollars, you could buy anything you wanted.

A car pulled up beside her and a voice said, "Hi! It's Barbie

44

Korman, isn't it? I'm Father DiAnni. Maria introduced us after the play last year."

She looked at the priest and smiled. "Hello, Father. What are you doing here?"

"I'm on my way back from Beachmont." He gestured toward the small Irish enclave a few blocks west. "Some old guy wouldn't have anything but an Italian priest. He doesn't think Father Kelly's the real thing."

Barbie didn't entirely understand the joke, but she grinned anyway. She wanted to keep Father DiAnni talking because he was a link with Maria. "I didn't think there were any Italians living in Beachmont."

"A few," he said, smiling. Barbie noticed how white his teeth were and how they gleamed against his dark skin. His black curly hair fell over his forehead and made him look very young. Maria had said he was too handsome to be a priest. She was right. "Hop in," he said. "I'll give you a lift home."

"I don't live very far."

"It doesn't matter, I'd enjoy a chance to talk to you. I'll be visiting Maria soon. She'll be glad if I can say I saw you."

Barbie looked around hastily, but the night was cold and the men who hung out at Izzy's had deserted the street corner early. No one would see her getting into a car with a Catholic priest.

"How have you been?" Father DiAnni asked. "If I remember rightly, Maria told me you were going to secretarial school."

Barbie nodded. She too was remembering something Maria said. If you told anything to a Catholic priest, he could never repeat it. Even if you said you murdered someone. If he did it was a terrible sin and he went to hell. She took a deep breath and made up her mind. "Can I talk to you?" she whispered. "Even though I'm not a Catholic?"

"WHAT'S THE MATTER WITH YOU THESE LAST COUPLE OF DAYS?" The pastor eyed his young curate with concern.

"Nothing, Father. A little tired, maybe."

"At your age that's hard to believe. Tell you what, take the evening off. I wasn't going out anyway. I'll stand by."

DiAnni was embarrassed. "I don't want to put my responsibilities on you."

"I'd rather have them than your bad temper. Go on, get out of here. Go see your mother or something."

DiAnni grinned. "Or something," he said.

"Moderation in all things, Father," the pastor called after his retreating back. "That way almost nothing's a sin." He was about to emphasize the *almost,* but the young man was already gone.

DiAnni considered himself lucky to have this particular pastor. A lot of the guys told unbelievable stories of spite and ego, but Father Pasco wasn't bad. For one thing, he kept this beat-up old Chevy going, as well as his own Olds. It was intended for parish business, but the pastor didn't object to it being used for other things.

The Mystic River Bridge carried DiAnni into Boston's North End and he turned right onto Hanover Street. Not until he parked did he realize he wasn't going to see his mother.

JOSEPH DiANNI WAS NOT, LIKE SOME, SPAWNED TO THE priesthood. He was born in 1932 in Boston's North End, amid a network of Sicilians who brought with them to the New World their intense tribal loyalties and feuds, and continued to play out the bloody drama of their island legacy in the area around Hanover Street.

Young Joseph was, however, the son of a man somehow apart from his fellows, a man who wrote lyric Italian poetry when he returned from working in his father-in-law's cheese factory, and dreamed of a new order being created in America. The senior DiAnni was not religious in the usual sense of the word. His cravings were for justice and human dignity, and he saw those things as unrelated to the plaster saints before whom his wife knelt with such fervor and regularity. When three men arrived in the cheese factory demanding to be paid for protection, DiAnni was terrified. He knew well the consequences of refusal. But that his aged father-in-law opened the cash drawer and paid without a murmur filled DiAnni with bitterness and rage.

For a month he argued with the old man. "If we pay them there can be no end to it. They will make us animals who crawl on our bellies and eat garbage to stay alive."

"They will kill us if we refuse," the other man said simply.

"Maybe that's better," DiAnni murmured. "What kind of life do they offer instead?"

The cheese maker thought his son-in-law to be speaking inane pieties, making himself feel more a man by talking. He didn't expect that when the Mafiosi arrived to collect their second monthly payment, DiAnni would face them with a knife and a refusal. The results were predictable. DiAnni was blinded by acid, the old man beaten until he was crippled for what remained of his life, and the cheese factory all but destroyed.

Neighbors summoned Joseph's mother and his grandmother to the scene of carnage and took the nine-year-old boy away until the women had tended their wounded. A week later Joseph was returned to his mother in the flat on Hanover Street. That same afternoon they had a visit from a tall man in his forties, with the smell of power clinging to his clothes and his skin.

"Come in, Don Stefano," Signora DiAnni said, and seated the caller with a glass of red wine and some fresh-baked *biscotti*.

"How is your husband?" the don asked.

"He's improving. They say he'll be home from the hospital at the end of next week. He won't never see again, though."

"Ah, that is a shame. And your father?"

"He can't walk. But they're gonna let him out of the hospital tomorrow."

"A shame," Don Stefano repeated. "And the bills for all this medical care? Such things are very expensive in America."

"Father Lucci says he will help."

"Yes, of course, Father Lucci. But the Church doesn't have so much money here in the North End. It will be difficult for the good Father to pay the doctors and support your son and your blind husband and yourself indefinitely. Is that not true, Signora DiAnni?"

He finished his wine, and Joseph's mother refilled the glass while the boy stood in the corner and watched and listened. "Yes," she admitted tonelessly. "It's true."

"Good, I'm glad you understand. That is why I have come. I have instructions from my *padrone*, a fine man who wishes you well. He is not pleased that the cheese factory should be closed, and that there should be no income for your old parents or yourself. He proposes to make you a present of the money to pay the hospital, and to restore the damage done at the factory."

"And what does your sainted *padrone* get in return?" Signora DiAnni was a small woman, dark and fierce, tempered by the two sorrows of being barren since her only son was born, and being married to a man who wrote poetry and dreamed impossible dreams. She was not a fool. "How could I repay the *padrone* for such wonderful kindness?"

"He has the welfare of all our people in his heart. He be-

47

lieves it is good for all if the factory operates again. You and your mother can take over running it, now that your husbands are so unfortunately made invalids. In return, the *padrone* will place you under his protection, and claim a small percentage of the money the factory earns."

Signora DiAnni turned and stared at her son cowering in the corner. "What about him? I have a child. How will he manage if I work in the factory all day?"

"You have friends, relatives, neighbors. He will be looked after."

"No." She spat out the word with sudden passion. "It is not good enough. Not for Joseph. Tell the *padrone* I will do as he says, if he also pays for my child to go to the school of the Don Bosco Fathers. He can live there during the week and come home on Sundays."

So was it arranged.

In later years DiAnni recalled little about his first months in the boarding school; they faded into a haze of loneliness and misery, were overshadowed by the memory of his suddenly shrunken father staring at nothing through sightless eyes. The details of only one incident remained vivid for Joseph. It occurred six weeks after he'd become a Don Bosco pupil, when he came home to spend Sunday on Hanover Street; home to his blind father seated in the small, cluttered front room. He'd fled the presence of the damaged man, seeking comfort in the kitchen where his mother was ironing.

"I never knew Papa had such a fancy shirt." Joseph reached over to finger a freshly laundered silk sleeve.

"Don't touch!" Signora DiAnni growled the command, as if the boy's small hand could permanently damage the shimmering cloth. Or maybe the other way round. "Besides, it's not Papa's shirt."

Joseph's eyes widened in surprise. "Then whose is it? Why are you ironing somebody else's clothes?"

"It's Don Stefano's." She bent closer to her task and didn't raise her face when she spoke.

He felt ashamed. It was wrong that his mother should do something so intimate for a stranger. "Is he giving you money to do it?"

She didn't answer immediately. With infinite care, almost tenderness, she finished pressing the collar, then stood her iron upright on the edge of the board. It was a new iron, a shiny electric thing, not heavy and black like the old one. Joseph's mother stroked the handle lightly. "I do him a favor, that's all.

He's been good to us, to you and to your papa." She didn't meet his eyes. "Don Stefano ain't got no wife. She died. Nobody to take care of him."

In that moment Joseph somehow understood that his mother's world was totally changed since the evil day at the cheese factory. And that in her new world he had little part.

He stumbled from the kitchen and went to kneel beside his father's chair. The older man put his hand on his son's head and softly spoke trivial, unthreatening words, but Joseph was conscious only of the muted sound of the expensive new iron skimming over luxurious silken shirts.

Later there were other things. Boxes of small black cigars appeared in the house, despite the fact that Signor DiAnni didn't smoke. Sometimes the cheroots were on the kitchen table or on the big console radio in the front room. Once he noticed one of them in his parents' bedroom.

Joseph said nothing. The incident with the shirt was the only time he ever asked a direct question about Don Stefano. But the man's presence grew ever larger in their three lives. The DiAnnis seemed to hover in Don Stefano's shadow. For Joseph he was a ghost who haunted the small apartment. Soon the Don Bosco School became Joseph's comfort and refuge. Hanover Street was a place of torment he visited because he was made to do so.

On one such visit, when he was twelve, Joseph saw that a narrow bed had been crammed into the kitchen. "For your papa," Signora DiAnni said. "It's easier for him. Closer to the toilet."

Joseph stared at her, and this time she stared back. A fire burned behind her eyes. He could not bear the heat of her gaze, and he swiveled and stared across the hall at the open door of the bedroom with its big double bed. It seemed to Joseph that the imprint of Don Stefano's head was still on the pillow. "It's not right," he muttered through a throat choked with tears. "It's a sin before God."

Signora DiAnni lurched forward and with one hand spun her son round, then with the other she slapped him hard, once on each cheek. Joseph could taste blood running from the inside of his lip into his mouth. "Don't talk to me about sin!" she hissed. "You know nothing. Stupid little boy who will grow up to be a stupid man. Like him." She jerked her head toward the room where his father sat alone.

Joseph ran out of the house and wandered the streets, but an hour later he came back. He said nothing to his mother, only went to his father and took his hand. "Come for a walk, Papa. It's nice out. I'll hold your hand. It will be all right, you'll see."

When they were alone, the man said to his son, "Joseph, it's my fault. If I didn't try to fight them, nothing would be like it is. Your mother—"

"Don't talk about her." Joseph realized he was shouting, and made himself be calm for Papa's sake. "It's just you and me out here now."

"Okay," his father said with a sigh. "However you want, Joseph."

Thus was a pattern established. Joseph and his father went for walks every Sunday afternoon, whatever the weather. They left the house, the older man using his son's eyes, and went to the waterfront, which was deserted on the sabbath. There they sat in the shelter of the warehouses and talked. After the first few times, the conversation always opened the same way. "Tell me 'bout the game," Joseph's father would say. The game to which he referred was baseball.

By the time he was twelve, Joseph had his full height of six feet two inches. He was not, however, built like a football player. The priests responsible for his care and education early recognized that Joseph's long, lean body and well-coordinated hand and eye indicated other things. They made him a pitcher, and the boy displayed not only the physical stamina and control required, but an aptitude for the psychology. He took his place on the mound and went slowly through motions calculated to unnerve the opposition, modeled on those of his unlikely black hero, Satchel Paige. Whether Joseph won games by his ability to outwit the batter, or because he had a masterful, and undetectable, change-up fastball was impossible to say. But he did win them. The Don Bosco priests rejoiced, Joseph was gratified, and his father insisted that every Sunday of the year they begin their conversation by talking about baseball. He never quite understood that Joseph's team only played during the spring.

When this homage to the ways of his son's native land was complete, DiAnni would speak of other things. He told his son how it could be if men were different, stronger, more willing to stand together against oppression. DiAnni could no longer read, but he listened to the radio, and in America things were said on the radio that were not even whispered in Sicily. In America, change was possible.

Joseph kept all these lessons in his heart. When he told his father he was going to the seminary to be a priest, he explained that it was the many Sunday afternoon discussions that had shaped and confirmed his vocation.

"You want to save men's souls," his father protested. "I want to first save their bodies and their minds."

"It's not like that, Papa. Not that strict a line. If the poor are to be helped, it must be the Church that helps them." Joseph had come to terms of a sort with the situation in his home. Poverty, he was convinced, had caused his father's blindness and his mother's infidelity. Poverty allowed men like Don Stefano to bend others to their will. "Only the Church has enough power to stand against evil," he added.

"Then why has she not done so?" DiAnni asked.

"You speak of the past, Papa. Old men who didn't understand what was possible in America. Now it will be different. The guys who go to be priests now, we'll be different."

"Who tells you these things?"

Joseph mentioned the priest who was his mentor, a man he'd met by chance one Saturday afternoon in Fenway Park. The Red Sox lost that day, but Joseph didn't. "I'm going to be like him. Not a teacher, not a Don Bosco Father. I'll be a diocesan priest and some day work in the parishes with the people. For them."

"I hope so," DiAnni said.

Joseph did not, however, go immediately to the seminary. When he was graduated from high school, it was June of 1950. On the twenty-fifth of that month, North Korea invaded South Korea. Joseph went into the army. Two and a half years passed. During that time, his father died, Don Stefano moved permanently into his mother's flat, and Joseph was made a lieutenant because, as one of his superiors put it, "He's not the least bit worried about dying, but he understands people who are." Joseph came home to Boston with a piece of bone missing from his hip and a deeper understanding of how the world was, and how it should be. They gave him a steel pin to replace the bone, a citation for bravery, and a purple heart. He threw the medals in the ash can in front of his mother's house and took himself and his barely perceptible limp into training for the priesthood.

In 1959, when he was twenty-seven and newly ordained, Joseph was assigned to St. Anthony's parish in Revere. There he preached sermons on justice and self-help and old Father

Pasco listened and shook his head. But he did not report the young man's radical ideas to the chancery office because he knew him to be earnest and sincere, and a good priest at heart.

IN THE NORTH END JOE WALKED THROUGH THE FAMILIAR rabbit warren of streets lined with Italian restaurants and grocery stores. At six on a Monday evening, they were quiet. It was too early for the restaurants and too late for the shops. Dusk was coming quickly, the gray light blotting out most of the filth of the streets. It was the craziest damned neighborhood in the world, he'd always thought that. Rich and poor lived side by side in conditions distinguished only by the size of their television sets and cars. And everybody threw their garbage in the gutter.

The pizza place he turned into was narrow and dark. It boasted no booths, just long, scarred tables and ill-matched chairs. The floor was covered in sawdust. Tattered travel posters praising Roma and Firenze and Pisa were tacked to walls stained with soot and grease. A few candles were stuck in fat, straw-wrapped chianti bottles and a dessicated string of onions hung by the door. It was there to ward off witches. A bar occupied one corner of the room, and a woman stood behind it. "Hi, Mama," he said.

"Hello, Father Joseph. What you here for? You see your mama yet?"

"Not yet. I will later."

"Okay. You hungry?"

"Not now. Thirsty."

She nodded and poured some zinfandel from a gallon jug into a water glass. *"Salute."*

"Salute," he said. He studied the woman while he drank. Mama Lorenzo had been behind this bar ever since he could remember. She'd always looked just the way she did now. Enormously fat, with bright red lipstick that ran into little lines around her mouth, and thick white powder caked in the crevices of her many chins. She was an ignorant, superstitious old woman who wouldn't hesitate to rob a blind man's cup, but she made magnificent pizza and she knew everything that went on in the North End. He finished his wine. "Tony Cig been around lately?"

"Tony's always around." She refilled his glass. "Not like a boy who get himself a fancy collar and don't come see his mama."

He knew she meant not herself but his own mother. "I go when I can, Mama. Priests don't have a lot of time off."

"No, too busy stealing." She spat on the floor to indicate her opinion of the clergy.

"I need to see Tony."

She glanced at the clock on the wall. It was a neon-lit pizza with bulbous olives to indicate the hours. "He should be in soon. Sit. I make you a pizza."

Mama buried her short, fat fingers in a roll of dough. Joe watched her and sipped his third glass of zinfandel. It grew dark and a few more customers drifted in. They were strangers from other parts of the city, cognoscenti who knew where to get the best pizza in the North End. Joe was wearing civvies so they paid him no attention. Finally the man he was waiting for arrived.

Tony went straight to the bar and kissed Mama. She said something, and he searched the gloom until he spotted Joe. When he came over, he carried a bottle of beer. "Hi, long time no see. What's up?"

"I need a favor."

"I'm listening."

"I want information."

Tony Cig took a notebook and a pencil out of the pocket of his shapeless jacket. He was the same age as Joe—they'd grown up together—but he'd looked fifty since he was fifteen. His real name was Antonio Pasquale Cigliocherra. That was too much of a mouthful, even in this neighborhood, so he became Tony Cig. He was a ferret, a man who knew things and could flush them out if he didn't. His methods and his sources were his secret, but his information was always accurate. Every newsman in Boston, and half the cops, paid Tony Cig.

Joe posed his question, consulting his notes to make sure he got the name right. "How long will it take to find out?" he asked after Tony wrote everything down.

"A day, half a day maybe. Meet you here tomorrow night and tell you what I got."

"No can do," Joe said. "I can't leave the rectory two nights running. Call me as soon as you can." He gave Tony the phone number in Revere, then reached for his wallet.

Tony made a dismissive gesture. "No charge. Call it a clerical discount."

"Thanks."

"Okay. Say a Mass for my father, how's that?"

"Fine, I'll do it." Tony Cig's father had been a brute who

beat his wife and kids regularly. When he died, his family made a novena of thanksgiving to St. Jude. It did not, however, surprise Joe to be asked to say a Mass for the repose of the old man's soul. He started to inquire about the rest of the family, but Mama arrived and slammed a metal pizza tray on the table between them. She shoved a stack of napkins closer and waddled back to her ovens.

The two men stopped talking and ate. The pizza was a symphony, a work of art. The crust was yeasty and thick, the tomato sauce subtle. It was topped with real scamozza cheese, the kind stored in a barrel under water, a sprinkling of anchovies, and rings of previously sautéed green pepper. A rich and fruity olive oil had been applied with liberality. When they lifted the slices to their greedy mouths, the oil ran over the backs of their hands and down their arms. "It's better'n sex," Tony said sighing contentedly. "S'cuse me, Father," he added. "When you ain't wearin' your collar I forget."

"It's okay. Sometimes I forget, too."

TONY PHONED THE NEXT AFTERNOON AT FOUR. THE housekeeper called Joe away from a meeting of the Little Flower Society to take the call. The priest listened silently, thanked Tony, and hung up. Then he stood by the phone for a few moments, trying to figure out how he could see Barbie. He decided he'd have to wait until Friday night when she was working at the theater. Even in civvies he'd be conspicuous if he called at a house on Shirley Avenue.

He was waiting for her when she finished work. "Barbie, it's me, Father DiAnni. I want to talk to you."

She got into the car, but didn't close the door. Neither did she look at him. Joe had parked in the shadows. He knew that Barbie would be embarrassed to be seen with a Catholic priest. "Shut the door," he said. "I'll drive down to the beach. There's no one around there now. We can talk."

He drove beyond the section they called "punk's corner" to a spot across from the main bathhouse. The beach was deserted, the stands all boarded over for the winter. A few cars were parked nearby, but neither Barbie nor Joe paid any attention to the couples necking in the dark. "I've been thinking about what I said to you last week," Joe began. He didn't look at her, just stared out the windshield toward an ocean swallowed by night. "I couldn't help thinking maybe I was wrong."

He'd told her to avoid the Wentworths as if they carried the

54

plague. He'd warned her that the world they represented was fraught with moral danger, and that sticking to her plan to be a secretary was the best thing she could do. Then he'd gone home and played the conversation over in his head and realized that he sounded like a two-bit prig who didn't know what life was really like in places like Shirley Avenue and Revere Street. Only he did know. And he hated himself for spouting the party line and equating poverty with virtue.

"I've done some checking," he said. "This Mrs. Wentworth is just what she said, a former model who now acts as a model's agent. Her business seems to be perfectly legitimate and aboveboard. I guess there's no reason you shouldn't give it a try if your folks agree. But you've got to tell them about it."

Barbie spoke for the first time. "I already have," she whispered.

"Told your parents, you mean?"

She shook her head. Her auburn hair glowed in the moonlight. "No, I haven't told them yet. But I'm giving it a try."

Joe smiled. "So you didn't take my advice."

Barbie turned and grinned at him. "You mad at me?"

"No. It was only a suggestion. Everyone has to make up their own mind in the end. But I still think you should tell your mother and father. Deceiving them's a rotten thing to do. That really is wrong."

"I know," she said. "I'm going to tell them this weekend. Helene said I had to. Anyway, I haven't quit the secretarial school yet. I've just been talking to Helene during my lunch hours."

Joe thought of the one disturbing thing Tony had reported. He swallowed hard and said, "Listen, Barbie, there's something I want to warn you about. Some people, men and women both, . . . well, they have funny ideas about love. It's not their fault, they're sick. But they prefer other women or maybe men . . ." He stumbled hopelessly, knowing he wasn't being clear, not knowing how to be.

"You mean queers?" Barbie said. Her voice betrayed no shock. "I know about fags. But Helene's husband is anything but that. He's a dirty old man, Helene hates him. She never lets him stay around when I'm in the office."

"Good. But that's not exactly it."

"She's butch, Father," Tony Cig had told him. "A real les. Other than that she's okay. And the way I hear it, she keeps her personal and professional life separate. Doesn't seduce little girls or anything like that. Has a regular woman friend and goes to the dyke bars in the Combat Zone when she wants some action."

Now Joe looked over at the girl. She was leaning back on the seat, and the moonlight limned her perfect profile. Her beauty took his breath away. It wasn't a carnal thing; she was too much a child to be a threat to his celibacy, but she was exquisite. Her looks seemed to him to give glory to God. And they were her passport out of the ghetto. Who was he or anyone else to say she shouldn't use the gift she'd been given? Joe DiAnni knew well that rich was better than poor. You could be a saint or a sinner in either case. She was still waiting for him to speak.

"Women can have unnatural desires too," he said.

She giggled. "I don't."

"I know that. I mean Mrs. Wentworth."

Her head jerked around and she stared at him. "Helene! That's crazy. She's gorgeous. You should see her."

Joe sighed. "Okay. I only wanted to alert you. If there's anything suspicious, anything at all, you call me right away. Will you do that, Barbie?"

"Sure. You going to see Maria soon?"

"The Sunday after next is visiting day. I'm taking her mother to see her."

"Give her my love. I couldn't write a letter for you to bring, could I?"

"I'm afraid not. It's against the rules of the convent."

"Okay. But you tell her I miss her." She paused and added shyly, "Tell her maybe I'm going to be a famous model."

He promised, and made sure she had his phone number. Then he drove her home.

SOPHIE CAST AN APPRAISING EYE OVER THE INTERIOR OF Steuben's Restaurant. It was dim and expensive-looking. "The food's good here?" she asked.

"It's very good," Helene Wentworth assured her. "The filet mignon is excellent, and so's the lobster."

Sophie suspected she was being bought off. "That's too much for lunch," she said, and ordered a mushroom omelette.

Barbie and Helene both had steaks. Sophie winced when the blonde asked for hers to be served rare and Barbie said she'd have the same. When she saw their bloody steaks, Sophie had to look away. Sometimes nowadays she ate bacon and even pork chops, but old habits die hard and bloody beef epitomized for her all that was *goyishe.* She made herself ignore the food. "So what you got in mind for my Barbie?"

"I asked you to lunch so we could talk about that," Helene said. She took a sip of her daiquiri before continuing. "I want to make her a model. She's a knockout, and when I get finished with her, she'll be the most talked-about face in America."

"What do you mean, finished with her? What are you starting?"

Helene wiped her lips delicately. She wore a red shantung coat dress that Sophie put at something over a hundred dollars. Even if she got it in the basement. The pearls could be real too. But pretty as she was, this Mrs. Wentworth was no competition for Barbie. Sophie compared the two with satisfaction, and waited for the other woman to speak.

"I'll spend a few months getting her in shape," Helene said. "Teaching her how to walk and move, that sort of thing. Then I'll book her some modeling jobs." Helene motioned for the waiter and ordered another drink.

"What do you mean, 'getting her in shape'? And what kind of modeling jobs?"

"She needs to lose ten pounds," Helene said. Then, over Sophie's protests, she added, "Of course she's not fat. But the camera adds weight. And I want to emphasize those bones. Look." She reached across the table and took Barbie's chin in her hands, turning her face from side to side. "Her cheekbones are her best feature. We want them to show."

"I think her eyes are her best," Sophie said defiantly.

"They're wonderful," Helene agreed. "But the cheekbones are more unusual. Besides, when they're played up as they should be, they'll make her eyes more outstanding."

Sophie had to admit that was probably true.

"People are staring at us," Barbie said.

Helene took her hand away and laughed. She had a low, throaty laugh. Barbie was trying to imitate it, but she hadn't achieved the same sound yet. "Relax, baby," Helene said. "We're going to have everyone in America looking at you pretty soon."

"What kind of modeling jobs?" Sophie asked again.

"Magazines and, to start with, maybe catalogs," Helene said. "Advertisements. Nothing but the best. Barbie's going to be a photographer's model. And she's a Cadillac, we're not going to act like she's a Ford."

"No painters," Sophie said firmly. "I don't want my Barbie

should be like those girls in the movies who take off their clothes and pose for artists."

"That's a different kind of modeling altogether," Helene said patiently. "It's nothing to do with what I have in mind for Barbie."

Sophie narrowed her eyes and peered at the blonde. "And what do you get out of it? I'm not a sophisticated woman, Mrs. Wentworth, but I wasn't born yesterday. Nobody does nothing for nothing."

"Nobody does," Helene agreed quietly. "Least of all me. I get ten percent of every dime she makes. Barbie's going to make me rich, Mrs. Korman, I don't deny it. But she's going to be richer than I am."

Sophie was silent for a moment. Then she said solemnly, "Okay. If Barbie wants it and her father agrees, I say okay."

Barbie yelped with delight. "I do want it, Mama! And Daddy will do whatever you say. He always does."

"So maybe I have a little influence with my own husband. What's wrong with that?" She smiled coyly at her daughter and Helene, and they smiled back.

"One other thing," Helene said. "I want Barbie to use the name Cole professionally. It's better than Korman. She objects because she thinks it will hurt your feelings and that it's disloyal."

"Don't be stupid, Barbie," Sophie said immediately. "Korman sounds too Jewish. In this world you get further if you've got a *goyishe* name. Excuse me, Mrs. Wentworth, no offense."

"None taken, Mrs. Korman. I worked under the name Helene Rand, but I was born Helen Reachey."

Sophie didn't know what kind of name Reachey was, but she said, "There, that's what I mean. And you can call me Sophie."

"Good. I'm Helene to all my friends."

The two women shook hands solemnly.

"It's Lebanese," Helene told Barbie, handing her the strange flat bread. "So am I."

Barbie tasted the bread. "It's good. Where do you get it?"

"There's a Lebanese bakery nearby. I think a few supermarkets may carry it. I'm not sure. Maybe I could get you a supply once or twice a week."

"Don't bother. My uncle Arthur has a grocery store. I'll get him to order it. This is better for me than other bread?"

"It's very low in calories," Helene explained. "And so is

this. Try it." She pushed a bowl of something that looked like sour cream across the table, and Barbie followed her example and dipped a corner of the bread in it.

"Ugh!" she said. "It's bitter. I'm sorry, I don't mean to be rude."

Helene laughed. "You're not. Yogurt is an acquired taste. But it's very good for you, and also low calorie. You'll get to like it. Yogurt, this bread, raw vegetables, and lean meat, that's all you can eat until we get those ten pounds off."

"My mother will die."

"Sophie's all right. You tell her I said it was for the sake of the cheekbones." Helene got up and crossed the small living room. It was furnished with two sofas upholstered in a rich dark print, and numerous jewel-colored cushions. There were two oriental rugs on the parquet floor. Barbie noted that although they didn't match each other or the furniture, everything looked great together. She also admired the many plants. Helene had greenery everywhere, even in the bathroom. "This is a super apartment," Barbie said.

"Thank you. I like it. It's small, but convenient." It was on Charles Street, and in good weather Helene could walk across the Public Gardens and the Common to her office. Actually she was thinking of giving the office up. She couldn't really afford the rent if she was going to forego all her other clients and concentrate on Barbie. They could work just as well here. She opened a closet and brought a large leather hat box to the kitchen table. "Come in here," she called to Barbie. "This table's better to work at."

Barbie went behind the partition separating the kitchen from the living room, then cast a nervous glance over her shoulder.

Helene understood the gesture. "He's gone," she said. "He won't be back. I threw him out yesterday."

"Oh, Helene, I'm sorry." Barbie had a terrible feeling that it was her fault the Wentworths had broken up.

"I'm not," Helene said. "He was a loser from the day I married him. I don't know why I did it anyway."

"Are you getting a divorce?"

"Why bother? It's expensive, and it only matters if you want to get married again. I don't."

"Not ever?" Barbie asked. "You just feel that way now," she added, answering her own question. "You'll change your mind when you meet someone nice. You will, too. You're beautiful, Helene."

Helene smiled and laid her hand on Barbie's cheek. She could hear Frank's voice screaming at her before he left. "You lousy bull dyke! You're throwing me out because you've got the hots for the little Jew-girl. I hope she bites your cunt right through!" It wasn't like that; Frank was wrong. She got wet between the legs whenever she looked at Barbie, but she'd never seduced an innocent in her life and she didn't plan to start now. If there was going to be anything like that between them, it would have to come from Barbie, not from her. Helene took a deep breath and made herself concentrate on business.

"Lesson number one," she said. "Skin care. You can't make a bad skin look good, no matter how much makeup you apply."

BARBIE LOST THE TEN POUNDS IN A MONTH. FOR HER SAKE Arthur started carrying Syrian bread—that's what he called it, though Helene insisted it was Lebanese—and yogurt. Sophie not only didn't object, she became a watchdog. "No flanken," she pronounced. "It's too fat." Barbie objected that it was beef, and that she wouldn't eat the lima beans her mother always cooked with it. "Fatty meats have more calories than cake," Sophie insisted, waving the dieter's handbook she'd bought. The eating habits of the entire family changed.

"She's too thin already," Moe said after the first week. "You want she should lose more?"

"The camera adds weight," Sophie said with the authority vested in her by Helene.

"So okay, I'm not worried by any cameras. For God's sake, make me a blintz!"

"Not until we've lost the weight."

They did. All the Kormans slimmed down, and Shirley Avenue watched with awe. Everybody knew that Barbie was going to be a model. Sophie strolled the street graciously accepting the homage that was her due. The day Barbie registered one hundred and eight on the bathroom scale, a celebration was decreed. "Invite Helene for supper," Sophie said. "Friday night. No, wait a minute, Sunday is better. About two, we'll eat at three." She wanted the blonde to come when it was light and the neighbors would see her. Sophie Korman had always welcomed her daughter's *shiksa* friends; she was an American. Now she was reaping her reward and it wouldn't hurt the others to know.

"Mama wants you to come to our house on Sunday afternoon. We'll eat about three."

Helene was wielding a fine-bristled brush dipped in eye shadow. "Pay attention. You're supposed to be able to do this for yourself. The white needs to go just under the brows to emphasize the bone structure. You have to be careful or you'll look like a clown."

"All right. Can you come on Sunday?"

"Sure, I'd love it. We have to be back here by seven, though."

Barbie was surprised. Usually she didn't come to Helene's on Sunday. "Why?" she asked, making faces at herself in the mirror to see if the eye shadow was correctly placed.

"There's a hairdresser coming. He's an old friend just back from Paris. I've been looking for the right stylist for you. I think Larry is it."

"I'd like my hair to be like yours," Barbie said. Helene wore her blond hair slicked back from her face and coiled into a tight French twist.

"It's too old for you. And it won't do a thing for the image we're working on."

"You always say that, about my image. What's it supposed to be? I never really understand."

Helene stepped back and studied her protegée. "No, you don't. That's bad, because you can't project it for the camera if you don't know what it is." She crossed the room, selected a record and put it on the phonograph. It was Beethoven's Moonlight Sonata. "That's you, baby," she said softly after the first few bars. "All flowing and soft, but with a tinkle in the background, a touch of the street urchin. Do you see it?"

Barbie shook her head.

"Close your eyes. Let it wash over you. Move with it."

Barbie was stiff at first, then more fluid. She bent and swayed and twirled. I'm going to die, Helene thought. If I can't touch her, I'm just going to die. She reached out her hand, but Barbie, eyes still closed, moved in the other direction.

"This feels great," she whispered. "Have I got it right?"

"Yes, baby. You've got it fine." The words came out husky, through a throat constricted with desire. The music came to an end. "Don't open your eyes," Helene commanded. "Wait. You're many different things. Just wait." She went to the phonograph and put on Tchaikovsky's Capriccio Italien. "Show

61

me what this makes you feel," she said in the same husky voice.

The primitive beat contained within the classical structure jerked Barbie into motion. Helene moaned, but if Barbie heard she didn't react. The girl was lost in a world that contained only herself and the music. Helene watched the look of ecstasy on Barbie's face, and clenched her hands into fists held stiffly by her sides. "Take off your blouse," she whispered. "Feel the music on your skin."

Barbie was wearing a cotton-knit shirt. She pulled it over her head and flung it away. Her small, hard breasts were completely hidden by a white cotton bra. "Take the bra off, too," Helene said. "Here, I'll help you. No, don't open your eyes." She stepped close to Barbie and unhooked the bra, letting her hands trail over the girl's arms as she took it off. Barbie's breasts weren't too small. They were perfectly proportioned for the narrow midriff and tiny waist that rose above her blue jeans. The music reached a frenzied crescendo. Barbie stretched her arms over her head, arched her back, and twirled. Helene came, with a sudden shuddering convulsion that soaked her underpants and made her knees weak.

The music stopped. Barbie fell on the couch, panting for breath. Helene lowered herself gingerly into a chair. She was still shaking. "That was great," Barbie enthused. "Hey, you must think I'm awful!" She reached for her bra and blouse. "I don't feel embarrassed with you," she said, suddenly serious. "You're just like a big sister to me. I don't know how I'll ever thank you, Helene."

Helene regained her composure. Thank God for that orgasm. Now she'd get through the rest of the day without doing anything stupid. She could blow everything if she wasn't careful. "You were terrific," she said. "Just remember what you felt like and project it, that's all the thanks I want."

They spent the rest of the afternoon on exercises and walking. "Let that gorgeous ass move," Helene told her. "But not too much. Don't give it away, baby. Make 'em pay for it." Then, just before Barbie left, Helene asked for directions to her house.

"Take the Orient Heights line to the Revere Beach stop," Barbie said. "I'll meet you there."

"Okay. Anything I can bring?"

"No, nothing but yourself." Barbie paused for a moment and bit her lower lip. "Listen, Helene. Our house isn't very

62

fancy. Daddy doesn't make a lot of money and my folks are kind of old-fashioned . . ."

Helene grabbed her arm in a grip so tight it cut off the rest of the words. "Don't you ever apologize to me or anybody else for what you come from! Not ever, do you hear me!" Barbie nodded. Helene still didn't let go. "This business you're going into, it's tough and lousy. Most of it stinks. The money's great and it's a super ego trip, Barbie, but if you let it change you, then none of that's worth it."

"I won't," Barbie said. "I'm sorry for what I said."

"Okay. Just remember the kid who didn't want to change her name from Korman to Cole. That's my Barbie. I don't want her to go away."

SUNDAY WAS A BITTER COLD DECEMBER DAY. HELENE GOT OFF the subway car wearing a fitted black coat with a mink collar and hood. She carried a mink muff and wore black suede ankle boots with mink cuffs. She looked like nothing that had ever walked up Shirley Avenue. Barbie escorted her past Izzy's and Arthur's Creamery and the Shirley Drug and wished the stores were open so more people would see her beautiful friend.

Helene seemed to read her thoughts. "I thought Saturday was the Jewish sabbath. I expected everything to be open here today."

"None of the people here are Orthodox," Barbie explained. "At least very few. Mostly we're all pretty Americanized." She hesitated, then screwed up her courage. "Do you mind if I ask what religion you are? I know you said you were Lebanese, but I'm afraid I don't know what that means."

"It can mean either Christian or Muslim. My family are Christians."

"Are you a Catholic?"

"Me? Hell no. I gave up being anything years ago. My family are Catholics, though. Maronite rite."

Barbie didn't bother to ask what Maronite rite meant. She told Helene a little about Maria instead. The other woman was astounded that young girls still entered convents. "I thought that all went out years ago," she said.

Sophie greeted her guest effusively. Moe tried to keep his eyes from popping. "Take Helene's things," Sophie said. "Put them on the bed."

Moe did as he was told. Helene handed him her muff as well as her coat, but she hung on to the wrapped bottle that had been cached inside it. "Barbie said I wasn't to bring anything, but my mother would roll over in her grave if I came to your house for a meal emptyhanded."

Sophie smiled in understanding and took the gift. It was red wine, and she graciously served it with the eye roast and potato *kugel*. She didn't like the wine, however. It wasn't sweet like Jewish wine. *Goyishe* taste, she thought. But she was too polite to say anything.

Moe didn't like the wine either, but he drank three small glasses almost automatically. He hardly tasted it or the food. Finally Sophie made him a decent meal again, and he was so distracted he couldn't enjoy it. Women like this he didn't see even in Filene's shoe department. "Do you mind if I ask where you got your boots?" he asked at one point. "It's a professional question, you understand. I'm in the business."

"Bonwit's," Helene said. Then she grinned at him and reached across the table to pour more wine. Her knitted dress had a V neck and when she bent forward Moe had a view of her breasts. "I shouldn't admit to buying from the competition," Helene said. "Barbie told me you're with Filene's."

The way she said it made him feel like a big shot. "Yes," he agreed. "And next time you need shoes you come to me. For you there'll be a discount."

By five o'clock it was dark, and Sophie put the lights on in the living room and they left the kitchen and went to sit on the faded furniture she'd bought secondhand when she first got married. "Let me help you with the dishes before I go," Helene said.

"Forget it. We'll do them later. Barbie and I get through them in no time."

Helene looked questioningly at Barbie. The girl said, "Mama, I told you I have to go back to Boston with Helene. The hairdresser's coming. Remember?"

"Yes, of course. I'm a little dizzy from that wine."

"Boston?" Moe asked. "So how will you get home? It'll be late."

"It's all right, Daddy. I'm a big girl now."

"It's not all right you should ride the subway alone late at night."

Helene took a deep breath and held it. Then she spoke. "I've been thinking the same thing," she said softly. "But this hairdresser is someone special. And it's the only time I could get him to come." That was true. She hadn't planned all this, it just happened. "I wonder if you'd allow Barbie to spend the night with me at my place? She can come home tomorrow afternoon at the usual time."

Sophie looked doubtful; she never slept properly until she knew Barbie was in her bed. But Moe spoke first. "Good idea. If you wouldn't mind, of course."

"I wouldn't mind," Helene said.

Moe smiled at his wife. The presence of the blonde and the wine combined to make him feel like a young man. Just as well if Barbie was out of the house tonight.

"SHE WAS MADE FOR THE SASSOON CUT," LARRY SAID. "GOD! Look at those bones."

Helene smiled. "If you weren't one of the girls, I'd say she turned you on," she told him. They looked at each other and laughed.

"I know she turns *you* on," Larry said. He saw the expression on Barbie's face and realized that most of the banter was over her head. "You're gorgeous, darling," he told her. "And I'm going to make you even more so."

"I don't know, Larry." Helene crossed the room and lifted Barbie's heavy bronze hair in her hands. "It's so spectacular. Maybe we shouldn't go for anything so short."

"Nonsense. Redheads are on every agent's list. Her quality is something else. She doesn't need long hair to emphasize it."

In the end Helene bowed to his skill, and Larry started cutting. Barbie sat very still with her eyes closed, afraid to look in the hand mirror Helene had put on the kitchen table. He cut it wet, then took an electric hand dryer out of his small suitcase. "Now for the blow job, darling. Are you ready?"

Barbie's eyes opened wide in shock. Helene was surprised that she understood. "Don't pay any attention to him," she said, taking Barbie's hand. "Larry's got a filthy mouth."

He danced around her with the dryer and the brush, humming softly under his breath. Finally he was finished. "Jesus," he said. "Even I don't believe it."

Her hair was a shaped cap that clung to her head like a metallic helmet. A small fringe kissed her forehead and her tiny flat ears. The amber eyes and the yard-long lashes stood out in startling relief, as did the high cheekbones. "I didn't realize before, but her mouth is a little too wide," Larry said. "It's a good thing. It makes her look real. Otherwise she'd just be too perfect."

"It's sexier," Helene agreed. "Larry, you're a sonofabitch, but a genius."

"Can I look?" Barbie asked.

Helene handed her the mirror. Barbie stared for a moment. Then her eyes filled with tears. "Thank you," she said softly.

"Don't cry, darling. It's hell on your looks." Larry started putting away his tools.

"Leave them," Helene said. "We need you at nine-thirty tomorrow morning."

"Sorry, love. No can do. I've got another appointment. There's a divine boy whose hair I've promised to style."

"Screw him," Helene said.

"I intend to."

"Larry, please. John Kramer's going to do her first shots tomorrow. I want you to go over her hair before we leave for his studio. It'll only take half an hour."

"Okay," he agreed reluctantly. "But only for you. And only so Barbie will remember me when she's big-time."

After he left, Barbie turned to Helene with a look of dismay. "Were you telling him the truth or was it just a story so he'd come?"

"About Kramer, you mean? It's the truth."

"Oh, God!" Barbie sat down and doubled over, holding her hands across her stomach. "I can't, Helene, I'm not ready. I get so nervous before things like this. I told you that."

"Yes. That's why I didn't warn you before." She knelt beside the girl. "You'll do fine, baby. You're ready, trust me."

Barbie put her arms around Helene's neck and leaned on her shoulder. "I'm scared."

Helene was trembling. She made herself pull away. "C'mon. A good face scrub and then to bed. You need your beauty sleep. I'll make you some camomile tea for a nightcap."

Barbie came out of the bathroom a few minutes later. She'd brought a pair of baby-doll pajamas with her. Her legs appeared to start somewhere around her waist. Helene looked at them with something like awe, and at the little fuzz of hair that showed below the brief pajama pants. She needed to do a bikini strip on Barbie, but she kept putting it off because she didn't trust herself. "Here." She handed the cup of tea to the girl. "You take the bed. I'll sleep on the couch."

The bedroom wasn't really separate, just a sleeping alcove divided from the living room by a screen of silver beads. Barbie looked over to it and said, "Sleep with me. It's a double bed." She heard Helene's sharp intake of breath, but misinterpreted it. "Please," she said softly. "As if we were sisters,

Helene. I like to pretend that. And I don't want to be alone tonight."

Helene put on the Mother Hubbard flannel nightgown she only wore if she had a cold or menstrual cramps. She scrubbed her face and creamed it and poured hot oil on her hair and wrapped it in a turban. I'm not seducing her, she said to herself grimly. I'm not. When she went into the alcove, Barbie was already in bed with the down quilt pulled up to her chin.

Helene got in beside her and lay rigid, afraid to touch any part of Barbie. She could smell the child's scent. It was composed of lemon and vanilla in equal parts, like an infant's.

They put out the lights. Helene willed herself to go to sleep.

"Is Larry a queer?" Barbie asked suddenly. Her voice was a sibilant whisper in the dark.

"Yes," Helene said through clenched teeth.

"I'm sorry about that. I like him."

"What?"

"I don't mean like a boyfriend. I mean he's nice, so I'm sorry he's sick."

Helene rolled over on her stomach and gripped the pillow. "He's not sick. He's perfectly happy. There's no goddamn crime in being gay."

"I know this Catholic priest. He told me—"

"Shut up!" Helene said. Her fury almost choked her. "Don't tell me what any goddamn celibate says about fucking. If they weren't all afraid of being queer themselves, they'd never become priests."

Barbie was used to Helene's language by now. It didn't shock her anymore, but the thought that Father DiAnni might be queer did. She thought about it for a while, then decided it wasn't possible. "Helene, are you asleep?"

"No, but I'm trying."

"I want to ask you something. I've never had the courage to ask anyone before. What's a blow job? I know it's something dirty, but I don't know what."

Helene groaned. "Forget it," she whispered. "You're too young, you wouldn't understand. Go to sleep."

"I can't, I'm too nervous." She reached out a tentative hand and found Helene's. She needed human contact, warmth to make the demons in her stomach go away. "Feel this," she said, pulling Helene's hand on to her belly. "It's rolling as if I'd eaten three hot fudge sundaes. That always happens when I get scared. It'll be like that tomorrow. I know it will."

Helene felt the taut muscles of Barbie's stomach; the

warmth of her skin burned through the thin cotton pajamas. "Baby, listen," she said. "There's things you don't understand. About men and women, about me. I want to protect you, but I don't know what the hell you really want."

"I want to be like you," Barbie said. "I've never met anyone like you before. You're so beautiful and so sure of yourself." She rolled onto her side and pushed her body against Helene's. "I wish I could sleep," she said. "I know I'll look terrible if I don't. I'm just so nervous."

Helene swallowed hard. "I know a way to relax you. I'll give you a massage." She allowed herself to stroke Barbie's buttocks. They rose from the hollow of her back with a kind of insouciance, two proud little hills that told the world, I don't give a damn. Helene slid the pajama pants down to Barbie's knees and pushed the top up to her shoulders. Careful, she told herself; this is therapy, nothing more.

Barbie sighed appreciatively. "That feels wonderful."

They'd cracked the window, despite the cold, and left the curtains open. Outside a neon sign flickered and made intermittent bands of light across the bed. Helene studied the texture of Barbie's skin and watched her hand moving over the elegant buttocks. Her own skin was drenched in sweat beneath the flannel nightgown. "Turn over," she whispered. "I'll do your tummy."

"That's where I feel the worst," Barbie said. "I've got this lump right in my stomach."

"Tension," Helene said. "Hold on, I'm going to try something." She fumbled in the night table drawer and a few seconds later Barbie heard a faint electronic humming.

"Hey, you're using the vibrator, the one we use for facials. What a great idea. It feels marvelous."

She relaxed and her thighs opened slightly. Helene saw the delicate pink flesh surrounded by bronze curls. In the dimness she couldn't be sure, but she thought she saw a little moisture dewing the flared lips. Her tongue darted out of her mouth and she longed to flick it gently over the precious area her ministrations had exposed. Instead she let the vibrator move down and touch the insides of Barbie's thighs. She waited, but the only thing Barbie did was sigh.

"Baby, I want you to try something. Here, take the vibrator." Helene pushed it into Barbie's limp fingers. "Use it yourself. Move it around to wherever it feels best."

Barbie held the vibrator against her belly, moving it in widening circles. "I've never felt anything like this before. Boy, you sure have ideas."

Helene placed the tips of her fingers lightly over the back of Barbie's hand. Not guiding, not influencing in any way, just waiting and feeling. "Can I ask you something personal?" she murmured.

"Sure, anything you want." The voice lazy and soft, fogged by incipient sleep and a growing sense of pleasure.

"When you were little, in the bathtub maybe, or in bed, did you ever touch yourself between the legs?"

Barbie turned her face to Helene's, trying to see her in the darkened room. "No, I never thought of it. Do most little girls do that?"

"Lots of them. It's perfectly natural. It's a great way to relax. I just thought, well, since you get so tense and nervous, maybe . . ."

"Yes," Barbie whispered. "I understand what you mean, but I don't even know how."

Gently, Helene guided Barbie's hand a little lower, causing it to bring the vibrator in contact with the tender skin between thigh and pubis. Barbie shivered. "Take it easy," Helene said softly. "You're not doing anything wrong. Only relaxing. It's harmless. Put it over to the right a little. Here, like this. Not inside. You're still a virgin, aren't you, baby?"

Barbie nodded. She was unable to speak. She didn't understand what she was feeling, only that it was different from anything she'd ever felt before. And that she couldn't stop now.

"This has nothing to do with what men and women do," Helene said. "It's not screwing, don't worry about that. It's just a woman thing. A nice thing, that's good for you." Her voice was a caress. Her lips were almost on Barbie's cheek and her hand was surer now, more firm in its guidance. "Move it up," she whispered. "It's your clit you want to touch. That's where the best feelings are."

Barbie didn't know what a clit was, or that she had one. She only knew that when Helene positioned the vibrator where she wanted it, there was a sudden, extraordinary surge of feeling. Barbie gasped aloud. She would have moved the vibrator away, but Helene was holding it firmly in place now. "Trust me," Helene whispered. "Trust me and let yourself go. You're going to come. Be a good baby and let it happen."

And in a few seconds, she did. Shuddering and gasping and feeling as if she were going to burst right open, and afterwards

69

more relaxed than she'd ever been in her life. And embarrassed. "Do you think I'm awful?" she asked in a small voice. "I don't know what happened to me."

"Just what's supposed to happen," Helene told her. "It's perfectly natural, like I said." She had trouble controlling her own voice because she'd come too, just watching. And she felt a little ashamed, because it was a kind of seduction, no doubt about it. But it wasn't a crime, goddamn it. And it *was* perfectly natural.

She took the vibrator away and pulled up the bottoms of Barbie's pajamas. "Go to sleep, baby. You're beautiful and I love you. And the whole world is going to love you pretty soon. Just go to sleep."

Before she dropped off, Barbie remembered what Father DiAnni had said about Helene. He was right, but he was wrong. There wasn't anything sick about it, and it felt good.

3

HELENE WOKE BARBIE AT SIX A.M. AND SUBJECTED HER to a bikini strip, using hot wax to remove any pubic hair that showed where her thighs and torso met. Again Helene longed to taste that gorgeous virgin pussy, but she wasn't going to push her luck. Not today of all days. Last night was enough. It was more than she'd hoped for and it would last her for a while. She remembered what she'd been told by the first woman who went down on her: "One suck doesn't make you gay." Maybe Barbie would develop a taste for woman-love, and maybe she wouldn't. Helene was determined that it would be the girl's own choice.

She dressed Barbie in a russet-colored leotard that exactly matched her eyes. Larry came in and looked at her and whistled. Barbie glowed with pleasure, and he glanced from her to Helene, then gave a knowing wink. "Just do her hair," Helene said.

"Be nice to me," Larry whined. "If you're not I'll tell Ann and she'll scratch your eyes out."

Helene winced. He hadn't been in town a week and he already knew the name of the lover she'd put on ice while she concentrated on Barbie. "I'm working," she said. "Ann understands that. Now for chrissake do her hair. We're supposed to be at Kramer's place in forty-five minutes."

The photographer's studio terrified Barbie. She took one look at the vast space and the assortment of lights and cameras, and blanched. "Okay, baby," Helene said, taking her hand. "Don't let me down. Get hold of yourself." To Kramer she said, "She works great with music. Put something on."

"What's your pleasure, gorgeous?" he asked Barbie.

"I don't know. What's the piece you played for me, Helene?"

Helene went to the phonograph and flicked through the stack of records. The Beethoven sonata wasn't there, but she found a Chopin nocturne. "This'll do fine," she said.

They waited in silence. Then Barbie started to move.

The photographer watched her for a moment, his eyes narrowed and his fingers tapping a nervous counterpoint to the rhythm. "Right," he whispered. "Oh yes, right." He reached for a camera, screwed on a Nikkor wide-angle lens, and murmured. "Over this way, gorgeous. That's it. Just keep doing what you're doing." He didn't stop shooting until the music ended. "She's fantastic," he told Helene. "Let's see what this does for her." He changed the record and the raucous new sound of the Chubby Checkers hit "The Twist" filled the studio. At first Barbie seemed confused, then she caught the beat and swayed with it. Kramer moved with her, two figures in a tribal rite.

"I'll have the proofs ready day after tomorrow," he told Helene.

"You think they'll be good?"

"Good? She's the greatest thing since Vaseline. Every cock in the U.S.A. will grease up for her."

In March Barbie had her first modeling job. It was for a brochure promoting the virtues of Boston as history city. She posed under signs identifying the Freedom Trail, walked along India Wharf in a trenchcoat, stood outside Faneuil Hall wearing a sexy version of Pilgrim dress, and finally climbed to the top of the State House to be photographed in silhouette against the dome. She hadn't eaten for three days before the job started and when it was over she retched her empty insides into Helene's toilet for half an hour. Finally she was calm—and starving. Helene made steaks and went out and bought chocolate milk shakes at the ice cream place on the corner.

Barbie finished her steak in five minutes, then took her shake and perched on the windowsill so she could look down on Charles Street. The weather had turned unseasonably warm, and the window was open. The sounds and smells of the city filled the apartment. "I love Boston," she said. "I never want to live anywhere else. I don't even want to stay in Revere. Why can't I move in here with you?"

Helene was afraid to speak. There had been a few more "massages" ending with the vibrator, but she still hadn't gone any further with Barbie, and she still didn't think the girl understood what was happening. To Helene it seemed that Barbie regarded their activities as beauty therapy, like a facial or a manicure, something to relax her when she got nervous. But Helene was wrong; it wasn't like that.

So many new things were happening to Barbie. She had little time to sort out her reactions. She'd always known she was pretty, gorgeous even. That's the word her family always used. Barbie's gorgeous, they said. Now strangers, *goyim*, who should know about such things, used a different word. They said she was beautiful. Beautiful meant like in movies and magazines. Beautiful meant a world entirely different than anything she'd ever known or envisioned in her future. It implied a kind of responsibility, dramatic things to live up to. Sometimes she thought that her newly wakened sensuality was part of that. More often she knew it wasn't. The things she felt when Helene touched her were of a different order and had little to do with her looks.

At least she couldn't get pregnant. That's mostly what Sophie's dutiful sex education had taught her. The man sticks his thing in the woman and it's nice and it feels good, but you can get pregnant from even just once and that's why you mustn't do it until you're married. And if you let a boy pet with you, he'll lose control and want to do it and say you're a tease. And afterwards he won't have any respect for you. And if, God forbid, you shouldn't be a virgin when you get married, your husband will throw it in your face every time you have a fight. All this wisdom Barbie had assimilated and understood. But nothing Sophie ever said prepared her for Helene, or for her own suddenly demanding sexuality.

Sometimes she tried to imagine a man—tall, dark, and handsome, naturally—doing the things to her that Helene did. Would she prefer that? Would it feel different? Better? She didn't know, and not knowing was scaring her to death. But each time Helene caressed her, she forgot her fear in the pure pleasure of her feelings. Maybe she had what Father DiAnni called unnatural desires.

Barbie thought of discussing it with the priest, but the mere idea made her choke with embarrassment. The reality would be impossible. Maybe if Maria were around . . . No, she probably couldn't even talk to Maria about this. Certainly not to Sophie. Her mother would be hysterical and demand that Barbie immediately end her relationship with Helene. So there was nobody to talk to, she'd just have to muddle through on her own.

"What are you looking so dreamy about?" Helene asked. "Stop building fairy castles about Boston. You're headed for the big time, baby. The cover of *Vogue,* a four-page spread in *Harpers Bazaar.* Just you wait. New York, that's where you're going to be."

Barbie had almost forgotten what they were talking about. Helene's words jerked her back to reality. "New York terrifies me! Will you come? I won't do it unless you come too."

"I'm your agent, I go where you go."

And that's the problem, Barbie thought. Aloud she said, "That's all right then." Which was also true. Sex aside, she couldn't go on with her career without Helene. It was unthinkable. And if she wasn't a cover girl, what would she be?

The phone rang and Helene went to answer it, then came back beaming. "What did I tell you? That was Mary Starkman at Bonwit's. They're doing a special photographic window display for Easter. Big blow-ups. And whose pictures do they want to use?" She reached over and wrapped Barbie in an enormous hug. "My baby's, that's whose."

Two days after the pictures went on display in Bonwit's windows, Barbie was summoned to an interview with Jason Gilbert. Helene was ecstatic. "He's a big agent. Right now he's representing Saks Fifth Avenue. He thinks they might want to use you for their winter catalog. They're going to shoot it next month in South Dakota."

"Next month is only May!" Barbie said.

Helene laughed. "Baby, you've got so much to learn sometimes even I'm astounded. We meet with Gilbert next Wednesday afternoon."

Only it wasn't we, as it turned out. Barbie had to go alone. Tuesday morning she got to the apartment to find Helene running a fever of a hundred and three. There was a doctor's office next door, and Barbie went and brought him back. "Flu," he announced. "But on its way to being pneumonia. You stay in bed and drink plenty of fluids, and take these." He wrote out a prescription and handed it to Barbie to have filled. "If you try anything foolish, Mrs. Wentworth, you're going to be a very sick lady. Maybe a dead one."

Helene sent Barbie home and told her to stay there until she went to Gilbert's office the following afternoon. Flu was contagious. "Just let him do the talking and look at you," Helene said. "Tell him I'm sick, but I'll call him Thursday morning. Tell him I make all the business arrangements."

Barbie agreed and reluctantly left. Helene telephoned Sophie and told her what had happened. "You get her dressed for the appointment, Sophie. Have her wear the beige knit dress. That's a Saks model, isn't it?"

"Yeah, twenty-two dollars in the basement. With the Saks label still in. You think I should go with her?"

Helene considered the idea and rejected it. She loved Sophie, but Jason Gilbert wasn't ready for her. "No. She's got to learn to do it alone sometime. Don't try and make her eat anything tonight or tomorrow. She only throws it all up. Just tea until after the interview. Then she'll eat like a horse."

GILBERT'S OFFICE WAS ON ARLINGTON STREET. BARBIE GOT AS far as the corner, then decided she couldn't go on. Not just yet. She wasn't due at the place for fifteen minutes anyway. She went into a drugstore and asked for an Alka-Seltzer. After it came she realized she shouldn't drink it. She might sit at Mr. Gilbert's desk and burp all through the interview. She stared at the fizzing liquid; fear was a knot of ice in her stomach and a clammy feeling all over her skin.

When she turned away from the soda fountain, she found herself looking into a pair of blue eyes that were openly and avidly staring at her. That's how she met Normie Gold.

"I'm at B.U.," he told her. "A junior."

"And you play, let me guess, football." She eyed his letter sweater. It had to mean football. Normie Gold was something over six feet, with shoulders nearly as broad. And good looking. Brown wavy hair to go with the blue eyes. Only the nose and the name proclaimed him Jewish.

"Yeah, football," he agreed. "And what do you play?" He moved closer and propped one muscular buttock on the stool next to hers. The boy behind the counter approached. "Two cokes," Normie said quickly. Then he turned back to Barbie. "Okay? Would you rather have something else?"

"Nothing for me, thank you. I'm a model. I'm on my way to an appointment right now. I have to go."

She started to leave, but Normie extended a hand to stop her. "You're the most gorgeous thing I've ever seen. You can't just walk out. What time is your appointment?"

"Three."

"It's only ten of." He looked at his watch, but didn't show it to her. "Just take a minute more and tell me your name."

"Barbie."

"Barbie what?" The blue eyes continued to devour her.

Barbie giggled. She couldn't help it, he was like a puppy. In a minute he'd be licking her hand. "Just Barbie," she said, not knowing why she was bothering to flirt.

"Magic. A princess from fairyland. Only mortals have last names."

"They teach a pretty good line at B.U.," she said, still laughing. "Now, Mr. Football, I have to go. 'Bye."

This time she did get off the stool and walk to the door. Normie Gold followed her, still pleading. "Hey, please wait! You've got to tell me your phone number. At least your address."

Barbie glanced up at the clock over the door. It said five after three. Oh, God! "No time," she called over her shoulder and ran into the street.

Gold started to follow her, but the voice of the boy behind the counter stopped him. "Hey, bud! You ordered two Cokes, you gonna pay or what?"

Gold could feel the accusing eyes of everyone in the crowded drugstore. Reluctantly he turned back, fished some coins from his pocket, and flung them on the counter. "Keep the change," he said louder than necessary. Then he rushed outside.

Arlington Street was a surging tide of shoppers and students, but the girl was not among them. Cursing softly under his breath, he stood where he was for a moment, poised on the balls of his feet, ready to run after her if only he knew the direction she'd taken. Finally he saw a flash of red hair about two blocks ahead and plunged into the crowd. But seconds later he was cut off by half a dozen shavenheaded men wearing orange robes and banging tambourines.

"Hare Krishna, Hare Krishna, Krishna Krishna, Hare Hare," they chanted, seeming to surround him. It was weird, like some damned foreign movie with meaningless symbols and obstacles. And nobody saying anything in plain English.

"Get out of my way!"

The robed figures melted to either side, opening a path, but there was nothing ahead of him. Barbie, if it had been her, had disappeared. "Shit!" Gold said. He turned belligerently to face the religious kooks, but they'd disappeared too, as suddenly as

76

they'd arrived. He could hear their tambourines and their chant, but they'd turned a corner and passed out of his life. Like the exquisite creature he'd been pursuing.

Gold cursed again and started to walk away, but a woman stepped into his path. "Wait," she commanded.

Normie stared at her. He couldn't tell her age or what she looked like because she was dressed entirely in black, with a black kerchief covering her hair, and very dark sunglasses. "Wait," she repeated. "If you want to see her again, wait."

The woman seemed to have a foreign accent of some kind, but Gold couldn't identify it. He kept staring at her, but she wasn't looking at him, she was fumbling in her bag for paper and pencil. Something about the whole thing mesmerized him and he stood there mute, unable to guess what might happen next.

"Here," she said finally. Again the intimation of an accent, but only that one word. Gold looked down at the scrap of paper she'd thrust into his hand. BARBARA KORMAN was written across the top in block capitals. Underneath was an address in Revere.

"How do you know her?" he demanded, looking up. He was talking to himself; the woman was gone. For a few seconds he felt dizzy and disoriented. The last half hour had been some kind of dream sequence, a drama manufactured entirely in his head. Maybe somebody had put something in his Coke. Only he had the piece of paper, didn't he? It was real. And so was the information it contained. The princess was real too. She was Barbie Korman of Revere. And she lived on Shirley Avenue. That was a good omen. She had to be Jewish, with that name and address. Which meant that she wasn't entirely out of his realm.

Gold folded the paper carefully and put it in his pocket. Then he walked away whistling.

"I DON'T BELIEVE IT," HELENE SAID. "YOU MET SOME JOCK AND because of him you didn't keep the appointment?"

"Not exactly." Barbie's voice was a faint murmur. Her hands were balled into tight little fists. "It wasn't his fault. We just got talking and I forgot the time. Afterwards, when I realized, it was after three o'clock. I ran all the way to Mr. Gilbert's office, but they said he'd left for the day."

Helene's face was as white as the pillowcase, and faint lines showed around her eyes. She looked tired as well as ill, old, and used up. When she didn't say anything, but just kept staring, Barbie added, "You know how nervous I get, Helene. I guess maybe I was just looking for an excuse not to face the interview."

"Jesus," Helene muttered through clenched teeth. "I still don't believe it. You're kidding me, aren't you, baby?"

Barbie shook her head in misery.

"You little cunt, you lousy cock-sucking little whore! How could you do it to me? After everything I've done for you, I crap out one day and you blow it all!" The curses were delivered in a rising crescendo. "Why?" she screamed finally. "Just frigging why?"

Barbie didn't say anything. She started to cry, but even her tears were silent.

Helene watched her for a moment, then reached for the phone. The call didn't do any good. Gilbert's secretary said he'd already left for South Dakota. They were starting to shoot early because a thaw was setting in and the snow was melting. The secretary promised to tell Mr. Gilbert that Mrs. Wentworth had called. Helene hung up and left her pale hand on the receiver, staring at it as if it belonged to someone else. "My nail polish is always chipping," she said tonelessly. "I think I'd better change my brand." Barbie looked up, unsure what change of mood the remark signaled.

"You blew it," Helene said. "Gilbert's shooting the catalog with his original choice of model. You were just a possible last-minute addition because he was impressed after the Bonwit's thing. You blew it, Barbie. A chance that half the women in the world would sell their clits for, and you fucked it up."

"I'm sorry, Helene; what else can I say?"

Helene's tone was conversational, as if she was discussing the weather. "Tell me, did you fuck the jock, or just talk to him for half an hour while you bitched up my life?"

"Helene! Don't, oh, please don't." Barbie's voice was a wail, a lament that echoed round the room. She doubled over, gripping her stomach and sobbing in loud gasps. Helene watched her for a moment, then sighed and struggled out of bed to take the girl in her arms.

"Okay, baby. Okay. It's over and done with. We'll forget it and move on to better things." She stroked Barbie's hair and her cheeks, pulled her closer and fondled her breasts and her buttocks. Eventually she put her hand under the girl's skirt and began rubbing her pubis gently while she crooned wordless noises of comfort.

NORMIE GOLD TELEPHONED BARBIE FOUR DAYS AFTER THEY met. "Hi, remember me? The guy in the drugstore."

Barbie remembered. She shuddered slightly and hung on to the receiver. "How did you get my number?" She'd only told him her first name.

"I've got sources," he said with a smug laugh. "I'm not likely to let a chick like you get away, now am I?"

"I don't know what you're likely to do. I don't even know you."

"That's why I'm calling. We should know each other better before I ask you to marry me." Despite herself, Barbie chuckled. It was a line, but an amusing one. "Besides," Normie continued, "I didn't tell you what time I'm picking you up Saturday night."

"That's because you're not," Barbie said. "I'm a model. I work hard. I don't date."

He pleaded and cajoled for a while, but she was adamant. "I have an exercise session Saturday afternoon," she told him. "I don't get home until after six and I'm exhausted by then. Thank you for calling, Norman, and good-bye."

"Wait," he yelled. "Don't hang up just yet. Say my name again. Just once more, please."

"Good-bye, Norman."

"That's terrific," he said with a sigh. "Everybody else calls me Normie; when you say Norman it's terrific. Good night, sweetheart. I'll be seeing you soon."

"Who was that?" Sophie demanded when she hung up.

"A guy I met in Boston."

"What guy? You didn't tell me."

Barbie had told her mother nothing of the fiasco, just allowed her to believe that she didn't get the Saks job because Mr. Gilbert didn't hire her. "Just a guy, Mama. It's nothing, don't make a big deal out of it."

"His name's Norman?"

"Yes, Norman Gold."

"He's Jewish?"

"I suppose so. He's a junior at B.U. He's on the football team."

Sophie looked skeptical. "You're sure his name's Gold?"

"No, Mama." Barbie sighed. "I'm not sure. I don't really care what his name is. You were listening. You heard what I told him."

That was true. "Yes," Sophie said with satisfaction. "I

heard. Probably he's a *shlemiel*. You don't need him, you've got your career."

Moe had listened too. Later he said to his wife, "Barbie's a young girl, a baby yet. You think it's good for her she doesn't see any young people, have any fun?"

"For a career like Barbie's gonna have, you got to make sacrifices," Sophie said. "Helene knows what she's doing. She loves Barbie."

Moe was silent. He went into the living room and opened the newspaper. Moe was a great reader of newspapers. He got both the *Globe* and the *Record* and they remained for months in a stack in the corner by his chair. Moe never threw out a paper until he was sure he'd read every word. Now he put down today's edition and reached into the pile for a November Sunday issue. He found what he wanted on the sports page. It was a description of a game B.U. played against Rutgers. B.U. lost, but in the line-up Moe found the name N. Gold listed as playing right tackle.

SATURDAY NIGHT WHEN SHE GOT OFF THE SUBWAY, HE WAS waiting for her. Barbie saw him lounging by the exit. Normie saw her at the same moment. "I told you I'd see you tonight," he said, reaching her side in three long strides.

"And I told you I'd be tired. Go away and leave me alone, Norman."

"No chance. I love you."

"You're crazy."

"Maybe. I still love you." He took her hands and held them away from her sides. "You're the most beautiful thing I've ever seen," he said, studying her.

Barbie's face was scrubbed free of any makeup. She wore the long-legged black leotard she'd worked in all afternoon and a black cotton poplin trenchcoat belted casually over it. She had on sneakers and no socks. It was a warm night, warmer than usual for the first week in May. Sometimes on Saturday evening she went back to Helene's after her exercise class. When she did that she usually stayed the night. This week that plan was canceled because Helene was still not feeling really well. And because Helene had remained cool to her since the argument. Barbie was being punished. She knew and understood it, but she still felt rejected and miserable.

"I meant what I said, Norman," she told him. "I'm a very hard-working girl. I don't date."

"Okay, but what are you going to do right now?"

"Go home, have a bath and something to eat, and go to bed."

"I'll drive you home. My car's across the street."

She looked at him. As well as a marvelous build and that nice wavy brown hair, he had a thin but perfectly shaped mouth. If it wasn't for the nose, he'd be a pretty-boy type. "Okay," she sighed. "I don't live far. But you're not coming in."

For answer Gold grinned and escorted her across the subway platform and up to the street. His car was a Thunderbird. It was bright red with a lot of chrome and the seats were covered in fake leopard skin. There was a *mezzuzah* hanging on a silver chain from the rearview mirror. He wore jeans and a white shirt open at the neck. Tonight the B.U. letter sweater was tied nonchalantly around his shoulders. When he bent to help her into the car, she saw a gold Star of David swinging around his neck. Helene was right: a jock. But a Jewish jock. Sophie needn't have worried.

He started the Thunderbird with a roar, but didn't obey her instruction to turn up Shirley Avenue. Instead he headed north on Ocean Avenue. "Hey," Barbie said, "you're going the wrong way."

"You're being kidnapped, relax and enjoy it."

She hunched into the corner and nursed her anger in silence. There was no point in arguing with him until he'd played out his silly little game.

After a few minutes he cut onto the boulevard and continued until he was in the section close to the Lynn border known as Point of Pines. It was a small enclave where expensive houses had been built by Revere Jews who made their money in the days before they were comfortable in towns farther up the coast like Marblehead and Swampscott. "Do you mind telling me what you have in mind?" Barbie asked stiffly.

"Just what you asked for, a bath and something to eat," he said, grinning. "At least that's the part I'm willing to admit." He turned right down a narrow lane as he spoke. For a moment Barbie thought he was going to drive them straight into the ocean. Then he stopped, and she saw two houses built side by side almost on the beach.

"Do you live here?"

"No, I don't." Normie was suddenly serious; she could see his pale eyes looking at her intently in the fading evening light. "I live in Chelsea, Barbie. This is my uncle's house."

Chelsea was a world away from Point of Pines, it was like Shirley Avenue. Barbie understood what he was trying to say. For the first time she felt kindly toward him. "Okay, I've got it. What will your uncle think of us arriving like this?"

"Nothing, he's not there. He and my aunt and the Cohens from next door are on a cruise. I know where the key is, though."

"I don't know," she said hesitantly.

"It's okay. We're not doing anything bad. They leave the key specially for me. So I can work out in the pool."

Reluctantly, too tired to argue, she followed him into the house. He had a big paper bag in his arms and when they got inside he wagged his head toward a door on the right. "You'll find everything you want in there. I'll drop this stuff in the kitchen."

She didn't move. "What is it?"

"Some things for supper. I figured you'd be hungry." He tried to make it sound like bravado, but it came out sheepish.

Knowing he'd planned the whole thing made her smile. He was like a little boy, and he had gone to a lot of trouble. She still didn't move toward the door he'd indicated. "I've got to call home," she said. "My mother will be frantic."

"There's a phone in there too."

She told Sophie she was with Norman Gold, at his uncle's house in Point of Pines. She even gave her the address and the telephone number. "I'll be home before midnight, Mama, don't worry." She didn't report that the family who owned the house was not at home.

Only after she hung up did Barbie inspect the room. It was a bedroom, but it looked impersonal. A guest room, probably. The furniture was finished in antique white with gold trim, the walls were covered in wallpaper with a gold embossed design, and there were red velvet bedspreads on the twin beds. She opened another door and found herself in a bathroom tiled in red with matching fixtures. The shower curtain was gold lamé over a plastic liner. Taking it all in, Barbie couldn't decide what she thought. Everything was all very expensive and luxurious, but the room didn't please her eye the way Helene's flat did. She pushed away the thought of Helene and stripped off her coat and her leotard and turned on the shower.

When she came out of the shower, she noticed a white terry cloth robe hanging nearby. She wondered if Norman's planning had included coming here in advance and putting the robe where she'd find it. Maybe that's why there had been fresh towels stacked in the bathroom. He knocked on the door while she was pondering this. "How do you like your steak?"

"Rare," she called back. Like so many other things, it was a taste Helene had taught her.

"I'm in the kitchen when you're ready," Normie said. "Just follow your nose."

The kitchen was straight out of *House Beautiful*. There were acres of oaken cabinets to match the beams in the ceiling. Even the freezer and the refrigerator had doors of oak. The stove top and the sink were set into a center island, also oak, and there were two wall ovens. The lighting fixtures were red glass with brass trim, and the floor was carpeted in red shag. Barbie had never seen a kitchen with a rug. "Your aunt's got some taste," she said.

"Yeah. Later I'll show you the whole house. She had a decorator from New York. The kitchen's supposed to look like an English pub. That's why the bar's in here." He gestured toward a high counter with an oak top and black-upholstered leather sides. A bottle of red wine stood beside two elaborate stemmed glasses. "I opened it. You pour while I finish being chef," he said.

Barbie sipped the wine and made a face. It was very dry, like the stuff Helene drank. She still wasn't used to it. "What does your uncle do?" she asked, while Norman reached into a cupboard for a couple of plates.

"Wholesale ladies' blouses. He and Abe, that's Abe Cohen from next door, started the business twenty years ago. They've got a big place on Kneeland Street now. They do all right."

"So I see. What about you? Are you going to sell ladies' blouses wholesale when you graduate from college?"

"Not exactly." He served the steaks and the salad and put them on a tray with a large bag of Wise Potato Chips. "I didn't take the time to make potatoes," he apologized. "Will these do?"

"Sure. I don't eat potatoes anyway; they're fattening."

She took the wine and the glasses and followed him out of the kitchen into a huge living room. There was no red in here; it was an all-white room with touches of brown and orange. "Who cleans this place?" Barbie asked, looking at the white rug.

"Aunt Sally's got a *shwartze* from Lynn. She comes in three days a week. Besides, they've got no kids. It doesn't get very dirty." He turned and saw that she still held the wine bottle and the glasses. "You didn't have to bring those; look." He opened a shuttered partition and the bar in the kitchen became part of the living room. "They didn't miss a trick in this place. When they started building, people said they were crazy. Nobody ever built on the water side of the street before. But they did it."

"What happens in a storm?" Barbie sat down on the floor by the coffee table—it was glass and chrome and at least six feet square—and attacked her steak.

"Nothing. They built their own breakwater."

She giggled. "Your uncle sounds like he doesn't take no for an answer."

"Neither do I," he said. They both laughed.

"What exactly?" When he looked at her questioningly, she explained, "You said you weren't going to sell ladies' blouses, exactly."

"Oh, that. I'm supposed to go to law school after B.U. My uncle says the business needs a lawyer, not another salesman."

After that they were silent until he said, "You're not eating any potato chips."

"They're greasy. Bad for the complexion."

He reached across and stroked her cheek with the back of his hand. "There's nothing wrong with your complexion. It's like silk."

Barbie didn't answer. She was startled by the strength of her reaction to his touch. Boys had been trying to paw her since she was thirteen. None of them ever made her feel a thing before this. But Norman did. So maybe whatever Helene had awakened in her was transferrable to a man, just as she'd hoped. Barbie trembled slightly, a mixture of relief and hope. She gulped down some wine to cover her feelings, and Normie poured her another glass.

"C'mon," he said when they'd finished eating and put the plates in the dishwasher. "I'll show you around."

They didn't tour the house, though. Instead they walked out to a redwood deck facing the ocean. There was a big pool on one side, Olympic size, Normie explained, and tables and chairs on the other. "I work out here three times a week."

"Because you're on the football team?"

"Yes. I got a football scholarship. Uncle Charlie would have paid my tuition, but the scholarship came up and I took it."

"You wanted to do it on your own, right?"

"Right. Besides, they always say Jews aren't good at sports. But I am. I can do anything with a ball. I'm fast too, even

84

though I'm big. Do the hundred in under eleven seconds." He stopped and looked sheepish. "I sound like a real blowhard, don't I?"

"No, I understand. What does your father do, Norman?"

He turned away from her and stared out at the water. She could see his profile, he wasn't as good-looking that way. He hadn't much chin, and the big nose was dominant. "He's a butcher. That's why the steaks were good. I know all about meat."

Barbie heard the bitterness in his voice. "It's hard work being a butcher. My father sells shoes in Filene's. Upstairs."

Normie faced her and put his hands on her shoulders. "I meant what I said before. I love you."

"You can't love me. We hardly know each other."

"I don't care. I do. I loved you the first second I saw you. Before I spoke to you even."

She almost told him what had happened because he spoke to her, but she didn't. Instead she lifted her face and waited for him to kiss her. She wanted him to, so it would blot out the memory of the consequences of meeting him in the drugstore. He didn't come on hard, the way she half expected him to. His mouth was gentle on hers, and he didn't grab for her the way boys usually did.

The kiss ended quickly. It was almost as if he was afraid. "Would you like to swim?" he asked.

"Won't it be too cold?"

"No, the pool has a heater. I turned it on when we first came in."

She giggled. "You're like your uncle, you think of everything. But I don't. I didn't bring a bathing suit."

"So what? Please, Barbie, I won't hurt you."

She guessed that there were probably bathing suits in the house, and that he knew it as well as she did, but she felt reckless and flushed with the wine. The thought of swimming naked was suddenly irresistible. "Okay," she said. "Turn around until I get in."

Then they were both in the pool, not touching until they'd completed a few hard laps and were lying in the water breathless with exertion. That's when he swam up next to her and put his arms around her waist. "God, you're beautiful," he said.

"How do you know? It's dark, you can't see me."

"I can feel you."

She could feel him too. His body was rock hard and heavy

85

muscled. She liked the sensation of his bigness next to her and she leaned against him for a moment, then she pulled away. "It's getting late. I've got to go home." He started to protest, but she said, "You promised. And if you don't behave, I won't see you again."

He swam to the edge of the pool, pulling her after him, and climbed out. In the moonlight she could see that he had a white tan line. And it was only May. He must use a sunlamp. He bent down and picked up a big towel and spread it open in front of him. "Here, climb up. I'll close my eyes."

"You're a liar, you won't," she said. But she got out of the pool anyway and let him wrap the towel around her and hold her close. He rubbed her briskly for a moment, then his motions changed and he was kissing her again. The towel slipped between them and fell unheeded to the deck.

This kiss was different. He probed with his tongue, and her mouth opened and permitted him access. He was fingering her nipples with one hand; the other was low down on her back, touching her buttocks. After a few seconds she pulled her head away. "I don't put out," she said. She was sorry as soon as the words were spoken. They sounded cheap and teenaged, and not really like her at all.

"Don't you think I know that," he whispered. "I know what kind of a girl you are, Barbie. That's why I love you, and that's why it's okay."

She sighed. A line again. Just when she'd thought maybe he really was special. "I've got to go home." She moved out of his embrace toward the bedroom where she'd left her clothes.

After she was dressed, she went back to the living room. He was waiting for her, looking miserable. "I'm sorry. I wanted it to be terrific and I loused it up."

"It's okay." The look on his face was pitiful. Barbie crossed to him and put her hands on his cheeks. "Really, Norman, it's okay. I understand. And it was a super evening."

He didn't kiss her again, just laid his head on top of hers and held her close for a moment. Barbie felt herself trembling. His tenderness aroused her in a way that groping did not. Once more he was making her feel the way she felt when Helene gave her a massage. Even her thighs were getting sticky. She pressed against his leg. He held her tight, not saying anything. She wanted a lot more, the intimate touch that would result in the explosion of sensation Helene could cause, but she knew better than to indicate her need. That could lead to his doing the other thing. Then she wouldn't be a virgin anymore. Worse, she might get pregnant. Barbie moved out of his embrace and Normie looked at her for a few seconds, then said, "C'mon, I'll take you home."

Before he let her off in front of her house she asked, "How did you really get my telephone number? You never told me."

"It was crazy," he admitted. "After you walked away a woman came up, handed me a piece of paper, and said something like, 'If you want to see her again, here's her address.' "

"What woman? Who was she?"

"No idea. Somebody foreign, I think. With a funny accent, and all dressed in black. As far as I'm concerned she was an angel of mercy. Who cares who she was?"

Barbie shook her head. It was a wild story, he was probably making it up. "You're nuts. Good night, and thanks for everything."

"When will I see you again?"

"I don't know. You can call me."

That night she slept with her hand pressed between her thighs. She felt warm and loved for the first time in days—the first time since Helene started giving her the cold shoulder.

THERE WERE A FEW MORE MODELING JOBS IN THE NEXT WEEKS, some magazine ads and a catalog for a national chain of sports equipment stores, but none of them seemed to recompense Helene for the aborted job with Saks. The older woman was sullen and withdrawn. For three weeks after she recovered from the flu she didn't ask Barbie to spend the night. When the invitation finally came, it occurred on an evening when Barbie had arranged to meet Norman. She refused. "Suit yourself," Helene said coolly. "Just make sure you're here by eight tomorrow morning. We're supposed to be at the studio at eight-thirty."

"I'll be here," Barbie said. She was doing a spread for the *Sunday Globe Magazine.* John Kramer had arranged the booking and was doing the photographs. A feature on winter fashions, and it was May. Barbie knew it would be hot as hell under the lights. "I wish modeling jobs weren't always out of season," she said. "We could be doing bikinis on a beach tomorrow."

"I never told you it was easy." Helene crossed to her small desk and took an envelope out of the drawer. "Here's your earnings so far this month. Nine hundred and thirty dollars. If you'd done the Saks job it would be something like four thousand."

Barbie didn't say anything, just took the check and left. Despite Helene's disparagement, the money thrilled her. She'd earned over three thousand dollars in four months. She wanted her parents to take at least part of the money, but they wouldn't hear of it. Except for the small amount she used for carfares and clothes—and Sophie still bought those for her in the basement—it was all sitting in a post office savings account. In her name. Barbie didn't know what she was saving for. She couldn't think of anything she wanted that cost that much money, but having it gave her a lot of pleasure.

Now she tucked the latest check in her bag and went to meet Normie. He was parked two blocks away, waiting for her. A few times she'd thought of having him come to the flat and meet Helene, but she always rejected the idea. She still hadn't found a way to tell Helene that she was dating Norman Gold.

They went to Jack and Marion's. It was the ultimate delicatessen, specializing in enormous sandwiches—one was actually a foot high and anyone who managed to eat it all got his name added to a plaque on the wall—and incredible desserts like huge bowlfuls of strawberry shortcake or a portion of cheesecake so large it was served on a platter. Jack and Marion's wasn't just somewhere to eat, it was an event, a place frequented by people who laughed a lot and talked about their trips to Miami Beach or Nassau in the Bahamas.

Barbie watched men in silk suits with large cuff links showing beneath the sleeves, and bottle blondes with mink coats draped across the back of their chairs even though it was spring. She knew she was attracting attention without a mink or a big diamond ring, and that Normie was aware of it and enjoying it. She took a slice of dill pickle from the bowl on the table and nibbled at it. Normie was watching her mouth. Almost unconsciously Barbie exaggerated her movements and let her tongue flick out between her lips.

"What are you going to have?" he asked. He was flushed; there was a faint sheen of perspiration on his forehead.

"Hot pastrami on a roll." The hell with the calories, she was hungry. "And afterwards a hot fudge sundae with coffee ice cream and marshmallow."

"You must have a tape worm all of a sudden," Normie said. "I've never seen you eat so much."

"I usually don't dare. But I'll sweat off three pounds tomorrow morning." She told him about the booking and how hot it would be in Kramer's studio.

"Barbie, tell me the truth." He leaned forward and studied her intently. "Do you really like what you're doing? Do you honestly want to be a big-time model?"

Automatically she started to assure him that she did, then she paused. "I don't know," she said slowly. "I make a lot of money, Norman. I feel safe because of that." She took out the check and showed it to him. She'd never mentioned her earnings before. She expected him to be impressed, but he just looked at the check then passed it back to her. "That's only for one month," she said. "I've got more than three thousand dollars in my savings account."

"Okay, the money's good. But that's not all there is to life for a girl like you."

"No," she agreed. "Parts of it I hate. Sometimes before I do a job I'm so nervous I'm sick. I used to be like that always, before I met you. Helene wouldn't believe that I'd eaten a meal like this the night before a date."

"This Helene," he said. "She doesn't own you, you know. The way you talk about her makes it sound like she's God almighty."

"She's my agent. And she discovered me. I'd be some jerk's secretary right now if it wasn't for Helene. Whatever I think about modeling, it's better than that."

"Better than being married?" he demanded.

She put down her ice cream spoon and stared at him. "You're crazy. What's being married got to do with it? Of course I'll get married someday."

"How about now? To me."

She laughed. "Norman, you are something else. A romantic proposal in a deli. And you not finished college and me just starting on my career."

He didn't answer, just called for the check. When they got in the car, he still wasn't talking. They drove to Revere through the Sumner Tunnel, and when they came out he headed not for her house but for the beach. His aunt and uncle were home from their cruise—he'd taken her to meet them the previous Sunday afternoon—so she knew they weren't going there. Instead he drove halfway down the boulevard and parked in the dark with the other "submarine watchers." Wordlessly he reached for her and kissed her hard. She pulled away and said, "Stop coming on like gangbusters. You know I hate that."

"I know what you hate and what you like," he said. He dragged her back into his arms and gripped both her wrists with one hand while he dropped the other between her legs. He kept kissing her and stroking her until she was panting with excitement, then he stopped. "I've got needs too," he said gruffly. He guided her hand to the front of his trousers, and she felt his swollen hardness. "Do something for me for a change," he said savagely.

She did because she didn't know how to refuse him, and because in a way she owed him. Norman had made her stop worrying about being strange, about what her relationship with Helene really meant. So she moved her hand the way he wanted, and after a few moments she liked it. It was exciting to hear him moan with pleasure and to realize that she was the source and the master of his feelings. When he reached down and undid the zipper on his fly, she liked the feeling of his hot flesh in her cool palm. It occurred to her that she would like to kiss him there, but the idea seemed to her too preposterous to put into practice. It didn't matter anyway; he came in her hand just then. As soon as he stopped shuddering, he reached into the glove compartment and found some tissues and gently wiped her palm.

Barbie lay back on the seat. Her lips were parted and she was breathing hard. His climax had made her feel peculiar. She wanted him to touch her between the legs, the way he had a few minutes ago. And at the same time she was afraid. But wanting was acting on the fear, corroding it like powerful acid. She could sense his eyes on her, but she didn't look at him.

She was wearing jeans, and he reached over and fumbled with the buttons. "No," she said quickly, almost automatically, knowing in her heart that she meant yes.

Normie echoed her thoughts. "Yes. I'm not going to rape you. I couldn't just now anyway. I'm going to give you what you really want. Take your pants off."

He sounded cool and masterful. Nobody had ever talked to her like that. It was even more exciting than stroking him had been. She undid the buttons of her jeans with trembling fingers, then he pushed her hands away and slipped the jeans and her underpants down to her knees. He put one arm around her and pulled her into a half-lying position across his lap. "Your snatch is all wet," he said. "Vaseline would go out of business if all women were like you." He touched the insides of her thighs, then wound his fingers in the soft curly hair between them. Then, very lightly, he let his thumb brush her clit. Barbie gasped and started to come almost immediately. But he didn't stop. Instead he suddenly jammed his fingers into her, pumping them in and out and keeping it up until she was writhing and biting back screams. At last she stiffened in his arms and was still.

Normie reached for the Kleenex again. This time he turned on the dashboard lights and made her look. There was blood on his index finger. "Either you've got your period or I just broke your cherry," he said.

"I haven't got my period."

"I didn't think so."

She was still half naked on the seat beside him and he kneaded her buttocks tenderly while he spoke. "We're getting married, beautiful. As soon as the wedding can be set up. If you say no I'm going to knock you up. Then you'll have to give in."

"What about your education?"

"It's finished. I got the word two days ago. I've flunked out." She started to say something, but he wouldn't let her. "Don't be sorry; I'm not. I've never been much of a student. B.U. just let me in because I can play football. I've already talked to Uncle Charlie. I'm starting in the business next week."

"But you won't be a lawyer."

"No, I won't. He's a little disappointed, but he'll get over it. I'm the closest thing to a son they've got. It's all going to be mine someday, you know that."

"Yes."

"So when are we getting married?"

"I don't know. I'll have to think about it."

I'm normal, was what she was thinking. At least with Normie I'm perfectly normal! It was a triumphant shout in her head.

THE WEDDING WAS SCHEDULED FOR AUGUST 15.

Sophie was a problem for a few days. She cried a lot, and kept talking about Barbie's career and what she was giving up. "And what about Helene? Look what she's done for you, what are you going to tell her? Answer me that."

"For God's sake, Sophie, shut up!" Moe slammed his newspaper on the kitchen table and looked from his daughter to his wife. "For almost nine months all I hear in this house is Barbie's career. Nine months! You can make a baby in that time. So what have you made? A gorgeous girl into a nervous wreck, that's what. So scared she doesn't eat before each time they're gonna take her picture. Look!" He grabbed Barbie and turned her toward her mother. "Look! Skin and bones you made. Now she wants to marry a nice boy, a Jewish boy with a good job and a future. He's even been to college. And you object. What's the matter with you, Sophie, have you gone crazy? Whose career are you worried about, yours or Barbie's?"

Sophie stared at her husband. In twenty-two years of marriage he'd never spoken to her thus. The kitchen was silent for long seconds. Barbie started to cry. Finally Sophie picked up the newspaper Moe had been reading. She folded it carefully and handed it back to him. "Maybe you're right," she said quietly. And to Barbie, "Don't cry, *mamele,* it makes your eyes red."

Dealing with the problem of Helene was more difficult. There were three modeling dates the next week, all connected with an unimportant catalog for a minor mail-order house. Helene was ill pleased and crotchety. Barbie kept trying to find the words to explain, and failing. On Saturday she went to the apartment on Charles Street determined to get it over with, but Helene greeted her with a bear hug and a broad grin. "We've done it, baby. The big break at last!"

Barbie managed a weak smile. "Helene, I've got to tell you something. A few months ago I—"

"Not now, for chrissake. Get in here and sit down and listen to me. This is the big one, don't you want to hear about it?"

It was an ad for Charles Jourdan shoes scheduled to run in the September *Vogue.* "John Kramer's got the commission, and guess who his model is going to be?"

Barbie closed her eyes, trying to imagine herself in the incredible role of a *Vogue* model. The only thing she felt was terror. "I don't know, Helene, I don't think I'm ready. I never will be probably, because—"

"Shut up, and stop running yourself down." Helene grabbed her shoulders and shook her gently. "Listen, baby, it's not just your career that's about to take off. Old Johnny boy has been angling for this for months. He's screwed his way through three secretaries and God knows how many assistant editors to get this job. Do you know what it means to a photographer to introduce a new face? A face that's going to set the whole damn country on its ear? Well, I do, and so does Kramer. So you just be a good girl and do what Helene tells you. Okay?"

"Okay." There really wasn't anything else she could say. A number of factors had conspired to give Kramer his chance with *Vogue*. Not all were based on his sexual prowess. The Jourdan company had decreed a Boston setting for the autumn ad. The city was shedding its staid brahmin image. Both Lord and Taylor and Saks were about to open stores in the new Prudential Center. Boston had always been wealthy, now it was to become fashionable. "The old Ritz Carlton Hotel," someone said. "That's the place to shoot. If they'll agree." Kramer, it turned out, had once bedded the married daughter of a man on the hotel's board of directors. Since the gentleman was of a generation that preferred such things kept quiet, permission to take pictures at the Ritz was forthcoming—and the choice of photographer assured.

They met in the Grill Room, fully set up for dinner but empty now. Kramer dressed Barbie in stiletto-heeled black satin shoes with a rhinestone buckle and little else except a diaphanous length of bottle green chiffon. Then he belted her waist tightly in a broad black satin belt that rose to a point between her small high breasts.

"Perfect," Helene whispered.

Kramer nodded. "Turn on the fans."

Helene moved carefully among the cords and wires of the portable floodlights, maneuvered around a tilted white umbrella that would reflect back the intermittent beams of a bounced strobe, and switched on three strategically placed fans. Barbie moved into the current of air. The green chiffon swirled around her long legs.

"Let's see the shoes, honey child," Kramer said softly. Barbie put one foot up on a chair. She leaned over and stretched out her arms, offering herself to the camera as if it were a lover. A second later she was bending over another table, then moving nearer the dark-paneled oak walls, then sitting on the corner of the buffet table. Kramer moved with her. He was using a Hasselblad with a Zeiss eighty-millimeter lens, and the shutter opened and closed in a barrage of shots. The dozen different images Barbie projected were reflected in heavy silver and gleaming crystal and stiff white napery. She flowed, she strutted, she smiled like a virginal waif and wiggled her ass like a whore. A gamin let loose in a Victorian dream, Barbie was superb because she knew it didn't matter very much anymore.

"Fantastic," Helene said when they were finished.

"Amen, amen." Kramer hugged Barbie and kissed her. "Even sweaty you're delicious. How do you feel?"

"Fine, John. Really good. I'm glad you got what you wanted."

"It's what we want too," Helene crowed. "John's just made our fortune, baby."

Barbie opened her mouth to tell them she was getting married and her husband-to-be expected her to give up modeling. No words came. She went home and wrote Helene a letter.

"THE BITCH, THE LITTLE COCK-SUCKING KIKE WHORE! I'LL KILL her, Ann. I'll go to her house and throw acid in her face! No, I'll do it after the wedding, and see who wants her then. The stinking little cunt."

The stream of invective went on and on. The letter was shredded into a million tiny pieces in Helene's sharp-nailed fingers. "I could have warned you," Ann Jessup said quietly, "if you'd only told me who she was. If I'd realized early on, before you got in too deep, I could have told you that she was one of my students and I knew what she was like. Why didn't you trust me?"

Helene looked at her lover with dull eyes. "I gave up my office and my other clients and lived on my savings. I even threw Frank out. All for her. Because she was so beautiful. She was special, Ann. Really special. She could have gone right to the top. I'd have taken her there. Now Kramer's shooting the *Vogue* ad again with another model. It's no good to him, introducing somebody who's not going to work again. Barbie's thrown everything away for some jock and I have nothing. Nothing." She collapsed on the couch, shaking with sobs, and Ann crossed the room and gently caressed the back of her neck.

"There," she crooned softly. "There, darling, don't do this to yourself. She isn't worth it. You have me, and I love you."

Helene flung her arms around the other woman and buried her face in Ann's breast. "I just don't understand how it went so far without my knowing about it."

Ann made comforting noises and held Helene and rocked her gently. It felt so good, and it had been so long. Worse, it had almost been permanent. She could have lost Helene forever. She closed her eyes to blot out the pain of such a desolate vision of the future, and when she did she saw Shirley Avenue and Barbara and all Barbara's kind. Invaders, cheats who took what was not theirs. But in the end there would be justice. Ann would make sure of it.

NORMIE'S AUNT SALLY ARRANGED FOR THE TWO FAMILIES TO meet at her house. "We'll keep it small," she told Barbie. "Just your folks, my sister-in-law and her husband, and of course the Cohens. You understand, Barbie, they're like family." Barbie nodded. It wouldn't have mattered if she didn't understand. Sally Rothstein was a dynamo of energy and opinions. Nothing deflected her from any goal she happened to choose. Not even the vodka she drank all day.

"I think maybe a Sunday brunch," Sally added. "It's better than a big dinner at night. Next Sunday. Please God it doesn't rain. We can eat by the pool."

The Golds and the Kormans arrived simultaneously. Normie drove his folks and Charlie picked up Sophie and Moe and Barbie. They pulled into the driveway at the same time, and introductions were made while they were still outside.

Sally ran out to greet them. She was thin to the point of emaciation, her skin was tanned to the quality of leather, and her bikini hid little of it. Sophie tugged at her flowered cotton sundress with a slight sense of discomfort, then she looked at Rita Gold, also wearing a sundress, and at Barbie, in a dark amber pure silk one-piece maillot with a matching skirt, and she felt better.

They ate lox and bagels and cream cheese, and onion omelettes. The men talked business, with Normie ostentatiously included, and the women appraised each other warily. "It was a big surprise to us," Rita Gold said. "We didn't know Normie was serious."

"To us, too," Sophie agreed. "But these kids today, who knows what they're going to do?"

"She's gorgeous, your Barbie. When Normie brought her to meet us, I could understand. She always wears beautiful clothes. Maybe it'll be hard for her with Normie just starting out."

Sophie took a sip of her orange juice. She was afraid Charlie had put some vodka in it, even though she told him not to. "You shouldn't get the wrong idea, Rita," she said. "My Barbie buys everything in the basement, or upstairs with a discount. She knows how to shop. I taught her."

At that point Barbie got up and moved to Norman's side. She took his hand and held it tight, and he put a protective arm around her shoulders. "You kids come with me," Charlie said suddenly. "I got a surprise that's just for you."

He led them through the house and outside, then up the

lane to the boulevard. "Look over there," he said. "You see the vacant lot between the two white houses." They nodded. "It's yours. I bought it. For a wedding present Sally and me are building you a house."

Barbie felt Normie tense. "No," he said softly. "Thanks, Uncle Charlie, but no."

"What the hell do you mean, no? You're my flesh and blood, Barbie I love already like a daughter. Who says I can't build you a house?"

"I say." The boy turned to the older man and looked at him pleadingly. "Please, you've got to understand. I can't just have you give me everything. I need help, I know that. If it wasn't for you giving me a job we couldn't even get married. But I have to do some things for myself."

"Like the scholarship," Charlie said. "Like giving those *potzs* a hold over you so they could flunk you out. It wouldn't have happened if you were a paying student, you know that?"

"Maybe."

"But you're not sorry, are you?"

"No, I'm not sorry."

The older man managed a smile. "Okay, have it your way. So where are you gonna live? In Chelsea over the store?"

"We saw a house in Peabody. In a new development. It's small, but it'll be good to start out with. We need to borrow the down payment. I thought I'd go to the credit union. Barbie's uncle runs it."

"Now you listen to me," Charlie turned to Barbie, who had not spoken throughout the exchange. "I don't mean any disrespect to your Uncle Arthur, darling, I know him and I like him. But this is your responsibility, Normie, not hers. You're the man of the family. You borrow the down payment from the business. From me. A regular loan with interest, not a gift."

"Okay," Normie said.

THE ENGAGEMENT WAS ANNOUNCED IN THE REVERE *JOURNAL*. They used one of Barbie's professional photos and gave the story a two-column spread because the girl was marrying Charlie Rothstein's nephew. Two days later Barbie received a congratulatory note from Father DiAnni. She was surprised and pleased, not least because he mentioned that he would let Maria know and that he'd already brought her the pictures of Barbie that ran in the *Sunday Globe*.

"I want to invite him to the wedding," Barbie told her mother.

"A Catholic priest? What will people say?" Sophie saved her best ammunition for last. "Besides, where would you put him? What table can we sit a priest at? With your old Aunt Bessie maybe?"

"I don't care what people say. He's my friend. Maria can't be there, Mama. Having Father DiAnni kind of makes up for it, like a link with her." Sophie's expression softened and Barbie added, "Anyway, we can put him at the table with Norman's friends from the football team. Most of them are Catholics."

Sophie had to agree it was a perfect solution. Certainly it was proper to invite the B.U. football team. Everyone would assume that the priest had something to do with them.

The seating was only one of the problems attendant on the wedding. They'd chosen a hall in Brookline, right near the Chestnut Hill Shopping Center. It was called Leffert's Plaza and it was new. "For a bride that looks like you, darling, and because we're just getting started," Mr. Leffert told Barbie and her mother, "we'll do everything at cost." The fact that the groom was related to Charlie Rothstein didn't hurt either. This wedding would bring him business. Mr. Leffert intended to make a profit on it, but he was willing to make some concessions.

"The fountain out here runs water for ordinary affairs," he said, pointing to the three-tiered edifice in the lobby. It contained a statue of Cupid spitting forth a gushing stream, and artificial roses floating in the oval base. "For you it'll be champagne."

"How much?" Sophie demanded. Barbie's savings were paying for the wedding, but Sophie was the chief negotiator.

"Nothing, Mrs. Korman, a pittance. I told you, for her—"

"I know what you told me, so how much?"

Leffert hestitated. "Four hundred. California, you understand. For that price even I can't do French champagne."

"For that price you should give us liquid gold."

"So who'd want to drink it?" He smiled at the joke. "Okay, three-fifty." He moved them across the room to a curved bay hung with blue velvet drapes. "In here we have the bar and the hors d'oeuvres. You want shrimp?"

Sophie made a face. "You can get sick from shellfish. I read it in the paper. Maybe no shrimp."

Leffert understood. They'd told him it wasn't to be kosher, but some things still made the older generation uncomfortable. Not the kids. For them he could serve salami sandwiches on white bread with butter. But the kids didn't pay the bills. "You know," he said, cocking his head and studying his clients, "I think what you should have is what we call half kosher."

"Mr. Leffert," Sophie said. "If you can't be a little bit pregnant, tell me please, how can you be half kosher?"

He laughed. "Not really, of course. But we'll do chopped liver molds and miniature potato latkes and knishes for starting. Then we'll make sure the roast beef is well done, and oven roast potatoes, not baked with sour cream. A few things like that. Maybe it's better for the groom's people. Mr. Gold's a butcher, isn't he?"

"Not a kosher butcher," Barbie said.

"All the same," Sophie interrupted quickly. "I think Mr. Leffert has a point. We can have the ice cream and cake for dessert, though. The rum cake with the real butter frosting. I mean, we're not saying it's a kosher wedding, are we?"

A COUPLE OF WEEKS BEFORE THE WEDDING, BARBIE AGAIN began taking long walks by herself. Sophie was worried, but she wisely said nothing, and Barbie did not discuss her feelings. She just walked and walked and made her mind a blank. If she was tired enough, she would sleep. She couldn't have explained her behavior to her mother if she wanted to. She didn't understand it.

Most of August was hot, but three days before the wedding it turned cool and overcast. Barbie walked as far as Orient Heights and the enormous statue of the Madonna of the Universe. Looking at the figure made her feel strangely calm and detached. She stood there for a long time and finally said aloud, "Why am I doing this? What do I really want?" The answer was born in her mind instantly. I want to be safe, that's why I'm marrying Norman.

At first she'd thought she agreed because she was grateful to Norman for convincing her she wasn't queer. But knowing that was enough; she didn't have to get married because of it. Only it wasn't just sex. It was all the uncertainty that Helene's world represented. She'd really rather be Mrs. Norman Gold, a married lady with a house and a husband, surrounded by people and value systems she understood. That was the why of it.

Now, staring at the alien statue that represented yet another unfamiliar world, she was also cheered by the fact that she'd been fitted for a diaphragm. The idea of pregnancy was scary. This way she could take her time and not have a baby until she was ready. Norman had agreed it was the best thing.

"I'm going to make love to you three times a day at least. Better you shouldn't have a big stomach right away." She smiled because she liked the idea of Norman making love to her. What they did in the meantime was pretty good, but she was looking forward to having him put something bigger than his fingers inside her. Looking forward to it so much that any lingering doubts about her normalcy were utterly dispelled.

As for Helene, she never answered the letter Barbie sent, just mailed Barbie's last check in an envelope without a return address and without a note. Barbie felt awful about it. She went to the flat to try and see her, but the super said that Mrs. Wentworth had moved out. He didn't know where she was living. There was no forwarding address, so she couldn't even send Helene a wedding invitation.

THE WEDDING GOWN WAS SOPHIE'S MAJOR TRIUMPH. SHE'D brought it home one afternoon when she'd gone shopping alone. "Mama," Barbie had protested, "how could you buy it without my seeing it! Can it be returned?"

Sophie shook her head. "No, it was a final markdown." Her voice was tremulous. "I know I took a chance, but wait. Don't say anything yet." She opened the dark purple box with shaking fingers. Barbie couldn't see anything but tissue paper. In the basement it was unusual for them to put tissue paper in a package. The gown must have come off one of the racks, not a table.

"Look at this first," Sophie said. She tugged free a cluster of tickets held together with string and metal clasps.

The smallest tag was pale yellow. It was imprinted with the words BERGDORF GOODMAN DESIGNER SALON. Underneath was the price, nine hundred and fifty dollars. "My God," Barbie breathed softly. She pushed the Bergdorf ticket away and studied those attached by Filene's. There were quite a few of them. The garment was a size five, one explanation of its having remained in the basement long enough to undergo all the automatic markdowns possible. The final price, the one Sophie had paid, was one hundred and eighty-two dollars. No wonder they put tissue paper around it.

"Don't say anything until I get it all out of the box," Sophie commanded. With shaking hands, she extracted a long cream satin sheath. It was like a slip, with thin shoulder straps and no decoration, but it was beautifully made, and lined with silk. The fastenings were hand-sewn hooks and eyes. The fabric was soiled in a few places, but Barbie knew that didn't matter. There was a French dry cleaners in Boston to whom Sophie always brought such problems. They'd never failed her.

"That's the underneath part," Sophie explained. "Here's the top." Barbie looked at it and gasped with delight. Her mother was holding a cloud of gossamer sheer tulle embroidered at intervals with butterflies, each pair of delicate wings re-embroidered in tiny seed pearls and beads. The gown floated from a high chinese collar also made of seed pearls, and had long fitted sleeves. Each ended with one of the butterflies. When she had it on, they would appear to float on the backs of her hands. "Could I let it go?" Sophie whispered.

"No. Oh, Mama, thank you! It's the most beautiful thing I've ever seen. What's this?" She delved into the box and pulled out another piece of satin.

"The headpiece," Sophie explained. "It came with, because the gown's a designer original. A whole look." She made Barbie sit down and try on the headpiece first. "Perfect!" Sophie said triumphantly. "I knew it would be."

Barbie's hair was completely covered by a helmet of cream satin edged in bejeweled butterflies that framed her face. "No veil and no train," Sophie said with satisfaction. "What do you need with them?"

THERE WAS NEVER A BRIDE TO MATCH HER, EVERYONE SAID SO. Joe DiAnni was inclined to agree. He was stuffed with food and awash in liquor. His head was filled with the raucous, raunchy humor of the brash hulks with whom he was seated, but when Barbie and her new husband came to their table, Joe sobered up immediately. He felt a catch in his throat just looking at her. It wasn't only that she was beautiful; he'd seen beautiful women before. It was the exquisite vulnerability of the girl that reached into Joe's gut and twisted some emotion he'd never realized he possessed. "Please be happy, Barbie," he begged her.

"I will," she promised.

4

FOR MARIA, LEARNING TO BE A SERVANT OF BETHLEHEM meant cleaning toilets. It also meant getting up at five-thirty and waiting in line to wash at one of the two sinks in the novitiate hall. Then going to the chapel and saying a lot of prayers in Latin and in English, followed by Mass at eight, and coffee, toast, and corn flakes in the refectory.

The toilets filled her morning after that. There were eighteen of them in different parts of the building. She carried a bucket and rags and scouring powder from one to the other and scrubbed and flushed.

"Don't lose the opportunity for prayer," Mother Bridget told her postulants. "Remember, Our Lord said to pray without ceasing." Maria dutifully repeated every prayer she could remember while she made her rounds. "Hail, Holy Queen . . ." Scrub and flush, then scrub again because there remained a spot of feces on the white porcelain. "Come, Holy Spirit, and fill the hearts of Thy faithful . . ." Scrub and flush, and don't forget to check for stains under the seat.

At eleven a bell rang and a line of nuns formed in the corridor outside the chapel door. The black-garbed postulants headed up the procession, at the front so the community could observe them. Their black dresses contrasted with the sky blue capes of the professed sisters. Blue for Our Lady, of course, as the booklet had explained, worn over a white dress to symbolize purity and virginity. "When the sisters are working in their

101

schools," the nameless apologist had added, "they wear a black dress because it is more practical."

In this, the provincial house of the order, there was no school—the house existed to house the elderly and infirm and to train the entrants—so everyone behind Maria and her fellow postulants was in white and blue. They said prayers until noon. The Little Office of the Blessed Virgin in Latin, the Rosary, and a perpetual novena to St. Brendan, to whom the Foundress had a particular devotion. After that they ate dinner, the main meal of the day.

It was adequate food, but not good, and for Maria, certainly not familiar. Mostly it was vegetables that had been boiled too long, and strange tasteless meat. The quality of the food mattered little to Maria. She was so tired after the toilets and after serving the others in the refectory that she ate almost nothing. Mother Bridget noticed. "You know, child," she said one afternoon as the postulants and novices sat sewing at their hour of "recreation," "we judge a true vocation by many things. Including a postulant's willingness to eat heartily and keep up her strength to serve."

Maria felt a chill of fear. The judgment referred to held far more terror than any final examination of her soul by the almighty. It was the vote of the community on whether or not a postulant would be clothed and allowed to progress to the next rung and become a novice. For some seconds she was paralyzed and didn't answer. The thought of failure, of being sent home in disgrace, was overwhelming. She could see the faces of her parents and neighbors, of Father Pasco and Father DiAnni. Suddenly she became conscious of silence. Around her the needles flew busily, but the chatter had stopped. Maria turned crimson and trembled. She had compounded her fault by not responding to the novice mistress's implied rebuke. Quickly she jumped to her feet. Her stool fell backwards with a loud clatter.

"I'm sorry." This was mumbled while she righted the offending furniture, and dropped to her knees beside Mother Bridget. "I confess my fault and beg you and my sisters to pray for my soul." The formula recited, she sat down and the others began talking again.

A few weeks later, the subject of her fitness to continue in religious life came up once more. Mother Bridget summoned Maria to her office. It was a cubbyhole at the corner of the novitiate wing, tucked in between the storerooms where the mountains of soap flakes and scouring powder were stored.

Enough to scrub all the toilets in the world. "You sent for me, Mother," Maria said.

"Yes, child. Sit down."

Maria was kneeling beside the woman, as was customary. The invitation to sit was decidedly the opposite. She felt the familiar chill of terror, but she rose and took a chair. She was careful not to lean back. "Nuns lean only on God," Mother Bridget had told her charges.

"Are you well, Maria?" the novice mistress asked.

"Yes, Mother, very well."

"You're quite sure?" The woman laid down the pen she was holding and looked long at the girl. "There is no sin in finding that one does not have a vocation, Maria," she said softly. "Many are called but few are chosen."

The quotation was meant as a kindness. It made Maria begin again to tremble. She clenched her hands in her lap and felt her nails biting into the soft flesh of her palms. "I believe I am called, Mother." She said it with as much force as her chattering teeth allowed.

"And you wish to be chosen." Mother Bridget smiled. She had long teeth. They reminded Maria of the horse that the rag man drove by the house when she was little. The thought distracted her. Another lapse of charity to confess. When she brought her attention back to the moment, the novice mistress was saying, "You realize that the vote of the community is based largely on my recommendation?"

"Yes, Mother."

"Very well. That will be all, child. You may return to your work."

At this hour of the day her work consisted of peeling vegetables for tomorrow's dinner; the toilets were sufficiently sanitary after her morning's labors. Maria scraped carrots with shaking hands and wondered about her fate. That night, she couldn't sleep. She cried instead.

The next morning, the prayers seemed interminable. The chapel was icy with winter, and outside the December wind howled and blew wet snow against the windows. Maria prayed only that the novice mistress wouldn't notice her reddened eyes. "Please, Lord, please don't let her send me away." Around her the Little Office of Our Lady was being chanted in a toneless singsong. She moved her lips out of habit, but she didn't see the words on the page.

Instead, there was a kind of silence building inside her, a whiteness that matched the world outside the convent. And then, suddenly, a singing, an exultant peace, a certitude, a knowledge. Arriving of its own accord, it settled over her like a feather quilt, with infinite comfort and endless warmth. Maria relaxed into it as if it were the most familiar thing in the universe, though it was unlike anything she had felt before. When she next became aware of the chapel, they were forming ranks to process to breakfast. Mass was over, and she had gone through all the motions, even received Holy Communion, unaware. She felt no guilt, nothing but quiet joy. Outside the snow had ended and the sun shone, brilliant on the purified earth.

ON THE FEAST OF THE PURIFICATION, FEBRUARY 2, 1961, SHE took the habit along with ten of the eleven postulants who had entered with her. One, the blonde with the enormous bosom, had been found unsuitable and had left during the night so none of the others would witness her shame. The rest were dressed in white wedding gowns. These were donations to the congregation from former students, now married, who gave this last symbol of their forfeit virginity to these who would guard the treasure for a lifetime. Maria's was of satin and lace. It was a bit too big, and had a long train she had to hold gathered up in her hand until the Mass was half over and the postulants were led out. They returned garbed in the white dress and blue cape of the congregation.

The cutting of their hair was the public part of the ceremony. Mother Bridget snipped it off of first one head, then the next. Brown, red, and black locks fell together in an egalitarian heap. As she finished shearing each sacrificial lamb, Mother Bridget handed the chaplain a white veil to bless. Then the starched wimple was pulled over the novice's head and the veil pinned in place.

Maria felt the weight of the unfamiliar headdress with satisfaction. She had not been found wanting after all. She had never worried about it since that morning of peace in the chapel. The sensations of that experience had not returned, but the certitude had remained.

"And now, dear new Sisters," the chaplain said, "you will receive your names in religion, to symbolize that the old Eve is dead and you are born anew in Jesus Christ."

Maria was conscious of her mother and father and Father DiAnni, behind her in the chapel with the other parents and friends. She had tried to make this moment easier for her parents. She couldn't yet know if she'd been successful.

"She wishes to be called Maria in religion," Mother Bridget had reported to the council who dealt with such matters. "Not Mary."

"But it's the same thing," Sister Francis had said. "Just the Italian form. Very understandable, I should think."

Mother Bridget had said nothing, but Mother Rose had sniffed. "Ever since Mother Columkill founded the Servants of Bethlehem we have all had Mary as part of our names. It is the custom."

"But that's because we were an Irish order originally," Sister Francis persisted gently. "You remember how we all said it was wonderful that an Italian girl should ask to enter. How it made us more American to have an ethnic mix."

"I recall that you said that, Sister."

Sister Francis blushed and stared at the table. Her degree in psychology didn't impress the Provincial. Mother Rose considered overeducated women a threat to Christian virtue. "All the same, I think we must be understanding of different cultural traditions," the younger nun said quietly.

"Of course, Sister." Mother Rose's voice dripped honey. "I'm sure you're right. We will give her the name Mary Anthony. Isn't St. Anthony much venerated among the Italians?"

"Her parish church was St. Anthony's," Mother Bridget added.

"Maria Trapetti," the priest said now, "henceforth you shall be called Sister Mary Anthony." Maria tried not to look at her mother when the new novices filed out of the chapel.

IN ONE WAY SISTER FRANCIS' EXPERTISE WAS RESPECTED. SHE administered the tests that determined whether a novice was trained as a teacher or assigned to the general housekeeping work of the convents and the schools. She looked over the scores earned by Maria, and smiled. "You will certainly make an excellent teacher," she told the girl sitting across the table, her delicate face dwarfed by the starched and pleated wimple and the white veil. "We plan to send you to Salem Teachers' College. Is that what you want?"

"I'd like to teach," Maria said shyly. "But I'll do whatever I'm told."

"Of course you will. I don't question your obedience, dear. I just want to know whether teaching really appeals to you."

"Yes." Maria felt a sudden urge to confide in the pretty young woman opposite. This was the first time she'd spoken to Sister Francis. She seemed quite unlike the older nuns. "I entered with that in mind. My mother wanted me to go to the Ortoni nuns."

"Good! Then teach you shall. On Saturday you go to our convent in Beverly. You'll live there and attend classes at Salem during the week. You understand, of course, that many things are different in Beverly. It's a smaller community, for one thing—only fourteen sisters. And there's a parish school attached."

Maria nodded. It would be blissful to live with something less than fifty women.

THE CONVENT OF THE HOLY CHILD IN BEVERLY WAS different indeed. The horarium was adjusted to the teaching schedule. That meant shorter morning prayers, earlier breakfast, and only one period of prayer during the day, from three to four P.M. Moreover, the general atmosphere was leavened by the involvement of the nuns with the parents and children of the parish. Maria and the other two novices who were students at the college saw little of the parishioners. They took an eight A.M. bus to classes in neighboring Salem, making the trip in silence as the rule constrained, and returned to do the housework of the convent. The professed attended to the teaching and related duties. But the formality of the Lynn house was a thing of the past. The young sisters began to know each other as human beings.

Maria had one other special pleasure during the two years of her tenure in Beverly. In the middle of the second winter, Father DiAnni brought Barbie to see her. The first Sunday of every other month was visiting day, and the nuns were allowed to spend an hour with one or two relations or friends. "Barbie and her husband live nearby in Peabody," Father DiAnni explained. "I'll bring them in February."

On the designated day, Maria woke to a howling blizzard and a sense of poignant disappointment. She had not realized how much she was looking forward to the visit. By noon the snow stopped, but the sky remained gray and threatening and the roads looked impassable. It always took a lot of time to get the plows in operation after a Sunday storm. "No parlors today, from the look of it," one of the sisters said.

"We can hope," another replied.

Maria and Sister Patrick, one of her fellow novices, shoveled the convent walk just in case, but the appointed hour came and went, and no cars pulled up by the front door. Maria and Patrick stood on the porch and looked at each other sadly. Then they spied a couple walking toward them up the deserted street. Maria recognized Father DiAnni instantly, but it took her a moment to realize that the woman with him was Barbie.

"Wow!" Patrick murmured under her breath. "Is that your old chum? The Jewish one?"

"Yes," Maria whispered. "Oh, yes, it is!" She broke from the porch and ran down the walk, her white veil flying free over her shapeless black winter coat, and intercepted Barbie with a bear hug. "It's you! It's really you! How did you get here through the snow? How did you get to look like a movie star? Where's your husband? What's he like?"

"One question at a time," Joe DiAnni laughed. Barbie didn't try to answer any of them. She couldn't because she was crying.

Finally they went inside and Maria took the priest's poncho and Barbie's hooded fur coat and hung them in the hall and led her guests into the stiff and ugly parlor that had been reserved for them. "We've got this room to ourselves, *mirabile dictu*," she said.

"What does that mean? Why are you so thin? I love the color of your cape." Barbie's words tumbled over themselves in a high-pitched girlish stream.

"It means 'miraculous to be told,' " Maria said through her laughter. "We have four parlors and fourteen nuns, so usually you have to share. But Mother Superior told me we could have this one to ourselves."

She did not add that the superior said it might be better to entertain her friend alone, since she was a Jewess. Or that she had bitten back the comment, Don't worry, it's not contagious. Instead she said, "I'm not as thin as you are. And the blue cape is traditional with our sisters. It's for Our Lady. Which you don't understand, but never mind. How did you get here?"

"The main roads are open," Father DiAnni explained. "We left the car on the highway and walked. Nothing was going to keep Barbie away, even if she had to hire a dog sled."

"I'm so glad," Maria said, then impulsively hugged her friend again. "Now sit down and tell me everything. I'm supposed to bring you tea, but I don't want to take the time."

"Oh, no, don't go," Barbie said. She produced a box and handed it to Maria. "Mama sent this. Her apple strudel, the kind you always liked, with raisins. Have it later. There's enough for an army; you know Sophie."

"She's still in business, from the look of it." Maria eyed the other girl. She wore a shirtwaist dress of taupe silk jersey. It was buttoned to the neck and had long sleeves, but it didn't manage to make Barbie look like a suburban matron. "Let me guess, Filene's basement?"

"Yes, with the label still in!"

They dissolved into peals of laughter, and Joe relaxed in his seat and lit a cigarette and watched them. He felt rather like someone visiting a patient in a hospital, and he realized that coming to see Maria always gave him that impression. Maybe when the council now meeting in Rome had done its work things would loosen up a bit in convents. It was ridiculous that friendship should be rationed by a rule designed in the nineteenth century.

There was a knock on the door and another young nun entered with a tray. "Tea and coffee," Sister Patrick said. "I didn't know which Barbie liked." She turned to the redheaded woman with a radiant smile. "I'm Sister Patrick. I've heard all about you. But none of it did you justice."

Maria thanked her for the tray, and introduced them. Sister Patrick left quickly. "Why aren't you drinking anything?" Barbie demanded after Maria poured two cups of coffee.

"It's against the rules for us to eat between meals or with laypeople. Crazy, huh? But that's how it is."

"Can't you have the strudel either?"

"Oh, I'm sure we can. I'll give it to Mother Superior, and she'll have it served in the refectory. I bet I can get permission to write a thank-you note to your mother, too."

"Okay," Barbie said softly. There was an awkward silence after that. Maria hastened to bridge it by asking about Normie.

"He's away on a sales trip," Barbie explained. "He has to make a lot of them. I figure he's been on the road eight of the eighteen months we've been married. But he'll want to hear all about you when he comes home. I've told him my best friend's a nun." She stopped and looked long at Maria. "You still are, you know. Nobody could ever take your place."

Later that's what Maria remembered about the visit. The wistful, almost lonely quality in Barbie's voice when she said that. And the surprising fact that she was perfectly at ease with Father DiAnni and called him Joe. Maria began praying for her friends with renewed fervor.

Maria enjoyed her time in Beverly, and was a little sorry when she was awarded her primary teaching certificate and faced with the prospect of returning to the Provincial House.

"Don't you wish we were getting a regular assignment?" she confided wistfully to Sister Patrick.

"I'm not sure," the other girl said.

There was more gravity in her voice than Maria expected. She looked up quickly. "Why not?"

"One of the kids at Salem gave me this." Patrick produced a magazine from her pocket. Reading magazines was forbidden. Certainly accepting them from laypeople was a grave violation of the rules. All reading matter was vetted by the superior, and carefully selected articles were clipped and left on the table in the common room.

"What is it?" Maria tried not to sound shocked. She didn't want to seem judgmental. In her head she was hastily trying to decide if she was bound to report this lapse at the weekly chapter of faults.

"It's a Catholic magazine," Sister Patrick said quickly. "It's approved by the bishops. And the editor is a priest." Her defense was impressive. "Besides, the girl who gave it to me is a good Catholic. She's head of the Legion of Mary in her parish."

"What does it have to do with going on a teaching assignment or returning to Lynn?"

"Will you read this?" Patrick answered by way of answer. "Please. I need to talk to someone about what it says. You're the only one who might understand."

It was an article about the "Document on Religious Women" being discussed at the Second Vatican Council now meeting in Rome. Maria took it reluctantly, but with a curiosity she couldn't suppress. She read the story with shudders of mixed horror and excitement, but she refused to share her reactions with Sister Patrick.

IT WAS CALLED THE "CANONICAL YEAR" AND CONSISTED OF twelve months of instruction in the faith, and in the constitutions of the Servants of Bethlehem, as well as lengthened prayer life. By tradition and law the Canonical Year was spent in almost total seclusion in the Provincial House. Maria went through it with a kind of stoicism that masqueraded as piety. She was determined to erase the doubts raised by that glimpse of apocalypse she had seen reported in the respectable Catholic journal of opinion.

Besides, there were other things to be concerned about. For instance, it was during her Canonical Year that she discovered she would never really be a nun. Nuns were strictly enclosed contemplative religious who took solemn vows. Until a mere few hundred years ago they were the only kind of women religious in Christendom. Then the needs of the poor inspired St. Vincent de Paul to found the Sisters of Charity, whose "cloister will be only in their hearts," and a new species of being was born. Sisters were "active religious" who took simple not solemn vows—the difference was fraught with canonical minutiae—and did work in the community such as teaching or nursing.

"We, of course, are a mixed congregation," Sister Francis explained. She taught the novices the history of the Servants of Bethlehem. "Mother Columkill envisioned a way of life in which traditional monasticism would be united with the apostolic zeal to serve. St. Thomas Aquinas teaches that this is the highest form of Christian life."

Maria felt some sadness at the thought that she had not quite kept the promise made to the crucified Lord in St. Anthony's church on that long ago Saturday afternoon. "I will be a nun," she had told Him. Until now no one had ever explained that she wasn't just that. On the other hand, she couldn't see herself as a cloistered contemplative, and it was doubtless divine providence that had led her to the sisterhood.

In June of 1964 she made her temporary vows—they bound her to be chaste, poor, and obedient for one year—with relief, because now the boredom of life as lived in the Provincial House would be mitigated by a classroom full of lively youngsters in a new convent to be established in the town of Wrentham. She was twenty-two years old and had been three years a Servant of Bethlehem; the prospect of teaching was light at the end of a very long and very dark tunnel.

THE PARISH OF THE HOLY SPIRIT IN WRENTHAM WAS LOCATED on the outskirts of a small rural community. It had been created when numbers of Italian-Americans began taking over the dairy farms in the area. The Cardinal Archbishop of Boston bought a huge tract of land and built a church that resembled nothing so much as a bomb shelter with windows. It was his favorite kind of architecture. His Eminence was not, however, insensitive to the needs of his flock. He wanted an Italian-American priest for the new parish. The likely place to secure one was among the Franciscans, so he consulted with the Provincial Superior of that order. The latter ate his fill of the Cardinal's excellent food, drank his ten-year-old Irish whiskey, and agreed to supply a priest to Wrentham. It would have to be a young one, he warned. They were stretched pretty thin, and vocations were down. "So long as he's sound," His Eminence said.

It was this young but sound priest, Father Francisco, who requested some Servants of Bethlehem to come and teach in his newly formed parish school. And the fact of Sister Mary Anthony's ethnic difference, and the queer discordance of her presence in the two convents in which she'd lived, which made Mother Rose agree to the new foundation.

For the Mother Provincial this was the sign from heaven for which she'd been praying. Not only because of Sister Mary Anthony; there was also Sister Patrick, a worry because she was too clever, and Sister Emily, who promised never to grow beyond teenage. Both could be sent to Wrentham along with Mary Anthony, the girl the Provincial thought of as her black sheep. Given the peculiar makeup for the new community, the choice of Mother Elizabeth as superior was obvious. Mother Elizabeth was sixty-seven years old. Fifty of those years had been spent as a Servant. She was yet young and healthy enough to teach, and old enough to keep a rein on the neophyte religious who would be under her. A satisfactory arrangement all around, Mother Rose decided.

The newly appointed superior had her doubts. She struggled bravely to conform to the rule, but the circumstances and the nature of her infant community made it difficult always, and sometimes impossible. Then she saw a youngster named Eda Martello praying before the stark crucifix that was the only piece of devotional art in Holy Spirit church, and Mother Elizabeth was imbued with new hope and faith. She would produce a vocation for the order from this enclave of foreigners; thus would be confirmed the blessing of God on the new foundation, and her own noteworthy talent for leadership.

Indeed, the girl was luminous with piety. Her neck was hung with medals, and she had a rapt look on her face at the parish novena on Wednesday nights. So the Mother Superior of the Wrentham convent singled out Eda as "the first fruits of the harvest." In fact, spotting her had made Mother Elizabeth feel better about her decision to allow the sisters to attend the parish devotions. It had nothing to do with Maria's reason for requesting permission to do so.

111

"We're such a small and new community here, Mother," Maria had said. "Don't you think it might help to establish a bond with the local people?"

The superior had intended to refuse. She understood quite well the spirit that vivified Sister Mary Anthony, and she knew she must extinguish it. Modernism was an old heresy, long ago condemned; that it continued to be born anew was merely evidence of the devil at work. Well, he would find no fallow ground in her convent. Nonetheless, when she opened her mouth to say no, yes came out instead. Mother Elizabeth escaped to the tiny chapel of the house transformed into a convent to pray for guidance, and Maria dashed to the kitchen to tell Sisters Patrick and Emily she'd won.

So on Wednesday nights the four Servants of Bethlehem donned their white dresses and blue capes and walked in silent decorum across the road to Holy Spirit church to join the Wrentham Catholics in perpetual devotion to St. Francis. "Maybe we should wear our black," Emily had ventured timidly. Their startling blue and white was a remarkable bit of bathos among the ordinary working folk of the parish.

"I agree," Maria had said immediately. "That's a great idea. We won't stick out like sore thumbs."

Patrick had laughed and tugged at the starched and pleated folds of her wimple. "You mean we'll be penguins rather than peacocks. *Rarae aves* in any case."

The conversation took place during recreation. Mother Elizabeth found it extraordinary and disturbing. Her three sisters sounded as if they were putting the decision to a vote. "The Rule states clearly that we wear our blue and white to prayer." Her voice was firm, her embroidery needle didn't falter.

"Unless the demands of the apostolate interfere," Maria said.

"I know the Rule, Sister. I have lived it since before you were born." The reproach solidified in the air of the common room. A stalagmite with a sharp and pointed tip.

"I confess my fault and beg you and my sisters to pray for me," Maria murmured mechanically. She didn't kneel.

They wore their pastel plumage—Emily's phrase—to the novena. Permission to attend might well have been withdrawn after that first sortie—Mother Elizabeth was in agonies of doubt about the rightness and wisdom of her decision—except for Eda, the girl with all the medals and the saintly smile.

"Mother Superior has her eye on the Martello girl," Maria

told Father Francisco. She grinned when she added, "If her parents are anything like mine, you've got your hands full."

"If Lizzie succeeds, you mean," he said. He always called the old nun Lizzie to himself and to Maria. To her face she was always "Reverend Mother."

"I rather think she will. Eda brought some ravioli to the convent the other night and stayed to chat with me and Emily. She's definitely got the itch."

The priest pushed aside the textbook they were examining and smiled. "Is that how you describe it among yourselves? An itch?"

"Depends on who 'ourselves' are at the time. For some of us, sure 'tis a holy call to be a bride of Christ." Her Irish brogue was pronounced and accurate. Maria had a good ear for patterns of speech and Ann Jessup of the old Dramatic Club had trained her well.

"What about you," Father Francisco persisted. "Do you think of yourself as a holy bride of Christ?"

Maria grimaced. "Not holy, certainly. As to the rest . . . I don't know. It's a dated image, perhaps. Tied up with a lot of nineteenth-century claptrap."

"Tied up with a mania about human sexuality," he said. "The Manichaeans we shall always have with us."

"The body as evil, yes, I suppose that's part of it." She was more serious than his remark warranted. "I want to talk to you about that."

"Go ahead."

"We have to do something about sex education for the children."

The priest leaned back and clasped his hands behind his head. His brown cassock was frayed under the arms. Maria wondered who did his mending. "Yeah," he said. "I've been thinking about that. And scared to death to mention it to the good sisters."

"These kids are being fed a lot of myths," Maria said. "I know them all; I was raised on the same vicious folklore."

"So was I, more or less. The version for boys, at least. In East Boston. Where was your cradle of iniquity?"

"Revere."

They grinned at the shared experience implicit in the geography. "How old are you?" he asked suddenly.

"Twenty-two."

"How'd you get so smart so young?"

"I have a terrible unconfessed sin," she told him. "I read."

"Dangerous." He leaned forward and pulled the book they'd been looking at back to the center of the table. *Living Your Faith, A Catechism for Today's Young.* "This is dangerous too. Do you think we dare?"

Maria shrugged. It was a gesture almost lost in the folds of her heavy black serge gown and black veil. "I think we'd better dare," she said. "Otherwise kids like these will grow up into a world that will destroy their faith before they have a chance to live it."

MARIA HAD TOLD THE PRIEST THE TRUTH. THESE DAYS SHE read everything she could get her hands on, and she no longer had scruples about the rule. Mother Elizabeth put a small selection of books and articles in the tiny common room every month. Maria read them all, but she read a great deal more besides.

She acquired her literature from the racks outside the church and from a friendly clerk in a nearby drugstore. "Take what you want, Sister. No charge, just bring it back when you're done." She became adept at bringing her cadged supplies in and out of the house undetected. If anyone had looked under her bed they'd have found the evidence. At any given time there was a stack of such magazines as *Commonweal, America,* and *Jubilee* as well as *Time* and *The Saturday Review of Literature.* A few times she even had copies of *The New Yorker,* and she always had three or four newspapers. All this was vastly informative, but it didn't satisfy her hunger for knowledge. Maria yearned for real books, and tried desperately to subdue the longing by prayer.

Mother Elizabeth was many things, but she was not a snoop. No one knew of Maria's craving or the way she partially satisfied it, but the changes wrought in her by such reading as she managed to do were bound to become apparent.

"SISTER ANTHONY, I HAVE JUST HAD A LONG SESSION WITH THE mother of Thomas Pittanzi. She is most disturbed."

"About what, Mother?"

"About what she thinks you are teaching her son in his catechism classes. She says Thomas came home and told her the Rosary was a lot of nonsense."

"Tommy is very flip, Mother. Like most thirteen-year-old boys. He says things just for their shock value. I'm sure his mother understands that."

"Apparently he was most insistent. How did he get such an idea, Sister?"

Maria took a deep breath. "I expect it's a result of a conversation in class last week. Someone asked me what was meant by the Teachings of the Church. I tried to explain the differences between revealed truth and devotions."

"And you cited the Rosary as not being revealed? But Our Lady herself gave the Rosary to St. Dominic."

"That's a popular legend, Mother; it may be true. But it's not part of the defined dogma of the Church."

"I do not require catechesis, Sister," Mother Elizabeth said softly. "Your students do. And you have an obligation before God and your lawful superiors to pass on to them the full body of the faith."

Maria tried to recite the formula of apology. She couldn't make the words come. The older woman watched her struggle for a few seconds, then turned away. "You may go, Sister. I would like you to prepare a talk on the beauty and value of the Rosary for your class. Including the fact that it is held in the highest esteem by the Pope himself. Please bring it to me before you give it to the children."

IN THE PROVINCIAL HOUSE IN LYNN, SISTER MARY FRANCIS also kept abreast of the changes in the Church as announced and explained in the journals of Catholic opinion. But while Maria acquired them by stealth, Sister Francis read them because her superior told her to. The echo of approaching thunder was still a distant thing, perceived as a mere tremor in the solid earth beneath the sturdily shod feet of the nuns, but it could be sensed.

"There are no applications for the postulancy this year," Mother Provincial announced at the July 1965 meeting of her council. The news was greeted with silence. There had been no time in living memory when the novitiate was empty of black-garbed postulants. Apparently it was to be so this year.

"The Lord will provide," Mother Bridget said finally.

"The Lord has charged us with providing," Mother Rose answered tartly. "I suggest we examine our consciences and see how we've failed Him."

No one spoke for a few moments. Then Sister Mary Francis cleared her throat tentatively. "I think, Mother, that it's a reaction to all the changes. Young girls don't know what tomorrow will bring, so they're reluctant to make a commitment."

"The labor in the vineyards goes on," Mother Rose said. "Nothing the Bishops decide in Rome is going to change that."

"I know, but . . ."

"But what, Sister? Please speak frankly."

"We must prepare ourselves for new approaches to the apostolate. The Sister Formation Council in Washington is very clear about it."

"Prepare ourselves how? Please be specific."

"There are so many things," Sister Francis said quietly. "One hardly knows where to begin." She looked at the faces of the old women around the table and told herself she must move slowly. "I think the first priority is getting more education for some of our sisters." She swallowed hard and prayed for wisdom. Half a dozen pairs of eyes studied her and waited. "We are amateurs in education. If we are going to continue running schools, we must become professionals."

"We are professionals in loving the Lord," Mother Rose said softly. Sister Francis started to answer, but the old nun stopped her. "Never mind, Sister, I know what you mean, and I agree. I do not like the implications of the decision, but I don't see any choice. I've already spoken to the Jesuits at Boston College. They are prepared to admit two of our sisters to a degree program."

A great deal of discussion followed. In the end it was determined that Sisters Mary Patrick and Mary Anthony would be withdrawn from Wrentham the following month and sent to B.C.

SELLING LADIES' BLOUSES WHOLESALE WAS OKAY AT FIRST. Normie enjoyed it. He got to travel to places he'd never seen and eat out on an expense account, which was kind of a kick. And when he walked into an office with his suit perfectly pressed and his big grin polished for the occasion, the girls behind the desks always smiled back. Inevitably Normie would put his sample cases down and talk to them for a while. Nothing important, just chat. But sooner or later it always led to something about the buyer he was there to see. Normie noted these gems of information and filed them carefully in his head. By the time he got into the buyer's office he had an idea about the best approach to use. His orders were always good. Sometimes they were terrific.

Not until being on the road so much became a drag did

Normie make an effort to get friendly with some of his clients. Soon he had a regular few he could count on to share an expense account lunch or dinner. Usually the evening meetings ended with the other man offering to introduce Normie to a girl. He was lonely, wasn't he? All salesmen were. "Not my problem," Normie would say smoothly. He'd take out his wallet and extract a picture of Barbie, one of her professional shots. "This is my wife."

The man across the table always looked at the picture silently for a moment, then he'd whistle or sigh and say something like, "No kidding? This is really what you got waiting at home?"

"No kidding," Normie would say with pride. "So there's not much point in playing around, is there?"

These incidents always made him feel doubly good. Not only was his ego stroked, he felt virtuous. But after a while all the men knew that Normie Gold had a knockout former model for a wife and that he didn't play around. So they stopped asking and Normie had no more opportunities to flash Barbie's picture and think about the dumpy broads the other guys were probably married to. Then they had nothing to talk about but sports or, for a while, the terrible events in Dallas. Or ladies' blouses. By the end of 1963 it had all become very boring. Nonetheless, it was his job and Normie continued to do it without complaining. But he was ripe for a bit of excitement. He found it in a rather unlikely place, at the barbershop in Boston's Hotel Touraine, where he regularly got his hair cut.

The Touraine had been a nice place once, back before the lower end of Tremont Street became the border of the area known as the Combat Zone. Charlie Rothstein had taken his nephew to the Touraine for the most important haircut of his life, the one just before his *bar mitzvah*. That day Normie had believed himself made privy to the true secret of manhood. Never mind what the rabbi was telling him about his first call to join the men of the peoplehood of Israel in reading the *torah*. Being a man was getting your hair cut in a shop in the lobby of a fancy hotel, and seeing elegantly suited customers lie back with hot towels on their faces and a manicurist holding their hand. Nothing like that ever happened at the barber's next door to Pa's butcher shop in Chelsea. On that momentous day Charlie had introduced his nephew to Johnny Casatano, the shop's owner, and Normie had known for sure that when he grew up he too would be a regular customer of Johnny's, and get the same deferential treatment Uncle Charlie received.

But by the time Normie was working in Boston, the Touraine had become a citadel of sleaze. Johnny Casatano still ran his barbershop in the lobby, because, he said, he was too damned old to change, but the clientele were not the same. "All greasers and fast-buck artists," Johnny complained. "Even your uncle don't come in here no more. I don't blame him. Who the hell wants to walk through a lobby full of hookers in order to take a haircut? Old-bag hookers at that," he added. "If they was good-lookin', maybe it wouldn't be so bad. But this place, it don't even attract a decent class of whores now."

"Never mind, Johnny," Normie said. "I don't notice them. You still give the best trim in Boston, right?"

It was loyalty not to the barber he barely knew, but to his childhood dream. And Johnny beamed and treated young Mr. Gold like a prince. A new customer was a rarity, something to be treasured. "Siddown," he said. "I give you a cut will make even your mama weep for joy."

So Normie went to the Touraine every few weeks and ignored his uncle's suggestion that he try a wonderful Greek barber in the Prudential Center. And that's how he got involved with Maluchey, and how come Charlie Rothstein didn't find out.

The first time was an accident. It was a few days before the Golds' second wedding anniversary in August of '63. Normie was waiting for Johnny to finish another customer, a still beefy old man who had once been touted as the next heavyweight champion of the world. Suddenly the old geezer jumped out of his chair and rushed to flag down a guy who was passing the door. The two looked like Mutt and Jeff. The stranger was no more than five feet tall and must have weighed two hundred pounds. The prizefighter peered down at him and muttered earnestly. Some money changed hands. Then the obese little man went away and the old fighter returned to Johnny's ministrations.

"What was that all about?" Normie asked when it was his turn in the chair. "Who was the pint-sized greaser?"

"Maluchey, you mean? He makes book. He's got this whole neighborhood wired; nobody else can muscle in. But he's okay, Maluchey. Don't welsh on nobody. Even if you have a big win. You play the ponies, Mr. Gold?"

"Nope. Don't know a thing about them."

The old barber laughed. "What's to know? You hear a little something here, a little something there. Pretty soon you know who to believe and you make yourself a few bucks extra."

"Like what do you hear?" Normie asked. "From who?"

"From me maybe. Tellin' you, since you is such a good customer, that La Traviata is a sure thing in the third at Hialeah today."

"A sure thing?"

"Guaranteed. Mr. Gold, with a name like that, can the horse lose?" Johnny hummed a few bars of Violetta's first-act aria.

Normie knew less about opera than he did about horses, but on his way out of the hotel he saw Maluchey again, and on impulse he stopped and reached tentatively for his wallet. The little man moved closer. "You're a regular customer of Johnny's, right?" Maluchey tended to whisper, and his eyes kept darting around the derelict lobby.

Normie nodded. "That's right. Johnny tells me there's a horse named La Trav something running this afternoon."

"La Traviata in the third at Hialeah," the other man said quietly. He wore a pinstripe suit that was too tight across his massive stomach and a purple-flowered tie half hidden by the numerous folds of his chin. When he spoke, gold caps flashed from his back teeth. Normie had to choke back a laugh. It was all like some old Jimmy Cagney movie. The bookmaker said, "There's a lot of smart money on La Traviata, but the jerks don't know it, so she's still seven to one."

Normie took a five-dollar bill from his wallet and passed it to Maluchey with exaggerated caution. "To win?" the fat man asked.

"Yeah, sure, why not?" Vaguely Norman remembered having heard something about win, place, and show; but he didn't know what the words meant, and five dollars was enough to throw away on a joke.

La Traviata came in first by two lengths. When Normie collected his forty dollars, he felt a surge of adrenaline that seemed little related to the actual cash. The whole crazy thing was a kick. Meeting Maluchey, picking a horse, betting and winning; it wasn't actually the money, and it certainly wasn't sport. He had no desire whatever to go to a track and see a race. It was just the outrageous seediness of the thing. He, Normie Gold from Chelsea, betting with a greasy-looking little bookmaker in a shady hotel. Like he was Jimmy Cagney.

Betting with Maluchey became a regular part of Normie's life.

When he was in town he started going to the Touraine for coffee every morning around eleven. If he was away on a sales trip, he looked forward to getting home and laying a few bets. A kick. Nothing more. Something to brighten the everyday routine. For over a year the sums were small, never over twenty bucks. But the time came when Normie had six wins in a row. He told himself he was crazy not to cash in on his streak, and he upped the ante. By late '64 he was regularly laying down fifty-dollar bets. In the winter of '65 he made it a hundred, because he'd started losing and wanted to make it back.

The day came when he ruefully shook his head as the bookmaker approached him. "Nothing today. I'm broke. First of the month. It's mortgage time. And this is April. Uncle Sam's looking for his cut."

"So what?" Maluchey spread his short arms expansively. "Your credit's good with me, Mr. Gold. Any friend of Johnny's . . ." He let the words hang in the air and did not add that Johnny had told him Normie Gold was Charlie Rothstein's nephew and heir. Everybody knew Charlie Rothstein was a very wealthy man.

"Thanks, but I don't think so." Normie started to walk away, feeling let down and empty inside because he wouldn't have a bet on today, nothing to look forward to.

"Well, okay, if you say so," Maluchey stage-whispered after him. "But you're missing a good thing. Pretty Barbara's running in the seventh at Rockingham. The smart money says she's due. Thirteen to one."

Pretty Barbara! Now there was an omen. Normie turned around. "Tell you what, you stand me a hundred each way." He knew about win, place, and show now. "Barbara's my wife's name," he added. Maluchey nodded, and Normie left the hotel with a spring in his step. Pretty Barbara was going to put him back in the black. Only she ran seventh in a field of nine. That's when Normie started dipping into the petty cash in the office.

There wasn't a hell of a lot to be had that way, not without raising awkward questions. As a source of betting funds it dried up pretty quickly. But Maluchey made it easy to continue. "Like I said before, Mr. Gold, your credit's good with me. You're a regular customer, right? Only thing is you gotta lay down some big money, so you can make a killing and get even. Now there's this filly runnin' in the fifth at Rockingham tomorrow, My Joy, she looks real good. Say five hundred each way?" Normie swallowed hard and nodded. The next day he caught the Rockingham results on the car radio. My Joy had been fourth. Normie pounded the steering wheel with his fist. So close. So goddamn close. Take it in stride, he told himself, your luck's got to change soon.

After that there was Jim Dandy and Custer's Last Stand and Philip's Blue Boy, and a dozen others. But none of them ran in the money, and Normie began having nightmares and waking in a cold sweat and doing sums in his head. No matter how many times he did them, they came out the same. He owed Maluchey over twenty thousand dollars. Jesus! Even the house wasn't worth twenty thousand dollars. And where would they go if they sold it? Would Charlie re-open his offer to build them something in Point of Pines? After Normie did a stupid thing like piss away twenty thousand dollars?

"What's wrong?" Barbie started asking. "How come you're so nervous lately?"

He wanted to tell her, but he couldn't. Gorgeous Barbie with her incredible amber eyes. What would he read in those eyes if he told her he'd plunged them into twenty thousand dollars of debt, just because he'd been acting out a kid fantasy. "Nothing's wrong, goddammit. Stop nagging. Where's that bottle of scotch? There was a full one in here last night."

"Yes, there was last night," Barbie agreed. "You drank it."

At which point he'd leave the house and drive to the liquor store in the Peabody Shopping Center and come home with a fifth of some cheap house-brand whiskey. At least he didn't drink outside, Barbie consoled herself. And he didn't waste money on good scotch when he was only going to pour it down his throat as if it were water.

THAT SUMMER OF '65 WAS HOT AND HUMID, NOT EVEN THE nights cooled off. In Peabody the shallow lawns in the new developments burned up and died, and no amount of watering would bring them back. Barbie looked at hers with pain; it was so damned ugly she hated to go outside. Sometimes she was even reluctant to answer the front door and gaze at the parched vista beyond. She always did, of course. When the chimes Norman had installed—they played "shave and a haircut, two bits"—sounded one Sunday afternoon, she opened the door and saw Father DiAnni. Her face lit with pleasure, despite the awful grass. "Come in, Joe, we weren't expecting you."

121

"I know. I came to say good-bye."

Barbie's eyes clouded. "What do you mean? Where are you going?"

"To Chile, I think. Maybe Peru." He walked into the house and closed the door. The sound of voices floated from the backyard, but the house itself was silent. Joe noticed, as he always did, that the place was no setting for Barbie. It had been furnished with the advice of Sally Rothstein and her friend Myrna Cohen, and it was vulgar and crude. A reflection of their personalities, not Barbie's. "I've joined the Society of St. James the Apostle," he explained.

"What's that? Why do you have to go so far?" Barbie took a cigarette from the reproduction colonial coffee table and lit it with shaking fingers.

"You're smoking too much," Joe said softly. "You promised you'd cut down."

"I have. I only smoke when I get nervous. You haven't answered my question."

"It's an organization founded a few years ago by the Cardinal. Priests from the Boston Archdiocese can volunteer to go and work in South America. 'From each according to his ability, to each according to his need,' " he quoted. "Good Marxist stuff, but Christian too."

"I need you here," Barbie said. Her lower lip quivered slightly. Joe felt the familiar wrench in his gut. As much as anything that's why he was going. "I won't have anyone to talk to if you go away," Barbie said. "Norman's getting worse."

"Did you speak with Charlie about it?" He'd told her weeks ago to mention Normie's moodiness and drinking to his uncle.

"I tried. He doesn't listen to me. Charlie thinks I'm a dumb broad. His words."

Joe sighed. "Listen, kid, I've thought a lot about it. It's the best thing. And it's what I became a priest for. To help people. I'm tired of saving the saved. You'll be all right. You're a ginger cat, you'll always land on your feet."

"I guess I will," she said, forcing a smile. "And you have to do what you want. I'm happy if it makes you happy." He started to say something, but she stopped him by laying one finger across his lips. "We won't talk about it anymore. Norman's outside with some of the neighbors. Come and have a beer and a hot dog."

The neighbors, all Jews, were accustomed to the peculiar

fact that the Golds had a Catholic priest for a friend. He was wearing jeans and a T-shirt, but everyone said, "Hello, Father."

Joe told them about his impending departure—he expected to be leaving in a couple of weeks—and they wished him luck. Normie even pumped his hand vigorously, as if he'd just won a lottery or a promotion. Pretty soon the conversation turned to the Red Sox and their desperate bid for the pennant.

By four Normie and Barbie were alone in the house. She loaded the dishwasher and fed the garbage disposal in the sink. He opened another beer and poured himself a shot of scotch to accompany it. "You've had enough, Norman," she said wearily.

Normie was at least twenty pounds overweight, all the football muscles had become fat, and he had pouches under his eyes. He was twenty-four years old and he looked like fifty. "I say when I've had enough, not you and not anyone else."

"I'm only thinking of the fact that you're supposed to make a seven A.M. plane tomorrow," Barbie said. "You always say it's hell flying with a hangover."

"Yeah," he agreed. "I know one way to be sure I feel good, though." He put down the bottle and the glass and eyed his wife. "Come in the bedroom."

"It won't work, Normie. You've had too much to drink."

"Don't call me Normie. You know I like you to say Norman."

She sighed. "Okay. Just wait till I finish cleaning up the kitchen."

"What the hell kind of thing to say is that? What a turn-off. 'Wait till I finish cleaning the kitchen.' "

Barbie left the dishes and followed him into the bedroom. She felt neither excitement nor desire, because she knew exactly what was coming. She removed her blouse and her bra, but left her shorts on. There was no need to take them off. Normie wasn't interested in anything but her breasts.

He stripped and lay down without bothering to turn back the spread. It was quilted satin and required dry cleaning and Barbie wanted to say something, but she didn't dare. Instead she went to the bathroom and got a couple of towels. Then she sat up next to him and took his head in her hands and guided his mouth to her nipple. Normie sucked avidly and at the same time took his flaccid penis in his own hand and began masturbating. Barbie crooned to him softly, the way he liked, and when he came he yanked his head away from her breast and whispered, "Mama, Mama, Mama." Over and over again, like a litany.

When he fell asleep, she went back to the kitchen and finished cleaning up, ignoring the tears that ran down her cheeks.

Sex had been good with him the first year. In those days he couldn't get enough of her; he thrust himself into her body at every opportunity. Moreover, he'd had staying power. Myrna Cohen had confided in one fit of liquorish intimacy, "There is nothing more important than staying power." After that Barbie realized that before they were married, Norman had balled Myrna a few times. However, she was pretty sure he wasn't doing it anymore and she put it out of her mind. Not even Norman could screw her as often as he did and still have something left over for Myrna Cohen. As newlyweds they made love in every room of the house, in their car, in his office, and once in the Rothsteins' pool while everybody was sitting around and talking. He'd grabbed her at the far end and pulled off her bikini bottom.

"Are you crazy!" she'd whispered. "It's broad daylight. They'll see."

"Ssh. They aren't paying any attention. They think we're just horsing around." Under the water she'd felt him squirm himself inside her. "Good, isn't it?" he'd said, clasping her around the waist and moving slowly. "Keep smiling, baby. Just keep smiling."

She'd thought she was going to die. The water lapped at her bare buttocks and his cock filled her and everyone was talking and laughing and not noticing a thing. "I'm making it now," he'd whispered into her ear. Then he'd withdrawn and it was over. He had to dive to the bottom of the pool to reclaim her bathing suit bottom. By the time she pulled it on she was sure Charlie was watching and knew what had happened. Besides, a globule of sperm was floating on the water.

Soon after that incident, things started to change. With her, first of all. Norman was away more and more frequently, and Barbie resented it. Besides, she was lonely. That was one reason she saw so much of Joe. Barbie wasn't comfortable with the young wives of the Peabody development. Mostly they only talked about their kids, and they looked at her in a funny way she recognized as jealousy.

In those early years she never examined the implications of her friendship with the priest. Not until one time when Norman was home and making love to her. Barbie caught herself imagining that it was Joe lying over her and humping her so powerfully he took her breath away. She felt terrible about that, guilty and ashamed and not a little surprised. She hadn't realized she felt that way. Imagining Norman was Joe seemed the height of disloyalty. But she didn't have long to worry about it. Soon afterwards her husband gradually lost interest in sex and didn't touch her for weeks at a time. In answer to her tentative probings, he said he was tired and worried about business. Barbie didn't want to nag.

When eventually he again made sexual overtures, it wasn't her vagina that attracted him. Normie had worked out the ritual that comforted and satisfied him, and Barbie didn't know how to object to it. Or how to decipher the cause of the fear she recognized behind his actions.

When her husband was away on sales trips, Barbie took the vibrator to bed. At least it kept her sane. At first she indulged herself by pretending Joe was her lover. Then an extraordinary new reality entered her life. It was something she mentioned to no one and couldn't explain to herself, but it was more important than sex.

All the same, everything that had happened today depressed her. The thought of Joe's leaving was a lump in her throat, and the last ten minutes with her husband had made it worse. Maybe if she knew what was bothering him, if she could get him to talk, things would improve. But she'd repeatedly tried and failed, and Charlie didn't want to face what was happening to Norman.

Barbie blinked away the persistent tears. Crying never helped. It just made her eyes red, like Sophie used to say. She turned on the dishwasher and went outside.

The fading light masked the ugly, stunted growth of the lawn and the evergreens they'd planted in the backyard. Barbie sat down on an upholstered redwood chair and closed her eyes. She started to relax almost instantly, feeling her breathing deepen and her muscles lose their tenseness.

In a few seconds she wasn't conscious of any of the painful events of the day. She knew only love.

IT HAD HAPPENED THE FIRST TIME DURING THE PREVIOUS winter. That experience was unlike those that followed. It was shrouded in both mystery and fear.

The first time, she'd been alone on a December day of lowering clouds that promised snow, and hating the thought of increased isolation brought on by a blizzard. So she'd puttered around the house, cleaning things that were already spotless, and wishing it was the weekend and Norman was home. Despite his depression and his drinking, he was company of a sort. Only he was off on another goddamn sales trip, and she was alone. She turned on the radio, got bored with the music and the disc jockey's patter, and shut it off. When she was a kid the words of the songs seemed to express her innermost thoughts, but they no longer did that. These days she didn't believe in love forever after.

The house had two bedrooms. One, intended for the child they might have eventually, contained only a chair and a table and some homemade shelves. She was increasingly interested in plants and flowers so she'd had made it into a growing area. Her latest experiment was germinating seeds in tiny earthen pots filled with soil she bought in plastic bags from a nearby greenhouse. These days she seldom thought of Helene, but she'd never forgotten the plants that filled the Charles Street apartment. Maybe someday she'd open a florist shop, have a career, so she wouldn't be so dependent on Normie for something to do with her life. Someday. But the thought wasn't much help right now. Better do something, no point in brooding.

She walked toward the closed door of the extra bedroom, intending to repot some tiny seedlings. Then, when she reached for the knob, it happened. She knew that something was waiting for her inside that room. The knowledge came with stunning clarity, and panic came with it. Barbie stretched out her hand, but could not make herself open the door.

For a few seconds she attempted to control her fear, then she gave up and went to the kitchen and made a cup of tea. She sat at the table with her hands clasped around a yellow ceramic mug, a careful match for the breakfast dishes in the colonial-style maple hutch. The tea grew cold and formed a scum across the top. Her arms were too heavy to lift, and her legs seemed unlikely ever to move again. But despite her outward stillness, there was a great maelstrom of activity happening inside her. No coherent thoughts, just a pulling and tugging to whatever was waiting down the hall.

For a few seconds Barbie closed her eyes and let herself sink into the vortex of that interior storm. Come through and there is peace, something or someone said. Come deep into the heart of yourself and find me, for I am waiting for you, longing for you, loving you. There is nothing to fear from love.

"Nothing to fear," Barbie whispered aloud. But she was afraid. Even so, she made herself rise and walk from the kitchen to the hall and toward the closed door. The aura was stronger than ever. It pulled her out of herself, out of shadow into reality. She was unaware of turning the knob and crossing the threshold. She knew only that she had passed from darkness into a shimmering, luminous effulgence, without beginning or end. There was no table or chair or shelves or plants. There was only radiant light, and the sweet sound of welcoming laughter.

A woman waited for her with outstretched arms. Though neither of them seemed to move, Barbie felt herself enfolded in those arms, and held with infinite tenderness and total acceptance. Slowly she understood that the woman was no stranger, that she had seen her before. I know you, she wanted to say. But there was no need for words, no need to explain, to find the beginning of either the experience or the knowledge. There was only the nowness and the oneness, and being a part of everything that was, or is, or will be. There was no time to the event, but when it began to fade Barbie knew it. She was afraid again, this time with the fear of unbearable loss. Wait! Don't go! she cried out in silence louder than speech. And in the answering silence there was the promise of return, and she was comforted. Then she was alone in the spare room with the table and the chair and the plants, and so tired she lay down on the rug and fell instantly asleep.

After that the Lady came frequently, and Barbie did not have to go into any special place to find her. She would simply look up and the beloved was there. When she didn't come, Barbie sometimes tried to dissect the experience.

Did she really see the Lady? Or did she just know she was there? Barbie wasn't sure. The only certitude was that somehow there were moments when she crossed into another dimension, another way of being. In those moments she was with the Lady. She was afraid to push the questions any further for fear of destroying the very thing she analyzed. That would be a disaster, because when she was with the Lady Barbie had, for the first time in her life, the perfect security she'd always sought.

Because she identified the Lady with a statue and a shrine she knew as Catholic, Barbie occasionally wondered if the visits were a sign that she must convert to the Catholic faith. The idea was awful—because of Sophie and Moe, and because she was not in the least drawn to the practice of any formal religion. Still, she'd do it if the Lady asked. The Lady never did.

One day, a few weeks after the first time she saw her, Barbie drove to Orient Heights to look again at the great bronze statue she'd happened on before she was married. The area surrounding it had been turned into a shrine. There were wooden benches and loudspeakers and lots of candles and strings of colored lights. Barbie sat in the rear of the area, gazing at the towering figure. It was indeed her Lady, but it wasn't. This one was only an inanimate representation. Her Lady was real and alive.

She waited, but the presence did not happen and she remained alone with a handful of praying people and the bronze figure. There was nothing for her here, neither joy nor explanation. Chilled with winter cold, Barbie rose to go. It was then she saw the rack of printed literature and picked up a small pamphlet that told the history of the shrine.

There was a metal box with a slot at the top, and Barbie forced a dollar bill into it, then went to sit in her car. She read the pamphlet before she drove away. It said that the statue had been sculpted by an Italian Jew, as a gesture of gratitude. The order of priests who ran this home for the aged also had a house in Rome, and during the war they had hidden the sculptor from the Nazis. "Oh, I see," Barbie whispered aloud. And from then on she was at peace about the whole incredible thing.

NORMAN GOLD HAD NO IDEA OF HIS WIFE'S MYSTICAL experiences, but he was praying a lot these days. Not that he understood anything about God or prayer. He only knew that he was sinking into a morass of pain and desperation, and the only way out involved paying a price he could not pay. To get out he'd have to tell Barbie about Maluchey and the debt. Worse, he'd have to tell Charlie. And he couldn't do that, he just couldn't.

"You don't look so good today, Mr. Gold," Johnny said. "A little pale. The heat, maybe. A summer flu. Them's the worst. Maybe I give you a face treatment. The hot towels make you feel better."

"I don't think so, Johnny. I'm supposed to make a plane in an hour."

"Fifteen minutes. That's all it takes. Trust me, you'll feel like a million." The barber was already busying himself with the steam cabinet and the white linen towels. He was pretty sure there was nothing odd about his voice. So maybe his hands shook a little. What the hell, he was an old man. Too old to argue with thugs and crooks. "Lie back, Mr. Gold. Just relax."

Normie lay back and thought about the plane and wished he was on it, leaving Boston behind at a few hundred miles an hour. Maybe he'd never come back. Just disappear. It was a big country, right? Wrong. Not for him. He couldn't face that any more than he could face the thought of Charlie knowing about his stupidity. That's why he had canceled his seven A.M. flight and booked a later one. Because last Friday Maluchey threatened to go to Charlie Rothstein and demand that he make good on Normie's debts. When Normie pleaded, the Lebanese showed a little mercy. He'd give Normie the weekend to come up with the dough. "I'm not an unreasonable man," Maluchey said. "I don't ask for the whole amount at once. You give me ten thousand and we'll go on as before. Who knows, maybe you'll have a big hit. You're due for a hit, Mr. Gold."

As if saying ten thousand made any difference. Ten thousand was as unavailable as twenty. But maybe he could borrow it. From one of the buyers he'd see this week. Yeah, that was an idea. He had a smart line of talk, didn't he? He'd think of some scheme the other guy should invest in. Maybe it would work. But he'd need more time. So on the way to the airport he made up his mind to talk to Maluchey again, and he canceled his early flight and booked a later one and came to the Touraine. He didn't really need a haircut, but Maluchey wasn't around and he had to kill time. Now he lay back in the chair and felt the warmth of the towels soothe his shattered nerves. Relax, he told himself, it's going to be okay. You'll work it out. Relax.

That's what the strange voice said too. "You just relax, Normie, and no one's gonna get hurt."

"What the hell." Normie struggled to free himself from the linen shroud that covered his face, but it wasn't possible. The towels were being held in place by strange hands. And the voice was strange too. Not Johnny's voice.

Something was clamped over his nose and his mouth. He couldn't breathe. His chest begun to burn, and soon there was a red haze in front of his eyes and a crazy ringing in his ears. He was dying. Oh, God. Oh, shit. Dying in a barber's chair in the sleazy lobby of the Hotel Touraine. Jimmy Cagney didn't die in the end. He always came out a winner. Oh, God. *Baruch atah Adonai* ... Not the right prayer. He didn't know any other prayers.

"Now you listen good, Normie. Maluchey wants you should understand that it has to be tonight. Not the whole thing. You owe thirty-one thousand two hundred and seventy dollars, but Maluchey, he's reasonable. You gotta pay just ten thousand. Less than a third. But it's gotta be tonight. Five o'clock here in the lobby. That way nothing's gonna happen to you or your pretty little wife, and your big-shot uncle don't have to know anything."

The numbers penetrated the physical agony. They heaved in his chest along with the struggle for breath. Thirty-two thousand dollars. All along he'd thought it was twenty. The darkness began to close over his head and the pain in his heart reached a point beyond endurance. Then it was over. The towels were off his face and the hand that had held them in place was gone. Gasping and choking for air, Normie struggled back to consciousness. The barbershop was empty. Johnny wasn't there and neither was anyone else. He dragged himself from the chair and staggered to the door. It was closed but not locked, and he yanked it open and began to run. The tired old whores in the hotel lobby ignored him.

Normie wandered through the streets of the Combat Zone in anguished oblivion. When he finally looked at the clock, he saw it was after noon. He'd missed his plane. And sometime in the last couple of hours he'd wet his pants. There was a dark stain down the front of his trousers. He'd have to go to Kneeland Street. He always kept an extra suit in the little office Uncle Charlie had assigned him. Yes, Kneeland Street. He'd have to talk to Charlie. There wasn't any other way now. "Nothing will happen to your pretty little wife," the voice had said. They knew about Barbie. Maybe they'd already gone to the house in Peabody and done something terrible to her. Acid in her face. So she wouldn't be beautiful anymore. Oh, Jesus!

He ran all the way, but when he arrived nobody was there. Everybody had gone to lunch except the switchboard operator, and she didn't notice him come in. Normie scurried to his office in the back, a rat bolting into its hole. He'd have to locked the door if he could have, but it didn't have a key. Instead he pulled the curtains over the window and crouched in the dark on the floor behind the desk. For endless minutes he just shivered and whimpered, and tried to think of how he'd tell Charlie what a mess he'd made. The picture got more and more horrible the longer he imagined it. Too horrible to be borne.

130

THE DAY AFTER HIS SUNDAY VISIT, JOE RETURNED TO Peabody. He'd promised to come and tell her the latest news, so Barbie wasn't surprised to see him. "When do you go?" she asked.

"I don't." Joe's voice was harsh with pain and anger. "I got word this morning that my appointment's been scrubbed."

"But why? I thought it was all set."

"So did I. They say it's because of the steel pin in my hip. That's a load of crap. I told them about it first thing, the doctor said it didn't make any difference."

"Why should it? You ski and swim and do everything. The only time I see you limp is if you're really tired." She took his hands, and drew him over to the sofa. "Sit down. I'll get you a beer." When she handed him the glass she said, "I'm so sorry, Joe. You really had your heart set on going, didn't you?"

He took a long swallow before he answered. "My head, if not my heart. It seemed like a good idea."

"And you really don't know why they changed their minds?"

"I can make a guess. I have a reputation as a radical. I preach sermons about civil rights and justice. Crazy modern ideas like that. Somebody at the top got wind of my application and red-penciled it. The monsignors in the chancery don't like priests who make waves."

"What are you going to do?"

Joe didn't have time to answer. The phone rang; it was Abe Cohen calling from Boston. He sounded hysterical and he didn't make a lot of sense. As far as Barbie could tell he was saying something about Normie. But Normie wasn't in Boston. He was in New Orleans selling ladies' blouses wholesale. Barbie tried to figure it out, then she gave up and handed the receiver to Joe with an expression of mystification.

"Hello, this is Father DiAnni speaking. What's wrong, Mr. Cohen?"

Joe listened for a while. Then he murmured, "Yes. Thank you," and hung up. When he turned to Barbie he was white-faced and his eyes were full of sorrow. He pulled her roughly into his arms and said softly, "Bad news. Get a grip on yourself, kid."

WHEN BARBIE AND JOE ARRIVED AT KNEELAND STREET, THE showrooms were empty and dark. In the back, where the offices were, the lights were on and a half dozen police were milling around. Two white-coated men stood to one side with a stretcher. They were waiting patiently. Charlie Rothstein was sitting on a folding chair in the hall and weeping. Abe Cohen was nearby, grim-faced and silent. He was the first to spot them.

"Hello, Father, thanks for coming. Barbie." He turned to the girl. "Barbie darling, what can I say?"

"I want to see him." Barbie's voice was cool and controlled.

"There's no reason for it," Abe said. "Better you shouldn't, darling. Remember him the way he was."

A red-faced Irish cop in plain clothes appeared. "There's no need for you to identify the body, ma'am," he said gently. "Mr. Rothstein's already done that."

"I want to see him," Barbie repeated. She turned to her companion. "Joe, please. I have to see him."

Joe tightened his grip on her arm. "I think it's what she wants, Officer. Only for a moment."

"If you say so, Father. But I warn you, it ain't pretty."

He led them to a small office at the end of the corridor. It had been Norman's since he came to work for the company. Silently, the policeman opened the door. Three men were busy taking pictures and making notes. "The widow would like to view the deceased," the Irishman said. The men in the room stopped their work and stepped aside.

Barbie took one step over the threshold and stood still. Beside her Joe stiffened, then exhaled in a long, sad sigh.

Normie was hanging from the overhead light fixture. It had started to come loose from the ceiling, but not fast enough or far enough to prevent him from accomplishing his own death. He had used his belt and a chair. The belt still remained around his neck, his head lolled at an unnatural angle, and his face was splotched purple. He'd bitten his tongue most of the way through, and blood had dripped from his chin onto his striped blue shirt front. The chair lay in the corner where he'd kicked it.

Joe tightened his arm around Barbie, but she didn't act as if she was going to faint. She stared at her husband for a moment, then closed her eyes. Joe saw her lips moving, but he didn't know what she was saying. After about ten seconds, he drew her back into the hall, and the officer closed the door.

"We didn't even know he'd come back," Abe said. The words had a used sound, as if he'd already repeated them a number of times, a droning litany of sorrow and shock. "First thing we knew was when one of the girls went in there to put some papers on his desk, and screamed. Charlie and I went out for lunch, see? The girls, too. Only the switchboard operator was here from noon until one. Normie must have come in then, but she didn't see him. I just don't get it. Why? Somebody's gotta know why."

Barbie ignored him. She turned to DiAnni. "Joe, please. Say the right prayers. I don't know what they are."

Abe Cohen put his hand on her arm. "Don't worry, darling. We've called Slotnick's Funeral Home. They'll take care of everything. There'll be a rabbi. All the right prayers will be said."

She kept her eyes on the priest. "Joe," she whispered again.

"Here." DiAnni pushed her gently toward the other man. "Look after her, Mr. Cohen. I won't be long." He disappeared into the room with the corpse, and when he returned Barbie and Abe were still standing where he'd left them. "It can't hurt, Mr. Cohen," Joe said with a small smile. "I don't imagine God cares much whether it's Latin or Hebrew."

The fatuousness of his own remark made DiAnni gag, but Abe nodded gravely and said "Thank you" in a dignified voice. The policeman said something to the white-coated attendants, and they went into the office and came out a few minutes later carrying a stretcher covered with a hospital-green sheet. When they walked past Barbie, she began for the first time to cry.

THE POLICE KEPT THE BODY A FEW DAYS, SO IT WAS MONDAY before they buried him. Joe went to the funeral and was shocked to discover how alien and sterile he found it. Nobody was promising Norman Gold immortality. On the other hand, neither did they deny him religious rites on the grounds of suicide. Watching Normie's bewildered, grieving parents, Joe was grateful for that. Barbie was stiff and solemn in a black suit and a black pillbox hat with a veil. She looked as Jackie Kennedy had looked some eighteen months earlier, as if someone had determined on the model to be followed in these circumstances. Joe tried not to think of her as an actress costumed for an important role, but the resemblance wouldn't go away.

"You all right?" he asked in a brief moment of privacy following the interment in Chelsea. Barbie nodded her head, but he still thought she looked like she was sleepwalking. He couldn't say any more because Sophie Korman joined them.

"We'll be going to the Rothsteins' now, Father," she said,

133

taking her daughter's arm and starting to draw her away from the priest.

Barbie followed her mother, then turned back to Joe. "We'll be sitting *shiva* at Charlie's house all week," she said. "Come any time if you want to."

Joe watched until the funeral cars were out of sight, swallowed by the filthy narrow streets of the town. It was an ugly thing they'd done, burying a young man who had been overcome by a despair none of them understood, and they'd picked an ugly place to do it. He wondered for the dozenth time what demons had beseiged Normie, and felt guilty because he hadn't tried harder to answer the question while the kid was alive. He wouldn't go to the Rothsteins' during the official mourning period. He'd intruded his otherness into the lives of these people too often. It was time to let go.

DiAnni turned and looked back at the grave. Two men were shoveling the last of the dirt over the coffin. "Good-bye, Normie," he said quietly. *"Requiem aeternam dona eum, Domine."*

THE SUNDAY FOLLOWING THE FUNERAL, JOE SAID THE EIGHT-o'clock Mass. At the nine and the ten he assisted with communion. At ten forty-five he started to return to the rectory for a second cup of coffee, but one of the kids from his youth group cornered him and they talked until it was time for his second Mass at noon. It was close to one before he let himself into the rectory through the kitchen. A cauldron of spaghetti sauce was simmering on the stove, and the spicy aroma made him realize he was starved. "Some woman, she keep calling you, Father," the housekeeper told him. "I tell her you no come back until dinnertime, but she keep calling. I put the message in the box."

He ran into the hall, Barbie's name a chant of fear in his head. Something had happened to her and she needed him. Her thin veneer of control had cracked. The messages were not, however, from Barbie. They contained only the word "call" and a telephone number. It was the number of his mother's apartment in the North End.

He dialed with trembling fingers. For years he'd had a recurrent nightmare. In it Don Stefano lay dying and Joe was summoned to give him absolution and the last rites. He couldn't make himself do it, and his mother's eyes looked into his with a condemnation so terrible he woke in a cold sweat.

The phone rang only twice before it was answered. "It's me, Mama, what's up?"

"Come right away."

He felt as if he was drowning, the nightmare was real. "Why? What's the matter?"

"He wants to talk to you."

"Is he all right?"

If she was surprised at his solicitude she didn't say so. "He's okay, but he wants to talk to you. Come now."

He apologized to the housekeeper about dinner and drove to the North End.

Don Stefano was sitting at the kitchen table. It was covered with an oilcloth that had been scrubbed so often the blue-and-white checks were worn away. A pack of thin black cheroots was open on the table, and a lit one was clutched in the old man's yellowed fingers. He was nearly seventy, and his voice was a harsh whisper because he had cancer of the larynx. "I have information for you," the don rasped.

"What information? Why should anything you know be important to me?" They were old enemies who did not pretend friendship. They didn't need it; mutual hate was a stronger bond.

"It's important," the old man said. "Before I tell you, you gotta make me a promise."

"I don't have to do anything. You tell me what you know and ask me what you want. If I can do anything about either, maybe I will."

"Talk respectful," his mother said. She was hovering in the background, refilling Don Stefano's wine glass whenever it was empty, like she had that first day. "You owe him," she reminded her son. "Talk respectful."

Joe started to protest, then gave it up. "What do you want?"

"You gotta promise, when I die, you get me buried from the Church. You say Masses for me."

Joe lit a cigarette with shaking fingers. "Why me? Go see a priest here. Go to confession. Anybody who's sorry for his sins can have absolution. Even you."

"You're her son," the old man said in his hoarse whisper. "It's gotta be you."

Joe stubbed out his cigarette and stood up. "I have to go. There's nothing for us to talk about."

"My information concerns the Jew-girl."

DiAnni was halfway across the room. The words hit him in

135

the back like an expertly thrown shiv. He turned around and took a step nearer the table. "Anything you know about her, you tell me. Now!" He grabbed the don's white shirtfront, and part of his mind registered the truth that there was nothing but fragile skin and bones beneath it. All the power had been eaten away by the cancer. "Talk," he hissed. "Talk or I'll kill you myself."

Don Stefano looked at him with calm eyes. "Let go of me." A thin smile showed stained teeth. "You think you can scare me?" He laughed as loudly as his disease permitted. "A threat from a little boy priest is supposed to scare Don Stefano?"

Joe released him and stood still. "God forgive me," he whispered. "Please, Don Stefano. She's only a kid. She hasn't done anything to anybody. Please tell me."

"Thas better. Thas respect, like your mama said." He selected another cheroot and took his time lighting it. "What about your promise?"

"Okay."

"Okay what?"

"Okay, I promise."

"Good. I believe you. The girl's husband killed himself because he was into Maluchey for thirty gees."

"Who's Maluchey?"

"He makes book. Works from the lobby of the Hotel Touraine. Same place the Jew-boy got his hair cut."

Don Stefano made it sound completely logical. A man went for a haircut once, maybe twice, a month and ran up a debt of thirty thousand dollars. Joe felt hollow and sick inside. All that fear and desperation, Normie lived with it until he could bear no more—a limited capacity for pain because of all his other limitations. He hoped Charlie Rothstein need never know he could have bought his nephew's life with thirty thousand dollars. "Okay," he said finally. "So it's done. The boy's dead. Why tell me now?"

"Maluchey don't think it's done. Thirty gees is a lot of money." The mouth of Don Stefano barely moved when he talked. The little cigar remained clasped between his teeth. "Word is that Maluchey's gonna have the girl snatched and get his money from her rich relatives."

Joe knew it was true. All his life had been spent in a world governed by such truths. He'd told his father he was going to fight it; instead, he merely ran away. "Who is Maluchey?" he asked again, in a voice dead with fear and shame.

"Like I tell you, he makes book. A small man, a Lebanese.

Not a *padrone*. But a lot of people owe him favors. Nobody'll stop him, long as he don't step out of his territory."

"What about you? Why can't you stop him?"

"Why should I?"

"Because of me. Because of my promise."

Don Stefano nodded. "Yes. I would do that if I could. Because you're her son." He jerked his head in the direction of Joe's mother. She remained where she'd originally stationed herself, behind her lover. "But I'm retired," the old man continued. "Besides, I'm dying. Nobody owes me favors anymore. Nobody but you."

"What should I do? Call the police?"

"Don't be stupid. Get her out of town for a while. I'll ask around. Perhaps I will learn a little more."

Joe turned and ran out of the house and down the stairs, fumbling his car keys out of his pocket as he did so. When he got to the street, he realized he was still being stupid. There was a pay phone on the corner and he ran toward it. The directory had been vandalized long ago, and he had to get information for the Rothsteins' number. It took forever, and he'd made himself calmer by the time a woman answered. He recognized Myrna Cohen's voice, they'd met a few times. He announced who he was, then he asked for Barbie.

"She's not here, Father. She left this morning to go back to her own house. I tried to talk her out of it. But she insisted she wanted to be alone."

He thanked her and hung up and called the Peabody number. The phone rang and rang, but there was no answer. Finally he gave up and dashed to his car.

He wasn't conscious of any coherent thoughts on the drive up Route 128, just a terrible panicky fear in his gut. He couldn't even pray. In Peabody, Barbie's neighborhood looked calm and ordinary, like it always did. Her living room drapes were drawn and the front door was locked. DiAnni started to ring the bell, then changed his mind and ran around to the backyard. She was sprawled on a redwood chaise lounge with her hands folded across her breast and her eyes closed. For one terrible moment he thought she was dead.

Then she opened her eyes and sat up and smiled a wan and tired smile. "Hi, Joe. I thought I heard someone come."

THEY WERE ON ROUTE 2 HEADING WEST BEFORE SHE ASKED, "Where are we going, and why? You promised to tell me once we were on the road."

"I'm taking you to Vermont, to the chalet."

The chalet was a ski lodge he'd bought into the year before. It cost thirty-six thousand dollars, but the bank advanced a ninety percent mortgage and Joe and the three other priests who were his partners needed to come up with only nine hundred each to make the down payment. Paradoxically, it was the self-indulgence represented by that purchase that had finally made DiAnni apply to go to South America.

"You should have explained before we left," Barbie said calmly. "I would have brought more sweaters." She knew the chalet well. She'd used it a few times with Norman. The priests never had weekends free, so they took turns lending it to their families and friends on those days. "It's always cool up there at night, even in the summer," she added. Joe hadn't given her much time to pack anything. His urgency had been so compelling she'd only thrown a few things into her big tote bag and gone with him. "Why?" she asked now.

He took a deep breath and said, "You're in danger. A guy wants to kidnap you."

She squirmed on the seat so she could face him, and her sorrowful eyes filled with doubt and disbelief. "Are you crazy? Who'd want to kidnap me?"

He told her, and she was silent for a while. When she spoke, her voice was full of sadness. "Poor Norman. Poor baby. Charlie would have given him thirty thousand dollars. He just couldn't ask."

"Yeah, I figured that. I hate it that we couldn't make him tell us what was wrong."

"No," she said with sudden vehemence. "Don't blame yourself and don't blame me. Normie was the way he was. He couldn't be any different."

"I don't blame you," he said. "I'm the one who's supposed to be trained to help people."

Barbie couldn't bear the sound of guilt in his voice. "Listen, I told you how peculiar Normie was lately. I didn't tell you everything." She explained about the weird sex, too intent on making him understand to feel embarrassed.

After that they lapsed into silence, until finally, seeing Joe's grim expression, she managed a grin. It was a mark of her basic disbelief in the melodrama of the moment. "Are you sure they're not following us, just waiting their chance for an ambush? Like on television."

"I'm sure. I've been watching."

The hardness of his tone made the episode more real. "Joe,

how did you find out? How do you even know about such things?"

"You know where I grew up. It shouldn't surprise you."

"It does," she said. "I grew up with bookies too." She told him about renting the pantry to guys who wanted to use binoculars to see the tote board at Wonderland. "I never heard of them kidnapping anybody. They weren't crooks, just bookies."

He sighed and started to deliver a lecture on organized crime, then stopped. "Forget it. It's nothing to do with you. You'll stay in Vermont a few days, that's all."

"How will I know when it's safe to go home?"

"I've got someone checking. I'll know."

"Okay." She dozed for the rest of the trip. He kept sneaking looks at her incredible profile and the way her gorgeous body indicated serenity, despite everything. "You're a marvel," he whispered once. But she was asleep and didn't hear.

JOE WATCHED THE SUPERMARKETS IN ALL THE TOWNS THEY passed through, but because it was Sunday, everything was closed. It was after five when they got to Wilmington. The chalet was four miles farther on, midway between Mount Snow and Haystack, and Wilmington was the nearest town. "I wish there was someplace we could buy some food," Joe said. "There's no way to tell what's left in the house. It's seldom used at this time of year."

"There's a little store attached to the gas station," Barbie said. "I think it's open on Sundays." It was. She filled a basket with groceries and insisted on paying. "I'm loaded. Charlie made me take some money this morning." She opened her wallet and he saw a stack of tens.

"That's good," he said. "I'm broke, as usual." He'd stopped on the road and changed his black suit and dog collar for the pair of jeans and sweatshirt he kept in the trunk. The priests all made a determined effort not to be identified as clergy by the locals. Now Joe blended easily into the late summer casualness of the village. In a few weeks the foliage display would begin and the place would be crammed with tourists, and shortly after that the snow birds would arrive. For the moment, Wilmington was at peace. "Any place we can make a call?" Joe asked the woman who was serving them.

She directed them to a phone in the rear, behind the restrooms. Everything was spotlessly clean. "Just dial the number you want. Don't forget the area code. After you're finished the exchange will call back and tell you what it cost. I'll be inside."

"Who are we calling?" Barbie asked.

"Charlie and Sally first. They'll be worried if they try to get you in Peabody and there's no answer. Just tell them you're going away for a few days. Don't say where."

She looked at him peculiarly, but she did as he said.

"What about your folks?" Joe said when she came out of the booth.

"I asked Sally to call my mother. I don't want to talk to her just now."

"Good girl."

The phone rang and he answered it and found out what they owed. Then he placed two more calls. Barbie stood a distance away and looked at the pine-clad mountains turning blue in the dusk. "All set?" she asked when he came toward her.

"For the moment. I don't think the pastor believes my story about a sick friend. But it will do for now." He didn't add that Don Stefano had no new information.

THEY FOUND A BOTTLE OF VALPOLICELLA IN THE HOUSE AND drank it with the steaks they'd bought. The evening turned cool as Barbie had predicted, and Joe made a fire. Then they put a Louis Armstrong record on the phonograph and took their coffee to the fireside. That's when she realized he was going to make love to her.

After all the fantasies, the reality turned out very different from what she'd imagined. Joe was slow and shy and inexpert. At first he tried to keep himself in check because he didn't want it to happen, then he was worried about hurting or shocking her. "I'm not fragile, I won't break," she whispered in his ear. His mouth came down over hers very gently and stayed so until she opened her lips and invited his tongue to taste more of her.

It was she who opened the buttons of her blouse and loosed her bra and offered her breasts to him. He touched them with wonder bordering on awe, and she guided his head into position and felt her nipples swell when his tongue flicked over them. They remained so until the record ended and Barbie moved out of his arms and turned off the phonograph and took off the rest of her clothes. He was lying on the couch with his eyes closed and his hands folded behind his head when she returned. "Look at me, Joe," she whispered. "Don't be afraid."

He opened his eyes and stared at her luminous skin lit by the dancing fire and he groaned, then reached for her and drew her close. Barbie knelt over him, doing things she'd never done before, with no motive other than that she wanted to do such things here with him. She offered her womanhood to his mouth and he suckled greedily and she moaned with pleasure. "I want to taste you," she said at last. So finally he unbuttoned his jeans and she pulled them off of him and buried her face in his crotch and took the swollen tip of his penis tenderly between her lips and bestowed gentle kisses on the insides of his thighs and his heavy balls and the sensitive blue-veined skin stretched taut and throbbing over his organ.

"I can't," Joe whispered.

"Can't what?"

"I can't stop."

She thought he meant he was going to come right away and she wanted him inside her when he did that. She wanted to swallow him and be swallowed by him. She wanted her love to reach out and possess him so he would always be hers. She lifted her head and knelt over him once more, letting herself down easily and guiding him inside her with one hand. The muscles of her supple body responded to her need. She grasped the essence of him with the essence of herself and moved up and down and managed to bring her clitoris into contact with his skin so that the friction excited them both and sent shock waves between their joined flesh.

"Oh, my God!" Joe screamed through clenched teeth. He grabbed her shoulders and pulled her down so that she lay over him and his arms were around her while he shuddered and shook with the force of his orgasm and of hers.

"I love you," she whispered. "I love you so much, Joe. I never knew how much until tonight, but I'm never going to stop."

SHE WENT INTO THE BATHROOM AND CAME OUT WEARING AN old flannel bathrobe she'd found there. Joe had put his jeans back on and he was standing by the stove in the little kitchenette that was part of the living room, waiting for some water to boil. "Coffee or tea?"

"Tea, please. I never drink coffee late at night."

He brought the drinks to the sofa and sat down beside her

and took her hand and kissed the palm gently, then took his own hand away. "Thank you," he said. His voice was so soft she had to strain to hear him. "Thank you now and thank you always, for the rest of my life. It was the most beautiful thing that's ever happened to me, Barbie. But it can't happen again. Not ever."

"Because you're a priest and you're going to go on being a priest. I know. I've always known. But it doesn't change anything. I love you."

He didn't answer, and they sipped their drinks in silence for a few moments until she said, "There's something I've got to tell you. I never mentioned it before, but I think you should know now." He still didn't say anything, but she knew he was listening. He had a way of cocking his head to the side and waiting, which meant you had all his attention.

"I think you should know," she repeated. She didn't understand why. A gift of self perhaps, like that which had preceded. "The Madonna of the Universe, I've seen her."

He looked blank, unable to decipher the information, then he said, "Oh, you mean the statue? The big one in Orient Heights?"

She laughed softly. A tinkling sound that came and went in a moment, but left its echo in the room. "Not the statue, silly. The Lady. I saw the statue first, of course. That's how I recognized her."

Alarms started buzzing in his head. "Listen, honey, you have been through a hell of a lot, not just the last couple of weeks, but all those months when Normie was acting so peculiar. It's natural if you—"

Barbie didn't know whether to laugh or cry. "Oh, Joe! You think I'm nuts, or tripping out like the college kids. LSD, maybe? Don't be an idiot. She is real, you know. And just because I'm not a priest or a nun doesn't mean I can't see her. I love her, that's why she comes to me."

"Of course she's real," he said quickly. He didn't know what to say after that. The Blessed Virgin Mary was real, and visions of her were part of the long history of Christendom, but what did that have to do with Barbie? She wasn't a saint; she wasn't even a Christian. He fastened on that thought. It was something he could understand. "Listen," he said slowly. "I've never tried to convert you, you know that. But would you like some books to read? About the faith, I mean. Or I can try to answer your questions if you want."

"What questions?"

"The teachings of the Church. The dogmas relating to Our Lady, for a start. If you want," he repeated hastily.

Barbie shook her head in wonder and frustration. "You're the one who's acting nuts. I'm a Jew because my parents are, because it's how I was brought up. Part of my genes, I guess. But that's got nothing to do with loving the Lady. She's beyond all that, bigger, more important. Don't you understand?"

It was his turn to shake his head. "What did she tell you?" He was thinking of Lourdes and Fatima and messages to rock the universe, and thoughts of such things connected with Barbie made his stomach churn. The Church needed no more bleeding Jesuses, and Barbie needed no notoriety.

Barbie's eyes went dark with anger and her jaw set in a way with which he was familiar. "Nothing. She tells me nothing. You don't understand at all. Maybe you're a little anti-Semitic, Joe. Just around the edges where it doesn't really show."

"I didn't mean anything like that. You should know better. I'm just trying to figure out what you're talking about."

"And you can't." Her voice and her expression softened and she leaned over and kissed him lightly on the cheek. "Forget it. It doesn't matter, and I was silly to bring it up." She rose and stretched her arms over her head. The old robe gaped open, and she hurriedly closed it. "I'm going to bed." She was halfway across the room before she turned and smiled. It was a smile lit with radiance and knowing and wisdom that banished some of his confusion by its splendor. "Good night, Joe darling. Sleep sweet, because in the morning we're going to be the same people we've always been. The same friends. Tonight never happened."

Joe might have called her in-bed thoughts prayers. Barbie knew she was simply talking to the Lady, not really surprised by her presence in the room. "Always a priest," she whispered. "Yes, I understand. It hurts, but I understand."

After Barbie left, Joe sat and watched the dying fire for a while. Then he stepped out onto the deck and looked at the sky alight with stars, and at the black velvet mountains lit by the moon.

"O my God, I am heartily sorry that I have offended thee . . ." he began. The rest of the act of contrition wouldn't come. He was sobbing too hard to formulate the words.

The next morning they went back to Wilmington and Joe made another phone call. Barbie bought more food and a heavy cardigan at the one boutique open during the off-season. When they returned to the chalet, they talked little, and pointedly did not touch. The day passed slowly, until shortly after four, when a dusty blue Volkswagen came up the driveway.

"Who's that?" Barbie's voice betrayed her tightly controlled fear.

Joe put his hand on her shoulder and left it there for a few reassuring seconds. Then he drew away. "Don't panic, kid. It's a friend of mine. I called him this morning. I've got to go back and you can't be alone."

She didn't say anything, just watched a big redheaded man climb out of the car, then get some things from the trunk. When he moved toward the house, he was carrying a small suitcase, and something else. Suddenly she recognized the second piece of luggage. "He's got a gun!"

"A rifle," Joe said easily. "He's the original great white hunter. Deer, things like that."

In fact, Father Lou Wisnovski had taken some persuading. "You're nuts, boyo. It's not the hunting season," he'd said on the phone.

"Listen, Lou, don't argue. Just bring a gun. I don't think there's a chance in hell they'll find her up here, but you never know. That's why I thought of you."

It wasn't the only reason. Wisnovski had been a faculty member when Joe was at the seminary. The Pole taught ethics and moral theology, and he deviated from the party line enough to make the rector uncomfortable. Eventually both men had agreed it would be better if Father Wisnovski returned to parish life. It was a particularly spiteful gesture that caused him to be appointed a curate rather than a pastor despite his fifty plus years. Lou said he didn't mind. "Less responsibility," he insisted. "More time to do the things I like." So he joined the younger men in the cooperative purchase of the ski lodge, and in the months when there was no snow, he hunted and fished and sailed. He also continued a lifetime practice of working out regularly at a Boston gym. When he hauled his six foot four of brawn into the living room of the chalet, Barbie stared at him openly.

"I guess Joe figures you'll scare the bad guys away," she said with a small frightened laugh.

Father Wisnovski produced a mock snarl. "I'm good at it. Besides, there are no bad guys. Just misguided boys who had an unfortunate childhood. We'll use psychology."

Her laugh was a little less tense the second time. While he spoke, the priest hefted his rifle. It was very big, like him, and

144

it glittered with deadly beauty. "This is excellent psychology," he said, patting the polished stock. "It's a 30-30 Winchester. Good if you're going after big game in brush country." He switched to a western drawl. "Shoot the head off a bear at fifty yards, ma'am, don't you worry none." He slipped back into his normal tone. "You don't by any chance play gin rummy?"

Barbie grinned at him. "I do. There's only one problem: I always win. Are you a sore loser, Father?"

"Not so you'd notice."

"I'd better go," Joe said. "I'm probably on disciplinary suspension already."

"No you're not." Lou took a pipe from his pocket and put it unlit between his teeth. "I'm an obnoxious nonconformist, but I've still got some friends among the movers and shakers. I made a call and somebody else made a call. As far as your good pastor is concerned, you smell like a rose. He'll greet you like the prodigal son returned."

The two men walked together to Joe's car. Lou carried the Winchester over his shoulder and the pipe still in his mouth. He looked like Davy Crockett, at least the way Crockett should have looked. "How's she really handling it?" he asked. "From what you tell me, she's had a lot of shocks in the past few days."

"Yes, but she's tougher than I thought. I've known her a long time, since she was a kid in high school, but I think I've been misjudging her." He didn't look at his old friend when he said, "Thanks for everything. I owe you; I won't forget."

"What kind of horseshit is that? Didn't you learn anything in my classes? You owe me nothing. Take care, and don't worry about the girl. Neither of us is going to budge from here until you give the word."

Joe nodded and put a hand on the car door, then he paused. "One more thing. I'd like you to hear my confession before I go."

Wisnovski nodded and looked around. He spotted a granite outcrop halfway up the hill behind the house, and they climbed to it and surveyed the scene. They could see all four sides of the chalet and about half a mile of the approach road. "Looks okay," the older man said. He unslung the rifle and propped it against a boulder. Then he reached into his hip pocket and produced a purple stole. "I had a hunch you might ask," he said.

Joe called the don as soon as he got back to the rectory, but there was still no news. "Tomorrow morning, I think," the hoarse voice said. "You come see me tomorrow morning."

Whatever Father Pasco had been told, he apparently believed it. He made no objection when Joe said he needed to go to Boston the next morning. "Of course, Father. I'll take the eight o'clock Mass if you wish."

"No, sir, thank you, that's not necessary." He shook his head in awe. He'd give a lot to know what story Lou had cooked up. A secret mission for the Holy Father, maybe. Nothing less seemed adequate for the reaction. For a while he could see the humor of the whole episode. It was black comedy, but it was funny.

He stopped laughing when he entered his mother's kitchen and smelled the familiar dark cheroot. Since he was a kid he'd hated the odor of Don Stefano's cigars. They were a sign of his presence and his rule.

"Sit down," the old man rasped. Joe's mother gave both men tiny cups of thick black coffee, then retired. The don drank his in one gulp and returned to nursing his ever-present glass of wine. "It has been difficult, but it's done," he said finally. "The girl won't be touched."

Joe felt the tension leave his body. It seeped away like water through a sieve and left him feeling drained and empty, but relaxed. "Thank you," he said.

"S'all right. It was good to find someone who remembered that I am due respect. Not all the young ones have forgotten how it used to be. One of them spoke with the Lebanese and explained my wishes."

Joe got up to go. "Thanks again," he said.

Don Stefano raised a restraining hand. "One more thing you should know. The reason it was so complicated, there was another woman involved. I don't know the details, but it took much influence to stop the *fragazza.*"

Joe nodded and started for the door. He'd thanked the bastard twice. It was enough. And he didn't want to know more of the twisted and ugly convolutions in the old man's world.

"Joseph." The voice arrested him with his hand on the doorknob. "You will not forget your promise."

It was a statement, not a question. "I won't forget," Joe said.

Downstairs he stood undecided for a moment, then headed for the Western Union office in Park Square. The little post office in Wilmington could be counted on to deliver a telegram. "Come home," he wrote on the yellow form. "All is forgiven."

I N T E R L U D E

THE LADY

Circa 4,000 B.C. to A.D. 375

HER ROOTS ARE OF BARELY IMAGINABLE ANTIQUITY,
buried in the ceaselessly moving sands of the
Arabian desert. In this vast emptiness, bounded
on the east by the Red Sea and on the west by the Nile,
salted by starlight and blazoned by fiery sun, the tale of
the Lady begins. For there is here some genius, some
primeval knowledge carried on the wind, some key to
the quest. This is a place where God speaks and the universe trembles in response. Here are found the ancestors
poised on the edge of now.

First a pair, a man and woman united by their mutual
need, that uniquely recurrent hunger for each other's
body; alone among all creatures in this desire to mate in
season and out. Soon offspring, eventually the partners
of the offspring. Thus a clan. Coalescing, bonding, remaining together for comfort and safety, they evolve
into a tribe, and finally into many tribes. Inevitably the
tribes battle to possess those isolated places where animals can graze, where crops can grow, and where can be
found that thing more precious than all things, water.

The struggle is without quarter. There is no end to the
wars, the movement, and the migrations. Yet some of
the nomads settle. Around them great civilizations are

147

born and die and are born again. The tribes of the desert lay claim to territory and acquire names by which other men may know them. The Ammonites, the Edomites, the Moabites, the Hebrews—they are the Semites.

Others trek onward, still seeking security, grazing . . . and always water. They move west to Africa, to yet another desert, the Sahara. Now this separate branch of the ancient stock also divides and is named. Mysterious spawn from that place of ferment and holiness, they call themselves Shelloh, Sus, Zouave, Tuareg. To the rest of the world they are Berbers.

THE DARK WAS NOT THAT OF THE DESERT BEHIND THEM, IT WAS washed gray, lightened by the glow of the city. The man shaded his eyes with his hand. Deep in the desert and in the mountains of the Rif he could see as well by night as by day; here, the enemy blinded him. His nose twitched. They stank, these foreigners. The stench of their great marble houses and amphitheaters and temples wafted across the deep wadi and assaulted him. Behind him he sensed the revulsion of the others of his party. Sensed too the lust of battle stirring their blood. He raised his arm, a signal to them to wait. A woman named Talama crept closer; her wooden spear touched his shoulder to signal her presence. "Why do we delay?"

For answer he pointed to a shadow on the path between them and the city. Two men strolled casually in the night, talking, unaware of the presence of the avengers. Talama caught her breath in pleased surprise. The leader felt her spear move, and he put a restraining hand on her arm. "Wait," he breathed softly in her ear.

The men came closer.

"Antoninus, you lied to me. I expected a dull outpost. Tangis is a city."

The taller of the two laughed softly. "It's not Rome."

"No, but you're not as bad off as I thought, after your pleading letters for transfer."

Antoninus stiffened at the choice of words. "I'm not pleading, Clodius."

"A prefect belongs in the field of battle, my friend. The Third Legion controls all of Africa. Where can you better serve the Emperor?"

Antoninus shrugged and didn't answer. They walked

on, seduced by the soft spring night and the smell of desert flowers blooming after brief winter rains. For a moment the tall prefect thought he caught some other, foreign scent, then it was gone. Not here, not this close to the city with its mighty praetorium housing five hundred infantrymen and two dozen cavalry. He dismissed the idea. "Speaking of the Emperor, is it true he's coming here from Tarragona?"

"With the wandering Hadrian, who knows? But there is a rumor. He bores easily, you know. I suppose a year in Hispania is enough. Africa beckons. Just a moment; these new sandals are chafing me." Clodius paused and bent down.

Antoninus turned his back on the older man and gazed at Tangis. Clodius called it a city, but only Rome was worthy of that name. In the moonless night he could just make out the roof of his house. It seemed small and insignificant, dwarfed by the surrounding desert. He despised it almost as much as the folly that made it necessary for him and his legion to remain. Harsh taxes, tribute extracted at swordpoint—a little less greed and they could govern without arms.

And while Clodius adjusted the lacings of his shoe and the prefect mused on the workings of the Pax Romana, Talama loosed her spear.

Antoninus knew when it sliced the air. He didn't hear or see it, only felt the breeze of its lethal passage. With a startled cry, he turned back to warn his friend. There was only one moment to take in his open-eyed stare of death—and the shadowy cluster of bodies pelting across the wadi. His hand dropped to his waist. One dagger against so many. The prefect grasped the still quivering shaft of the spear lodged in Clodius' heart and pulled it with a savage jerk. The wooden tip broke off in the wound. That was always the way with the weapons of the desert tribes. Antoninus cursed and judged the distance between himself and the attackers. For a fraction of a second he turned his head and measured the road that led back toward the city. His decision was instantaneous. Flinging the now useless spear at the enemy, he turned and ran.

For weeks the memory of that flight sat sour in his belly. And the knowledge that of the twenty-seven who attacked, only five were killed. The rest got away. One of them even managed to take the vexillum, proud banner of the legion, from its post outside the praetorium. The centurion responsible for that dishonor was beheaded the day after the raid, but that didn't satisfy Antoninus. When Hadrian proved the truth of the rumors by arriving in Mauretania, it was Antoninus who suggested they send a major force into the desert and subdue once and for all the rebellious tribes. Hadrian seized on the idea, and announced that he himself would lead the legion into battle. Antoninus was a seasoned politician as well as a soldier, and he knew better than to protest. It was only after the brief but hard fought campaign ended in victory that he again asserted himself.

"Death is too good for them," Antoninus told his Emperor.

"What then?" Hadrian looked at his prefect through narrowed eyes. Ambitious, this one; longing for the taste of Rome.

"Banishment," Antoninus said. "Permanent banishment of the entire tribe, not just the raiders. That way we're rid of all of them."

The Emperor moved to the door of the tent and faced the endless expanse of the Sahara. "It should be impossible to find any more isolated or inhospitable place for them."

"With respect, it's no longer isolated." Antoninus pointed to a map lying on the table. The great cities of the empire were clearly marked. From Carthago and Utica in the east to Tangis in the west they formed an arc along the Mediterranean to the shores of the Atlantic, surrounding the great desert of the interior. "Here," Antoninus said. "Here, we'd be forever rid of all of them." His finger came to rest on a tiny scattering of marks off the Atlantic coast.

Hadrian bent his head and studied the map. "The Fortunate Isles."

"Yes, described by King Juba and by Pliny. Deserted, according to both of them. Sufficiently distant for people with absolutely no knowledge of ships or navigation."

The Emperor smiled and put his hand on the prefect's shoulder. "Well said, Antoninus. Do it. But there's something else: we don't wish to be seen as weak rather than merciful. Among these barbarians the women fight too, but the men are the leaders. Let's devise something special for them."

Antoninus waited. Hadrian paced and thought. Finally the Emperor spoke. "I can't come up with any particularly novel ideas at this hour," he said ruefully. "Just cut out their tongues before they're loaded aboard the ships."

"Only the men?"

Hadrian made a dismissive gesture. "Yes, I suppose so. And Antoninus." The prefect paused in the doorway of the tent. "When all this is over, I want you to join me in Rome."

Hadrian watched the younger man walk away. He knew the prefect was pleased. So was he. A man so ambitious was better where he could be watched.

Antoninus was conscious of Hadrian's eyes on his back, and careful not to let the degree of his elation show. But it surged in him, ran in rivulets down his spine and made the ends of his fingers tingle. Escape from the heat and the barren sands, a place in the Emperor's entourage, and, above all, Rome. He walked on, needing movement to express his excitement. A sentry saluted smartly and Antoninus nodded in response, turning his face from the glow of the soldier's torch so his broad grin wouldn't show.

A few yards to his left, the women prisoners were roped together, lying on the ground. The prefect approached one of the guards. "All quiet?"

"Yes, sir. We've whipped the fight out of them."

Antoninus grunted and lifted a pole topped with burning pitch from where it had been plunged into the sand. He carried the light closer to the captives. They sprawled over each other, a tangle of arms and legs seeking protection from the cold of the desert night. He could smell their festering wounds. The stench eliminated any eroticism from their nakedness. He thought of how they had looked in battle, short, fierce women with blood lust in their eyes. Now most of those eyes were closed in defeat and exhaustion.

But not all. One woman stared up at him. Impulsively, Antoninus reached down and hauled her to her feet. The cord around her neck yanked two others awake as well. And it kept her from standing upright. She squatted in front of him, staring at the ground.

The sentry came quickly to his side and took the torch. "Shall I have this one cleaned up and brought to your tent, Prefect?"

Antoninus hesitated. A woman might be useful tonight. A way of dealing with his surging emotions. He looked at her more closely. Good breasts and a flat belly, muscular legs and arms. Filthy hair, but it might be blond once it was washed. He was tempted. Except that tomorrow would be a long day. Better he conserve his strength. "No, I don't think I've the stomach for anything so primitive."

The sentry lifted his foot and shoved the woman back into the heap of her fellow prisoners. Then he guided the prefect back to his tent.

Talama watched them go.

SOME OF THE PEOPLE FROM THE GREAT TEL BETWEEN THE Moroccan Rif and the Sahara were banished to the easternmost of the Fortunate Isles. Seventy-two of them were put ashore on that barren island. Thirty-one mutilated men, sixteen women, and twenty-five children, a few sheep, some goats, two barrels of water, and a dozen sacks of grain. When the ship bearing the other members of their families, clans, and tribe sailed away, the women fell to the ground. They beat their foreheads on the desiccated earth and wailed. The children took up the mournful dirge, and the combined cries echoed from the surrounding peaks beyond the shore. Only the men were silent, ashamed to make the pitiful, strangled cries that would come from their tongueless mouths.

For three days the exiles cowered in the lee of the cliffs, screaming with fear when wild dogs came near. They ignored the sheep and the goats, and the animals wandered off in search of grazing. The sacks of grain were immediately ripped apart and left open. Anyone could grab at will a handful of the only available food. On the fourth day, at sunrise, Talama came to her senses.

Though she had been married for ten years, Talama was still almost young. Her husband was dead, but four of her daughters were with her in exile. When she looked at her children, Talama knew she must find strength. "We have finished our grieving." Talama's voice was a thing of certitude in the dawn. "We must plan. And we must live."

"What if the soldiers come back?" another woman demanded.

"Then they'll come back. At least it won't be so easy for them to find us." Talama turned to the stark bare hills. "We must move inland for security. You," she pointed to one of the mute men. "Gather up the grain. Be careful to get every bit that spilled." He looked at her with bitter resentment. Women didn't issue orders to men. But since he could make no reply he had little choice except to obey. Besides, he knew she was right.

So did the others. Talama had no special status among them. Until now none of them had thought her any different from themselves. But she alone was willing to face the future, any future, and first grudgingly, then gratefully, they followed her lead.

They assembled their small supply of stores, moving stiffly, still oppressed by terror. A little boy pointed to the second water barrel. It had burst its staves and no one had thought to salvage it. The other barrel had already been drunk dry.

"It's stupid to move from here," someone muttered. "We'll die of thirst whatever we do." Others took up the refrain.

"Look." Talama commanded them. Her strong, full body straining toward the hills, she stretched out her arm. In the distance was the faint silhouette of a scrawny tree. Talama moved her pointing finger and they noticed others. "If there are trees, there must be water in the ground. We'll find it. Now come."

All day they walked, a straggling caravan of despair without destination and without hope. Only Talama was sure of her goal; the rest followed because it was easier than arguing or being left behind.

By nightfall the children were wailing their fatigue and hunger and thirst. Opposition to the forced march grew stronger. "You're crazy, Talama. You don't know where you're going or why. This is a strange place. Evil. Those trees get farther away the more we walk. The place is cursed and so are we. I'm not going hungry any longer."

Talama had denied them food all these long hot hours. Now the woman who spoke made a lunge for the sacks of grain.

"Wait!" the self-appointed leader cried. "We can't just

stuff our mouths. That's all we have. It has to be divided carefully. We must save some for seed."

No one would have listened to her except that again one of the children startled them all. "Look!" he shouted. "Water! Talama has brought us to water!"

The crowd ran to where he stood. Beneath them was a depression in the stone. A trickle of moisture was just visible in the dying rays of the sun. Scrambling over each other in their haste and thirst, they fought to dip their fingers in the precious fluid. Talama ignored them. Summoning the last of her own waning strength and determination, she half-crawled behind the outcrop of the cliff.

As she suspected, the source of the water was there. It was neither a stream nor a spring, only a great hollow stone basin, but it was full of water. Talama realized that some time in the recent past it had rained, and miraculously, this depression had not allowed the water to seep away.

She hurried back to the others, still warring over the trickle of moisture. "Stop! There's plenty for everyone. Come and see."

They saw and drank their fill, and ate the handful of grain Talama allowed them. Then the wanderers slept. In the morning they decided to remain where they were. Not only was the water a sign from heaven, a short distance away they discovered a flat plane with deep soil still moist from the same rain that had filled the natural cistern. Here they could plant, as they had done for a few months each year in the old land.

"But we have no tents," someone complained. "No shelter."

"There are caves," Talama said firmly. "And stones that we can pile up to make huts."

The others nodded agreement and slowly began to organize themselves into work parties. Talama saw with satisfaction that a small supply of hope had come into the hearts of her sisters. Only the men were doing nothing. They stood apart and silent, watching the women work. Talama approached them. "Go into the hills and find the goats and sheep that wandered away the first day. Without them we can't survive."

She didn't expect to be refused. Of course she knew that men did not obey women in the old days in the desert, but she knew too that everything was different now. What use were men who couldn't speak? They had no choice but to do as they were told. She turned aside. Suddenly the strongest of the former warriors dashed forward and hit her hard on the side of the head. Talama stumbled to the ground.

She remained on her knees for a moment, her breasts heaving with pain and surprise. The other women stopped working and stared at the unfolding drama. Slowly all the men moved closer together. Soon they were ranked in opposing lines: the women and children on one side, the silent men on the other, Talama on her knees between them.

For long moments the only sound was the wind in the hills and the distant cawing of the gulls on the shore below. Finally, Talama rose to her feet. "Very well," she said softly, "you don't choose to sacrifice your dignity, even if it might save all our lives." Turning to the watching women and children, she beckoned her daughters.

The eldest of the four was nine; the youngest, three. "Go into the hills and find our goats and sheep," Talama told them. "Don't come back unless you bring them with you."

Wordlessly they stared at her and knew she would not recant. When they left, the littlest one was struggling on her short, stubby legs to match the stride of her sisters. "Among us from now on only small girls will care for animals," Talama said. The others looked at this unnatural mother with fear, but they went on with their tasks.

A week later the children returned to the makeshift settlement. Talama hadn't really expected to see them again, though she spoke confidently of their imminent return and ordered a corral of stones built to house the livestock. Now she gazed at her daughters with joyful wonder. The youngest, held in the arms of her sister, was obviously dead, but Talama made no cry of mourning. "You've done very well," she told them. The girls drove seven sheep and nine goats into the newly erected enclosure.

Talama took the body of her dead child and carried it to a tiny cave above the camp. One of the silent men had been a priest in former days. He raised his arms to the one God the tribe had long worshipped, but since he could chant no prayers over the small corpse, a number of the women supplied his voice and sang the burial song.

TALAMA'S YOUTH FLED QUICKLY. WHEN FIVE SUMMERS HAD come and gone, she was an old woman. She made herself a hut a little way from the village and spent her days alone, in prayer and in thought. Many wonders had come to pass on the island they now called Tyterogaka. The soldiers of the cruel prince had never returned and the people were free to live as they wished. Some of the things they'd done would have been taboo in the old days, but everything had a purpose in this strange place.

Because there were so many more men than women, it had been obvious that they must share. At first this caused bitter enmity, but eventually Talama decreed that each woman must take three husbands. That had kept the peace for a while, until the men began fighting over whose turn it was to lie next with the wife they held in common. "One passage of the moon," Talama said. "From one full moon to the next a woman lies with her first husband, then the next moon with her second, and then the next with her third."

This arrangement prevailed not only because Talama's words usually became law, but because it pleased the women. The thing they liked least about giving themselves to three men was the uncertainty over the fatherhood of their children. Now they could be reasonably sure which man had sired which infant. To keep peace they gradually stopped calling their sons ben—son of—anyone, but they knew which seed had produced which fruit, and this allowed them to direct their domestic affairs with confidence.

By itself this arrangement didn't end strife. In the past they'd always had a chief, but no chief had been among the men deposited on Tyterogaka. The women felt this lack as much as the men. Talama's rule was accepted as a necessity, but it wasn't in the nature of things for a female to lead.

In time-honored tradition the men fought to establish dominance, and five of the youngest and best males died as a result. Everyone realized this was foolhardy in such a small community where so much labor was required to survive, but no one had a solution. Then the answer came to Talama, in a moment's insight based upon a fortuitous accident.

Zoma ben Yasef had been a child when they first came to the island. Now he was a strong and virile young man. Often he roamed by himself among the high mountains to the south and to the north. One afternoon, when the great heat of the third summer was on the land, and the village was still except for the buzzing of flies and the occasional baaing of the sheep, Zoma ben Yasef returned carrying a stone that was black on one side and glittering green on the other. Everyone clamored for a closer look and demanded to know what it was.

"I found it lying among the rocks high in the mountains," Zoma ben Yasef explained. Proudly he held up the amulet and turned it so they could all see the way the sun made sparks of light bounce from the crystalline green surface.

Talama too stared at the jewel. Then she had her inspiration. "Zoma ben Yasef is our chief," she cried out. "The Holy One has given this sign that he is to rule." Talama fell to the ground and made obeisance. Within seconds the other women did likewise. There was a pause, then the men too knelt. They weren't fools; they knew the fight for dominance couldn't go on forever. Besides, Zoma ben Yasef was young and able, and he could speak. That would help keep the women in line, which was a necessity obvious to all of them.

"Zoma ben Yasef is our chief," Talama repeated, raising her arms to God. "His son will rule after him and their sons after that. We are blessed by the Holy One." With careful ceremony, she took the black-and-green stone, tied it with a leather thong, and hung it around the new chief's neck.

Now, old and worn out and awaiting death, Talama sat in the little hut she had made for herself and prayed, and thought about the many strange things that had occurred in her life.

ONCE MORE THE TERRIBLE VOICE OF GOD HAD SPOKEN IN THE holy desert. And the Word became Flesh. Once more the nucleus was rent asunder and the awesome power of that division cast fire and sword upon the earth and reverberated through all time that was, and is, and will be.

157

From the burning vortex of that cataclysm spun fragments apparently unrelated, but parts of a whole.

AFTER THE BRIEF CAMPAIGN IN AFRICA, ANTONINUS TRAVELED always with Hadrian. Eleven years later they stood together surveying the smoldering remains of Jerusalem, that once beautiful city on the hill. "Too bad," the prefect murmured. "These Jews are such fools."

The Emperor nodded in agreement, but his eyes were sad. This wasteland of devastation was not his choice. Hadrian had been charmed by Jerusalem when he first saw it three years earlier. Not by the city it was then—a handful of Hebrews living in hovels amid the ruins left by the seige of Titus sixty years before—but by the beauty of the site. "I'll build a great Roman city here," the Emperor had promised. "Over there I'll raise a temple in honor of Jupiter." He'd pointed to the ruins of Solomon's Temple to the one true God. But the Hebrews refused his offer to make them a city where commerce could thrive and there could be light and music and learning.

I am the Lord thy God, thou shalt have no other God before me.

In reply to Hadrian's generosity, the Jews, that small, tattered remnant still quivering in the agony of their last defeat, again took arms against the mighty Roman army.

"How do they last so long?" Hadrian had asked throughout the thirty-six months of that imbalanced campaign. Antoninus, who always knew the details of such things, mentioned Rabbi Akiba, great scholar turned revolutionary, and his sponsorship of a messiah called Simon Bar Cochba. "Another messiah," Hadrian had sighed. "They'll never learn."

To teach them, the Romans destroyed 985 towns in Palestine, they killed over half a million men, a greater number perished of starvation and disease, and Bar Cochba fell while defending Bethar. In the aftermath so many Jews were sold as slaves that their price fell to that of a horse. To escape slavery, thousands hid in underground channels and died of starvation, while the living ate the bodies of the dead.

Jerusalem, Jerusalem! thou which killest the prophets and stonest them which are sent to ye. How often would I have gathered thy children together and ye would not.

Hadrian looked at the emptiness that had once been a city, and in the purple dusk he turned to Antoninus. His voice was hard. "Never again. They will not rise again."

Circumcision he forbade, and the observance of the Sabbath, and the public performance of any Hebrew ritual. No Jew could enter Jerusalem except on one fixed day each year, when they might come and weep beside the ruined wall of their Temple.

While all this was accomplished and plans made for the great Roman city of Aelia Capitolina that would rise upon the ashes, Antoninus reported word of yet another uprising among the Sahara tribes around the cities of Roman Africa.

"It's been put down, I trust." Hadrian sounded weary. "We don't have to go back and lead the battle?"

"The rebellion is ended," Antoninus assured him. "I'm told another few hundred survivors have been deposited in the Fortunate Isles."

And neither man recognized that the enemy was one and the same. The Hebrews and the tribes of the Sahara were bred in the same cauldron of God.

WHEN THE ROMAN SHIP LANDED YET ANOTHER BAND OF DAZED half-dead exiles on the shores of Tyterogaka, Talama was dead and Zoma ben Yasef had grown into a strong and wise chief. His scouts excitedly reported the new arrivals. They were impatient to go to them as soon as the ship had disappeared, but Zoma made them wait. "They must first realize what this place is that they've come to. They have to understand what they face here."

Five days later, Zoma ben Yasef appeared on the beach, surrounded by a retinue of his strongest followers. The newcomers were totally desolate. No wise Talama had risen among them to bring order out of chaos, and their food and water were nearly gone. They stared at Zoma in wonder, their eyes transfixed by the shining green medallion round his neck. Zoma stared back. Finally he spoke. "I am ruler in this place. We will not kill you if you swear to accept our ways and obey our laws."

He spoke a language much like theirs, and the survivors remembered stories of another banishment a decade earlier. They realized that this man was one of themselves, but changed and transfigured by this strange land. Without exception they swore allegiance to their new chief and went to live among his people.

The newcomers numbered forty-one. Combined with the original community, which had known both births and deaths, they made a total of just under one hundred and fifty unwilling settlers in a place of both beauty and desolation.

They were now heirs of the last glacial age, the latest period of geological history. They lived among low, rounded pleistocene mountains, volcanic cones that had once spewed forth the fire that shaped this world. The thin, scorched soil in which they struggled to grow grain was the remains of an ancient lava field, pounded to dust by millennia. Grazing for their sheep and goats was a minimal layer of scrubby thorn bushes that overspread the slopes and valleys of the mountains.

For a few weeks in most years, after the annual rains, there was a sudden flowering of succulent green plants on the plains, progeny of seed carried on the trade winds that continually swept the island. This lush carpet lasted a brief time, then burned dry in the perpetual sun. The exiles learned to let their animals feed voraciously while the plants lived—ah, but the milk was sweet in those days!—and to harvest and dry all that they could not eat.

The yearly rain was not just important for the livestock; the impervious stone and crusted earth of the island kept the rain from draining away. In natural hollows and laboriously hewn cisterns the people stored all the water they would have for at least twelve more waxings and wanings of the moon.

The rains were a beneficence beyond price, and the old priest who had been among the first settlers indoctrinated a few young men into his mystic secrets, in silent lessons where his trembling old hands were more eloquent than speech. They learned to offer sacrifice in petition and thanksgiving for the incalculable blessing of water.

A hard land indeed, in its way harder than the desert that had spawned them, for here a few days' walk in any direction brought them to the sea. Nomads used to wandering incalculable distances, they were now imprisoned on their small island. Of boats they knew nothing, nor had they materials with which to build. A few young visionaries dreamed of skimming across the waves to other islands they could sometimes see in the distance, but it was an idle fantasy. The crashing waves filled them with fear, and no history of sea-faring lodged within their blood and sinew to give them courage.

But they were not unhappy. The clear and penetrating light of Tyterogaka, that light that limned each mountain peak in bold strokes and flowed over the land like golden honey, illumined them. Truth shimmered on Tyterogaka, and the people knew themselves to be children of the Holy One.

A CENTURY LATER, IN THE PLANTING TIME AFTER THE RAINS, A GIRL was born on Tyterogaka. Her mother was the five times great-granddaughter of Talama and her father was the woman's middle husband, Figo. The woman, called Saysay, was placid and quiet, but Figo was always nervous and anxious. No one believed him when he ran through the village shouting, "The child is born in a burial robe."

The men scoffed, but a few women were curious enough to go to Saysay's cave and see for themselves. They found the mother crouched in a corner, staring at an infant still tied to her body by the life cord. It was Figo's job to assist in his wife's delivery, no one else was permitted to be present, but now he was outside screaming in terror and Saysay was alone and exhausted by pain. The women drew close and peered at the child.

"Your womb has come out," one said. "You'll be barren from now on."

"I never saw such a thing," another said. She was very old and somewhat wise and with one bony finger she prodded the thin mucous membrane that shrouded the infant. Instantly it burst, and water spilled to the earthen floor. The baby lay still until the old woman prodded again, then the child gave a faint cry.

"She's alive!" Saysay exclaimed. Swiftly she reached for the sharpened stone Figo had thrown down in shock. With one stroke she severed the cord linking her body to that of her daughter. She picked up the baby and sucked the mucus from her mouth and spat it on the earth, and wrapped the child in a goatskin and lay down, still holding her close.

The women went away, muttering to themselves

about strange things and saying the child would never be like everyone else. In that they were correct.

Saysay and Figo named their daughter Fala. She had the flaxen hair that some among them had, and eyes the color of the stormy sea, and she grew up strong and healthy, except that she always preferred to be alone. When seven summers had passed since her birth and she was sent out to shepherd her parents' flocks, she led the animals high into the mountains far above the village and remained away for days at a time. Once she told the priest that a man accused of theft was innocent, even though everyone believed him guilty. To prove her words, the man survived the ordeal of the smoke cave and didn't suffocate but lived.

"Fala is different," the villagers muttered. They remembered the circumstances of her birth, and waited to see whether her difference would prove good or evil.

When Fala completed her fourteenth summer, it was time to find her first husband. That's when Saysay realized that the others were reluctant to enter into a marriage contract with her daughter. "It's been a bad year of no rain," they said by way of excuse. That was true, but it was not the whole truth. Saysay grieved in silence for her ostracized child. After all, she herself had cut the cord between them; that was a special bond. Besides, she bore no more children after Fala, just as the old crone had predicted.

The drought persisted for another twelve cycles of the moon. The village knew desolation; starvation killed both people and animals. Repeatedly the priest offered sacrifices from among the few ewe lambs left to them, but the Holy One did not hear. Still the people did not lose faith. Once more they gathered in the shelter of the great semicircular walls they had built as a praying place—in their tongue, a tagoror.

But when the priest raised his arms to pray, something very strange happened. It was not his voice that sang out the ancient chant. The priest was an old man who made only a thin, reedy sound. On this night the chant suddenly burst forth in clear, sweet notes that rose like birdsong toward the full orange moon and filled the tagoror with a beauty that made many weep. On and on the chant went, untiring and never halting. The priest remained with his arms upstretched, the people hardly breathed, even the ewe lamb tied to the altar stone did not bleat. None of the worshippers spoke, but they all knew it was Fala's voice that carried their petition to the heavens.

When at last the girl stopped singing, the priest lowered his arms and with one slashing motion drew his sharpened stone across the neck of the lamb. Blood spurted over him and the altar, and the people bowed their heads. When they looked up, it had grown dark. Dense clouds had suddenly swept in from the north and covered the moon. A few seconds later, the first heavy drops of rain fell.

"Fala!" the people shouted. "It's Fala's doing! She's a goddess come to earth. Remember how she was born."

The girl heard and became frightened. Before they could catch her, she dashed out of the tagoror toward the hills. It seemed to her that she ran for hours, hidden from her pursuers by the clouds and the storm. Finally, when she could run no more, she fell to the ground and slept.

In the morning the sun rose on the washed earth. When Fala looked down from her place high in the mountains, she saw the reflections of many great puddles of water in the crevices and folds of Tyterogaka. She looked around her, still dazed and afraid, and saw the entrance to a cave that had been veiled by the night.

The cave was fifty paces deep and twenty paces wide. Its floor was smooth rock and its walls higher than her head. In its farthest end, where no light penetrated, Fala found a stream trickling from a rock and she dipped her fingers in the water and put it on her tongue. It was sweet. She drank greedily, thankful that the rain had penetrated into this mysterious place. Then she sat down to think.

Fala didn't know what had prompted her to sing the priest's chant the night before. Now she regretted that overpowering impulse, even if it helped to bring the rain. Fala knew the old tales that all mothers told their children. She knew of the evil prince who had banished them to Tyterogaka, and of the men whose tongues had been cut from their mouths. She knew that when the great and wise Talama buried her youngest daughter, the mutilated priest could not utter the burial prayer and the women had chanted it for him. Maybe that memory had made her sing. But now the people were saying stupid things. She was no goddess. There was only the Holy One, whom they all worshipped. Trembling, Fala closed her eyes and leaned her head against the smooth wall of the cave.

For a long time she sat still and silent. Then God spoke to Fala and told her what she must do, the message she must carry to the village. At first she resisted, but the Holy One was not to be denied. The great outpouring of love and peace that filled her heart gave Fala courage.

When the sun was directly overhead, she rose and left the cave, pausing for a moment while her eyes adjusted to the blinding light. Fala put a hand on the side of the cliff to steady herself, but the cliff was not smooth like the interior walls. It was marked somehow. She looked and saw a long spiral as tall as she was, carved into the face of the rock. Then she knew it was a holy sign, and that this cave was a holy place.

When Fala entered the village, the people ran to meet her. Only Saysay hung back, awed by this shining presence who had been her child.

"Wait!" Fala cried when the villagers fell to their knees before her. "Don't bow to me. I'm no different from you, except—" She paused and prayed for courage. "Except that today I spoke with the Holy One."

The people murmured in shock. Maybe they wouldn't have believed, but wasn't the ground beneath their feet soaked with the blessed, miraculous rain? "Tell us, Fala." The old priest stepped forward. "Tell us what the Holy One told you."

"I must go to live in the old hut, the one where Talama died. I must lay with no man, take no husband, and bear no child. I must have a robe of pure white goatskin, and if ever I pass a day when I do not offer thanks and adoration to the Holy One, it will turn black. When we go to pray in the *tagoror*, I must walk alone. I must sing the chants while the priest offers sacrifice or admits young men to manhood or binds men and women in marriage." Fala paused and looked at those around her. It was obvious that they understood and she knew they would agree.

"There's something more." Fala walked close to the chief, a descendant of Zoma ben Yasef whom they called King Tomen, and pointed to the glittering medallion he wore. "Look into the heart of the green stone."

The people looked. There were markings in the stone, but they'd always been there. No one knew what they meant or thought to question them. Now Fala showed them that the pendant had a long spiral carved into its heart. "That is the mark of the Holy One, of God whose name I have been told. The name of God is Acoran, and that is the symbol of the name."

For a few seconds the crowd was silent, then they began to chant, "Acoran, Acoran, Acoran. Acoran is our one and only God who made all that is." And they drew spirals in the moist earth.

Soon afterwards, all was done as Fala had directed.

FALA LIVED A LONG TIME IN THE HUT THAT HAD ONCE BEEN Talama's, which the people rebuilt for her. She never ceased to pray, and she was shown many ways to bind the people close to Acoran. Secretly she returned to the cave of the revelations and learned that there, even when no rain came, water could always be found. She took some of this water back to her hut. When a child was born it was brought to Fala and signed with the special water that it might be a child not only of flesh-and-blood parents, but of Acoran as well. At all the ceremonies in the *tagoror* Fala chanted the prayers. When she was growing old and her voice wasn't as strong and pure as once it was, she decreed that, if they chose, other young women could come and live with her. Three joined her in the hut and vowed to share her consecrated life. To commemorate this great thing that would ensure continued blessings, the people built a wall around the place where the virgins lived. Because all things must have a name, they called the praying women *hamagadas*.

When Fala died, seven *hamagadas* lived with her. They elected one of their number to take her place. "Henceforth you will be our Holy Mother and we will obey you as if you spoke with the voice of the blessed Fala, who learned the name of God."

Even the king revered the *hamagadas*. He made a law that said that no matter how terrible a crime had been committed, the guilty party could claim sanctuary behind the wall where the consecrated women prayed.

Once a man murdered his enemy, not entering

through the front door in daylight as was lawful, but sneaking in through the rear in the night. When he realized that his crime was known, he fled to the *hamagadas* for safety. But the Holy Mother was wise. She didn't shelter the man. "Sanctuary can only be claimed if we accept the fugitive," she said. Everyone agreed that this was just. The brains of the criminal were bashed out upon the killing rock near the sea, and justice was seen to be a thing good in Acoran's eyes.

The man who thus died had been the slaughterer of animals for meat, and the people murmured among themselves that it was the man's closeness to blood that had made him a criminal. Hearing these whisperings, the king declared that henceforth only that man's son and his sons after him could kill animals for food. Thus they would isolate those whose work might lead them to break the laws by which they all lived.

Some years after Fala's death, a terrible siege of sickness came upon the newborn infants and small children of the village. Their tiny bodies were wracked with pain and their bowels poured out water, and many died. The *hamagadas* prayed, and eventually they said that it was the thinness of the mothers that made the infants ill. After that, all girls went to a special cave to be fed by the *hamagadas* and fattened before marriage.

The cave chosen for this rite was near the one where the sacred water flowed, but it was not the same. The precious cave marked by Acoran was a secret known only to the *hamagadas*, and they told no one of its existence. Then, in the twentieth summer after the death of Fala, another discovery was made, and of this all the women of the village were to learn.

A young *hamagada* was sent to the holy cave to bring back some of the sacred water, and after she had prayed and purified herself, she entered and pressed her clay vessel to the wall down which the water flowed. She had filled it and was about to leave when, despite the darkness, she spied an object on the floor.

Thinking that someone had entered and perhaps defiled this sacred place, the *hamagada* bent to examine the strange thing. It was a small lump of rock. Hesitantly, she carried in into the sunlight. It was made of pitch-black stone, cleft down its length with a seam of the same green jewel that formed the pendant of the king.

The girl brought the stone back to the enclosure and gave it to her Holy Mother.

The Holy Mother held the small stone in her palm for some moments, and closed her eyes in prayer. When she opened them, she said, "This is a blessing for the women of Tyterogaka. See, it is formed in the shape of a woman. When the young girls come to the bride caves, we will show them this and press it to their bellies and they will be blessed and fertile. Because Acoran, who is God, has given us this thing."

5

I N OCTOBER OF 1965, TWO MONTHS AFTER NORMAN'S death, Joe attended a series of seminars for priests of the diocese and met the Franciscan in charge of Holy Spirit parish in Wrentham. As far as Joe knew, Maria was still teaching there.

"She's not with us anymore," Father Francisco said. Joe looked startled. The brown-robed friar laughed. "I don't mean she's dead. Her provincial sent her and the other sister with brains to get a college degree. I don't blame her; all the sisters are getting educated these days. I just wish I had something better to work with than the old rejects who've taken their places."

Joe wrote to Maria the next day. She answered with a note saying she was always free on Wednesday afternoons and that if that was still one of his days off duty, maybe he'd come and see her sometime. He went the following week.

The Jesuits had assigned a small house on their campus as living quarters for the numerous women religious now among the students. Joe rang the bell and was admitted by a tall, raw-boned lady wearing thick glasses, a denim skirt, and a B.C. sweatshirt. "Hello, Father. I'm Sister Sarah Lee, what can I do for you?"

He had to struggle against a grin. She didn't look like anyone who should be called Sarah Lee. Maybe all this return to baptismal names wasn't such a good idea. He wondered whether he should ask for Maria or Sister Mary Anthony. He decided on the latter; the Servants of Bethlehem hadn't shown much enthusiasm for renewal as yet.

"Oh, yes," the woman calling herself Sarah Lee said. "She's probably in her room." She showed him into a parlor furnished in dentist's office modern and decorated with macramé and arty inspirational posters. "Make yourself comfortable. There's a bottle of scotch and some glasses in the cupboard over there. I'll tell Sister you're here."

He heard her calling "Tony!" as she climbed the stairs. He didn't feel like a drink so he ignored the scotch and studied the posters. They bore messages like "Smile, God loves you." The books on the tables and shelves were more interesting. They represented every shade of opinion. Thomas Aquinas shared shelf space with the *Bhagavad Gita* and Kahlil Gibran. A treatise by one of the Berrigan brothers had pride of place on the coffee table.

In a few minutes Maria came in. They shook hands in a slightly formal way. At first Joe didn't know why he felt uncomfortable. The setting, maybe. It was so unlike the rooms in which he'd visited Maria during the past four years. No, that wasn't it. She looked different. He cocked his head and studied her. "What happened to the technicolor habit?"

"As of last month we only wear it in the Provincial House. Not that we're getting too modern too fast. This is the prescribed alternative."

"This" was a black dress with a high neck and long sleeves, and a broad black belt cinching a formless skirt that ended midway between knees and ankles. The white wimple was gone too. It had been replaced by a short veil attached to a narrow white band. A small amount of Maria's brown curly hair showed, but that was the outfit's only redeeming feature.

"You look like a fugitive from the thirties," Joe said. "Who thought up this get-up?"

"A committee, naturally. I wasn't on it. Not on the one that decorated this room either. Come on, let's get out of here."

It was a bronzed autumn afternoon, golden with sunshine and crisp with the tang of burning leaves. They walked to a deserted end of the campus, and Maria told him that she was studying literature and languages. She really wanted to specialize in linguistics and she hoped it would be possible to do a masters in that after she got her B.A.

"Foreign languages, you mean?" Joe asked.

"Not exactly. The origin of language itself. The role of words in the development of cultures. It's probably a pipe dream. I doubt that Mother Provincial will see any value to the congregation in a degree in linguistics."

Her tone wasn't bitter but neutral; still, it made Joe aware of an undercurrent. "Are you okay?" he asked. It occurred to him that he put that question to his friends frequently. He wasn't sure what it was supposed to mean.

"I'm hanging in," Maria said slowly. "I'm not quite sure why or how, but I'm hanging in."

It was more honesty than he'd expected, and he didn't know what to say. Maria filled the gap in the conversation by adding, "I struggled a bit before I made my final vows last month. But I made them."

"I didn't know you were having a tough time," Joe said. "I was awfully busy; I'm sorry." Last month he'd been trying to come to terms with his feelings for Barbie and forget the way he'd felt when she was in his arms. He spent every waking moment avoiding occasions of sin—such as ever seeing her alone—and every sleeping one dreaming of her. It hadn't occurred to him to get in touch with Maria during that period.

As if she read his thoughts she asked, "Have you seen Barbie lately?"

"Not for a while. I've talked to her on the phone a couple of times. She seems okay."

"Poor kid. My mother wrote me about it and I got permission to send her a note. I don't imagine it did much good."

"She was happy to hear from you. She didn't know you were here, though. Neither did I." He told her about meeting Father Francisco.

"He's an all-right guy. A good priest. I miss him. And by the way, I wasn't here when I wrote to Barbie. That was in August. I was at the Lynn convent. If I'd been here I wouldn't have needed permission to write to her. And I could have gone to the funeral. That's one of the big changes. We've got that all-flavors-of-ice-cream convent you saw back there, and as much personal freedom as our individual conscience allows. I think that's why I'm still in possession of most of my marbles."

Joe grinned at her. "You're one of the sanest people I know. You always have been." On impulse he added, "I want to ask your advice about something."

"Things really are changing when a priest asks a sister for advice. Let's sit down."

They found a bench under a maple tree and a tapestry of tawny leaves drifted to their feet and settled incongruously on Maria's ugly habit. "So ask," she said.

He hesitated for a moment. "I don't think she'd mind my telling you," he said finally.

Maria felt a twinge of panic. There were things she suspected about the relationship between Barbie and Joe which she definitely did not want to discuss. But he wasn't talking about anything like that. He told her instead about Barbie's supposed visions. "I don't know what to make of it, or if it's necessary for me to do anything at all. She's such a funny kid. Sometimes she seems to live in her own world with a scale of values I don't in the least understand. The only thing that worries me is that this may be some kind of indication that she needs psychiatric help. What if I don't do anything and it turns out to have been the warning I should have heeded and didn't?"

Maria said pensively, "You say she seemed to think it was perfectly ordinary? That everybody had visions?"

"Priests and nuns. She implied that you and I must see the Blessed Virgin every day. Twice on Sundays."

"So she wasn't, what's that horrible phrase, making herself singular."

"No, nothing like that."

Maria exhaled loudly. "I don't know, maybe she does have visions. I'm too unsure of everything these days to come down on one side or the other."

"I thought maybe I'd suggest she come talk to you about the whole thing. There's no one who'd make her feel more relaxed. She loves you a lot."

"I love her, but I can't talk to her about the faith. Certainly not about her mystical experiences. I'd be useless. I'm too jealous."

THE JESUIT WHO TAUGHT CHURCH HISTORY, FATHER William Hapsburg Rolles, had a face etched with pain. His skin was brown and taut. It stretched over a long and scrawny neck across a rounded hairless skull, and all of it was creased and gullied with the scars of sorrow. But it was dry and somehow sterile pain, as if the wounds had been inflicted long before, when the flesh was new and impressionable. He never explained how he came by his distinguished middle name, nor the source of his mask of suffering. He spoke of agony nonetheless.

171

His classes were an endless catalog of the sins of the institution he served. The burning of heretics, the maneuvering for political gain, the destruction of whole cultures by so-called missionaries, the corruption of power, from the Edict of Constantine to the apparent Vatican silence while six million Jews perished—he left out nothing.

Maria approached him after one class. "Didn't anything good ever happen?"

The Jesuit was assembling his notes with slim, elegant hands that protruded from the jacket of an exquisitely tailored black silk suit. "I beg your pardon, Sister?"

"Didn't the Church ever do anything good?"

"I teach history," he said. "I don't invent it."

She would not be silenced by his glibness. "But you make it sound so unrelievedly bad. Surely it isn't just that."

He looked at her in silence for a moment. His eyes were watery blue. They conveyed nothing. "The judgment is yours," he said finally. "Not mine."

For a while Maria skipped his class. Then she felt childish and guilty, and she returned. The priest made no mention of her absence, he spoke only that litany of sin and destruction that was the fruit of his learning. For four consecutive weeks he lectured on the support the seventeenth-century Jesuits gave to the institution of human slavery.

"Do you believe no good has come from any missionary activity?" Maria asked him after yet another recitation of horror.

The priest sighed. "I am not the judge of good and evil, Sister. Thank God I've been spared that burden."

"Why are you a Jesuit then?" she demanded in frustration.

He stared at her as if he'd imagined her impertinence. Then he picked up his papers and walked away.

"You're destroying me," Maria whispered to his back. His step didn't falter. She believed he had not heard.

That night she did not sleep. She spent the hours from ten to six sitting on her bed and studying the notes she had taken in the Jesuit's class.

Across the campus, in his comfortable book-lined room, the priest didn't sleep either. He passed the night as he passed most of them, kneeling in prayer. Two days later he sent Maria a note asking that she come to his office.

Maria expected him to apologize for upsetting her, perhaps try to mitigate some of the damaging things he'd said. But it was too late for that. She was already convinced he'd been telling the truth; any recanting now would be more hypocrisy.

As soon as she entered the office, she realized it wasn't to be like that. There was another man present. Maria judged him to be in his late twenties. He wore jeans and a wrinkled tweed jacket and had a somber and preoccupied manner. He didn't rise when she came in. The Jesuit introduced the stranger in the same noncommittal voice he used in class. "This gentleman is another Jesuit, despite his unorthodox costume. I believe you two may be of use to each other. Now, if you'll excuse me, I have an appointment. There's no need to lock the door when you leave." He walked out of the room, leaving Maria and the strange priest to appraise each other.

"Have you any idea what this is all about?" Maria asked when the silence became uncomfortable.

"I think so. Detective work."

"What?"

"Literary detection of a sort. Old languages. It's my subject. At least it's what I'm doing at B.C. at the moment. Actually, I'm an archaeologist." The priest took a pipe from the pocket of the disreputable jacket. His shoulders were oddly angular and the material seemed to have stretched itself over them at the expense of the sleeves. They ended a few inches above his bony wrists. "Do you mind?" he asked.

"I don't know whether I mind. I still don't understand what it has to do with me."

"I meant the pipe," he said, with a sudden grin that settled over his craggy features like a benediction.

"Oh, no. Go ahead and smoke. But I'd really like to know why your work involves me."

"Father seemed to think you'd be interested in helping me." He jerked his head in the direction of the older man's desk. "According to him, languages and semantics are your long suit."

Maria was startled. "Well, they're what I like best. But how did he know? I only take Church History with him."

The priest sucked on the stem of his pipe. "There's not much he misses. He's a saint, you know."

"No, I don't know that."

"He was seven years in a communist prison camp in China," he said quietly. "Subject to some of their more refined methods of 'reeducation.' How old do you think he is?"

Maria shrugged. "Sixty, maybe sixty-five."

"He'll be forty-four his next birthday." Then, when she

gasped, he added, "If you ever let on I've told you, he'll skin me alive."

"I won't let on. How do you know?"

"He's my uncle. My name's Hank Rolles."

"Why are you telling me about it?" Maria demanded. The contradictions raised by the tale made her very uncomfortable.

For a while Rolles looked at her in silence. She noted that his eyes darkened when he was concentrating. "Damned if I know," he said at last. "What about this work I mentioned—are you interested? And is it true that you speak French, Italian, and Spanish?"

She hesitated for a moment. "Yes, that's true, but mostly I've taught myself. I don't have any training in linguistics. I probably couldn't be much help."

"It's drudgery at this point. A lot of sifting of details and checking one thing against thirty others. Perhaps you'd find it boring."

"No, I doubt that. I'd be interested if I thought I could be of use."

"Let me be the judge of that," Father Hank Rolles said, with another of his rare grins.

AROUND THAT SAME TIME JOE DiANNI RECEIVED A SHORT letter from Barbie. In it she explained that she was moving away from the Boston area. She'd sold the house in Peabody and realized a ten-thousand-dollar-profit, so he wasn't to worry about her. She said nothing more; it was left to Joe to read between the lines and understand the reasons for her flight.

He felt rotten about it for a while, then he decided that she'd made the best choice for both of them. He had his priesthood, and a girl like Barbie was bound to find a good man to love and marry. He destroyed the letter and resolved to put the entire episode behind him.

What Barbie had not told him was that she was three months pregnant.

WHEN MARIA BEGAN WORKING AS ASSISTANT TO THE YOUNG Jesuit Hank Rolles, he made one rule. "I can't stand being called Father. Hank's the name." Other than that he said little, just issued terse instructions. At first Maria was in awe of him, and of what she heard of his reputation as a genius of sorts. She crept meekly into his office, did the jobs assigned to her, and crept out again. Eventually curiosity and courage meshed, and the situation changed.

It took her about a month to decide he wasn't forbidding and cold behind his customary scowl, merely immersed in his own world. So on one afternoon in that winter of early 1966 she tentatively cleared her throat and said, "Listen, Hank, maybe I'd be more effective if I knew what I was doing."

"You're looking for Hamitic linkages," he murmured without looking up.

That was supposed to explain everything. Maria sighed and watched him. Pale January sun spilled across the oak table he used as a desk, and highlighted dust motes dancing in the air. The room was tiny and cluttered, but right next to the main library—just one of the numerous perks granted Rolles. Because he was not merely another researcher, much less a student, he was a fellow Jesuit. He belonged to the New York province, not Boston, but in the subtle stratification of the college society, religious took precedence over layfolk, and Jesuits over everyone but God. Maria sighed again, but Rolles continued to ignore her. After a few seconds she went back to work.

She was examining closely worded pages of text, a photocopy of some ancient document written in Arabic script. Maria couldn't read the alphabet, much less understand the words, but that didn't matter. All she had to do was go through the thing letter by letter and search out certain characters and groups of characters. Each time they occurred, she underlined them. It was painstaking, difficult, and boring, just as Hank Rolles had warned it would be, but coming three afternoons a week to this little office had swiftly become an important part of her life. Because he was so uncommunicative, she had no clear idea of what Hank was doing; nonetheless, his palpable sense of mission and suppressed excitement communicated themselves to her. Maria felt as if she were participating in a mysterious adventure.

They worked on in silence for nearly an hour more. Finally Hank stood up, stretched his arms, and yawned loudly. "Enough for today. I'm beat and half blind; you must be too."

Maria's eyes were red-rimmed and watering, but she smiled when he looked over her shoulder and whistled softly. "Hey! That's great, you've struck a rich vein." He was noting the many times her careful pencil marks indicated that she'd recognized the special characters he was seeking. "I'd no idea," he added. "You didn't say anything." This last was slightly accusatory, as if she'd been keeping an important discovery to herself.

"I didn't know," she said, with a mixture of amusement and annoyance. "I've no idea what the norms are, so I can't tell what constitutes a 'rich vein.' "

Rolles perched on the edge of the table, swinging one leg and grinning his rare grin. "No, you don't, do you? Sorry, I've been pretty oblivious to everything but the work itself. I should have explained more." He glanced at his watch. "It's six o'clock. C'mon, I'll walk you home and try to fill you in a bit."

They left the office just as it was. Rolles worked in apparent chaos that was comprehensible only to him. Mountains of books and files and cardboard boxes filled every inch of space. They seemed to be in no order, but he could instantly put his hands on exactly what he wanted. At first Maria had expected to be asked to tidy the place, but she quickly learned that Hank Rolles would have considered such an effort heresy. So they simply locked the door behind them and walked through the silent library to the winter-dark street. Ice crunched loudly beneath their feet as they started across campus.

Students hurried past them, most headed for the mass civil rights meeting scheduled as that evening's contribution to campus ferment. A few spotted Maria's black veil and paused to say, "Good evening, Sister." Bomb throwers and activists perhaps, but at bottom well-bred Catholic children. Schooled in places like Queen of Heaven Country Day School and nice suburban parishes where, however much else changed, respect for the good sisters was bred into blood and bone.

None of the students greeted Rolles, who wore a turtleneck sweater under a down parka. He ignored them too, but for once he was paying attention to Maria. "Do you know what I mean by Hamitic linkages?" She shook her head.

Rolles stopped to light his pipe before he continued. "It relates to Ham, Noah's second son according to the Bible. The accuracy of that is unimportant; for linguistic scholars it's become a code word for an ancient language root. What laymen seldom realize is that by the time the Jews and the Babylonians and the Egyptians appeared on the scene, that part of the world we call the Holy Land, specifically from the Arabian desert across the Red Sea to the Tigris–Euphrates valley, had been the scene of the birth and death of countless civilizations. Today we speak of them as comprising two main groups, identifiable by their language roots." He stopped abruptly. "Am I boring you?"

"Absolutely not! Go on, please." Unconsciously she slowed her walking pace, wanting the conversation to continue, not wanting to face the sterile dinner hour. The assortment of nuns with whom she lived had made an effort to find some sort of conventual format for their evening meal. Since they couldn't agree on what that should be, or whether it should be at all, they'd evolved a compromise in which the first part of the meal was eaten in silence, and they talked over coffee and dessert. Like most compromises, it was unhappy and stilted. Maria pushed the thought of it away and paid attention to Hank.

"One verbal strain is the northern class of Semitic languages, including Chaldee, Syriac, and Aramaic. That last was the lingua franca of Galilee in Christ's time, by the way."

"Yes, I know that." She was pleased to be able to say she knew anything at all.

"Good. The second strain is Hamitic. That's the African linguistic group. There's even a legend that all the black races are descended from our friend Ham. Be that as it may, the Hamitic language group is made up of Egyptian, Libyan, and Ethiopic. The Libyan strain includes Berber, Tuareg, and Guanche, among others. What I'm doing is trying to trace the history of tribes of Berber-speaking Algerian nomads, trying to learn something about their origins. That's what you were doing today."

"I was with you until the last sentence. How was I doing that today?"

Rolles chuckled and the sound carried in the cold, crisp evening. "That document you're working on is part of a Berber history recorded around the year 426. I'm looking for links between that and some of the small religious sects in Palestine in the first century. Like the followers of John the Baptist, for instance. The kind of isolated fringe communities that always exist. The radicals, the kooks, the visionaries. The sort who are usually hounded from place to place by the establishment."

"Nothing changes very much, does it?"

"Not very much," the Jesuit agreed. "Anyway, one way to make the connection is through language. I think this document contains traces of pure Aramaic, and I'm trying to prove it."

"And if you do?"

They were almost at the door of her residence and the porch

light cast a glow over Rolles unhandsome but oddly attractive face. "If I do, I can maybe scare up funding for a dig." He smiled at her. "You can come along if it works; you'll have earned it."

She lifted a hand to her veil. "I wonder what Mother Provincial would say to that." She was laughing, but he wasn't.

"Yeah, I forgot. I don't usually think of you as a nun, despite the get-up." With which enigmatic remark he turned and strode off into the night.

MARIA WORKED WITH MORE ENTHUSIASM AFTER THE PRIEST'S long explanation. Now each repetitive task had meaning. She realized that she had caught a glimpse of the lure of scholarship. It wasn't dry and dusty and dead once you understood it; it was magic. Like the detective work the Jesuit had first called it. Like a maze that had many dead ends, but a tantalizing prize at its hidden heart.

That attitude was responsible for her discovery. Maria was sensitized to mystery now, and when, searching an old subject index for any resource she and Hank might have missed, she came across a particularly cryptic reference, she knew it for an anomaly. Guanche-J-X-32S.106. Hastily she copied the information onto a scrap of paper and brought it to Hank. "Look at this and tell me what you make of it."

He studied the code for a moment. "Guanche is one of our language types, of course. J probably means it's a journal of some sort. As for the rest, I don't know."

"Neither do I, but I mean to find out."

Maria located Monsignor Walsh, the head librarian, in his office. He was a spare, gray-haired man with sharp, ascetic features. Typical of one type of Jesuit. "Yes, Sister, can I help you?"

"I hope so. I'm working with Father Rolles on his linguistic research. We wondered if you could decipher this for us." She passed the slip of paper across his desk.

The priest didn't look at it immediately. "Linguistics? Father Rolles?" He sounded doubtful, then his gaunt face brightened. "Oh, Rolles the Younger, you mean. Yes, of course."

Maria grinned at the in-house joke. "Do you call Father William, Rolles the Elder?"

"Not exactly. He's known as Rolles the Martyr. Not very consistent, are we? Some would say that's quite jesuitical." Father Walsh pushed his wire-rimmed spectacles higher up on his nose, as if to repair a barrier breached by momentary humor. He studied the reference she'd brought him. After a few seconds he sighed warily. "Is this important, Sister?"

"I don't know. Maybe, but maybe not," she admitted.

Walsh seemed to fight a private battle, which integrity of scholarship finally won. "You can't ignore it, of course," he murmured. "Not if it might be important. This bit of cataloging was done by Father James McClintock, the college's first librarian. Sometime around 1870, probably. During the first decade of the library's existence. The letters FC indicate that."

"What do they mean? I've never seen them in the catalog before."

"Florentine Collection. It was the first important collection the library acquired. That's how I know this is McClintock's work. The entire Florentine Collection was cataloged by him."

"I see. Father Rolles thinks that the J indicates it's a journal of some sort, but there's no location code. X doesn't refer to any of the stacks, does it?"

"Not exactly." The priest sighed again, then took off his glasses and looked at her through watery blue eyes. "I imagine you consider yourself one of the new breed of nuns, don't you? Not easily shocked and all that. Am I correct?"

Maria was startled. "I suppose so. But what can be shocking about something to do with the Guanche language strain. That's the subject heading, after all."

"Quite," Father Walsh agreed. "But apparently my honored predecessor considered the material inappropriate for the perusal of students. The X means it's locked in the library crypt. Come along, I'll show you."

They descended deep into the bowels of the building, through narrow corridors lit by low-wattage bulbs that flickered on for a few moments when a switch was pressed and turned off automatically seconds later. There were three locked steel fire doors between them and whatever they were seeking, and the librarian opened each of them with a rusty key selected from a huge ring dangling at the belt of his black cassock. Maria had visions of being buried alive in these endless cellars and wondered how long it would be before Hank came out of his customary preoccupation and realized she was missing.

Finally they came to the end of a low-ceilinged corridor and were in a large chamber of sorts. A heavy wrought-iron gate separated them from its dark depths. The faint hum of machinery was the only sound, but when Monsignor Walsh turned on these lights they remained lit, and illumined banks of metal shelves with books and cartons and file cases stacked three rows deep.

"We have climate control equipment down here to avoid any damage or deterioration. That's the whirring noise you hear. But I'm afraid no one has done much work with these resources for a long time. Never enough staff or money or time," he added apologetically. While he spoke he unlocked the metal gate. It swung open with a faint protest that died quickly in the dead air. Despite the humidity and temperature control, there was a musty smell.

Maria took a step forward, tantalized as much by the surroundings as by her original curiosity, then hesitated. This was the librarian's domain; it was up to him to lead the way. He moved ahead of her to the shelves on the right. They weren't actually shelves, but cabinets. Another set of locks had to be opened before their contents would be revealed.

"Cabinet 32S contains mostly nineteenth-century rubbish. The pornography of its day," the priest explained. "Things with titles like *Maria Monk* or *Priests, Women, and the Confessional.* Scandalous tales of illicit carryings on and babies buried in the walls of convents. That sort of thing. All unsubstantiated muck, of course. But inflammatory in old Father McClintock's view."

"It's a wonder that such things are even part of the library collection," Maria said.

Walsh smiled his thin-lipped smile. "The demands of scholarship, Sister. Father McClintock worried about the reputation of the Church, but also about having a library worthy of the name. Here we are, number 106." He withdrew a dun-colored cardboard envelope, untied it, and lifted the flap. They both peered inside. The contents consisted of one small leatherbound book. It was black with age, and bore no inscription on the cover. "Go ahead," the priest said. "Have a look."

There wasn't any sense to it, but Maria's scalp was tingling and her hand trembled. Monsignor Walsh did not seem to notice her agitation, but merely waited for her to remove the book from its innocuous buff case. Finally her fingers closed over the volume. The inexplicable sense of having taken a momentous step increased, then faded as abruptly as it had come. Reality as antidote to both dreams and nightmares.

The journal was approximately eight inches long, five inches wide, and half an inch thick. The black leather cover was stained in the bottom right corner, but thanks to careful storage, the hide remained soft and flexible. Maria opened it carefully. The paper was a rippled, soft parchment type, with the ruffled edges that were a hallmark of paper cut by hand. It was unlined and sewn to the binding with heavy black thread. The thread showed. Not a thing of elegance or wealth, just a workaday notebook of its time. And as they'd suspected, it wasn't printed but handwritten.

"Can you read it?" the priest asked, peering over her shoulder in the harsh glare of the unshaded bulbs.

"I think so. The ink is very faded, but it's a clear and well-formed hand."

It was impossible to say what color the ink had once been. Now it was a uniform yellow-brown that almost blended with the tarnished ivory color of the paper. Whatever had stained the cover had soaked through to the first page, and the bottom half was unreadable. But the opening words were clear. *El día dos de Noviembre, en el año del nuestro Señor mil siete cientos treinta y tres. Hoy día he llegado en la isla de Lanzarote. ¡Dios ten misericordia a mi!*

"You read Spanish?" Monsignor Walsh asked.

"Yes, reasonably well. This is very formal and old-fashioned, however."

"Not surprising, since the date is November 2, 1733. About a hundred years after Cervantes, but the language would still be quite different than anything spoken today." He eyed her speculatively, a scholar sizing up an aspirant to his most exclusive of clubs.

"Yes," Maria agreed. "But that will only mean more patience, it's not impossible. Where is this island of Lanzarote he speaks of, have you any idea?"

"One of the Canaries archipelago, called the Fortunate Isles in classical times, off the coast of Africa. They've been part of Spain since, let me see, around the early fifteenth century, I believe."

She looked again at the impassioned cry that opened the journal: Today I arrived on the island of Lanzarote, God have mercy on me! "The writer didn't seem very happy about Lanzarote."

Walsh smiled. "I rather think the Canaries have been considered the back of beyond by Spaniards for some time. The political philosopher Unamuno was exiled there in the beginning of this century. Not Lanzarote, one of the other islands. There are seven of them. I forget which one Unamuno was sent to, but I remember what he said about it."

"What was that?"

The Jesuit reddened. "To be frank, Sister, he called it the, er . . . world's posterior."

"Asshole of the world's what he said," Hank corrected later. "Posterior. That's pretty good. Poor old Walsh, he must have choked."

"Well, I think the writer of the journal shared Unamuno's opinion. Anyway, he was a priest. Must have been a Dominican because he speaks of living in a priory in some place called Teguise. A village, apparently. And of traveling to other outlying villages to say Mass and hear confessions."

Rolles peered over her shoulder at the yellowed pages. "How far have you gotten? Damn! I wish I knew Spanish."

"I'll make a translation for you. It will take a while; the language is old-fashioned and a lot of the spelling looks peculiar to me. I've just read the first three pages so far. He says there was a volcanic eruption taking place in the south of the island, only it seems to go on and on. Is that possible?"

"I think so, yes. We can ask somebody in the science department. I expect the great Jesuit order can produce an expert in vulcanology."

Maria nodded, less concerned with the natural disaster than the human one she'd begun to glimpse. "My guess is that this is essentially a record of the conversion to Christianity of the natives. He seems to be questioning people about what had happened three centuries earlier when the first Spaniards came. And about what their ancestors originally believed. Monsignor Walsh says the Canarian natives spoke a form of Guanche, that's why the journal was cataloged under ancient languages."

"Mmm, okay. But why did old McClintock lock it up with the hard-core porn? Any ideas about that?"

"Not yet. Monsignor Walsh doesn't know either."

"Well, maybe you'll figure it out. Lately you're becoming a pretty good scholastic detective."

Coming from Hank Rolles, that was high praise. Maria felt her cheeks warm. He ignored her blush and picked up the diary. "Know what I think? This stain on the cover is salt water. I bet it fell into the sea at some point."

"Lanzarote is an island," she said tartly, "so that's not very surprising or much help."

Hank grinned. "Right. I leave it in your hands, then. When you've got it all psyched out, come and tell me."

Maria painstakingly translated the pages of the journal, giving Hank the English version each time she completed a separate entry. They followed no particular pattern; they were merely a series of old legends, and stories of the conquest of the native population by representatives of the king of Spain in 1402. There was nothing to explain either the Dominican's interest in the subject or why the first librarian locked the diary away.

True, the journal spoke at length of the destruction of the island's native religion, but no one of Father McClintock's generation would have seen anything scandalous in that. The pagans were being introduced to the true faith. Indeed, that attitude permeated the writing in the journal. "Forty-six men and women were killed on the day of the first landing, but the remaining population were all eventually baptized," the Dominican had written with apparent satisfaction.

"So what was McClintock hiding?" Maria asked in frustration after she'd been working on the diary a week.

"No idea," Hank muttered. "And it doesn't matter. We may have struck another kind of pay dirt. Here, look at this." He pointed to a group of words in the primitive glossary of the island's original language. The diarist had carefully noted any non-Spanish words he heard. "That's not Guance," Rolles said softly. "That's pure Berber."

Maria looked at him. His face glowed and his eyes were bright with excitement. "So what?" she asked.

"So nobody knows very much about the origins of the original people of the Canaries. According to Pliny, the islands were uninhabited in the first century. Then thirteen hundred years later the conquering Europeans arrive and find a whole civilization. Where did it come from?"

"I've no idea."

"Neither has anybody else, but if their language was Berber derived, then we have a clue." He said no more, but went back to poring over the carefully typed translations she had provided. "Keep working on this, will you," he muttered. Maria wondered if he realized that she had her own class work to do, as well as acting as his assistant, but she didn't say anything and she knew she would go on translating the diary. Hank might be fascinated by the linguistic clues; for her part, she had found another source of excitement in the journal of the long-dead priest.

IN EARLY MARCH, HANK LOOKED WITH SATISFACTION AT THE final stack of translations of the Lanzarote diary. "This deserves a celebration. Do you have to go back to your ersatz convent for dinner tonight?"

"No, I suppose I don't have to. We're all pretty much free agents. What did you have in mind?"

She knew she sounded wary. Certain things about her relationship with the Jesuit were unsettling. It wasn't quite like any friendship she'd had with a priest in the past. Hank never wore clerical garb, for one thing. For another, not only did he refuse to be called Father, she'd never seen him performing any sacramental function. Maria guessed he said Mass early mornings in the chapel of the residence where he lived, and he'd once mentioned hearing confessions in a local parish on Saturday afternoons, but she'd never actually seen him doing those things. Somehow that truncated her view of his sacerdotal role. And sometimes she caught him looking at her in a way that was outside her experience, but which triggered a lot of instinctive feelings and fears. More and more frequently these days one heard of priests and nuns kicking over the traces and running off to get married. Maria was repelled by the stories and determined not to become one of the statistics.

"What I have in mind," Rolles said in answer to her question, "is Chinese food. Do you like it?"

"I've never tasted it."

"That settles it, then. We're going out and have a Chinese feed."

"I don't know," she said hesitantly. "There's still the problem of giving scandal. Even if you're absolutely innocent, it's no good if you don't look as if you are."

Rolles grinned. "Sister Mary Anthony, conscience of the western world. I thought of that. If you wear your black coat you just look dowdy, not like a nun. And you can put this on over your veil." He tossed her a thing she didn't at first recognize as anything but a bit of bright red wool.

It turned out to be a knitted hat, the kind girls wore to cover all their hair and their ears in defense against the Boston winter. Maria felt decidedly odd when she handled it. She hadn't worn anything red in over five years. And the presence of the hat in Hank's office meant he had plotted this outing, which somehow made it less innocent. "I don't know," she repeated.

"Please," he said, and the way he looked at her was both touching and painful. Maria dropped her eyes, but she didn't return the red hat. Instead she shoved it deep into the pocket of the black coat Hank had pronounced as dowdy, but unidentifiable.

BOSTON'S CHINATOWN WAS COMPRESSED INTO A DENSE fretwork of streets bordered by Kneeland on one side and the newly extended Mass. Turnpike on the other. Maria and Hank took the subway to State Street and walked from there. It was a balmy evening, extraordinary for March, and Maria felt hot and silly in the red wool hat she'd pulled on over her veil. She thought of taking both things off and going bareheaded, but the idea struck her as dishonest. Besides, beneath the veil her hair was shorter than Hank's, and ugly. She simply hacked it off every couple of months with a scissors and no mirror, the way she'd been taught to do when she was a novice. Some of the sisters with whom she lived had started having their hair done at beauty parlors near the campus. Maria was appalled by that. Besides, the Servants of Bethlehem expressly forbade it.

"Here we are: Tyler Street." Hank took her arm as they turned the corner.

The immediacy of his touch broke into her reverie about appearances. His grip was strong and sure, and very masculine. Maria moved away a few inches. He let go instantly.

"Funny," he said, "in New York the Chinese restaurants all have names. Itsi Woo's, Gung Ho's, stuff like that. Here they're known by their numbers. Velly glad you come to exotic Number Twenty-Five Tyler Street, foreign devils. Come eat our velly tasty shaved bamboo."

She laughed. "You're kidding, aren't you? There isn't a restaurant called Gung Ho's, even in New York."

"Don't know. But there should be. Maybe we'll run off and open one. You be the cook. Gung Ho's, serving the best Italian food in town."

They were still giggling when they turned into the restaurant. It was on the second floor, reached by a steep narrow staircase that smelled exotically of incense and jasmine and unknown spices. Upstairs, the decor was a disappointment. Plain wooden tables and chairs, lighting from Woolworth's, and only one red enamel screen to lend an oriental air. The enamel was chipped.

"Speaking of ethnic verities," Maria said, looking around, "is it true your family is related to the Hapsburgs?"

"Yup. Back in the distant past, but it's true. Great Grandpa fled to America because of some intrigue involving Bismark and King William I, according to the legend. All pretty heavy stuff. And who cares."

Unconsciously Maria started to remove her coat, then remembered and left it buttoned. "I've been thinking about old sins of late. Because of the diary. Don't you think history, our personal history, matters?"

A waiter approached. Maria glanced at the menu and found it incomprehensible. She was grateful when Hank said, "Let me order, since you're a neophyte."

He was serious about it, conferring with the young Chinese lad for some minutes before a seemingly long list of dishes was decided upon.

"So much?" Maria said when the waiter was gone.

"The stuff doesn't fill you up. You'll see. And I do think our personal history is important, but not more than grace and free will, if you'll forgive a bit of doctrine."

"But that's part of it. The things that have been done to people in the name of religion, don't you ever worry about that?"

"Nope. I worry about sin, all kinds. You're just detailing one particularly virulent and nasty form."

The conversation was interrupted when egg rolls and pork strips arrived. Hank showed her how to dip them in soy sauce and duck sauce and hot mustard and eat them with her fingers as he did. Maria was an instant convert. "Fabulous!" she pronounced.

"Wait till you taste the rest."

And to lend weight to his words, the main dishes came. Fried rice, and chicken in a delicate sauce with almonds and pineapple, and shrimp in something wonderfully garlicky called lobster sauce, though it had no lobster. They ate with gusto and it occurred to Maria that this was the first meal she'd truly savored since she entered the convent.

"I haven't enjoyed anything so much in years," she said when the dishes were cleared away and they were left with a fresh pot of green tea to drink from little handleless cups that felt sensuous and warm to her palms. "Thank you."

"My pleasure. What did you mean before, about the diary

making you think of old sins? There's nothing new in that stuff about converting people with swords and bullets."

"No." She shook her head, and caught a peripheral glimpse of the red hat bobbing in a mirror on the opposite wall. "Not that. I mean the story about the girl and her lover and how they died."

Hank knew the entry to which she referred. The Dominican had written at length about a couple who came from different clans. They broke a taboo of their people and died for it. "I wonder if the old boy knew any Shakespeare," Rolles said. "Romeo, Romeo, wherefore art thou, Romeo."

"True," Maria said. "The Montagues and the Capulets. It's all been done before, but still . . ." She let the words trail away, embarrassed to say more.

"Done how? Are you talking about a book?"

He was more perceptive than she'd given him credit for. "Yes, sort of. It just seems to me that the whole thing, the old legends and the Dominican himself, they'd make a terrific novel."

"Maybe they would. I'm not much of a novel reader myself. Are you thinking of writing it?"

She touched the hat, calling his attention to the veil underneath. "I don't expect it would be allowed."

Rolles stared at her for a moment. "That matters to you, does it? Still?"

She realized the import of his question and returned his gaze. "It still matters. I realize that seems to be the minority view these days, but I've been in the minority before."

"Okay, but why? Have you an answer for that?" He leaned over and refilled their tea cups, giving her time to formulate a reply.

"Because," she said slowly, "I don't think you can go through life breaking promises."

Rolles was silent for some moments. Finally he said softly, "That's not good enough. It won't get you through the hard places."

"It has so far," Maria said. He looked as if he might pursue that subject. To head him off, she asked if he'd been raised in New York.

"Scarsdale, in the bosom of Westchester County. All the best schools and country clubs, in fact all the right moves. And my father is a doctor. You get the picture."

"I'm not sure. It's a world I've read about, but never been part of."

"You haven't missed much." He poured the last of the tea into their cups. It was cold and bitter, but neither of them seemed inclined to move.

"Do you resent your background?" Maria asked.

"No. Resent is too strong a word. Actually, I think my family is pretty great, and we like each other, which is rare. It's just that having everything so easy . . . Well, it kind of scared me."

"Scared you into the priesthood, you mean."

"Perhaps. It's not what keeps me there, however."

Back to square one again. Only it was her turn to ask the question. "What does keep you there?"

"It's a quest," he said quietly. "I haven't come to the end yet."

"And your work? What does archaeology have to do with being a priest?"

"In general, nothing. That's probably why I'm a Jesuit. It has to be the Jesuits or the Dominicans if you want some kind of intellectual life. There's another connection, though." She waited and he stared at the teacup, avoiding her eyes. "Being a priest keeps me a member of the human race, not just another academic in an ivory tower."

They left the restaurant and walked in companionable silence all the way to the Common. The civil rights meetings had spilled off the campuses and coalesced here. Masses of young men and women were listening to someone talk about the Boston Massacre that took place on this same spot two hundred years before and made a black man the first casualty of the revolution. The speaker and his listeners were all white and middle class and very earnest. After a few minutes the crowd joined hands and started singing "We Shall Overcome." Maria and Hank slipped down the stairs into the subway.

THREE WEEKS LATER, SHE CAME INTO HANK'S OFFICE TO FIND him packing all his files and books. "Transferred," he said before she had a chance to ask. "To Jerusalem University, as part of a special study group on migrations of early nomadic tribes."

Maria waited a moment to get her breath and cope with her unexpected sense of loss. "Congratulations," she managed after a few seconds. "That sounds great."

"Yes, it is." He turned to her then and they looked at each other for the space of a few heartbeats. "Better all around, no doubt," Rolles added. "My guardian angel working over-time."

Maria looked away and pretended she didn't know what he meant.

Hank Rolles was gone three days later. Maria deeply regretted the loss of her work as his assistant, and the easy friendship they'd come to share, but she realized that his manhood as such was no threat to her commitment as a Servant of Bethlehem, and that it never had been. Whatever she felt for Hank, it wasn't a man-woman thing. He had instead been her safety valve, a way of dealing with the problems she'd come to see in his uncle's history classes. Getting absorbed in Hank's work had helped to sublimate those concerns, and gradually, almost without realizing it, she'd evolved an answer for herself. It was extremely simple. She'd made a promise and she would stand by it. The whole world would come unstuck if people stopped doing that. Maybe the idea that she could affect the destiny of the world was ludicrous; nonetheless, it was the anchor to which she tied her life and her determination to honor her vows.

That June she received permission to stay on at B.C. during the summer and take some extra courses. Mother Provincial's reasoning was that Sister Mary Anthony would gain her degree more quickly thus; Maria's was that her fragile grip on what she'd once called her "vocation" wouldn't stand up to the pressures of the Lynn convent.

The summer courses proved fairly undemanding and she had a lot of time on her hands. More and more she spent that time thinking about the Lanzarote journal and the story of the thwarted lovers. Sometimes she even made notes about how the material could be fashioned into a book. She always gave it up after a little while, knowing it was a futile waste of time, but she never threw the notes away.

One day soon after the start of the summer term she received a note requesting she go to the head librarian's office. "I've finally had an opportunity to spend some time with the librarian's personal files," Monsignor Walsh explained. "Fortunately, they're intact right back to Father McClintock's day. I've solved the mystery of the suppression of that old journal. The one about Lanzarote. You remember, don't you?"

Maria had a complete copy of the diary, though she had not said so when she returned the original. Instead she'd quietly looked up the laws of copyright and discovered that something as old as the journal, and anonymous besides, was in the public domain. "Of course I remember the diary," she said.

"Well, in 1869 Father McClintock had some correspondence with a Dominican archivist in Spain. It seems that around 1740 the priest who is the likely author of the journal took himself off Lanzarote and out of the order. No explanation of any sort, though it was rumored he'd had an affair with a local woman. She was supposed to be descended from the original people on one side, and high-born Spanish on the other. So it would have been a great scandal. More so in those days," he added somewhat lamely. It seemed a little silly to talk about such things as a scandal in the atmosphere of defection in which he and the young nun before him were living out their religious lives.

"I see," Maria said. Her head was buzzing with ideas about how that information could fit into the novel, but she said nothing except, "Thank you for telling me. It does seem an excess of discretion on Father McClintock's part. There's nothing in the diary about any of that."

Monsignor Walsh smiled. "It wasn't just discretion. The Dominicans wanted the journal. McClintock refused to let them have it. He promised instead that he'd lock it away where only serious scholars would have access to it. It was a nice jesuitical compromise between Christian charity and a librarian's notorious greed of acquisition."

A YEAR LATER, IN JUNE OF 1967, MARIA WAS AWARDED A Bachelor of Arts degree from Boston College. She had acquitted herself with honor and even been invited to become a member of Phi Beta Kappa. Mother Provincial did not feel it appropriate that Sister Mary Anthony join what had first been a secret society established on the heretical campus of William and Mary. Maria tried to explain that it was a purely intellectual commendation these days, but to no avail. So she did not obtain the little gold token that was so valuable in the world of scholarship. Neither was she permitted to go on and take a master's degree in linguistics. If she'd thought to make a way of life for herself in the safe haven of academia, such thoughts were swiftly proved futile. Instead, she was required to return to the Provincial House in Lynn and accept a teaching position in a local high school. The Servants of Bethlehem were experimenting with sending their sisters out to teach and bear witness among non-Catholics.

In order to take the job, Maria had to give up wearing any

habit, however modified. In its stead Mother Rose provided her with a spartan wardrobe of dark woolen skirts and white cotton blouses. Maria also stopped wearing a veil, although her hair was still cut very short. She was yet required to cut it herself with a kitchen scissors, but in deference to new realities she was allowed the use of a small hand mirror. One other concession was made, not just for her but for all the sisters, except the old ones who did not wish to change. Dormitories were abolished and chipboard partitions were erected, which gave each woman a relatively private space of her own.

That bit of privacy seemed at first enough to sustain Maria. Sometimes she even used it to look over the notes for the novel she'd thought of. But she did nothing about them. Teaching first-year Spanish and advanced Italian filled her life, or at least her hours. Luckily, some of her students were bright and eager, and being outside a totally Catholic environment was refreshing. That nothing really challenged her intellect or her imagination she tried to ignore. After all, she reminded herself, her spiritual life was supposed to do that. Except that it didn't exist.

She faced that truth one day in 1968, specifically on her twenty-sixth birthday. She was in the garden of the Lynn convent on a mild February Sunday, pushing old Sister Mechtilde's wheelchair up and down the path that ran between beds filled with winter-dead flower stalks. Sister Mechtilde was nearing ninety and while her body was crippled and worn out, her mind was still sharp. Moreover, kindness and content still lit her faded eyes. Maria quite enjoyed taking the old nun out for a bit of air.

"Look!" the dry and ancient voice said suddenly. "Is that a flower?"

"It can't be, not in February." Maria bent to examine the spot of color that had caught Sister Mechtilde's attention. "A robin," she said, lifting the lifeless form. Its red breast glowed against the frozen earth. "Dead I'm afraid, poor thing."

Sister Mechtilde wore knitted black mittens and her shriveled form was wrapped in layers of blankets, but she freed one arm and stretched it toward Maria. "Let me see."

Maria placed the bird on the wool-covered palm. Its intense color burned bright against the black. "Not a sparrow falls . . ." Sister Mechtilde quoted softly, and smiled her toothless smile. "I expect that goes for robins, too."

Maria grinned and didn't answer, feeling the cold rise from the damp concrete where she crouched beside the wheelchair.

The old woman tipped the bird out of her palm onto her lap and lay her mittened hand on Maria's head. "As for you, the very hairs of your head are numbered. You do know that, don't you, Sister Mary Anthony?"

Maria stood up briskly. "Come along, old dear, we can't stay out here chatting while you get a chill." She pushed the wheelchair toward the house. When they passed the large compost heap behind the shed where the summer furniture was stored, Sister Mechtilde made her stop and toss the robin's body on the pile of refuse that would make garden fertilizer next summer. Always put everything to the best possible use and waste nothing—one of the tenets of nunship, as interpreted by the Servants of Bethlehem.

For the rest of the day Maria thought about Sister Mechtilde's question, and her inability to answer. That night after evening prayers, she stood by the window of her ugly six-by-eight-foot partitioned cubicle and examined the realization that she did not believe the very hairs on her head to be numbered by some benevolent and immanent creator. She had no sense whatever of the presence of God in her life, and the practices of religion in which she participated were, for her, devoid of meaning. It was not simply that the practices had changed, and in changing lost much of their old beauty and mystery. No, she had changed. The girl who knelt in St. Anthony's church, sustained and uplifted by a set of unquestioned certitudes, didn't exist anymore. The only thing that existed was a commitment to this community, to some kind of human service, and to the notion that there was value in continuity and loyalty. I promised, she reminded herself. A coldly reasonable voice in her head said, "Promised what to whom?" but she silenced it firmly.

Maria did not want to look at her community with new eyes, to examine the nature of the entity to which she'd pledged her allegiance, but it was impossible not to. Because if continuity was one of the virtues of the Servants, it was also one on which they clearly had but a tenuous hold. In four years there had been only one new entrant, and she'd barely lasted the six-months' postulancy. On the other hand, somewhat miraculously, the congregation had yet to suffer any defections. They were shrinking in numbers because the old nuns were dying and not being replaced, not because of the mass exodus that convulsed so many other sisterhoods. Thus Mother Rose continually exhorted her daughters to be of good heart. They had done what the second Vatican Council commanded, changed and modified many of their nineteenth-century customs. God would reward them by sending new novices as soon as things settled down. "Have faith," she told them. Maria tried to at least go through the motions.

Then, in May, Mother Rose had a heart attack and died. In her honor the sisters donned their vibrant blue capes and white dresses for the funeral; a few even wore their former wimples, coifs, and veils. It was briefly a thrilling experience. The demonstration of solidarity and unity with the past had been unplanned and undiscussed and yet, without exception, all thirty-eight Servants appeared in their old habits on the day they buried the woman who had been Provincial of the congregation for thirty years. When they walked in colorful procession from the cemetery back to the chapel, Maria had tears in her eyes, and a sense of purposeful determination.

But Mother Rose's passing signaled an end, not, as they'd hoped, a beginning. The tightly coiled spring that held them together had lost its tension, and the bits and pieces that formed the whole began dropping one by one into a void, leaving nothing solid in their wake.

On the day that the high school in which she taught closed for summer vacation, Maria returned early to the Lynn house. The place was very quiet, but that was normal. She put her books and papers on a table by the stairs and went to the kitchen for a cup of coffee, thankful that the Rule allowed such small freedoms now.

At her first sight of Sister Bridget, the cook, Maria knew something terrible had happened. Sister Bridget's mouth was twisted with pain and her face was swollen with crying. "What's wrong?" Maria demanded, moving to the old woman's side. "What is it?" Maybe the Pope has died, she thought. Just like Sister Bridget to weep over that.

"Sister Mary Francis is going away."

At first Maria couldn't take in the words. "Going away where? What do you mean?"

"She's leaving the convent," Bridget said between sobs. "Not the Church, she says. But it's the same thing, isn't it? She's leaving us. After twenty-three years, she doesn't want us anymore."

Maria instinctively understood the many mixed emotions betrayed by those words, but she could not deal with them. She felt as if someone had flooded her stomach with ice water. Inside she was cold and cramped and suddenly very frightened. With no word of comfort for the weeping woman, Maria turned and ran through the silent halls where once she'd been taught to walk always with decorum and downcast eyes.

Sister Mary Francis's cubicle was three doors from her own. Maria ran to it and entered without knocking. Francis was standing beside an open suitcase folding a black cardigan. She looked up at Maria without surprise.

"Is it true?" Maria asked, despite the evidence before her eyes.

"It's true." The other woman put the sweater on top of the others in the suitcase, then she sank onto the hard, narrow bed. She wasn't pretty anymore, but the eyes Sister Mary Francis turned toward Maria were still warm and lively. All the charm and vivacity that had attracted a young girl in the long ago days of her novitiate remained.

Maria could not bear to let it go without a struggle, without even an explanation. "Why? After so many years, after making a commitment. How can you just walk out now?"

"In conscience I have no choice," Francis said quietly. "My commitment was to serve Jesus Christ. Now I can do that better elsewhere. We have become an irrelevancy. The hungry, the homeless, and the dying are still in need, but we no longer answer that need." She broke off. "That all sounds very pompous. I'm sorry. I can't explain."

No more could Maria understand. She went away speechless and broken-hearted. Not just because Mary Francis whom she'd admired was betraying something Maria clung to as important; but because in doing so the other woman was affirming belief and trust in God. Which meant that her road was utterly closed to Maria.

Three weeks later, Sister Mary Patrick announced that she was leaving too.

"Where are you going to go?" Maria asked, because that was an easier question than why.

"I'm taking an apartment in Boston. With two other women."

"Nuns?"

Patrick shook her head. Maria noticed that she had a lot of gray mixed into her brown hair. And Patrick was her age. "Not nuns," she said. "Women I met through the consciousness-raising group I joined." She'd been teaching math at an exclusive girls' school farther up the North Shore. Apparently they bred more than debutantes these days. "Look," she added, pulling a book off her night table and handing it to Maria. "Will you please read this."

It was something called *The Feminine Mystique,* by a woman named Betty Friedan. Maria remembered that Patrick had been the one to give her the forbidden magazine and its news of the apocalypse brewing in Rome. A lifetime ago, when they were at Salem Teachers' College. She replaced the book on the table.

"Don't you see it yet?" Patrick's voice was harsh with intensity. "The whole thing's a put-up job. A way of keeping women down. We're the alternative to barefoot and pregnant. Eternally virginal and subservient."

Maria remained wordless, as she was so often these days, and Patrick softened enough to take her hand. "Sooner or later you're going to wise up and be as brilliant as everybody says you are," she told her. "When that day comes let me know, I'll help as much as I can."

After Patrick, five more left—not just young ones, there were two women in their sixties among them. The edifice Maria had built to take faith's place was quickly crumbling, and she realized she was simply marking time.

Perhaps it was to stave off the moment of decision that she finally began writing the book she'd envisioned after she read the diary. She also found herself frequently looking at the handful of cards she'd received from Barbie over the past few years, as if they were a link with the Maria who once was and was no more.

She had three cards from Hank, too. The first had come from Jerusalem a few months after he left. The picture was a lurid reproduction of a painting, Jesus straining to carry his cross along the Via Dolorosa. Hank's message read "Having a wonderful time, wish you were here." It was unsigned but she'd hidden it for fear someone would see and be scandalized. Another had come in '67 from Damascus. "On a dig here, but nothing looks like turning up." That one he'd signed H.R. Last year he'd written from Tangiers. "Definitely think Canary people rebels banished by Rome. Will publish and await Nobel Prize." She'd heard no more since then. For quite some time she'd also had no word from Joe DiAnni. Now she tried to get in touch with him, but that proved impossible.

INTERLUDE
THE LADY

A.D. 1336 to A.D. 1480

IN THE DARK CENTURIES WHEN EUROPE WAS RID OF THE domination of Rome but found little to put in its place, no one whispered of the Fortunate Isles, those Islae Canaris of the wild dogs, and the sun, and the mountains. The people of Tyterogaka were gifted with nearly a millennium of peace. Then, in the great world beyond the island, men made for themselves the compass, the rudder, and the quadrant, and ventured in pursuit of knowledge and riches. In the year 1336 a Genoan named Lancelotto Malocello reached Tyterogaka and claimed it for his prince. Malocello's claim would have meant little, except that now Tyterogaka appeared on the new maps of the Europeans, marked with the arms of Genoa and named Lancerotus in honor of the "discoverer."

Thus identified, the island fell prey to slavers, who came with increasing frequency and took live booty away to the flesh markets of east and west. The children of Acoran called them the robbers of people. Except for these devastating raids, the next thirty-nine years passed in calm. No one discerned the approaching holocaust.

* * *

HER NAME WAS URTAYA, AND IN THE SUBTLE CREAMS AND ECRUS and browns of the landscape her pale blond hair and dark-tanned skin blended well. Behind her lay the village of Teguise, where her people and their king lived and grew their crops; ahead, the mountains. Urtaya was lithe and slim. Unmarried, oddly unbetrothed despite her seventeen years, she had not yet gone to the bride caves to be fattened. Now she placed her hands on her narrow hips and felt the bones. They were a mark of rejection, perhaps a sign that she was unworthy. Still, she liked the feel of her thin body. She was perverse, in this as in so much else. That's what they all said.

She sighed and shaded her eyes against the blazing sun. Goats were spread almost as far as she could see, patient and untiring in their search for food. The heat was unbearable, but Urtaya bore it. Goatherding was for children, little girls. It was by choice that she was here. "Let me go out with the goats," she'd told Agul, her mother. "A few days alone. After that I will give you my decision."

"There is no decision. You must do as all women do. There's nothing to brood about. This thing you think of, that boy . . . It's madness." Agul did not speak in anger, only with quiet certitude.

"A few days," Urtaya pleaded. "By myself. Please."

"Go then. But nothing will be changed when you return."

So she had taken food and a milking bag, borrowed the staff of her young sister, and gone. The time was almost up; tomorrow she was expected back in the village. Then Agul would be proved right. Nothing would be changed.

Thinking these things, Urtaya did not hear the boy until he stood behind her. "Hello," he said softly. "I have been looking for you."

She did not turn around, but her heart began to beat hard in her chest. She could feel it hammering, and feel the skin of her goatskin dress rise and fall over her breasts. "Why did you come here?"

"I told you, I've been looking for you."

"You mustn't. It's madness."

"Those aren't your words, they're Agul's."

"Perhaps. They're true anyway."

The young man, whose name was Zanis, dropped to his knees beside her and reached for her hand. "Look at me, don't turn away. Look at me and say 'Zanis, it's wrong for us to love each other.'"

Urtaya stared mutely off into the distance, but she didn't remove her hand from his.

"You can't say it," he said. "You know it's a lie."

"Yes, but that makes no difference. It's not what you or I want that matters."

Zanis stood up. "Yes, it is," he insisted. "I've decided. I won't go through with the ceremony. We'll get married and go live by ourselves somewhere up there." He nodded in the direction of the higher mountains to the north. "Just you and me, Urtaya. I have a few goats of my own. We can take seed with us. Years ago I found a cave below the great cliff; we can live there. No one will bother us, no one will care. Why should they?" His voice was thick with the urgency of his pleading and his hunger for her.

Urtaya looked at Zanis's dark eyes and dark hair. He was made like all the men of his clan. "They will care," she told him. "And they will bother us because you're from the king's cave, one of the clan of Zonzamas. You aren't permitted to marry the daughter of one who slaughters animals."

Zanis couldn't prevent himself from shuddering. "Don't say that. Your mother has three husbands. It's just as possible you're the daughter of one of the others."

Urtaya shook her head. "I am his," she said. "I'm not ashamed of my father. He's a good man, who does what's necessary for everyone. We must have meat to eat."

Zanis turned away, averting his eyes from the white goat beside them. "I don't want to talk about meat, or about your father. I came here to talk about us."

"There's nothing to talk about." Urtaya moved closer to the goat and lay her hand tenderly on its back. "A coat fit to make a robe for a *hamagada*," she murmured. "All white, without a blemish."

"Is that what you want?" Zanis asked angrily. "To be a consecrated *hamagada*? Never to lie with a man, with me?" He moved toward her and put his arm on her shoulders. "I know you want to be my wife, Urtaya, I see it in your eyes whenever I look at you."

She saw things in his eyes too. They made her resist his arguments about defying the law. Zanis's eyes showed weakness and a love of ease. He was of the cave of the king, accustomed to having what he wanted. Otherwise she'd gladly stand beside him in rebellion. As it was, she dared not. To fight and not to win meant a life forever ruined. If Zanis first revolted, then capitulated to his clan, she might as well be dead.

Urtaya said nothing of this because she really did love him. "I want to belong to you, but it's impossible. Go home to your clan, Zanis. The ceremony will take place in the *tagoror* at the next full moon. You'll forget about me once you are a man."

"I don't need their ceremony! I'm a man now." Suddenly he bent his head and kissed her. Very hard and full on the lips, as only the betrothed may kiss.

Urtaya tried to pull away but his arms around her waist held her fast. She didn't struggle, only remained quietly in his embrace. After a moment, he released her. "You're a fool, Zanis. It can't be." Her words were like bitter sea water on her tongue.

"I'm a fool for you. I must have you, Urtaya. If I don't, it doesn't matter whether I live."

She looked at him in silence for some seconds. So long she'd fought this battle, so long she'd hoped, and told herself hope was pointless.

"You're thinking of something," he said. "Tell me." His words were tender and cajoling, calculated to move her.

"There is one way," she said finally. "It might work."

"Tell me," he repeated.

"At the ceremony the priest will ask you three questions, won't he?"

Zanis stared at her, noting the way her blue eyes slanted and her full mouth turned up slightly at the corners. He could taste her mouth still; he longed to taste it again. "Three, yes," he said softly, drugged with looking at her. "He will ask have I ever prepared food; looked after, milked, or slaughtered an animal; have I ever acted wrongly toward a woman."

"And you'll tell the truth?"

"Of course, I must swear by Acoran."

Urtaya nodded. "Yes, you must. So what will happen if you admit to acting wrongly with a woman?"

"But I haven't! Just now, when I kissed you, that was only because I knew you wanted it."

She raised her hand and lay her finger over his lips. "There are other things men and women do. Not just kissing. If we did those things, the priest couldn't make you a nobleman, or give you the *magada*. Perhaps then your clan wouldn't care if we ran away to the north."

Zanis turned away. "I'd be in disgrace. They'd shave my head."

Urtaya lifted her hand and touched his dark hair. "It would grow again. You'd forget."

For a few moments there was silence. Then, wordlessly, he turned and pulled her to him. Urtaya pressed her body against his. She was ready to yield. Despite all her forebodings—her sure knowledge of Zanis's weakness as well as his strength—she was ready. The secret place between her thighs was wet with wanting him, her breasts trembled and the nipples were swollen and hard. So was the male thing he was thrusting against her now.

Zanis fumbled with the shoulder ties of her dress. Finally they came apart. The skins slithered down between them. The hot sun burnished Urtaya's nakedness.

"PLEASE," URTAYA PLEADED WITH AGUL. "IT IS ONLY A SHORT time."

"Almost thirty risings of the sun," her mother said. "With each of them you'll grow further from the bride age."

"Please." The girl's voice was a low whisper, hoarse with urgency.

Agul sighed. "It can't make any difference. In the *ta-goror* Zanis will become a man, son of a chief. He will be as far from you then as he is now, as far as the stars. You're a foolish child."

She broke off and looked away. Pato, the girl's father and Agul's second husband, walked through the place where the women sat. He made no sound. It was the time when Agul lived with her third husband and Pato was servant of the household. At the next full moon the roles would change.

Urtaya avoided looking at her father, and he didn't look at her. Agul studied them both in the brief moment when Pato's short, sturdy body moved past the fire. His shadow on the circular stone walls was large. It hovered over Agul and her daughter, then was gone. The woman sighed again. When she took Pato as her husband, the village had not approved. He was the son of a slaughterer of animals, fated to the same work. He and his kind were shunned. But Agul loved him and married him, and secretly he was her favored husband. Urtaya, only child of that peculiar union, was her favored daughter. "Very well," Agul said at last. "I'll do what you want. It won't make any difference, but maybe you'll be easier in your mind after Zanis has the *magada*. Promise me that when we leave the *tagoror* you'll go to the bride cave."

Urtaya nodded solemnly. "I promise. If Zanis is given the *magada*, I'll go."

It took longer than Agul had predicted. The full moon that should have seen Zanis become a man was obscured by clouds, and there was no ceremony. "My mother says it's an evil omen," he told Urtaya when they met in secret behind the fortress of Zonzamas the king.

"Do you think so?"

"No, a good one." Zanis spoke firmly. "Each day I'm more sure of what I'll do. I won't fail." He stretched out his hand and touched her cheek. Urtaya placed her own small hand over his big one and pressed his palm to her skin.

"I trust you, Zanis, and I have a surprise." She looked away as she spoke, suddenly shy.

"Tell me. Tell me your surprise." His smile was full of love.

She clasped her hands below her thin waist. "I have life growing in me."

Zanis swallowed hard, then nodded. "Good. Acoran has blessed us. Our child will be blessed."

The time of the manhood ceremony came. The moon rose low behind the peaks surrounding the *tagoror*, its blue-white light shimmered on the ranks of kneeling people, on Zonzamas the king, and on his wife Queen Fayna. It shone too on Zanis, standing between his mother, Tisa, and his father, Gadafo. Gadafo was the queen's brother.

Lost in the crowd of onlookers, Urtaya kept her head bent and her eyes closed. She was trembling, terrified lest her fear be seen. I trust you, she shouted repeatedly but inwardly. I swear by Acoran that I trust you, Zanis. You won't fail me or our child.

The sound of chanting broke the stillness. From a place near the foot of the mountain a line of *hamagadas* approached, singing their hymn to Acoran. The moon shone on their white gowns and illumined the decorated wooden staff they carried before them. This was the *magada* that would soon belong to Zanis. It would mark him as a member of the ruling clan and a full-grown man.

The *hamagadas* entered the walls of the great *tagoror* and were joined by the priest. Still singing, the procession approached Zanis and his kin.

"See the *magada!*" the priest cried out.

Urtaya could not watch. I trust you. She sent her thoughts across the open ground to Zanis. I trust you, you won't betray me, beloved.

Zanis raised his hands to the heavens. His head was thrown back and the fire made his face bright. "I see the will of Acoran," he intoned. "I see the *magada*."

The *hamagadas* raised their hands in prayer and joined their supplications to those of Zanis. Always since the blessed Fala their sacred chastity had sweetened the plea and bent the ear of Acoran to the people.

No one moved. The voice of the priest stabbed the silence. It mounted to the top of the walls and the mountains, it raced toward the moon and the stars. His chant was wordless, its meaning was in the notes and the pitch and the rhythm, and understanding was in the flesh and blood of the listeners. For more than a thousand years the children of kings had been thus marked out by Acoran and received to manhood.

At last the chant ended. "Kneel before Acoran who made you," the priest said. "Acoran who made all that has been made." Zanis knelt. "Zanis, son of the woman Tisa and her husband Gadafo, who is brother to Fayna, wife of Zonzamas who is our king; Zanis, do you swear by Acoran to answer truthfully?"

Urtaya was far away at the back of the arena, near the wall, as befitted the daughter of the man who slaughtered animals, but it seemed to her she could hear Zanis breathing. "I swear," Zanis said. "I swear by Acoran."

Urtaya clenched her fists and pressed them into the flesh of her belly.

"Three things must be known," the priest said. "Remember that you have sworn." He took a step closer to the boy and raised the *magada* over his head. "Zanis, kinsman of Zonzamas, have you prepared food for anyone else to eat?"

"By Acoran, I have not."

"Zanis, kinsman of Zonzamas, have you looked after, milked, or slaughtered an animal?"

"By Acoran, I have not."

"Zanis, kinsman of Zonzamas, have you acted wrongly with a woman?"

"By Acoran . . ." There was a pause. Everyone waited but no further sound came. In the silence, surprise was born. It danced across the indrawn breath of hundreds of onlookers, flitted over the faces of the parents of Zanis, and came to rest in the eyes of the high priest.

"Zanis," he intoned once more, "kinsman of Zonzamas, have you acted wrongly with a woman?"

Urtaya's heart was singing. Now, she told herself, it will all come to pass as I have dreamed it and as he promised.

Some more seconds passed. "By Acoran," Zanis repeated at last, "I have not!"

The *hamagadas* began the hymn of praise and thanksgiving to Acoran. A sigh of relief murmured around the *tagoror*. "Arise," the priest said in a loud voice. "Take the *magada*, the symbol of your dignity and service to the people."

"No! No, he can't!" Urtaya's voice rang over the heads of the crowd. It echoed from wall to wall of the *tagoror*, and overcame the singing of the virgins. "No, no, no."

Everything stopped. The hymn died away; hundreds of eyes turned to stare at Urtaya. Only Zanis didn't look at her. He stared into the fire.

"Come forward!" the priest called out. "Speak the truth in the name of Acoran."

Urtaya couldn't move. Agul began to weep. Urtaya saw her mother's tears, and she stood up and walked toward the priest.

He studied her in the firelight, then looked at Zanis. "Tell me why this boy cannot take the *magada*," he said.

"Remember that you're speaking in the presence of Acoran who made you."

"I remember." The silence was absolute. Urtaya's small voice carried around the *tagoror*. "Zanis and I love each other. We want to marry."

"You're the daughter of Agul, and of Pato who slaughters animals," the priest said patiently. "It's forbidden."

"I know. We both know." She swallowed hard, didn't think she could go on, and knew she must. "But still we love each other. We have lain together." There was a gasp of unbelief from the assembly. Urtaya lifted her head and looked straight at the priest. "I have his child growing here in my body." She pressed her hands over her stomach. "Ask Zanis if this isn't true."

The priest turned to the boy. "Zanis, kinsman of Zonzamas," he began.

Zanis didn't wait for him to finish. "It's true," he said, then repeated the words in a louder voice. "What Urtaya says is true."

For many breaths no one moved or spoke. Then, with a loud cry, the priest raised the *magada* over his head and brought it down to split in two over his knee. With another cry, he hurled the pieces into the fire.

Zanis dropped to his knees again. He hung his head and waited for the shaving of his hair to begin. After that would come the pronouncement of banishment. He knew. He'd always known. Only for a moment had he dreamed again the dream of his childhood before he knew Urtaya, of the moment when he'd receive the *magada* and take his place among the men of Zonzamas's cave.

Urtaya wanted the earth to open and swallow her. She wanted to throw herself into the fire that was devouring the *magada* that was to have belonged to Zanis. She only stood in silence. After a moment she felt a hand on her shoulder, pulling her back out of the priest's sight. She turned and looked into the face of Ico, Holy Mother of the *hamagadas*.

Ico didn't say anything, but Urtaya read sympathy in her eyes, and a warning. She allowed Ico to ease her into the ranks of the virgins. They closed around her without seeming to move at all. Most still had their hands raised skyward in prayer. Urtaya wanted to raise her hands too, but she was afraid even to pray.

The priest approached Zanis with a sharpened stone in his hand. He reached out to begin the shaving of the boy's head.

"Wait!" The voice of ultimate authority broke into the silence. The king stepped forward and faced his people. The oval pendant hanging round his neck was lit by the fire, and its green brightness reflected in his strong face. "It is not enough," the king said. "Banishment is punishment for breaking the laws of manhood, not for lying after you've sworn by Acoran to tell the truth." Zonzamas addressed his words to the priest. He didn't look at Zanis or his parents.

"You speak truly," the priest said at last. "To lie in Acoran's name means . . ."

"Death," Zonzamas supplied.

"Death! Yes, death!" The crowd took up the cry. Soon it was an incantation, a chant like the one sung by the now silent *hamagadas*. "Death! Death! Death!"

Urtaya opened her mouth, but instantly a hand was clasped over her lips. "Be silent," Ico whispered in her ear. "For the sake of your child."

The priest led Zanis from the *tagoror,* the boy walking as if he could neither feel nor see. The people followed, led by Zonzamas the king. Slowly they all moved toward the sea. Only Tisa and Gadafo, the parents of Zanis, remained alone in the *tagoror* with the bitterness of their grief.

The sands of the beach were white. The calm ocean reflected the moon, and the night was as day. In the brightness the deathrock stood out, high above the tides, its flat surface dry and clean, a thing both innocent and lethal.

Urtaya kept close to the Holy Mother, and Ico did not let her go. When the virgins began to chant the death prayer, Ico didn't raise her arms, she kept them around Urtaya.

Four men came forward and led Zanis to the rock. At last the boy woke from his trance. He tried to pull away but it was too late. The men held him fast and spread him on the blue-gray stone. The priest held up his arms and prayed for a few seconds. Then he stopped to pick up another stone. He approached Zanis with measured steps. There was nothing more to say. The vengeance of Acoran was swift and wordless.

A few minutes before the priest had lifted the *magada*; now, he lifted the instrument of death. When the rock dropped onto the head of Zanis, the only sound was the smashing of bone and flesh. There was not even time for the victim to cry out. Zanis died in silence.

"No, by Acoran, no!" Urtaya could be still no longer. Her protest howled into the night, her shrieks tumbled into the sea.

"The girl," someone called out. "The girl! She has to die too! She violated the sacred law."

A hundred voices took up the refrain. The reek of blood was in the air and the smell entered their nostrils and filled their mouths and their throats; it became a seductive taste on their tongues. "Take her to the fire cave! Make her breath the smoke! Let her die by choking!"

The priest looked around him hesitantly. It was for Zonzamas to decide the fate of Urtaya. Only the king could pass sentence.

Zonzamas opened his mouth to speak. Swiftly Ico stepped to the edge of the cluster of *hamagadas*. Her daughters moved closer to her and to Urtaya. Now each one of them had their arms raised to Acoran. Each white gown shone in the moonlight. "The girl is ours," Ico said in a loud voice. "She had claimed our protection and it has been given. See, she's here among us. She has sanctuary."

The king looked at the Holy Mother and nodded his head. "True, that is our law. Since she has claimed your protection, the girl Urtaya is yours. From now on, to me and to her parents and to all our people, she is dead." He raised his *magada* and plunged it into the sand. "I, Zonzamas, have spoken."

In the place of the *hamagadas* Urtaya was safe from physical danger, but nothing could lighten her sorrow. The months passed, and Ico often spoke to her with a mother's love and compassion, but it helped little.

"You mustn't remember," Ico said. "You'll harm the child. You must be peaceful and full of joy."

Urtaya looked away. She no longer remembered what peace and joy meant.

One day Agul came to speak to the Holy Mother. She bowed low in obeisance to the other woman's station.

"Forgive me, but I fear for my daughter."

"Why? She's safe here in the enclosure of the *hama-gadas.*"

"No," Agul said. "Tisa and Gadafo, the parents of Zanis, haven't forgiven her. They plot Urtaya's death. You've given her sanctuary according to the ancient law, but they're powerful people."

Ico studied the brown earth at her feet, and when she looked up her face was thoughtful. "I see. Perhaps I was foolish not to guess. But tell me, don't they care about the life of their grandchild?"

"They say Zanis can't be the father, he'd never have broken the law. They say Urtaya lied out of spite. There are some who believe them, men who are loyal to Gadafo."

"But Zanis admitted that Urtaya told the truth."

Agul shrugged. "He was their only son. They see and hear what they wish."

"Yes, I understand. Thank you for telling me these things, and don't worry about Urtaya and the baby. We'll keep them safe. And my sisters and I will pray to Acoran for all of you."

Agul bowed again and went away.

A FEW DAYS LATER ICO LOOKED FOR URTAYA, AND FOUND HER by the water pit. It was nearly empty, and Urtaya was cleaning the deep sides with coarse sand.

Ico looked at the sky, bright blue with no trace of cloud. "We will pray to Acoran and offer sacrifice and it will rain, just as it does each twelve full moons. All life goes on, Urtaya. You must forget your sorrow and live. It's Acoran's will."

The girl whirled round as fast as her heavy body would allow. "Why didn't you let them kill me? Then it would be over and I'd be at peace."

"You're guilty of nothing that deserves death. You and your child are entitled to as much life as Acoran grants you."

"No guilt," Urtaya repeated. "Forgive me, Holy Mother, you speak foolishness. Zanis is dead because I convinced him to lay with me. Don't you understand? I tempted him and he gave in."

Ico touched the girl's blond hair. "Poor child. You're too young to carry such burdens. Zanis didn't die because he lay with you. Only because he lied after he had sworn to Acoran to tell the truth. Otherwise his only punishment would have been to forfeit the *magada* and be banished."

"I know the law. But I knew Zanis too. I knew he was weak. It was too much to ask him to be shamed in front of everyone. I knew that, but I asked him just the same. And now he's dead."

Ico saw that it was pointless to argue. "Very well. Even if what you say is true, the child of Zanis is alive. You must think of that."

The daughter of Urtaya and Zanis was born on the night the rains came. They came as they usually did on this island, with suddenness and incredible ferocity. Great sheets of water flung from the sky, an outpouring of life from Acoran. Everywhere the cracks and crevices of the earth were filled. Every hollow place shaped and cleaned by the hands of the people caught and held the precious gift. And on this night of beneficence, the life of Urtaya's child began. She opened her legs and spewed forth a girlchild in the time between sunset and the rising of the moon.

The storm continued all through the next day and night. In the morning, when the sun rose again, Ico went to Urtaya. "The rains have ended. Acoran is good. Every place that can hold water is full."

"Yes. Acoran is good."

Urtaya was nursing the baby. The infant had Zanis's black hair, and eyes as blue as Urtaya's. "She'll be a beauty," Ico said.

"Yes, I think so." Urtaya smiled, and there was a look of peace on her face for the first time since the night in the *tagoror*.

"What will you call her?"

"Zana."

"I see. It's a good name."

Ico went away and thanked Acoran for yet another miracle.

In the year known to those not of the island as a.d. 1377, the child Zana was two years old. Her birthday was accompanied by the rains, as it always seemed to be. Everywhere was freshness and new life, and Urtaya looked at her daughter and her world and felt joy. It was good to be here with the *hamagadas*. Today was sweet, and she'd stopped worrying about tomorrow. Acoran had brought them this far; her future, and Zana's, was in Acoran's hands.

Urtaya was working among the cooking pots and the little girl was playing nearby when the noise began. A dull sound at first, then a mighty roar of voices and shouting and strange, sharp cracklings. Urtaya picked up Zana and ran to the wall of the enclosure. Ico and the other *hamagadas* were there too. "What is it, what's happening?"

"Strange men with mighty weapons have come across the water," Ico said.

"The people robbers," Urtaya said.

"Yes." Ico looked at the girl thoughtfully, then made her decision. "Here, give me Zana." Without waiting for agreement she grabbed the child and thrust her into the arms of one of the *hamagadas*. "Take her to the altar in the temple," she told the virgin. "Stay there until I come for you."

Urtaya had no time to protest. Ico pulled her to a little gate at the rear. "What is it?" Urtaya asked when she caught her breath. "Why have you taken Zana, Holy Mother? Why are we here?"

"Urtaya, listen carefully. There is very little time. Do you remember Tisa and Gadafo, the parents of Zanis?"

"How could I forget?"

"They've plotted revenge. All these many risings and settings of the moon have passed, but they've never forgiven. A band of men are with them, their kin, and they've sworn to avenge the death of Zanis."

"But we're safe here. They wouldn't come inside the enclosure of the *hamagadas*! They wouldn't dare to violate sanctuary!"

"They would if they thought no one would know. Hatred poisons the hearts and minds of men and women, Urtaya. It distorts their reason. The coming of the robbers of people will give Tisa and Gadafo the opportunity they've been waiting for. Our people will fight the strangers and while that's happening the others will come here. That's why I sent Zana to the altar place. Not even men half crazed will violate Acoran's altar. I'm sure of it. But if you yourself were there . . ."

"Yes, it will be safe for Zana, but probably not for me," Urtaya agreed. "I understand."

"You must hide, Urtaya. High up in the mountains where no one can find you. When the strangers are dead or gone it will be safe for you to return."

Urtaya's fear showed in her face. "I've never been high up in the mountains. I don't know them."

"Behind this gate is a path. If you follow it until the sun is straight overhead, you'll come to a climbing path. Go up until you can go no farther. At the end you'll find a cliff with the mark of Acoran cut into its side." She traced the spiral symbol of God on the girl's palm. "You know the mark. Look carefully where the symbol ends and you'll see a tiny entrance to a cave. Inside there's a stream where the *hamagadas* go to get the holy water for our ceremonies. Only we know about it. You'll be safe there, and you can look down on the sea. When the strangers have gone, you can come home. Remember, stay away until they're gone or until I come for you."

Urtaya nodded solemnly. "I'll do as you say, but shouldn't I take Zana with me?"

"You're grown and strong, Urtaya. You can live on what food you find. Zana is only a child. Leave her with us. I promise you no harm will come to her."

"Very well. Give me your blessing, Holy Mother."

Urtaya knelt, and Ico laid her hands on the girl's head. Then she reached beneath her white gown. "I give you something more. A symbol of Acoran, a holy thing to protect you." She pressed the small black stone figure with its jeweled green seam into Urtaya's hand. "Now, go quickly. Acoran be beside you."

Ico's forebodings were well founded. Gadafo and his men appeared soon after Urtaya fled to the mountains, while the sound of fighting rang round the island.

"Where is she? We claim a life for a life!"

"You have no right to the girl's life," Ico told him. "Zanis didn't die because of her. He died because he lied in Acoran's name."

Gadafo was not interested in logic, only in blood. He grabbed Ico's arm and looked around the empty courtyard. "Where are the others? Where's the child?"

His lance was at Ico's throat; already she could feel its tip piercing her skin. But Ico was not afraid of death. "We are at prayer in the place of Acoran's altar. If you violate the sanctuary, blood will be on you and your children and their children. You'll bring catastrophe to the whole island."

"I'm not interested in your legends and superstitions, woman. I want what's my due, the death of that vicious girl. And I want her child."

He had relaxed his grip while he spoke and Ico stepped back slightly and looked at him, trying to understand. "You want to murder an innocent child?"

"No," Gadafo said slowly. "My wife wants the child. She's convinced herself the baby is part of Zanis."

"She is," Ico said solemnly. "She's your grandchild, and Urtaya is her mother. Don't make more tragedy, Gadafo. Go away and leave us in peace. Go do your duty, fight beside your king and kinsmen."

With a savage cry, he grabbed her once more. "Inside," he shouted to the restive men behind him. "They're all in there! Get them!"

It was over in a few minutes. The men returned to the courtyard carrying Zana. The little girl was covered with blood and she was sobbing, but she was unhurt. "Where's the mother?" Gadafo asked.

"Not there," one of the men answered. "Not anywhere. We looked."

"My sisters," Ico whispered. "In Acoran's name, what have you done?"

There was no answer. Two or three of the men looked away from her. As if they already felt the shame of their terrible deeds.

Ico was silent for some seconds. Then she looked at Gadafo. "The thing you have done today will never be forgotten. All our people will pay for the sacrilege you have committed." She lifted her hands in prayer and began the death chant. Gadafo plunged his spear into her heart before the prayer was ended.

NEVER IN THE MEMORY OF THE ISLANDERS HAD THE STRANGERS who came to rob people stayed longer than a few risings of the sun. Urtaya knew she wouldn't have long to wait. From her vantage point on top of the mountain she could look down and see the fighting, and the people herded into the moving thing on the water. The following sunrise she tried to see if the strangers had gone, but she couldn't find the shore. A fierce, sand-laden wind swept the island and obscured her view. It was the red wind of the west, and it did not end after two sunsets or even three. It went on and on.

Urtaya lost count of the days. She drank from the stream in the cave and ate the roots of scrubby plants growing nearby. Every morning she looked down and considered returning to the *hamagadas*. But she couldn't see anything, only the red haze carried by the howling wind. Urtaya was terrified. Amid the chaos Tyterogaka and the holy place of Acoran seemed as empty as a tomb.

"Zana," she whispered over and over again. "Zana, Zana, Zana. O Acoran, protect my child!"

She was torn between whether it was better to go or to stay where she was. Which would help Zana more?

"Stay until I send for you or until the strangers have gone," Ico had said. Urtaya decided she must obey the Holy Mother. Only by so doing had she and Zana survived until now.

Time passed. Urtaya became weak and feverish. Maybe there was some poison in the roots of the plants, something that didn't harm goats but was bad for humans. Urtaya stopped eating them, but she grew too ill to notice when the red wind ended.

She clung to the gift that Ico had given her, the little statue. It reminded her of a *hamagada* in her long gown. Urtaya ran her fingers over it and found comfort. The statue was holy, a symbol of Acoran, as Ico had said. No matter how weak she was Urtaya never loosed her grip on the figure. She kept it pressed close to her heart.

She was very ill when the Lady came, so weak she could barely see. But she heard the soft, sweet voice that said, "Come, Urtaya, it's time. I've come to take you home."

Urtaya couldn't focus on the visitor. It wasn't Ico, she was sure of that. It wasn't Ico's voice, though it was true and kind like hers. "Who are you? Did the Holy Mother send you?"

"I came because it's time," the Lady said. "The Holy Mother is waiting for you."

Urtaya felt the Lady's hand take her own. It was soft and cool and the moment it touched her she felt full of hope. The touch was a promise. "Is Zana safe?"

"Yes, she's safe."

"Oh, thanks be to Acoran!" The girl tried to sit up, but

she was too weak. And the Lady took the holy figure from her hands. "You mustn't," Urtaya said agitatedly. "I have to bring it back to the Holy Mother. It's hers."

"She doesn't need it now. Neither do you. We'll leave it here."

Through the mists that veiled her eyes, Urtaya saw the Lady study the little statue. She saw her smile and run her fingers over the symbol of Acoran. Then the Lady laid it on the ground, near the entrance of the cave. "We will leave her here. She'll be found later. Come, Urtaya."

Suddenly Urtaya felt strong. She rose easily, as if she had eaten and slept. She'd never moved so freely in her life. There were no restraints. Urtaya knew she could do anything, even fly like a bird if she wanted to. But when she looked back, she saw a heap on the ground. It was almost as if she'd left her body behind. It didn't matter. She was herself, whole and well and free. The strange Lady was waiting for her. "I'm coming," Urtaya said.

She began to move toward the Lady, then, just for a moment, she turned and looked at the little statue still lying on the ground. It had a face now, a beautiful face where the woman had touched it. "How strange," Urtaya said.

The Lady laughed. It sounded to Urtaya like the joy of the whole world.

TISA, THE MOTHER OF ZANIS, TOOK THE CHILD ZANA INTO HER cave. But Tisa knew that she had gained the child in blood, that death was the purchase price for the small, dark-haired figure who was flesh of her flesh. First the death of Zanis, then the terrible dying of the consecrated women. Tisa wept for these things.

"Be quiet, woman," Gadafo told her repeatedly. "Be quiet and forget."

"I can't forget. None of us can."

The people of Tyterogaka grieved and muttered about the evil that Gadafo had done, and about the curse he had brought on the island. They did nothing more because Gadafo was the brother of Fayna, the queen.

More and more frequently the robbers of people came, and a new evil as well. Sometimes there were islanders who cooperated with the strangers and led others into traps. Worse, some of the strangers didn't leave when they had taken their captives. They made trouble even in the cave of the king. It was said that Queen Fayna's youngest daughter was the child of one of them. When Zonzamas died, there was no clear agreement as to who was the next lawful king.

All this happened while Zana grew to ripeness and Tisa became an old woman. But Tisa did not allow the passing of time to dim her memory or blot out her duty. Often she told Zana the story of her birth, and of the death of her parents. "You must know the truth, Zana; it must not be a weapon others can use against you. Zanis, your father, died on the killing rock, his brains spilled by the priest. Urtaya, your mother, disappeared into the mountains. She died somewhere up there. Alone."

As if these terrible stories were not enough, Tisa took Zana to the deserted place where once the *hamagadas* had lived. Where Gadafo had killed them. "He was crazed with grief," Tisa explained. "We had only one son, only Zanis. My husband didn't know what he was doing."

Together the two women roamed the empty, decaying enclosure of the consecrated virgins. Zana tried to remember something of the early days of her life when, according to Tisa, she had lived here with the holy women. No recollection came to her, and that always made her sad.

Tisa looked for other things. "There was the altar." She pointed an aged, wrinkled finger at the spot. "That's where the *hamagadas* prayed to Acoran when our people were at peace. Where are they?" she would wail as if she didn't know. "Where have the holy ones gone?" And she looked for something else. "There was a little figure, made of black rock and of the green sacred stone. The same stone as the pendant of the king. I saw it when I was a bride. Ico, the Holy Mother, showed it to me. It was beautiful and Acoran was in it. Where can it be?"

Tisa searched, but she never found the thing. Each time, the grandmother and grandchild would leave the enclosure without answers.

Zana became a beautiful young woman. When more strangers arrived, in the year that outsiders called 1402, she was twenty-seven. By then Zana had two husbands, a daughter, and three sons. Tisa was dead. But not her stories. Zana told them to her daughter, the child she'd named Urtaya.

When this second Urtaya was ten, the strangers built a fortress and claimed to be rulers of this place they called not Tyterogaka but Lanzarote. Urtaya was not surprised; by now such things had come to be expected.

The conquerors were Normans, men named Bethencourt and de la Salle. They remained during all of Urtaya's lifetime. When she was an old woman they and others of their clan were in possession of the best growing lands and all the places where water could be stored. They were indeed rulers. There were many of them, and they lived in great houses built above the ground. The people of Acoran served them, were subject to them, and were told of a God named Jesus, said to be the only God. The priests of the strangers said that Acoran was an idol, an evil thing to be despised. To pray to Acoran or to offer sacrifice in Acoran's name was forbidden and punishable by death.

Urtaya, the daughter of Zana, lived a very long time and saw much. When she died in 1480, there were two names to be feared on Lanzarote. That of Jesus Christ who was a God-man, and his representative, the king of distant Spain who was said to be their king now. The people who had once worshipped Acoran didn't know why their God had deserted them, and few of them cared anymore.

But Urtaya told the old stories to her daughters and they to theirs. The tales were whispered in secret at night, when none could overhear. "We are of the clan of Zonzamas who was king, it is our duty to remember," the old ones told the young.

It was a legacy passed from woman to woman; no sons were told of the days past. Not for them to mourn the *hamagadas* and the lost symbol of Acoran, the little stone figure Tisa never found. It was an inheritance to be guarded by the mothers and daughters, as they guarded and passed on life.

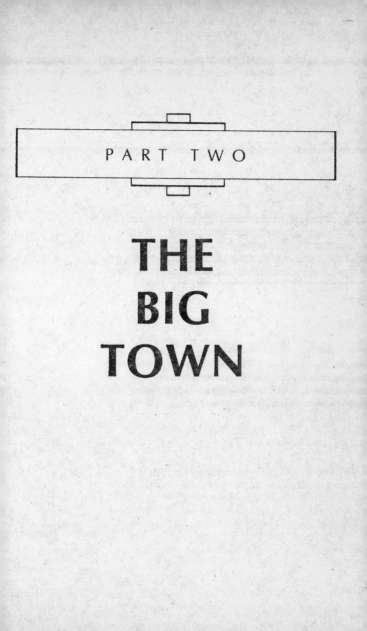

PART TWO

THE
BIG
TOWN

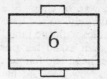

6

A T TWENTY-FIVE BARBIE STILL LIKED TO WALK, although the miles-long tramps of her teenage years were no longer possible. That was but one of many changes worked in her life by the birth of her daughter. Barbie considered them all a small price to pay for Norma.

The little girl was a year old, and every day of her brief life had been a gift, a blessing bestowed by providence. Because whatever else happened or didn't happen, Barbie could see Norma, touch her, kiss her, nuzzle into that incredibly sweet-smelling warm neck, watch the smile on that chubby little face, feel the tiny fingers that gripped her own with perfect trust and confidence. No longer did she worry about her own security, she was charged with providing security for this small being who, miraculously it seemed to Barbie, had grown in her body and come to fill her life.

Which was not to say she was either a perfect mother or completely happy. Norma, like any baby, could be wearing, and the isolation Barbie felt compelled to maintain in their lives could be very lonely. That's why she'd invested in a sturdy stroller and why she pushed her daughter through the streets of Manhattan whenever the weather was good. In this spring of 1967 her customary route was from her apartment on West Sixteenth Street to Washington Square. There Norma could toddle at will and Barbie could observe the constantly changing scene.

The Square was actually a park, part of New York's fund of green and open spaces, a link between fashionable lower Fifth Avenue and Greenwich Village. Often these days the inhabitants of these different worlds met in the Square to protest the Vietnam war. A less belligerent blending took place around the chess tables in the park's southwest quadrant. Barbie had no interest in politics, war, or chess. She did enjoy watching people concentrate intensely, so she usually gravitated to the squat cement game tables with the inlaid marble squares.

"Do you play?" a man asked her one Sunday afternoon.

"No." She shook her head and felt peculiarly shy. In nearly one and a half years in New York she had spoken to few people except shopkeepers and neighbors. Many men looked at her, a phenomenon to which she was accustomed, but she never returned their attention.

"That's your little girl, isn't it?" His voice was low and friendly and Barbie liked his looks. He was tall and angular, with an action-ready tautness that showed however casually he moved. His jaw was square, the facial skin molded to a hard-edged frame, the nose high-bridged and aggressive. It was the face of a man in his mid to late thirties, but his crew-cut hair was a startling pure white. It didn't look like a color gone gray; white was its color. His eyes too were remarkable, a pale, glittering gray, framed by white brows and lashes. Against his dark tan the effect was arresting, attractive, even sensual, but at the same time austere. So Barbie was amazed when he squatted on the grass and held out his arms to Norma.

"Hi, my name's Phil, what's yours?"

Barbie smiled at the ploy; the baby ran to her and hid. "She's shy with strangers." The gray glance demanded more. "Her name's Norma, mine's Barbie."

The man stood up and held out his hand. Like his voice his touch was firm and pleasant. "Hello, Barbie."

Had he pushed, that would have been the end of it. He didn't. A chess game ended, the loser stood up and walked away. The winner turned toward Phil. "You on?"

The white-haired man nodded, sat down, and was instantly engrossed in chess. But when Barbie and Norma left, he waved farewell.

On weekdays Phil was never in the Square and Barbie's visits remained devoid of human companionship. There was a wall around her she herself had erected, and people respected

220

it. But on Saturdays and Sundays it was different. Phil and Barbie chatted a bit when he wasn't playing. If he was, she stood and watched. His moves were never hurried and seldom wrong. Eventually he'd murmur, "Check." Soon something like "Check and mate in three." At which point his opponent would usually tip over his king with a despairing gesture.

In the casual talk they shared before and after his games, Barbie told Phil she was a widow. Apart from that they spoke of nothing personal; they didn't even exchange surnames. Then, one Saturday in June, Phil accompanied her when she left the park. It was an easy and natural gesture, and had about it no air of forethought. He simply walked beside her past the empty circular fountain with its customary quota of mismatched protesters to the Fifth Avenue arch, and remained at her side when she started uptown.

Suddenly it grew dark and an east wind rose. "It's going to pour. Do you live far?" Phil glanced anxiously at the child in the stroller.

"Not far. Sixteenth Street." Barbie pushed the carriage a little faster.

"Let me." He replaced her grip on the handle bar. Then, to Norma, "Hold on, honey, we're going to run." The child didn't understand, but she giggled with glee when the pace increased to a fast trot.

Barbie adjusted her stride to keep up. They reached Sixteenth Street just as the first big drops splatted on the sidewalk, and a few seconds later they were level with the converted brownstone where she lived. There was a flash of lightning, followed immediately by a wicked clap of thunder. The heavens opened and sheets of water poured from the sky. "In here?" Phil yelled.

"Yes!" Barbie dashed up the steps to open the door to the hall and Phil hefted child and stroller together and rushed both to safety. "Thanks so much," Barbie lifted Norma into her arms. She was on the verge of asking him to come up for a cup of coffee when he spied an empty taxi heading east.

"I'd better grab that," he called over his shoulder as he ran down the stairs and flagged the cab. "See you next week."

The following Saturday, Barbie found herself watching the clock and counting the hours until it would be time to leave for the Square. She also dressed more carefully than usual. It was a hot day and she put on a chino miniskirt that hugged her hips and displayed her long, tanned legs. The white blouse she wore with it tied at the waist and she left the top button open. She didn't analyze her feelings or intentions, just enjoyed the pleasant sense of anticipation.

Phil wasn't in the park. She waited until nearly six, but he didn't come. Neither did he appear the following day. Barbie was upset and disappointed, and she was short-tempered with the baby. She was very annoyed with herself for that, and not sorry that on Tuesday she was scheduled to go to Boston for her biannual visit with Sophie and Moe.

There both sets of doting grandparents would overwhelm Norma with love and attention, and renew their pleas that Barbie leave New York and "come home." The Golds would be as insistent as the Kormans, and Barbie would listen patiently to all their arguments and say little. She would also nod her head in agreement when they remarked, as they always did, that little Norma looked like her dead father. Then, after two weeks had elapsed, Barbie would bring her daughter back to the apartment on Sixteenth Street. It was all totally predictable. In Revere she always managed to conceal her tension. Certainly she never contacted any of her old friends, least of all Joe. But by the time she left she'd have lost a few pounds, there would be circles under her eyes, and she'd have a headache that would persist for days. Nonetheless, she didn't begrudge these visits. Under the circumstances, it was the least she could do for her family.

BARBIE AND NORMA RETURNED TO NEW YORK ON THE FIFTH of July. The city was a blast furnace by day and stifling by night. The child slept badly until, on the morning of the seventh, she succumbed to exhaustion and fell into a deep sleep right after breakfast. The flat was a large studio on the top floor; only one room with a curtain of wooden beads separating the sleeping from the living quarters. Now Barbie tied back the beads so the makeshift bedroom would get the maximum air, and made herself another cup of coffee. She was just going to drink it when there was a knock on the door.

The bell hadn't rung so Barbie expected a neighbor. Theoretically no one from outside could get in without identifying himself through the speaker; it should have been someone who lived in the building. It wasn't. It was Phil. In the dim light of the landing his white hair and silvery eyes looked eerie. A messenger from another universe.

"Hi. Where've you been? I was worried."

"I went to Boston to see my folks."

"I see. Everything's all right, then?"

"Sure, fine." She was conscious of his high-charged vitality. And of the fact that she wore only a disreputable man's shirt that reached to somewhere around the middle of her thighs, and no makeup. Also that there was a tone of genuine concern in his voice that absurdly made her want to cry. "Come in." She stepped aside. "But be quiet, Norma's asleep."

Phil followed her into the apartment. She saw his gray glance sweep the small interior and take in everything. All at once her efforts to make the place attractive seemed pitiful. "It isn't much," she said defensively. "But it's comfortable."

"It's very nice. I like all your plants."

She flushed with pleasure. "Thank you. I've grown most of them myself from seed. I enjoy it. Coffee?"

"Thanks. Black, please." And when he took the mug from her hands, "I hope you don't think it presumptuous of me to come. I really was worried. You didn't say anything about going away. Not that it's any of my business."

"I would have told you, but you weren't in the Square the weekend after the rainstorm."

"No, I know. Something came up. Business."

She had no idea what business he was in and didn't feel she could ask. All at once there seemed nothing to say. "I have a little garden on the roof," Barbie stammered after a few seconds. "Would you like to see it?"

Phil smiled and nodded and she ushered him out to a tiny steep staircase that led to a skylight. It was propped open because of the heat, and they emerged onto a flat, tarred surface four stories above the street. In one corner was a kind of pergola made of bamboo shades stretched over white painted poles. Beneath it was an assortment of flowerpots containing a variety of outdoor plants. The section of roof under the pergola was covered with a dark green straw rug and there were a couple of chairs slung with beige canvas. "Did you do all this yourself?" he asked.

Barbie grinned. "Yes. I'm outrageously proud of it, so you'd better say something nice."

"It's fantastic, I mean it. And a lot cooler than the apartment."

They sat in the beige chairs. Barbie could see down the stairs into her flat and she would hear her daughter if she woke. The strangeness between them faded. They chatted easily about nothing for a few minutes, then Phil looked at his watch. It was a thin wafer of gold and it occurred to Barbie that it was probably very expensive. So were his clothes, now she came to think of it. He wore simple dark slacks and a white sportshirt, open at the neck. But the outfit was perfectly tailored. "I've got to go, I'm afraid," Phil said.

They stood up. Barbie was again aware of how she looked—or thought she looked—and she tugged at the rolled-up sleeves of her shirt. It had belonged to Normie. The color had long since faded and the collar and cuffs were frayed. "I'm sorry." She giggled nervously. "I should have made you wait while I changed."

"That wasn't necessary." His eyes spoke more than the words and she was conscious of the way he was studying her. "Look," he added, "can you get a baby-sitter sometime?"

"One of my neighbors looks after Norma once in a while. I don't go out much."

"I thought not. But will you go out with me? Say Friday night? Dinner and a show?"

She hesitated only a moment. "I'd like that."

HE WAS SUPPOSED TO PICK HER UP AT SIX-THIRTY, BUT WHEN the buzzer rang it wasn't Phil but a uniformed chauffeur who appeared.

"Good evening, ma'am. Mr. Williams was unavoidably detained and he asked me to bring you uptown." The chauffeur was elderly and appeared harmless. But Barbie took the note he handed her with a sense of unease. The casual friend she'd made in the park seemed suddenly strange and threatening.

"Sorry," the note read, "but I can't get away for another hour, so I've sent Harris. Please don't be alarmed. He's worked for me for many years. I've asked him to bring you to the Pierre. Meet you there. Don't disappoint me." His handwriting was small and precise. The kind that gave nothing away. Barbie folded the note and put it in her bag. Mrs. Gretzman from the first floor was sitting on the couch with Norma. They were looking at a Dr. Seuss book.

"I won't be late," Barbie said.

"Don't worry, darling, we'll be fine. Have a good time." Mrs. Gretzman was favorably impressed by Harris.

The limousine was a black Mercedes-Benz and had a glass partition between the driver and the rear seat. Barbie felt as if she'd stepped into a movie, but at least she knew she looked the part. Her dress was one of Sophie's latest finds, mahogany-colored pure silk with a straight skirt and a slightly bloused bodice ending in spaghetti ties over the shoulders.

There was a matching short-sleeved jacket lined with orange print. If you looked closely you could see that the pattern of the print was composed of the designer's initials. Lately Barbie had been wishing her mother would stop buying her clothes; there wasn't room for them in the tiny apartment, and besides, she never went anywhere. Now she smoothed the rich silk over her thighs and was comforted.

Phil was waiting for her in the bar at the Pierre. "I'm sorry. I just couldn't get away."

"It's all right. Your chauffeur's very nice."

"Would you like a slightly rushed dinner now, or a more leisurely one after the theater? I've got tickets for *Hair*. If you've seen it, we'll skip it, of course."

"I haven't seen it. But I don't think I'd better have dinner after the show. It will get me home too late."

He nodded and signaled to the man behind the bar. "Tell Jacques I'd like a table for two in the grillroom in ten minutes. Steaks with whatever else he recommends. And a bottle of the '52 Mouton. Okay?" he asked, turning to Barbie.

"Okay."

She asked for a martini and he passed on the order, specifying Beefeater's. Then he turned back to her. "I've very glad you came. I was a little worried you'd balk because you didn't know about Harris."

"Apparently there's a lot I don't know. Not even your last name, until Harris spoke of you as Mr. Williams. Who are you, Philip Williams?"

"Not Philip, Philocles. And it was something unpronounceable before it became Williams. My parents were Greek. I'm an attorney."

"A very rich attorney."

"Yes, I guess you could say that."

"Why do you hang around Washington Square?"

"I like to play chess. It relaxes me."

"Are you married?"

"No, a widower in fact, so we have something in common." He reached over and touched her hand. "Scout's honor, I'm not lying. Go on, ask anything else you like."

She was embarrassed. "Sorry. I suppose none of it's any of my business."

He shrugged. "Why not?" He seemed about to say something else but a waiter appeared and announced that their table was ready.

After the show Harris drove them to Sixteenth Street. Phil

came upstairs with her and waited until Mrs. Gretzman left. "I suppose I should have left too," he said. "Now I've compromised your reputation."

"After the chauffeur it doesn't matter. She was here when he came—and suitably bowled over."

They both laughed, softly because the child was sleeping behind the beaded curtain. Phil moved a step closer and took Barbie's face in his hands. "I want to make love to you." It wasn't a demand but a request. Spoken simply, even gently.

"I know."

"And do you want me to?"

"I'm not sure."

He leaned forward and kissed her softly, then he stepped away. "I'd rather wait until you are sure. See you in the park."

DURING THE FOLLOWING WEEK, BARBIE THOUGHT ABOUT PHIL a great deal. Then, on Thursday afternoon, she came home from shopping and found two men working in her apartment. The janitor had let them in and they were installing an air conditioner in the window overlooking the street. "I didn't order an air conditioner," Barbie protested.

"It's all paid for, lady. You're Mrs. Gold, ain't you? And this is the top floor at Five West Sixteenth Street, ain't it?"

She nodded and he showed her a receipt and an order for installation. It was signed by P. Williams.

"You shouldn't do things like that," she told him Saturday afternoon.

"Why not? I can afford it and you can't. Besides, it's better for Norma."

"I know, but—"

"But nothing. I don't think you're for sale, Barbie, and I don't think I'm buying."

"I didn't mean that."

"What then?"

She shrugged helplessly. "I don't know. It just doesn't feel right."

"Very well, I won't do it again. You'll keep the air conditioner though, won't you?"

She could tell he was hurt. "Yes, if you'll let me say thank you. Come to dinner tomorrow evening. I'm not a bad cook. Do you like Italian spaghetti?"

For a moment she thought there was something odd in the way he looked at her. Then he laughed and said he loved spaghetti.

It was a pleasant evening, and when it was over Phil left without even attempting to kiss her. Barbie knew, however, that the relationship must soon move either to intimacy or dissolution. She still wasn't sure which she preferred.

TWO DAYS LATER SHE GOT A NOTICE IN THE MAIL SAYING HER rent was being increased forty dollars a month. Barbie went to the drawer in the kitchen table where she kept her papers and took out her bank book. Of the ten thousand dollars she'd had when she came to New York, there was three thousand left. She had thought to make the money stretch until Norma was old enough to go to nursery school. Then she could look for some kind of job. What kind was uncertain.

She didn't think it likely that she could go back to modeling. Even with her looks it was too tough a field to break into, and she'd forfeited her toehold years before. She couldn't be a secretary because she'd never finished the course in typing and shorthand. A receptionist maybe, or some kind of sales clerk. In a florist shop perhaps, so her interest in plants would be of some use. But it wouldn't do yet. Not while Norma was still so young. She'd promised herself she wouldn't leave Norma until the little girl was at least four. It was tied up with a lot of earlier decisions.

When she first learned she was pregnant, Barbie had agonized about what to do. She'd considered keeping the birth a secret and giving the child up for adoption, but she couldn't do it. So she'd made her choices and hoped for the best. Now she was frightened. For a few minutes she stared at the bankbook, then she put it away. She'd just have to find a cheaper place to live.

Mrs. Gretzman watched Norma while Barbie tramped the streets with the real estate section of the *Times* folded under her arm. Each place she looked at was worse than the one before. She couldn't move Norma into a hovel with a toilet down the hall and a bathtub in the kitchen. She could borrow some money from Charlie Rothstein, of course, but if she did it would have strings attached. Charlie would press her to move back to Boston with the baby. He wanted that as much as her parents and the Golds did. For Charlie too Norma was the balm that healed the wound Normie had made. So Barbie knew she couldn't do that either.

Twice she went to a small Catholic church on Twenty-second Street where she often visited. She loved the dim, cool interior, and found something oddly comforting in the chipped pews and the garishly painted statues. But now, as had been the case for over a year, she sat in the church alone. The Lady didn't come anymore.

Friday afternoon she picked up the telephone and dialed the number she'd looked up the day after the dinner at the Pierre. There was only one Philocles Williams listed under attorneys in the Yellow Pages. At an address on East Fifty-ninth Street. There was no listing in the white pages, so she didn't know where he lived. A voice answered by repeating the telephone number. "This is Barbara Gold speaking," she said. "I'd like to talk with Mr. Williams, please."

"Hello, Barbie," he said a few seconds later. It was the first time they'd spoken on the phone, but he didn't sound surprised.

"Phil, I'm sorry to bother you at your office, but I'd like to speak with you. Tomorrow in the park doesn't seem the best place. Could you possibly come here this evening?"

"No, I'm sorry but I can't. Not tonight. Tell you what, I'll send Harris for you in the morning. Will Mrs. Gretzman look after Norma?"

"Yes, I'm sure she will."

"Fine. Ten o'clock then. Good-bye, Barbie."

He hung up before she had an opportunity to ask where Harris was going to bring her.

She was downstairs waiting when the Mercedes pulled up. Harris jumped out and ran around to open the door. "Good morning, Mrs. Gold," he said pleasantly. That was all he said, and Barbie couldn't make herself knock at the glass partition and ask where they were going. She'd dressed carefully, a tailored suit of heavy slubbed cotton, the color of unripe cantaloupe, with the jacket buttoned and no blouse. Tiny gold earrings and her wedding ring were her only jewelry. Now she toyed nervously with the ring.

It turned out to be the East Fifty-ninth Street address listed in the telephone book. Another of New York's ubiquitous converted mansions, but the resemblance to her building ended there. This conversion had been made without thought of money and with every concession to beauty and comfort. His offices were on the ground floor. She could tell because his name was lettered discreetly on a brass plaque next to the door. Harris, however, ignored that entrance and led her to an elevator at the rear of the foyer. "Mr. Williams is waiting for you upstairs, Mrs. Gold." He pressed a button and disappeared back into the foyer. The elevator rose noiselessly.

When it stopped the automatic door slid open, and she was in a large hall with a black-and-white marble floor and walls upholstered in dull green brocade.

Phil was waiting. He grinned at her and took both her hands in his. "I know you must be sick of men saying you're beautiful. I promised myself never to do it but I can't resist. You're incredibly lovely, Barbie Gold."

"Thank you. Frankly, I made a special effort this morning, and I'm so nervous I'm shaking. There, I feel better for saying that."

He cocked his head and studied her. "I'm intrigued. I thought we were friends. You're not supposed to be nervous with me."

That gentle voice—it always seemed such a contrast to his hard-edged exterior. It disarmed her. "I need help," she blurted out. "I've never done anything like this, taken the initiative, called a man . . ."

"Forget that. If you need help that's what friends are for. C'mon. We'll have some breakfast first, then talk."

He led her out to the terrace. It was roofed with an awning of yellow-and-white-striped canvas, and magnificently planted. "This is my garden, but I can't say I did it all myself."

Barbie blushed and he chucked her under the chin and laughed at her. "You deserved that."

There was a table laid with heavy white napery and gleaming silver, and he poured freshly squeezed orange juice into shimmering crystal goblets. Barbie took the glass from his hand and their fingers touched momentarily. In that instant she knew that Phil had engineered her presence in his home, and her reason for coming. He was behind the sudden increase in her rent.

The knowing was a mysterious alchemy of instinct and intuition, but she was accustomed to both. She sipped her juice slowly and savored its sweetness. When she put down the empty glass, he took her in his arms and she raised her head and parted her lips, waiting for his kiss. She understood that she had acquiesced to his vision of the future, but she didn't really mind. His arms were strong and supportive and she relaxed in his embrace with a sense of relief.

The kiss was gentle, like his voice, a question not a demand. When it ended, he put his palms on either side of her face. "Listen, there's no quid pro quo involved. I suppose you need money. Okay. But as I told you before, I don't think you're for sale or that I'm buying."

It wasn't true, but it wasn't a lie. She realized that he probably believed it. "I know. I usually know things. Most people don't realize that." She looked long at him. The opaque gray eyes were unwavering. "Take me to bed, Philocles Williams. I want to see what you're really like."

He was wonderful. Barbie realized it was going to work.

The next two years passed quickly. They were often exciting and never unpleasant, and Barbie didn't regret her decision, even though it had been manipulated.

7

THE DOORMAN WAS BORED. GUARDING THE PORTALS OF the shiny new building on East Seventy-second Street entailed long periods of doing nothing, interspersed with bouts of tending to the niggling demands of a dozen assorted tenants. He divided his charges into those who were good tippers, whom he styled okb's—okay bastards—and those who weren't—ngb's, the no-good bastards. Neither category was particularly active just now. It was lunchtime, but he couldn't go and eat until his relief came in half an hour. So on this May morning in 1969 he did what he always did to amuse himself. He watched the women in the street.

One woman had held his attention for the last ten minutes. Thirty-eight, twenty-six, thirty-eight, he'd decided. *Zaftig,* the way he liked them. A great *keister* probably, but hard to tell because she was wearing a girdle under her tweed skirt. He hated girdles. Bras were okay, but dames who shoved their *keisters* into a tube of elastic didn't realize what a disservice they did to guys like him. So okay, she was tight-assed and not the best-looking broad in the world—skin kind of sallow and hair pulled back into a tight bun. Still, there was something about her. He kept watching.

She had arrived on the block between Third and Second avenues with a battered suitcase in tow. It was heavy, judging from the way she carried it. She'd parked it by a streetlight

231

and stood staring at number 227 for a while. Every few minutes she'd pace up and down in front of the door, then she'd go back to staring. The doorman was fascinated. Number 227 across the street was a house that interested him. That's where the redhead lived.

The ground floor was the redhead's shop, the place where she sold plants and flowers; the upper floors were where she lived. The redhead was one of the compensations in his job. Looking at her was pure pleasure. True, she wasn't exactly his type—tall and slim, not *zaftig*. But gorgeous. A looker. He'd long ago decided she must be an ex-model; her clothes indicated it too. He didn't like her friend, though. The guy with the chauffeured Mercedes, who regularly called on the redhead, had odd coloring, a tan, but with white hair. And a way of moving, like a tiger maybe. Smooth and lazy on the surface, lots of power underneath. Dames probably fell all over him, but he made the doorman nervous. So what did this new broad have to do with the two of them? Maybe she was just waiting for the plant shop to open up after its lunchtime break. Nah, unlikely. With a suitcase? And that scared rabbit look?

A buzzer sounded and he had to leave his watching post. Six C, one of the okb's. "Yes, Mrs. Hall, what can I do for you?" Mrs. Hall wanted to talk about a Bloomingdale's delivery that hadn't taken place. It occupied him for three or four minutes, and when he went back to the door the broad and her suitcase were gone. He wondered if she'd gone away or gone upstairs, but when his lunch relief arrived he forgot about her.

MARIA CRUMPLED THE LITTLE SLIP OF PAPER AND SHOVED IT into the pocket of her cardigan. Then she retrieved her suitcase and climbed the four stairs to the front door. Her choice had been between Barbie and a YWCA; the addresses of both were written on the paper she'd clutched all the way from Boston. Barbie had always seemed a better alternative than the impersonal Y, but Maria was scared. She hadn't written, and they'd done little more than exchange Christmas cards since Barbie moved to New York. What was Barbie like now? What was her little girl like? And what would be the reaction to the sudden appearance of an ex-nun?

She needn't have worried. Barbie opened the door, her amber eyes opened wide in surprise, and she stared for a few seconds. Then she grabbed Maria in an enormous hug.

There were a lot of questions at first, all jumbled together and none getting answered. Then Barbie drew Maria inside toward a sofa upholstered in flowered chintz. "Sit right there, don't move. No, don't drag that heavy suitcase any farther. I'll get someone to take care of it later. Just give me ten seconds to buzz Angie."

She went back into the foyer and Maria heard her talking on what sounded like an intercom. "Open up without me, please. A very old friend has just arrived." There was a pause and Maria heard another voice. It was too distorted for her to make out the words but she heard Barbie answer, "Yes, that's fine. And if the tulips aren't here by three, you'd better let me know. I'll call KLM." Then she returned to the living room.

"God! Let me look at you. You look exhausted. When did you get in? Do you want a drink?"

"About an hour ago. Twelve-thirty at Port Authority. I'd love a glass of milk if you have it."

"Port Authority! You took a bus. No wonder you look dead. Of course I have milk. Wait a minute, I'll get it." She disappeared again but her voice still carried into the living room. "We're on our own at the moment. Stella, my housekeeper and sort of nanny, is out with Norma. A puppet show in the village. Then they were going to Schrafft's for ice cream. Norma's a Schrafft's freak. She calls it Traf's and she's the best three-year-old customer they'll ever have. Aha! I knew that was in here. This damn refrigerator is so full I can never find anything."

She returned carrying a tray, which she set down in front of Maria on the glass coffee table. "Milk and cold chicken," she said softly. "Did you bring your homework?"

Maria looked at the tray and its burden of ivory china edged in raised pink strawberries. "We're a long way from Shirley Avenue," she said. When she raised her head, her eyes were full of tears.

"Not such a long way." Barbie gestured with her hand at the spacious room and its elegant evidence of a life-style neither of them could have imagined ten years earlier. "This is nice," she said. "But it's just stuff. You and me, we're the same as we were."

"No," Maria said. "We're not."

Barbie inhaled deeply and held her breath for a moment. "Okay. Not exactly," she said finally. "But not really changed in the ways that matter. At least I don't think I am." Her friend didn't answer right away. "What's going on, Maria?" Barbie asked. "What are you doing here?"

"I've left the convent. I'm not a Servant of Bethlehem anymore."

Barbie didn't flinch. "I see. I've read that lots of nuns are doing that these days. So okay, you're not a nun anymore. Since when? And why did you come to New York? I'd like to think it was to see me, but I doubt it."

Maria took a sip of milk before she answered. "I left yesterday afternoon. I came to New York because I have business here. I almost didn't get in touch with you at all. I was going straight to the Y. But when I got off the bus, all those people, all that hustle and bustle . . . I needed to see a familiar face."

Barbie nodded. "Right, so far so good. First of all, forget the Y. You're staying here with me. Second thing, if you left yesterday you must still feel rotten. That's not a lot of time to adjust." She studied Maria through half-closed eyes. "You do feel rotten, don't you?"

Maria folded her hands in her lap and looked at them. "Not the way you mean. I'm not guilty or undecided. I've known for months I was going to do it." She paused before she continued. "The truth is, what I feel is scared."

Barbie got up from the couch where she sat and crossed the few feet to its twin. She knelt down on the creamy shag carpet and pried Maria's tightly clasped hands apart, taking them into her own. Peripherally she noted that Maria's nails were bitten down to nothing. "Don't be scared right now, honey. Put it off until later. Right now you need to rest. Eat your chicken. C'mon, what would Sophie say if it was wasted? I'm going to run a bath for you." She had a sudden thought. "Where did you sleep last night?"

"I didn't really. I was waiting in the bus station at Park Square."

"That's what I was afraid of. Okay, a bath and then a nap. After that we'll have a good long talk."

Barbie was gone for at least ten minutes and Maria had a chance to study the living room. The print on the furniture was in shades of pale yellow and acid blue. The colors complemented the ivory rug and the whole was brought into focus by the many tones of green of the myriad plants that were everywhere. These weren't the potted geraniums or poinsettas with which Maria was familiar. Barbie had at least a dozen varieties of growing things, even a tree with delicate trailing branches and small shiny leaves. Everything was in its own pot, but the pots weren't the ordinary clay color, they were the same warm ivory tone as the rug. Maria remembered Barbie arranging tunafish cans in a pattern on the kitchen table because they looked nicer that way. "A long way from Shirley Avenue," she whispered aloud.

"Yes, maybe," Barbie said from behind her.

"I didn't hear you come back."

"That's why I have big thick rugs. Come along, your bath's ready."

The guest room was on the third floor. It stunned Maria more than had the living room. The walls were painted a smoky lavender color behind a covering of heavy white lace. Everything else in the room was white as well, except for a tumble of lavender silk cushions on the white lace spread, and an enormous bowl of dark purple irises on a table by the window. Barbie didn't give her long to admire the room. She shepherded Maria into the adjoining bathroom, then left her alone in a haze of fragrant steam. "Have a good soak and then a rest," she called from the next room. "Whenever you wake up, just press the buzzer by your bed. Oh, and don't worry about your suitcase. Stella's strong as an ox; she'll bring it up later. Meantime, I left a nightgown and a robe in the bathroom for you."

Maria stripped off the tweed skirt and the dark serviceable cardigan. Underneath she had on a tailored cotton full slip. The kind of clothes that two years ago had replaced the shapeless black habit. Now she hung them behind the door. Then she saw a blue velour bathrobe and a matching batiste nightdress and touched them briefly. They were the softest things she'd ever handled. Impatiently, she pulled off the slip and the rest of her underclothes and stepped into the bath. It was thick with rich, creamy bubbles, and the heady scent of roses swirled in the steam above her head.

Maria sank down and let her taut muscles relax.

THE LUMINOUS CLOCK BY THE BEDSIDE SAID SIX. SHE'D SLEPT almost four hours. Outside the open curtains the sky was a dusky blue-gray. Her first instinct was to get dressed and go downstairs, but Barbie had told her to ring the buzzer. She decided to comply. Barbie's voice responded almost instantly. Apparently the whole house was linked by some kind of elaborate intercom system. "Hi! You okay?"

Maria thought she had to find the speaker and direct her words at it. She looked around but couldn't see where she was supposed to reply. "Just talk normally," Barbie's voice said again. There was a laugh in it, as if she were picturing the other girl's confusion.

"I'm fine," Maria said. It felt very odd to speak into thin air and wait for an answer.

"Hungry?" the disembodied Barbie asked.

"Well, yes, as a matter of fact I am."

"Good, so am I. Just stay put. The food and I will be up in twenty minutes."

She made it in eighteen. Barbie came into the room pushing a wicker tea cart loaded with covered dishes. It looked very elegant until she lifted one elaborate silver lid to display a steaming pizza. "Pizza and beer. To hell with the calories."

Maria laughed for the first time that day. "I haven't had a pizza in years."

"No, I figured that. This came from a really good place around the corner." She was opening a bottle of Löwenbräu as she spoke but Maria shook her head.

"No beer for me. I never developed the taste."

Barbie had brought wine as well, and milk. Maria chose milk. "You'll get fat drinking so much milk," Barbie admonished as she poured a huge glass of it. Then she spread four turkish towels over the blankets, and the two girls curled up on the bed and ate. "When you're ready to talk, I'm ready to listen," Barbie said when they finished.

"Okay. Is my suitcase nearby? I want to show you something."

"Right outside the door. I'll get it."

She went out and came back with the case. Maria opened it. There was a cardboard box on top, the kind that contains a ream of typing paper. That's what was in this one, but they weren't blank sheets, they were closely typed. "My manuscript," Maria said.

"A book? You've written a book? That's terrific."

"Not exactly. It hasn't been accepted yet. Here, read this." She took an envelope from the top of the box and passed it to Barbie. It was from Oakes and Randolph, one of the more prestigious New York publishers.

Barbie read in silence for a while, then she said, "This sounds pretty encouraging to me."

"Yes, that's what I think too. And I believe it's unusual to get a letter like that. I've read that normally they send a form letter saying thanks but no thanks."

"Yes, don't call us, we'll call you. That's not what this says. 'Extraordinary promise and worth further work. . . . I hope you'll let me see it again.' That's not just a polite brush-off." Barbie read the letter a second time. "I don't understand the specific things she's telling you. What kind of book is it?"

"A novel, but based on fact," Maria said. "You see, I did a lot of work on old documents at B.C. I was helping a young Jesuit archaeologist, and I hoped to get a degree in linguistics."

"Did you?"

"No, I was sent on a teaching assignment instead. In Lynn, so I was living back in the Provincial House. That's probably what brought everything to a head." Barbie looked questioning.

"Never mind all that now," Maria said. "I'll explain it some other time. But one of the old manuscripts haunted me. I couldn't get it out of my mind. In 1733 a Dominican priest was sent to Lanzarote, one of the Canary Islands. They're off the coast of Africa, but they belong to Spain. Anyway, this priest got friendly with the few remaining islanders who traced their lineage back to the original race living on Lanzarote. Most of them had been slaughtered by the European colonists, but in the eighteenth century there were still a few left. The Dominican was trying to learn about their religion before they had been forced to become Christians. What he heard was a tale, mostly just bits and pieces, of a young couple who loved each other and wanted to marry, but they were from different clans and it was taboo. Eventually both lovers died, and the destruction of the island religion was connected with that."

Maria paused for breath. Enthusiasm animated her pinched and drawn face. "The story seemed to me a natural novel. And it's related to things I know about. So I started writing it. Late at night in my room. No one else knew. That was one of the good things in the changes at the Provincial House," she added parenthetically, "we had private rooms and didn't sleep in a dormitory anymore."

"So you've come to New York to do more work on this story, to be a writer?"

"Yes," Maria said shyly.

Barbie sucked in her breath with a sharp sound. "You've picked a tough field. Everybody thinks it's easy. It can't be, the world would crack apart from the weight of the books." She was sorry after she spoke; she didn't want to destroy Maria's small store of hope.

She hadn't. Maria spoke with conviction. "I know. But I've got to try."

"Besides," Barbie said firmly, "you have this super letter from a real editor. It's different. Tell me something: have you got any money?"

"A hundred and seventy dollars left after the bus fare. I borrowed a couple of hundred from a girl who quit the convent last year. She was Sister Patrick. Maybe you remember her, you met her once." Barbie made a negative gesture and Maria let it pass. "I figure I can get a job of some kind, perhaps teaching, and work on this in my free time."

Barbie was quiet for a few moments, obviously searching for words. "Look," she said hesitantly, "this is May. If you get a teaching job it probably won't start until September."

Maria nodded. "Yes, I know that. I hope I can find something else to tide me over the summer. Anything, I don't care what. I can get a room at the Y for twenty-two dollars a week."

"Forget that," Barbie said. "And forget about a summer job. Stay here with me. Take the summer to work full time on your writing. Why not?"

"Because it isn't fair. Why should I be a burden on you? I didn't come here for that, Barbie. I was just down and scared, and I needed to spend a little time with a friendly face. I'll move to the Y tomorrow. I want to. It will be better all around."

"No it won't. It's silly. Maria, listen, I make a good living. Very good. You saw my shop downstairs. It's *the* place to buy plants and flowers, the most popular place of its kind in the city. You won't be any burden."

"I can see from this house that you're doing well. But I can't take charity. Not even from you."

"What's charity? I'd love to have you here. Say it's just for three months. Only until September. Please, Maria." She grabbed the other girl's hand and held it tight. "There's so much I'd like to talk to you about. You're the only person who might understand."

Maria started to protest again, but just then there was a knock on the door. "That must be Stella." Barbie jumped from the bed to respond to the summons. "I told her to bring Norma up as soon as she'd had her bath."

She opened the door, and a small pink-and-white explosion burst into the room. Three-year-old Norma flung herself at her mother. Barbie snatched her up and kissed her loudly. The tight hug bespoke her passion for the child, and her pride. "This is my daughter. Norma, say hello to Auntie Maria."

" 'Lo. I went to Traf's today. Do you like Traf's?"

"I've never been to Schrafft's, I'm afraid." Maria stared at Norma and Norma stared back. The child was looking at her with Joe DiAnni's black eyes. Her face was his, made young and female.

"You'll stay, won't you?" Barbie's tone was pitched low and she retained the possessive, protective hold on her daughter. The eyes of the two women met across the top of Norma's dark curly head. "As I said," Barbie said, "there's a lot for us to talk about."

DURING THE NEXT THREE WEEKS, MARIA WORKED VERY HARD. She spent many hours in the lavender-and-lace guest room. Strewn about were her bulky manuscript, the editor's critical but encouraging letter, pages of handwritten notes, and a stream of pages issuing from the portable typewriter set up on the table beneath the window. Maria felt both anxiety and a terrible sense of urgency. They combined to keep her apart from the life of Barbie and her household. Either out of respect for Maria's work, or some motive of her own, Barbie didn't again seek the opportunity for intimate talk. Maria was glad; she was too emotionally battered to want to bear the burden of Barbie's confession. She wanted to make her own.

Under the word "Jesuit" the telephone book had a cross-reference, "See 'Society of Jesus.' " Beneath that heading there was half a column of entries. The Provincial Office was listed at 46 East Eighty-third Street, fourteen blocks from Barbie's house. Maria walked there on an afternoon that wore spring like a smile. In these rarified days the city was charged with excitement. All the Tin Pan Alley myths—"I'll take Manhattan . . ." "New York, New York, it's a wonderful town . . ."—came surging up from the pavement and eddied around her in the sparkling air. Slim and elegant women, hard men with hard eyes, taxis and limousines—a gray granite version of some ancient forbidden city, wherein reigned the twin gods, money and power. Maria was simultaneously attracted and repelled; it was in some ways terrifying, but in this place at this time, New York was a sensuous caress.

She had not known what to expect at the address of the Jesuit Provincial, but whatever she might have imagined fell short of the reality. The office was part of a complex that filled an entire square block. At its heart, fronting on Park Avenue, was a great stone church with a neo-classical facade and the letters "A.M.D.G." carved above its enormous doors. *Ad Majorem Dei Gloriam,* motto of the Jesuits. To the greater glory of God. Well, perhaps. Here too was a massive temple raised in solemnification of power, as telling as those that surrounded it. A different sort of power? Maybe.

Maria fought back the impulse to leave. Two thousand years of control was distilled into the vital plasma that had vivified her life and still ran unwelcome in her veins. In the huge edifice before her it seemed to reach out and haul her back. Ridiculous, she told herself, and walked up a short flight of steps to the door of 46 East Eighty-third.

"Yes, may I help you?"

He was young and probably Irish. Red hair and heavy horn-rimmed spectacles perched on a much-freckled nose. The black cassock he wore was clean and new. A recent ordinand perhaps, or maybe a senior seminarian marking time behind a desk in the Provincial office. "I'm trying to locate a priest of this province," Maria said. "Father Hank Rolles. Last I heard he was traveling in the Holy Land with a special study group. That was a couple of years ago." He asked her to spell the name and she did, adding unnecessarily that he was an archaeologist, and that she had known him at Boston College. Maria sensed reluctance warring with ordinary good manners as the young man turned to a bank of card files and methodically flipped through one drawer. "Yes, Father Rolles is in England now," he said finally. He faced Maria and held the card in his hand, but he didn't volunteer any more information.

She understood, because it was impossible not to. These days they all had their guard up, the young ones often more than the old. She was female, and therefore a threat in a way that would once have been unimaginable. Or at least less readily acknowledged. "We were working together on some research," she explained. "Eighteenth-century documents relating to Lanzarote in the Canary Islands. I have some additional information." As if that nullified her sex, or the possibility that she would seduce Father Hank Rolles into forsaking his vows. She wanted to tell the redhead the threat was long past. It had been exorcised years before. But probably he wouldn't believe her if she said, "We faced the enemy over egg rolls and pork strips and vanquished him." The thought made her giggle. The boy looked at her warily, as if

240

she was slightly demented. Then he looked again at the card in his hand.

"Oh, yes, I see here that he's working on something to do with the Canary Islands."

Maria wondered if Hank's entire life was contained on the five-by-seven card. It was pink. Probably that signified something. And the notations were doubtless in some code known only to Jesuits. Something they were taught to decipher at ordination. Secret knowledge bestowed by the laying on of hands. It would probably make it worse if she explained that she was an ex-nun. So she waited in silence and finally he said, "At Cambridge University in England. Doing research." Reluctantly he added, "He's living at St. Edmund's House."

"Thank you," Maria said. "I can write to him there. I suppose that's enough information."

He looked slightly chagrined and scratched some notes on a piece of paper. "Here's the full address." His tone and his manner were reminiscent of Pilate washing his hands. Be it on your own heads.

Maria thanked him again and took the paper and left. She walked down Madison Avenue slowly, looking in all the shop windows, agog at the extent and variety of the lure of mammon. Chic little boutiques with witty presentations of high fashion rubbed shoulders with shops full of exquisite china and others where one painting on an easel made an expensive understatement. Expensive was part of it; she wasn't so innocent that she didn't know you could spend a million dollars without trying in just one block. But the operative word was beauty. Whatever else these places might be, they were dedicated to beauty. She'd never seen so much splendor in one locale. By the time she reached Seventy-second Street, Maria felt drunk with it.

She turned east and walked the three and a half blocks to Barbie's. Looking at it now, she realized that the house and the shop were part of a larger reality. They were of the world she'd just been exploring. Barbie's world. Could she ever enter it? Did she want to? She shivered despite the warmth of the sun and realized she was frightened. Because if the answer to that question was yes, she had to face the fact that she might try and fail. Then what? What world could she inhabit? She had fled a carefully structured reality, one in which her place was absolutely clear, and arrived at nothing. She was a thing floating on the tide, with no idea where she might wash up.

All at once she was conscious of being watched, and turned her head. Across the street the doorman of a stridently modern apartment house was staring at her. He was short and scrawny and even at this distance she could see that he had terrible skin. Unbidden, the thought came that giving up nunship meant competing for men. Quickly she looked away and climbed the stairs.

Barbie was standing at the door of the shop saying good-bye to a customer. She put out her hand to restrain Maria and when the customer was gone she said, "Do you realize you've never been inside this place? Aren't you curious?"

"I'm sorry," Maria said. "You must think I'm terrible. I'm so wrapped up in my own concerns I've not shown any interest in yours."

"Creative geniuses are like that, I'm told," Barbie said lightly. "But come see now."

Barbie led her into a fantasy world of wicker and pottery and green and growing things. "No wonder you're doing so well," Maria said in awe. "It's positively incredible! I've never seen anything like it."

"It is nice, isn't it?" Barbie's pride was justified. "Look, aren't these great? They're a new addition this year." She was pointing to a group of waist-high terracotta urns with a series of planting pockets staggered along their gracefully curved sides. In each such opening was a strawberry plant dotted with tiny red fruits. "Strawberry jars have been known in England for ages. They're less common here," Barbie explained. "These plants are a variety called Baron Solmacher. A type of true French *fraises des bois*. No runners, so they work well." She plucked one miniature berry. "Here, taste it."

Little prickles of flavor happened on Maria's tongue. "It tastes like the essence of strawberry. How can you keep them growing in this light? I would have thought they needed a lot more sun."

"They do. These are on order for a solarium in a house on Fifth Avenue. It's quite amazing how these concrete-bound New Yorkers manage to find places to grow things."

The plants Barbie provided to satisfy the city dwellers' desire for greenery ranged from full-size orange trees, growing and fruiting in enormous wicker baskets, to tiny rock plants in decorated china eggs. The shop was called Green Gold, and apparently it represented more than a play on Barbie's name. "We don't do cut flowers as such, except when someone wants a large quantity of something special for an important party.

Three hundred white tulips, say, or a gross of yellow calla lilies. Those we fly in directly from European growers. But we make a specialty of forced bulbs."

Scattered throughout the shop were bowls and troughs and pots and baskets of flowers. Irises and tulips and daffodils and crocuses and lilies, and half a dozen things to which Maria could put no name, sprouted from an endless variety of containers. "Growing flowers last four times as long as cut ones," Barbie explained. "We have special lighting and temperature-controlled units in the cellar. That's where we bring the bulbs into bloom. So it can be spring every month of the year. Angie and I do it all ourselves."

The assistant to whom she referred stood nearby, smiling shyly. Angie was short and burdened with too much weight, mousy hair, and dull, close-set eyes. It wasn't hard to see why she satisfied a hunger for beauty in the plant shop, or that she was devoted to her employer.

"I can't take it all in." Maria shook her head in wonder. "How did you get started with all this? Where did you learn about it?"

"Pretty good for a nonagrarian Jew, huh?" Barbie laughed, and the bell on the shop door tinkled in counterpoint. "Customers. We'll have a bull session tonight if you like. I'll tell you all about it."

"I HAVE A PARTNER," BARBIE EXPLAINED. "YOU'D HAVE MET him before now, but he's out of town." She was curled up on her enormous bed wearing a tattered man's shirt, an incongruous contrast to the sophisticated bamboo print that covered the walls and furniture of her bedroom. Pots of orchids filled shelves in one corner, indirectly lit from someplace overhead. They glowed with incandescent colors.

Maria trailed her bare foot over the thick, dark green pile of the carpet. "Did your partner teach you about plants?"

"No, I did that myself. I got interested years ago, when I was modeling in Boston. I had a friend whose apartment was full of plants, and I fell in love with them." Barbie wondered what Maria would say if she told her about Helene, but she had no intention of doing so. Helene was a long time ago. Phil was now. "My partner put up the money. It took an enormous amount of capital to make all this happen. I couldn't have done it without Phil Williams."

"Does he work with you?"

"No, he owns a half interest in my business, but he doesn't

work in it. He's a lawyer." She paused. "That's not all. This better be up front between us, Maria. Phil's my lover."

Maria noted that the lamplight made a blazing helmet of Barbie's bronze hair. It looked almost like a halo. "Do you expect me to be shocked?" she asked.

"I don't know. That's just it. I don't know where your head is anymore. Not since we were kids and thought we mustn't let a boy feel us up because we were good girls."

"I'm not sure myself," Maria said softly. "I don't have many moral certitudes these days." She took a sip of the chilled white wine they were drinking. "Are you going to marry this man?"

"Don't you start too! He asked me that every day during our first year together. No, I'm not going to marry him, or anyone else. I've been married. Once was enough."

"I see. You're not in love with him, are you?" Maria waited for an answer. For some time now she'd wondered what it meant to be in love, and whether she ever would be, once she stopped being a "bride of Christ."

Barbie rolled over on her stomach and propped her chin in her clasped hands. "No, I'm not in love with Phil. He's in love with me. In a practical way, it comes to the same thing."

"I wouldn't have thought so."

"In a practical way, I said. Loving somebody, wanting him so bad it hurts, that's something else. I don't want to feel that ever again. I don't think I could."

Maria took a deep breath and held it. Now it would all be said. She knew whom Barbie loved in that way.

Instead the other girl asked, "What about your work? How's it going?"

"I'm not sure. I have lots of words, tons of them, but I don't know if I've improved the book." Maria heard her own voice from a distance, while part of her mind grappled with the problem of what to say about Joe if Barbie raised the subject.

"Well, stick with it," Barbie said. "You'll get it right, I'm sure you will." She got off the bed and stretched. "I'd better get some sleep. I've got a busy day tomorrow, and Phil will be here for dinner. Please join us. I want you two to meet."

BEFORE SHE WENT TO SLEEP, MARIA TYPED A LONG LETTER TO Hank Rolles, telling him she'd left the convent and was writing that book they'd talked about so long ago and did he think it was okay to use history as a basis for a novel, or was she making a mockery of scholarship? She also told him what Monsignor Walsh had reported about the Dominican who'd written the journal—that he'd become involved with a woman and ultimately left his order and his priesthood. She addressed the letter to St. Edmund's House in Cambridge, England, and left it sitting on her desk. She'd mail it first thing tomorrow.

But in the morning she held the envelope in her hands for a long time, and finally she ripped it up and dropped the pieces in the wastebasket. Hank might misunderstand, think she was suggesting something, seeking him out for reasons other than the true ones. Besides, she wanted to concentrate on the future, not wallow in the past. And her days of asking for absolution were over. Her conscience was her own to judge. The scholars in their sterile purity would not be disturbed by any small ripple she caused in their deep and ancient pond. Not even Hank Rolles, who, by his own admission, never read novels anyway.

She looked at the pile of manuscript and smiled wryly.

It wasn't a novel yet, it might never be. So there was no point in borrowing trouble. Maria carried the wastebasket to the incinerator downstairs and consigned her confession to the flames.

IT WAS DIFFICULT TO DECIDE WHETHER OR NOT SHE LIKED PHIL WILLIAMS. His extraordinary coloring and his controlled vitality made him a very attractive man, but there was something else, something hard, almost threatening, beneath the charming surface. Maria felt unnerved, and tried to allay the feeling with small talk. "What kind of law do you practice, Mr. Williams?"

"Call me Phil, please. Barbie tells me you two are very old friends. Tax law, mostly. I advise clients on corporate investments. Rather dull, I'm afraid. Nothing like Perry Mason. Nothing to interest a writer."

"I don't deserve that title. I'd like to be, but I'm not making much progress."

"Maria's feeling discouraged because she's having a hard time with some revisions," Barbie interrupted. "I keep telling her all writers have times like that. They do, don't they?"

"That's what one hears," Phil agreed.

Maria had to force herself to pay attention to his words because his voice was so seductive. It caressed her; it was like velvet. She realized he'd asked her what her book was about. "It's set on the tiny island of Lanzarote. At least that's its name now. When my story starts it's called Tyterogaka. That's in the fourteenth century. The book ends two hundred years later, after the European conquest and the conversion of the islanders."

"Unusual. How did you come to decide on such a subject?"

Maria guessed that he knew she was a former nun; Barbie would have told him. Warned him, was probably the apt phrase. "It's not the missionary part that interests me. At least not in the way you may think. I'm not beating the drums for Christianity. It's just a good story."

Phil nodded and turned to Barbie with some comment about his recent trip to the Bahamas. For the rest of the meal Maria had little to say, and she excused herself right after coffee.

Phil watched Maria leave. "Your friend's a bright girl, but does she have to look like such a frump?"

"I told you, she just came out of the convent."

"Not far enough out, judging by appearances."

"She needs time to adjust. I don't want to push."

"Okay. I'm feeling pushy though." He pulled her close. "I've been without you too long. I'm starving."

"You don't have to push. The door's always open."

"Only for me, I hope." He held her while he spoke and nibbled her ear between words.

"Only for you."

"Let's go to bed."

They climbed the stairs with their arms around each other and their bodies touching, learning anew the landscape of their particular union. "I dreamed about you every night," Phil said. "Then I'd wake up with this terrific hard-on and nothing to do about it."

"I don't believe that. There must have been dozens of women in the Bahamas."

"No. Not at my conference. My clients don't approve of wanton living. Anyway, I didn't want any other woman, just you."

He took her quickly the first time. His eagerness enveloped her like a quilt, filling her loins with his need, leaving her little of self and reducing her to that which satisfied his hunger. But only the first time. Afterwards, there was more pleasure. He was gentle-handed and soft-mouthed, and there was always that somehow paradoxical tenderness that was more a relinquishment of control than the explosion of climax.

Barbie's skin came alive under his touch and her muscles

and nerves spasmed in response to his knowing fingers. "Slow and sweet," he whispered. "The way you like it." He probed deep inside her and she moaned. "Not yet, I'm not going to let you come yet." He withdrew his hand.

"I'll lose it," she muttered.

"No, you won't lose it. I won't let you."

Then his mouth was on her, sucking her breasts until the nipples were swollen and throbbing and her hips writhed their own rhythm of demand. He rolled over and effortlessly lifted her on top of him and she screwed herself down onto the hard thing that was available for her gratification. Phil's hands cupped her buttocks and he laughed softly, while in the dim light of the bedroom the bowls of orchids shimmered and her perfect skin was sheened with the sweat of desire.

Barbie felt her orgasm begin between her legs and climb into her belly. She closed her eyes tight and retreated into the fantasy that always waited for her. Joe, her mind cried out in silence. Joe, Joe, Joe . . .

Later he said, "I might be able to help your girlfriend, if you'd like."

"I'd like. What do you have in mind?"

"A guy I know, a writer. Maybe he can give her some advice. I'll set it up."

┌─────────────┐
│   │
│   8   │
│   │
└─────────────┘

O NE HUNDRED AND SIXTEENTH STREET, THE SCLEROID artery of Spanish Harlem, was lit by high-intensity arc lamps. Intended as a deterrent to crime, the bright light caught mostly despair in its blue-white glare. The man heading for the subway station on the corner seemed indifferent to both the squalor and the prospect of mugging. He was a big man who walked with his leonine head hunched into wide shoulders, muscular arms swinging free. A taxi detached itself from the curb across the road and drew level with him.

"Hey, you gringo bastard! Don't be so cheap. Take a cab." The driver leaned over and unlocked the door on his right. The big man peered in, smiled, and slid his bulk into the front passenger seat.

"How goes it, Jimmy?"

"Lousy. Been out for four hours and *nada.*"

"How come you're hanging around up here? The money's burning holes in the fat cats' pockets in midtown."

"Yeah, Si, I know. But I thought I'd cruise the *barrio* for a while. Look around, you know."

Simon Shore sighed. He did know. "She's not on the streets. Not since she tied up with El Diablo. Stop being a schmuck. You're only wasting time, it won't make any difference if you do find her."

The cabby was small, dark, and wiry—a Hispanic supplied by Central Casting. He slammed the wheel with his fist.

"What do I tell my kids, hey? You got any smart ideas about that?"

"None whatever," Shore said tonelessly. "I have to go to Sixty-eighth and Park. You taking me?"

"Yeah, sure. Why not?"

The cab pulled into the street, but the driver didn't lower his flag and the meter stayed silent. They did not speak again of the man's wife. A few weeks before she had deserted him and their two small children and joined the stable of whores managed by a pimp called El Diablo. She'd done it to get money to support the heroin habit she'd ostensibly kicked when she married Raul Jiminez, the cabby. Since the cure didn't stick, the girl had determined to get out while she still had sufficient looks to turn a trick. Smart of her, in a way. Both men knew that; there was no need to discuss it.

"Sixty-eighth and Park's the Armory," Jiminez said. "Why you goin' down there? You callin' out the National Guard to protect your shithole?"

"I'm getting an award from His Honor the Mayor. I'm a big *macha* tonight, Jimmy boy. Talk nice to me."

"I wondered about the threads." Jiminez jerked his head at Shore's suit and tie. "How come you're kissing ass for those mothers?"

"They're giving me fifteen hundred bucks along with the medal, for service to the great city of New York. For fifteen hundred bucks I'll kiss ass."

"Yeah."

The wide streets rolled on. Shore watched Spanish Harlem become first the Upper East Side, then the golden strip that was Park Avenue from Eighty-sixth Street south. Eventually the block-square Seventh Regiment Armory appeared on the left. Skillfully Jiminez maneuvered his cab through heavy traffic to the front door. "Thanks," Si said, unfolding his length onto the crowded sidewalk.

"Nothin' to it. You go tell His fucking Honor what's really going down. Maybe somebody'll listen."

"Don't bet on it. See you around."

A fare climbed into the back of the taxi and Jiminez dropped his flag and gunned into the street. Shore looked after him for a moment, then turned and struggled through the hordes into the Armory lobby.

He'd lived with anger and frustration for some time now, and he nurtured both emotions, knowing that if they left he would too, but inside the Armory Shore came under attack.

Plunging into the midst of men and women from a once familiar world was like sinking into a hot bath. Comfort stroked him, and caught him unaware. The suit and tie began to feel right, and he smoothed back his longish brown hair with his palms, knowing that it curled over his collar in the back and made him look like the professor he used to be.

Once upon a time Simon Shore taught social psychology at Amherst College. Then, he astounded his family, friends and colleagues by suddenly giving up his tenure, moving to Spanish Harlem, and opening a youth hostel. That was four years ago. Raul Jiminez and his girlfriend had been among Shore's early successes, back when he still thought success was possible. By the time the shit hit the fan in the Jiminez household Si knew that success was an illusion, and that he wasn't willing to quit on that account. Now he stood in the Armory foyer, getting his conflicting feelings under control and looking for his elder brother.

Tom Shore was a writer who lived in the village, a fact he acknowledged as a case of arrested teenage romanticism. Tonight he had promised to come and lend moral support to Si's exercise in compromising principles for money. Tom didn't think the youth hostel made much sense, but the late Sadie Shore of Brownsville in Brooklyn had raised her two boys to look out for each other. Most of the time they still did. So Si craned his neck to see over the top of the crowd, spotted Tom, and pushed through the throng to his side. "Glad you made it."

"Wouldn't miss it for the world," Tom said loudly. More softly he added, "C'mon, let's go inside and get this farce over with. Mustn't disappoint all the liberals waiting to jerk off just knowing their hearts are in the right place."

The brothers moved through the sea of tables that filled the vast expanse of the Armory's drill floor. Pubescent usherettes, carefully chosen to represent all the city's ethnic minorities, periodically looked at their tickets and directed them ever deeper into the cavernous interior. Eventually they reached the front, near Mayor Lindsay and the other pols and churchmen who presided over the brawl. Tom said something about benign *genii loci,* but Si couldn't hear him over the din. A tiny Chinese girl wearing a ribbon of office across her small, pointed breasts separated them, firmly shoving Si in the direction of the dais reserved for the evening's honorees.

"Stay cool," Tom said. Si watched him being shown to a table. It was close enough so Si could see his brother stiffen and scowl before he reluctantly sat down. Which was odd, because Tom was seated next to an exquisite redheaded creature gowned in a sliver of black silk. She had a face like the young Garbo, only better. The redhead was talking to a man with a dark tan and white hair. The man greeted Tom as if he knew him, but got only another scowl in return.

The indifferent meal of chicken and green peas was followed by interminable speeches, and finally the awards. There were twelve of them, and the program indicated that Si was the eighth. The seventh winner was a contractor who gave a gym especially equipped for the handicapped to a local school. As well as being very rich, the contractor was fat and red-faced. When he took his award he had tears in his eyes, and he clutched his shield-shaped wooden plaque to his chest as if it were a heart transplant. After the contractor sat down Lindsay talked about the hostel for a few moments, using words like determination and courage and vision. Si felt sick. He stood up and made his way to the microphone. An acceptance speech was called for, but he had no idea what he would say.

About twenty feet separated Shore from the mayor. Slowly he negotiated the cramped aisles between the tables, conscious of his bulk, and of the hungry eyes of some of the women. Certain types of females always looked at him like that, those who found a touch of the Don Quixote syndrome a turn-on. Finally he was close enough to take the plaque from Lindsay's hands. Deliberately he turned his back to the photographers and leaned down to the mike. "I just want to tell the caterers that after they scrape the plates I'd be glad to take the leftover chicken uptown."

He sat down in silence. The audience tried to decide if he'd made a rather tasteless joke and maybe they should laugh. In the end they only managed a smattering of applause, which was expressive of Shore's own ambiguities. But when he caught Tom's eyes, his brother gave him a thumbs-up sign and Si felt better. He noted the redhead looking at him, but her eyes were not avaricious and Si smiled at her. At the same time the man with the brush-cut white hair said something to Tom and got a one-word reply. Then Si's attention was distracted by more photographers.

Later he saw the couple again. He and Tom were standing on the sidewalk outside the Armory, preparing to separate and return to their disparate worlds. A large black Mercedes managed to sidle up beside them. The rear window slid down effortlessly and Si saw that the man's eyes were opaque gray. Hard eyes, that belied his soft voice. "Drop you someplace, Tom?"

"No, thanks."

"Very well. You won't forget the little matter I mentioned." It was a command not a question, issued low key, but unmistakable. The man didn't wait for it to be acknowledged. Instead, he turned to Si. "Congratulations on your award, Mr. Shore." Again he didn't wait for a reply, just drew back into the plush interior of the limousine. Si caught a glimpse of the woman, shimmering in a kind of glow of her own, before the Mercedes pulled away with a surge of silent, controlled power.

"Who is that guy?" Si asked.

"Philocles Williams."

"Am I supposed to know the name?"

Tom smiled slightly, just with his mouth; his eyes and his heart weren't in it. "You don't, do you? Which would be funny if it wasn't so damn sad. Go home to your windmill, brother mine. Tilt nobly and be not concerned with the face of your foe."

"Sorry, you've lost me."

"A long time ago," Tom Shore said softly. He raised his arm in a casual salute and moved off into the crowd.

CARMINE STREET GAVE MARIA AN INTENSE SENSE OF *DÉJÀ VU*. She walked along the sidewalk skirting the displays of eggplant and tomatoes and peppers that spilled from dark and fragrant shops. A pushcart full of fish was trundled across her path, and a woman with a moustache and a black dress argued volubly with a storekeeper. But number thirty-nine didn't seem to fit. It was a modern concrete building five stories high. There was a board in the hall listing the tenants. Most of them seemed to be businesses of some sort or another. For a moment she thought she'd gotten the address wrong. Then she spotted the words "Fifth floor—Thomas Shore."

The large carton she carried made it difficult to climb the four flights of stairs, and the June heat didn't help. When she reached the door at the top, she was panting. It opened before she had a chance to knock. "You're Maria Trapetti?" the man asked.

"Yes."

"Well, come in. Put that thing down over there." He gestured to a table that was full of books and magazines. Maria had to push some of them to one side to make room for her carton.

"Are you Mr. Shore?"

"Tom. 'Mr. Shore' makes me feel like an old man. Care for a beer?"

"No, thank you. It's very kind of you to agree to see me. I'm sure it must be an awful bore for you."

"Maybe," he said, turning and studying her openly. "Maybe not. Depends. Anyway, one doesn't say no to Philocles Williams. Sit down. And don't look so scared. I won't bite."

"Why?"

"Why won't I bite?"

"No, why doesn't one say no to Phil?"

Shore laughed softly. "Lady, if you don't know, I'm not going to be the one to tell you." He seated himself across from her in a large black leather chair and put his feet on a nondescript coffee table. "You're a friend of his girlfriend, I hear."

"A friend of Mrs. Gold's," Maria said stiffly.

"And an ex-nun. It shows."

Maria pleated the fabric of her denim skirt with nervous fingers. "I suppose it does. Look, I'm sorry about this. I gather you agreed to see me under some sort of duress. I'll just go and we can forget all about it. I'll tell Phil you were very helpful. That's what you want, isn't it?"

"What's your hurry? You look like you could do with something to drink. If you won't have beer, how about some iced tea?"

"That would be very nice, thank you." She watched his retreating back as he went behind a screen that apparently concealed a kitchen. He was of medium height, about five ten or eleven, she guessed, with a stocky build that might have been fat, but wasn't. When he came back with a tray and two glasses, she noticed that his eyes were very blue. And he had a dark complexion and gray-streaked hair. She took a sip of the tea. It was delicious, very cold and tangy with mint. "This is wonderful!" Her voice betrayed her surprise.

"Glad you like it. Now, tell me why you think you can write a book."

"I don't know if I can. I just know I want to. And this gave me some encouragement." She reached into her bag and took out the well-thumbed letter from the editor.

Shore read it in silence. Then he took a long pull of his beer before he said, "Maybe you can. She's pretty complimentary. That doesn't happen often in this business. Rejections come preprinted and without adjectives."

"That's what I thought. It's why I had some hope."

"Had?"

"Yes. I've been trying to change the things she points out as weaknesses, but I just keep getting deeper and deeper into a quagmire. Lots of words and little meaning."

"Good. If you see that, it's a good beginning. Is that all of it?" He gestured to the box she'd left on the table.

"All seven hundred pages."

"Okay. Leave it with me. I'll read it and let you know what I think. Can you come back in a few days—say Thursday?"

"Yes, of course. But it still seems like a terrible imposition. You must have work of your own."

"I'm between books. Like an actor between engagements." He grinned, and Maria noticed that he looked younger when he smiled. Less intense. "Stop worrying," he added. "I'm really quite interested. I've never played Pygmalion before."

On the way home Maria stopped at Brentano's. They had three paperback editions of novels by Thomas Shore. She couldn't really afford the five dollars, but she bought them all.

When Maria returned to Carmine Street, Shore met her at the door with three days' beard blueing his jaw and her manuscript in his hands. "Here, take this. I haven't got time. Sorry." He slammed the door in her face. Maria left. There didn't seem anything else to do.

Two days later he telephoned. "Sorry about the other day. Come tomorrow if you can. Bring the opus."

"I don't know," she said hesitantly. "Are you sure? I don't want to be any trouble to you."

He chuckled. "Too late for that. Anyway, it's no trouble. Come at noon, we'll have lunch before we go to work."

"Oh, no, really. That's too much bother."

"Jesus! Will you stop apologizing? See you at twelve." He hung up before she could object further.

"Was that your neurotic author?" Barbie asked.

"Yes, he wants me to come for lunch tomorrow. I think he's insane. Listen, you don't know how Phil happens to know him, do you? I mean, some of the things he says are very strange."

Barbie shrugged. "Phil knows everybody. Besides, if this Shore is a creative genius, he's entitled to be strange." She held up a pot of ivy. Its green leaves were mottled with unexpected gold. "*Hedera canariensis,* from the Canary Islands. I thought I'd put some in your room for luck. Because of the setting of your book," she added when Maria looked blank.

"Oh yes, I see. Thanks, that would be lovely." Maria didn't look at the plant, just kept staring in puzzlement at the telephone.

"Stop worrying. If he can help you what difference does it make if he's a little crazy?"

"None, I guess."

"Right. Maria, look there's something I better tell you. My folks are coming for a visit next weekend. My mother-in-law, too. You're welcome to be here, but I don't know if you want to be."

Maria shivered slightly. The reaction was brief and she controlled it quickly, but she knew Barbie had noticed. "I don't think I'm ready to see anyone from the old days. Except for you."

"What about your parents? I never thought to ask you before! Maria, do they know where you are?"

"I wrote them. They know I'm in New York."

"But you haven't seen them, have you?"

"No." Then, when Barbie started to say something more, "Look, I don't want to talk about it, if you don't mind. And I'll make some arrangements about next weekend. Maybe I'll move to the Y."

"Whatever you do, it's just for the weekend. So you won't have to make a lot of explanations to Sophie and Moe. Don't start that business about living somewhere else again."

Maria smiled gratefully. "I won't."

"Good. Because there's a lot we haven't talked about yet."

LUNCH WITH SHORE WAS A REVELATION. HE DREW BACK A curtain and revealed a round dining table set in front of a long, narrow window that looked out across the rooftops of Greenwich Village. "I hope you're hungry. You're not on some kind of permanent ex-nun fast, are you? Penance for your sins, or something like that?"

"Nothing like that. As a matter of fact, I'm starved."

They began with a delicate chilled soup of palest green. He brought it to the table in small white bowls and grated fresh nutmeg over the top before he'd let her taste it. "Cream of avocado," he explained. After the soup he produced a huge quantity of steamed clams and they ate them with their fingers, sucking the last of the juice from the shells then chucking the empties into a pail he provided for the purpose. "A friend brought these down from Cape Cod this morning. They were dug yesterday. An unexpected beneficence."

"I've eaten clams before," Maria admitted. "But I've never tasted any as good as these."

"They're steamed with a lot of fresh tarragon and a little dry vermouth. Makes all the difference."

"Where did you learn to cook?"

"From my mother, first of all. Sadie Shore of Brooklyn was a very good cook. Then I branched out."

"You're Jewish, aren't you? I knew you must be when I read *Herschel's Hope*."

He grinned. "I wrote that a lot of years ago. I guess I was Jewish then."

"Not now?"

"Not the way you mean. In other ways, it's not something you stop being. Nothing to do with theology, though. I'm antitheological."

"So am I, I think."

He looked surprised. "A very ex ex-nun, is that it?"

Maria shrugged but she didn't have to answer, because he got up to clear away the debris and bring a salad of romaine lettuce and raw mushrooms and a large piece of ripe brie. They drank only water because Tom said you couldn't drink wine then work. When they'd finished the salad and the cheese, he made a pot of coffee and let her wash the dishes in his tiny sink while he cleared a work space for them on the table by the couch.

"Okay," he said finally, "let's get to it. First of all, I've written a critique of your craft as craft. Nothing to do with substance, just stylistic things you don't know and have to learn."

Maria ran her eye over the three closely typed pages he handed her and realized that before returning her manuscript he had read it thoroughly, the five-hundred-page original and the two hundred plus pages of revision. "I'm appalled," she said. "This must have taken a big chunk of your time."

He waved her objection away with his cigarette. "If we're going to do it, let's do it right. Writing is hard, slogging work, that's the first thing you have to learn. Don't try and read all my notes now. You can do that better by yourself later. Let's talk about the essentials, the characters and the plot."

"I don't know how to talk about them. Everything I've got to say I've said in there." She pointed to the pile of manuscript.

Tom studied her for a moment through narrowed eyes. "Yes and no," he said at last. "You've said a lot, but you haven't said everything. That's just it. It's a very superficial book. Facile, sometimes deft, and often almost interesting. Most of the time you bored me."

She sat there, staring at him and not knowing what to say. She was devastated. "You think I ought to give up the whole thing, don't you?" she whispered at last.

"I didn't say that. If I thought it, I wouldn't have bothered with that critique or this session."

"That's why you threw me out when I came the other day," Maria said, as if she hadn't heard his last remark.

"No, the other day had nothing to do with your manuscript. Forget about it, please." He leaned forward and stubbed out his cigarette, then he reached for her hand. "Listen, Miss Ex-nun, there's a story in those pages just waiting to get out. You wrote them, so I have to assume the story's in you. Your kind-hearted editor thought so too. That's why she wrote you that encouraging letter. But neither she nor I nor anyone else can free the story. Only you can do it. You've got to peel away the protective layers everything's wrapped up in. Your characters and their conflicts, we never see them bleed. We never really care. What you don't tell is like a blanket stifling what you do. Do you understand what I'm saying?"

"I'm not sure." Maria was conscious of his hand still holding hers and she pulled away. A strand of hair had come loose from her bun and she tried to tuck it back into place, anything to break the tension of the moment and ease the pain he was making her feel.

"Why do you wear your hair in that God-awful style?" he demanded. "It makes you look forty."

"It's convenient," she said stiffly.

"It's awful. Take the damned pins out. Go on, do it."

Her hands were shaking but she did as he said. Her hair still wasn't long, the way it had been before she entered the convent. She'd only started letting it grow a few months earlier, after she made up her mind to leave. Now the dark curls came to the level of her chin. She shook her head, and her hair formed itself into a nimbus around her pinched, wan face.

"Better," Tom said. "A lot better. Stop looking terrified. I know if this was a soap opera here's where I'd seduce you. I'm not going to. Bringing sexual awakening to ex-nuns isn't my personal fantasy."

"Stop it. I don't know how to talk to you. You say outrageous things and I don't know how to answer. I am, as you keep reminding me, an ex-nun. I haven't any experience with situations like this. I'm not glib and sophisticated, and you scare me to death."

"You're scared of your characters, too," he said. "That's why they're boring."

She realized that he was still trying to help with her book. That's what it was all about. The lunch, the business with her hair. Everything. It had nothing to do with her personally. She was an obligation Phil Williams had thrust upon him. Shore was simply trying to do his best. He confirmed that assessment with his next words.

"Have you read any D.H. Lawrence?"

She shook her head, conscious that her hair brushed against her cheek. It had not done so for many years.

"I'm thinking of *Lady Chatterley's Lover*. Not his best, but the one that created all the furor and ultimately changed the censorship laws. You really don't know it?" She shook her head again and he continued. "Lady Chatterley takes a lover, just like the title says. A gamekeeper, well below her station in life. At one point after they've made love he touches her and says something like, 'This is where you shit and this is where you piss and I wouldn't have a woman who didn't do both.' That's what's wrong with your characters. We never believe they really shit and piss. You do, don't you?"

She stared at him, wide-eyed, and didn't answer.

"Well, don't you? C'mon, Maria, answer me!"

"Naturally," she whispered. Her voice could barely be heard.

"Naturally indeed," Shore said with a sigh. "The most natural and basic human functions. You do them, just like everyone else. So you can write about them, about the way people with such primary needs feel. Here." He ruffled through the pages and pulled a page out. "Right here, where the missionary meets his first islander . . ."

After that, they worked over the book for a long time. When they were both too tired to continue, he insisted on taking her out for something to eat. "Lunch was five hours ago. I'm hungry even if you're not."

They went to a small, dark place, a sandwich bar rather than a restaurant, where Shore was greeted like a relative by the old Italian man behind the counter. "Mama, Tommy he's here! Come say hello."

A small, skinny woman whose black dress was covered by

an apron came out and kissed Tom, and when she heard the name Trapetti, looked approvingly at his companion. "An Italian girl. So you got some brains for once. Wait, I make you something to eat."

In a few minutes they were each eating half a loaf of bread stuffed with eggplant parmesan. They drank a few glasses of chianti, and there was a lot of talk and laughter. For the first time, Maria knew that she had really left the convent. She could feel freedom on her skin. Later Shore put her in a taxi and told her to return in ten days with a couple of rewritten chapters.

Maria began another draft of her novel, with Tom's critique propped up in front of her and his words ringing in her head. She wasn't revising this time, not patching up something already done. She was making up something new, and she had the faint hope that this time it was coming out the way she'd first felt it—with all the urgency and reality of the moment when it originally took shape in her head.

Her plan of going to the Y while the Kormans were visiting was altered at Barbie's insistence. Phil had a beach house in Montauk at the far end of Long Island, and his chauffeur drove Maria there on Friday morning and promised to return on Tuesday. The house was at the edge of an isolated point and had steps leading down to a small private beach. It was perfect in every detail of design and furnishing. The freezer was full, and a local woman who came in to clean kept the refrigerator stocked with fresh food. For the first hour of her stay Maria wandered about the house, trying to discover something about Phil in its spacious interior. Eventually she decided it had no clues to offer. After that she put aside the mystery that was probably of her own devising and worked and lay in the sun and swam in the beautiful blue water. That weekend, she achieved a tan and forty pages. She'd never felt better in her life.

Late Tuesday afternoon Harris returned her to Seventy-second Street. Maria wanted only to go to her room and continue writing. The cadences of the book were clear to her now; she seemed to breathe in rhythm with them. Whole scenes chased themselves across the landscape of her mind like speeded-up film strips; lines of dialogue played constantly in her head.

Angie met her in the front hall, stepping out of the shop to intercept her. "I thought you'd want to know right away, Miss Trapetti. Little Norma's very ill. Mrs. Gold and Stella are at the hospital with her. They've been there since noon." Maria dropped her suitcase and the package of manuscript and ran back to the street to prevent Harris from leaving.

New York Hospital was on the East River, a few blocks downtown. The chauffeur had her there in ten minutes. Then she had to bully half a dozen indifferent attendants before she found Barbie in the isolation unit, separated from her daughter by a glass window.

Norma looked lost in the big hospital bed, the tiny form obscured by a maze of tubes and bottles and machinery. "What is it? What's wrong with her?" Maria remembered the happy healthy child she'd said good-bye to Friday morning.

"They don't know," Barbie said dully. "She raised a fiendish temperature this morning right after everyone left. I thought it was just overexcitement, but in half an hour she couldn't breathe. I tried to call the doctor but the line was busy. Busy, busy, busy. I tried to get through for ten minutes. It was a nightmare. Finally I just bundled her into a cab and came straight here."

Barbie was gowned in green, like the nurses and doctors on the other side of the glass with Norma. Also like them, her hair was hidden by a green turban. Beneath it her skin was sickly pale. "Have you eaten anything?" Maria asked. She realized she sounded like her own mother. Whatever the problem, better you should eat. Barbie's look revealed the inanity of the question. One of the doctors detached himself from the busy group in the isolation room and stepped into the corridor where they stood.

"She's holding her own," he said. "I can't say more than that just yet, Mrs. Gold, but your little girl's a fighter."

"What about the fever?"

"Still very high, I'm afraid. We've sent blood samples to a special lab that deals with rare diseases. Hopefully we'll know more when the reports come back." He turned to Maria, as if to forestall any more questions from the distraught mother. "You shouldn't be here. Immediate family only."

"She's my sister," Barbie lied swiftly. "Please, I need her here."

The doctor looked from parent to child and back again. "Okay," he said. "But you'd better get suited up, miss."

Someone brought Maria an isolation outfit and she put it on. "What a rotten color," Barbie muttered. "It makes everyone look like a fish." She turned again and watched the movements behind the window. There was a lot of activity, but no layman could make sense of it. Norma didn't move. There was a tube inserted in her nostril. It made an ugly brown streak across her chubby cheek.

Stella had gone for coffee. She returned with two cups, apologizing to Maria because there wasn't a third. Maria shook her head and took Barbie's hand. "Come sit down and drink your coffee. Stella can watch here for a few minutes."

Barbie let herself be led a few feet away to a vinyl-covered armchair. She sat down but didn't drink, only held the paper cup in limp fingers while scum congealed on the top of the coffee. Maria watched her, trying to think of something to say. Visions of permanent brain damage engendered by sustained high fever replaced in her mind the fictional dramas that had lurked there an hour before. Barbie's eyes were closed and her lips were moving. She was praying. Maria tried to pray too, but nothing came. It was years since she'd been able to pray.

Farther along the corridor an elevator door slid open and Phil stepped out. He came to them and knelt beside Barbie's chair, taking the coffee cup from her fingers and folding both her hands in his. "What happened? Why didn't you call me earlier? Harris told me you were here."

Barbie shook her head and didn't answer. Maria told him as much as she knew, as much as any of them knew.

"Who's the doctor in charge?" Phil demanded. "Is he the best? We've got to make sure she has the best."

Barbie's face suddenly came alive, encouraged by the thought that maybe there was something more they could do. "His name's Cohen. That's all I know."

"Okay. That's enough to start with. I'll go make some calls. Be back as fast as I can." He mocked a punch to her delicate chin. "Hang in, baby. The marines have landed." He spent a few seconds studying Norma through the window, then he disappeared into the elevator.

Barbie rose from her seat and went to resume her vigil by the glass. Behind it nothing appeared changed.

Phil returned in less than half an hour. This time he was followed by a young nurse and he was wearing a green outfit, like the rest of them. Again he went straight to Barbie and put his arm around her shoulders. "It's okay. This is one of the best units in the state for this kind of thing. Cohen's well thought of."

"Is there anything else, Mr. Williams?" the nurse asked.

"No. Thank you, you've been very helpful."

She turned to go but paused and said, "We've arranged a room for Mrs. Gold on the floor below. So she can get some rest. And the cafeteria will send up a tray whenever she's ready to eat something."

"Thank you," Williams said again. Then, to Barbie, "It's not a bad idea, you know. You need some rest and something to eat. It won't help Norma if you collapse."

Maria wondered how he managed to command such a response from the big impersonal hospital. It disturbed her, but for Barbie's sake she was grateful. "Phil's right," she said. "Let me take you downstairs. Just for an hour, Barbie, just a little rest."

Barbie shook her head vehemently and Maria was about to argue when the doctor appeared. "Her temperature's down three points," he said with a broad smile. "It looks hopeful."

"Thank God!" Barbie said, clinging to Phil and sagging a bit.

"Who's this," Cohen asked, "a brother?"

"Philocles Williams," Phil said, keeping one arm around Barbie and extending his other hand to the doctor. "A friend of the family."

"You're not supposed to be here." Cohen ignored the outstretched hand.

"I cleared it downstairs." Phil mentioned a name that caused the other man's eyebrows to raise. "You can check it out if you like."

"I haven't got time to check out what they do downstairs." Cohen's voice was sour with fatigue. He looked at Barbie. "Get some rest, Mrs. Gold. Go home for a couple of hours." He didn't know about the VIP treatment and the room on the floor below. "She's stable now. I promise you. I haven't said that before, have I?"

"No, you haven't," Barbie said. She managed a weak smile.

"So you know it's the truth," Cohen pressed. "Now listen to the doctor and get out of here for a little while."

Phil pushed her gently toward Maria, like a baby being passed to another set of arms. "Take her downstairs. I'll stay here until you come back."

Cohen took their green gowns and hats and deposited them in a wheeled cart marked ISOLATION on all four sides. Then he shepherded them to the elevator.

Once inside Barbie said, "Not to that room, wherever it is. I want some air. Let's go for a walk."

Outside, the late June heat accosted them, rising in noxious waves from the pavement. It was after seven but still stifling. They turned a corner and headed for the river. To get across busy East River Drive to the embankment they had to climb a long flight of stairs and navigate a narrow pedestrian overpass. "I hate heights," Barbie said. "They make me dizzy. Stairs like these, with just treads and no risers, they're the worst."

Maria took her hand and they descended to the strip of park fronting the river. It was a little cooler. There were benches, but they ignored them and hung over the rail, gazing at the turgid water and watching a barge make its leisurely way uptown. "You know she's Joe's daughter, don't you?" Barbie said.

"I guessed as much. She looks a lot like him."

"It was just one time," Barbie said. "Only once. A short while after Normie died."

"Maybe we're imagining things." Maria didn't believe it, but she said it anyway. "Maybe she's your husband's child."

"No. Normie hadn't touched me in months. That was one of the symptoms of how mixed up his head was. Anyway, I'm glad she's Joe's. I love him very much and he loves me."

Maria noted the use of the present tense. "Do you see him?"

Barbie's amber eyes were startled. "See Joe? Of course not. He doesn't know I have a child, certainly not that she's his. Everything I've done since I knew I was pregnant was to make sure he'd never find out."

"Even Phil?"

"Especially Phil. I had to stay in New York, make a life for us here. Joe's a priest to the tips of his fingers. He'll always be a priest. One moment's weakness mustn't be allowed to spoil all that."

A vise of pain squeezed Maria's heart. Coming from someone else the words might sound grandiose and phony, but Barbie was speaking the truth. "When did you last see Joe?"

"Years ago. Right after Norma was conceived. Since then I've made it my business not to see him. Before I got the house and the business I sometimes went home to visit my folks. I had to do that, but I never went near Revere Street. Just stayed on Shirley Avenue, like a nice Jewish girl. It's a lot easier now that they come here."

"I see." Something in Maria's voice betrayed her.

"What is it?" Barbie demanded sharply.

"What's what? I don't know what you mean."

"Yes you do. Come on, Maria, I know you too well. What aren't you telling me? It's something about Joe, isn't it? What's happened to him?"

"I don't know." Her voice was a faint whisper barely audible above the sounds of the river. "About three years ago he disappeared."

"Disappeared? What the hell does that mean?"

"What it sounds like. He just dropped from sight. Walked out of the rectory one day and never returned. I thought it was funny when none of my letters to him were answered. I called his pastor but got a lot of vague nonsense, so I asked a friend of mine, another priest. He finally found someone at the chancery willing to tell him what little there was to tell. That Joe had simply disappeared."

"Maybe he was hurt or kidnapped or something," Barbie said desperately. "Didn't they check?"

"Of course they did. They even had the police make inquiries. There was nothing to indicate any kind of, what do they call it, foul play. Joe went AWOL because he wanted to. It's the only explanation. It's been happening a lot in the last few years. Plenty of guys have waked up one morning and realized they've been sold a bill of goods." Her voice was bitter.

"Not Joe," Barbie said.

"How can you know that? You said yourself you haven't seen him in years."

"I have it on excellent authority." Barbie turned and began walking briskly toward the hospital.

A WEEK LATER, NORMA WAS PRONOUNCED CURED AND released. Except that she was a little pale, she didn't seem at all a child who'd had a brush with death. The doctors still didn't know what had attacked her; they called it an unidentified virus and assured Barbie that any recurrence was a million to one shot against.

"Can we go to Traf's?" Norma asked as soon as she was in the back of Phil's Mercedes and on the way home.

Phil looked inquiringly at Barbie, and when she shrugged and nodded he leaned forward and pushed aside the partition separating them from Harris. "Take us to the Schrafft's at Fifty-ninth and Madison."

Harris nodded, and in the rearview mirror Maria saw him grin. "Could you let me off here?" she asked on impulse. "I'd really like to go home and get on with some work."

"Sure." Phil passed the instructions on to the chauffeur. "Maria," he said before she got out of the car, "I've been meaning to ask, was that fellow Shore any help to you?"

"An enormous help. I should have thanked you before this."

"No matter. I'm just glad it's been worthwhile."

She waited until the car was out of sight—why she couldn't say—then walked the five blocks back to Barbie's house. Inside, she went straight to the telephone and dialed Tom Shore's number. She was startled when a woman answered. "I'd like to speak to Mr. Shore, please. This is Maria Trapetti."

The woman on the other end didn't bother to muffle the mouthpiece. "Tom," she called. "It's for you. Maria somebody."

Sounds of music and laughter filtered through the receiver. Maria glanced at her watch. It was noon. Early for a party. She heard a voice that could be Tom's shout, "I don't know any Maria."

"What did you say your last name was?" the woman asked.

"Trapetti. Maria Trapetti. Never mind. I'll call back later."

Just then she heard Tom say, "Yes, I do know a Maria! The ex-nun with the book." There was a moment's pause, then his voice was closer and more distinct. "Hi. How've you been?"

"Okay. But Mrs. Gold's little girl was very ill. That's why I haven't called before now. You said ten days and it's been two weeks. I thought I'd better let you know."

"Ten days? Oh, to bring teacher some new work, you mean. That's all right. How's it going?" His words were a little slurred, as if he'd been drinking.

"Very well. At least I think it is."

"Good, glad to hear it. You let me know when you're ready and I'll have another look." He hung up, and Maria felt deflated and hurt. Which was ridiculous. Thomas Shore couldn't be expected to fill his life with her and her book. She went upstairs and put a clean sheet of paper into the typewriter, but no words came. The urgency of the days preceding Norma's illness was gone. No voices spoke in her head, and no rhythms poured through her blood to spill themselves onto the typewriter keys.

She was still sitting and looking at a blank page two hours later when the intercom in her room buzzed. Barbie sounded excited. "Maria, I don't care what you're doing, you have to stop and come down to the shop right away. I just got home and found the most amazing surprise."

Maria recognized the woman as soon as she pushed open

265

the shop door. Ann Jessup was older, but not changed. She smiled when she saw the second of her former students.

"Maria too. How extraordinary!" She put out her hand, and Maria shook it and returned the warm smile.

"Mrs. Jessup just happened in to buy a plant," Barbie explained. "An hour earlier and I would have missed her."

"Actually, we have missed each other at least once," Ann Jessup said. "I've been in before. I have a friend who is very fond of houseplants. I had no idea this was your shop, Barbie. I didn't even know you were living in New York."

"No, how could you? I take it you live here too?"

"Yes. The lure of the big city. I've got a job with a small dramatic school." She looked from one girl to the other. "Is this a joint venture?" She indicated the display of plants.

"Oh, no," Maria said at once. "It's all Barbie's. I'm just staying with her for a while." An effort to remember flicked across the older woman's face and Maria added, "I was in the convent. When I left, Barbie invited me to spend some time with her." Better to have it out in the open. Besides, Mrs. Jessup wasn't a Catholic. It would be a matter of indifference to her.

The woman confirmed that opinion by nodding toward two large plants sitting on the counter. "I can't decide between these. What do you think?"

"This one is *Myrtus communis microphylla,* a dwarf form of true myrtle," Barbie said. "The leaves have a lovely scent when you stroke them. But it needs full sun at least half a day. The other's a type of *Aglaonema* called White Rajah. It will do well in a north window. What exposure can your friend provide?"

Ann Jessup studied both plants carefully. "You know your stock, don't you? And you're still as beautiful as ever."

"I couldn't run this place if I didn't know my stock," Barbie said. She didn't understand the non sequitur, or the vague hostility she sensed. For a moment she was annoyed, then she decided she'd imagined it, because the former teacher turned to her with an exuberant smile.

"I can't resist the myrtle. We should be able to give it enough sun. My friend and I share an apartment." She said it quickly, as if she'd been caught in a lie.

Barbie watched while Angie wrapped the plant, then reached for a pale yellow crockery bowl full of nodding white flowers. Their perfume was heavenly. "*Narcissus poeticus.* I'd like you to have them. A little gift for old times' sake."

"Why, thank you, Barbie. That's very kind. I know my friend will be delighted."

BLACKNESS SURROUNDED HER. THE SUNLIGHT COULD NOT burn it away. Ann Jessup's legs trembled and the plants weighed heavy in her arms. She started for the bus stop on Lexington Avenue, decided she hadn't the strength, and flagged a cab.

"You want I should go downtown on Second, lady, or try the East River Drive?"

Ann stared at him, not registering the words, and he shrugged and presumably made his own choice. She didn't care, she was only grateful for the support of the seat and the relative quiet. All these years, and Barbie had come back. She'd thought it was over, but it wasn't. Maybe it never would be. Destiny. There was no other explanation.

Ann sighed softly and took a handkerchief from her bag and wiped her eyes. She'd have to get a grip on herself. Destiny wasn't something you could fight. You had to face it. You had to recognize that some things, some terrible things, were inevitable.

I N T E R L U D E

THE LADY

A.D. 1733 to A.D. 1863

WIDE AND DEEP RUN THE CONVERGING CURRENTS, obscure and diverse are the threads of the tapestry. Their pattern can be discerned only from the distance of years. In the tumult and the anguish that was Catalonia at the dawn of the eighteenth century there was yet another—a vital—link.

"YOUR FAMILY HAS ARRIVED, FRA IAGO." THE LAY BROTHER delivered his message and faded into the shadows of the dusk-filled garden. The young priest closed his book and stood for a moment, marshaling his strength for what must follow, then strode purposefully through the cloister into the public rooms of the priory.

His parents were waiting. Don Jesús Ramirez de Martín was a short, squat man. He stood by the window, staring at the great city of Barcelona spread below. Fra Iago paused and examined the stolid figure. Don Jesús blotted out the light, as the great battles and political upheavals of the past twenty years had blotted out Catalonia's independence. Iago's mother, Doña Dolores, came to his side, flinging her arms around his neck and weeping.

Don Jesús turned. Above the head of the sobbing

woman his eyes met those of his son, and they communicated silently for some seconds. Then the older man spoke. "Hush, woman. This grief doesn't become you. We've long since given our son to the Church and the Dominicans. They'll send him where they will."

Doña Dolores patted her eyes with a linen handkerchief and sat down heavily in one of the stiff wooden chairs ranged along the wall. Iago and his father clasped hands, held each other for a moment, and separated, seating themselves near the woman. "What time do you sail?" the father asked.

"With the dawn tide."

"And to reach this island of which I've never before heard, how long?"

"Three weeks, a month perhaps. It will depend on the winds of God."

Don Jesús grunted. His wife and his son might believe in such divine intervention; he knew this exile was the choice of men. "Had I been less open in my allegiances they would not send you so far," he muttered. It was all the apology he could manage, for he was a proud man, descended from a proud line.

"Not necessarily," Iago said quietly. "I too have spoken openly."

Indeed he had. While France and England and Spain warred over Catalonia, while the province tried vainly to protect its autonomy, Fra Iago de la Cruz had preached eloquently about corruption and license and the obligations of rulers. Eventually those sermons reached the ears of powerful men and a discreet word was passed to the superior of the Dominicans in Barcelona. "This Order has had its Savonarola," the Prior told his young monk. "We have no wish to repeat the experience. And neither, I'm sure, have you."

Fra Iago had bowed his head in acceptance, while in his mind's eye he saw the stake and the flames that had claimed the life of the long-dead monk to whom he'd been compared. "I am your obedient child, Father Prior," he said. "I will do as you command."

So had he agreed to the exile that began tomorrow, preceded by this painful scene with his family. "Where is Teresita?"

"Outside, waiting." His mother rose, opened the door, and beckoned her youngest child into the room.

Iago clasped his small sister to his chest and held her a long time. She was the one he would miss most. Between himself and the twelve-year-old girl there existed a rapport that gave both joy. Finally he pushed her a little away. "Let me look at you, Teresita. I must fill my eyes so that your image will stay with me."

The girl neither wept nor smiled. She gazed steadily at her elder brother and in that lengthy look they made their farewells. The silence was broken only by Doña Dolores's sobs, muffled by her handkerchief, and the heavy breathing of Don Jesús. Then the tolling bells of the priory church summoned the friars to prayer. "I must go," Iago said. "It's time for Compline."

The family of the priest surrounded him for one moment more, pressing close to share their breath and their heartbeats and their love. Then they parted. Iago walked with them to the door. As they spoke their final goodbyes, Teresita pressed a gift into his hand. He didn't open the package until much later, after the prayers of Compline were over and he was alone in his cell. It was a notebook, a simple thing of dark leather and blank pages. Teresita had enclosed a note saying he was to record his experiences therein, and someday when they saw each other again she would read it and it would be as if they'd never been parted at all.

"¡DIOS TEN MISERICORDIA A MÍ!" IAGO WHISPERED AS THE SHIP docked in the harbor of the tiny port of Arrecife. A pall of smoke hung over the island of Lanzarote. It blotted out the sun as far as the eye could see and the stench of fire burnt his nostrils and choked his throat.

Those were the first words he recorded in Teresita's journal. ¡Dios ten misericordia a mí!

Fra Iago de la Cruz had arrived on Lanzarote in the middle of the massive and sustained eruption of the volcanos in the south, on the second day of November 1733. This storm of flame and molten lava, this endless shuddering of the earth, this triumphant roar of the power of evil was to fill his world and that of all the islanders for three more years, until the sixteenth of April 1736. While it continued it imprisoned them in a surreal universe, a palpable hell. When it ended, eleven villages had ceased to exist and a once fertile valley had become a smoldering no-man's-land. The entire island was now beneath a shroud of black volcanic ash. Henceforth this ebony covering would be Lanzarote's most notable characteristic, legacy of the volcano they called Timanfaya.

From his Priory in the ancient northern town of Teguise, Fra Iago wandered the island, preaching and consoling and administering the sacraments, as did his brother priests. But in the face of such catastrophe their words seemed hollow and their actions ludicrous and inadequate. The faith of many was tried in those terrible days. Iago de la Cruz was among those found wanting. Eventually he believed in nothing at all, and to make tolerable the desolation left him after the death of faith, he succumbed to the advances of a beautiful and equally unhappy woman, Doña Urtaya Immaculada. She was the wife of a fat and rich farmer many years older than she, and she was barren. Those two sorrows provoked her into seducing the handsome young Dominican.

"What kind of a name is Urtaya?" he asked one afternoon when they lay together in the ruins of the Castle of Santa Barbara, which was the scene of their assignations.

"A very old name." She traced the length of his supple spine with one finger. "On my mother's side I'm descended from the original people of this island. When it was called Tyterogaka, before the Spaniards came."

Fra Iago wanted to ask her more, such things interested him, but her busy fingers drove all thoughts from his mind. Instead of talking, he pulled her voluptuous body closer and fed on her ivory breasts and felt the strong muscles of her belly and her buttocks expand and contract beneath his exploring hands. When he could delay no longer, he mounted her and drove himself into the warm, moist depths of her womanhood and spilled his seed with moanings of ecstasy and release.

Afterwards he was, as always, overcome with self-loathing and regret. He moved away from her and sat with his head between his knees and nursed his futile self-pity and remorse.

Urtaya hated this mood that often came upon Iago. He was all she had of happiness or pleasure, and she feared that one day he would conquer his desire for her and make his confession and return to his vow of celibacy. Now she went and knelt before him and took his limp hands in her own. "Don't be sad, my love. Surely God is long accustomed to the weaknesses of men and women." He raised his head and looked at her with dull eyes, and Urtaya had a sudden inspiration. "That book you have, the notebook in which you always record things, is it with you?"

Iago nodded. Teresita's gift was never far. He carried it in the pocket of his habit.

"Get it, then," Urtaya commanded. "I'll tell you the story of my namesake and you can write it down."

Iago's curiosity was piqued and he did as she said. But having succeeded in finding a ploy to keep him a little longer in the ruined castle, Urtaya was suddenly reluctant and afraid. "What's wrong?" Iago asked.

"I'm breaking a vow." She stopped speaking and looked at him. So many vows they had broken together, how could she explain this one, or tell him why it was more sacred than the rest? But she must, for she hoped that knowing what an ancient taboo she violated for his sake would bind Iago to her yet more strongly. "For countless generations the women of my family have told this secret story to their daughters. My great-grandmother told it to my grandmother and she to my mother and my mother to me. If I had a daughter I would tell her. But I don't and never will have, so I'll tell you." Urtaya hesitated, and Iago waited. Finally she began.

"In the last days of Tyterogaka, before the conquerers came, the king was named Zonzamas and his wife was Fayna and she had a brother named Gadafo who was married to Tisa and they had one son called Zanis . . ."

Urtaya spun out the tale of her namesake over many months and many stolen hours of love, and Iago wrote down everything she said. But to protect them both, he made it seem as if the story was told him by the village people he met in his travels across the island, and he interspersed it with other legends and bits of ancient history he'd heard in less compromising circumstances. At last the day came when his lover could tell him no more, and Iago thought back over what he'd heard and found it strangely unsatisfying, a story without a proper end. "But didn't anyone ever find Urtaya's body, or the statue Tisa looked for?"

"No one. I think Urtaya must have come down from the mountains and drowned in the sea, and her body was washed away. Or maybe she fell into one of the volcanos and was burned to nothing."

"And the statue?"

The woman shrugged her beautiful shoulders. "Who can say? Maybe it never existed; maybe Tisa only imagined such a statue. I can tell you no more. That's the story my mother told me and her mother told her and so on." She rose, restless and tired of talking.

Iago went to her side. "Good-bye, Urtaya."

She looked at him in surprise, for there was something final and sad in Iago's voice. But she was afraid to ask him if they would meet again so she only kissed him quickly and slipped away.

That night, while the Priory slept, Iago took off his white Dominican robes and put on the rough fisherman's clothes he had been saving for this inevitable moment. Then he went out into the dark and made his way to the harbor, where a boat was waiting. The captain had agreed to take Iago to Africa. He took the priest's money and five days later put him ashore in the ancient Roman town of Tangis, now called Tangiers. All Iago had with him of his old life was his violated priesthood and Teresita's notebook. The former he made himself forget, but the latter he kept always on his person.

TEN MORE YEARS PASSED AND THE FALLEN PRIEST ROAMED TWO continents, bitter and beggared. He died of starvation and exposure in a Florentine alley in 1750. Those who found him discovered among his rotten rags the journal he had preserved through so many years and vicissitudes. Eventually the journal, being such a thing as excited the interest of certain kinds of collectors, made its way to a noted private library. More than a century went by until, in 1863, that library was purchased by the Father General of the Jesuits. He sent the books to newborn Boston College in America, to celebrate the founding of that institution.

Six years later, Father McClintock made his bargain with the Spanish Dominicans and the journal was locked in the library crypt, to await the coming of Sister Mary Anthony.

9

WHEN IT WAS OVER, JOSEPH DiANNI REALIZED IT WAS not the business with the old man that soured his priesthood; the dying of Don Stefano was only a catalyst. "Come," his mother's voice over the telephone said. "Come right now, like you promised." So was he summoned to the enactment of his nightmare.

"He's dying," she said when he entered the flat on Hanover Street.

"Did you get in touch with your pastor?" She shook her head. "Why not? You should do that. He's supposed to be the one you call." And while he spoke, he felt sick. A human being was dying in the next room and he, Joseph DiAnni, priest of the holy Catholic Church, was standing here arguing protocol.

Signora DiAnni fixed her hard black eyes on her son. "He's in there waiting for you. Stop talking and go."

Don Stefano lay beneath a shiny red satin quilt, a ludicrous anomaly in the dim and dingy bedroom. His face wasn't white like those of others whom Joe had assisted out of this life, it was yellow. Even his eyes were yellow. For a few moments they seemed open but unseeing, and Joe wondered if the man was already dead. Then the don spoke. "Good. I knew you would come. Do what is necessary." The words came out rasping, but with surprising firmness.

Joe reached into his pocket with clammy fingers and took

out a stole. It had nothing to do with any promise made to Don Stefano; the imperative was an earlier vow. Ordination laid this burden on him; hatred could not obviate it. He knelt beside the bed, and his face was level with that of the dying man. "The sacrificial death of Jesus Christ made reparation for all sin. Our Lord created an infinite reservoir of forgiveness. To drink from those living waters we need only be sorry for our sins and ask the forgiveness of almighty God."

The stiff textbook words came hollow from his constricted throat and rang in his ears like lies, although he had always believed them true. The don said nothing. "Are you sorry for your sins?" Joe whispered. The whisper too was a lie. He wanted to shout obscenities. He wanted to accuse, to chant a litany of the vicious carnage for which the old man had been responsible: the widows and orphans he'd made, the thievery that created grinding poverty, the countless men whom he'd sent to violent, unexpected deaths. Who had heard their last confession? What priest was called to ease their end? Instead he only repeated, "Are you sorry for all your sins?"

"Your papa," Don Stefano rasped. "I didn't do that job. The *padrone,* he never told me till it was over."

As if that exonerated him, cleansed him of the stink of the manure heap in which he'd spent his life. Joe closed his eyes. Minutes passed. He prayed not for the dying man, but for himself. Lord, let me leave the judgment to you. Footsteps. His mother had come into the room. Still he could neither look at the creature in the bed nor speak the words the occasion demanded.

Signora DiAnni drew one sharp breath. "He's gone." She dropped to her knees beside her son, and Joe made himself look at the face of his enemy. Don Stefano's eyes had rolled back in his head and his jaw hung slack. Rosary beads clicked softly through his mother's fingers. Then she spoke. *"Confiteor Deo omnipotenti, beatae Mariae semper Virgini . . ."* The Latin words learned by rote in childhood slipped off her tongue. When the *confiteor* was ended she recited the act of contrition in the gutteral, fruity Italian of Sicily. Then she waited.

His muscles were quivering with tension. The pressure building inside him had to be released. Either he must do what his priesthood demanded or run. It was as if his mother read his mind. "Do it," she hissed through clenched teeth. And again, "Do it."

His body leaned forward, wrenched by some power beyond both understanding and hate. Almost of their own accord, his anointed hands made the sign of the cross. His fingers barely touched the sere skin of the old man's forehead, and the words of the conditional absolution called for by the circumstances forced themselves through his frozen mouth. "May Almighty God have mercy on you and forgive you your sins and lead you to everlasting life. . . . May our Lord Jesus Christ absolve you and, if you are yet living, I by His authority absolve you from every bond of excommunication and interdict in so far as I can and you need. . . . May the Passion of our Lord Jesus Christ avail you for the forgiveness of your sins and the reward of life everlasting."

"Why you speak in English?" his mother demanded when he at last pulled the quilt over the old man's face.

"That's the way it's done now. Since the council in Rome." He didn't wait to see if the explanation satisfied her, but went out to the kitchen and found a bottle of whiskey behind the many bottles of wine and poured himself a stiff drink and swallowed it in one gulp. He heard his mother's voice on the telephone, calling the undertaker. Then she came and stood beside him.

"Now you go to the church. You tell the priest it's okay. You tell him Don Stefano can be buried proper."

And that too he had to do. The tired old pastor of the parish listened gravely and shook his head. "Thank you, Father. It was good of you to come and explain all this. Thank God you were there at the right time." Joe saw the relief in the other priest's eyes and understood that he was grateful to be spared the need to take on principle a stand that would displease the powerful forces that ruled the North End.

A misty rain fell on Hanover Street when he returned to his mother's flat. It blurred the Christmas window displays that announced the advent of December, and dimmed the colored lights strung across the road. Upstairs, Signora DiAnni still sat alone in the kitchen. The neighbors would arrive when the undertakers did, alerted to the events of the afternoon by the familiar black van in the street. There was an abstemious glass of dark red wine by his mother's elbow and next to it an unopened box of the don's cheroots. There was also a tattered manila envelope. Her hand lay protectively over the dull brown paper. "It's all right?" she asked.

"Yes. The pastor will be around to see you later. Everything's arranged."

She sighed deeply. "Good." Her eyes were clear and no tear stains marked her cheeks. Joe could not guess what she was thinking or feeling. He could understand little of what had happened in this place for the past two decades, and even less of the drama of the last hour. The whiskey churned in his stomach and he felt ill. "What will you do now?" he asked.

She shrugged as if the matter was of no importance. "Here," she said instead of answering his question. "This is for you. I been saving it." She held out the manilla envelope. He hesitated and she added. "It wasn't his, it belonged to your papa. Today, what you did for me . . . I want you should have it now."

The envelope contained a spiral notebook. It was ivory with age, and the edges of the sheets were marked both by time and the occasional thumbprint. He had to tip it to the light of the window to read the faded ink. Then he closed the book with a gesture of pain. It contained poems written by his father. Joe knew that once, before he was blind, his father wrote such things, but he had seen none of them until now.

There was a respectful knock on the door. Before Joe could move or speak, Signora DiAnni shrugged again and rose. The somberly clad men from the funeral parlor entered the house, and behind them came the neighbor women, their customary black dresses proclaiming their readiness for this familiar duty.

Joe let himself out without saying good-bye. He took the notebook with him.

LOU WISNOVSKI WAS ASSIGNED TO ST. THERESE'S PARISH IN suburban Wellesley. His rectory, like the homes of his parishioners, was decidedly upper middle class, a universe removed from Revere and the North End. Joe sat on a piece of black canvas slung over a heavy wooden frame and faced the Pole across a coffee table of glass and chrome.

"How long ago did you say this happened?" the big red-headed man asked.

"Three weeks."

"And you've been eating your guts out ever since, right? Boyo, you've got a problem. Maybe nobody told you: they just ordained you, son, they didn't make you pope. Nobody's given you the keys to the kingdom. You don't bind and loose in heaven."

"Leave it to God, you mean," Joe said. "That's what I told myself for a while. But it's too glib, too slick. I hated him, Lou. He was filth, scum, the dregs of the earth. All right, it was only a conditional absolution, but I gave it to him, not because I wanted to save his soul. I did it because he'd made me promise. At least I think that's why. I'm not really sure."

"So what? You think you bought his way into heaven in spite of himself? Fooled God, maybe? Your theology stinks. The absolution was conditional because you thought he was probably already dead. That's how it should have been. But the critical thing is that it carried the same condition that all absolution does. If the old bastard wasn't sorry for his sins, no words of yours could erase them."

Joe poured himself another beer and took a long swallow. "By the numbers. That's how we do things. Everything precisely defined and carefully thought out and hedged about with rules and regulations. How many angels can dance on the head of a pin? That's what stinks."

Lou said other things, but they didn't reach Joe and he knew they didn't. Eventually the two men left the rectory and went to an obscure bar on Arlington Street, a section of Boston where neither was likely to meet anyone he knew. They switched from beer to scotch and got quietly drunk. The liquor didn't make the problem go away, but it succeeded in covering it over for the time being.

The meeting with Wisnovski took place a few days before Christmas. After it Joe was involved in the many holiday demands of his parish. On New Years' Day, Father Pasco called him into his office. "Something for you, my young friend," he said as he said every year.

It was customary for a pastor to make a present to his curates of a part of the money collected at the Christmas Masses. Father Pasco's habit was to make the payment in cash. Joe took the wad of bills and shoved them into his pocket, mumbling his appreciation.

Later he counted the money. It came to seven hundred dollars. He didn't take it to the bank and put it in his checking account, which, as usual, had a balance of three dollars and seventy-two cents. Instead he put the money in his bottom drawer, beneath his two pair of clean jeans.

The following Tuesday was his day off duty. He rose at six A.M. and dressed in one of the pairs of jeans, heavy hiking boots, and his ski jacket. Then he put a few more clothes into the battered rucksack he'd had since seminary days and divided the seven hundred dollars between his wallet and his pockets. He left the rectory before the housekeeper arrived to make breakfast, looked once at the Chevy, which belonged not to him but to the parish, and set out on foot.

It was a cold January morning and grimy hard-packed snow squeaked beneath his boots. That was the only sound in the street. His elegy, he thought. Appropriate. The day his father and grandfather were attacked had been just like this. He remembered the same dingy snow on the sidewalk when he watched the ambulance men emerge from the cheese factory with two stretchers. Now he carried in his rucksack his father's belated legacy, the little notebook of poems. His mother's bequest he carried in his heart. It lodged there beside his failed sense of purpose, a conviction that he was a sham unwilling to go on living a fraud. He'd become a priest to lift himself above the dung heap that spawned him, but it hadn't done that, just hurled him back into the excrement.

A God that demanded he exorcise the sins of a man he despised was beyond his understanding, and no longer real to him.

A LARGE MAJORITY OF THE MEN THEN LEAVING THE priesthood did so formally. It was representative of the times that they grasped the lifeline thrown by the learned Catholic journals and distinguished Catholic theologians. Suddenly certain things were possible not just in canon law, but in practice. A priest could give up his function without giving up his Church. That same climate of opinion ensured that those who sought the dispensation usually got it. Maybe because the bishops were in paroxysms of guilt over the many apparently unsuitable candidates they'd ordained in preconciliar days.

So a great number took off their roman collars and struggled to find a way to make their unique education and skills productive in secular society. They had extraordinary problems, and various organizations were formed to help them. Joe DiAnni contacted no such organization and applied for no dispensation.

The first seven months he bummed his way south, following the sun, picking up odd jobs as he went. He was a dishwasher in Connecticut and New York, a parking lot attendant in New Jersey, and a night watchman in Maryland and Virginia. Few people asked him questions he didn't want to answer, and those who did were subjected to such silent hostility that they soon retreated. He made no friends, and for thirty weeks he spoke no personal word to any other human being. Eventually he got to Florida. He'd been in Miami three days when he met Pete Chiarra.

The meeting took place behind a bar in a narrow, fetid alley on the edge of the Cuban district. Three men were systematically working over a fourth. DiAnni didn't think, he just responded. The intended victim was a hulk of a man with massive fists and a huge, totally bald head set on enormous shoulders. Once the odds against him were marginally improved by DiAnni's intervention, the fight ended quickly. The attackers fled down the alley, and DiAnni and the stranger were left to appraise each other.

"Thanks," the bald man said as he wiped the blood from his face.

"You're welcome. Who were they?" Joe checked himself over. He seemed unhurt except that his eye was rapidly closing and his jacket was torn.

"Never mind who they were, they're not worth talking about. My name's Pete Chiarra." He stuck out one enormous hand.

"Joe DiAnni," Joe said while he shook it.

"No kidding? A fellow wop. I shoulda guessed. C'mon, I'll buy you a drink. It's the least I can do."

Joe picked his rucksack off the ground where he'd thrown it and followed Chiarra to a small bar. It was the kind of place where their battered appearance would pass without comment; still, they took their drinks to a table in the rear. "You from around here?" Chiarra asked.

"Nope. Boston. I've been working my way south. Got to Miami the day before yesterday."

"Least it's warm," the other man agreed. Then he nodded in the direction of the rucksack. "You got a place to put that down?"

"Not at the moment. I was looking for a rooming house, or maybe just a park, when I spotted your friends."

"I got a boat," Chiarra said. "You want, you can bed down on her until you find something better."

"That would be great. Thanks."

"Don't mention it. I owe you. Besides, you're a *paesan,* right?"

The boat was an unlikely thirty-foot cutter with a small cabin that slept two. When morning came Joe noted that Chiarra's *Bella Donna* was the best-looking thing in the rather seedy marina. Her teak decks were immaculate and her brass was polished mirror bright. "She's a beautiful lady, all right," he commented.

"Yeah. And the source of all my trouble."

"How's that?"

"I took a loan to buy her. Figured I could maybe get some charters. I'm no good at it, though. Don't kiss ass good enough. So I fell behind with the payments."

Joe took another bite of bacon and egg and watched Chiarra for a few moments. Part of him said, leave it alone. Entanglements were what he'd come all this way to avoid. But he instinctively liked the bald giant, and he'd been without human contact for a long time. "I gather those guys last night were trying to collect."

"Yeah, that's it." Chiarra's voice was muffled behind his mug of coffee.

"Which means your loan didn't come from any bank."

"First off it did. But I had to get money someplace else when the bank wanted to take the lady away. I'm into those *sporchi* for ten gees, but she's mine. I don't plan to give her up."

"Loan sharks don't give up either," Joe said. "We got rid of the three collectors last night. But there'll be others."

"Yeah, I know."

"What do you plan to do about it?"

"That's what I don't know."

"Why not just get out of here?"

"Can't. My inboard's in the repair shop. It'll take three hundred bucks to get her out. Might as well be three million as far as I'm concerned. The bastards know that."

Joe kept on eating and didn't say anything. He had four hundred and seventy-seven dollars in a money belt around his waist. He'd made few inroads in the original seven hundred; mostly he'd managed to earn enough to pay for his limited needs. "Where you figure to go if you could get away?" he asked finally.

"I dunno. West Indies maybe. You can do a bit of fishing, sell your catch. Make enough to eat that way."

"Would you consider taking a crewman?"

"You?" Chiarra eyed him warily. "Look, I owe you, I know that. And I don't usually ask a lot of questions, but you don't add up, mister. You don't look or sound like any road bum I ever met."

Joe let this remark pass without comment. He was just about deciding to take his rucksack and go before there was any more trouble when Chiarra asked abruptly, "You runnin' from the cops?"

"No. I'm not running from anybody. Not the way you mean."

"That's straight?"

"Yes, it's straight."

"Okay, I believe you. Not that it makes a hell of a lot of difference. Without the motor I'd never get far enough to matter. With or without a crewman."

"What if I said I knew where to get the money to reclaim the motor?"

Chiarra grinned, a broad smile that split his big, ugly face. "I'd say, welcome aboard."

THEY HAD THE MOTOR IN TWO HOURS. WHILE THE BALD MAN worked at installing it, DiAnni kept watch. Neither of them thought the hoods likely to come in daylight, but it paid to be cautious. It was August, and the air was a crucible even on the water. Stripped to the waist and wearing a pair of cut-off jeans, DiAnni sat on the deck, swatted mosquitos, sipped a can of beer, and waited. It was after five when Chiarra emerged from the tiny hold. "Okay, she's ready to go."

"Do we need to get provisions, anything like that?"

"Yeah, but I don't think it's a good idea to do it here." He looked at the sky. The sun was moving west and dusk was approaching. "We better put some miles between us and Miami before we stop for provisions. That is, if you still want to go."

"I want to."

"Okay. I'll get the motor going. You cast off."

"What does that mean?"

Chiarra stared at him incredulous. "Cast off. Let go the mooring lines. Ain't you never been on a boat before?"

"Nope. I never even saw one close up until last night."

"Sweet Jesus," Chiarra said. "This is gonna be some trip."

IN THE ENSUING TWO YEARS, DiAnni LEARNED A BIT ABOUT sailing and a lot about peace. Lying naked on the deck, that was the way to be; it was the essence of the whole damn thing. Today the teak was warm and smooth beneath his buttocks. Overhead was blue sky and a yellow sun to warm him, while a gentle breeze dried the sweat on his flesh as soon as it formed. He was the color of the wood, a dark russet brown, and he blended with his environment as if he'd been born to it. The North End, Revere Street, the crazy climactic swings of Massachusetts and the equally erratic swings of his psyche, all were warmed out of him. There was the sea, the sky, the beauty of the earth—and the few days fishing each week that

282

earned enough for him and Pete to buy all they needed. Nothing else. He didn't want anything else ever again.

A quarter mile away was a scene straight off a picture post-card. By long tradition these were called the Out Islands, though at present there was a government move to rename them the Family Islands. Whether Family was better than Out depended on your point of view. For Joe the old name did fine. The *Bella Donna* was anchored off Eleuthera, in the lee of Cupid's Cay, first permanent settlement in the Bahamas. She'd been there three weeks, and as far as the two men were concerned, she might stay there forever.

Joe lazily sat up, stretched, and reached for another beer. The hillsides around the tiny town of Governor's Harbour blazed with bright red poinciana. The elaborate homes of the very rich were lapped by tongues of fire. He looked idly at the houses for a moment; bright white pleasure palaces where the beautiful people came to escape the harsh winters of their money-making cities. They were all empty now. It was late May, and the jet set frolicked elsewhere. Only one place exhibited any sign of life. A black man was expertly wielding a machete on the velvet green lawn of one fine house close to the shore.

Joe watched the man's skilled movements for a few minutes, then he sank back on the deck and returned to his reverie of nothing. Eventually Pete would return with the supplies, later they'd have a meal and a few drinks. Maybe they'd go ashore and look at lovely women with thrusting breasts and strong buttocks and wide, welcoming smiles. Maybe they wouldn't. Tomorrow they'd probably fish. The choices were limited and the election of one option over another was purely a matter of whim and mood, and of little import.

Vaguely he was listening for the put-put sound of the rubber dinghy's outboard. It would signal Pete's return. A different sound reached him half an hour later and caused him to grab for the pair of cut-offs lying on the deck. A powerful motor was approaching the harbor; it could only be attached to a large boat.

Large indeed; a couple of hundred feet long and some thirty feet wide, spewing white foam behind her twin screws. Her hull was satiny black and she entered the harbor with an easy diminution of speed that bespoke power in the hands of a master helmsman. Joe watched her in admiration. Two and a half years with Pete Chiarra hadn't made him an expert sailor, but it had taught him to appreciate men who were, and to respond to the beauty of a superb vessel. The name etched on her side was *La Contessa*. Flying from a small mast above the bridge was the courtesy flag. It was a Union Jack because, though recently granted something called autonomy, the Bahamas were still a British colony. Joe looked toward the flagstaff, aft on the starboard side. The flag of registry had a quartered red, white, and blue field with one red and one blue star. So the yacht was Panamanian. Joe grinned. Judging from the marinas and harbors he'd seen, there must be at least one yacht per person in Panama.

The *La Contessa* came gently to rest in the water. She was some fifty feet astern of the lady, and Joe saw the nattily uniformed man who dropped the forward anchor. But the yacht was abeam of the cutter so he didn't see the tenders lowered, or get a good look at their passengers. He considered going below for binoculars, but it appeared that the dozen or so people being carried ashore were all men, hardly worth the trouble. A business conference of some sort. And to be held in the mansion that had had its grass trimmed an hour earlier, judging from the direction in which the small boats headed.

He was still watching the new arrivals when he saw Pete returning. The lady's dinghy skirted the yacht's tenders cautiously at first, then Chiarra put on a burst of speed and roared up to the cutter. He flung a line and Joe caught it with more than usual skill. Just as well; Chiarra's great round face was red with rage. "Fucking bastards," he muttered. "Lousy cocksucking *sporchi*. Why the hell they gotta come here?" He swung his huge frame onto the deck with a lithesome grace that never failed to startle.

DiAnni reached for the sack of groceries. "Who? The guys from the yacht?"

"Guys! They ain't guys. Not normal people. They're lice, monsters, crawling things."

Joe's eyes narrowed and his glance flicked from his friend to the men now landing at the private dock below the fine house. Only one species of being was able to evoke such passion from Chiarra, those who threatened to take his lady from him. "How do you know?" he asked quietly.

"I came right by 'em, didn't I? I saw him, that's how I know."

"Saw who?"

"The boss man from Miami. The one I owe ten gees." He

284

was working while he spoke; and it was obvious he was preparing to sail.

"Hold on," Joe said. "You got one fast look. Maybe you're wrong."

"I ain't wrong."

"You recognize any of the others?"

"No. But they gotta be the same kind. Lice only mess with lice."

Silently Joe went below and came back with the glasses. The last tender was unloading at the dock when he got the newcomers in his sights. There were thirteen of them. Nothing unusual to look at. Middle-aged men dressed in expensive sports clothes and basking in the sun that warmed their chilled northern bones. Only one figure stood out. A tall, slim man who seemed ageless. He moved like an athlete despite his crew-cut white hair.

"Jesus!" Chiarra exploded. "You gonna help me get underway, or you just gonna watch while they come get us?"

DiAnni dropped the glasses and started stowing loose gear.

THEY FOUND A SECRET AND SHELTERED INLET, ONE OF THE countless number that existed in the hundred thousand square miles of water occupied by the Bahamas, and anchored just as the sun dipped below the horizon. A school of groupers bumped and nuzzled the cutter's bottom and came to the surface to catch the bits of food the men flung over the side. The fish were brown, flashed with red, and their strangely human faces seemed to Joe to be questioning his presence in this hidden sanctuary.

"What you figure they're doin' here?" Pete asked. He wasn't referring to the fish.

"Not looking for you. Get that out of your head. That part of it was just one of life's unpleasant coincidences."

"What then?"

"A business meeting, I suppose. These are British islands, so they're free of the feds. Ship's Panamanian registry. God knows who owns the house. Nobody likely to be connected with the Mafia, you can bet on that."

Chiarra spat over the side and just missed a large grouper whose staring eyes accused him of treachery before they disappeared below the water. "Some business," he said. "Some fucking lousy business."

That night Joe lay on the deck, but he didn't sleep. He

stayed awake and wrestled with a lot of demons he'd thought banished many months past. Below, in the snug locker where his few personal possessions were lodged, his father's notebook was carefully stored. Once in a while he took it out and laboriously translated a bit of the old man's Italian scrawl. It was bad poetry. Sentimental and mawkish mostly, except for an occasional line that caught at his heart and bespoke a talent that might have been, had it been nurtured and trained. One of these lines lived in his memory. "We cannot go where beauty dwells," his father had written. "Beauty must come to us and if she choose, sign with her silvered breath our lives, a thing for her to use."

Beauty was in these islands, in the great stretch of warm, shallow sea that he and Pete had been exploring for over two years. But being in proximity to physical beauty didn't sign a man's life. It didn't touch the raw core. And by itself, it didn't heal. Joe held up his hands and looked at them in the moonlight. Priest's hands. What the hell would Pete Chiarra say if he knew he had a spoiled priest on his boat?

Joe grinned in the dark, but the grin faded quickly. What was he going to do with these hands for the forty or so more years he'd probably live? He'd never again use them to transform bread and wine into the body of Jesus Christ, of that he was sure. What then? They were hard and callused now, transformed by hauling on sheets and fishing lines, but that was something alien that had been superimposed on his flesh. He was no fisherman. Once he'd been a fisher of men, but he was that no longer. Just as he was no longer a celibate.

Funny how he still thought in those terms. One minute he told himself he was an agnostic, the next he was responding to all the old symbols. Who was it who said "Give me the boy and I'll give you the man"? Yeah, the Jesuits, talking about Catholic schools. Maybe they were right. An innoculation that took, and conditioned your responses no matter what. So how come he didn't feel guilty? Maybe that's what the seminary had done for him. Laymen thought the whole structure was built on guilt. He knew that, on the contrary, it was based on forgiveness. And that was the thing he couldn't live with. Which was why he was lying here thinking about the future and about women and feeling sad, but not guilty.

There had been many good, sweet, and loving women in the years he'd been with Chiarra. Some with tawny brown skin, some as white as moonlight, even one of yellow-ivory with hair the color of midnight. He had enjoyed them and learned from them and, for a few minutes at least, he had loved them all. But just as his calluses were a disguise, so too were the ladies he had taken to his heart for a short space out of time. They were not part of him, not of his essence. Only one was almost that, and she was far away and he hoped she was happy.

He allowed the memory of Barbie to surface in his mind, a thing he almost never did, and for a moment the sweetness of it filled him with a strange and sad and paradoxical joy. Then he pushed away the vision of her and sealed it deep below his consciousness with the discipline of long practice. One thing only he came to know with certitude during that long night. His time with Pete on the *Bella Donna* was drawing to a close. It had been good and necessary, and he was grateful for it. But something was urging him to move on, and he would not long be able to ignore it.

Finally he slept. His dreams were less controlled than his waking thoughts. In them Barbie came to him as she had that night in Vermont and he tasted her sweetness and both lost and found himself in the perfection of her beauty.

AFTER THE TIME ON THE PHONE WHEN TOM SHORE BARELY remembered her, Maria decided not to call him again. Then, when she was finished, she was so drunk with creation, so crazy with words, that she dialed his number at six in the morning. A second before he answered she got nervous and started to hang up. "Hello, who the hell is this?" His voice prevented her from breaking the connection.

"It's Maria Trapetti. I'm sorry. This is an awful time to call you."

"It is that, lady."

At least he seemed to know who she was. And he'd answered, not some woman sharing his bed. "I'm sorry," she repeated. "Go back to sleep. I'll call you later."

"Jesus, you've got a nerve. Now that you woke me up, you damn well better tell me why you called."

"I just finished the book. That is, I finished it a few hours ago. I spent the night reading it and ...." Her voice trailed away. Too shy to say what she really thought.

"It's good, huh?"

"I think so. Of course I'm probably no judge." She took a deep breath and didn't plan to say more, but her mood overcame her discretion. "I think it's very good," she added defiantly.

"Okay, that's great. Bring it over. I'll put the coffee on."

"Now?"

"Sure, now. If it's good enough to wake me up, it's damned well too good to wait."

When she arrived on Carmine Street, it was barely sunrise. The smell of perking coffee filled the landing outside his door and the door itself was ajar. "That you?" he called. "Come on in. Be right with you."

The apartment was still cool. In these dawn hours August was just teasing. Maria put the box of typescript on the coffee table and looked around. Tom wasn't in sight. The apartment was much neater than when she last saw it, and she wondered if some woman had been cleaning it for him. To confirm her suspicions there was a pink chiffon scarf folded and left on the table by the door, as if waiting for its owner to come and re-claim it. Maria sat down and pressed her legs together. She smoothed the fabric of her denim wrap-around skirt over her bare knees and wished she'd worn nylons, despite the weather.

"Breakfast in three minutes," Tom said, emerging from the bathroom wearing nothing but a towel. Maria averted her eyes from his nakedness and concentrated instead on the wonderful aroma. "Croissants," he said as he disappeared into the tiny kitchen. "Do you like jam or marmalade?"

"Whatever you have, it doesn't matter."

"My God, you're irritating! Of course it matters." He stuck his head around the screen and she was conscious of the way his silver-speckled hair, wet from the shower, swept back from his forehead. "I don't serve croissants to people who don't give a damn whether they have jam or marmalade."

"Jam, please." In chagrined tones.

The rolls were like nothing she'd ever eaten, flaking in her fingers and melting in buttery goodness in her mouth. The jam, a rich conserve of whole strawberries, was an embarrass-ment of riches. The croissants and the milky, mellow coffee were perfection by themselves. "Did you make these since I called?"

He chuckled. "They take twenty-four hours to get ready for the oven. I buy them from a little French lady whose name I guard as if it were the holy grail. Freezer to table in less than twenty minutes. For special celebration breakfasts."

"I hope you think there's something to celebrate." Her high had evaporated and she was terrified that the book was a dis-aster and he was going to tell her so.

"I probably will," he said. "When a writer feels the way you do after something's finished it's usually with good cause. The lousy ones leave you sick to your stomach."

"I'm not sure I'm a writer."

"Yes, I think you are. That much showed the first time."

He began clearing the remains of their feast. He'd replaced the towel with a pair of track shorts and a shabby T-shirt. Maria's newly opened novelist's eyes saw that his legs were tanned and loose-muscled, as if they'd once been in running trim and now the bulges had disappeared beneath the surface, from whence he could summon them at will. If her eyes were opened, however, his were not. They were wary, secretive eyes. She'd thought them blue; now, in the limpid early light, they looked green. "Let me do the dishes." She jumped up and took the tray from his hands.

"Okay. I'll start reading, shall I?"

"No! I mean yes," she amended in a whisper that betrayed terror.

He smiled a sympathetic smile and lit a cigarette before he lifted the cover from the box of dreams.

When she came out of the kitchen he was reading and making a careful, neat pile of the pages he finished, as only people who respect manuscripts do. He didn't look up. Maria curled herself on the sofa. She wouldn't interrupt until he got to the end of the first chapter. She hadn't slept in twenty-four hours, so she put her head down and closed her eyes. When she opened them, midday sun was pouring through the windows and she was soaked in perspiration. The first thing she noticed was the ashtray full of cigarette ends; the second, a three-inch pile of typed sheets, turned face down.

"I'm sorry. I must have dozed off."

"Slept the sleep of the dead, more accurately. It's almost one." She opened her mouth to say something, but he forestalled her. "Please don't say you're sorry again. I'm getting tired of hearing it. Why don't you take a shower?"

She looked from him to the manuscript and back again. Her dark eyes met his, blue again now, and the question she was afraid to ask was transmitted without words. "Go take a shower," he said again. "Let me get my thoughts clear. I just finished."

She half ran to the privacy of the bathroom, choked with disappointment and ashamed for him to see her tears. If it was good, even half as good as she'd thought, he'd have said so right away. Instead, he was groping for a way to let her down gently. At first she only turned on the shower so he wouldn't hear her crying. Then she was seduced by the sound of water splashing in the tub and she stripped off her clothes and stepped behind the curtain under the spray.

His words startled her because they came from only a few feet away and she knew he'd come into the bathroom. "Don't panic, I can't see a thing," he said over the noise of the shower. "I brought you a robe and a clean towel."

When she turned off the water, she was calm—resolute was the word she thought of. She reached for her bra and underpants, but rejected them because they were still damp with sweat. The robe he'd provided was thick terry cloth, blue lightened by numerous washings, and too big for her, but an improvement over the clothes she'd slept in. Physical comfort seemed suddenly very important, a barrier against attack.

There was a cold beer waiting for her on the coffee table and she grabbed it and drank a large swallow, forgetting that she disliked beer. "Go ahead, tell me," she said when she put the glass down. "I can guess, but you might as well say it."

"Okay, I will. Congratulations. You're going to make a lot of money."

"What?" She sat down, knees trembling, stomach doing flip-flops, unable to take in his words.

"It's a bona fide, rip-roaring, authentic piece of commercial fiction. Destined for best-sellerdom as sure as God made little green apples. I'd suggest you take it to your friendly neighborhood editor's office right away. Then start figuring how you're going to spend the advance."

She stared at him, neither believing what she heard nor understanding the tone of voice in which it was conveyed. "I don't know whether to weep or say thank you," she said finally. "You're not teasing me, are you?"

"No," he said gently. "I'd never make a rotten joke like that."

"But if you like the book, why are you looking at me that way?"

"I said it was going to be a huge success. I didn't say I liked it."

The elation that had started to return drained away. "Oh, I see," she whispered. "At least I think I do."

He watched her for a few seconds, then ran his fingers through his hair in a gesture of frustration. "Oh, shit! Look, like everyone else I've got my hang-ups and sometimes I kid myself and call them standards. There's no reason for you to be measured by them, least of all by yourself. I thought you were trying to do one thing and it turned out you were attempting something else. And that something else you did to perfection, if I'm any judge. Hell, it's nothing to cry about. C'mon, smile, you're going to be rich. Like the man said, it's better than poor."

Maria used the sleeve of the blue robe to wipe away her tears. "Are you?"

"Am I what?"

"Any judge?"

"Yes, as a matter of fact I am. I only threw in the disclaimer to be polite. I was an editor for years before I quit to write full time. I've wet-nursed half a dozen books that sold over a million copies in paperback. This is better than anything I ever unearthed. Like I said, your tame editor is going to be a very happy lady."

"But that's some kind of crime? Selling, what did you say, a million copies?"

"In paperback. That's where the big numbers and the big bucks are. And no, it's no crime."

"So why do I feel like a criminal?"

"Beats me."

He leaned back and lit another cigarette and watched her over the flame of the match. She was staring at her bare feet, her hair was free of the bun thanks to the shower, and her eyelashes cast a long, dark shadow over the warm olive tones of her cheek. "Maria," he said, leaning forward to flip the match into the ashtray. "I'd very much like to make love to you." Her head jerked up and she stared at him. She opened her mouth, but no words came.

"Okay," he said as if she'd spoken. "It's probably a lousy idea. I have no experience in deflowering virgins. And I'd hate it if you agreed out of some sense of obligation."

"You are the most egotistical man I've ever met," she said finally.

"I'm a writer. It goes with the territory. Only a colossal egotist can sit down, stare at a blank page, and attempt to fill it with words someone else will want to read. Pretty soon you'll realize you have the same disease. Ego is *sui generis* in this game."

"You think everything's a game. Especially me. Two months ago, when I called and that woman answered, you didn't even remember my name. I was some annoyance you'd managed to forget. Now you tell me all kinds of wildly contradictory things about a piece of work I've poured my heart

and soul into, and you finish up by inviting me to your bed."
She stopped because he was laughing.

"So that's it. You're angry because I'm not pretending that
I've been sitting here unable to forget you. My little ex-nun,
you've got a lot to learn. This morning, before you telephoned,
I'd also have been hard pressed to remember your name. All I
remembered was the story you first brought me to read, and
the intimations of genuine talent I thought I saw. As for inviting you to bed, I'm a man and you look like a woman. At this
moment you look like an appealing, attractive woman. I
thought maybe we could make some good things happen for
each other."

Maria shook her head. "Stop it. You confuse me. You always confuse me."

"Okay. Tell you what, it's not three yet. Get dressed and
we'll go together and drop this thing off at your editor's office.
Then we'll go out and find a superb meal by way of consolation."

"Consolation for what?"

"Oh, I don't know. I guess mostly not screwing."

"You get dead that way," he said, and she looked at
him, a little sick to her stomach. No, more than that. Very
sick. Because she'd asked him straight out why he'd first
agreed to help her and he'd repeated the same thing he'd said
the first time, that it was difficult to say no to Philocles Williams. Only now he'd elaborated. "You get dead that way."

"You're joking, aren't you?" Maria knew he wasn't.

"I told you before, I try to avoid really rotten jokes."

"I don't understand. He's a lawyer, an influential man."

"A lawyer for thugs, hoodlums, the mob. You know what
those words mean, don't you? Oh, yes, your name's Trapetti. I
forgot."

"You think every Italian is tied up with the Mafia?"

"No. Not you certainly. But at least you can translate the
words. *Cosa nostra,* our thing. Sounds almost benign put that
way, doesn't it?"

She didn't answer, only said, "Phil isn't Italian."

He laughed softly and took another bite of his ham-
burger—they hadn't gone for a super meal after all, neither of
them had enough money. "Yeah, with that name I expect he's
Greek. That make you feel better?"

"No. I feel awful. Barbie doesn't know."

"Barbie? Oh, the paramour, you mean. Hell she doesn't.

You may have just left the convent, kid. Mrs. Gold's been around."

Maria shook her head. "No, she hasn't. Not the way you mean. Have you ever met her?"

"I saw her at a big party once. Some half-assed testimonial arranged by the pols. I went because my brother was getting an award." It was the first time he'd mentioned having a brother. "Williams and your girlfriend, or I should say his girlfriend, were there. She's some looker."

"Yes, I know she's very beautiful. But that doesn't make her the sophisticate you think she is. Barbie's one of the world's innocents. Don't look at me that way. It's true. I'm more worldly-wise than she is, whatever you think."

"Okay, what difference does it make? I'm not sitting in judgment on the lady. No doubt she has her reasons for tying up with Williams. Just don't kid yourself about him. Beneath that whitened exterior beats a black heart. Sorry, lousy metaphor. Or whatever it is. He's a bastard, though. If she doesn't know, you'd better warn her."

"How do you know so much about him?" How come he knew about you, was what she wanted to ask, but she didn't have quite that much nerve.

He sat back and lit another cigarette and took his time about answering. For a while she thought he was going to change the subject, then he said, "I live in an Italian neighborhood. That tell you anything?"

"You mean about the power base of the mob or the Mafia or whatever it is?"

"Not the power base, the most likely victims. Loan sharks, for instance, don't do so well on Park Avenue. If you don't really need the money, any bank's glad to lend it to you. The people in my end of town need it sometimes. When they do, they go wherever they can get it. Meeting the payments can be tough."

"Does Phil collect the debts?"

He laughed again, with even less humor than before. "Don't be an idiot. Williams isn't a collector, he wouldn't get his hands that dirty."

"Your talking in riddles. I don't understand."

"The old man and his wife, the couple that run the submarine shop, you remember them?" She nodded. "They borrowed four thousand to pay their grandson's medical bills. Then Signora Contini got sick and they had to close the sandwich bar for a few weeks. Disaster. They got behind in the payments. The old man told me one day. He wasn't whining. He was just desperate to talk to someone. 'Pretty soon,' he tells me, 'they gonna come in here and break the whole place up. Maybe break me up too.' So I tried to help."

Maria pushed away her half-eaten sandwich and took a drink of Coke. "Could I have a beer?" she asked suddenly. Tom seemed glad of the interruption. He got another beer for himself and one for her. "Go on," she said when the drinks were served. "Tell me what you did."

"I took as much of the payment as could be found and smelled around until I knew where to bring it. Not the bimbos who walk the pavements. The bigger brass, middle management, you might say. Next day, Williams called me. Wanted to know what made me presume his client Mr. Important had anything to do with the criminal elements in society, et cetera. The short of it is that somehow the Continis were given all the time they needed to repay. And I went on Williams' list of people who owe favors."

The beer was bitter and unpleasant in her mouth, but she liked the way it warmed her inside and settled her churning stomach. "That's where I come in, isn't it? One of the favors."

"You might say. But only initially."

"Why did you send me away when I came back the first time?"

"Did I? Oh, yes, I remember. One of my turning-over-a-new-leaf days. Screw them all, I'm no lackey. Bad melodrama. It's one of my failings."

After that they walked in the summer dusk. They were near the office where she'd dropped off her manuscript. Tom showed her an adjacent block that was still old Murray Hill; intact and unchanged since the early days of the century, despite being a stone's throw from Park Avenue South. Maria listened to his explanations of the architecture and the history and felt clumsy and stupid and abominably naive. She also felt frightened and alone.

"I have to decide, don't I?" she said, apropos of nothing.

He looked at her warily, as if he'd picked up her thoughts in the humid air between them. "Decide what?"

"What world I want to belong to."

"I guess maybe you do, now that you're going to be rich and famous."

"Don't keep saying that. It may not be true."

"It's true."

"Then I guess, yes. That's part of it."

"And the other part?"

"I'm scared. And sort of weighed down with the past."

They'd walked downtown as far as Madison Square and she paused for a moment and looked at the dusty trees. She noted masses of pigeons and wondered where they roosted during the night. "Can I come home with you?" she asked, concerned not about the pigeons but about herself and the man beside her, but him only peripherally, only as far as he met her needs of the moment.

"And get rid of your past, you mean? Lose your encumbering virginity?"

"Yes. That's what I mean."

"Okay, if you want to."

"I want to."

THE SEX WAS EMBARRASSING AND AWKWARD THE FIRST TIME, A little better the second, and surprisingly good thereafter. "You have a talent for it," Tom said, stroking the rich curve of her hip and letting his blunt finger trace the delectable join between thigh and pelvis. "Ishtar reincarnated."

"Who or what is Ishtar?"

"Babylonian goddess of love, better than a vestal virgin."

"Vestal virgins have their place."

"Yes, I suppose so. But you're not one of them."

"Not anymore." She giggled softly, amazed at herself because she felt no guilt. Maybe it would come later. Right now she was still aquiver with the almost-orgasm she'd achieved half an hour earlier. She might not have recognized it as such, except that Tom explained. He was a gentle lover, slow and thoughtful once his first hunger was appeased. Just what she needed. A part of her brain ticked over and accused her of using him. She giggled again because that was ridiculous in the circumstances.

"Tell me what's funny." His hands were busy even while he spoke, loving her almost of their own accord.

"I was feeling guilty about you."

He hooted. "That's a twist. Why?"

"I don't really know. I'm mixed up. I feel right here with you, comfortable and easy. And I'm enjoying myself. Somehow that doesn't seem fair."

"Not to worry. I kind of like it too."

He propped himself on one elbow and stared into her eyes. The bedclothes were rumpled with the activities of the last thirty-six hours—they'd spent two whole nights and one entire day in bed—and a vague half-light at the window announced the coming of a second dawn. "Listen," he said. "I hate to sound corny, but we'd better get something straight. I'm not good at serious relationships. Worse, I don't want to be. I enjoy you, all of you, including your body, and I'd like us to go on together for a while, if you want. But it won't ever be more than that. Okay?"

"Okay." She agreed without thinking, more conscious of his hands cupping her breast than of the import of his words. She was fascinated with all her physical reactions, a whole new unexplored world loomed.

Why, for instance, did her nipples stiffen and swell when he touched her? Why did she enjoy the sensation of his sucking on her breast, as he was doing now? She sighed deeply and let the theory be stilled by practice. It felt very good. Suddenly he withdrew his mouth and went into the bathroom. She lay still with her eyes closed, enjoying the things she felt and waiting for him to come back.

But when he did, he didn't lie down beside her. Instead he scooped her up and carried her into the bathroom and sank her unceremoniously into a tub full of steam and bubbles. Then he climbed in too. "Hmm," she said. "What new perversion is this?"

"Inspiration by association. Goddesses and baths of asses' milk and stuff like that."

"Asses' milk?"

"Not really. Just water and bubble bath. Very expensive bubble bath, I might add. Left behind by a lady with a taste for things French that smell of *muguet des bois*."

She felt a twinge, utterly illogical considering what she'd been thinking earlier, at the notion of the many females who had doubtless preceded her in his bed, but she didn't show it. She was smart enough to recognize a test when it appeared. He waited a moment, then said, "Move over a little, you're lying on the loofah."

Maria retrieved it and scrubbed his back, enjoying the breadth of it and the fact that his skin was smooth and there was no spare fat on his frame. Next to him she looked blowsy and overfed. Or so she thought. He didn't.

"You have a fantastic shape," he said when he took the sponge from her and reversed their roles. "God, you're like something out of a Rubens painting."

The water floated her breasts, the smoky brown aureoles peeping up from the bubbles, and beneath it his hand kneaded the flesh of her belly. He kissed her and she loved the taste of him, mingled as it was with the innocent scent of the *muguet des bois*. The bath began to grow cool and he clambered out and lifted her from the tub into an enormous bath towel, a little rough from the laundry, and she let herself be rubbed dry, then carried not to the bed, but to the big shag rug in the middle of the living room. He went to the window and drew the curtains and sunlight streamed in, benignly warm now, not the punishing thing it would be later.

When he returned to her side she reached up her arms, but he disengaged them from around his neck. "Don't do anything. Just lie there and be done to."

The next time she felt his exploring fingers they were slick and slid over her skin with a seductive, consuming ease. She realized he'd produced some sort of cream from somewhere, but that was her last analytical thought. After that it was just feeling. Whole symphonies were playing in her belly, a string section executed vibratos on the soft insides of her thighs. *"Con brio,"* he said. As if the analogy had a physical presence of its own, to be plucked at will from the ether.

His fingers moved faster, his mouth suckled, his weight imprisoned her deliciously, freeing her from any need to protest that might be dredged up from a recalcitrant subconscious. The first soporific sensations were replaced with new tensions. Like wires strung throughout her body, quivering and straining and causing her to strain with them. She was reaching, reaching . . . pulling herself inward and tightening every muscle in a desperate effort to achieve . . . what? His lips were against her ear. "I'm going to enter you now," he whispered. "Deep, deep inside. And you'll feel me all the way. And you're going to come."

He knelt between her legs and drew them up to his waist and drove himself into her, deeper than any time before. She felt him as he'd promised. He filled her entirely. The soreness that had lingered after the first piercing was gone and in its place was only this new unbearable tension. Her lips parted and she moaned, then moaned again and whispered, "Please . . ." but didn't understand what she was asking for. "Please, please, please . . ."

"Yes."

He drove even deeper. But slowly. In full and fantastic control made possible only by the fact of numerous ejaculations over a short space of time. "Talk," he commanded as he slithered in and out of her in long pulsing strokes. "I want to know what you're feeling." Maria opened her mouth to obey but no words came. Only a long and strangled scream that accompanied a thunderous implosion of sensation she could not have described in any case.

A few hours later he said, "Go home now. Something's working."

She didn't understand, and when she looked her question into his eyes, he laughed and tweaked her nose. "I've got an article to do. I'm a week over the deadline now. All of a sudden I think I can write it. Understand?"

"Of course." She dressed and marveled that the clothes she'd put on four days ago still fit her body. Everything seemed so changed, it was extraordinary that the skirt and blouse weren't too small or too big, or in some other way representative of the truths she knew.

"I'd give a lot if you'd stop wearing a girdle," Tom said when she came out of the bathroom. "That's the most gorgeous ass in New York and you stuff it into a rubber harness."

She blushed, although she knew it was absurd. Too late for blushes now. Except it was different. The spoken intimacy had the power to embarrass because they'd closed off a portion of their personas, left them waiting while they resumed other identities. "Call you in a couple of days," he said, kissing her lightly. He made no mention of taking her home, and Maria was slightly piqued by that. Another absurdity. She had to laugh at herself.

"Okay," she said. "Don't call us, we'll call you. I get it."

"Right. By the end of the week probably."

In the house on Seventy-second Street Barbie kissed her lightly too, the way Tom had, only this was hello not good-bye. Hello and welcome to the club. Barbie knew, even though when she called to explain her absence that first night Maria had said she'd be tied up on business for a few days. "How goes it?" Barbie asked.

"Good. Fine, I mean," Maria added shyly. "Tom thinks the book 'very salable.' For him that's not the same as good, but I'm happy about it. We took it to the editor's office."

"You'll be interested in this, then." Barbie held out an envelope with the return address of the publisher. "It came by messenger this morning. I'd have called Shore's flat tonight if you didn't come home."

The letter was enthusiastic and full of the excited phrases Tom had promised. Maria read it quickly and gave it to Barbie. Then she sank into a chair and inexplicably began to sob.

After that they hugged each other and finally went into the kitchen and drank cold milk and ate left-over chicken. It seemed to grow in Barbie's refrigerator, the way it had in Sophie's. Maria mentioned that and they laughed, and talked about old times and new dreams, and surprised visions of delight danced in Maria's head.

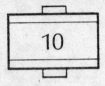

10

BARBIE'S ACCOUNTANT CAME EVERY TWO WEEKS, A SMALL
balding man named Murphy with a diffident manner
and a high falsetto voice. Murphy's voice annoyed her
until she learned to ignore it. He balanced her checkbooks and
made entries in two sets of ledgers, one relating to Green Gold
and the other dealing with her personal expenditures. He also
prepared quarterly statements and tax returns. Like the ledgers, the statements dealt separately with her business and the
personal accounts.

From the beginning Barbie had given Phil a copy of the
quarterly report on the shop. After Green Gold began showing a profit, she included a check. The money represented
partial repayment of the loan he'd originally made her, as well
as his share of the profits.

As the amounts grew, so did Barbie's self-esteem. She didn't
object to being Phil's mistress, nor to the fact that it was common knowledge. Even Sophie and Moe understood that it was
so, although they never mentioned it. But had she been what
she still thought of as a "kept woman," she'd have been uncomfortable. She wasn't. The ledgers and the reports and the
checks freed her to indulge a growing affection for Phil. He
was kind to her and to Norma, in his own way he was fun to
be with, and sex was good with him; what else mattered? She
was a little distressed by the intensity of his feelings for her, a
truth she couldn't help but recognize, but like Murphy's ob-

jectionable voice, it was something she learned to live with. Once in a while she considered what might happen if she ever fell in love with someone else and wanted to leave Phil. Probably it would mean a lot of melodrama. But that didn't worry her because she wasn't going to be in love with someone else. At least not someone she could make a life with. She had been in love once only. It didn't have anything to do with Phil.

A FEW DAYS AFTER MARIA GOT THE LETTER FROM THE publisher, it was time to give Phil the latest quarterly report. Barbie always hand-delivered them. Often he was at her house that same evening, but the money and the analysis of Green Gold's income and outgo she took to him. "At his office," she explained to Maria with a self-deprecating laugh. "Maybe I'm schizophrenic, but it's important to me. A symbol, I guess."

"Of what?"

"I'm not sure. My independence, I suppose."

Maria failed to see how the gesture created independence from the man she knew Barbie's lover to be. She wondered for the dozenth time if she should repeat what Tom had said about Williams. It was easier to put off that decision. Especially since Barbie was already hurrying out the door. "Don't forget, the Plaza at noon. Second floor," she called as she left.

Barbie was taking Maria to her hairdresser, something she'd wanted to do for weeks. Maria had resisted until yesterday. Barbie thought it was her arguments about an author's image that changed Maria's mind. It wasn't, but Maria hadn't bothered to explain. "I shall hate every minute of it," she said now. "But I'll be there."

"WHY HAVE YOU HIRED A FIRM OF PRIVATE DETECTIVES?" Phil's face and his tone were grim. There were little white lines of tension around his mouth. They made a marked tracery on his tanned skin. His hand, long and elegant and well cared for, lay over the envelope containing the statement. He'd not opened it. He'd simply taken it from her, then asked his question.

Barbie stared at him. Her first reaction was surprise. The checks to Barton Associates were drawn on her personal account. They had nothing to do with the business. "How do you know about it?"

"Never mind that. I want to know why."

She flushed with anger. "None of your damn business!

What I do with my personal money is no concern of yours."

"Yes, I'm afraid it is. Please tell me, Barbie. It will save a lot of trouble." His voice had gentled and she had the distinct impression he was humoring her.

She was sitting across from his desk in a chair of polished mahogany and delicate brocade, and she gripped its arms with cold hands. "Do you keep track of everything I do?" Her voice was a whisper, harsh with pain and dawning knowledge. "It must be Murphy, I suppose. He reports to you, doesn't he?"

"Yes." No apologies or explanations. Just the single word.

"That stinks. That's the lousiest thing I ever heard of."

"No." He shook his head slightly, not wasting too much energy on the gesture. "It's not what you think. I look after you because I love you. You know that."

She took her hands from the chair and wrapped her arms around her torso, shivering with cold. Phil rose and adjusted the air conditioner in the window. Then he went to the Queen Anne table in the corner and poured her a cognac. "Drink this, you'll feel better."

"Nothing will make me feel better. We had something good and you've spoiled it."

He held out the drink. She didn't take it, so he tossed back the pale amber liquid himself, then put the crystal snifter on the table and sat on the corner of the desk. He was closer to her now, not separated by a width of polished rosewood. His opaque eyes studied her face. "Beautiful girl," he said softly. One slim finger reached out to trace the line of her cheek. She was too frozen with shock to pull away.

"Listen, whatever you think this means about you and me we can talk about later. I'll make you understand, I promise. But first I have to know what you've told this guy Barton. Why have you hired him? What is he doing for you? What is he supposed to do? Everything, my love. I can't compromise on that."

"I'm not your anything," she said woodenly. "Not if you'd do a thing like this."

He waited silently. Not moving, not taking his eyes from her. After a few moments she said, "I know about you. That is, I don't know but I suspect. I have for a long time. It doesn't matter to me."

"What doesn't matter?"

"That you're a lawyer for the mob, for racketeers. I don't give a damn about things like that. It's all just money. Money only matters if you don't have any."

"Barton Associates. Why?" he repeated.

"Because a friend is missing. I hired them to find ... my friend."

"You started to say him. Your friend is a man?"

Barbie sighed. This was the one thing she'd always feared. A pitfall more real and better understood than anything to do with Las Vegas and gambling and what they called laundered money. "Yes, my friend is a man." Hopelessly, knowing she'd tell him whatever he asked because his will was stronger than hers, and that in the end he'd be the one to suffer because of it.

"Where did you meet him? How long has he been 'missing,' as you put it?"

"I've known him since I was a kid in high school. He's from the town where I grew up. That is, he worked there. Actually he's from Boston, the North End."

Phil's eyebrows raised slightly. "Interesting. How have you kept in contact with him?"

How—because I know everyone you see, every place you go. That statement wasn't made, but they knew it was true. Both of them knew it now.

"I don't," Barbie said. "I haven't seen him in years, not since before Norma was born." She was sorry she'd mentioned Norma. That part she wouldn't ever tell him. But it was done; she'd spoken her daughter's name as part of this ugly scene. It seemed a desecration. She needed to cover it with more words. "He's a priest. Three years ago he walked out of his rectory and was never heard from again. I know him very well, and that doesn't make sense. I want to find out what happened to him and if he needs any help." She choked over the last words. "I'd like that drink now, please."

Phil moved from the desk and got it for her in silence. After she took the first sip he walked to the window, hands folded behind his back in a characteristic gesture. "It begins to make a crazy kind of sense. This mysterious friend is a priest and Maria is a former nun. So I suppose Maria told you about his disappearance."

"Yes, that's right."

"How come you never mentioned it to me? Aren't I a logical choice of confidant? What do you know about private detectives and tracing missing persons?"

"Very little. But it's my affair. It has nothing to do with you."

He turned back to her. "Yes, it has. But not the way I first thought, apparently. I'm sorry; none of this would have been necessary if you'd told me about it at the start."

"Murphy could have kept his cover. Isn't that the word in your circle?" She couldn't keep the bitterness from her voice.

"I think that's more to do with spies. There's nothing cloak-and-dagger about my work or my clients. I'm no spy."

"Yes you are, you spy on me." She stood up, gathering her handbag and her briefcase from the floor beside the chair. "I have to go. I'm meeting Maria."

"Very well. I'll see you tonight."

She started to shake her head, then stopped. There was little point in it. She would see him tonight. That's how it was. "Yes," she said as she left the office. She didn't want to think about what she was affirming.

Phil stared at the door that closed behind her. His pulse was racing but the anxiety didn't show. After a lifetime's training, his feelings seldom did. But he could sense the blood surging through his body, a tingling composed of the terror of possible loss, and the swift flood of relief when it turned out to be different than he'd suspected. He sat down heavily, put his head in his hands for a moment. He'd disappointed her, made her unhappy, when all he'd ever wanted from the first day was to have her and protect her—protect both of them, Barbie and Norma. Sorrow was a stranger, an enemy he'd kept at bay for nearly twenty years. One great sorrow, and then he'd outlawed that emotion from his life. Now he didn't know how to deal with the lump in his throat or the empty feeling in his belly. He jerked himself upright and savagely pushed the buzzer that summoned his secretary.

She appeared instantly. "Call that food store on Ninth Avenue and Forty-first," he told her. "The Italian place. I want them to deliver some things to Mrs. Gold this afternoon. Some of their special goat cheese, and those olives and sausages she likes. And a couple of bottles of the Frascati red, the '65. She likes that too."

The secretary knew the Frascati red was a rarity; usually only the white was exported. But she'd find some. That was how she kept her job. That and her English accent and equally English discretion. "Will that be all, Mr. Williams?"

He nodded. It wasn't enough, in this situation nothing could be, but it was a start. A way of saying he was sorry, that he loved her. The only way he knew. There was one other thing, but he'd do it himself. He spent the next hour on some business that couldn't wait, then walked round the corner to

F.A.O. Schwarz on Fifth and Fifty-eighth. He'd seen the thing last week and rejected it as too crazy and extravagant. Today he didn't think so. It was still there. A giraffe in tawny plush, with incredibly lifelike and soulful brown eyes. Allowing for the elongated neck it stood five feet tall. And it cost three hundred and fifty dollars, because it was motorized. Buried in the realistic pelt at the shoulder were three buttons; one propelled the creature forward, one back, and the third caused the head to dip and turn. Maybe in real life giraffes weren't beasts of burden, but Norma could actually ride this one.

When he'd arranged for it to be delivered, he felt much better.

WALKING TO THE PLAZA, BARBIE TRIED TO IMAGINE LIFE without Phil. It was a surprisingly unpleasant thought. She was used to him, that must be it. And he and Norma adored each other. But could it ever be the same again? Would this shattered, betrayed feeling go away? She walked into the hotel and waited for the glamour of the place to give her the usual buzz. It didn't happen. Most times she thought to herself, here I am, Barbie Korman from Revere, hobnobbing with the elite. That's why she had her hair done here rather than someplace closer to home. Today the magic was tarnished and the music flat and tuneless.

Maria was waiting for her by the elevator. "I was afraid to go up without you. I've never been in a beauty parlor in my life. What's the matter? What happened, Barbie? You look awful."

"I'm okay. I'll tell you about it over lunch. Let's go. Dimitri gets hysterical if he's kept waiting."

The hairdressing salon at the Plaza wasn't particularly elegant. It should have been, of course, given the decor of the rest of the hotel. But somehow this particular enclave had been forgotten in the periodic refurbishings undergone by the landmark lady on the edge of the park. Instead the salon was a smallish place with half a dozen driers and only three combing-out stations. Dimitri was small too, a sort of miniaturized man with a sycophantic air and a twittering manner. He kissed Barbie enthusiastically on both cheeks. "Darling, you are too gorgeous for words. The dress is divine."

It was pale ivory with a silky sheen and a tight brown suede belt. The skirt ended six inches above her knees and flared slightly around her long, perfect legs. When she put it on that morning, the first time she'd worn it, Barbie had been pleased with the effect and anticipated just such a comment from Dimitri. Now she hardly heard him. "This is my friend Maria Trapetti. She's just written a best-seller."

"Barbie!" Maria couldn't get used to Manhattan hyperbole. It was a game, of course, but one she didn't know how to play. "I hope it will be a best-seller. I don't know if it will be."

"Of course it will be," Dimitri said. "And you need a new image, right?" He reached up and fingered her thick, curly hair. "Something that will be easy to take care of, and look terrific when you're on television and signing autographs."

"That's it," Barbie said. Maria sighed in resignation and allowed herself to be led to the sink for a shampoo. Later Dimitri and Barbie conferred, standing behind her so she could only see them in the mirror.

"The temptation is to cut it short and just let all the curls go natural," the little man said. "On you, of course, the shorter the better." He turned to Barbie and touched her dark red hair with a proprietary gesture. "But for Maria, I'm not so sure."

Barbie concentrated on her friend's appearance and ignored the dull ache that remained in the pit of her stomach. "It's so thick. That's the problem."

"Yes, but if we cut it properly that will be an advantage." Dimitri studied Maria's reflection in the mirror, putting his tiny hands on either side of her face and tilting her head to the side. "She has classical features. A nice oval face and a good chin. I think we want to frame all that, soften it."

Maria felt like a specimen in a zoo. She closed her eyes when he started to cut and only opened them when she felt the warmth of the blow dryer and the tugging motions of his brush. Even at that early stage it was possible to see what he'd done. Her dark hair was now a little below chin length, not much different than it had been before. But it was shaped in layers that molded her head, and somehow he'd made the tight curls into gentle waves. She'd always admired Barbie's bangs and secretly hoped she might have them too, though she'd been too intimidated to say so. Dimitri hadn't given her bangs, he'd swept her hair back from her forehead and exposed the strong widow's peak from which it grew. Because it was so thick and because he was skilled, there was a natural lift and buoyancy to the cut. Maria was very pleased and embarrassed by her pleasure. She wondered what Tom would say.

They left the hairdresser's and went down to the Palm Court. Every table was taken, or so it seemed to Maria. Barbie

306

spoke to the headwaiter, who obviously knew her, and the two women were at once ushered to a small, well-placed table. A waiter appeared instantly. Barbie asked for a cognac to come before her spinach and bacon salad and Maria was surprised, but didn't comment. "Perrier water for my friend," Barbie said. Maria smiled her thanks. She'd been wondering if she dared ask for a Coke in such a setting. Perrier water. She'd have to remember that.

"You're certainly well treated here," she told Barbie.

"Phil gives the maitre d' enough *vigorish* in the course of a year to guarantee it." Barbie was surprised to hear herself say that so casually. As if Phil and her connection with him wasn't a pain in her stomach and a cold feeling around her heart.

"What's *vigorish?*"

"Yiddish for graft, small bribes. Like *baksheesh,* as the Arabs say. A word for it in every language."

The drinks came, and the salads. Barbie finished her cognac quickly and called for another. "What's wrong?" Maria asked, looking at her friend's untouched plate. "Do you want to tell me?"

Barbie started to shrug, but it turned into a shudder. "I just found out that my accountant spies on me for Phil. So he knows everything I do with my money. And he keeps watch over me. He didn't admit the last part, but I know it's true."

"How did you find out?"

"You don't sound surprised," Barbie said instead of answering the question.

"I'm not. Tom told me some things about who Phil really is."

"About being a lawyer for crooks, you mean. I know that, it's not what I'm upset about. I didn't think he let any of that touch me, that's all. I was a fool, I guess. But I didn't think so."

Again Maria remembered the bookmakers in the pantry. She was always trying to fathom Barbie's amorality, and always failing. "What tipped you off?" she asked once more.

Barbie told her. Maria toyed with her fork, her own appetite gone. "Did you learn anything about Joe from the detectives?"

"Not yet. I won't give up, though. I'm going to find him."

"Maybe he doesn't want to be found. Have you considered that?"

"Yes. I won't necessarily get in touch. I just want to know he's all right."

"I see. And what about Phil? Where does that stand?"

"No place different," Barbie said softly. "I don't know if I can explain. I'm not walking out on him or anything like that."

Maria was astonished to feel relief at those words. Then she realized that she'd been afraid Barbie would incur some terrible punishment if she attempted to break with Phil. "Okay, you don't have to explain. I just wanted to know."

"He'll be at the house tonight. Don't say anything about all this, please."

"No, of course I won't. Anyway, I won't be there." She smiled shyly. "Tom called after you left. We're going out."

Barbie looked up and suddenly said, "Maria, I've got to ask, are you on the pill?"

"Birth control? That's what you mean, isn't it?"

"Naturally. I know Catholics aren't supposed to, but—"

"What Catholics are supposed to do doesn't seem very important to me lately," Maria interrupted. "I'm not on the pill, as you put it. I don't know anything much about it. But I should be, I guess."

"Yes. You should see a doctor and get a prescription. I'll make an appointment." Barbie looked around for the waiter. She surprised four different men who were staring at her. "Let's get out of here," she said. "Let's go across to Bergdorf's and spend a lot of money."

"I don't have a lot of money. And I can't just keep letting you do everything for me."

"Don't be an ass. You're going to have plenty of money pretty soon. You can pay me back. Besides, you're in love and I feel lousy. Buying clothes is good for both conditions."

"I'm not, you know," Maria said.

"Not what?"

"In love. I like Tom. I like what . . . well, what we do together. But I don't think I love him. I don't know what I feel."

"Welcome to the club," Barbie said.

THE DAY SHE SIGNED HER CONTRACT WITH OAKES AND Randolph, Maria met Si Shore for the first time. Tom had mentioned his brother once or twice but Maria didn't expect him to be at the restaurant. She'd thought she was meeting only Tom for lunch after the morning session at the publishers. But she knew who Si was as soon as she saw him. He was sitting next to Tom and the resemblance was real, however hard to pin down. The two men were deep in conversation and neither saw her come into P.J.'s, where, according to Tom, they served the best hamburgers in the world. She took a moment to study them.

Si was a head taller than Tom, he carried the stocky build they shared with more assurance. And his hair wasn't gray, it was sandy colored and fell in a boyish shock over his forehead. Maybe he was younger.

"Yeah, by four years," Tom said after the introductions were complete and she'd asked the question. "But Si was born a serious old man. Forget him. How'd your meeting go?"

Maria reddened with pleasure. "I probably shouldn't say so, but marvelous. I felt like a queen. Everybody made a fuss over me. And the rewrites they're suggesting are simple. Nothing very major."

"Good. Sheila Wayne's a good editor. I don't know her personally, but I've asked around. She's okay. You can trust her. Not that any writer should trust a publisher too far. Speaking of which, did you get the money?"

"Not yet. They said they'd mail the check in a couple of days."

Si grimaced and spoke for the first time. "The check's in the mail. It's got whiskers."

Maria looked blank.

"That's what people say when they're avoiding bill collectors," Tom explained. Then, to his brother, "I warned you, one of the world's innocents. Just escaped from the cloister."

Maria had tried to tell him what a cloister was, and that she'd never been in one, but he persisted in using the word in its popular sense. She decided to ignore it. "I'm interested in your work, Si. Tom never talks about it."

"That's because he's ashamed of me. He thinks Spanish Harlem's a lost cause and my little operation is pointless."

"Mental masturbation," Tom said. "Kidding yourself that you're getting something done, when what you really have to do is change the system so there aren't any more goddamn Spanish Harlems."

"There you have the well picked over bones of an old argument," Si said. "Not worth resurrecting. You don't look like any nun I've ever seen. No wonder the publisher made a fuss over you."

The non sequitur startled her for a moment, then Maria became aware of her appearance, as she did so often lately, and was glad the food arrived so she didn't have to acknowledge the compliment.

She was wearing the suit Barbie made her buy at Bergdorf's. It was heavy white linen and at first she'd complained about how impractical it was, but Barbie assured her that these days what looked like linen was really synthetic, at least partly so, and could be thrown in the washing machine. Maria wasn't likely to throw this outfit in the washing machine. It cost two hundred dollars and had a loose boxy jacket lined with printed scarlet silk worn over a matching blouse, and a linen skirt that hugged her buttocks and needed a discreet slit in the side to allow her to walk.

"It was made for you," Barbie had enthused. She was right.

After Maria bought the suit she steeled her courage and changed from a girdle to panty hose. She'd been rewarded with the kind of looks that Barbie always got from men—something she never expected to experience, and was slightly ashamed of enjoying it quite as much as she did.

Tom was grinning at her, as if he'd followed the whole sequence of thoughts in her head. "My little caterpillar has turned into a butterfly recently," he told his brother. "Helped by her gorgeous girlfriend. You can look, but don't touch. I saw her first." They laughed together and ate the hamburgers, which were as superb as promised. Toward the end of the meal Tom withdrew a newspaper from behind him on the seat. "Have you seen this?" He handed it to Maria.

A picture of Philocles Williams was on the front page. He was coming out of a federal courtroom walking beside a man who was shielding his face from the cameras. Williams wasn't hiding his. He'd stared at the photographer with a look of eloquent disdain. "Lawyer Gets Bail for Man Reputed to Head Professional Hit Men," the caption read.

YEARS BEFORE, DURING THE RIPENING OF THAT PHENOMENON known as the Jazz Age, a young woman named Patsy Williams was sent to a finishing school in Switzerland. She was eighteen years old, youngest member of a clan long the doyens of Chesapeake Bay, laden with old money and old sins. The family Williams reaped the rotten harvest of 1929 at approximately the same time that daughter Patsy finished her expensive education and was ready to come home and come out. Since cash was suddenly in short supply, albeit the base of the Williamses' fortune was land and not seriously affected by the crash, her father decreed that Patsy should embark on a "grand tour." It was cheaper to keep an heiress in Europe than in Maryland in those days.

Patsy didn't mind. She and Cousin Emily, chosen as companion by virtue of being over forty and genteelly poor, said good-bye to the dour Swiss. Then the attractive Miss Williams set out to "do" the Continent. It did her, as it happened, but at first that wasn't apparent. London fascinated, Paris charmed, Brussels and Amsterdam were boring, but the Riviera was delightful. When the autumn winds of 1930 blew cold and wet and the pleasures of Nice began to pale, Patsy and Emily wandered south in search of the sun.

They crossed into Italy at Genoa, took one look at it, and boarded yet another train for Florence. Patsy decided that she adored the Italians, but that Florence was not her kind of place. Too wearing. Aggressive beauty that accosted one at every turn with incessant demands for appreciation. So, restless, homesick, and chilled to the marrow by the unheated marble corridors and high ornate ceilings of the Renaissance, the woman and the girl moved on to Rome. The city on the Tiber did not disappoint; a practiced whore, she knew exactly which face to show the soul-sick Americans.

December turned inexplicably balmy, the low rays of the sun at its nadir gentled the faded yellow magnificence of the architecture, and the Romans, elated by their false spring, left their drafty houses and began once more living in their natural habitat, the street. Patsy Williams was ravished by Rome before she was seduced by Alexandros Manos; the one event made the other easy.

"It's for *Natale,* signorina. To think of Christmas. *La Madonna e Jesus.*" The young man bounded up the Spanish Steps alongside Patsy, his long legs taking two steps to every one of hers, so he was always just in front of her, waving the lurid picture of the Virgin and Child under her turned-up nose.

"No, thank you. No, *grazie.*" Patsy kept shaking her bobbed blond head, but the would-be salesman pretended not to notice.

"You *Americana,* no? This very good picture for *Americana* lady. I sell cheap. So I can go home visit my poor mama in Greece for *Natale.*"

Patsy narrowed her blue-gray eyes and studied him. Beautiful. There was no other word for such a boy. And Greek, not Italian, which added the pleasure of the unexpected. "What are you doing in Rome?" He looked at her blankly. "Why are you here?" she repeated.

The boy shrugged and managed to make the gesture look elegant. "I study the art. And the English. I speak good, no?"

"Not bad," Patsy conceded. "Did you paint that?" She pointed to the picture he was trying to sell. They'd reached the top of the steps near the mellow facade of the convent of

Trinità dei Monti; behind them, the lush gardens of the Villa Medici, below, the joyous jumble of the Piazza di Spagna. And though it was December, the smell of oleander scented the morning and birds sang with spring exuberance. Patsy sighed deeply and settled on a bench. The stone was warm to her buttocks, she could feel the heat through her heavy tweed skirt.

"Me!" The boy spoke with indignation. Patsy had difficulty recalling her question. Oh yes, the picture. "I no paint this garbage," he was saying. And to prove his point, he ripped the garish thing in two. "Soon I go to America. Become great painter and have many dollars. My name it is Alexandros Manos. You remember my name, pretty *Americana* lady. You never gonna forget you meet me."

Which was true.

Soon Patsy left to meet Emily at the nearby English Tea Room, where they hoped to pay homage to the ghosts of Byron and Shelley and Keats. Whether the poets saw them is debatable. Manos definitely did. All that day he followed the two women. By evening he knew the location of their hotel and had a fairly sound idea of their habits. It had been time-consuming, but Manos judged it worthwhile. Rich American girls did not often come so tantalizingly close.

Thereafter, Alexandros dogged the women's footsteps. Finally Patsy and Emily agreed to have dinner with him. One thing led to another and Rome, fickle courtesan that she was, obliged by becoming wet and stormy. Emily caught cold and was confined to her room. So Patsy went along to meet Alexandros at the church of Santa Cecilia, where he had promised to show them a particularly beautiful painting.

"Now, *cara mia,* you will do me the honor to look at some of my paintings. It is not far from here my studio."

He led her through the narrow streets of picturesque Trastevere and Patsy noted only his broad back, his narrow hips, the way his dark hair curled in the drizzly rain, and how white were his teeth when he turned and smiled at her. "But I didn't realize!" She protested when he unlocked his studio door. "This is where you live, Alexandros. I can't come here alone." Her eyes fastened on the big bed in the center of the room.

"Ah, *cara,* you are not alone, you are with me. And only I want you to see my paintings. I want you to know I don't lie when I tell you that someday I am famous."

Patsy let him lead her inside.

When this art exhibition finished up in Alexandros' bed, both were surprised at how easy it had been, albeit for different reasons.

For a while Patsy was besotted with her Adonis and conspired with him to create opportunities for lovemaking away from the watchful eye of Emily. Then, in February of 1931, she realized she was pregnant, and infatuation turned to fear and dislike.

Manos gallantly offered to marry her; such had been his intention from the beginning. Patsy might have agreed out of desperation, but Emily was neither as stupid nor as blind as the lovers supposed. She had fathomed the realities of the alliance some weeks before and sent for aid. Mrs. Williams arrived in March, took one look at the man who had impregnated her daughter, and sent him away with a check for five hundred dollars and a threat of legal action should he ever attempt to presume on the acquaintance.

The redoubtable Maryland matron was dismayed that the pregnancy had progressed beyond the point where a simple operation could swiftly terminate it, but true to her heritage, she coped. Patsy was sent to a convent near Frascati. The discretion of the good sisters was ensured by a large emolument, should Christian charity prove insufficient.

The son of Patsy and Alexandros was born in September 1931. He was an infant extraordinary in only one particular. The blond hair of his mother had been transmitted to him as pure white. A few weeks after birth the light blue of his eyes began to assume the silvery cast they would have all his life.

The name Manos appeared nowhere on the birth certificate; Mrs. Williams saw to that. But she could not prevent her daughter from naming the child Philocles, a bit of whimsy that, without explanation, Patsy insisted upon. Shortly thereafter, the three women and the infant took ship for America.

Patsy's mother suggested adoption, but perversely, the girl would not sign the papers. Instead she agreed to an arrangement whereby her son and his "Aunt Emily" were installed in an apartment in Trenton, New Jersey. Trenton was chosen because Mrs. Williams had inherited property there.

Once having made her stand for motherhood, Patsy ceased to be interested in the fruit of her Roman winter. A check was sent monthly to a Trenton bank, and it was as large as it needed to be to provide Emily and the boy with those things deemed necessities by people such as the Williamses. Thus there was money for an excellent private education, but very little for clothes, movies, records, or any other of the accoutrements of the good life in thirties and forties America.

Philocles was raised to believe that his parents had died at sea shortly after his birth and that Aunt Emily supported him on the proceeds of the insurance. "I must tell you the truth, my dear," Emily said the evening of his seventeenth birthday. "I don't like to hurt you, but I've thought about it and prayed, and now I believe you must know before you go to Yale next month."

So did the boy learn that his father was a Greek fortune hunter who had dismissed Philocles' existence as having no bearing on his life, and his mother a wealthy Chesapeake Bay socialite, now married, with other children whom she did acknowledge.

A few days after the revelation Philocles went to Maryland, determined to confront the woman who had borne him and dismissed him with equal ease. He watched daily outside her great mansion, unknowingly imitating the way his father had stalked her earlier in Rome. Patsy usually rode in the early morning, so eventually the boy's vigil was rewarded by a moment when he faced his mother alone, beyond the heavy iron gates of the estate. Emily had already telephoned Patsy and warned her of what she'd done and what the consequences were likely to be. Patsy wasn't truly surprised when a tall, white-haired young man stepped out of the shrubbery and stood waiting in the middle of the road.

She was astride a handsome roan too well trained to shy at the appearance of the stranger. The horse merely stopped and waited. Patsy stared at Philocles and he stared at her. Had she been in any doubt as to his identity, his extraordinary coloring would have convinced her. But there was no doubt. Mother and son faced each other across the abyss of their separate pain. Patsy opened her mouth to speak, but no words came.

Behind the boy was the great house, silhouetted by morning, growing lighter and more real against the dawning sky. Her life, the life she'd made for herself on the ruins of impetuosity and stupidity, was at risk. Philocles still said nothing, only stared at her. Patsy felt as if she were drowning in his silent accusation. Then he stretched out one tentative, seeking hand. "Mother, why—"

Patsy did the only thing it seemed possible to do. She lifted her riding crop, struck out wildly to drive him from her path, and spurred the horse on in a gallop.

For some moments the bastard child remained in the rhododendrons where he'd fallen when the thong of his mother's whip lashed his cheek. Eventually, he rose, and brushed himself off, and returned to Trenton. Emily, who realized that she had loosed Armageddon with her tongue, remained silent. So did he. They never spoke of the matter again.

At Yale, Williams was a satisfactory student. He might have been more, for he had keen intelligence, but he chose to put the greater part of his energy into earning money rather than grades. Opportunities for enrichment were not rife on the New Haven campus. Most of the undergraduates had no need of them. Williams, however, discovered a fact that was to serve him many times. The rich were miserly by nature.

Philocles made a connection in town that allowed him to buy cigarettes at a dime less than the normal price, from a gentleman who offered no explanations about the source of his supply. They were eagerly bought by his fellow students at a nickel below par. This didn't earn Williams huge sums, but it eased his straitened circumstances somewhat and allowed him to develop a social life for the first time. He knew that he was participating in an illegal activity, but this only made him cautious. It hardly seemed a moral question. Those who purchased the cigarettes were equally guilty, but they wouldn't even be charged if the operation were uncovered.

As much as anything this perception of justice in America shaped Williams's decision to become a lawyer. The fees for law school, he knew, would be paid without question by the family in Maryland; the rest he would take care of himself. Along with this ability to make choices based on reality, Philocles developed another talent. He created for himself a fantasy peopled with Greek parents and innumerable relations and some dark political maneuverings that had caused him to be sent to safety in America, to live with a distant relative and assume the protective coloration of the name Williams. This make-believe world he shared with his new friends and acquaintances, until eventually he believed in it more than he believed in the naked agony of the morning he had met his mother.

Such were the skills and attitudes he took to Harvard Law School in 1951. They served as well in Cambridge as they had in New Haven. Nickel profits on packs of Camels ceased to be sufficient for his needs, so Williams organized a service just as necessary to his fellow students, and one for which they were prepared to pay more. He engaged the services of a former professor whose brilliant career had been cut short by drink. This gentleman was willing to write papers for the price of a bottle of Riesling. Williams rewrote the themes in such a fashion that they could not be detected as coming from the pen of a legal savant, and sold them for many times their cost. It did not surprise him that he had no shortage of customers.

In 1953 two things happened. Philocles Williams married Betty Jane Chase, beloved only daughter of the senior partner of the Wall Street law firm of Chase Fulham and Winston, and he was admitted to the bar in the state of New York. The two events were not unrelated. The following week, Emily, her task apparently completed, had a heart attack and died. Philocles felt a genuine sense of loss. Now he was truly a man without any ties to childhood or ancestry, but he envisaged a future of ease that would compensate.

Then Betty Jane, chosen for her ability to ensure his success, spoiled everything. On a summer night when they were driving home from Cape Cod, where they'd gone to celebrate their six-months' wedding anniversary, Williams suddenly blacked out behind the wheel. He had never experienced anything similar and he had no warning of the event. He simply lost consciousness for a few seconds, the car went off a bridge into a river, and Philocles's young bride drowned. He emerged unhurt.

Mr. Chase blamed his son-in-law for his daughter's death, though there was no evidence of negligence. Unfortunately for Williams, Chase had not yet bestowed any sizable wealth on Betty Jane, so there was little for the bereaved husband to inherit. And certainly Philocles could no longer count on a future with Chase Fulham and Winston.

It occurred to Williams to look for a position with another established firm, but the antipathy of the senior Chase indicated that most such doors would remain closed to him. So he used his meager resources to open an office on Fourteenth Street. Then, after hanging out his shingle, Philocles consulted a doctor. No tests showed any explanation of the strange fainting spell he'd had while driving home from Cape Cod. He dismissed any worry about his health, but he took to using taxis and public transportation. Moreover, he decided not to own another automobile until he could afford a chauffeur. It was his intention to hasten that day.

Since Fourteenth Street was in a less desirable part of Manhattan, it was perfect for Williams's purposes. Most among the trickle of clients who came to him were connected one way or another with what is called "the criminal element." Those who were not perpetrators were victims. Williams lawyered for them as well as he was able, and spent more time on the guilty than the innocent. After eighteen months of sleeping in his office and penny-pinching so he could spend money where it would do some good, the opportunity for which he'd been so carefully planning arrived.

THE PHONE KEPT RINGING. WILLIAMS HAD TO ACCEPT THAT IT wasn't a dream. He rolled off the lumpy, narrow couch and staggered to the desk. "Hello, what the hell time is it?"

"Little after two A.M. This Williams?"

"Yeah, I think so."

"You think so? What kind of shit is that? I wanna talk to Williams, the shyster."

"Okay, it's me." He was fully awake now. And he recognized the voice on the other end of the line. He'd been giving the cop fifty bucks a month for nothing but promises. This was the payoff. He could feel it coming, and excitement made his belly tighten. "What have you got, O'Rourke?"

"Kid named Mark Zandino. You know who he is?"

"I know. What's the charge?"

"Morals. I ain't gonna say nothin' more. Just get your ass in gear and get down here in half an hour if you're interested. No longer or we gotta let him call the lawyer he's screamin' for."

"It'll take me an hour. I have to make a stop on the way." Fifty-seven minutes later Williams, carefully shaved and impeccably dressed, met O'Rourke in the precinct lobby. Williams handed over a manila envelope. "This is the bail order. Where's the bondsman?"

O'Rourke jerked his thumb toward a man dozing on a bench in a corner. Williams shook him awake, signed the proper papers, and handed over two hundred dollars. O'Rourke was still looking at the judge's order. "How'd you get to him so fast?"

"Same way I made sure you'd call when the right thing came up." The cop looked blank. "I was prepared, O'Rourke. Careful planning, it's the secret of success. Where's Zandino?"

"Upstairs; let's go."

They climbed two flights. The concrete steps were worn in the center by thousands who had gone this route before them. On the landing outside the third floor, Williams handed

O'Rourke four hundred-dollar bills. That was the absolute end of his money. If this failed, he wouldn't eat for a few days. But he probably wouldn't need to eat. Dead men didn't.

O'Rourke led him down a corridor that smelled of piss and desolation into the room where Mark Zandino waited. "Okay, cutie pie." The policeman spoke in a high falsetto. "Some smart-ass shyster just got you bail."

"Jesus," Williams breathed softly. The boy facing him was about five foot two and exceptionally slim. He had brown eyes that seemed sunk into his head because tears had made his mascara run in black streaks over his heavily rouged cheeks. He was wearing a black ruffled blouse and a tight gold lamé skirt that ended just above high-heeled gold sandals. His waist was cinched by a wide black velvet belt with a rhinestone buckle, and a curly blond wig lay on the table beside him. Williams took it all in while O'Rourke stood and grinned.

"Ain't he a pretty little bugger? And the word is he's got the tightest asshole this side of Brooklyn. Real popular, our Marco."

"Shut up," Williams said softly. And to the sobbing boy, "Come on, Mark, we're getting out of here."

They stopped at the desk in the front hall and a smirking cop handed the boy an innocuous-looking brown tote bag. They both checked the contents and agreed everything was intact. "I have to find a washroom and change," the boy said as soon they were past the desk.

"No you don't, son. We haven't got time for that." Williams hustled his client down the stairs and into a cab. He leaned forward and gave an address in Brooklyn Heights.

"No! I can't go home like this. Who the hell are you anyway? Did my father send you?"

"I'm Philocles Williams, your lawyer. And you might say your father sent me. After a fashion." He reached into the brown bag and took a ten-dollar bill from the wallet in the zippered side pocket. He'd need that to pay the cab fare.

"Give me that." Mark pulled the bag into his lap and began rummaging for things to clean his face. Williams saw the jar of cold cream before Mark had a chance to use it. He took it and the bag and put them on the far corner of the seat. The boy's limp fingers offered little resistance. Mark stared at the lawyer for a moment, then began to shiver and soon to cry.

Forty minutes later, Williams was facing his reluctant client's father. The boy stood between them, still shivering, still crying. His finery glittered in the dim light from a shaded desk lamp. "Marco," the old man said in a tormented whisper. "Marco, how could you do this thing? It's a frame, isn't it? The police did this to you to get at me."

Enrico Zandino, head of one of the most powerful underworld networks on the East Coast, waited for his youngest son to take the escape route he'd been offered. The boy only whispered, "I'm sorry, Papa."

"It's not a frame, Mr. Zandino," Williams spoke with an authority that forced the old man to look at him. "There are a dozen witnesses prepared to swear that your son is a frequent customer at the drag bars in the Village. He is a homosexual, isn't that so, Mark?"

Again the sibilant apology. "I'm sorry, Papa."

The senior Zandino stared at the lawyer and at the grotesque caricature that was his son. A roar of anguish and fury spewed from his throat. It was the cry of a wounded animal and it ended in a stream of maledictions. Finally his rage was spent. "*Infamate.* Get out of my sight." He stumbled across the room and held open the door, and the boy half ran, half crawled into the hall.

When Enrico Zandino turned back to Williams, he was calm. "What do you want?"

"To help you deal with this situation."

"Are you offering to kill my son?" The shrewd, hooded eyes studied the face of the lawyer. "What other solution is there for such a problem?"

"A private clinic, Mr. Zandino. In England, perhaps. With discreet psychiatrists who are experienced in dealing with such things. If I make the arrangements, your name will be kept entirely out of the matter."

The old man walked slowly across the room and seated himself behind the desk. "But you will know my name." He spoke in a conversational tone, inviting the stranger to examine with him the necessity of his own murder.

"Yes," Williams agreed. "But I am trustworthy."

"How do I know that?"

"Because I came here immediately. I did not take what I knew to your enemies. I didn't allow Mark to continue to deceive you. Besides, I am more than normally intelligent. I didn't arrange all this, but I made sure I'd know immediately if an occasion arose when my services would be of use to you."

Zandino looked long into the opaque eyes of the man across

from him. Philocles thought about how many times in history kings had dealt with evil news by killing the messenger. Finally the old man spoke. "You want to work for me?"

"Yes. I will cost you a great deal of money, but I'll earn it."

"You are a lawyer. I have many lawyers."

"I'm better than they are. I'm not just a lawyer, Mr. Zandino. I'm creative. I'm perhaps best described as an expediter."

"Very well. To start with, you can expedite my disgusting son out of my house and into this clinic you spoke of. Fortunately his mother is away tonight. If she ever finds out the truth, I'll kill you myself."

The future of Philocles Williams, Attorney at Law, was assured. It was not quite the same as that which he'd envisioned when he married Betty Jane Chase, but in terms of financial reward, it was perhaps even better.

11

THE SALESGIRL IN JONES'S ON THE PLAZA IN KANSAS CITY
kept ogling DiAnni. She had lank blond hair and a gap-
toothed smile. She was pretty in a way, but Joe was only
half-conscious of her surveillance. He was thinking instead
that Middle America is a state of mind and a loaf of white
bread, maybe whole wheat.

Such impressions had matured during this long blue-and-
gold autumn of 1969. Now, as well as contemplating such
deathless truths, he was dreaming of a tuna sandwich. And
realizing he'd have to settle for white or whole wheat bread;
nobody in Kansas City served rye or pumpernickel. That's
really what the nation's heartland was about. It was insulated
from the edges, and from their ethnic lumps in the melting
pot. Somebody had wrapped a hazy gauze curtain around the
central states, so all the impurities from the coasts would be
filtered out. He sure as hell was one of the impurities. Nonetheless seven months earlier he'd slipped through the scrim,
and come to Missouri by way of Mississippi and Arkansas.
Pete Chiarra and the *Bella Donna* he'd left in Biloxi, a bitter-
sweet parting both men understood as necessary, but regretted.

Ever since, without admitting it to himself, DiAnni had
slowly wended his way north, and planned to turn east.

Kansas City was a slight detour. A guy in St. Louis told him jobs were easy to get in Kansas City. They weren't in St. Louis when Joe was looking, so he'd headed west to the town the natives called "Kanscity," as if it was one word. Since September he'd worked in a dry cleaning plant downtown near the stockyards. Now the smell of chemicals permeated his clothes and clung to his flesh. He tasted carbon tetrachloride in the back of his throat and he longed hopelessly for a submarine sandwich on crusty Italian bread, stuffed with hot sausages and dripping tomato sauce. He'd found a place called Luigi's on the lower end of Walnut Street, but the people who ran it weren't real ginnies. They spoke with a Missouri twang and didn't put garlic in their food.

"You want something, mister?" The salesgirl had finally decided to speak, but her question was breathless and a little nervous.

DiAnni wondered if she identified him as alien to the environment. He grinned at her. "Sorry, I was daydreaming. Yeah, sure. I want a newspaper."

The blonde handed him a copy of that morning's *Star* and he paid for it, adding another grin as well. The girl smiled back her gap-toothed smile. Won over by my fatal charm, DiAnni thought as he escaped to the coffee shop across the road. He passed up the tuna sandwich and settled for a jelly donut. At least they knew about jelly donuts in Kansas City. The memory of the girl lingered.

In the Bahamas the casual alliances he'd formed with women had seemed appropriate and acceptable. But he hadn't continued the practice after he left the boat. The girls in America struck him as sad. Maybe it was just his own sadness, echoing back to him in the tentative smiles and the hungry eyes of the women. Sighing, he pushed the thought away and glanced at his watch. One-thirty. He had an hour and a half to kill before he was due to work the graveyard shift at the plant. Three to eleven. Hours for someone like him, with no family and no social life, hours for a corpse. He ordered another donut and opened the paper.

It was two-twenty when Joe paid his bill and folded the paper. Columns of legal notices covered the back page. He looked at them unseeing, then caught his breath and looked again. The announcement was almost obscured by the centerfold. Only the name DiAnni showed. It was enough to arrest his attention because he'd been a non-person for nearly four years. He hadn't received even a piece of mail in all that time.

Now his name was on the back page of the *Kansas City Star*. "DiAnni, Joseph—late of Boston and Revere Massachusetts. Contact atty D.G. Soldi re inhrtnce . . ."

Joe stared at the notice. The abbreviated word had to mean inheritance. From his mother. She was the only possibility, and that had to mean she was dead. He felt a pain in his gut, then suppressed it. He'd spent a long time forgetting she was alive; it was too late to mourn her death. And what would she have to leave him that she had not already bestowed? Money. Nothing else would cause an attorney to take an interest. From where, he asked himself, and thought of the little apartment on Hanover Street and of the cheese factory, long since sold. He thought too of the don, and the pain came churning back into his stomach.

Carefully Joe folded the paper and left the coffee shop. He'd missed the bus, so he had to thumb a ride downtown, and he was an hour late for work. The foreman gave him a dark look, but didn't say anything. Joe punched his time card and mentally subtracted two dollars and twenty-five cents from his pay. Not very important. He lived cheap, in a furnished room with a gas ring and a toilet down the hall. He wouldn't miss a couple of bucks. Soon the familiar smell of chemicals overwhelmed him, and for a while they drove away the memory of the notice in the *Star*.

He didn't allow himself to think of it again until he lay in his narrow, uncomfortable bed, watching the neon sign flash on and off across the street. He'd pulled down the paper windowshade, but it was full of holes, so the light came in anyway and made a flickering pattern on the worn blanket. Intermittently it showed up the back of his large hands. Tough hands now, but still capable of reminding him of things he didn't want to remember. He shoved them under the cover. Anointed hands were a burden in a life like his. They weighed him down, were baggage he wanted to jettison but couldn't. And why hadn't the ad spoken about them? "Reverend DiAnni" would have been a more certain identification. So maybe it didn't mean him. Nobody knew he was in Kansas City. Why should he be the same Joseph DiAnni the lawyer was looking for? Because the phrase "late of Boston and Revere" made it a near certainty. Maybe D. G. Soldi was a sensitive type who didn't want to tell the world that the man he sought was an ex-priest.

The question kept him awake a long time, and when he finally slept it was a restless and dream-ridden slumber. At eight he awoke and realized that the decision was made. The paper lay on the battered bureau where he'd left it. Last night he'd underlined the Boston telephone number; now he went to make the call.

That afternoon he told the foreman at the dry cleaning plant he'd be quitting at the end of the week. The man only shrugged. Joe spent the next few days thinking about his conversation with D. G. Soldi. He'd been asked the name of his mother and father, his former "profession," and his mother's address until her death three months earlier. He gave all the information in simple declarative sentences, didn't say that he'd been unaware of his mother's dying, and asked no questions either about that or the mysterious inheritance.

"Well, Father," the lawyer said at last. "You seem to be the man I'm looking for. There's a bit of money waiting for you if you care to come and claim it."

DiAnni winced. "I left the priesthood some time ago," he said stiffly. And knew himself a fool to say this instead of all the more important things.

"Yeah, okay. I forgot, sorry. Do you plan to return to Boston in the near future, Mr. DiAnni?" The "mister" was emphasized in a way that seemed insolent.

"How did you know I was in Kansas City?"

"I didn't. I've been running ads in all the major papers across the country." There was a pause and Soldi added, "Standard procedure in cases like this."

That wasn't entirely true, but Joe didn't know it. "I see. Okay, I'll come see you sometime next week." When he hung up, he'd felt dizzy and nauseated because it suddenly hit him that his mother was really dead. All that anger and savage will was ended at last, or released. He didn't know which. Neither did he know why he'd agreed to go to Boston, how much money was involved, or why he wanted it. Finally he told himself this was just something he had to do, and gave notice at the plant and began making preparations to go home. Except that he didn't call it that in his head. He thought of it as going back.

For the lawyer, the telephone conversation was a more satisfactory thing. He waited for the priest to click off the line, then depressed the button on the phone, released it, and dialed the area code for Manhattan. He was charged with nervous energy born of elation. When you produce results for a man of

Mr. Williams's stature, the future might hold any manner of promise.

AFTER THE PAINFUL REVELATIONS THAT TOOK PLACE THE DAY Barbie learned the truth about her accountant, Phil began giving her presents. Expensive things like a set of Louis Vuitton luggage, a string of matched pearls from Tiffany, and an exquisitely decorated china egg in the style of Fabergé. He'd given her lovely gifts before, but only on occasions such as her birthday or Christmas. These offerings were different, and she recognized it.

"Why do you let him keep giving you all this stuff?" Maria asked. "He thinks he's buying you."

"No," Barbie said softly. "He's just trying to soothe his conscience. It matters to him that I was angry about the spying." She adjusted the position of the china egg on her dressing table. The stem of violets that encrusted the top caught the sunlight, and the tiny topaz chips at their hearts winked up at her. "It's beautiful, isn't it?"

"Yes, of course. But aren't you angry?"

"Not anymore. I was at first. Then I understood. It's the only way he knows. The way he always does things. It was stupid of me to expect anything different."

Maria shook her head, and her thick chestnut hair punctuated her remarks. "It's stupid for you to go along with it. You're getting awfully deep into something I don't think you understand."

"Of course I understand it. Besides, I'm already in deep. I have been for years. And Phil's helping me find Joe." Maria's eyes widened in surprise, but Barbie ignored them. "Phil knows how to go about things like that. If anyone can find Joe, he can."

Maria shifted her position on the foot of the bed and spoke slowly and cautiously. "Honey, I know it's none of my business. But I love you and I love Joe, and I'm scared to death. Say Phil does locate him; what's going to happen then?"

"I'm not sure." Barbie's voice was hesitant but unafraid. "He won't hurt him. Don't worry about anything like that. Phil isn't crazy and he's not insanely jealous."

"Damn it! How can you be so innocent? Phil's a crook. How in hell can you know what he will or won't do?"

Barbie giggled. "Tom Shore's had a big affect on your vocabulary. You don't sound like an ex-nun anymore." Then, before Maria could reply, "Phil's not a crook. He represents crooks. It's not the same."

Maria sighed in frustration, then made a wry face. "You're right about me, anyway. If Lizzie could see me now."

"Who's Lizzie?"

"Mother Superior of the convent in Wrentham. Mother Mary Elizabeth, but we called her Lizzie behind her back. She was a narrow-minded bitch, but I suppose she meant well."

Barbie looked hard at her friend. Maria had changed more than her language, her hairstyle, and her clothes in recent months. She was different in ways that weren't so easy to catalog. "Do you ever miss your old life?"

"Hell, no!" With so much emphasis, the certitude seemed an affectation.

"You're sure," Barbie pressed. "Nothing about it?"

This time Maria hesitated before she answered. "Not what it was," she said finally. "Maybe I miss what it was supposed to be, what I was looking for when I entered."

"Did you ever find it?"

"Once or twice, perhaps," Maria admitted softly. "Not often enough to make the rest of it worthwhile."

Barbie nodded. "Yes, I can understand that." A few times she'd almost spoken about the Lady, believing she could tell Maria if anyone. But something always held her back. The memory of Joe's incredulity perhaps, despite the fact that he was a priest. Or just because it was painful to talk about something that had been so extraordinarily wonderful and wasn't anymore. Barbie hadn't seen the Lady in years. "I do understand," she repeated now. But she didn't say more.

Impulsively, Maria reached out and hugged her. "Darling Barbie. That seems to be your role in life. Understanding people who probably don't understand themselves." She pulled back from the embrace and their eyes met and held. "Be careful, please. I don't trust Phil; he frightens me."

Barbie started to answer but there was a knock on the door. It was Stella, with a question about Norma's regular visit to the doctor that afternoon. After she left, Barbie seemed preoccupied and the mood of girlish confidences was broken. "I've got to get dressed." She opened the closet with a pout of dissatisfaction and stared at the long rows of clothes. "What are you doing today?"

"We're supposed to be going uptown to see Si's youth hostel. Tom's been promising to take me for weeks and I finally pinned him down to a definite date."

"If uptown means Spanish Harlem, you're the one who'd better be careful," Barbie said.

WHEN SIMON WAS FOUR AND THOMAS WAS EIGHT, THEIR father was killed by a streetcar that veered off the track and onto the sidewalk at the exact moment Mr. Shore was locking the door of his small shoe-repair shop in the Brownsville section of Brooklyn. Sadie announced the fact of their loss to her sons with quiet dignity, and without tears.

"What will we do now, Mama?" Tom asked.

"We'll do things right. Take care of ourselves and get along. You'll both be the best at everything. You're his legacy, you'll do it for your father's memory." Sadie addressed her words to Simon, although it was Tommy who had asked the question, as if she already knew which of her sons was more likely to do things right.

Tom Shore was early marked by his particular genius. English teachers sent home ecstatic reports, other teachers bemoaned the boy's lack of application and interest. Si was different. All his grades were equally good. He didn't shine in one thing, the way Tom did. Si worked harder than anybody else and got top marks in every subject. In this he was a product of his mother's influence. She worked twenty hours out of every twenty-four.

The streetcar company paid compensation, a settlement made hastily out of court because it was obvious there had been negligence in the maintenance of the track, and Sadie used the money to buy the tenement in which she and her sons lived. Thereafter their income came from rents. To ensure that those were adequate, Sadie kept her six apartments in excellent condition. She did everything herself: plumbing, carpentry, painting—only the occasional electrician was hired help. That was her way of doing things right and thus honoring her dead husband's memory, and Simon watched and understood, and wished that his brother did not cause his mother so much worry.

"Writing books you can't make a living, Tommy," she told the older boy when he quit college at the start of his junior year. To Simon she need make no such protestations.

Si majored in sociology at Columbia and graduated *cum laude* the same day that Tom, recently back from Korea, got a job as a junior editor with a publishing house and moved to Manhattan. Si envied Tom the independence, but that did not alter his own plans. He proceeded to Harvard to take a master's degree in psychology, and remained to get a Ph.D. in behavioral science. If Sadie worried about the practical value of so much education she never said so, perhaps because his lengthy academic career kept her younger son out of the army.

The summer after he was granted his doctorate, Si acquired two more new things: a wife, and a position on the faculty of Amherst College in rural western Massachusetts. The wife was a slender, long-haired Bennington girl. Arty and committed, as such types usually were. The pair were bedded and wedded two months after they met, and since she was nominally Jewish, Si was still doing things more or less right. But by the time he'd been three years a husband and a college professor, Si was bored with both his marriage and his job.

The intensity of conviction that first drew him to the girl proved to be a superficial thing, centered on causes he never judged particularly important. They were thin and brittle and fragile, like her body, liable to shift with any changing current of air. Instructing the youth of privilege who were at Amherst preparing themselves to take over the banks and insurance companies of their fathers was equally without meaning. Occasionally Si pondered the possibility of siring a child upon his wife's angular loins, but this seemed wholly unlikely, and in fact proved to be so. He thought of writing a paper on boredom as a method of contraception, but never quite got around to it. When the girl left him, he almost didn't notice. However since Sadie was ill with a terminal cancer, he kept her from knowing about the separation and subsequent divorce.

"My fault," he told Tom. "I wanted her to lubricate my life, but you've got to ooze your own juices."

When Sadie died, Si stood beside her open grave in the humid torpor of a July midday and listened to the bearded rabbi intone his arcane chants. He did not think of the meaning of the words, nor of his mother's life, but of a class he was scheduled to teach in the autumn. It was listed in the course catalog as The Patterns of Assimilation of Ethnic Minorities in America, 1880–1950. His gaze shifted from the coffin to the sliver of torn black ribbon pinned to his lapel. It was there in acknowledgment of the biblical injunction that he rend his garments in mourning. Si wanted to laugh but he knew no one would understand, not even Tom, and he suppressed the urge.

The moment came for Sadie's sons to recite the *Kaddish,* and Si was comforted to find that he could still read the Hebrew alphabet he'd learned for his *bar mitzvah* and had not looked at since. He found it oddly reassuring that he had no need to refer to the left-hand page that contained a transliteration of the mourner's prayer.

After the funeral, Si returned to Amherst. Next day he drove forty miles to the town of Holyoke, the nearest place with a Jewish community of any size, and located the orthodox *shul*. It was an ancient ramshackle building where the women still sat upstairs on a balcony separated from the fragile old men, who could be found muttering half to themselves and wholly to God in the early hours of each morning. Every day for the next year Si drove to Holyoke to say *Kaddish* for his mother. He had to rise at five to accomplish this before his first class, and after a while the rabbi, astonishingly a man approximately his own age, said it was not necessary. Under the circumstances the professor could say the prayer in the privacy of his home. Shore was not interested in this dispensation and did not avail himself of it.

On the first anniversary of Sadie's death Si returned to Brooklyn for the unveiling of the headstone that marked her grave. Afterwards, he told his brother that he'd given up his professorship. "What'll you do now?" Tom asked. It was almost the identical question he'd asked when their father died. Si promised to let him know. He didn't, until after his scheme was in place and operating.

MARIA HAD BEEN WARNED ABOUT THE NEIGHBORHOOD, BUT IT was many times worse than she'd imagined, and the gray December afternoon didn't help. "It looks like the aftermath of a war," she said.

"Wrong. The aftermath of a battle. The war's still going on." Tom's tone was weary.

"I don't see how Si can stand it." Maria looked at decrepit buildings defaced with spray-painted slogans, windows devoid of glass, broken doors spilling filth and garbage. She could almost hear the soft, slurred sound of rats moving their furry bodies amid the decay. "How does he face this every morning?"

"Either he's a saint or he enjoys pissing in the wind. Take your pick."

"Neither," Si said later. Tom had gone to stare moodily at a huge mural painted on the wall of the narrow entrance hall, and Maria and Si were alone in his tiny office. "I just think somebody's got to try to do something. Somebody's got to give a damn about these kids," he added. Then he clamped his teeth shut and looked grim. "I hate myself when I say things like that. All the liberal, bleeding heart clichés. Step right up, folks, and hear the lecture. Doesn't mean much, but you'll feel good and noble for listening, and I'll get a hard-on from talking. Cheap jollies."

"Don't," Maria whispered. "Don't denigrate yourself or your work like that."

"Oh, Jesus, you're really ready to get the true religion, aren't you? All set to throw yourself on the barricades. How touching."

His bitterness curled around her like whips; it made her cheeks tingle. "What do you want me to say! Isn't this fun? Isn't it great that all these unfortunate boys are here so people like you can vent your do-good instincts!"

A flicker of something like respect passed across Si's face. "So you can fight back. I've wondered. And yeah, maybe that's what you should say. Maybe it's true. I sometimes think the reason neighborhoods like this exist is because we nice middle-class folks need them."

"Do you need this one?" she demanded.

He didn't have a chance to answer. Tom appeared in the doorway. "Have you taken a good look at that picture your sweet little charges painted out there?"

"Yeah, lots of good looks. What do you think of it?"

Tom lit a cigarette and held it between his lips while he spoke. "It scares the shit out of me. I've never seen so much hate plastered on a wall."

"You've got it, brother mine," Si said quietly. "They put the message up there for you to see and you saw. An A for sensitivity."

Maria pushed by both men and ran to look again at the mural. It was superficially innocent, a depiction of the scene outside. There was the street, full of nineteenth-century brownstones encrusted with filth and crumbling from decay. The technique was crude and inexpert, but the colors were bold and the lack of perspective somehow made the picture more savage and immediate. The street in the picture was, like the real one, full of garbage. But in the mural three obviously Hispanic youths were shoveling it into a wheelbarrow. Self-help, she'd thought. Something like that. Only the barrow was pointed at the left-hand corner, and when Maria looked carefully she could see there a tiny representation of the Statue of Liberty. It was so small and poorly done she hadn't noticed it at first. Now she saw that the barrowload of rotten garbage was about to be pushed toward the statue. And a blob she hadn't identified before revealed itself as a pair of rats sitting atop the refuse and looking hungrily at the symbol of the American dream.

Tom came up behind her and laid a gentle hand on her shoulder. The tenderness of his touch contrasted with the ugliness on the wall. "Take a good look at the faces."

The boys in the picture had bloodlust in their dark eyes. The anger poured off the wall and threatened to engulf her, and Maria wondered how she had managed to avoid it when she looked at the mural earlier. "Promise of apocalypse," Tom said. "Do you think Si's little sandbag operation up here is going to hold that back?"

She shivered. Just then, two boys who could have been models for those in the painting walked through the hall. One made a point of brushing up against Maria. She stiffened and felt ashamed in the same instant. *"Follable,"* one of the boys muttered.

"He said you were fuckable," Si translated. He was leaning against the door of his office watching her. Maria couldn't look at him.

"Let's get out of here," she said.

Tom's grip on her arm tightened. "Yeah, let's."

Maria turned back to Si. "Come with us," she said. "Let's all go downtown for dinner." She knew she was pleading and she waited for some sign that Si understood, and had exonerated her. His expression remained pleasant and noncommittal and disinterested.

"No can do, I'm afraid. I'm the only one on duty this evening."

"Oh." Maria felt deflated. She looked away from Si, but that forced her to look again at the mural. She couldn't bear it, and turned back to the office. Si had taken a step toward her. Without warning, he leaned over and kissed her on the cheek. "Thanks for coming," he said.

Maria saw his face in a sudden, revelatory flash. There were crinkles of laughter at the corners of his eyes, which were almost navy blue, and his nose was a little crooked, which was somehow appealing. She didn't speak, but she smiled at him and touched his face with the tips of her fingers. His skin was taut and cool, and the brief tactile contact gave her an unexpected tingle of pleasure.

Tom stared at them both, then pulled Maria toward the door. He didn't say good-bye to his brother.

* * *

It was almost Christmas in Boston. DiAnni realized that he'd returned two days short of the fifth anniversary of Don Stefano's death. It was an ugly, unpleasant coincidence, and it didn't make his homecoming any easier.

Soldi's office was on Friend Street. Removed from the North End, but close enough so he could retain contact. As soon as they met, Joe knew that the little overweight lawyer in the shabby suit was part of the world he'd been running from all his life. He wanted to turn around and run again, but he'd promised himself he wouldn't. All during the long bus ride east he'd chewed at the problem and examined it, and finally he'd concluded that he would take the money his mother had left him and, if there was enough, use it to get a degree in sociology. Twenty years ago, when he was eighteen, he'd promised his father that he was going to help people. Maybe it was time he started. Maybe he could finally grow up enough to stop avoiding all the unpleasant truths he found so distasteful. Maybe he could stop studying his navel and start thinking about something besides himself. The priesthood hadn't changed him; maybe sociology would.

"Seventeen thousand, six hundred and thirty dollars after taxes, the cost of the legal notices, probate charges, and my fee." Soldi pushed the check across the desk. Like the desk, his hand was scarred and grimy. The whole operation was definitely second-rate, maybe third.

"Thank you." DiAnni took the check without looking at it. "Tell me, how did my mother come to you originally? I gather she had you make out her will."

Soldi raised both his hands in a gesture of dissent. "No, nothing like that. I never met the lady. Her legal affairs were handled by a colleague on Hanover Street." He began shuffling through papers, as if he were going to produce the colleague's name.

"Then how did you get involved?"

"The court. I make a specialty of this kind of thing. Finding missing heirs for ten percent of the inheritance. A standard charge in matters of this type. It's all there in the accounting I gave you."

Joe glanced at the paper that had preceded the check across the desk. "Yes, of course." He folded the check and the bill and put them in his wallet. "I'd like to talk to my mother's original attorney, if you'd give me his name."

"Sure, sure. Just a minute." The papers in the top drawer of the desk were scrutinized further. Suddenly Soldi looked up with a grunt of surprise. "Damn! I must be getting old. Forgot to give you this." Another item was pushed across the desk. This one was a sealed envelope with "Joseph" written on it in handwriting DiAnni recognized as his mother's.

"Thank you," he said again. He held the letter in his hand. It was grimy and well-thumbed, as if it had spent time in many drawers before coming to this one. It weighed down Joe's palm, seemed to him to smell of cheroots and rough wine. He rose to leave, thoughts of the nameless attorney who'd prepared his mother's will driven away by her tangible presence. He had to turn back to shake the little man's outstretched hand. "Thanks," he said for the third time. Soldi merely nodded.

Outside the sun was shining and the air was sharp and clear. He walked up Milk Street past Government Center, then down Tremont toward the Park Street subway station, where he could get a trolley to Brighton and the furnished room he'd rented the day before. But when he came to the subway, he changed his mind and turned right into the Common. The usual Christmas manger scene was in place. Numbers of small children were standing beside earnest parents who pointed to the figures of the nativity drama and made edifying explanations. Joe stood watching for some moments, then walked deeper into the park and sat beneath a leafless maple tree.

Eventually, he took the envelope from his pocket and opened it. His mother had never learned to write the Sicilian she'd spoken as a child. This was a note printed in English, in block capitals. The syntax and the sentiment were so much hers that she seemed to speak aloud from the page. "The money come from selling the factory. Nothing from him. No blood is on it." He read the message over a few times until the letters blurred on the page because his eyes were full of tears. After a few minutes he stopped his silent weeping and tore up the message and the envelope. He walked a few paces to a litter basket and disposed of the pieces of paper, then he looked up. He was facing the entrance to the chapel of the Paulist Fathers across the street.

The sanctuary was deserted because it was mid-morning and this church served the working faithful who came before nine and during their lunch hours. DiAnni stood in the back and stared at the flickering candle next to the tabernacle. He wanted to pray for the repose of the souls of his dead—his mother and father and maybe Normie Gold and even Don Stefano. But no prayers formed in his mind, and his mouth was dry, as were his eyes. Eventually he left, and took the subway to Brighton. Later in the day he realized that he had automatically genuflected before leaving the church.

The room he'd rented was in a big wooden frame house owned by a tough peroxide blonde who took gentlemen boarders; the last of a dying breed. She demanded payment in advance and didn't serve meals or allow kitchen privileges. During the time he spent there Joe never saw any of his fellow tenants. Of course there were men to be seen coming and going on the street, but it did not occur to him to wonder who they were or to imagine that they had any interest in him.

He found a small restaurant nearby with a pay phone and he made that his base of operations for eating and conducting other business. By the time a week passed he had contacted the New School for Social Research in New York and obtained by mail admission forms and information about the course in which he was interested. He had also made all the necessary banking arrangements. It was now the twenty-second of December, and he had no reason to remain longer in Boston.

Next morning he left the Brighton house with his packed knapsack on his back and the New York bus schedule in his pocket. He intended to go at once to the Greyhound station at Park Square. Instead, he impulsively made one last call from the restaurant on the corner.

"St. Therese's Rectory." The woman spoke with an Irish brogue, straight from the secret farm where they bred priests' housekeepers.

"Good morning. I'm trying to reach Father Lou Wisnovski. Last I knew, he was assigned to St. Therese's."

"Sure he still is, bless him. I'll be after ringing his room if you'll wait a moment."

It seemed an omen of sorts. And Lou's voice sounded the same on the telephone. Right down to the enthusiasm when he said, "Well hello, boyo! It's been a long time. You okay?"

"Yeah, fine. You?"

"Older, but fine. Where are you?"

Joe told him and they arranged to meet for lunch near the bus terminal. Wisnovski expressed no surprise when he learned that Joe intended to leave Boston the same day.

The first few minutes, they were awkward with each other, each noting the changes nearly five years had wrought, wanting to say a great deal, saying very little. Finally, Wisnovski broke the ice. "That was some exit scene. And not one word since. What the hell were you playing at? A lot of people worried."

"I know, and I'm sorry. At the time there didn't seem any other way to handle it. Then it just seemed to get further and further away and matter less."

"What mattered less? The people you left behind, or yourself?"

"I don't know. Both, I guess."

"And now?"

"Now I'm going to go to New York and take courses in sociology. I think maybe I've still got something to offer, and maybe it's not too late."

Wisnovski ordered another beer. "Maybe it isn't," he agreed. "Why sociology?"

"Because I've had a long time to think and it seems to me that's what we've all been doing right along. Becoming priests so we can serve the poor and all that, only I no longer think that's how to do it."

"Screw the poor." Lou didn't wait for DiAnni's shocked protest. "Maybe that's why you became a priest. Not me. And if so, it's a damn good thing you left. Please God the recent mass exodus has rid us of the servers of the poor and downtrodden."

"I take it you're trying to make me mad. What do you mean exactly?"

"Exactly that the priesthood is not an institution for bringing about equality of man, or ending oppression, or any other Utopian fantasy guys like you get in their little pin heads. It's for worshipping God and administering the sacraments. That's not very popular talk at the moment, but it's true."

"Says you." DiAnni lit a cigarette and was surprised to find that his fingers were trembling. He wasn't angry. It was some other response that he preferred not to identify.

"Says me and two thousands years of Church history and teaching and theology and experience. You want me to cite chapter and verse, I can."

"In your words, screw the chapter and verse."

"Okay, but you used the whole thing, boyo. The whole institution. It fed you and clothed you and educated you and held you up as something the slob in the street could respect. You dumped on all that, and that stinks."

Joe slammed his glass down hard. It slopped over onto the paper placemat. He'd wanted to talk to Lou about his mother and the money, and the morality of taking it. Face it, he

335

wanted sympathy and the pat on the head Lou always gave him. Instead he was getting the party line. "What the hell could I do? The way I felt it was the worst kind of hypocrisy to stay in."

"Nobody wants you in, boyo. Least of all me. Not the way you were thinking, not the way you're thinking now. But the institution deserved a little respect. You should have done it right. You want to be laicized, you can be. But by the rules, without leaving a lot of people swinging in the breeze. A little respect—you owed that."

"A little respect," Joe said softly, all the anger drained out of him. "That's what the don always said. A little respect."

Wisnovski shrugged. "So because a villain said it, the words become villainous? You think the Church and a Mafia don are the same thing?"

"No, I don't think that."

"Okay. Then do what's right."

"Still teaching ethics, aren't you?"

"Damn right."

"Say I agree." Joe's voice betrayed his hesitation and ambiguity. "How the hell would I go about it after all this time?"

"No sweat. You make application to the chancery. You're still a priest of this diocese, boyo."

"And when the chancery processes the correct number of forms and the Cardinal gives his *imprimatur,* I won't be?"

"You won't be a priest of the diocese, no."

"But?"

Wisnovski paused before replying. "You know my answer to that."

"A priest forever, according to the order of Melchizedek. An indelible mark on the soul."

"You got it," the older man said softly.

"I don't want it. I don't believe it."

"The first point's irrelevant, the second is between you and God."

Neither man said anything for a while. Eventually Wisnovski stubbed out his cigarette and stood up. "Go get your bus and become a social worker or a sociologist, or whatever the hell you're planning. Meanwhile, if you want, I'll start the laicization process with the chancery. Later you'll have to carry the ball yourself, but I can get things moving."

"Might as well," Joe said after a time.

Lou grinned. "Good boy. Hey, I forgot to ask, you seen your mother?"

"She died a few months ago. I came to Boston to collect the money she left me. That's how come I can afford to go back to school."

"I see," Lou said softly. If Joe expected more criticism, he didn't get it. "Tough," the older man said. "I'll offer my Mass for her tomorrow."

ON CHRISTMAS DAY 1969, THERE WAS A BLIZZARD IN NEW York. Ann Jessup didn't mind. It was nice to be in the cozy apartment with just Helene. They'd been going to a party on Jane Street but that was way over in the West Village, the end of the world on a day like this. Outside Ann's building on East Fifth Street the drifts were piled as high as the first-floor windows by noon, and the storm showed no sign of letting up.

"Frig it," Helene said, glancing at the snow-filled street. "You go if you want. They'll have to celebrate the joys of the season without me."

"Of course I won't go without you!"

Of late Ann's voice had developed a high-pitched whine. Helene wondered if she only did it at home, or if her students were subjected to it too. It was even more pronounced when Ann added, "Besides, it's nice having Christmas with just the two of us. I'll make a real holiday dinner. There are some turkey legs in the freezer. You sit here and be cozy." She indicated a large armchair by the tiny fireplace, which always smoked but which Ann insisted on lighting nonetheless. She shook out a knitted afghan while she spoke.

"Sweetie, I'm not that decrepit yet," Helene said with a sigh. "Go cook dinner if you want. I'm going back to bed and read."

Ann folded the afghan with exaggerated care and didn't say anything. At least Helene had called her sweetie. She seldom did that these days. A few minutes later she heard Helene's voice on the telephone and went into the hall and mouthed the words, "Who are you calling?"

Helene's gray eyes sparked. "Excuse me a sec," she said into the phone, and to Ann, "I'm calling Gloria to let her know we can't make it. Anything else you want to know?"

Ann shook her head. She felt rotten. Helene hadn't even covered the mouthpiece. Gloria had heard the tone of voice she used. It was always like that lately, for a long time in fact. If Ann was honest with herself, she had to admit it. This apartment, for instance. It was nice and the rent was reasonable, but they didn't really need two bedrooms. Helene said it was because she was a restless sleeper. That wasn't true, it was just an excuse because she was moody. They could have a one-bedroom place closer to midtown for the same rent. The school where Ann worked was in the eighties and Helene's magazine job was in the Village; midtown would have been equidistant and fairer. But Helene got her way in this as in most things. They lived at 29 East Fifth Street because the rent was cheap, and because Helene said, "We're among our own kind."

What did that mean, Ann wondered, while she took the turkey legs from the freezer and assembled the ingredients for Christmas dinner. It wasn't as if she and Helene were like those lesbians one saw in the streets, with their mannish clothes and their talk of "coming out." No, they were attractive middle-class women and their personal relationship was their business, it didn't have to be advertised. After all, they were both divorcées, more or less. They were entitled to call themselves Mrs., they didn't have to flaunt their difference. But Helene insisted she was through with all that. "I'm sick of kissing straight asses," she said. Ann didn't know what that was supposed to mean, either. She always wondered if Helene meant she was sick of kissing her too. God knows there was little of that these days.

Familiar tears of self-pity formed in the back of Ann's throat and she swallowed hard to drive them away. If Helene came in and found her crying again, she'd be furious. She wasn't patient anymore, the way she had once been. Sometimes Ann suspected that Helene wasn't faithful either. There was Gloria, for instance. The thought made her head ache and a terrible pain start in her chest. She couldn't bear to think of Helene's beautiful body naked and pressed up against Gloria's muscular gym teacher's frame. Gloria was one of those butch types Ann hated. The image was sordid and ugly, and nothing like what she and Helene shared in the good times.

There was a spider plant hanging in the kitchen window and its long tendrils tangled in Ann's hair as she brushed by. She pushed it away savagely and for a few seconds the pot swung crazily from its hook. Damn all the plants. They were Helene's passion. Not hers, even though she was the one who bought them. She'd told Helene there was a very nice plant shop near the school but she didn't say that Barbara Korman, who was now Barbara Gold and a widow, owned it.

Sometimes Ann told herself she was crazy to keep going back to Green Gold and seeing Barbara and talking to her.

Everything bad in her life was because of what Barbara had done to Helene. The change in Helene and her attitudes dated from eight years ago, when Barbara sent that despicable letter.

Of course some good came out of it. Soon after that Ann gave up her job at Revere High School and left her husband and she and Helene came to New York to live. At first it had seemed like a dream come true. Ann got a job with the drama school so she didn't have to teach typing and shorthand anymore; Helene went to work for a magazine called *Woman*—it was months before Ann realized it was a gay magazine—and they lived together, the way they'd always said they would someday. But it had never been as good as the dream, and Barbara Korman was to blame for that.

Ann sighed and poured herself a glass of cooking sherry and swallowed it in one gulp. Merry Christmas, she told her reflection in the window. Outside it was still snowing, large sporadic flakes now, and the wind had died down. They were passing through the eye of the storm, the lull before another furious onslaught. Just like her and Barbara. In the end, nothing would deflect the tempest. It would have to be played out to its final scene. Destiny, as she'd realized some time ago.

Ann began chopping onions for the bread stuffing. Each time the knife thwacked the cutting board, she told herself it was what she'd like to do to Barbara Korman's elegant neck.

THE NEW SCHOOL HAD A STUDENT HOUSING OFFICE THAT gave advice on apartments, matched up possible roommates, and generally tried to help with the almost impossible task of finding inexpensive shelter in Manhattan. Joe didn't want a roommate; at thirty-eight he was long past that. But he knew he needed advice. He explained his problem to a girl in a long gypsy dress. She had the earnest, no-make-up-long-hair appearance that characterized most of the female students.

The girl worked hard at maintaining eye contact while they spoke and took every opportunity to touch him. Not a come-on, Joe realized after a few minutes. Part of an attempt at "relating," a word of enormous importance with youngsters of her ilk. "There's one possibility, Joe," she told him after she'd flipped through her card file.

"What's that, Sue?" First names were a must.

"A groovy studio at 29 East Fifth Street. Two drawbacks, though. It's a fourth-floor walk-up, and it's only for six months. A sublet. But fully furnished, and one hundred and thirty a month. That's cheap for here, believe it or not."

"I believe it. I'll take it."

"Sight unseen?" She sounded incredulous.

"You bet. Last of the great risk takers, that's me."

He moved in on January 10. It was during the day, when most of his neighbors were at work, so he didn't see anybody and, as far as he knew, nobody saw him. That was okay. The last years had made him a very independent man who didn't need much in the way of human contact. The studio came with a hi-fi and a decent collection of records, as well as plenty of books. They would give him all the relaxation he needed. Not that he'd have much free time. He planned to find some type of part-time job soon, to keep his money from running down too fast. But first he'd take a few weeks to get acclimated and learn to be a student again.

DiAnni was whistling when he descended the stairs to find a supermarket and get some groceries. Life was beginning to make some sense at last. He didn't notice the man on the corner, because there were lots of men on lots of corners in the East Village in New York City.

IN THE COOL, YELLOW LIGHT OF EARLY MORNING, BARBIE watched Phil's face poised above her own. For this intense and fleeting instant he had shed his characteristic mask of disinterest. It was always thus; Barbie understood that when he made love to her, Phil ceased to be afraid.

"Barbie. Oh, God, Barbie." He spoke her name again and again, like a benediction. The throbbing, swelling, plunging part of him lodged within her was a bridge he crossed out of loneliness. Her fingers gripped his shoulders and pulled him closer, her hips writhed and strained to deepen and intensify the contact, not at this moment to abet her pleasure, but to assuage his need. Later there would be time for her. She tightened the muscles in her thighs and her pelvis, allowed him total use of her, and waited while the rhythm of his thrusts became short and choppy and very fast and finally melded into one long, involuntary spasm. At last he shuddered and relaxed, lying limp over her for a few moments, then raising his head. "You okay?"

"Mmm, fine." She smiled and he rolled to his side, taking his weight from her. She wriggled into a slightly changed position, which resulted in his leg lying beneath her buttocks and raising the lower half of her body. Phil put his hand over the triangle of bronze hair, as yet not moving or probing, just letting her feel the promise of his touch. "Nice," she said.

"You're beautiful and I love you." The words soft and moist breathed against her ear, his tongue running along the line of her jaw then tracing her lips, his hand still motionless upon flesh that his exertions had dampened. She felt warmth spread from his palm, encompass her thighs, creep inside her. She began to tremble with anticipation. "Tell me what you want," he whispered.

"Love me some more." Her voice was very low, for him alone. "Make me come. Please."

"Soon," he promised. He flexed the leg beneath her and raised her lower body higher and his hand began a slow, gentle stroking of the places he'd thus exposed.

Barbie closed her eyes and floated into just feeling. His fingers were tracing lines of fire on her skin. She strained to open the secret places deep inside her and waited for him to touch them too. His head lay on her belly now, his tongue was licking and probing and moving to where she longed for it to be. When at last that exquisite kiss came, her buttocks were cupped in both hands and held with strength and she could not move away from the hunger of his mouth, which was her hunger, too. Little wordless sighs and sounds were born in her racing blood, adopted the cadence of her pulse, and trembled on her lips. More and faster and better, until she was almost there. And then he stopped, laughing lightly at her gasp of dismay. "Soon," he said again. "But I want to watch you and feel you."

Once more he entered her, still amazingly hard, or hard again. She never knew for sure. It didn't matter. The wonderful length of him went deep inside and filled her. Long, slow, sure strokes intended only for her pleasure and her need. He did not lose the rhythm nor alter it when he knelt upright and pulled her legs around his waist, and the strokes continued when he put his hand on her once more and drew small, tight circles with his thumb and said, "Now, my love. Now."

"Yes," she answered. "Oh, yes, yes, yes . . . now." The last word drawn out with her breath until it became a sound of joy and satisfaction, and an echo of the crescendo of feeling below her belly.

He shuddered once more, a pale imitation of the torrent that had shaken him earlier, and at last he withdrew. "Good?" he asked finally, lying beside her, skin pressing skin, hands intertwined.

"Wonderful."

"I'm glad."

"I know." She raised herself on her elbow and looked at him. Their eyes held for a moment, "Thank you," she said.

He stroked her cheek with his knuckle. "For what? I enjoyed it."

"For loving me."

The mask dropped into place once more and he rolled away, then stood up and padded into the bathroom. Barbie pulled the embroidered Porthault linen sheet over her nakedness. It was one of half a dozen he'd given her recently. She listened to the sound of the shower. When Phil emerged he wore the dark, pinstripe trousers of his business persona and he quickly put on the white shirt and dull red tie that went with that image.

"Phil?" Her voice pierced his preoccupied silence. He adjusted his cufflinks and didn't answer, just waited for her to continue. "Have you heard anything from the detectives? Or the lawyer in Boston?"

"Nothing yet," he said easily. "These things take time. I warned you, remember?"

"Yes, I know. I just wish he'd turn up." She got out of bed and walked to the window, unconscious of her nakedness or her beauty. "I only want to know where he is and if he's all right. I've told you that."

"Yes, I understand. Don't worry, it will be okay."

She didn't acknowledge that claim, only said, "It looks like snow again."

"Middle of January, what can you expect?"

MONTAUK IN JANUARY. NOT EVERYBODY'S IDEA OF PARADISE. Not his, either. Phil shoved his hands deeper into the pockets of the down parka. The wind had died, but bitter cold attacked his face with slivers of ice. The ocean stretched flat and gray toward a darkening horizon. No salt smell, no gulls; the world had been put on hold, suspended in a deep freeze. He walked on, the only moving thing in sight. Even the sand was still and hard beneath his feet.

He'd come to think, but his thoughts weren't coherent. The gift of logical calculation was frozen too. A professional expediter who didn't know which way to turn. Assess the risks, determine the exposure, and decide if you're willing to pay the price of losing. That was the way he operated, a habitual mind-set carefully nurtured after he'd been force-fed on life's

342

less pleasant realities. Now none of it meant anything. Because he stood to lose either way, and that was not an acceptable risk, it was a ticket to hell. Barbie was a flame inside him, the only fire, the only source of warmth. Without her he was forever locked out here in the cold. But he had to choose one of the options. Doing nothing was just one more source of exposure; no matter how careful he was she could conceivably find out. That, too, was an unacceptable risk.

He turned back to the house, no longer visible in the encroaching dark, and quickened his pace. A light appeared in a downstairs window. Harris had returned to collect him, so it must be six. Harris was never late. Williams felt the wind rise at his back and heard the whisper of the stirring sea. The calm was ended, the elements were alive again. A few yards to his left, the surf of an incoming tide hissed softly over the frozen sand.

The house was at the end of the crescent of beach. When he reached the stairs only a narrow strip of shore remained dry. Harris had switched on the outside lights and there was a pool of yellow illumination at Williams's feet. He squatted for a moment, staring at the water, feeling the presence of his carefully constructed world behind him. Slowly he began to write with his finger on the compacted sand. *Joe. Barbie. Me. Tell her. Don't. Take him out.*

He scrawled the last quickly, his finger making little raised hillocks of sand around the letters. He stared at them for a moment, then deliberately wiped them away with the hard edge of his hand. Not possible. Not even if it guaranteed she'd always be his. It was one line he couldn't cross. He'd made the decision years ago and he was incapable of altering it, because beyond were suicidal depths and he was not a man prone to suicide. He wanted life. With Barbie and Norma.

The waves washed closer, and he rose and began to climb toward the house. When he reached the top of the stairs he turned and looked back. The ocean had already obliterated the list of his options.

THE WORKING TITLE OF MARIA'S BOOK, THE ONE SHE'D PUT ON the manuscript, was *Island of Dreams*. Too hackneyed, the publisher said. Lengthy meetings ensued in which new titles were suggested and put forth for Maria's opinion. She hated all of them. "You know, it really is the publisher's decision," Sheila Wayne, her editor, said finally.

"Is that true?" Maria demanded of Tom.

"I think so. You'll have to check your contract to be sure, but if I remember rightly it's in there."

"Damn! I shouldn't have agreed to that."

Tom leaned back in his chair. He'd been looking gray and tired lately and the gesture conveyed all that and more. "They were waving sixteen thousand bucks under your nose, you were ready to sign anything. I told you then you needed an agent."

"I know, you don't have to remind me." She'd been cautious, unwilling to give away ten percent of her earnings.

"Yes, I do, because it's still true."

"About the agent, you mean?"

"Yes, if you plan to write more."

She looked up at him, her head coming up in a sharp, surprised little movement that spoke hurt. "Of course I want to write more. Later, when I see how this book does."

"Okay," Tom said.

He was working on a new novel, but that was different. Tom was an established literary figure, not just a scared hopeful like her. "You don't approve," she said. "You think I should go ahead regardless."

"Sweetheart, I told you a long time ago, approving and disapproving's not my line. You're a free agent."

That wasn't wholly true. Maria was not, for instance, free to see more of Si, not the way she wanted to. True, these days Si came frequently to the flat on Carmine Street. He said he needed to get away from the hostel and that Maria's civilizing influence on Tom made his brother worth visiting. It was supposed to be a joke, but Tom got a tight look around the mouth whenever the three of them were together. Especially when Maria and Si laughed at the same old movies on the television. Tom didn't find either the Marx Brothers or Laurel and Hardy funny. "Si's got the hots for you," he said once. That too was meant to be a joke, but wasn't.

"Another guilt trip," Barbie said when Maria spoke about the triangular relationship in which she was suddenly involved. "You seem to attract them."

"Why should I be guilty?"

They were in the plant room in the basement and Barbie was potting white crocuses into pale yellow ceramic containers shaped like frogs. She wore a nondescript smock and rubber gloves and her brow was furrowed when she said, "No reason,

344

as far as I can see. You aren't married to Tom Shore. But you feel guilty nonetheless. It's written all over you."

"Maybe a little," Maria admitted. She picked up one of the bulbs; Barbie said they were corms but they looked like bulbs to Maria. The thing was hard and papery-dry in her fingers. Maria found it difficult to believe that something beautiful would grow from such unpromising beginnings. "Tom's done so much for me. And he's been feeling rotten lately. I don't want to make any waves."

"You still ought to cool the relationship," Barbie said. Her words were interrupted by the muffled sound of the shop bell ringing overhead and she waited until she heard Angie's heavy footsteps on the quarry tile floor before she continued. "Then you could see what develops with Si."

"I'm not sure I want anything to develop with Si."

Barbie laughed and took the corm Maria was holding and plunged it into a bed of peat moss. "Oh, yes you do. You get dreamy-eyed when you talk about him. You never reacted like that to Tom." While she spoke, Barbie wiped the nose of the china frog, then put it into a cold dark cupboard because the crocuses needed such conditions to trigger their growing cycle.

"I admire Si, that's all," Maria protested.

"Sure." Barbie shrugged off her smock. Lately she'd adopted the ethnic look. Today she was wearing heavy twill trousers and an embroidered tunic. A kind of cossack outfit. "I still think you should pull a little bit away from Tom."

"Maybe I will, when he gets over whatever bug is ailing him."

There were more footsteps overhead and Barbie hurried up the stairs to help Angie deal with the customers. Maria watched her disappear in a flash of dark green and purple, the red-gold hair shimmering above. She wondered if cossacks had red hair. Si's hair was almost red in some lights. The thought surprised her. She didn't want to admit that she noticed so much about Si.

Quickly she climbed the stairs away from the mysteriously vibrant and unnerving atmosphere of the plant room. As she passed the shop door Maria heard a familiar voice. Ann Jessup again. She came in frequently. Funny how old relationships changed. Now it sounded like Barbie was the teacher as she patiently explained some plant's requirements to Mrs. Jessup.

* * *

345

OVER BARBIE'S OBJECTIONS, MARIA STARTED LOOKING FOR her own apartment. "Why, for God's sake? There's plenty of room, and I love having you here. You can share some of the expenses, if that makes you feel better."

"I couldn't afford to pay a fair share of them," Maria insisted. "Besides, I'd like to have my own place. I've never had the experience."

Barbie couldn't quarrel with that, which pleased Maria, and it was true as far as it went. Moreover, it eliminated the need to say that she didn't enjoy living in a house where Philocles Williams came and went with such freedom. Nonetheless, Maria didn't immediately find something she both liked and could afford. Midtown and the Village were equally expensive, and the section they called the East Village appeared to Maria exactly what it was—a tumble of tenements and lofts glamorized with a trendy name, but otherwise little changed from the slum it had been.

The apartment search took a lot of Maria's time and the two women saw less of each other. So the morning Barbie had what she thought was a brilliant idea, she didn't know if Maria was home. It was nine when she went to the lavender-and-lace guestroom and knocked. There was no answer at first. Maria must have either spent the night at Tom's or left early to continue her apartment hunting. Barbie was about to turn away when a sleepy voice invited her into the room.

"I've got it," Barbie said, standing by Maria's bed and grinning. "I've never written a word, but I'm sure I'm right."

Maria stretched and tried to focus sleep-filled eyes. "Got what?"

"The title of your book. *A Lasting Fire.*" She paused and waited. Maria didn't say anything, just stared at her. "Well," Barbie said finally, "what do you think?"

"I think you're a genius. What time is it?"

"A few minutes after nine."

Maria reached for the phone and dialed. "Sheila's probably not in, but her secretary will be. I can leave a message."

Sheila Wayne was in. Maria repeated the title suggestion and waited in silence. Then her face split into a broad grin. "Right. I'll get back to you this afternoon."

"Does she like it?" Barbie demanded before the receiver was back on the cradle.

"She loves it. They're having a meeting this morning and she's going to try it on the sales manager. He seems to be the final authority on literary effort."

Three weeks after the title of the book was chosen, toward the end of February, Tom, Maria and Si were at Tom's place. They were watching one of the old movies to which Si and Maria were addicted when Tom said, "I have to leave for the airport in an hour."

Maria was astonished. "Where are you going? How come you didn't say anything before this?"

"To Detroit. What's to say? I'm going to have a look at the scene of the crime."

Maria knew he was researching a novel set in the thirties that had something to do with the Reuther brothers and unionizing automobile workers. It wasn't that which made a little knot of anger form in her chest. It was just the way he assumed no responsibility for their . . . their what?

She asked herself the question, but got no answer. Harpo Marx chased Groucho up a ladder. Neither she nor Si laughed. Tension was a palpable presence in the room. Tom went into the bedroom. She heard him foraging in the closet and knew he was packing.

For a while nobody said anything. Nonsense continued to flicker on the twelve-inch black-and-white screen and make shadows in the darkened room. "Si." Maria heard her own voice before she realized she was going to speak. "Can you use some help at the hostel a couple of days a week?"

He looked at her ruefully and shook his head. "Not your scene, baby, forget it."

"I decide what's my scene," Maria said. "Anyway, I mean office work, typing letters, that kind of thing."

"Yeah, I could use that," Si said quietly. "If you really want to do it."

"I want to."

Tom came out and looked at her hard, but he didn't say anything. He had a duffle bag over his shoulder and he didn't kiss her when he left.

The next day the bound galleys of Maria's book were delivered. She joined Barbie and Norma for breakfast and produced them with a flourish. "A LASTING FIRE by Maria Trapetti" was printed in black bold type on a buff-colored soft paper cover.

"Is this the book?" Barbie asked hesitantly.

Maria laughed. "No, don't look so disappointed. These are page proofs for me to correct. The book will be the way you expect it to look. Boards and a paper dust jacket with artwork."

"You're learning the lingo," Barbie said, grinning. "You sound very professional. What are boards?"

"Hard covers. I do sound like the real thing, don't I? Not like the phony I sometimes think I am."

"The last thing you will ever be is phony."

"I mean a phony writer. I'm scared stiff. I keep wondering if it's just a flash in the pan or if I can do it again."

"You can," Barbie said with the same love and admiration she'd lavished on Maria during their high school years. "You can do anything you want. Even Mr. Marcus said so."

"And Mr. Marcus was the fountainhead of all wisdom." Maria squeezed Barbie's hand and they laughed together.

Norma, who'd been ignored for a few moments, was about to spread orange marmalade on the cover of the galleys. Both women yelped at the same time and rescued the book. When Norma had been given a piece of toast instead, Barbie noticed Maria's clothes. "Where are you going dressed like that?"

"Like that" was a pair of jeans and a loose multicolored shirt. Maria looked down at them, slightly self-conscious. "I offered to spend a few hours helping Si at the hostel. They don't have anyone to do the typing and filing and he's been handling it by himself. I didn't know what to wear, so I bought this. Do I look ridiculous?"

"Not a bit. Like a love child. All you need is beads."

Si said something of the same sort. "Welcome to the Now Generation. Where's the bourgeois lady writer gone?"

"Not very far," Maria admitted. "This get-up's only a cover."

"Nice cover. I like you with your hair brushed loose and no makeup. Your gorgeous girlfriend always looks a little plastic to me."

"Barbie is definitely not plastic," Maria said coolly. "Let's agree not to criticize each other's life-style or friends, okay? Then maybe we can get something done in this disaster area."

"Okay," Si agreed. "You always surprise me when you show some spunk. The modest little ex-nun fools me sometimes."

Maria didn't reply. She moved to a desk littered with papers. Mostly they were forms Si had to fill in to get the state and city funds that supported his project, but she ignored them and took a copy of the bound galleys out of her tote bag.

Si looked at it and grinned. "Are you pleased?"

"I hate it!" Maria exploded in a burst of painful honesty. "It reads like the most amateur drivel I've ever imagined." Tears rolled down her cheeks. Admitting aloud her secret fears had broken a dam she'd carefully erected.

Si moved to her quickly. "Hey, don't do that! It's going to be fine, you'll see. You've just got author's nerves." He patted her shoulder ineffectually, and when that didn't stem the flood he murmured something comforting and wrapped her in his arms. She stopped crying after a couple of minutes, but Si didn't let her go.

"Sorry to be an idiot," Maria said against his chest.

"Don't apologize. It's a nice excuse."

They remained as they were, each recognizing the sea change portended by this moment. Maria was aware of the soft brushed denim of his shirt where it pressed against her cheek, and of his heart beating fast in her ear. He had his own distinct smell. Very male, but fresh, and free of the tobacco odor that characterized his brother. The thought of Tom caused her to stiffen slightly.

Si was the first to step away. He didn't say anything, just picked up the galleys and put them back in her bag. Then he made some comment about the forms she was supposed to deal with. The abyss on which they'd stood closed over.

Later, while they waited for the taxi that had been called to take Maria downtown, Si asked, "What does Tom say about the galleys?"

"He hasn't seen them yet. They only came this morning. He probably won't say much. Tom doesn't approve of my book. Too commercial."

"That bother you?"

"Only sometimes. Mostly I realize that Tom's is a kind of talent I can never aspire to, so I do what I can. It's okay. We can't all be geniuses."

"True. There's something else, though." He was interrupted by the entrance of a dark, emaciated boy with a sweatband around his forehead and a tattoo on his cheek.

"You clean, Diego?" Si asked, barring the boy's way.

The youngster couldn't be more than twelve. He looked at Si with a combination of scorn and insolence and kept his hand in the pocket of his leather jacket. It occurred to Maria that he might be carrying a switchblade or a gun. Probably both.

"What if I ain't clean? You goin' for the pigs, mother-fucker?"

"Nope," Si said quietly. "I'm just not letting you in here. You know the rules. You want a meal and a bed for the night, okay. But you don't bring any rat poison inside with you."

"Fuck you, gringo."

Diego feinted a punch and Si grabbed his fist before it made contact. He didn't let go and the boy didn't try to pull away. "Fuck you too. That's beside the point. Are you clean?"

Diego stared at him for a moment, then laughed. "Yeah, keep your pants dry, Mr. Honky Do-gooder. I'm clean."

Si released him and Diego disappeared into the rear of the house. Maria didn't know what to say. At that moment, the taxi arrived. Si took her arm—this time there was nothing intimate in his touch—and escorted her down the broken steps, across the garbage-strewn sidewalk, and into the cab. Only when she was inside with the door locked did he motion for her to roll down the window.

"Listen, there's something you should realize," he said. "A brilliant writer like my brother, sometimes he regrets not being able to do the ordinary stuff that Mr. and Mrs. America want to read. Don't forget that."

"I won't," Maria promised, though the notion hadn't previously occurred to her.

WHEN *A LASTING FIRE* WAS SOLD TO THE BOOK OF THE MONTH Club for sixty thousand dollars, Maria had cause to remember Si's words. Soon afterwards she learned that *Cosmopolitan* was negotiating for first serialization rights. If the deal went through, they'd run excerpts from the novel before its September publication. Oakes and Randolph would get half of the payments from the book club and the magazine, as well as from any other subsidiary rights sold, but it still came to more money than Maria had ever expected.

"Only the beginning," Tom said. "The overture for the big best-seller, twenty weeks on the *New York Times* list, just like I promised. Go buy a mink and a house in Bucks County." His words were stopped by a spasm of coughing, but not before Maria identified the undertone of envy in his voice.

"When nobody remembers my name they'll still be reading books by Thomas Shore," she said softly.

Tears were running down Tom's cheeks. It wasn't clear whether they were caused by the coughing fit, by sadness, or by the laughter welling up in his throat. "Oh, my little nun, you're something else. You tell it true, however. Sister Pollyanna, that's what I'm going to call you."

She had on the jeans she'd bought to wear to Spanish Harlem and now found the most comfortable things she owned, and she shoved her hands in the pockets and walked to the window. It was March, but spring seemed eons distant. New York was gray and cold and wet. "Let's spend some of the money," she said suddenly. "Let's go someplace where it's warm and sunny and have a vacation."

Tom didn't answer right away. He'd wrapped his arms around his chest, and when she turned to look at him, Maria realized he was in pain. "You can work on your book and get rid of that damned cough," she added.

"Do you mean it? You don't want to stay and be part of all the action? The paperback rights sale will be coming up soon. You're about to be lionized."

"I don't want to be lionized. I want to get out of here."

"What about Si?" He eyed her through half-closed lids.

"What about him? He's managed without us for years. The hostel won't fold up if I don't type his letters." Besides, she thought, he's one of the things I want to leave behind, one of the things I'm scared of.

"No, the hostel will continue in the service of man," Tom said, preferring not to specify what he'd really meant. "You'll have to pay for the whole trip," he added. "I'm in my usual state of financial embarrassment."

"What difference does that make?"

He shrugged. "None, unless you care."

"I don't care."

"Okay. Where will we go?"

She didn't hesitate at all. "Lanzarote. I want to see it."

He grinned. "Deal," he said.

They got their coats and went to find a travel agent who might be familiar with that obscure set of dots on the map that represented the archipelago known as the Canary Islands.

```
┌──────────────┐
│      12      │
└──────────────┘
```

THE FIRST POSTCARD BARBIE RECEIVED FROM LANZAROTE said simply that Tom and Maria had arrived and were getting their bearings. It sounded slightly disappointed, as if Lanzarote wasn't as Maria expected. A week later, there was a second card. It mentioned that Tom was working on his novel and feeling better; Maria was exploring and writing a bit too. In mid April, after they'd been away a month, there was a letter. A number of snapshots were enclosed, and the letter itself was dotted with exclamation points. The climate and extraordinary moonscape scenery were proving seductive. They'd moved out of the hotel and rented an isolated house by the sea. And in a P.S., "Guess what! A friend from Boston College days—Father Hank Rolles, a Jesuit—has turned up here. Not so surprising, since in a way he's the one who introduced me to the Lanzarote documents. Hank's an archaeologist and Tom finds him fascinating, so we see a lot of him." Barbie resigned herself to a long separation from Maria.

That evening she showed the letter and snapshots to Phil. He merely grunted, his interest centered on her: plummy sensuous mouth curved in a smile, batwing brows fluent and mobile, the Botticelli neck carrying his eye to skin sheened ivory in the subdued light of the dining room. She leaned forward to serve him a crêpe in orange sauce, and the brandy flared up anew. It sparked gold from her amber eyes. Phil took the crêpe from her hand. "Quite a meal. What are we celebrating?"

"Oh, I don't know; spring, maybe. Today there were daffodils in bud on Park Avenue."

"A con. They bring them in from greenhouses to fool the visiting firemen."

"I know."

She laughed and her breasts pushed at the thin fabric of the printed Indian gown. She wasn't wearing a bra, and her nipples made a clear outline in the sheer cotton. Phil reached out and traced them with one proprietary finger. She smiled, and finally he took his hand away. "What besides spring?"

"Must there be something else?"

"Yes, I think so. You're keyed up."

"As a matter of fact, I am." She rose—restlessly, he thought—and went to the sideboard. Like the table, it was glass and bamboo. An enormous bouquet of mixed flowers set to one side was reflected in the mirror across the room. Barbie adjusted the angle of one yellow iris and there was an indefinable improvement in the composition. "I had a brilliant idea today."

Her voice was suddenly too gay, too carefully casual. The back of his neck tingled. "What idea?"

"I don't know how I could have forgotten. I think maybe because the circumstances when I met him were rather unpleasant. So I blocked it all out."

"What circumstances? Met who? You aren't being clear." Because she didn't want to be, perhaps.

"Never mind the ancient history, I'll tell you about it some other time." In place of her confused and ugly memories of Norman and kidnapping plots, she substituted a name. "Lou Wisnovski. A priest friend of Joe's. I just remembered how close they were. I'm going to write to Father Lou. I'll send the letter to the chancery office in Brighton, because I can't remember the name of the parish where he was stationed."

Phil waited a moment, watched her fussing with the flowers, and took a deep breath. He had to choose now. He ached with loving her, and with fear. "St. Therese's, in Wellesley," he said quietly.

Barbie's spine stiffened and she stood very still, her hand hovering over a heavy spray of white lilac at the center of the bouquet. When she spoke, it was a harsh whisper. "You know about him because you know everything, I suppose?"

"Yes. It's my business to know things." He wanted to say so much more, to apologize, to beg understanding, to speak his love. He couldn't; the habit of defensive control was too strong.

"You bastard!" Barbie hissed. She turned to face him, all the color drained from her cheeks, trembling with rage, an icicle quivering in a gale, ready to drop and shatter at any second. "You rotten bastard! You promised to help and all you did was manipulate. The puppetmaster holding all the strings. Have you ever had a genuine emotion or spoken an honest word? Three years! Has any of it been real?"

"I love you." He managed the declaration through clenched teeth. "If you don't believe that, I don't know how to convince you."

"Love me! You don't know how to love anyone. I'm a possession. Another pretty and expensive toy that Philocles Williams plays with. Get out. I don't want to see you ever again." She was shaking harder now, clinging to the back of a chair to steady herself.

He stood for a moment, staring at her, trying to master his own pain and anger. Williams's body turned slightly, as if to obey her command to go, but he didn't follow through on the motion. "No," he said, more to himself than to her. "Not like this. Not so easily this time."

Barbie didn't know what he meant. She didn't care. She just wanted him gone. She watched his face and saw the familiar mask begin to crumble slightly at the edges. His jaw was rigid and his lips set in a thin, straight line, the metallic eyes dark with anguish. "Get out," she said again. Her voice was deadly quiet.

They stood so a few seconds more, facing each other across a chasm of feeling. Just when it seemed that one or the other of them must end this whispered violence, must scream or strike out, the door to the dining room was pushed open.

"I can't sleep, Mommy." Norma's high childish singsong vibrated in the tense air. "I came down to ask Uncle Phil to tell me a story." The little girl stood in the doorway with her dark curls tangled around her chubby face and a teddy bear held unceremoniously by one arm. "Appolonius can't sleep either," she added. Appolonius was the teddy bear, a present from Phil that Norma decreed must have "a funny name like your real one."

Barbie picked up the sturdy four-year-old body, hugging it close to protect and be protected. "I'll tell you a story, darling."

"No, not you. Uncle Phil, his stories are better." Norma squirmed in her mother's embrace and stretched out her arms to Phil. He reached for her, and wordlessly Barbie let her go, then stood watching while Phil carried the child from the room.

"Once upon a time there was a princess who lived on an island named Corfu . . ." She heard his voice trail away as they mounted the stairs. Finally she sat down hard, unable to support her own weight any longer. After a few minutes, she realized she was crying. She wanted to get up and go to her room and lock the door, but she couldn't. Sadness and disappointment pressed down on her and turned her legs to lead, and made her body a stiff, unresponsive thing that would not obey her commands.

She didn't know how much time went by. The crêpes were a congealed soggy mess in the copper chafing dish and the flame beneath them had long since burned out. Barbie idly picked up a knife and began slashing them into long, snakelike strips. She was still doing it when Phil returned. He watched her for a moment, then took the knife from her hand and pushed it and the crêpes away. After that he took out his handkerchief and wiped her tear-stained cheeks.

"She's asleep," he said. Barbie didn't answer. Phil put the handkerchief in his pocket and took one of her limp hands. "I'm sorry." The words seemed to come from far away, dredged up from his belly, forced through unwilling lips. "I'm very sorry. I don't know how to stop manipulating, as you call it. It's the only way I know to protect what I care about. I love you so damn much. Norma, too. I can't face the thought of losing either of you."

"Why do you always lie to me? Why? Why?" She repeated the word again and again until it choked in her throat and made the tears start once more.

"Because I'm scared," Phil said. The mask was completely shattered now. His thin, aristocratic face was naked and terrifyingly vulnerable. "Three years," he whispered. "Three years and you never once said you loved me."

"I never cheated on you and I never lied to you."

"I know. I've tried to think that was enough." He'd been holding her lifeless hand all this time; now he dropped it and reached into his shirt pocket. "Here, I've been carrying this for weeks, trying to decide whether to give it to you. It's DiAnni's address. He's in New York."

Barbie took it, but she looked not at the paper but at Phil. "Call off your watchdogs," she said tonelessly. "Off me and off him. Please, if you've ever loved me at all, do that."

He hesitated, then nodded. "When will I see you again?"

"I don't know. I need time to think. Leave me alone for a while. It's the only way."

Williams nodded again, and left the house.

BARBIE HAD NEVER BEEN IN THE EAST VILLAGE. FIFTH STREET was a dreary line of tenements, but the curtains and the plants in the windows indicated that it was a neighborhood slowly moving up. She studied the grimy brick facade of Joe's building and her eyes sought the top floor casements.

"Fourth floor studio" was written beside the address on the piece of paper Phil gave her. There were curtains up there, they appeared to be heavy beige burlap—elegance on the cheap—and they were open, but no familiar form walked by the windows. Barbie stood for a few moments more, inexplicably afraid to enter the building and ring the bell. It began to rain. She looked around and spotted a place called Nancy's Healthfood Snackery. Inside she chose a table that faced the street. There was a blackboard menu with an assortment of peculiar offerings. She ordered hot carrot juice and honey. It was awful so she just let it sit in front of her, and kept staring out the window.

She'd had a vague idea of being inconspicuous so she'd worn black slacks and a black wool poncho. But she saw the eyes of the boy behind the counter flick to her expensive gold watch at the same moment her own did. It was four-twenty. She'd wait until five. Setting a deadline made her feel less bizzare. If she saw Joe, she'd approach him; otherwise, she'd just go home.

"You want me to heat that up again?" the boy asked.

He had bleached hair and Barbie wondered if he was Nancy and if the restaurant's name was some kind of code announcing it was only for gays. He didn't seem hostile, though, and she was the only customer. "No," she said. "It's okay."

The boy shrugged and busied himself behind the counter. She went on watching the street. It was three minutes to five when she spotted him. He was walking quickly through the rain with a bag of groceries in his arms. The bundle almost obscured his face, but she'd have known him anywhere at any time. The same tall, muscular form, the same way of carrying his head. The black curls were a blur at this distance, and

Barbie wondered if they showed any gray. When he mounted the stairs, he fished in his pocket for a key, then tossed the hair out of his eyes with a gesture so familiar it wrenched her heart and made her gasp.

The boy behind the counter looked at her quickly and she dropped her eyes, as if to conceal some illogical guilt. When she looked up again, Joe was gone. A few seconds later she saw him in the top floor window. He stood for a moment, peering into the street before drawing the curtains. A light went on behind them, but it cast no shadows in the murky dusk.

Barbie rose, paid for her untouched drink, and left a quarter tip. She stepped out into the rain and hesitated, staring at number twenty-nine. There was a line of doorbell buttons beside the door. Her finger tingled as if she'd pressed the uppermost one and her throat constricted as she imagined herself answering the question that would follow. She'd have to speak her name into the dull metal grill next to the buttons. What would she say? "It's Barbie, I'm the mother of your child. Do you remember me? Will you let me in?" And what if he asked, "Barbie who?" Would she reply Korman or Gold? For a few moments more she remained where she was. No one passed her on the sidewalk, and the rain began to pelt down hard.

Barbie turned toward Third Avenue, where she could get a cab.

ANN JESSUP STOOD AT THE WINDOW OF HER FLAT FOR A LONG time after Barbara walked away. She was shivering despite the heat in the living room. The chill that had kept her home today, perhaps. No. It was the audacity of it. Seeing the little kike bitch come here to their street and stand and stare at their building, and sit in that health food shop and keep staring. She'd been there for almost an hour. Waiting for Helene, of course. But how had she found out? How did she know Ann's address, or that Ann lived with Helene? There'd never been any way to make the connection. Ann had been so careful all along.

She'd started being careful eight years ago in Boston. In those days she'd been the one waiting in the street, desperate to see who it was that Helene spent all her time with. She remained cautious when she began following Barbara, even when she gave Barbara's name and address to that ridiculous boy who tried to pick Barbara up in the drugstore. That had seemed to work at first—it brought Helene back to her—but still Ann never dropped her guard. She'd even been careful to pay cash for the plants, never a printed check. All these years, so much care and concern. But there was no escape from destiny. She was not truly surprised that Barbara was here, now boldly waiting for the woman she'd rejected so long ago, ready to come between them again.

Ann allowed the curtain to fall back into place and pressed her cold fingers to her throbbing head. The time had come. She must do something really final this time. Something that would be sure to work, not fail mysteriously the way her scheme to have Helene's bookmaker uncle take care of things had failed. She'd never known why that happened. He'd given her back the thousand dollars she'd paid him and said, "No go, lady. You and me, we both gotta take our losses. It was a good idea but it won't go down. The kid's got friends in high places." She'd not understood the words, but she'd never forgotten them.

So much time and trouble and planning. So difficult to keep Helene from ever finding out. Too bad, that. If only Helene knew what Ann was willing to do for her, how much she loved her. The pain in her head got worse.

Ann went to the kitchen to make a cup of tea and take some aspirin. She'd have to think of something better this time. Something that depended only on herself. But she couldn't think of it now. Her headache was too severe.

"YOU LOOK TERRIBLE, SWEETIE." HELENE PRESSED HER HAND to Ann's forehead. "You're feverish, too."

"It's just a virus. I'll be fine as soon as the weather gets better."

"A virus shouldn't last ten days," Helene said. "Neither should this frigging rain, come to think of it." She walked to the window and looked outside in disgust.

Ann jumped up and stood between Helene and the rain-sheeted windowpane. "Don't open the curtains! The light hurts my eyes." She'd been saying things like that for days, and keeping the drapes drawn whenever Helene was in the house.

"What light? Nine A.M. and it's dark as midnight. God, what weather." Helene dropped the curtain she'd momentarily pulled aside and studied her friend. "How about making an appointment with the doctor, say for tomorrow morning? It's Saturday, so I don't have to work. I'll go with you."

Ann settled back on the sofa. Her eyes were dull and

smudged with fatigue and her cheeks were sunken hollows. She saw Helene staring at her. Ann put her palms to her face, as if she knew how ill she looked and wanted to hide. "I don't know, it seems a waste just for a virus."

"Come on, baby," Helene spoke in soft, pleading tones. They warmed Ann's heart. "Be sensible. Do it for Mama. I can't stand seeing you like this."

Ann smiled tremulously. When Helene was kind to her, it was like the old days and she loved her so much her heart hurt. "Okay. If it will make you feel better."

"It should make both of us feel better." Helene busied herself plumping the cushions behind Ann's head and making sure everything she needed was within reach. "Don't get up any more than you have to. I'll pick up something for supper on my way home."

Helene let herself out of the apartment feeling a mixture of affection and exasperation. It was years since she'd had any passion for Ann Jessup, but one way or another they'd been together a long time. Ann's devotion could be a hell of a drag, but it was real and she never could bring herself to rebuff it entirely. Life, Helene decided as she walked down the empty street toward the bus stop, was shit. Most of the time, anyway. There were good moments, great ones even, but most of the time it was shit. And this damned rain didn't help.

From her vantage point in the window Ann watched until Helene had turned the corner into Cooper Square. She waited another few seconds before she pulled open the drapes with a savage tug on the cord. Her heart was pounding wildly. Barbara never came this early in the morning, but for each of the ten days since they'd begun their secret, simultaneous vigil, Ann had felt this same terror. If some morning Barbara came before Helene went to work, or failed to leave before she got home, they'd see each other and it would be too late.

"Kike bitch," Ann whispered aloud. "Frigging cunt whore." All day she kept up this chant of hate, sitting in the window, well back so she couldn't be seen from the street, shivering in the draft, neither eating nor drinking, only waiting and intoning her loathing. For most of the hours she watched alone. But each day at four Barbie came, and remained until a few minutes past five. Then she left. Ann discerned the pattern after three days, but she didn't trust it. She was sure of only one thing: Barbara was waiting for Helene.

Ann promised herself she'd do something soon, maybe today. Otherwise she'd have to endure another horrific weekend. She'd been in agony all the previous Saturday and Sunday because Helene was home and that meant surcease of the vigil. Ann watched Helene minute after long, painful minute, and thought how unprotected her love was during those hours when Ann wasn't on guard by the window. And what if the kike whore did something? What if she came and rang the bell or knocked on the door? Helene might answer, and see her.

Ann pressed her hands to her aching head. The headache was with her constantly now; it didn't subside with any amount of pills. And it had been worse last weekend. Now her temples throbbed harder with the memory. Oh, God, she couldn't go through that another time. She just couldn't. "Have to do something," she muttered to herself. Suddenly she declaimed in a loud stage voice, " 'And where the offense is let the great axe fall!' *Hamlet,* Act four, Scene five." The words echoed in the empty apartment, and Ann laughed softly. Then she began to cry.

But neither while laughing nor crying did she take her eyes from the street.

BARBIE STOOD IN THE DOOR OF GREEN GOLD STARING AT THE rain, sighing at the gray monotony of it. If only the sun would come out, maybe her mood would change. She thought of Maria on her island. There had been a long letter this morning saying that she and Tom had decided to stay another month or two on Lanzarote. It sounded marvelous. Sunny by day, because that was the way of the place, and candlelit by night, because their house had no electricity. Maria suggested that Barbie bring Norma and join them for a while. It was tempting.

"But not until I settle things," Barbie murmured. "Which I must do. Now. I am acting absolutely crazy, and if I keep this up, I will be crazy."

A customer climbed the three steps and Barbie opened the door, smiling as warmly as she could. Mrs. Creighton-Smith was expected, a regular client and a good one. They were meeting to plan the decor for her small June wedding. Like two of her three previous weddings, it would take place in her Connecticut country home. The job would produce a handsome profit, so Barbie could afford to take Norma and run off for a week in the sun. As soon as I settle things, she repeated to herself. Then she led the woman to the small office in the rear and they sat down to discuss the theme of white lilacs and pink tulips that the frequent bride had chosen this time around.

"There's a nice staircase, you remember." Mrs. Creighton-Smith was a brittle blonde with brittle eyes and a voice to match. "I thought maybe we'd do garlands. You know, along the banister."

"No garlands," Barbie said firmly. She'd done the flowers for two of the previous weddings and she knew her client's penchant for overstatement. "Too heavy and too much like Christmas. You want fantasy and froth. A spring garden, just as we discussed. Nosegays, perhaps, at discreet intervals. Just a single spray of lilac."

She wasn't giving the woman short shrift, she'd planned all this carefully some weeks before. But while she spoke, one part of Barbie's mind was occupied with her own inability to make a decision, and another was tabulating the number of times she heard Angie greeting other customers. Weather like this was good for business. People wanted something green and growing to cheer themselves up and remind them that spring would really come. "It's a question of the shade," the woman was saying. "Not that poison pink you used at Sarah Clement's dinner party last week."

Spiteful bitch, Barbie thought. Her voice betrayed no reaction. "Those were Fritz Kreisler tulips. I'm suggesting the variety Clara Butt for you. It's a much more delicate shade. There's some of them outside, I'll show you."

She hurried out of the office without waiting for a reply. Angie was wrapping a bowl of freesias for a man. He was tall and dark and his broad back was turned toward Barbie. She caught her breath and paused in midstep. Then he moved and she could see his profile. It wasn't Joe.

That was her latest fantasy. That he'd come and seek her out and take the decision out of her hands. But it wasn't going to happen like that.

She reached for an oval china dish filled with pale pink Clara Butt tulips and retreated into the office.

"Enchanting!" the woman exclaimed. "But they don't have any scent."

"Scented tulips are few and far between," Barbie explained patiently. "And none of them are the large hybrids we need for effect. The lilacs will provide all the perfume we want."

The bride-to-be left at three-thirty. "How does she think we're going to get five hundred tulips of one variety if she makes up her mind a month before the wedding?" Angie demanded.

Barbie laughed. "Don't worry. I ordered Clara Butt from a

Dutch grower six weeks ago. There wouldn't be a hope of getting them otherwise."

"What if she changes her mind?"

"She won't." Barbie was pulling on her raincoat as she spoke.

Angie looked at her speculatively. "You're going to catch your death of cold going out every day in this weather."

"Can't be helped."

It was the only explanation she'd offered either Angie or Stella, and while it was inadequate, it served to end the questions. She was the lady who signed the checks. "Don't stay open a minute past five-thirty," she told Angie. "You haven't had a chance to breathe all day. And be a doll and buzz Stella. Tell her to give Norma an early dinner, but not to put her to bed before I come home." Norma had been very difficult of late. She'd picked up her mother's mood, as children always do. And she missed her beloved Uncle Phil.

Miraculously, she found a taxi immediately. It struggled toward the East Village in fits and starts through traffic swollen by the fact that it was Friday afternoon and pouring. The slow trip gave Barbie plenty of time to think.

IN SO MANY WAYS NORMA WAS AT THE HEART OF THE PROBLEM. Phil and Joe and Norma and herself, four lives all tangled up together. But Joe didn't know his role in the drama. Maybe he didn't care. Perhaps that's why he'd never bothered to find her in all these years. Not fair. He knew neither that Norma existed, nor that she was his. Barbie couldn't accuse him of not caring. Sighing, she closed her eyes and leaned back. The taxi smelled of stale cigarettes and Coca-Cola. Someone must have spilled a can of soda on the seat. It was still damp. She started to move nearer the window, and suddenly she froze. She wasn't alone.

It was many years since she'd seen the Lady. Not since before Norma was born. But her presence was unmistakable. Slowly Barbie turned her head. The seat beside her was empty. There was no sound. So the Lady was not physically present, and she didn't choose to speak. This was different from previous experiences, but not to be confused with anything else. Barbie knew the Lady was with her. She felt the great outpouring of love. There was neither time nor place. She merely floated in the gentleness and the promise of the Lady's sustaining joy. Then it was over. She was by herself once more and the cab driver was pulling into Cooper Square.

Unseeing, Barbie walked the short distance to East Fifth Street. Her cheeks were wet, whether from tears or rain she couldn't tell and didn't care. She was remembering what she'd been told. Not told today; today the Lady had said nothing, only reminded her. But years before she'd said always a priest, and Barbie had known what she must do. She knew now too. The long period of doubt was ended.

The peroxide blond boy in Nancy's Snackery greeted her like an old friend and brought her carrot juice. She'd found it was drinkable if she had it cold and minus the honey. Barbie sipped and kept watch on the street. At five to five, Joe came home. Just as he had for the past two weeks.

This time she waited only until he put on the lights in the studio, then she crossed the street and rang the topmost bell.

"Such a long, long time," Joe said. He put his hands on either side of her face and turned it to the lamplight. "You're more beautiful than I remembered. Maybe just more beautiful." He leaned forward and kissed her softly on the forehead, then drew her farther into the room. "Come and get warm. It's lousy out there."

She'd said almost nothing since she spoke her name into the speaker beside the bell, and she still felt tongue-tied. Joe didn't seem to notice. He took her raincoat and got her a glass of wine and sat down on the chair opposite hers and leaned forward and watched her while she sipped her drink. When he took a cigarette for himself he automatically lit one for her and she took it, though she'd stopped smoking when she was pregnant and never started again.

"How the hell did you know I was here?" he asked at last.

"That's a long story," she managed to say. Being with him like this was taking her breath away, making her choke. Or maybe it was just the cigarette. "I live on Seventy-second Street," she told him. "I have a plant shop."

He nodded gravely. "Are you happy?" She stared at him, and he had the grace to grin. "That's a crazy question, isn't it? Who ever knows if they're really happy. Let me put it another way: are you content?"

He seemed to want an answer badly; there was no need to tell him of the turmoil of recent weeks. "I have a little girl, a lovely home, and a good business that I built myself."

"A little girl," he said with pleasure. Then he cocked his head in the old way. "You didn't mention a husband."

"No husband," Barbie said.

He smiled ruefully. "Then that must be the way you want it. I've given up the sin and morality business. I'm not a priest anymore. But you probably know that. Otherwise you wouldn't have come looking for me here."

"I know because Maria told me. She left the convent last year." Joe raised his eyebrows but Barbie didn't wait for his comment. "She's been living with me, but at the moment she's in the Canary Islands. She's written a book about one of them. It's called *A Lasting Fire* and she's going to be famous in a few months." She was chattering like a monkey and she took a hurried sip of wine, but still didn't pause long enough to let him speak. Instead, she said quickly, "You are, you know."

"I am what?"

"A priest. You'll always be a priest. The Lady told me a long time ago. That's really all I came to say."

Joe ran his fingers through his hair and stared at the floor. "Oh, Christ," he muttered. When he looked up, his eyes were suspiciously moist. "Do you still see the Lady often?"

She couldn't help it. She giggled. The concern in his face was the same as it had been the first time she told him. "Still think I'm nuts, don't you? Oh, Joe! You're an idiot. I just explained that I'm a mother, I have a business of my own, friends . . . Do you think I could do all that if I was a raving lunatic? Do I looked freaked out?"

"No, but . . ." He shrugged helplessly.

"Oh, forget it." She leaned over and took his hand, suddenly sure enough of herself and her feelings to make the gesture unself-consciously. "Tell me about yourself. What are you doing in New York?"

He told her about his studies and a little about the years with Pete Chiarra on the *Bella Donna*. Then he said, "Do you remember Lou Wisnovski?"

"Yes," she said slowly. "Yes, I do."

He paused for a moment, as if her tone had alerted him to some undercurrent of meaning apparent to her but not to him, then, when she said no more, he continued. "I saw him a couple of months ago. He started the ball rolling with the chancery. I'm applying for laicization. Just a formality maybe, but I've begun feeling good about it. I don't know why."

She shook her head. "You shouldn't feel good about it." She paused, embarrassed because she was preaching and that was outrageous, considering they hadn't seen each other in nearly five years. But the burden of her message was too grave to be ignored. "You can't ever stop being a priest, Joe. It's what you're supposed to be. If it could have been different, I'd never have left you."

That was a belly blow, and it took him a couple of seconds to recover his breath. Not because she was insisting on the immutable character of holy orders—she didn't even know what that phrase meant. Just because she'd reminded him that she'd loved him once upon a time. And because the thought of anything as exquisite as the creature sitting opposite actually loving him was stunning. And because he'd also loved her, and it suddenly occurred to him that given half a chance, he could again. "You're blowing my mind," he said softly. "Listen, let's go and have some dinner. There's a good Chinese place a couple of blocks from here." He needed a break in the intensity of the reunion, needed to talk with her someplace where there were other people and lights and noise, and some kind of ordinariness to temper all this raw remembering and feeling.

"Okay," she said. "But I'll have to call my house first and say good night to Norma."

"Norma?"

"My daughter." She had no intention of saying "our daughter." That was one of the things made very clear this evening. She could give him no more excuses to deviate from the path he must follow. It had been true five years ago, and it was true now.

"Norma," Joe repeated. "She's Normie's daughter, then?"

"Of course," Barbie said firmly. "I just didn't tell you I was pregnant when he died."

"Why not?"

She shrugged. "It made sense at the time. Do you have a phone?"

"No, I'm sorry. There's one here but it's disconnected. I haven't bothered to have it turned back on. There's a pay phone around the corner. It's on the way to the Chinese place I mentioned."

"Okay. Let's go, then."

He helped her into her raincoat and put on his own and opened the door into a hall that was surprisingly dark. "The bulb must have blown," Joe said. He started to reach for her arm so she wouldn't trip on the stairs, but suddenly there was something or someone hurling itself between them, and grunting and brandishing a knife with a long, thin blade that glinted in the eerie darkness.

* * *

IT WAS THREE O'CLOCK WHEN ANN STARTED SHARPENING THE knife, the same time that the conversation about Clara Butt tulips was taking place. Ann couldn't know that, or that she would cause the flowers to be a burden to someone with little idea of the effect Barbie envisioned—but it would have pleased her if she had.

The movement of the blade against the sharpening steel did please her. It was a Sabatier boning knife, half an inch wide and nine inches long, one of a matched set that Helene had given her the previous Christmas. An expensive gift, and a thoughtful one. Ann enjoyed cooking. She was good at it, too. She watched Julia Child on television twice a week. She'd learned to do her own butchering and boning when necessary, and how to wield the knife and the steel in opposite hands so the blade became razor sharp and burr free. Today Ann kept up the rhythmic motion for a long time. When she saw Barbara go into the snack bar across the street she was still sharpening the knife, and she continued to work on it when the kike whore came out and crossed the road and started up the stairs of the building.

Ann drew a sharp inward breath. It was the sign she had waited for. Until this moment she'd had no idea what she really intended. But now Barbie had crossed the line. Barbie wasn't going to wait any longer. She was going to lurk in the hall and accost Helene when she returned from work. Probably that's what she'd planned all along, she'd only been stalling while she got her lines clear in her head. Something like, "I'm the one who's loved you all these years, Helene. Look at me, see how beautiful I am. You don't want Ann Jessup anymore. She's over forty, an old hag. I'm the one you've been secretly dreaming about, and now I'm here."

Ann held up the knife and examined it critically. Barbara Korman had never been able to deliver a line decently. Too bad she couldn't wait and listen to the bitch make a shambles of her big moment. But she had to forego that pleasure. Helene must never know about any of this. Helene had to be protected.

Ann stood up and tightened the belt of her navy velour bathrobe. The handle of the knife felt very secure in her palms, and she wasn't shaking anymore. She was perfectly calm. Even her headache had subsided. That was because she'd decided to take action. It was what the situation required all along. Just like her Yankee mother used to say. "Better get up and do something. Don't just sit around and moan."

Ann put out all the lights in the flat and went to the door, pressing her ear against it and listening carefully. The only sound was her own breathing. Five-thirty, not much time. Helene would be home around six. Cautiously, allowing absolutely no noise, she slipped the chain from the catch and cracked the door. The hall was dim, but she sensed its emptiness. For a moment she was puzzled. She'd expected to see the kike waiting on the landing outside. Ann opened the door a little wider. After a few seconds, she took off her slippers. The halls weren't very clean, but this wasn't the time to be fastidious. She padded barefoot out to the stairs and peeked down to the first and second-floor landings. She couldn't see anyone, but that wasn't conclusive. There were corners hidden from her view. Ann slipped the knife inside her robe and was about to descend a few steps when she heard voices from the studio flat above.

The man who rented the top floor was away for six months and a little while ago the apartment had been sublet. Of course! She saw it all now! She should have realized earlier that Barbara would be clever. And she had plenty of money, otherwise she wouldn't have that glamorous florist shop and house. So she'd arranged for an accomplice, someone to move in over Ann and Helene and spy on them and tell the Jew cunt what they did and when they came and went, things like that. But she was smarter than either of them, Barbara or her hired informant. Smart enough to take the bulb out of its socket after she climbed the stairs and reached the landing outside the studio, and to crouch there in the shadows and wait as long as necessary.

Not very long, as it turned out. In a few minutes Ann Jessup heard the man and Barbara approach the door, and saw it start to open.

JOE RECOGNIZED THE THING COMING TOWARD THEM AS A knife a fraction of a second before it reached its target. He grabbed for it instinctively, and momentarily caught hold of the blade and felt the flesh of his palm open and pour forth warm wetness. There was no pain in that instant, only shock and numbness. Neither was there any noise beyond the stertorous breathing of the unseen assailant. Then Barbie said, "What is it? What's happening?" and there was a strange muffled cry and another thrust toward the sound of her voice.

Joe hurled himself between the wildly plunging knife and Barbie. His eyes were adjusting to the dark, and he saw a glow of white skin inches away. The attacker's flesh. He lunged for it as he screamed, "Go back! Get inside!" Then he couldn't say anything because he was struggling with a lunatic strength he recognized as such even as he fought it. The hand gripping the knife wouldn't let go. He held the wrist and squeezed and bent with all the weight of his two hundred plus pounds, but he didn't hear the clatter of the weapon falling to the floor. Instead he lost his grip, and an instant later his cheek seemed to have been seared with fire.

Barbie started to scream. He wanted to warn her again, tell her to run inside and bolt the door, but he had no breath for anything except for this epic struggle between himself and the person he was trying so desperately to separate from the weapon. At last he again got hold of the attacker's arm. He bent it back and back, away from him, away from Barbie, still screaming behind him. There was a red haze in front of Joe's eyes and a dizziness that came after him with the same determination as the knife. He was losing blood, and with it, consciousness. He gave one mighty heave, knowing it might be his last, praying that he'd topple the assailant down the steep stairs a few feet away.

Instead, the opposing body lunged forward and suddenly lost its footing. They crumpled to the floor together, and even as they fell Joe was aware that the knife had entered soft flesh and buried itself to the hilt. In the millisecond between that recognition and actually hitting the ground, he thought it was he who'd been stabbed. But by the time they lay together in parody of an embrace, he knew it was the other body that had swallowed the blade and expelled that oddly final gasp.

Joe tried to roll free, and didn't realize that his hand still gripped the knife arm until he felt it cut up and slice through the assailant's flesh as if it was so much whale blubber. A great wash of hot blood soaked through his clothes.

THE POLICE BROUGHT A DOCTOR, WHO SUTURED JOE'S CHEEK and his hand, but they hadn't yet allowed him to wash, or change out of the clothes that were soaked in the woman's blood. They had to take pictures first. Joe didn't object. He simply sat pale and silent while the detectives and the technicians went about their measuring and photographing. The activities were vaguely familiar to Barbie. It was like the day Norman hung himself. Only there hadn't been so much blood then, and this time Barbie wasn't worried about whether anyone said the proper prayers over the remains.

The police made chalk marks to indicate the place on the landing where the dying happened. Then they covered the cadaver with a sheet and moved it back a few feet. Into the living room. Barbie kept staring at the mound that was a corpse, and telling herself it really was Mrs. Jessup. She had recognized her instantly and told the police her name. That's when they'd begun looking as if something suspicious was going on. "You know the deceased?"

"Yes, she was my teacher in high school. And sometimes she came and bought plants in my shop. But I didn't know she lived in this building."

"You came here to see your boyfriend, right?"

"To see Father, I mean Mr., DiAnni, yes."

"Father? You a priest, bud?"

When Joe didn't answer, Barbie said, "He was a priest. He left some time ago."

"Oh, one of those." The detective was beefy and bald except for a fringe of red hair. His name was O'Shaughnessy. He made some more notes on his pad and was about to say something else when a blue-suited black man entered the room and whispered in his ear. A few seconds later, Barbie was gaping in disbelief. Helene Wentworth was ushered into the apartment, white-faced and sobbing. She didn't notice Barbie.

Somebody flicked the sheet back from the corpse's face and Helene gasped and dropped to her knees, despite the hold the black man had on her arm. "Oh, Ann, oh sweetie . . . How did it happen?"

"You agree this here deceased is Mrs. Ann Jessup?" the detective asked.

"Yes, oh yes. Ann." Helene's voice was muffled by sobs. The uniformed man drew her to her feet and covered Ann's face once more.

"Sorry," the detective said perfunctorily. "We had identification from Mrs. Gold here, but the deceased was your roommate, right?"

Helene nodded and looked around her for the first time. Her eyes met Barbie's and widened in astonished recognition. The first time Helene opened her mouth, no words came. Finally, she managed to whisper, "What the hell are you doing here?"

"I don't know," Barbie said. She couldn't think of any other answer. It was all too preposterous. She and Helene and Joe and the police, and Ann Jessup lying dead. It was a nightmare so grotesque it was almost funny. Barbie felt laughter start to bubble in her throat and she clamped her teeth shut, knowing that if she started laughing she'd never stop.

"You two ladies know each other?" The detective didn't sound surprised, only weary. Barbie nodded.

O'Shaughnessy surveyed them all in silence chewing on his lower lip and constantly referring back to his notes. Finally he said, "I think I better bring you all down to the station. I ain't chargin' nobody with nothin', but I'm gonna read you your rights."

Before he could begin that television-familiar chant about remaining silent and all the rest, Barbie swallowed her laughter and found her voice. "I'm not going anywhere, and neither is Mr. DiAnni, until I make a call."

The detective shrugged. "Sure, lady, that's your privilege, that's what I was going to say." He gestured to the phone on the table. "Call whoever you want."

Barbie remembered what Joe had said, a lifetime ago when they'd been on their way to a Chinese restaurant. "It's disconnected."

"Oh, is it?" O'Shaughnessy stared at her again, as if she'd confessed to guilty knowledge. One of the uniformed men said something. The detective nodded and the second man took Barbie's arm and started to escort her downstairs. She could feel Joe's eyes following her when she left, but he still didn't say a word.

They walked into the living room of the flat below. Barbie felt a shock of recognition. There were plants everywhere. Many of them she had herself sold Mrs. Jessup. So this had to be the dead woman's home. And Helene's too. Because the decor made it a duplicate of the little place on Charles Street.

Barbie stood and stared. The cop said something, but she didn't hear. She was back in Boston, loving Helene, getting her first glimpse of a world that wasn't Revere. Only what did it all have to do with Ann Jessup and knives and death?

"Phone's right here, lady," the black man said. He sounded bored.

"What? Oh, yes."

With an effort, Barbie wrenched her mind back to now. There were lots of facts and they fitted together and made a pattern, maybe even made sense. She was too numb and confused to find the key. She knew only one thing with certitude.

Her hand was steady when she lifted the receiver and dialed. And her voice didn't quiver when she said, "Phil, it's me. I'm at Twenty-nine East Fifth Street and the police are here. Someone's been killed, a woman I know." She didn't have to say more. She listened carefully while he told her to do and say nothing until he arrived. His voice was calm and controlled, and she'd never heard anything so reassuring in her life.

Only then, when she'd hung up and realized that everything was now going to be straightened out and explained, did she faint.

Barbie opened her eyes and saw Phil's face. Two faces, actually, hovering over her and watching her anxiously out of what appeared to be four silver-gray eyes. "Hello. I told you to remain silent, but you didn't have to knock yourself out to do it."

She couldn't laugh or smile, but Phil's two faces gradually merged into one, and through a mouth so dry it felt stuffed with cotton she asked, "Where am I? What time is it?"

"Not very original. It's morning. You're in St. Vincent's Hospital. Apparently you fainted after we hung up. When you fell, you hit your head on the table. A minor concussion, the doctors say. Nothing to worry about."

"I'm thirsty."

He held a glass of water and a straw to her lips, touching her face gently while she sipped. "Not too much the first time," he said, taking the straw away. "They're giving you something, that's why you're so thirsty and drowsy. Just relax, darling, everything's okay."

Barbie tried to nod, but it was too much effort. She felt herself slipping back into sleep, only there was something she had to ask Phil first. It was important, but she couldn't remember what it was. She couldn't remember anything and her eyelids refused to stay open. "Joe," she managed at the last second. The thing she had to ask was about Joe.

"He's all right," Phil said. "Go to sleep now. DiAnni's all right."

The next time she woke, she vomited copiously into a stainless steel basin held to her cheek by a starched and anonymous nurse. This time she remained awake long enough to glance out the window and see that it was night and that she was in a private room full of flowers. Then she went back to sleep.

In the morning, she remembered everything. The nurse

371

woke her early and said it was Monday. She asked how Barbie felt, and didn't wait for an answer but brought her tea and toast and her overnight case. Packed by Stella, no doubt.

Barbie ate the scanty breakfast and kept it down. The nurse left with the tray, and Barbie got up and half staggered to the bathroom, astounded at the fact that her legs were so weak. She felt better after she'd washed and brushed her teeth and splashed on some cologne. She was combing her hair when the nurse came back.

"Mrs. Gold! You're not supposed to get up alone the first time. What if you had another fall?"

"I don't make a habit of it," Barbie said, coming out of the bathroom in the plum-colored terry cloth robe that Stella had sent.

"That's a great robe." The nurse eyed her patient with frankly female appraisal.

"It was a Christmas gift from a friend. It's a gag, actually." Barbie turned around so the other woman could see the legend appliqued on the fabric. Angie had given her the robe last year. Across the back the name "Bloomie's" was writ large in aquamarine cord. "Not just for Bloomingdale's," Barbie explained. "For me, because I'm in the flower business."

The nurse laughed. "You're really feeling okay, aren't you? Mr. Williams will be glad to know that. He calls just about every hour."

Barbie sat down on the side of the bed. Her legs still felt a little wobbly. "I don't think I'm sick. I'm very confused, though. Someone attacked us in the hall outside Joe's apartment and it turned out to be my old high school teacher, then—" She stopped, realizing that none of this was any of the other woman's business. Besides, she wouldn't have any answers.

"I know," the nurse said sympathetically. "Not the details, they never tell us that. Just that you went through a horrible experience." She busied herself tidying the room while she spoke.

"The police want to see you, but Mr. Williams says they aren't to get in until he talks to you. He wants you to call him as soon as you can." She gestured to the phone beside Barbie's bed. "Better do it right away if you're able. The doctor will be in soon, and he's bound to tell the police it's okay to talk to you this morning." She moved discreetly to the door. "I'm specialing you until you're released, so I'll be right back. Soon as you're off the phone."

Barbie nodded. Phil's doing, of course. She didn't need a private nurse, or a private room full of flowers, for that matter. But that was his way. And the nurse was sure to be getting a generous bonus to ensure that she told Phil everything that happened in the hospital room. Barbie's lips pursed in anger, but it only lasted a moment. Phil was the person she wanted to talk to now, despite the surveillance.

He wasn't particularly informative on the telephone, just said that yes, Norma was fine, and he'd be right over to see her, and she wasn't to talk to the police until after he came. "That's your legal right; they won't argue."

"Okay. Where's Joe? How is he?"

"He's fine. He didn't want to stay at his flat so he's in a hotel. A small private place."

Arranged by Phil, too. No doubt of that either. "Thank you," she said. Her feelings were still confused, but gratitude was certainly among them. "I take it you explained things to Stella and Angie. You're sure Norma is all right?"

"Norma's great. I saw her last night. She thinks you had to go to somebody's house to arrange flowers. She sent you 'great big kisses.' Angie and Stella too."

When he arrived, he wasted no further time on loving messages. "Tell me about Vermont," he said immediately.

"Vermont? I don't understand any of this. I've been trying to figure it out, but nothing makes any sense. What's Vermont got to do with it?"

"According to DiAnni, he had to hide you away someplace up there. Right after your husband died. Because somebody was after you."

Barbie closed her eyes for a moment. Vermont: where Norma was conceived, where she'd promised the Lady she wouldn't try to take Joe away from his priesthood, and where Lou Wisnovski guarded her with a hunting rifle and a sense of humor. When she opened her eyes, Phil was still watching her and saying nothing. She took a deep breath before she began speaking. "Normie committed suicide, he hung himself. I told you about that." She had, soon after they became lovers, but she'd never elaborated. "Apparently the reason was that he was thirty thousand dollars in debt to some bookmaker."

Phil nodded. "According to DiAnni, a Lebanese named Maluchey. Maluchey's dead. I got the word on that this morning."

"If Joe told you everything, why are you asking me?"

373

"You might remember something he forgot." He touched her hand lightly. "Please, Barbie. It's important."

She nodded and didn't pull her hand away. "Joe said that this Maluchey wanted to kidnap me. Because Normie's uncle was rich and would pay a ransom to get me back. Somehow Joe got it all squared away, I never asked how."

"His mother was shacked up with an old Mafia don. DiAnni used influence. It's how most things get done."

"I don't see what any of this has to do with Mrs. Jessup and what happened."

"I'm not sure myself, but I have a hunch there's a connection. I'm working on it. Helene Wentworth's Lebanese too, you know. She was your agent when you modeled, wasn't she?"

"Yes. But that's insane, too. What's Helene's involvement? I didn't even know she knew Ann Jessup. Or that either of them knew Joe, let alone lived in his building."

"DiAnni says he never saw them before in his life."

Barbie agreed, then suddenly sat up in bed. "No, wait a minute! I just remembered. The night of the cast party, the night Maria played Katherine in *The Taming of the Shrew.* Joe came to the party. He must have met Mrs. Jessup then. She was the drama coach at the high school." She sank back against the pillows in defeat. "But that can't mean anything, it's crazier than all the rest of it."

"Crazy is the operative word," Phil said. "I think this Jessup woman was mad as a hatter. But I can't prove it. So far everybody who knew her says she was perfectly normal, in a manner of speaking."

"Why do we have to prove anything?" Barbie looked at him closely, trying to read more in his face than he might be willing to say, but the mask was securely in place. "Phil, it's all pretty hazy, but Joe killed her, didn't he? They were struggling for the knife after she attacked us, and he killed her. It was self-defense. Are the police trying to say anything different?"

Williams shrugged. "At the moment they're not saying much of anything. But the word is that they're considering a manslaughter charge. That means DiAnni would have a criminal record, even if he got a suspended sentence, which is likely. You can see their point of view. You all knew each other from years back. Suddenly the four of you are in the same building and somebody winds up stabbed to death. It doesn't sound like an accident."

"It was self-defense," Barbie insisted. "I hadn't the faintest idea that Ann Jessup or Helene Wentworth lived in that building. I'm sure Joe didn't either. I knew Mrs. Jessup was in New York because she sometimes came to the shop to buy plants. But that's all, not where she lived or with whom, or anything else. I haven't seen Helene since before I was married."

"Okay," Phil said. "That's what you tell the police. Don't get excited, and don't worry. They'll doubtless be in on my heels. Just answer truthfully any questions they ask, and leave the rest to me. Don't volunteer any information they don't already have. I can be present during the interrogation, if you wish, but I can be more useful elsewhere if you think you can handle it."

"I can handle it. Anyway, I don't have anything to hide."

"Good girl." He stood up, leaned over to kiss her, then apparently remembered how things were between them, apart from this emergency, and pulled back.

It was Barbie who tugged his head down to her face. The kiss was devoid of passion, but warm. "Thank you for helping," she said. "I know how you feel about Joe."

"No." He shook his head and looked at her sadly; the mask was slipping slightly. "You don't know. I feel nothing about DiAnni. I only care about you. And only since I met you." He paused for a moment, fighting his instincts, telling himself he had to open up. He couldn't be more vulnerable to her than he was already. "Think about this, will you? I didn't know about the Mafia or about Vermont because I never pried into what your life was before I met you. I could have, I just didn't. It didn't concern me. Only your safety. Only being sure that nothing could hurt you because of your connection with me. That's what you never understood. Probably I should have given you DiAnni's address sooner. I didn't because I was scared of losing you. And I almost did. Not the way I imagined, but what difference would that make in the end?"

When he stopped speaking, Barbie could find nothing to say to fill the silence.

As Phil promised, the police came a few minutes after he left. Their questions were perfunctory and easy to answer. They knew a lot less than Phil, and they didn't raise such disturbing conundrums.

In the afternoon she was released from the hospital. Harris

came to take her home, but when she got into the black Mercedes, Phil wasn't there. She'd thought he might be, and his absence caused her a swift pang of regret.

On Wednesday afternoon, Phil sent Harris to bring Barbie to his office. When she arrived, Joe was already there. Suddenly, without either of them apparently making the first move, they were hugging each other hard, clinging together in simple celebration of the fact that they were both alive.

"How are you feeling?" They asked the question simultaneously, then laughed and broke apart.

Barbie glanced quickly at Phil, but his face betrayed no reaction to the warmth of the meeting. "Would you both please sit down," he said. "We've a lot to discuss." Very cool, very professional.

"As I suspected," he continued, "the origins of this business go back a long way. Helene Wentworth and Ann Jessup were lovers in Boston." He consulted some papers on his polished rosewood desk. "From approximately June of 1959. They were both married at the time, but that didn't matter much. After about eighteen months Mrs. Wentworth wanted to cool it, although Mrs. Jessup didn't feel the same way. That coincided with Mrs. Wentworth's discovering Barbie and starting to manage her modeling career. So Helene used Barbie as an excuse for seeing less of her former girlfriend." Phil paused and glanced at his watch. "We're okay for time. Anyone want a drink?"

Joe asked for a scotch. Phil stepped to the bar to get it, and Barbie studied Joe. His cheek and his hand were heavily bandaged, but apart from that he looked unharmed. Except that his eyes were dull and he stared out the window a lot. She'd noticed him doing it even while Phil was speaking. When he got his drink, DiAnni swallowed it in one gulp and wordlessly held out his glass for a refill. He's killed a human being, Barbie thought. I've been thinking of everything except that.

She hadn't asked for anything, but Phil handed her Perrier water anyway. No ice and a slice of lemon, the way she always took it. Their fingers brushed momentarily when he gave her the glass, then he was back behind the desk continuing his narrative.

"Barbie, you decided to give up modeling in the spring of 1961, correct?"

"Yes. Because I was getting married. Normie didn't want me to go on working."

"Right. Well, it seems Helene Wentworth took that very personally. She was upset and turned for comfort to Ann Jessup, her old lover. Soon after that they moved to New York and began living together." Before he could say more, the buzzer on his desk sounded. Phil excused himself and stepped to the door.

Joe continued to stare straight ahead, but Barbie half turned in her chair. When Helene Wentworth entered the office, the two women found themselves eye to eye immediately.

There was a long pause, a moment when it wasn't clear if they were going to shout and scream, or just be cool and formal. Helene found her voice first, and altered the nature of the static bouncing between them. "Hello, baby," she said softly. "Long time no see, and this is a hell of a way to have a reunion. I just came from Ann's funeral."

There was warmth and friendliness and regret in her words. And an unspoken absolution. Forget all the guilt, her gray eyes said. None of it matters now. Barbie stood up and went to her, and held out her arms. They hugged, staying close for a moment. Neither of the men said anything. "I'm sorry, Helene," Barbie murmured after a while. "It must be rotten for you."

"It was an accident." Helene gently pushed the younger woman away. "I told those cop pricks the same thing, but they want to make themselves feel like big daddies. It's all so nice and juicy, full of the kind of people they like to lean on, a gorgeous broad who's the girlfriend of a super-rich lawyer, a couple of gays, even an ex-priest, for chrissake. The pigs think they've died and gone to heaven." She paused for breath and spotted the bar. "I could use one of those."

Phil poured her a hefty scotch. Helene took it and sat down. She wore a black suit and black stockings, and when she crossed her legs Barbie noted that they were as superb as ever. So was the rest of her body, although Helene's face had lines that Barbie didn't remember, and puffy circles under the eyes. What the hell, they were both almost ten years older.

"Mrs. Wentworth," Phil said, "I've told the story as far as your arrival in New York with Mrs. Jessup. Would you tell the rest again? The way you told me last night."

Helene shrugged and opened the top button of her jacket. The breasts were still high and firm. "It's not particularly interesting. I'd had it with the modeling business, so after we came here I got a job on a women's magazine. Ann became a full-time dramatics teacher, the thing she'd always wanted to do. The only tension came from the fact that I got less concerned with who knew what I was and how I got my jollies. Changing times and all that shit. Only Ann didn't change. She never wanted to be labeled as a lesbian, not even in her own head. That, and the fact that things were different between us, made her unhappy."

"Different between you how?" Phil asked.

"I didn't want to sleep with her anymore," Helene said coolly. Her eyes flicked to Barbie's face and she grinned. "I take it you understand about me now, baby? Grown up some, haven't you?"

"Some." Barbie knew it was too late to explain that she'd always known and it hadn't mattered. It was only about herself that she'd wondered.

"And you think Ann blamed Barbie for that changed relationship?" Phil asked.

"It's possible, maybe even likely." Helene turned to the younger woman. "I took it real hard when you cut out on me, baby. You could have been the most famous face in America, you know that?"

Barbie shook her head. "I'm sorry, Helene. I was just too young. I didn't really know what I wanted. I've always hated myself for that letter. It was such a gutless way to tell you."

"Old stories, kid. Water over the dam, as they say. It was all too long ago and life's too short. Ann should have realized that. I blame myself for not seeing how disturbed she was and getting her to a shrink."

They talked a little more—that is, Phil and Helene and Barbie did; Joe didn't say a word. Not even when Barbie explained her indecision about getting in touch with Joe. She didn't try to explain why, only that she'd been unsure she wanted to and that she'd gone to East Fifth Street every day for almost two weeks, but each time lost her nerve at the final minute.

"I can't prove the rest," Phil said, "but I'm sure I know what happened. Mrs. Jessup was home with the flu, so she saw you looking at the building and somehow construed your presence as indicating another threat to her relationship with Mrs. Wentworth. That's what pushed her over the edge."

"A woman," Joe said suddenly. They all stared at him. He shook his head as if to clear it. "When Don Stefano told me Barbie was safe after the kidnapping threat, he mentioned that a woman had been involved. He said it made it harder for him to call off Maluchey."

"Leontyne Maluchey? My uncle?" Helene's voice was incredulous.

"The same," Phil interposed. "He made book in Boston, and Barbie's husband owed him a lot of money." He explained what had happened to Norman Gold. And that afterward there was a threat to kidnap Barbie.

"Jesus!" Helene said. "You think I had a hand in that? I said a lot of crazy things when Barbie first took off, but I never meant any of them."

"Not you," Phil said. "Mrs. Jessup. I can't prove it, but I think she's the one that gave Maluchey the kidnapping idea."

"And gave Normie my address the first time," Barbie added thoughtfully. She'd been figuring it out while they talked. It all looked so clear now. The solution to the mystery she and Normie never understood. "The day I met Normie I only told him my first name. We were in a drugstore. According to Normie, after I left a woman came up to him and told him my last name was Korman and I lived in Revere. So he could find my phone number." She paused and bit her lip. "But I think he said she had some kind of accent."

Phil shrugged. "Mrs. Jessup was a drama teacher, wasn't she?"

Barbie nodded. "Yes, of course. The day it happened, I was supposed to meet the agent for the Saks catalog. Do you remember, Helene?"

"Oh yes, I remember." The two women looked at each other again. "Poor Ann," Helene muttered.

They sat silent for a few moments. Phil poured fresh drinks. Finally he said, "We meet with the D.A. on Monday. I'll tell him what I've got. Don't worry, they'll never go to a grand jury when they hear the whole story. Self-defense and death by misadventure. I think we can count on it." He turned to Helene. "Thank you, Mrs. Wentworth. We'd have had a much more difficult time without your cooperation. Mr. DiAnni and Mrs. Gold would have faced a lot of unpleasantness."

Helene rose and smiled. "For a face like that," she said, nodding toward Barbie, "I'd cooperate in almost anything. Me and all the rest of the schmucks. Good-bye, kid, and good luck. Maybe we'll have lunch sometime."

"MOMMY, ARE YOU GOING TO COME RIGHT BACK?" NORMA stood with her hands on her hips, looking and sounding as imperious as an almost-five-year-old could manage. "You won't be days and days, like last time?"

"Right back. Promise, promise, promise," Barbie said. "A three-times promise can't ever be broken, right?"

"Right!" Norma hurled herself at her mother and Barbie hugged her tight.

"You smell like chocolate cake," Norma said.

Barbie laughed and looked at the bottle of perfume on her dressing table. "I don't think that's what they had in mind. Okay," she said, disengaging herself. "You go have your breakfast. Tell Stella I said you can watch the cartoons until I come home. Then we'll go to Schrafft's for lunch."

"Good-o! Uncle Phil too?"

Barbie hesitated. "Maybe. We'll see."

"A yes maybe or a no maybe?"

"A maybe maybe. Now scat!"

She watched the child run from the room, then turned back to the mirror. A simple dress the color of bitter chocolate, because Phil said something conservative was best. But she was still pale from her bout in the hospital. She tied a daffodil-yellow scarf around her throat, and on impulse added a wide bangle of yellow enamel edged with thin gold braid. A piece of summer jewelry but what the hell, it was spring at last.

Barbie was humming when she left the house.

IT TOOK LESS THAN AN HOUR AND WAS AS PREDICTABLE AS PHIL promised it would be. When it was over, Joe looked only slightly less dazed. He shook Phil's hand and said something about his fee.

"No charge," Phil said. "Barbie was involved too."

Barbie waited to see if Joe would react to this proprietary declaration. He didn't. Joe still seemed to be moving through a fog, not really hearing or seeing anything. She reached out to touch him, to say something, but the gesture was stillborn because a man came up and said Joe was wanted in the next office, there were forms that needed signing. "I'll call you later," he murmured as he walked away.

Barbie stared after him for a moment, then Phil took her arm. "C'mon. I'll get you a cab."

They walked down the linoleum-floored corridor, footsteps tapping in unison. Barbie considered asking Phil to have lunch with her and Norma. She wasn't sure what the invitation would mean to either of them. Worse, she wasn't sure what she wanted it to mean. She turned to him, intending to say . . . what? Then it ceased to matter.

Harris stood before them. His face was flushed with worry

and his eyes were anxious. He held his hat in his hands and kept twisting it nervously. "Mr. Williams, sorry, sir. I thought I better come find you both. It's little Norma; she's been rushed to the hospital again. Another one of them crazy fevers. I got the car right out front."

DÉJÀ VU IN GREEN. THE NIGHTMARE REPEATED. NORMA'S small body, seen through a glass, pierced with tubes and instruments, and surrounded by figures swathed in green masks and gowns and turbans. Only their eyes showing, and those clouded with worry and fear. Barbie could smell the fear. It escaped from behind the observation window and infiltrated her skin through the pores.

"How? Why? They said it wouldn't ever happen again. They said she was perfectly well. Just last month the doctor said so. This morning she was fine and happy."

Phil kept his arm around her shoulders, supporting her. "They're doing everything, darling. All the medicines that cured her before. Once she's better, we'll find the best doctors in the country. We'll make sure it doesn't happen again." He stopped speaking, knowing the words weren't getting through to her and didn't make any difference anyway. Only the vigil mattered. Only standing here and holding on to Norma with their will.

The elevator door opened and closed. Barbie was vaguely conscious of someone taking her hand, and she momentarily pulled her eyes away from her daughter's face and looked into Joe's.

"I came as soon as I heard," he said. "What is it? Do they know?"

Barbie just shook her head and turned away. It was left to Phil to explain that this was the second such attack and that the doctors were hopeful they could control it the same way they had previously. Joe nodded and peered through the glass at the child he'd never seen.

Norma's eyes were closed, but he noticed the black curly hair. She didn't seem to look like either Normie or Barbie, but who could tell in conditions like this? He glanced at Barbie again, and saw the pain and the terror apparent in the set of her jaw. He noted too Phil's supporting arm.

A friend of Mrs. Gold's, that's how the lawyer had introduced himself the first time, that night when Joe was paying attention to nothing but his own shock and disbelief, telling himself he'd killed a woman and didn't even know why. He hadn't thought much more about Williams until this moment, beyond his being a good lawyer, a man who could make things a little smoother. He'd been too wrapped up in himself, in the terrible thing that had happened to him.

Now he saw that Williams was more than Barbie's friend. Her lover, perhaps. Maybe her daughter's father. No, Barbie said Norman was the child's father. She'd said it just before the horror happened, and that too he'd thought no more about till now. Joe tried to get a fix on things. Something was wrong, bothering him. Only he couldn't put a name to it. Too many shocks. His head was like swiss cheese, full of holes.

A nurse approached, and Phil moved aside so she could speak with Barbie. Suddenly something in the other man's stance rang a bell in Joe's mind. He'd seen Phil Williams before. That unusual coloring was hard to forget. But where? The association wouldn't come. Barbie's voice interrupted his musings. She was shouting, but in a harsh whisper, as if afraid to make a noise that might penetrate the barrier between herself and her child.

"What do you mean you've lost her records! How can you cure her if you don't have her records?"

"Not her medical records, Mrs. Gold. Just the admittance forms. I'm from administration, I told you that."

Not a nurse, a clerk, but suited up in green like all the rest of them. The only way anybody could get into this isolation unit. "I thought I'd just copy the address and date of birth from the earlier card, but I can't find it," the woman said. "I'm sorry. If you'll just give me the facts again I can stop bothering you. Mistakes happen, you know."

"Mistakes," Barbie said dully, staring at the woman.

"I can tell you what you want to know." Phil guided the woman a short way down the corridor. Then, a few seconds after he began murmuring to the clerk, he returned to Barbie's side. "Sorry, honey, I don't remember her exact birth date."

"May twentieth, 1966," Barbie said. She didn't take her eyes from the scene on the other side of the glass.

Joe heard the date and filed it. Maybe when the kid was better and life was normal he'd bring her a birthday present. May 20 was only a week away. Barbie's daughter, after all. And Normie's. What would she be, five years old? Yes, five. And when did Normie die? August '65. DiAnni remembered that it had been stifling hot when they buried Barbie's husband. And still August when he drove her to the chalet, a week after the funeral.

The memory of that night came back with sudden force. Barbie, pressed against him, loving him so openly, so generously. And himself, not feeling guilt or remorse until it was over. Just wanting the beauty and the wonder of her, taking her love for the priceless thing it was. That's when Joe remembered the rest of it. The drive up Route 2, Barbie telling him that she and Normie hadn't had normal sex for months before he died, so that Joe would understand how messed up Normie's head was, so he wouldn't feel guilty because he hadn't prevented the suicide.

DiAnni stood very still. He stared through the window at the child fighting for her life. It washed over him in slow, dull waves. Not shock, just a sad, sad ache. "She's my daughter."

Barbie didn't hear him. Phil was still in conversation with the harried records clerk. "My daughter," Joe repeated. He turned to Barbie and grabbed her arm, felt his fingers dig into her flesh. "She's mine, isn't she?"

Barbie's amber eyes were clouded and she was very pale, but it wasn't his declaration she was reacting to. "Yes," she said quietly. "She's yours." Then she disengaged her arm from his grasp, and gave all her attention to the life and death struggle that was the only thing that mattered.

DiAnni couldn't handle the quiet admission, the easy dismissal of his pain. "Why didn't you tell me!"

She waved her hand at him. "Not now, please not now."

Joe swallowed hard. He stared through the glass, trying to imagine himself a father, trying to convince himself that the child would recover, that he'd have an opportunity to know her. Of course he would. Anything else was unthinkable.

Phil finished with the clerk and rejoined them. "Any change?" Yes, Joe wanted to say. A big change. I know now. But he didn't, and Barbie shook her head, and the silent vigil went on.

It seemed an eternity, but it was less than half an hour. One of the doctors detached himself from the group by the child's bedside and came out. It was Cohen again. "We're winning," he said with a tight smile that betrayed tiredness. "The drug's taking hold. Just like last time. Her temperature's down a couple of points. Try and relax; I think it's going to be okay."

Barbie sagged against Phil's side, then straightened up. "Why did it happen again? You said it wouldn't."

"It was heavy odds against, Mrs. Gold, but in these cases one can never be sure."

"Is it just going to keep happening? There must be some-

383

thing we can do." Barbie's voice started to rise on the last few words.

Phil tightened his grip on her. "Hang loose, baby. It won't help if you go to pieces."

Cohen eyed Barbie. "Would you like to lie down someplace? I can give you something to help you sleep for a couple of hours." She shook her head, and he shrugged. "Very well, but you may as well get out of here and take a break. Later you can probably see her without the window." He walked away without saying more.

"C'mon," Phil said. "I'll take you home for a little while. We'll come back later."

Joe had been silent since the doctor emerged. Now he reached out one tentative hand and laid it on Barbie's arm and spoke her name. Just her name, nothing more. She turned her emotion-ravaged face to him and their eyes met and held for a few seconds, then she nodded.

"I need to talk to Joe for a bit," she told Phil without looking at him. "We'll meet you back here at four. Okay?"

Phil didn't say anything, but he dropped the arm that had been round her waist and stood and watched the two of them go to the elevator.

Barbie and Joe didn't speak during the descent. When they were standing in the lobby he said, "Where shall we go?"

"There's a cafeteria in the basement. I don't want to go too far."

It was long past lunchtime and too early for dinner; the cafeteria was nearly deserted and nothing in the steam tables looked edible. "Just coffee," Barbie said. She went and found a table in a far corner and waited. He came with a tray bearing two paper containers of coffee and two sad-looking cheese sandwiches.

"You've got to eat something," he said. And a few seconds later, "How come you told Williams to come back this afternoon?"

She was startled, her brain numbed by pain and fear. It took a few seconds for her to understand the question. "To see Norma, you mean? They adore each other. She'll expect to see him there as soon as she's awake. Phil's like—" She remembered and bit back the rest of the words.

"Like a father to her," Joe supplied. "Yeah, I thought so. Why, Barbie?"

"Why what?"

384

"Why didn't you tell me. When you left Peabody, you knew, you'd have had to. You were what, four months pregnant?"

"Three. And you know why I didn't tell you."

He toyed with the uneaten sandwiches and the bad coffee, studying his hands as if they could supply explanations. Which in a way they could. Anointed hands. "You can't play God," he said. "Whatever private revelations and visions you think you have, you can't make other people's decisions for them."

"There was no option." She reached for his pack of cigarettes, then remembered she didn't smoke. "I did what I had to do, Joe. What I knew was right. Okay, believed was right. For a time I thought maybe I'd give the baby up for adoption. Then when I knew I couldn't do that, I told my family and allowed them to believe she was Normie's child. It's what everybody believes. Thank God the timing worked out."

"And the other night? When you came to my place, were you going to tell me then?"

She knew what he wanted to hear, but she shook her head. "No, especially not then. You know why."

The control he'd maintained was stretched thin. He lit a cigarette with trembling fingers. "Listen, I want you to quit that. It's not your business, Barbie. I didn't leave because of you. I left for my own reasons. I told you I was being laicized. That part of my life is over. When she's better, I want to get to know my daughter." His voice broke on the words. His child, flesh of his flesh, fruit of his loins. All the old tribal buzz words, all the primitive truths. "Are you going to allow me that?" he asked.

Barbie put her hands to her temples. "I don't know. It's all happened too fast. Right now all I want is for Norma to be well. Can't we wait until later and talk about it then?"

An attendant came by with a wheeled rubbish bin and a broom. "Hey, mister. No smoking. Can't you read?"

DiAnni stubbed out the cigarette. "What about Williams?"

"Phil's not the point. Neither are you or I, if it comes to that. The only thing that matters is what's best for Norma."

"I have no argument with that."

"Good. Let's go back, shall we? It makes me nervous being away from her so long."

DiAnni reached over and touched her cheek. "Just a minute more, I want—" He stumbled, then found the words. "I just want to say I'm sorry you had to go through it all alone. I wish you'd felt you could come to me. But I think you were great to manage as well as you did."

She smiled, but didn't say anything. Silent again, they went back to the isolation wing and wrapped themselves anew in the sterile gowns and masks. The nurse beside Norma's bed saw them and came outside. "She's still stable. You can come in for a moment, Mrs. Gold." She stepped out of the doorway to let Barbie pass, but put a hand up to prevent Joe's following her. "Immediate family only, I'm sorry."

Barbie turned and saw the look of privation on his face. "He's her father," she said softly. Without thinking of what she'd committed herself to by the admission.

The nurse looked from one to the other and made a gesture of acquiescence. She moved away, and Joe and Barbie went to the child's bedside.

Norma was breathing deeply. Her long black lashes made shadows on her flushed cheeks. There was an intravenous set-up, and one chubby arm was taped to a board with a needle lodged in the pink flesh. The nurse came close and pressed the skin around it, then did something to the apparatus that controlled the speed of the drip. When she was satisfied, she moved a little distance away. Barbie took her daughter's free hand, and automatically the small fingers curled around hers.

Joe leaned forward, studying the child, drinking her in. After a few seconds, he lay a hand on her forehead. At that moment she opened her eyes. Joe drew back, startled and illogically afraid. "Mommy," Norma whispered.

"Right here, darling." Barbie leaned down to kiss the usually moist mouth and found it dry and hot. She glanced up at the nurse. "She feels very warm again."

The nurse came close and Joe moved out of her way, separated from his child by his own fear and strangeness and by a conspiracy of women. He saw the nurse reach for the thermometer, then place her competent fingers on Norma's pulse. "We'll just have Dr. Cohen come up and take another look at her," she said coolly.

"Her fever's up again, isn't it?" Barbie said in a voice ragged with fear.

"You'd best wait outside, Mrs. Gold." The nurse made firm motions of eviction. "We don't want her upset."

"No," Barbie said sharply. She pulled away and took Norma's hand. "How's my baby? I think you're just fooling me so you can watch television late tonight." Norma managed a small smile and the nurse looked at them once more, then let herself out of the room, moving quickly down the corridor toward an interhospital phone. Joe drew close to the bed again.

He was trying to think of something to say, something that would establish the first tentative contact between him and his little girl, when it happened. Norma's eyes suddenly went blank. She'd been looking at her mother and then she wasn't looking at anything at all. Her mouth opened and she was struggling for air, gasping and choking and writhing her tiny body. "Nurse!" Joe screamed, running for the door and yanking it open. "Nurse!"

The woman turned, looked at him, dropped the phone, and came running. Barbie had her back to both of them. She was hanging over the bed, holding on to Norma and shouting her name. "Norma! Don't go, baby. Mommy's here! Don't go!"

The elevator door hissed open. Phil Williams's face appeared in the window and Cohen and two other doctors ran into the room. They hauled Barbie away from the child and the nurse took hold of her shoulders and pushed her toward the door. "Please, Mrs. Gold. You've got to go outside now. It's better for Norma. Really."

Joe came out of his frozen stiffness and tried to put his arms around Barbie, but she struggled away from him. The three of them battled a few seconds more in the doorway. Behind them the doctors wheeled some kind of black box with long electrical leads to the bedside. Joe saw it out of the corner of his eye and saw Norma's small form arch once, then fall back. Williams had been watching too, but he wrenched himself away from the window and reached for Barbie. She sagged against him and let him take her into the corridor. The nurse pulled the curtain over the glass and closed the door. Phil was still holding her when Cohen appeared a few minutes later.

The doctor didn't have to say anything. One look at him and they knew.

13

IT WAS THURSDAY AFTERNOON WHEN MARIA GOT PHIL'S
cable, twenty-four hours after the funeral. Maria tried to
imagine the soft, warm, sweet-smelling body in a box
under six feet of earth, but she couldn't.

"What is it?" Tom looked at her pale face and the telegram
she held. "What's happened."

"Norma's dead."

"Norma? Your friend Barbie's kid? Oh, my God. How old
was she? Around four, right?"

Maria crumpled the pale blue piece of paper, but she didn't
throw it away. "Just five next week. I mailed her a birthday
present the other day." She sat down heavily, shivering despite
the hot sun. "Phil says it was the same high fever she had a
year ago."

"I take it he sent the cable?"

"Yes."

"Can you get there in time for the funeral?"

Maria shook her head. "No, that was yesterday." She
spread the paper over her knee, carefully smoothing out the
wrinkles. The words hadn't changed. They were just as ugly as
the first time she read them. "NORMA DIED TODAY, RECUR-
RENCE OF FEVER. FUNERAL TOMORROW."

Tom took the cable from her hand. "It's dated Monday."

"Yes, I saw that." She raised her face to him. "Tom, I've got to go home. Barbie must be . . . I don't know what word to use."

"There aren't any," he said. "No words at all. Shit! What a bummer. Her husband committed suicide, didn't he?"

"Yes."

"*Mourning Becomes Electra*," he quoted softly. "Life imitating goddamn art, or something equally banal. C'mon, I'll drive you into Arrecife and we'll see about getting you home."

"You don't mind?" she asked when they were in the old jeep that provided their transportation, bouncing over the washboard that posed as a road. They complained about the jeep, but it was faster than the burros used by the locals. The Canarian concept of time took some getting used to. Like a telegram that took three days to arrive.

"Of course I don't mind." Tom negotiated a savage rut. "Friendship is one of the few things that makes sense in this crapped-up world. I'm pleasantly surprised that Philocles Williams sent you a cable. I figured he'd want his paramour locked up like the princess in the tower."

Maria held on to her broad-brimmed straw hat, fighting the combination of wind and jouncing that struggled to dislodge it. "Phil can be okay sometimes. Listen, you don't want to go home too, do you? Maybe see a doctor about that cough."

"No, it's getting better. And I wouldn't be any use to Barbie, I'm practically a stranger. My work's going well, so I'll stay put."

"The rent's paid until the end of June. I'm sure to be back by then."

It was the first mention of her future plans and Tom shot her a sideways grin. "Glad to hear it. I'll be waiting."

In Arrecife they learned she'd be fairly lucky with connections. There was only one flight a week from the island to Madrid, but it was on Saturday afternoon. That made only two days to wait. Maria would arrive in Madrid too late for a flight to New York, but there was one Sunday morning. All in all, it wasn't too bad.

"TELL HANK I'M SORRY NOT TO HAVE HAD A CHANCE TO SAY good-bye." Maria looked away from the ramshackle building which served as the airport terminal and studied the arid dun-colored landscape. She found it strangely poignant.

"Will do," Tom said. "Too bad he hasn't been around lately." But the Jesuit was a frequent visitor, he was sure to

389

turn up. "If he offers to say Mass for the little girl, what do I tell him?" Tom added.

"Tell him thank you. It can't hurt, can it?"

He grinned and kissed her lightly. Most of their kisses were of that platonic sort lately. For the past few weeks she'd been trying to decide how she felt about her renewed celibacy. Today the problem seemed minimal. Only Barbie mattered, and what to say to her.

WHEN SHE GOT TO THE SEVENTY-SECOND STREET HOUSE Maria still hadn't figured out anything comforting to say. It was after five P.M. New York time, after ten for her. The city was prematurely hot and muggy, and the house so still she needed only to open the door to sense the presence of death.

Phil had sent Harris to Kennedy to meet her, but he hadn't come himself. Instead he was waiting for her in the front hall. He took both Maria's hands in his and drew her close, as if they were intimate friends. "Thanks for coming. I couldn't think of anything more important I could do for Barbie."

Williams's embrace was surprisingly welcome, an antidote to her feelings of inadequacy. "I don't know what to say to her. I've been trying for hours to come up with something that might help."

Phil shook his head. "You don't have to say anything. You and Barbie go back a long way together. Just go upstairs and love her a little. She's lying down. The doctor just left. He gave her something, so she may be asleep."

"Who else is in the house?"

"Only Mrs. Korman. Mr. Korman had to go back to Boston today. Stella's at her sister's in the Bronx. She's pretty upset too." His eyes suddenly filmed over and he turned away to hide his tears.

Maria tapped lightly on Barbie's door, but there was no reply. She opened it cautiously and peeked in. The drapes were drawn, but when her eyes adjusted to the dimness she could see Barbie's motionless form, covered with a sheet. An air conditioner hummed softly in the window, the room was very cool. Maria tiptoed to the bed and looked down. For a moment she thought Barbie wasn't breathing and panic seized her insides and twisted her gut. Then the other woman opened her eyes.

Barbie didn't say anything, just stretched out her arms. Maria dropped to her knees. They stayed close for a while, rocking slightly and hugging as tightly as they could. After a bit Maria's shoulder felt damp, and she realized that Barbie was crying. It was a soundless, sobless weeping, almost emotionless. It went on for a long time. Maria was crying too, but she was more aware of Barbie's tears than her own. Eventually she felt a relaxation of tension in the other woman, and thought perhaps the spent emotion had brought some relief. But when she released her, she realized that Barbie was in a deep, drug-induced sleep. She laid her back gently, covered her with a blanket, and turned down the air conditioner before leaving the room.

Downstairs, Phil wasn't anywhere to be seen. Maria wandered into the kitchen. Sophie Korman was standing at the stove, busy stirring and tasting.

"Hello, Maria darling. I'd know you anywhere. Just the same like when you were a kid. Smart and pretty shows all over your face." Then, after a quick kiss, "Sit down, I'll get you something to eat. You must be hungry after that long trip."

Maria wanted to say how sorry she was, how much she sympathized; Sophie was bustling and it didn't seem appropriate. Then, in the middle of pouring a glass of milk, the chatter stopped. Sophie still poured, but she stared unseeing as the glass filled and overflowed, first onto the counter, then the floor.

"Listen to me," she whispered, finally setting the empty milk carton down, but not bothering to wipe up the mess. "I'm a . . . what do you call it? A caricature. You know what I was doing when you came in? Making chicken soup. Can you believe it, Maria? My little girl's upstairs in so much pain we have to keep her doped up, and I'm feeling like somebody took a knife and cut out my heart, but I'm making chicken soup. Just like the jokes on television."

Sophie's face crumpled and she started to cry. Not silently, as Barbie had, but great wrenching sobs that shook her small, round frame and made her shoulders hunch and her breath come in hard, hurtful gasps. Maria crossed to her, thinking that this house was going to float away on an ocean of grief. The line of an ancient prayer flashed through her mind. "To thee I come, mourning and weeping in this valley of tears." Yes, indeed. She tried to put her arms around Sophie, but the older woman twisted away and wouldn't accept comfort. Instead she grabbed a dish towel and buried her face in that.

Maria sponged the spilt milk from the counter and the floor, and waited. In a few minutes Sophie regained control. "I'm sorry. Just when I think I'm not going to cry any more, the flood starts again."

She sat down heavily, talking not to Maria so much as to the wall. "Look, roosters she's got. From Portugal. All these tiles shlepped across an ocean, just so my Barbie can decorate her kitchen. You think the roosters make up for a husband and a child? You know, when Barbie was born, my mother, may she rest in peace, she tied a red ribbon to her wrist. It was supposed to ward off the evil eye, because everybody said how gorgeous Barbie was. You think she feels any better up there now because she's gorgeous?"

Maria didn't try to answer the question. She picked up the glass of milk and sipped it, just to have something to do with her hands.

"My Moe, he wanted another baby. Not me. Not smart Sophie. Could I maybe do it better a second time? Could I do it even as good? No, nothing could be more beautiful, so Barbie was enough. Only the red ribbon didn't work." Her voice kept climbing until it became a shrill, hysterical scream. "You up there! For what she's paid, you can take back the looks and the roosters!" Sophie flung herself from her chair and lurched across the room, drunk with anguish and crazy with grief.

Maria was paralyzed. This small, slightly ridiculous woman whom she'd known most of her life was a stranger, an avenging fury. Sophie's neck was rigid, her face bright red. Suddenly she spat full force at the tiled wall. "You hear me?" she shrieked. "That's what I think of Your roosters, and Your gorgeous, and Your fancy shmancy! Better You should have made her ugly and given her a little happiness."

This time Sophie didn't try to pull away when Maria put her arms around her and crooned wordless sounds of comfort. Eventually they sat together on the couch in the elegant living room. "Let's have a little brandy," Maria said. "We both need it." She poured two small ponies and smiled when Sophie tossed hers back like a veteran. She didn't even cough.

"Do me a favor, darling," Sophie said when she put down the empty glass. "Go turn off the lousy soup. No reason it should boil away and burn the pot. Maybe Phil will have some later."

Maria returned from the kitchen, puzzling over the ease with which Sophie Korman accepted her daughter's lover. The thought didn't prepare her for Sophie's next remark. "You tell me what I should think, Maria. You were always such a smart kid. A nun, even. Tell me what I should think about God, now that I've buried my son-in-law and my granddaughter and I don't know what to say to my daughter?"

"I don't know, Mrs. Korman. I wish I knew what I believed, then maybe I could help. But I don't know."

Sophie shrugged. "That's what I thought."

AROUND TEN-THIRTY, PHIL REAPPEARED. "JUST CHECKING IN," he told Maria. "Everything okay?"

She nodded. "Barbie's still sleeping, and I finally prevailed on Mrs. Korman to go to bed."

"What about yourself? You've had a long day."

Maria glanced at her watch. "I've got a second wind. My internal clock says it's early morning. Time to get up and get going." On Lanzarote she and Tom had become dawn risers, both starting to write by six.

Phil was busy heating cognac in a large crystal beaker. He waited for it to ignite, then doused the flame with more cognac. "Good for what ails you," he said, handing her a snifter.

"Thanks." Her second brandy of the evening. Some kind of a record for her. She didn't feel any effect, though. "Do you have a nurse for Barbie?"

"No. She insisted she didn't want one. About the only request she's made, so it seemed best to agree. The doctor will be here in the morning. He comes three times a day."

"You're keeping her sedated?"

"The doctor's idea. Just until she's over the worst of it."

"Over . . ." Her voice trailed away.

"Yeah. Sounds nuts, doesn't it."

He leaned his head back against the couch, and Maria noted that he was tired. Funny, she never thought of Philocles Williams as a tired man.

"It's been pretty hard on you, too," she said.

He didn't reply. Instead he said, "Do you know that Joe DiAnni is in New York?"

Her eyes opened wide. "No, I didn't know that."

"I suppose you couldn't. All the dying has come too close together." He told her the story.

"Oh, my God, Ann Jessup. . . . It's hard to believe. Poor Barbie, poor Joe."

"I haven't seen him for a few days." Phil sat up and pinned Maria with his metallic eyes. "He's Norma's father, isn't he?"

She wondered if she was giving him a new weapon, some

393

new hold over Barbie. It seemed a ridiculous consideration under the circumstances. "Yes, he is. But I don't think Joe knows that."

"He does now. They were arguing the morning Norma died. In the hospital. I thought that's what it was about." Phil told her how it had been. "I think DiAnni believes Barbie had no right to keep the truth from him."

"Maybe she didn't," Maria said tiredly. "She did what seemed best at the time. It wasn't the easiest way for her, just the one she thought was right. Joe's got no business holding that against her now. They weren't lovers, you know. Just close friends. Barbie told me it was a one-time thing. One fall from grace, is how she put it."

"I don't give a damn. I'm not sure you understand that. Or Barbie, for that matter. I couldn't care less what she did before I met her. How many lovers or who they were, it makes no difference. But if DiAnni tries to hurt her now, I'll squash him. Fast."

Maria knew it was true; it had to be, because Phil was not likely to make idle threats. Still, she wasn't protecting Joe when she said, "He won't hurt her. No matter what he thinks, Joe's not vengeful. He may disagree and be bitter, but he'll understand."

"Okay, let's hope you're right." Williams stood up to go, then turned back to her. "Do you know who Proteus was, by any chance? I've been meaning to look it up, but I haven't had time."

She took a moment to adjust to the abrupt change of subject, then to search her memory. Mythology wasn't one of her interests, but it was one of Tom's. He'd mentioned somebody called Proteus. "Some Greek god of the sea who could change himself into anything he wanted. I think he did it whenever somebody tried to catch him and make him tell the future."

"I see. It makes sense." She looked at him blankly and he continued. "The doctors said Norma had a proteus infection. Some kind of rare virus they were able to cure the first time. Then it metamorphosed and went into hiding. When it reappeared, it was immune to all the drugs."

Science and myth all bound up together. And nobody quite knowing where the dividing line was. Just like in ancient times. Some things never changed.

In a couple of days Stella returned to take over the household, and in a rare surcease of introversion Barbie persuaded her mother to go home. "Daddy needs you more than I do," she said.

Finally Mrs. Korman agreed. On impulse, Maria offered to go with her. "I haven't been home in a long time. Besides, you shouldn't travel alone." Barbie looked at Maria with gratitude for a second, then retreated to the private world of suffering behind her blank eyes.

Sophie and Maria caught the Boston shuttle from La Guardia that same afternoon. Mrs. Korman kept up a steady stream of chatter all during the fifty-minute flight. Nerves, Maria realized, but she was grateful. Maria wasn't sure what she wanted to do in Boston, and listening to Sophie kept her from thinking about it.

"He couldn't stay any longer, my Moe. Big *macha,* thinks Filene's shoe department can't get along without him. They probably can't. When Moe retires in six months, nobody's ever going to find anything in that place. Did I tell you we're moving to Florida? A gorgeous place in Miami Beach. A senior citizens community, all old fogies like us. To tell the truth, we like the idea. And we don't rent, we own. Barbie picked out the flat already. The furniture even."

Sophie didn't say so, but Maria guessed that Phil was behind the purchase of a condominium in Florida. Barbie made an excellent living, but she didn't have that kind of money. And certainly the Kormans didn't. Or the Trapettis. The thought of her own family came unbidden from the shallow depths of mind where it had been lurking. That's when Maria knew she was going to see them. So much grief and dying; it made her aware of mortality, and guilty about neglect.

She took Sophie to Shirley Avenue in a cab, and asked the driver to wait while she took the other woman upstairs. The Korman flat was unchanged, like the neighborhood. All the ethnic lifelines were present—anchors for the insecure, even after two generations. Only there were no bookmakers. Maria looked at the pantry and saw shelves of canned goods. A dream perhaps; unreal, as so much of her past seemed to be.

Sophie saw her glance and laughed. "You're looking for Nat and Sid. They've been gone for years. Too much trouble. Moe and me, we always thought that. We only did it that once. Just to have some extra money for Barbie's senior year." Her eyes filled with tears but she didn't let them fall. She put her hands on either side of Maria's face and looked deep into the dark eyes. "You're a good girl, darling. A wonderful friend. One lucky thing that's happened to my Barbie."

"I'm lucky too," Maria said. "When I needed Barbie, she was right there."

"Good. Now go, darling. Go see your mother. Don't be afraid. So maybe she doesn't understand, maybe she's hurt 'cause you're not a nun anymore. It doesn't matter. She's still your mother."

Maria folded Sophie in a quick, close hug, amazed at the perceptiveness behind the unsophisticated exterior. "Thank you," she whispered. "You give me courage."

It needed more than courage, it needed a lifetime of communication, which hadn't taken place and which couldn't be manufactured on demand, despite anybody's good intentions. Like Shirley Avenue, Revere Street was unchanged. The town itself had changed a great deal, whole new neighborhoods had sprung up, removed from the old laws and the old boundaries. But the seminal communities and their myths and ways of being were as before.

Maria was dizzy with the familiarity and frightened by her visceral anxiety. Old habits. An inoculation at birth, with a lifetime effect. The look on her mother's face made it worse. The door was locked and Maria had to ring the bell, and there was a moment when she realized that her mother didn't recognize her. It passed in a fraction of a second, but the memory came to lodge permanently in a cold place in the pit of her stomach.

"It's you! Come in, don't stand there."

Maria leaned over to kiss and be kissed, but the gesture was perfunctory. Uninvited, she followed her mother into the kitchen and sat down and watched while the older woman continued the interrupted job of making gnocchi. "You gonna stay?" she asked, while her fingers broke off bits of potato dough and transformed them into little curls that would enclose the sauce in their artless depths.

"Just for tonight maybe."

"Okay. There's plenty of room. Papa will be home in about an hour. I thought you were still on that island, what's its name?"

"Lanzarote." She'd sent her mother a postcard every couple of weeks. "One of the Canary Islands. The setting for my book. I came home last Sunday, to be with Barbie. Her daughter died."

Mrs. Trapetti nodded. "I read it in the *Journal*. A shame. Maybe somebody baptized the baby before she died. A nurse or a doctor maybe. I read someplace they often do that when a child's going to die."

Maria sighed. "I don't know, Mama. It doesn't matter. All that stuff about unbaptized children going to limbo, nobody believes that anymore." Mrs. Trapetti snorted, and Maria knew it had been the wrong thing to say. She didn't want to argue theology or confront ignorance; she hadn't come home for that. To cover up, she asked about her brothers and sisters.

"All moved out, like I wrote you. Except Celia's been staying here lately. With her baby."

"Where's her husband?" Celia was her youngest sister. She must be twenty now. Maria could hardly remember what she looked like.

"Her husband's gone," Mrs. Trapetti said. "Nobody knows where. Just as well. He treated her rotten."

For her mother to make that statement, Celia's husband must have been a cross between Bluebeard and Jack the Ripper. Maria didn't know what else to say. She watched her mother's clever fingers. A dish towel was spread to one side of the table, and rows of gnocchi filled it with incredible speed. Enough for an army, despite the reduced family. "Celia and the baby are using your room," her mother said. "You can stay in Nonni's."

"Okay, that's fine." Her room, Nonni's room—no matter that neither of them had lived in the house for over ten years. Immutable labels for changing realities.

There was the sound of a key turning in the lock and a young woman came in holding a little boy on her hip, her face sheened with perspiration brought on by the heat of the afternoon and the effort of motherhood. "Maria!" the girl squealed at once. "It is you, isn't it! Gosh, you look fantastic. What about your book? You got a copy? Sal, this is your Auntie Maria. The famous one in the family."

All the enthusiasm she'd hoped for, all the spontaneous affection, but from the wrong source. Maria kissed her sister and made appreciative noises about the baby. She saw Celia eyeing her clothes. Maria was wearing the white linen suit. She'd brought it along from Lanzarote in case she had any business meetings in New York. It had seemed the right thing to wear today. A respectful gesture. Now she said, "Hey, we're about the same size. Have you an extra pair of pants and a shirt by chance?"

"Sure. C'mon and we'll find something. Watch the baby, huh, Ma?"

Mrs. Trapetti nodded and the two girls went from the kitchen through the dark, narrow hall to the room on the second floor where Maria had grown up. A tiny cubbyhole of a room, but she'd had it to herself because she was the eldest. It even smelled the same. And the same plaster crucifix was hanging over the bed, with her crystal first-communion Rosary strung over one arm. The only thing different was the crib squeezed in beside the narrow bed.

Celia found a pair of jeans and a T-shirt and watched in fawning admiration while her sister changed. "Here," Maria said, "you keep the suit. It'll look great on you."

"Gee! You mean it? I don't know. Where would I wear a suit like that?" All the younger girl's desperation quivered in her voice. Twenty years old and nothing to look forward to but this room and premature motherhood.

"Listen, Celia, are you getting a divorce?"

"How can I? Divorce costs money. Besides, the Church says I'm married until I die."

"Do you believe that?" If she did, then Maria would back off. She didn't mean to destroy faith, if Celia had any.

"I dunno. I don't think much about it. What difference does it make?"

"That depends on you." Maria pulled a checkbook out of her bag and wrote hastily. She had to ask Celia's married name. "Here," she said finally. "This is enough to get you started on a divorce, if you decide you want one. Otherwise just put it in the bank and keep it for an emergency. Don't say anything to Mama or Papa. This is for you."

Celia looked at the check. "A thousand dollars," she said in awe. "You really are rich, aren't you?"

"I've been lucky. If you decide to get out of here, out of Revere, go back to school maybe, just let me know. I'll help all I can." Conscience money, she admitted to herself, an apology for leaving you all so far behind. Just like the monthly checks she'd been sending her mother since the book was sold.

"I gotta see how Sal is." Celia tucked the check in the pocket of her dungarees. Something in the gesture told Maria it wouldn't go for either a divorce or a ticket away from Revere Street. Clothes, probably. For her and the little boy. What the hell, she should know by now that everybody has to make their own choices.

Downstairs the gnocchi were simmering in a huge pan of

salted water. The scent of tomato sauce filled the kitchen. Tom would have been in ecstasy.

Carlo Trapetti came in and did the same thing he'd done every evening Maria could remember. He poured himself a glass of wine from the jug beside the sink, then left it to sit while he washed his face and hands. His greeting was somewhere between the coolness of her mother and the enthusiasm of her sister. Maria wondered what she could say to him. They had talked so little in their lives, what words could bridge that gap now? Before she could decide, the doorbell rang. Mrs. Trapetti started guiltily, then looked at her eldest daughter. "Go in the back bedroom," she commanded. "We don't want to bother with explanations."

Maria stood in the darkened room where her brothers had once slept and squeezed her eyes shut so the tears wouldn't spill over. Probably none of the neighbors even knew she'd left the convent. Probably her mother was living in terror in case any of them saw the name Maria Trapetti on a book and asked if it could possibly be her.

In a few minutes Celia came and said whoever it was had gone and she could come out. The girl had the grace to be embarrassed. "Don't take it too hard," she said softly. "You know how they are. And this neighborhood hasn't changed since the last century."

Maria nodded, but when she was once more in the kitchen with her parents she said, "Look, I forgot, I've got an appointment in New York tomorrow morning. It's probably better if I go back tonight. I just wanted a chance to say hello. And to see the baby," she added lamely. She'd not remembered his existence; she wasn't even sure she'd been informed of his birth. All the same, she hugged him fiercely and kissed him hard. Another generation. Maybe a better one. There was always hope.

"Yeah, sure," Carlo Trapetti said. "You better go now if you got an appointment. Never can tell how late them planes is gonna be."

"Don't you want some supper first?" her mother demanded.

Maria ate a helping of gnocchi and sauce, then she stood up and said she had to leave.

"You want me to call a taxi?" Mrs. Trapetti asked.

Maria didn't know what to reply. Another taxi arriving at the door would raise questions on Revere Street. Possibly no one had noticed the one that brought her, but they'd surely notice a second. She felt terrible about the pain she'd caused her family, was still causing them, and she just wanted to get away with as little fuss as possible. "Maybe it's better if I walk down to the subway stop," she said. "Probably quicker than a taxi."

"Yeah, it goes straight through to Logan, too," her mother said. Then, without warning or preamble, her chin came up and she got a strange, stubborn look in her eye. "C'mon, Maria," she said, "I'll walk you to the station."

They left together, walking side by side along Revere Street toward the beach and the subway stop that had come into existence shortly before Maria entered the convent. After a few minutes, Mrs. Trapetti linked her arm in her daughter's. They didn't speak until they reached their destination. "You take care of yourself," the older woman said finally. "I'm glad you look so good. You gonna get married, maybe?"

"Maybe," Maria said. It wasn't true, but she knew it would make her mother feel better.

"Good. You're not so old. You can probably have a couple of babies even. Take care of yourself," she repeated.

Then she turned and walked away.

"How did it go?" Barbie asked.

Maria leaned back in the chintz-covered armchair and pressed her fingers to her temples. They were throbbing. She felt terrible—exhausted, and unclean in more ways than a mere shower could remedy.

"God-awful. I made a mess of it. I just wish I understood." Then, realizing how her words could be construed, "I don't mean your mother! Sophie was fine when I left her. She's a lovely lady, Barbie. I think that's part of what I find so confusing. You've managed to keep a connection. A link or something. Some sort of guide rope you and your parents can follow back and forth into each other's worlds. I've never been able to do that. I went home, but we had nothing to say to each other. They're ashamed of me, and I resent it. To make it worse, I gave my sister Celia money to salve my conscience and I'm afraid it may do her more harm than good. Oh, I can't explain. Not to myself or you. What do you think?"

She stopped, waiting for Barbie to comment. If anyone could understand, it would be Barbie. But the other woman wasn't looking at her, she was staring at a fixed point in space. Maria realized that Barbie hadn't heard a word she'd said. Still drugged, perhaps. "Come on, honey. I'll take you up to bed." Maria tugged her gently to her feet and led her upstairs.

When they passed the door to what had been Norma's room, Barbie stopped, stiffened, then walked on. She's like a robot, Maria thought. A wind-up doll. She's slipping completely away from reality.

"You've got to stop sedating her," Maria told the doctor next morning. "She has to come to terms with her grief sooner or later."

The doctor was a white-haired man with a florid face and an air of bonhomie that struck Maria as forced. "Now, Miss Trapetti, we're just helping her over the worst time. Don't you worry."

"You're not helping her at all. She's losing her grip on the real world. And there's something else bothering me. What happens if you keep this up? Isn't she liable to become addicted to the drugs you're administering?" The man's expression said she'd found the way past his facade. She pressed her advantage. "That's possible, isn't it?"

The doctor busied himself arranging things in his black bag. Maria kept staring at him. Finally he lifted his head. "It's a possibility, yes."

"A near certainty if the treatment continues," she insisted. "Isn't that true?"

"Perhaps," he admitted softly. "But I'm following Mr. Williams's orders. He said to make her rest." His face grew redder and he didn't meet her eyes.

She didn't waste any more words on the doctor, just waited until he'd left, then took a taxi to Phil's office. She'd never been there before. All its wealth and elegance sickened her, and fueled her anger.

A middle-aged secretary looked up when Maria entered. Jeans and a sweat shirt didn't seem to impress her much. "Yes, can I help you?" A British accent. In keeping with everything else in the place.

"I'd like to see Mr. Williams right away. It's urgent."

"Mr. Williams is in conference just now. If you'll leave your name and telephone number, I'll just ask him to ring you when he's free."

"Ask him now." Maria spoke through clenched teeth. She leaned forward, rigid with fury. "If you don't buzz that damned intercom I will. Tell his crooked highness that Maria's here and that I'm coming in."

The secretary pulled back slightly, as if the fire in Maria's eyes could actually burn. "I don't think—"

"Damn you! You don't have to think anything. I've just

left Mrs. Gold. Now tell your rotten boss I'm waiting for him."

"Oh, I see! You should have said so right away. Mrs. Gold. That's different, of course."

Thirty seconds later Phil stepped through the door into the reception area. "What's wrong? What are you doing here, Maria?"

"I came to tell you . . ." Maria paused and looked from Phil to the secretary. She'd have no objection to publishing her opinion of Philocles Williams in the *New York Times,* but she didn't want Barbie soiled by any more gossip.

Williams understood her gesture. He led the way through another door into a conference room of some sort, a space as luxuriously decorated as the rest of the office. He turned to her. "What did you come to tell me?"

"That I'm not going to allow you to make Barbie into an addict." She tried to keep her voice as cool as his, to suppress her rage because she knew it was a weapon he could use against her.

"What the hell are you talking about? Where is she? What's happened?"

"She's home in bed. Doped up to the eyeballs by your tame physician. Too far gone to know her own name, let alone yours or mine or Norma's, God help her."

Williams stared at her. "I don't know what you're talking about. You're upset Maria, tired. It's understandable. I merely instructed that she be given something to help her rest. Just until the shock wears off."

"You son of a bitch," she cursed softly. "Do you think I'm going to succumb to your charm? I know what you are and what you're trying to do. That idiot doctor admitted it. If he continues shooting Barbie full of whatever he's giving her, she'll become addicted. Maybe she already is."

"Addicted? You think I'm trying to make Barbie into a junkie?"

"I know you are."

His control slipped. She knew it because a small tic started pulsing in his cheek. When he spoke his voice was still soft, but hoarse, as if his throat were tight. "What makes you think I'd do a thing like that?"

"She'll never get away from you then, will she? She'll need you in order to get her fix. Isn't that what you want? Isn't that how the Mafia does things?"

His hand flew up so fast she didn't see it coming. Only after her cheek stung with pain did she realize he'd slapped her. Then it was Williams, not she, who recoiled. He sat down on a rosewood chair upholstered in gray tweed to match the drapes and the fabric-lined walls. "I'm sorry," he said his voice as monochromatic as the room. "I don't know why I did that. What you're saying isn't true. And it's too ugly to be mentioned in the same breath as Barbie. All I wanted to do was help her get over the pain. The day of the funeral she was in hell. I've never seen anything like it; I couldn't stand it. I had to do something. I never meant for him to use strong drugs."

"Don't you see? The doctor thought you were being evasive. That you really wanted her completely doped up."

Williams looked stunned. "I'll have his license suspended."

Maria sighed. Stupidity, not evil, was behind the drugs. "No, don't do that. He was doing what he thought you wanted. It's your fault, Phil, not his. People like him are so scared of you, of your power, they try to anticipate your demands, guess what you mean. I don't care about him and neither should you. Barbie's the one that matters."

"What should I do?" The question was oddly poignant; he sounded like a lost child.

"Tell the quack he's not to see her again. And get another doctor. Someone legitimate and outside your sphere of influence. If you know any, that is."

"Of course." Phil's voice was more normal now, but his eyes pleaded with her when he said, "You'll stay with her, won't you? Until she's all right?"

"Until she doesn't need me anymore," Maria promised.

BARBIE CAME OUT OF HER DRUG-INDUCED FOG INTO A REALITY of pain. It was impossible to know how much of her agony was the result of grief and how much the physical hell of withdrawal symptoms. The new doctor, a woman whom Maria liked at first meeting and immediately felt comfortable with, said she thought it unlikely Barbie was an addict.

"Ten days isn't really long enough to set up a dependency syndrome. A start on one, yes, but not the full-blown agony you're describing."

Maria had reported holding Barbie for hours while she sobbed and retched and trembled. And all the while Maria was remembering Frank Sinatra in the movie *The Man with the Golden Arm* and being terrified to the point of physical sickness herself. The doctor listened quietly and didn't accuse Maria of melodrama. Her name was Tessa Ambrose, and she had tanned leathery skin, short iron-gray hair, and piercing green eyes that seemed to see through things. A very tough lady, but one both kind and smart. Phil had found her, and despite everything, Maria had to admit he'd come up trumps.

"Barbie's grieving." Dr. Ambrose said now. "It hurts like hell, of course. But it's necessary. Grief suppressed is the most damaging thing in the world. Some studies even indicate that repressed grief or repressed anger is at the root of a lot of the cancers we see. In women particularly."

Maria managed a smile. "Not very surprising. That it should be mostly women, I mean."

"Not a bit," Tessa Ambrose agreed. "So you be glad your friend isn't afraid to weep. And hang in there. I'll be back to-morrow."

The next day, Maria was able to report that the storm had calmed somewhat. "Good," the doctor said. "Try and get her to take a walk this afternoon. Maybe go into her shop down-stairs. Not for long. Just an hour or two. Just a way to get her out of the house."

The shop had reopened three days before. Angie had asked Phil's permission to take down the sign that said "Closed due to a death in the family" and open the doors. "We'll lose all our regular customers," she'd explained. "I don't think Mrs. Gold would want that."

Phil agreed, and now when Maria went downstairs she found Angie thumbing through a thick file. "What's that?" Maria asked, pointing to a sheet daubed with vibrant color.

"The plans for a wedding we're supposed to be doing. Clara Butt tulips, that's the pink bits, and white lilacs. Mrs. Gold was working on it when . . . everything happened."

Maria took the paper and studied it. "Has the customer said anything? Does she still expect Barbie to do the wedding?"

"Of course. Anyway, she's in Europe. A honeymoon before the ceremony. That's how it usually is with these people. Be-sides, the flowers were all ordered specially from Holland. Weeks ago. I was just confirming the delivery arrangements."

"When's the wedding?"

"June eleventh. That's a little over a week away."

"Right." Maria looked at the design sketch again. It made no sense to her but she recognized the scrawled notes as being in Barbie's hand. "I'm going to borrow this for a bit, okay?" Angie nodded and Maria took the file away with her.

She showed it to Barbie when she brought in the lunch tray Stella had so carefully prepared. Barbie looked blankly at the food, but her eyes flickered with life when Maria handed her the file.

"Mrs. Creighton-Smith, soon to be Mrs. Creighton-Smith Locksley. I forget all the previous names. This is her fourth wedding. A good customer," Barbie added with a wan smile.

"That's what Angie says," Maria added. "And she's worried about the arrangements. I told her you're sure to be well enough to do them, but you won't be if you don't eat something. Stella slaved for an hour on that spinach salad. It's your favorite dressing."

Barbie pushed the file away and lifted a fork. It seemed to weigh down her hand. She took a mouthful, but no more. "I can't. I'm sorry. It just chokes me." Tears welled up anew in the amber eyes, and Maria reluctantly took the tray away.

"What about a little walk this afternoon? Dr. Ambrose said it would be good for you."

"Whatever you want," Barbie said listlessly.

ON FRIDAY, MARIA REALIZED SHE HADN'T YET CALLED SI. IT seemed a peculiar oversight. On the plane from Spain she'd thought of him a lot, then he'd just disappeared from her head. Swallowed by grief, like everything else. Now she wanted desperately to see him. She phoned, and they agreed to meet for lunch.

The restaurant was obscure and quiet. Si listened impassively while Maria told him why she'd returned, and what had happened since. When she'd finished he said, "Life's certainly dumped on your girlfriend lately."

"I know. And I feel so helpless. What do you say to someone who's had so much pain? And there's something else." She explained about the sedation, leaving out her mistaken idea that Phil was deliberately trying to make Barbie an addict, just making it sound as if the first doctor was incompetent. "I keep wondering if she's still having some kind of withdrawal symptoms. She won't eat or take an interest in anything. She's like an automaton."

"Doesn't sound like withdrawal," Si said. "Besides, Tessa Ambrose is as good as they come. If she says Barbie's not addicted, she isn't."

"You know her?"

"Sure. She works in my neck of the woods a couple of days a month."

Maria wasn't surprised. "She's a very nice lady."

"The best." Si leaned forward slightly. "So are you. I admire your commitment to Barbie."

"My God! Don't you start that too. Barbie's my oldest and dearest friend. When I left the convent, she took me in. I couldn't have written my book without her support—emotional and financial."

"Okay. That makes you both good girls. If that's true, I like Barbie too. I tend to think of her as a jet-set beauty queen. Something to decorate Philocles Williams's arm."

"I told you before you had her all wrong."

"So you did."

After a bit, Maria told him about his brother. "He's working hard. I think the book is going really well. He still has that damn cough, though. And he gets tired very easily. I wanted him to come back to New York with me and see a doctor, but he wouldn't hear of it."

Si shrugged. "Tom's stubborn. He always does everything his own way. What about you? Are you going back to your island in the sun?"

"Yes. That is, I'd like to. But I can't leave Barbie just yet." Maria took another bite of her salad. "Will you do me a favor?"

"Sure, if I can."

"You can. Come to Barbie's house tonight. I want you to see her. I want to know what you think."

"Tonight's not possible," Si said. "Not tomorrow either. What about Sunday afternoon?"

"Fine. These days our social calendar is blank. Stella won't be there, but I'll fix you a meal. I'm not in her league and certainly not in Tom's; still, you won't starve." For a while they were quiet, then, almost accidentally, their eyes met. "What was your wife like?" Maria asked suddenly.

"Tom told you?"

"That you're divorced, yes. Wasn't he supposed to?"

"It's no secret. I just don't talk about it much." He sat back and sipped his indifferent wine. Finally he said, "My wife was skinny. Inside and out."

"Not very bright, you mean?" Maria found it hard to imagine Si married to a fool.

"No, nothing like that. She was smart enough. A Bennington girl. All their usual concerns with art and higher realities. She just never seemed very solid to me. It was so tenuous, her and her ideas and causes. Nothing you could sink your teeth into, or count on to withstand a big wind."

"I see. Why did you marry her?"

"The usual bad reason. I thought I loved her, and married seemed the thing to be. She left me, by the way, not the other way round. And she was right. I was a lousy husband. I was pretty skinny in those days too."

Maria looked at his heavy shoulders, deliberately twisting his meaning. "That's hard to believe. Did you ever play football? You look so much the type."

"Never. Too busy getting good marks so I could grab the next scholarship and the next degree. Then, after I got my doctorate, I got married. I'd just accepted a position on the social sciences faculty at Amherst and I arrived with my shiny new title and my shiny new wife."

"Then?"

"Then, I woke up after a couple of years and realized I was totally numb. So was she, as it turned out. The separation was predictably painless."

"How did the youth hostel come about?"

He told her about his mother's funeral and the class in the assimilation of ethnic minorities. "I looked at that damn bit of torn ribbon and realized that everything I was doing was something like that. A symbol of the real thing, a substitute."

"But what change can you achieve? It's such a vast problem." She stopped, conscious that she could be hurting him, not wanting to do that.

"A drop in the ocean, I know. But it's my drop. I bring it and dribble it in and at least it's wet. I'm not just talking." He studied her openly for a moment, then leaned forward and touched her cheek. "What are you doing, Maria? What's real in your life?"

"I don't know. Just that I don't want to be rubbed raw again." She spoke with sudden intensity, spitting out the words as if defying him to chide or contradict. "I don't want to be belly to belly with my fellow man, not anymore. I tried that for nearly nine years. A life of service and self-sacrifice. I don't want to sacrifice myself. I want . . ." She hesitated, then whispered, "I want to be saved."

For some moments he was silent. "What that means is open to a number of interpretations," he said finally.

She stood up. "When I figure out which one applies, I'll let you know."

* * *

THE CHALKED OUTLINE OF THE BODY IN THE HALL HAD LONG since disappeared. All the same, Joe saw it whenever he passed. And going inside and closing the door didn't help much. The vision of the sheet-covered corpse on the stretcher in the middle of the living room lurked behind his eyeballs. Every time he blinked, there it was. He spent a lot of time sitting on the couch trying not to blink.

The apartment downstairs was empty. Helene Wentworth had moved out a few days ago. As far as he knew, she hadn't lived there since it happened. Couldn't blame her for that. He'd go someplace else too, if he could. But he had a lease on this place, he couldn't afford a hotel, and he didn't know anyone in New York. Barbie, of course, but that was different. He didn't want to see Barbie.

DiAnni put his face in his hands. He could feel the stubble of beard, which told him he hadn't shaved in days. Not since the funeral, probably. Barbie hadn't noticed him at the funeral. When they buried Norma, Barbie had been beyond noticing anything. Not like that day in Chelsea when Normie was put into the earth. She wasn't playing at being Jackie Kennedy the morning of Norma's funeral.

The memory of Barbie's grief didn't move Joe to pity. Not even when it was superimposed on the picture of the warm, serene girl he'd once known so well. His pity was all for himself, and it was confused with rage. At least Barbie had known their daughter for five years; she'd denied him that.

He poured himself another glass of wine. It went down hard, through a throat burned raw by too much alcohol and little else. Whiskey would be quicker, of course. He wouldn't have to swallow so much of it to produce the desired effect. But it was too expensive. DiAnni managed to laugh at himself. For five years he'd lived from hand to mouth and never worried. Now he had over fifteen thousand in the bank and he was obsessed by thoughts of poverty. All of which proved he'd been crazy to leave Pete Chiarra and the *Bella Donna*.

If he closed his eyes he could see the trim cutter and smell the sweet, salt balm of the Bahamas. No he couldn't. All he saw was that goddamn corpse. A murderer. That's what he'd become. And to pay for his crime he had the vision of the daughter he'd never held in his arms, arching her tiny body in agony while her heart stopped.

Shit! He was losing his goddamn mind. He needed a psychiatrist, or a confessor maybe. He rose and began pacing and muttering aloud. "Bless me, Father, for I have sinned. It's nearly six years since my last confession. Since then I've committed numberless sins against faith and charity and I've fornicated more times than I can recall. Oh, and by the way, I murdered a woman a couple of weeks ago. And I found out that I had a daughter, but I didn't know she existed until the day she died."

DiAnni stood on the spot where the stretcher with the corpse had been, and listened to the echo of his voice. He remained where he was until the words faded from his mind, an act of conscious will. "Got to get a grip on yourself, Joe," he whispered. "Start looking for some kind of job for a start. Go back to attending classes. And get rid of this damned bug juice." He was still holding the glass of wine.

He walked into the kitchen and poured it down the sink with slow, deliberate motions. The dark purple liquid made a little puddle around the drain, a beautiful contrast against the silvery stainless steel. Once he and Pete had speared a fish, a barracuda, and its guts stained the aquamarine waters just that color. He'd been fascinated, and Chiarra had screamed bloody murder because he wasn't helping to land the thing. Memories of Pete flooded back. Sweet and good memories, almost strong enough to drive out his current demons, as they had exorcised the old ones.

Something tugged at the edge of his brain. Something he'd been trying to recall for days. The stainless steel sink was part of it. DiAnni stared at the sink. A series of pictures began clicking in his head, a film strip he could roll back or forward at will. Governor's Harbour on Eleuthera, shining white houses with green velvet lawns against a backdrop of glowing poinciana, himself on the deck of the lady, waiting for Chiarra to return with provisions, the dinghy racing up to the cutter, then pulling out as fast as they could because Pete recognized some Mafioso bastard among a group of men getting off a yacht.

That was it, it had something to do with that day. He'd gone below and gotten the glasses and trained them on the men landing in Governor's Harbour. And only one had been noteworthy. A man tall and slim, like himself, with white hair belied by youthful vitality and a dark tan. He hadn't seen the eyes, the binoculars weren't strong enough. Now he stared at the sink and he knew what color the man's eyes were. He'd looked into them numerous times of late. They were gunmetal gray. "Oh, God." It wasn't a prayer. More like a curse and a moan.

Don Stefano had reached out to touch him from the grave.

A WOMAN TOLD HIM MRS. GOLD WASN'T WELL, THAT SHE wasn't seeing anyone, but he pushed past her into a living room that immediately struck him as a movie set, glamor laid on with a palette knife. In the background there was the soft hum of an air conditioner, which only served to accentuate the silence. Barbie was sitting on a chair with a blanket over her knees. She looked washed out against the vibrant colors of the room. Faded. She wore a sweater although it was over eighty outside, and he saw her tremble, as if in pain. He thrust his pity aside. Whatever she was suffering, she deserved. "I want to talk to you."

"Hello, Joe. Sit down. Stella, get Mr. DiAnni something to drink, please."

He shook his head, warding off the attentions of the older woman. "I don't want a drink. I want to talk to you." Barbie continued to stare at him. He half realized that she didn't really see him, wasn't concentrating on his presence, but he didn't allow that to silence him. He had come to ask for an explanation. No, to say he had one, to accuse. He took a step nearer her chair.

"I've been trying to figure why you did it. Why you kept me away from her. This morning I worked it out." She raised her eyes to his face, but they seemed to look through him to some point on the wall behind his head. Joe clenched his fists by his sides, the only way he knew to keep from hitting her. "Tell me when you became a Mafia whore. When did you decide to bring up my daughter with filth and scum?"

"Get out of my house." The command was whispered, as if that was all she had strength for.

"Not until you tell me how you could do something like that! How could you become such a bitch!"

Then there was a voice behind him. "You heard the lady, DiAnni. Get out."

DiAnni turned. Williams was standing by the door. He wasn't wearing a coat or tie. He looked like a man interrupted while he was relaxing in his own home. "I think I'm going to kill you," DiAnni said very quietly.

"No. You're not the killing type, whatever's happened lately. In a contest I would kill you. But that's not going to

410

happen either. You're going to walk out of here now and not come back. Go where you want and do what you want, DiAnni, but if I ever smell you near either of us again, you'll be dead."

DiAnni stood still for a few seconds. He stared first at Barbie and then at Philocles Williams. And all of a sudden he wanted only to cry. "My fault," he muttered. "The whole stinking mess is my fault." He stretched a tentative hand toward Barbie. She flinched, and he dropped it heavily by his side.

"Get out," Williams repeated.

Joe moved toward the door. He was stumbling as if he was drunk. He'd almost made it to the exit when Maria walked in. He didn't recognize her at first, not until she said, "Hello, Joe. It's been a long time."

"Maria? It is you, isn't it?"

Williams's voice cut the air between them. "Mr. DiAnni was just leaving."

Phil's tone made Maria glance quickly at Barbie. "What's going on?" she demanded. "Are you okay, honey?" Barbie didn't answer, just kept shivering and staring at the wall. "Jesus!" Maria exploded. "I went out for a couple of hours to have lunch with a friend. What have you two managed to do to her in the meantime?"

Her anger was directed at both men, but it only reached Phil. By the time she turned around, Joe was gone.

"DR. AMBROSE PUT HER BACK TO BED FOR TWENTY-FOUR hours," Maria told Si on Sunday. "But today she's coming downstairs for lunch. Try not to look shocked when you see her. It's pretty grim."

"What were they fighting about?"

Maria went on setting the table. "I don't know. Phil won't tell me, and Barbie can't. Whatever it was, it set her back days. Just when I thought we were making a little progress."

"Have you seen the other guy, what's his name, Joe?"

"Joe DiAnni. No, I haven't seen him. I don't know where he lives and I don't think I much care. It's all too damn convoluted. Too many old ties and knots and heartaches. I want Barbie to look to the future. Me too."

"Hope is a tiny girl."

She paused with the dishes still in her hands. "What did you say?"

Si took the plates from her and put them on the table.

" 'Hope is a tiny girl,' " he quoted, " 'nothing but that little earnest of a bud, which shows itself at the beginning of April.' It's a poem by a fellow called Péguy, a Frenchman."

" 'God Speaks,' " Maria said. "I know it." She stared at him with sad and shining eyes, and because the moment was both very true and very painful she added, "What's a nice Jewish boy like you doing in a place like this?"

He grinned. "For a *shiksa,* sometimes you're pretty smart-mouthed."

Thus they bantered the moment away. When it was safely behind them, Si looked at the dining room table and asked, "Who's the fourth?"

"Phil maybe. In this house you never know. It's always better to be prepared."

"Lord of the manor."

"Something like that." She made a final adjustment to the wine glasses and started for the door. "Go pour yourself a drink. I'll see if I can get Barbie to come down."

Maria noticed that Si tried to obey orders. He worked at keeping shock from his face when Barbie came into the living room. Her eyes were sooty hollows in a white face and she didn't walk, she shuffled, like an old woman. Then she stumbled into a chair, as if the journey from the bedroom had exhausted her.

Maria left them alone while she went to the kitchen to finish preparing lunch. She heard Si attempt to get some talk started, but Barbie answered him in monosyllables if at all. Poor Si; none of this was his problem. But he's my problem, Maria thought. I am becoming a professional martyr. Still trying to be the nun with the saintly smile. Trying to be true to Tom. As absurd as everything else of late, and as sad. She ought to forget both brothers. But she couldn't forget Barbie, so she'd better get this lunch cooked and get on with her life.

She'd made gnocchi. Homage to her mother, perhaps. But her fingers were clumsy, and the little curls of dough were just blobs. When she put them in boiling water they disintegrated and congealed into a soggy mess. Oh, well, the sauce was good. Maria dumped out the failed gnocchi and took a box of spaghetti from the cupboard.

The fourth place was unnecessary. Phil didn't arrive until after they finished eating. Maria offered to heat something up for him—thinking of how much she sounded like Sophie or her mother—but he refused. Phil guided Barbie from the table to the living room, his arm around her as if he was afraid she'd fall, and Si helped Maria clear and stack the dishes in the dishwasher.

"Well?" she asked as soon as they were alone. "What do you think?"

"She's not a junkie. It just doesn't happen that fast, Maria. I wondered if she was getting stuff without your knowing it, continuing to take something, but she isn't. Not that it was very likely, with Tessa Ambrose on the job. Anyway, that's all beside the point. Barbie's not on anything. I'd swear to it."

"What's wrong with her then? She's like a zombie."

"Catatonic is the word," Si said.

"Oh, God, you think it's that bad?" Maria's voice was a moan.

"Not quite. But getting there. And the way it looks, she's enjoying the trip."

"Enjoying? You think Barbie is enjoying all this?"

"Not consciously. She's not trying to do anything consciously. But she's decided to stop fighting and living. The fact that you and Williams and whoever else is around hover over her just helps it along."

"What do you suggest we do then? Let her starve herself to death? Lie up there in that bed twenty-four hours a day until she stops breathing?"

"Absolutely not. Get her out of here. Out of this house, out of New York." He looked at Maria with sudden animation. "Why don't you take her back to Lanzarote with you? What the hell, it's someplace different. No memories for her."

For the first time in days, Maria was fired with enthusiasm. It made so much sense. She ran into the living room and flung herself on her knees in front of the chair where Barbie sat. "Listen, I've had the most marvelous idea!" She ignored the blank stare that greeted this remark, and just went on. "I'm going to take you to Lanzarote with me. It will be a complete change from anything you've ever seen or imagined. You remember, I've told you how weird it is, but beautiful. And we have the most marvelous house. You'll love it. You can swim every day. And the flowers! All kinds of exotics you've never seen before. What do you say?"

Maria waited, gripping Barbie's hands in hers, staring into her eyes. And no, she wasn't imagining it. There was a flicker of response there. Not much, but more than she'd seen since this nightmare began. Slowly Barbie nodded. "Lanzarote," she said, a child learning a new word. "I think I'd like that." Then she turned from Maria to look at Phil. "Can I go, please?"

Ice formed around Maria's heart. Like Norma asking if she could go to Schrafft's. I'm not responsible for me, you are responsible. Say the right thing, you bastard, Maria thought. Say the right thing or I'll strangle you.

"Why not?" Phil answered. "If you want to go to Lanzarote, Barbie, there's no reason not to."

It wasn't a bad response, but it didn't satisfy Maria. It sounded too much as if he was giving the permission she'd asked for. "You'll look after the shop, won't you, Phil?" Maria said, trying to make Barbie believe that's why she'd asked Phil if she could go.

"The shop's doing fine." Maybe Williams understood and maybe he didn't. In any case, he rose to the occasion. "Angie's got her cousin helping her, honey. They're going to do the Locksley wedding from your sketches. After that they won't take any more design commissions. Not until after you're well. But Green Gold will stay open. That's what you want, isn't it?"

Barbie nodded. "Yes, I want to go to Lanzarote with Maria."

A far place. That was the phrase she'd been hearing over and over in her mind. You must go to a far place. Barbie didn't think it was the Lady talking to her. She didn't believe in the Lady anymore. Because there wasn't any God and any goodness. If there was, Norma would be alive. So the Lady was a trick of her imagination. And the recurrent command that burned in her brain when the others thought she was thinking nothing was her imagination too. But now Maria was offering to make it come true, and the only certainty Barbie felt in the midst of her pain was that she must go. "Lanzarote far away," she whispered. She sounded almost gay.

Maria smiled, then turned to Si and mouthed him a silent kiss.

GIVING CELIA A THOUSAND DOLLARS HAD LEFT HER BANK account very low. Monday morning, Maria called Sheila Wayne and asked about the payments from the book club and the magazine serialization.

"Things are looking marvelous," the editor told her. "The paperback rights are going to bring six figures, we think. At least high fives."

"That's great, Sheila, but I need some cash now. I checked, but my bank says no deposits have been made to my account."

There was a pause on the other end of the phone. "Well, let's see, it's June. We close our books next month, and you should get a statement and a check within eight or ten weeks of that."

"But the sales were made in March," Maria said.

Sheila's voice developed a slight chill. "I know. But if you read your contract you'll see that we have the obligation to account and make payments semiannually."

When Maria hung up she was choked with frustration. The damned contract was in Lanzarote with her personal papers; nonetheless, she suspected Sheila was telling the truth. Still, somebody must be able to tell her if she was being cheated. She thought for a moment, then reached for the telephone directory.

"No pass-through clause," Saul Hill told her. "Nothing that obligates them to pay you your share when they collect. Instead they tack it on to semiannual royalty payments. Publishers get to play with a lot of money that isn't theirs that way."

He was Tom's literary agent, the only one whose name she'd ever heard, and the only person she could think of who might be able to tell her what was going on. "You're a close friend of Tom's, I know," Hill continued. "So how come he let you sign a contract without an agent?"

"I wanted to save the ten percent," Maria said, annoyed enough to be frank. "I had no idea the book was going to make so much money."

"And all that fine print didn't seem important. Just that they liked your manuscript." The agent sighed. "Honey, you tell Tom from me he's a schmuck, and a no-good louse to let you get taken like that. A genius yes, but a schmuck nevertheless."

"Tom has a thing about telling people what to do. And I was very stubborn." And Tom didn't want to get involved because he was feeling jealous and ashamed of himself for it, she thought, but didn't say. "Okay, Mr. Hill, what do I do now? I'm almost broke, despite all the money I'm supposed to be making."

"You've got no problem, honey. Any bank will give you a loan against what you've got coming. All you need to do is get a letter from the publisher."

"But it isn't fair," Maria wailed. "The bank will charge me interest. And it's my money."

"Yeah," Hill said with a small chuckle. "And maybe the interest will come to more than ten percent."

"Mr. Hill, will you help me? I know the contract can't be changed, but somebody should be able to squeeze some money out of Oakes and Randolph. And I'm working on a new book."

Hill didn't chuckle this time, he laughed aloud. "Lady, I like your style. I'll get back to you later today. Ten thousand carry you for a couple of months?"

"Yes, that's plenty."

"Okay. I'll worm it out of them. And from now on, you're my client. You don't sign anything without my seeing it first. Now, before you complain, you go take a good look at the option clause in your contract. Without me you'll get shafted worse on your next book." Then, with an abrupt change of subject, "Is Tom working?"

"Yes, he is. I haven't seen the manuscript, but he's working hard."

"Wonderful. From Shore it's not the quality that's the problem, just getting him to put the words on paper. Go sit in the sun, honey. You write and tell Tom to write. Leave the rest to me."

14

THE ECHOES OF THE ACCUSATIONS HE'D MADE FOLLOWED
Joe down the stairs. He didn't remember Williams's
threats, only his own impotent words. And when he was
outside, he could feel the house behind him. It was a malevolent presence, the place where Barbie entertained her Mafia
lover, and the place where she kept his daughter. The emana-
tions from the building ran up and down his spine. Crawling
spiders. A woman pushed by him to go into the flower shop.
He could smell the verdant growth of the plants in the moment when the door opened. Then it closed, and he smelled
only the corruption of the street and the house. The spiders
were still active. He was a hive of them, a nest, a host to the
insects of evil.

Once Pete Chiarra had told him a crazy story about a guy
who went to South America and got bitten by some spider
they had there. The bite wasn't poisonous, but what the spider
was really doing was laying her eggs under the man's skin. He
didn't know anything about it at first. Just that he had a boil
on his neck that took a hell of a long time to come to a head
and break. Then one morning he was shaving and he nicked
the boil by accident and dozens of baby spiders crawled out
and scurried up and down his face. According to Chiarra, the
guy went nuts and jumped out a fourth-floor window and
killed himself.

Joe didn't know if any of it was true. But he knew now that
you could be a host for evil and filth whether you wanted to or

not. You let it happen just by taking no action. Sometimes action was the only imperative.

HE FOUND FORTY-SEVEN DOLLARS IN THE POCKET OF HIS JEANS. It was enough. The cab to LaGuardia cost seven fifty and the one-way shuttle flight to Boston was twenty-nine. It was just after seven in the evening when DiAnni stood on the subway platform at Logan airport and waited for the train that would carry him into town.

Fifteen minutes later he got out at Park Street and began walking. He passed Government Center and turned north, and after a short while he was on Hanover Street. In all only four hours had passed since he'd stood in front of Barbie's house and identified the presence of the excrescence on his flesh, nurturing the spiders of evil. Now he had returned to the jungle where he'd been bitten. He was going to kill the adult spiders who had impregnated his body with their young.

Scaficci's bakery had been in the same location since before Joe was born. Among his earliest memories was going down to Scaficci's each year before Easter. His mother always gave him two dollars to buy a *pizza dolce,* a sweet pie of ricotta cheese and citron. Papa loved *pizza dolce.* Old man Scaficci made the best in the North End. So too his *panettone,* a traditional Christmas bread. But as the years passed, the old man's sons objected to laboring all night in the kitchen behind the store to produce holiday baked goods for a couple of dollars. After a while the younger Scaficci men bought such delicacies from factories, and spent their time on more lucrative pursuits. When Joe was in his teens the bakery was the central drop for the neighborhood numbers runners. During all the daylight hours a clutch of dark-suited figures could be seen at the single table in the corner, drinking thick black coffee laced with anisette.

Joe stood in front of the bakery. It was shadowed by dusk. He tried the handle of the glass door; locked. For a few seconds he stood and thought. The little spiders were very active in his neck at the moment. He could feel them gnawing at his flesh. They were in his spinal column, too. Probably they lived well off spinal fluid. DiAnni clenched and unclenched his fists, and remained undecided.

The block in which he stood was empty. Farther down he could see the lights of a restaurant, and overhead a faint glow behind the curtains of flats where people lived. But at ground level this particular stretch of the street was deserted. It was a place of daytime stores that closed their doors early. Now a gust of wind rattled the metal garbage cans waiting by the curb for dawn collection. The bent and misshapen cover of one flew off and swirled in the air for a moment before it deposited itself at his feet.

DiAnni smiled, then reached down and picked it up. The handle felt satisfying and firm in his grip, and the weight of the lid was exactly right for his purposes. He took a step back, cocked his head and ran his tongue over his lips, just like the old black Satchel Paige used to do, and went into his wind-up. A change-up fastball. The kind that was over the center of the plate before the batter knew it had left the glove. The glass of the door shattered with gratifying noise and Joe stepped through the jagged opening, wielding his weapon on the display cases that lined the walls.

"I AM SORRY TO DISTURB YOU WITH SUCH *BANALITÀ*, BUT THERE are things which make this not an ordinary matter."

The elderly *padrone* inclined his head and flicked a bit of ash from his cigar. "It is never ordinary if those who are under our protection are attacked. Tell me how much damage has been done, and what you know of the *ladro*."

"Not actually a *ladro;* nothing was taken. Only three stores broken into and smashed. Two of our *soldati* were eating at a restaurant nearby and they heard the noise and got hold of the man before the police came."

"Why did they not leave him for the police?" The *padrone* leaned forward and studied the face of his lieutenant. "You are telling me this is the start of a war? Someone has sent this piece of *merda* to announce that I am wished ill?"

"No, no. Nothing like that. Fortunately, one of our *soldati* identified the man immediately. He is Joseph DiAnni. The son of the woman who used to run the cheese factory, old Don Stefano's woman."

"That one! But he is a priest."

"Not anymore. You remember, a few years ago he took off his collar and ran away."

The *padrone* removed his cigar from his mouth and spat on the floor. "*Infamatà*. Another of these scum who calls himself a man but breaks his vows and puts on ordinary clothes and lies with women. It is a sin before God."

"Yes, but this one is also of some interest to your good friend from Brooklyn in New York." He spoke a name the other man knew well.

"What are you telling me? You make no sense. First you say it is not the beginning of a war on my interests. Now you insist the filth who has done this thing is sent by my respected friend from Brooklyn. You make no sense."

The younger man poured a glass of wine for the older and began again to explain. "I do not know why this DiAnni has come home and begun breaking the windows and doors of the stores in his old neighborhood. I know only that he is a priest who has left his priesthood, and that a few months ago he was being looked for by the man who is the lawyer of your friend from Brooklyn in New York. And there is something else. When old Don Stefano died, it was this one, this Joseph DiAnni, who arranged that the Church would give him a proper burial. He did this for his mother. I think you would want to know that."

The *padrone* sipped his wine and was silent for a few moments. "Yes, all these things I wish to know. Where is the *traditore* now?"

"Where he will do no further damage. He is unconscious and will remain so until you say what is to be done with him."

"Very good. Now go. I will make a telephone call and I will think. In a while I will tell you my decision."

When the decision came it was more generous than Joe had any right to expect, had he been sane enough and sufficiently awake to expect anything. Asked to offer an opinion, Philocles Williams had chosen not to be vengeful. Maybe just because the man had been Norma's father. "Crazy, but harmless," he decreed. "Not worth any trouble."

The *padrone* summoned his lieutenant. "Take this piece of filth to the office of the Chancery in Brighton. Leave him bound and gagged where the businessmen priests will find him when they arrive on Monday morning."

"It is Friday night only."

"I know what night it is. I know too that forty-eight hours will not kill such a one as this. He is the problem of the Church, they will decide what to do with him. But you must make them understand that if he comes again to the neighborhood of his birth, I will not be responsible for his safety."

Thus it was that at eight forty-five on a bright warm Monday morning in May the monsignor who was secretary to the chancellor of the archdiocese of Boston entered his pleasant office and found DiAnni trussed like a chicken, gagged and blindfolded, on the nice new red shag carpet.

* * *

420

"THE SHRINKS HAVE DECIDED YOU'RE NOT ALTOGETHER NUTS," Wisnovski said. "Just a little bit."

DiAnni leaned back in a chaise lounge on the terrace of the very private clinic and stared at June blue skies studded with puffs of cloud. A bird sang somewhere nearby. "A temporarily morbid reaction to stress. That's what they told me."

"Yeah," Wisnovski agreed. "But a mighty dangerous one, boyo. You stirred up a hornets' nest."

"I think that's rather what I intended at the time."

"You're lucky it wasn't fatal."

"Maybe I am at that." Joe lit a cigarette and looked pensive. "Luckier than you mean. Listen, Lou, it would be very bad for me to die just now. I am in one hell of a mess as far as the state of my soul goes."

"Oh, really? I thought you weren't much worried about that these days."

"That's what I supposed. But I've had some time to think lately. The problem is, I'm not thinking very clearly yet."

"What do the shrinks say?"

"Nothing. This isn't something you talk about with psychiatrists. At least I can't. I need to pray, Lou. But I seem to have lost the knack, if I ever had it. Besides, I'm not absolutely sure there's anything to pray to. I want there to be, but ..." The words trailed away. There were no words for his ambivalence and his fear and his wanting.

Wisnovski stretched and folded his massive arms behind his head. "Well, I'd say, 'get thee to a nunnery,' but you'd probably try and screw all the nuns. Is that the kind of thing you have in mind, boyo?"

"Not screwing, no," Joe said with a grin. "But maybe I should spend some time in a monastery. Something like the Trappists over in Spencer."

"Not them. They're all involved with guitars and gurus these days. I'd guess you need something a little more solid. Unless my traditionalist attitude offends you."

"No. I think it's exactly right."

"Leave it with me. I'll see what I can do."

THE ROAD RAN FROM MONTPELIER PAST STOWE. AT ESSEX Junction they turned north. Once they'd gone through Smuggler's Notch, civilization was only a memory. Wisnovski had all he could do to keep the ancient blue Volkswagen on the rutted Vermont track. Eventually the track ran out. "According to the map, we walk from here," Lou said.

The two men abandoned the car and went on foot through a forest redolent with the smell of pine and abuzz with the summer sound of small insects. The path was narrow, but not overgrown. Someone apparently kept it clear. Perhaps the same someone who had drawn the homemade map on the piece of paper Lou clutched in his hand. "We should be there by now," he said after they'd walked for twenty minutes.

Joe grimaced. "You can't prove it by me, you're the great white hunter. This place really exists, doesn't it?"

"Oh, yeah, it exists."

"Carthusians, for God's sake," Joe mumbled. "I thought they became extinct a few centuries back."

"A low profile, maybe that's why they're still around. Hold on, this looks like it."

He pointed to a log cabin set well back from the path, camouflaged by the dense growth. Only the eye of a woodsman prevented him from walking by it.

There was a small front stoop and a door with a knocker made from an old squirrel paw. Wisnovski manipulated the defunct squirrel. A few minutes went by; the two men grew uncomfortable and uncertain. Then the door opened. An elderly fellow with a partially shaved head appeared. He wore a threadbare white habit. It looked slightly askew, as if he'd pulled it on over ordinary clothes when he heard their summons. "I'm Brother Hyginius. You are expected. Welcome in Christ's name."

WHEN WISNOVSKI FIRST MADE THE SUGGESTION, JOE LOOKED up Carthusians in the Catholic encyclopedia. "An order of monks founded by St. Bruno in 1084, whose life is essentially that of hermits," he'd read. "On Sundays and feasts they meet in their church for the Office, in the refectory for two meals, and perhaps for a walk. The rest of the time each monk spends alone in a private cottage with provisions for prayer, reading, eating, sleeping, manual work, and a tiny garden. Meat is never eaten, and the night's sleep is broken into two periods, separated by at least three hours of the night-office. The order has both monks, who are priests, and lay brothers. Their numbers are very few in both Europe and America, but they have recently made a foundation in rural Vermont."

And so Joseph DiAnni came to the fastness of rural Vermont to be healed, to be cleansed of the spiders who had laid their eggs in his flesh and tormented him for so long. "A rare privilege, boyo," Lou had smiled. "These guys almost never take guests, and they leave the harboring of disciplinary problems and penitents to the Trappists. But they know a bit about prayer and being alone with God. That's what you want, isn't it?"

"That's what I want," Joe had agreed. "How did you get me in?"

"Ah, you don't think I'm going to tell you that, do you? Influence, lad, your old Uncle Louie's got influence."

Brother Hyginius offered them tea and they drank it from chipped crockery mugs, wishing it was whiskey, or at least beer, made awkward by their shared perception of being intruders. It was better after Lou left. "See you in a month, boyo. Send a carrier pigeon with an SOS if you need me before that." Then he was gone, and DiAnni was alone with the frail old man.

He noted the faint trace of an accent, vaguely middle European, but the Carthusian didn't speak enough for him to identify it. Instead they washed the tea cups in silence punctuated by smiles, after which Hyginius indicated that Joe should follow him. He insisted on shouldering the younger man's knapsack, again only with gestures, and led him deeper into the forest.

About a hundred yards down a narrow path they came to another log cabin. The Carthusian unlocked the door, then handed DiAnni the key. So this one was to be his. It was a single room, lovingly built and tended, but simple to the point of austerity. There was a narrow cot, a table, a few bookshelves, and one chair. In a corner across from the woodstove that served both for heat and cooking there was another small table. This one was exquisitely fashioned of hand-rubbed pine, with wooden pegs instead of nails. A master craftsman's work.

Joe took a step closer to the second table, drawn by its unexpected beauty in this place so unadorned. Then he recognized its function. There was a small altar stone let into its center, and two candles in brackets either side. A crucifix hung on the wall behind, and on the table itself was a linen cloth covering something. He saw the outlined shape of the things beneath the cloth and recognized them. A chalice and a paten. A stab of sudden, ferocious longing took him by surprise. Suddenly DiAnni wanted to say Mass so badly he ached with it, could taste it like hunger on the back of his tongue. For a few seconds he stood where he was, then turned away.

Perhaps Brother Hyginius saw his pain and chose to ignore

it. Perhaps his life of solitude had dimmed his eyes so he no longer noticed such human anguish. All he did was point to the schedule posted by the door and the clock ticking away on a shelf beside the bed. Then he left.

Joe knew he ought to unpack his few belongings, check the schedule so he'd be ready for whatever came next, get settled in. He did nothing, only rehearsed in his head the letter from the Cardinal Archbishop he'd received before coming here. It hadn't been unkind—the old fox wasn't a thunderer—but at the end there were the words he was remembering now. About his being forbidden to offer Mass or administer the sacraments in view of his recent laicization. The comment had seemed unimportant at the time. He hadn't expected anything else. Now it seemed as if some horrendous and permanent amputation had been performed on his person.

"Greetings," a voice said from the doorway. "I'm Bede Briars." The owner of the voice was a big, sunburned man of some forty years. He wore overalls and a plaid shirt, and only the shaven circle atop his tonsured head indicated that he was a monk. He looked like a farmer, and his Midwestern drawl reinforced the impression.

Joe introduced himself and shook the man's callused right hand. A six-pack of Budweiser dangled from the left. "Present from the Abbot," Briars said, handing DiAnni the beer. "We get one a week, for Sundays and feast days. A bottle of wine, too, but that's for saying Mass." He stopped speaking and his face got a little redder than normal. He knew, apparently. His next words confirmed it. "My cabin's about a quarter mile down that path. I say Mass at six-thirty every weekday morning. Come any time you like."

Come and I'll give you communion, he meant. Because Joe wasn't a priest anymore. At least not so you'd notice. An indelible mark on the soul, according to Lou Wisnovski, but the Archdiocese of Boston had covered it over, like the cloth covering the chalice and paten on the nearby altar. "Thanks," Joe said. "Maybe . . ."

Maybe what? He couldn't receive communion. Not the way he was now. Unshriven, fouled with the excrement of his sin. Not fornication, or even murder. He knew better than to be afraid of such mundane lapses. But despair was a solid lump in his belly and he didn't know how to make it go away. The sin against the spirit, the one Jesus said was unforgivable.

The act of charity that had bent his rule of silence completed, Briars turned to go, then he turned back. "I almost forgot, this belongs in here. I took it after old Father William died; this was his cabin. He went to God a week ago and I took the picture to repair the frame." He'd left a reproduction of the icon of Our Lady of Perpetual Help outside the door; now he gave it to DiAnni. Then he raised one hand in salute and disappeared into the trees.

Joe looked at the picture. It was a cheap imitation in colors too florid to resemble the original. He put it aside, but unbidden, the thought of Barbie came. "The Lady told me you'd always be a priest." Barbie's Lady. Her visions. Her certitudes. No, not just hers. The convictions of Lou Wisnovski and Brother Hyginius and Bede Briars, and those of all the other men unseen but near at hand. Including, probably, the dead Father William. He had some weird sense of having come to the fulcrum of the universe. One of them, at least. A place of tremendous power, maybe a place that kept the world from splintering into meaningless atoms and floating away in space. He could almost feel the pulsing beat of silent prayer and adoration that surrounded him in these woods.

It will take time. Be at peace, you are much loved.

There had been no sound, but he knew he'd heard the words. In his own head, perhaps. A message from himself to himself.

Except that the voice had been that of a woman.

PART THREE

THE
ISLAND

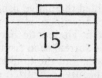

15

A ND THERE IT WAS, SEEN BELOW THEM AS A BROWN-
black sliver of land framed by the silver wing of the
aircraft, and seeming to stand upright in a perpendicu-
lar ocean. An optical illusion, a distorted view made common
since the coming of ships that sail not sea but sky; it was an
appropriate first view of Lanzarote.

Two aspects of one geological truth shaped the island. In
the north the Famara massif was formed of volcanos beginning to grow old, albeit not yet ancient, and surrounded by the
achromatic browns and ecrus of *los malpaises,* the lava bad-
lands. A placid creature, Famara, invoking subtle, half-for-
gotten memories.

Ah, but in the south was Timanfaya, the devil's lover; exotic, alluring, frighteningly beautiful. Timanfaya, a range of
volcanos so young as to be almost virgin, a bride still flushed
with excitement. Less than two hundred and fifty years had
passed since her defloration, that rupturing of maidenhead
that poured forth fire and annihilation on the valley of villages, and with molten lava reshaped a coastline into fantastic
coves and gorges and cliffs, trapping blue-green water in shining black basalt cups. Timanfaya still laughs with hot delight,
and fire still rumbles in her belly and dances just below her
skin. Her wedding garment remains fresh and exquisite, a covering of red and lilac and blue and black cinders encrusted to-

gether like shimmering sequins. Timanfaya is the teasing soul of Lanzarote. *Las montañas del fuego*—the Mountains of Fire.

"ABOUT A HUNDRED MILES NORTHEAST IS TARFAYA, A TOWN on the border between Morocco and the Spanish Sahara." Tom's outstretched arm directed Barbie's gaze across the glittering aquamarine sea. She listened quietly. Maria watched them, noting that Tom was brown and leathery and squinted in the sun. He resembled the native fishermen with whom he often chatted in the afternoon after siesta. Barbie looked somehow more herself. The exotic backdrop, perhaps. The white adobe walls, the surreal cacti rising from earth overlaid with black volcanic ash, and the tumble of vivid bougainvillaea suited her, as if beauty recognized its own.

"It's odd, isn't it," Barbie said. "Being so close to Africa, you wonder how the islands came to be Spanish."

Maria's heart tripped and beat faster. It was the most normal thing she'd heard Barbie say in weeks. And when Tom began to explain the history of the European conquest, Barbie listened attentively.

Maria at first had been the expert on Lanzarote, but between them, Tom and Hank Rolles had passed her. Hank had convinced Tom of his hypothesis that the original peoples of the archipelago were exiles from the Algerian Tell. The two men studied shards of pottery, the evidence of Berber traces in the original language, and Pliny's ancient description of the "Fortunate Isles." They had endless discussions of elaborate theories, which often bored Maria because they seemed to detract from the intense now of the island, the now of their lives here.

Tom was repeating an abbreviated version of the posited history, and if Barbie was bored, she didn't show it. She stood still and patient while Tom regaled her with facts, until Maria said gently, "She's tired, it's been a long trip. Come along, honey, I'll show you your room and Tom can educate you further over dinner." Barbie allowed herself to be led away, but to Maria it seemed there was a touch of less robotlike compliance in her movements.

"Not so much a Barbie doll," she told Tom later.

"Good. That's what you brought her here for, isn't it?"

Maria nodded. And she'd brought him here to get rid of his persistent cough, and to write his book, and to help her forget about Si. And only one of those objectives was achieved. He was writing—for that matter, so was she—but Tom looked

430

ghastly despite his tan. He was painfully thin, and she'd been struck by the tentative way he moved as soon as he met them at the airport. So probably she had two invalids to look after in this wonderful but impractical house. Tired as she was, the prospect was daunting.

"Go lie down for a bit." Tom touched her cheek tenderly with one finger, as if he'd read her mind. "Everything's okay. Have a rest. I'm going to make dinner."

"Oh, no!" she protested quickly. "I'll do it. You look tired. You must have been working all hours while I've been gone."

He turned aside. "I'm fine. You're imagining things. Besides, one of the fishermen brought us some *berberechos*. You'd ruin them."

Probably true. She didn't even know what the damned things were. Maria wearily walked round to the flower-filled rear courtyard and climbed the narrow twisting staircase that led to her room. Her bed was a built-in stone slab, piled with pillows and quilts. When she lay down she looked out an arched moorish window toward a chain of cliffs that marched across the near horizon to the sea. In the late afternoon sunlight they were tawny brown, flecked with salmon pink and marked by rivulets of erosion that seamed their flanks and made them look as if a giant child had scraped his oversize fingers from top to bottom.

Called Casa Capricho, the house belonged to an elderly English publisher whom they'd met during their first month on the island. They were staying in the Hotel Fariones in Puerto del Carmen—the beating heart of tinseltown, Tom called it. They'd run into the publisher in the bar. "Don't usually come down here," he'd explained. "Not my Lanzarote at all. Hope you've seen more of it than this village of tourists."

Tom and Maria said they had. At least they were beginning to. "It grows on you," the Englishman said. He was a tall, heavy-set man with twinkling gray eyes, fine straight hair swept back from a broad brow, and a quietly sincere manner beneath his proper British exterior. Good-looking in a sort of way, and somehow scholarly. Maria liked him at once. So did Tom, which was more unusual.

"We're finding that out," Tom said in reply to the other man's comments about the seductions of the island. "Maria's met an old friend, an archaeologist, and he's opened our eyes."

"Oh, the chap doing some investigations up near Teguise,

you mean? Forgive me, so few Americans come here. It's largely an English and Scandinavian holiday place, with a few Germans for good measure, so I couldn't help but connect you with the American Jesuit. What brought you to us? Plenty of warm islands closer to home, I'd have thought."

"Miss Trapetti's just written a book set on Lanzarote in the eighteenth century."

The publisher smiled. "Shop talk at last. Now I'll confess. I made an effort to meet you. I recognized you at once, Mr. Shore. And naturally one would wish to meet your charming companion." He'd twinkled in Maria's direction. Then he'd deftly turned the talk to Tom's British publisher, a long established imprint the Englishman, whose name was Robin Jewett, pronounced stuffy and unimaginative. Finally Tom suggested Jewett contact Sam Hill in New York.

"I'll tell him we've met and that I'd like him to consider any offer you make," Tom said.

"Good. I rather think that might be profitable for both of us. When are you planning to return home?"

They'd shrugged and said they weren't sure. "We're just beginning to feel as if we know Lanzarote," Maria explained. "And we'd like to know more. But . . ." Her gesture included the hotel and the sprawl of tourists' villas stretching out past the pool along the golden beach.

"But this isn't conducive to an extended stay," Robin Jewett agreed. "Tell you what, I've an idea. My house is going to be empty for the next three months. It's an odd place and fairly isolated. But perhaps you'd enjoy staying there a while. You'd be doing me a favor, actually. I don't like leaving it alone for long periods."

At first they protested, but in the end they'd agreed to discuss it further. Next morning Jewett collected them and they drove to the village of Playa Negra. It was a tiny pueblo south of Puerto del Carmen, nestled in a fold formed by the sea and a range of vaunting hills that insinuated their own strange beauty between the tiny settlement and the splendor of the black-velvet Mountains of Fire.

The road was terrible, a washboard dirt track, and at her first sight of Playa Negra, Maria was appalled. Oh, no! Not this for any length of time, she thought. The pueblo was ugly and dirty, a collection of jerry-built shacks surrounded by half-wrecked fishing boats and nets. There were swarms of flies lured by the outdoor latrines that served for sanitation, and a heat haze that almost obscured the black shingle beach.

Then she saw Casa Capricho. It filled a finger of land thrusting into the sea, a strange amalgam of planes and angles and levels that ran from a raised garden in the rearmost courtyard to a stone jetty that gave access to the ocean. Stark white except for the lush vegetation that hugged its unlikely corners, the house was a fugue, a series of repeated themes rising in rhythmic counterpoint above the sea lapping the jagged rocks.

"You probably know that *capricho* is Spanish for whim," Robin Jewett said. "It's well named. The builder was an old friend, a Frenchman and a bit of an eccentric. He intended the place as an investment, something to sell, but he designed it with nothing practical in mind. I'm probably the only fool he could have sold it to. Still, I'm inordinately fond of it. Silly to say that about a house, I suppose. All the same, there it is. Come have a look around and you'll see what I mean."

It was a rabbit warren, a glorious tangle of small rooms boasting extraordinary unexpected views, reached by preposterous stairways and corridors. At one side there was a rounded tower, fashioned like the old windmills that once drew the ocean into the salt-pans dotted across the island. The tower housed a curved staircase that led to a sheltered erie at the top, with a breathtaking semicircular vista of mountains and sea.

"I could work here," Tom said softly.

Robin Jewett smiled. "I rather thought you'd say that. How about it, Miss Trapetti? Could you tolerate the inconveniences?"

They were not imaginary. As well as the village and the terrible road, the house was burdened by having no electricity, only one bathroom, and the customary Lanzarote problem of almost no water. What there was was stored in an underground cistern, an *aljibe,* and pumped to the house by a temperamental old gasoline motor. Still, once she'd seen the place, none of that fazed Maria. "I would love to live here. But there's one thing we're firm about, Mr. Jewett: you must allow us to pay rent."

"No, please. I told you you'd be doing me a favor. You can see how isolated I am. Someone really should be here to keep an eye on the house."

Maria and Tom insisted. Finally, realizing perhaps that the fact of their professional overlapping made it imperative, Robin Jewett agreed to accept a nominal rent. So they paid for three months, which took them to the end of June, when the Englishman would probably return from London to spend some time in his whimsical hideaway.

Now Maria looked sleepily at the mountains and tried to calculate. Sixteen days, she made it. Then they'd either have to find something else or go home. But meantime, Barbie could bask in the sun and continue her climb back to normalcy. She herself could go on flexing her writing muscles, just practicing really, convincing herself she'd be able to do it again when she wanted to. And Tom? Tom could go on . . . doing what? Tom can go on dying, she thought.

And was suddenly, chillingly aware that he was doing exactly that.

It was after seven when Maria came downstairs. The long, gentle dusk of early summer crept across the land, and the sun slowly westered behind the incredible hills. Barbie was sitting on the low wall of the terrace outside her bedroom. She'd changed to white trousers and a pale cream silk blouse, with an angora sweater of the same shade over her shoulders. She looked better than she had for days. "This is a healing kind of place," she said softly when Maria approached.

"It is that."

"Look, I've never seen mesembryantheum growing like this." Barbie pointed to a carpet of spiky green finger-shaped leaves and flat orange flowers. They spread a lush undulating blanket of color from the terrace to the rocks above the sea.

"I never knew its name," Maria said.

"Endemic to South Africa, I think. Ice plant's the common name. It didn't arrive here by itself. I can't imagine that."

And I can't imagine that something's already piqued your interest, Maria thought. Aloud she said, "The house is owned by an English publisher. I think he planted the gardens."

"I've always wanted to see an English garden," Barbie said. "They're famous."

"Well, this can't exactly qualify." Maria laughed. "I don't think Lanzarote is anything like England."

"Maybe we can visit England before we go home," Barbie said. Then, as if the idea had suddenly dawned, "It doesn't matter how long I stay away, does it? I mean, without Norma, there's nothing to hurry for."

"There's your work, and Angie and Stella." She refrained from mentioning Phil.

"Yes, but there's no hurry. I have to get used to that idea."

Tom called them in to dinner. They ate in the tiny dining area that was little more than a narrow passage between the kitchen and one of the two sitting rooms. The table was a heavy dark wood slab on a trestle. Fat candles, looking as if they'd escaped from an altar, made provocative shadows on white walls. *Berberechos* turned out to be a kind of mollusk. "Cockles, near as I can figure out," Tom explained. He'd made them into a delicate sauce with garlic and olive oil and white wine, and they ate it on rice, colored pale yellow by a bit of turmeric.

"Delicious," Maria proclaimed, and noted that of her two patients, Barbie had eaten better. Tom barely touched his food.

She started to admonish him, thinking how much like her mother she sounded once more, but he interrupted. "Indalencio came with a letter while you were napping."

Indalencio was the local mailman. Two or three times a week he came on a burro and delivered the mail. In between those visits they could collect the letters at his small grocery shop in the next village. The letter he'd brought today was from Robin Jewett. It said that he couldn't get away until September and very much hoped that Tom and Maria would consent to stay in the house over the summer. "What do you think?" Maria asked.

"I'd like to stay," Tom said. His voice had none of his customary banter, and the naked longing on his face was a shock. "I'd like you to stay with me," he added.

Maria swallowed hard. To cover her confusion she took a sip of her wine, a local firewater called *malvasia*. "Of course."

Tom rewarded her with a wide grin. It looked macabre in his thin face. In the candlelight, he seemed to be wearing a death mask. But his manner wasn't grim. "What about you, Barbie?" he asked. "Think maybe you too can be seduced by our whim-house and this weird island?"

"Oh, yes," Barbie said solemnly. "I already am."

"Good girl." Tom set his wine glass down. Maria saw that his fingers trembled. His hearty manner seemed forced when he added, "Hank Rolles, Maria's tame Jesuit, will be along later. You can hear the exiled Berber theory straight from the horse's mouth."

LEGEND SAID THAT IGNATIUS LOYOLA, A FIFTEENTH-CENTURY Spaniard, found enlightenment in a cave. From that came the founding of the Jesuits. So maybe it was not coincidence that brought Hank Rolles to the caves in which he now labored. Maybe it was one of the mysterious grand designs of God. Rolles thought of that only intermittently. True, he had a hidden agenda, but he didn't quest after spiritual truth.

Officially he was seeking any pre-conquest sites on the island not so thoroughly vandalized as to be worthless from an archaeological point of view. He would then notify the Ministry of Culture in Madrid, and attempts would be made to ensure that the sites remained intact until money was available to excavate them properly.

Madrid's interest in the obscure little island was not the sign of some new empathy on the part of the government for one of the remaining outposts of empire. It was simply that the functionary from the ministry who gave Rolles his brief was a *conajero* by birth, a Lanzarotean. Like most provincials transported by luck and wit to the capital, the man harbored a belief that great treasures waited to be unearthed in the place of his birth, secrets that would give him the same pride of origin claimed by descendants of other ancient great peoples.

So convinced was he of this fact that he insisted Rolles required a cover story to mask his activities on the island. Surely thieves lurked in every *tapas* bar in Arrecife, waiting to plunder the island of priceless artifacts and sell them to the prestigious museums of Britain and points west. To outwit them, Rolles must claim to be working on the old Zonzamas dig. The cave of the last native king had been discovered years before, and abandoned soon after. Whatever there was to loot from the site was long gone. But the man from the ministry said Zonzamas would protect the new and greater discoveries Rolles was bound to make. So go forth, worthy Jesuit, and poke around.

Since this conversation took place in Cambridge, England, in the Cambridge Arms on King Street, surrounded by ancient halls of learning and lubricated by numberless pints of that fine local brew, Abbot Ale, it did not at first appear as far-fetched as it seemed in the cold light of later mornings. But Hank Rolles knew the answer to that. It was not the Spaniard met by chance who was sending him to Lanzarote. As a Jesuit, he had a special vow of obedience to His Holiness the Pope. Under God, it was His Holiness alone who could bid Hank come and go. There were, however, quite a few Jesuits, and the Pope couldn't look after all of them. So command was delegated to the Father General of the order, residing in Rome,

436

and from him to numerous Fathers Provincial. The one answerable for Hank Rolles resided in New York.

That Father Provincial sent Rolles to Cambridge because of Rolles' theory about the original inhabitants of the Canary Islands. He had published an article explaining his thesis and noting that in the second century A.D. the Romans could do pretty much what they liked, so a bunch of rebels with their tongues cut out, exiled to the deserted and little known "Fortunate Isles," was nothing unusual. However, Rolles' thesis didn't entirely please some members of the Spanish establishment. Nomads? Rebels? Criminals of a sort? And a mere fifteen hundred years ago? Really, Father.

The remark was echoed by the Father Provincial. "Really, Father, you should have been more discreet. It doesn't do to make enemies in academia. We'll give you some time in Cambridge. See if you can come up with any proof. Lots of stuff about ancient Rome in the libraries of Cambridge. Doubt it myself, but fine if you could. Quite a feather in our caps, wouldn't you say?"

So Rolles could take his pick of explanations. Meeting a vacationing Spaniard who turned out to be from Lanzarote, and also in a position to arrange a permit for fieldwork on the island, was a coincidence, or an act of God. Eventually, he put his money on the latter and despite initial incredulity requested permission from his superiors, as did the Spaniard from his. After that, the one returned happy to Madrid and the other went ecstatic to Lanzarote.

Only when he got to the island did the Jesuit realize that God was having a laugh at his expense. For surely He, in His omniscience, knew full well that Hank had been a little in love with Sister Mary Anthony a few years before on the campus of Boston College, and that the priest felt pleased with himself because he never gave in to the temptation into which he'd been led. So God promptly led Rolles into greater and more insistent temptation. Because on Lanzarote, where the priest thought to investigate his theories and make a splash in the weightier journals of archaeological speculation, he discovered instead Maria Trapetti.

Maria did not wear a shapeless dress, such as Sister Mary Anthony had worn. She garbed her curvaceous body in jeans that clung to an extraordinarily rounded bottom, and loose blouses that fluttered over a wonderfully full bosom. And her hair wasn't hidden under a veil, it was brushed back from an

437

elegant widow's peak he'd not known about, and hung in thick curls and waves, and danced its dark brown dance in the sun. And that same sun warmed the olive tones of Maria's skin and did marvelous things for her dark eyes and the nice oval shape of her face.

All these wonders Hank Rolles, S.J., noticed, despite his desire to ignore them. And it made it no easier that Maria was obviously shacked up with the writer, Thomas Shore, because Tom was a nice guy and very fine to talk to and drink wine with. More important, he was mortally ill, and though he wasn't a Catholic he seemed to want to discuss things spiritual with the Jesuit. So under the circumstances, Hank couldn't stay away from the whimsy house on the sea in Playa Negra just because Maria was living in sin.

Nor did it make any difference when he visited the night of Maria's return to Lanzarote and met her friend, Barbie Gold. Rolles realized that Barbie was one of the most beautiful women in the world, and probably quite the most beautiful he'd ever seen, but that didn't alter his much suppressed feelings for Maria. Barbie Gold was obviously cut to pieces inside. Her pain and her need cried out to the priest in him. Maria tantalized the man.

The four sat together for a while, but Barbie contributed nothing to the conversation and soon slipped silently away to her room. "She was much better earlier," Maria told Hank. "Now she's terrible again. Withdrawn and silent and all the awful things I thought she was getting over."

Hank looked at the little furrows of concern between Maria's wide-set eyes and longed to smooth them with his finger. "It probably isn't unusual for her to take two steps forward and one back," he said. "I think a shrink would call that normal."

DAYS PASSED IN HOT AND SUNNY SUCCESSION. THE THREE occupants of Casa Capricho seemed in suspended animation. Barbie spent most of her time in her room. It was a cantilevered mezzanine between two of the many levels of the house. The ceiling was of wood, a rarity on the desert island, according to Maria. It was painted pale turquoise blue and overlaid with gilt. Looted from some French church or chateau, Tom explained, brought over by the fellow who built the house. Barbie listened quietly while they interpreted the environment, telling her to see as if they assumed she was blind. But she saw too much. She saw everything, and it terrified her.

Pain eddied around Barbie, it was her invisible shroud, she was befogged by it. Norma's pain, Joe's pain, Phil's pain, her own. All the seeking and groping and wanting and needing was suffocating her. And now this. A new imperative so strange she could not cope with it, so strange she feared for her sanity, though she no longer knew where the line was between sane and mad.

Since her arrival, the island had started to possess her. Lanzarote was pressing in on her, stealing her breath, making her heartbeat erratic. There was the sun and the wind, and the startling tawny vista with its swathes of black volcanic ash spread about as if by the hand of a child, there was this house, white and sea-blue and green, and all of it was shouting at her, calling her name. You know me, Barbie, the island said. And more important, I know you.

She went for a walk—years since she'd done that—creeping out of the house so Maria wouldn't see her and make clucking noises about her health. It wasn't her body that was sick, not anymore, but nobody seemed to understand that. The washboard road hurt her feet in their rope-soled espadrilles, and she cut left, into a fallow field. She was on a wide plain rising from the sea, with the village at her back and the mountains beyond. Scattered white houses dotted the vista, little flat-roofed cubes that glowed in the sun. She didn't hear the other sound until she'd gone far enough to escape the roar of the sea.

A farmer was plowing in the distance. He wore a black fedora scrunched down on his head and a black suitcoat that flapped over nondescript rolled-up trousers. And he was hanging on to a wooden plow pulled by a camel. Tom and Maria had told her about it, but she was still unprepared. Besides, they hadn't mentioned the chant. The man was singing to the beast, a low, repetitive cadence punctuated by grunts and the wind. It was music older than time. She stood and listened and stared.

The animal was dun colored and mangy and had a single hump. A camel or a dromedary? She didn't know. Not that it made any difference; the beast of the desert nonetheless. She pictured long rows of them ridden by robed men with curved scimitars at their waists. Thank you, Hollywood. But behind the celluloid was a truth. It swirled around her in the hot, dry air and sang in the old farmer's chant; it was a long, long past, and it was hers. It was part of her semitic blood, an older part than the European *shtetl* and the ghettos and the bearded black-garbed men with their shaven-headed wives who took ritual baths. They were all recent history of a sort. This was older, more primitive. Had she been in Israel she would have expected to feel these things, but on Lanzarote? Yes, here. Because this island was part of it, and eventually she would know why, as she'd learned about the Jew who was hidden from the Nazis in Rome and made a sculpture of the Madonna of the Universe in thanks and sent it to America where she would see it.

So that's what she was doing here. She was waiting for some truth, something the Lady would come and explain. But that couldn't be. The Lady was a delusion, wasn't she? A thing Barbie had created in her own head, like Joe always thought. She shuddered, not wanting to think about Joe, not wanting to admit that maybe the Lady was real. Because how did you reconcile the Lady and her perfect, unquestioning love with a four-year-old dying in agony? There wasn't any way to reconcile them.

Barbie turned and walked back to the house, leaving the chanting farmer and the camel behind.

"SHE'S LIKE A GLASS DOLL," TOM SAID. "ONE WRONG MOVE and she'll shatter."

"I can't worry about it anymore," Maria said savagely. "I've done everything I know how to do. The rest is up to her."

"Oh, oh," Tom whispered, "thus passeth Pollyanna. Had enough of martyrdom, have you?"

"Everybody's got to make their own choices. Isn't that your line?"

"It is indeed." His eyes got greenish, the way they did in some lights and some moods. "Remember that, will you, pet? That's my only religion. Freedom of choice."

"Yes," Maria said after some seconds. "I'll remember."

"He's made up his mind to die," she told Hank later. "I'm supposed to sit and watch."

"I don't think that's exactly it. He's made up his mind that if he's going to die it will be his way. Not quite the same thing."

They were walking along the black shingle beach. The wind whipped Maria's hair into a swirl of curls around the nape of her neck and outlined the thrust of her breasts beneath the thin fabric of a vivid pink caftan. The priest averted his eyes.

"I feel like a character in a Greek tragedy," Maria said. "I'm living in the midst of conflicting dramas, all about death and dying."

"Not a character. You're the chorus. Anyway, you can always go home to New York. Doubtless a fawning literary audience awaits."

"You're a bastard," Maria said. There was little passion in the remark. Then, without warning, "How come you're still a priest? Even the Jesuits have joined the rush to laity, I'm told."

"Some." Hank took his pipe from his pocket and lit it, cupping his brown, capable hands against the wind. When it finally drew, he said, "It depends on what you thought when you started out, doesn't it?"

"Does it?"

"I think so, yes. I told you before, it's a quest. I'm not all that sure. I only know that I want to be. That's still the same."

"Self-delusion! That's a hell of a reason for being a Catholic, let alone a priest." Maria stopped walking and leaned back against a smoothly eroded cliff face, accessible only now when the tide was dead low. "I think you just wanted to live up to the image of your saintly uncle. All that melodrama about the communists and torture and loyalty unto death. It would seduce any kid. I think it seduced you."

"Maybe," Hank said mildly. "We'd better keep walking. We'll be cut off by the tide fairly soon."

When they returned, the terrace was full of noisy, gesticulating people. Everyone from the village was there, and Maria had some difficulty locating Tom in the throng. "Barbie's had a present," he explained when at last she found him. "So she's decided to give a party. This isn't it, by the way. This is just the group planning the party."

Phil had shipped in a crate of prime sirloin steaks from a ranch in Texas. They'd arrived at the airport during the afternoon and been rushed straight to Playa Negra, as the sender directed. Even on Lanzarote, Maria marveled. *Phil makes everybody jump, even here.* Along with the steaks there were five pounds of beluga caviar, an enormous quantity of fresh raspberries, and a case of French champagne. The need for a party was obvious.

Tom took charge of the barbecue pit, improvised under his direction by a few of the fishermen. Two village women prepared a salad and the tiny salted potatoes that were a local specialty. Barbie put the caviar in a bowl, and sliced some lemons and a huge quantity of the anise-flavored bread that was their daily fare. The caviar and champagne turned out to be the hors d'oeuvre; they demolished it while they worked on the main event. Hank stared in horror when a couple of the fishermen made caviar sandwiches and wolfed them down in between hauling chairs and tables from the house to the terrace.

"Fish eggs are fish eggs as far as they're concerned," Tom said. "Sturgeon doesn't impress them."

Neither did French champagne. When it was gone, someone fetched a few jugs of *malvasia*. By that time the steaks were done. They at least excited admiration. There were no cattle on the island and, until importations from Argentina and Africa began a few years earlier for the sake of the tourists, no beef. Certainly none of this quality.

Afterwards someone produced a *timple*, a kind of Lanzarote ukelele, and someone else a guitar. They clapped their hands to the repetitive Canarian melodies and sang, and a few of the women danced. Maria watched their heavy-set bodies sway in the moonlight and marveled at their sudden unexpected grace. It occurred to her that she'd not seen Barbie for a while; she'd half decided to go look for her when the other woman appeared.

Barbie stood in the doorway watching the dancers. Her face seemed to glow, and at first Maria thought it was the moonlight again, making all things magic, but after a while she realized that Barbie was lit from within. Something's happened, Maria thought; she's turned some corner. But she didn't dare to ask, in case it were a fragile thing.

Barbie went back inside and came out with the raspberries and let everyone help themselves. They ate them with their fingers, like candy. "A marvelous feast," Hank told her. "Many thank-yous."

Moonlight washed the ocean, and in its glow Barbie was very pale, but shining. She didn't acknowledge his thanks, merely asked, "Will you do something for me?" The amber eyes were two large jewels.

"Sure, if I can."

"I want to go up to the mountains around Teguise."

"Fine. They're beautiful, and I spend a good bit of time up there anyway. When would you like to go?"

"Tomorrow." There was an undertone of urgency in her voice.

"Okay, why not? Tomorrow it is, then."

Hank left soon afterwards, telling Maria that he'd agreed to take Barbie out the following day and she could come if she wished.

"No, thanks, I'll stay home and try to work." And keep an eye on Tom, Maria added mentally. He was exhausted, white and in a cold sweat, all from the exertion of barbecuing a few steaks. And he'd eaten next to nothing. Lately she watched every mouthful of food Tom took. The task was easy, because there were so few of them.

Maria spent a restless night. Too much rich food, perhaps, or just listening for hours to Tom's wracking cough.

Dawn was a gray promise when finally she slept, and when she woke, it was after nine. She could hear Tom tapping away at his typewriter in the tower. The noise was frantic at times, then there were long pauses of nothing at all. It was a creative rhythm she'd come to recognize, the kind that caused Tom to smile at lunch and say it hadn't been a bad morning, maybe even okay. There was no other sound in the house. Hank must have called for Barbie early.

The day was warm and sunny, the air velvet on her skin. There was jasmine in bloom, and it attracted softly buzzing bees and scented the morning. Maria's typewriter beckoned, its silence a reproach while the one in the tower clattered so persistently.

She had made a work area for herself beneath the shade of a tumble of bougainvillaea in the lee of one terrace wall. It was a lovely spot, but today she was reluctant to sit down and get started, fidgety, looking for excuses. Finally she made herself accept the discipline of the desk, and when she did, she knew immediately what she was going to do. She realized too that the decision had been fermenting for some time. Now it was taken, and she was in a tremendous rush.

With no further hesitation she wrote to Si, saying that she feared Tom was mortally ill, that he knew it and had decided to do nothing about it, and that she could not bear the responsibility of silent complicity in that decision. Si was a blood relation; it was up to him to take some action.

She addressed the envelope before she had a chance to change her mind and took it to the pile waiting to be collected by the mailman on his burro. Maria buried the letter beneath half a dozen others, so there was no likelihood of Tom's spotting it. Not that he'd say anything; jealousy seemed to be one of the many things he'd decided to eliminate from his life lately. Still, if she could, she'd have driven to Arrecife and mailed it. In frustration, Maria looked toward the jeep. Not knowing how to drive was yet another consequence of growing up on Revere Street and entering the convent at eighteen.

That aside, she felt better once the letter was written, relieved of some of the weight of responsibility she'd been feeling lately. Barbie was improving, too. It was a good sign that she'd asked Hank to take her sightseeing. Fleetingly Maria wondered if Barbie, with her beauty and her fragility of the moment, was a threat to Hank's priesthood. She had no answer for that, but the thought led to her novel-in-progress.

It was a story about a woman who married a man soon after he left the priesthood, then had to live with his excruciating guilt. She'd written only sixty pages, but already Maria knew this was a manuscript created mainly in anger. Perhaps it would be good because of that, or maybe in spite of it.

GASHED THROUGH THE CENTER OF THE ISLAND WAS A VALLEY buried deep in the ubiquitous black volcanic ash. "La Geria," Hank explained. "The grape-growing region."

Surely the most extraordinary vineyards in the world, with each vine sunk deep in an ebony hole and tossing its green tendrils across a wall of charred stone. But no more fantastic than the town of Teguise, seen from their vantage point. They approached along the narrow road that bisected La Geria. The pueblo seemed to Barbie a child's drawing, an infant's concept of what a town must be. Blobs of white, representing the houses, were splattered on the brown slopes of an ancient volcano. There was even an ostentatious rounded spire marking the presence of a church. In the crystal-clear air the edges of everything, mountains and houses alike, were stark and unblurred. Hard lines drawn with the side of a crayon.

"Nobody seems to know the origin of the name Teguise," Hank said. "The first Europeans are supposed to have found a capital of some sort here, inland to stay away from the slavers who plagued the coast, but I think myself it's not the original site. Back there behind us and a little to the east is the cave of Zonzamas, the last native king. I suspect the *conquistadores* simply built their European-style houses close to that." He broke off. Barbie wasn't listening. She was staring straight ahead. "Anything special you want to see?" he asked.

"The mountains above Teguise," Barbie said. Just as she'd said yesterday.

"Okay. We'll leave the car a short distance beyond the far side of town and hike. You up to that?" She nodded, and they didn't speak again.

When they started climbing, Hank worried a bit. She'd been

444

so ill, perhaps this wasn't a good idea. But Barbie scrambled ahead of him, almost as if she knew where she was going. She was wearing sneakers, and the path up the stark treeless mountain appeared to pose no problem. When they emerged on a plateau about a thousand feet above sea level, she stopped and looked around. "You can see the ocean from here." It was her first comment on the view.

It was spectacular. They were staring down across a great plain toward a natural harbor little changed from what it had always been. Hank started to comment on that, but Barbie forestalled him. "Wait, let me think. It's right around here."

"What's right round here?" A chill crept along the back of his neck. "What are you looking for, Barbie?"

Her eyes were half closed, as if she were hiding something. "Oh, I don't know. I've just been thinking about Maria's book. You know, the girl who's supposed to have died up here."

"The one the old Dominican heard about, yes, I know. But there's no proof of any of that. He collected some stories and wrote them down. Maria made a novel out of it. All well and good, but no proof. Don't get psychic on me, will you?" He grinned as if it was a joke. Barbie grinned back.

"No proof, of course," she said. "But it's interesting to look, don't you think?" And while she spoke she ran her hands over the sheer rock walls behind them. A *booboo* tree grew improbably in the angle formed by one strata breaking to admit another. *Booboo* was a local word meaning silly. A silly tree because it grew without soil and without rain, and had a long, deep root system that scurried impossible distances below ground, undermining any water cisterns and house foundations that crossed its path.

"A very lush *booboo*," Hank said. "Must be water somewhere beneath us." He pushed the scrawny, supple trunk aside as he spoke, and suddenly paused and audibly caught his breath.

"What is it? Tell me, Hank, I've got to know, it's important!"

He kept staring at the cliff face he'd exposed, but he reached out one hand and drew her closer. "Look. That marking there. What do you think it is?"

Barbie peered in the direction he indicated. "I don't see anything. Yes . . . wait a minute, I do! I thought it was a crack at first but it's not. It's something definite." Her finger traced a spiral about three feet long.

"The mark of Acoran," Hank said. His voice was very soft,

almost worshipful. "The pre-conquest people called God Acoran. The spiral was one of their religious symbols." Barbie stepped closer to inspect the face of the cliff, but now he held her back with purposeful strength. "Don't move, don't even breathe. We may have found something, and I've got to take pictures before anything gets disturbed."

"But I want to look for the cave," Barbie insisted. "I know it's here."

"There's no reason to suppose any cave," Hank said. "But that's beside the point. What matters now is that we destroy nothing by accident."

His professional concerns didn't interest her. Barbie broke away from his grasp and slid a few feet to the left, churning up the powdery soil as she did so. "Be careful, damn it!" Hank's shout didn't have anything to do with her welfare.

Barbie pretended she hadn't heard. She kept edging along the ledge until she reached a place where it was too narrow to allow her to walk at all. She had to lean her weight forward against the cliff to keep from tumbling off, and stretch out her arms to maintain her balance. Normally she'd have been terrified; now she knew only her inner imperative. Finally she felt the opening. It was long and irregular, and, as near as she could tell by touch, about eighteen inches wide. Just wide enough for someone as slim as she to squirm into.

Hank tried to follow her without doing damage to the precious site on which they stood, knocking her off the narrow ledge, or falling off himself. It was a large order, and he moved slowly and clumsily, cursing her as he did so. "Will you tell me why you had to go nuts up here with me? Barbie, for God's sake come back and let's get the hell down off this thing! I'll bring you up again once I've got things under control, I promise."

He had a bad head for heights and he kept wanting to shut his eyes in terror, but fought to keep them open and on the woman a few yards away. Only once did he give in. He closed his eyes, and when he opened them again she had disappeared. Oh, sweet Jesus! Frantically he looked down to see if her crushed body was lying below, but he saw nothing except the purple haze of his own nauseated vertigo.

HER BODY BLOCKED THE NARROW OPENING, MAKING THE light into a thin shaft that penetrated only a few feet before being swallowed by the hungry dark. She waited for her eyes to adjust, and was conscious of being in limited space, not a yawning cavern as she'd expected, and of the barely perceptible sound and smell of water. She was afraid to move, felt an atavistic need to crouch down, to curl herself into a ball and present a smaller target for danger, and she fought it. Finally she made herself stretch out an arm and swing it in a wide, slow half circle.

She touched nothing, not even a cobweb. There were no walls immediately in front or to either side of her; that fact increased rather than assuaged her fear. She could hear her own breathing, nothing else. She took one hesitant step to her right, running the toe of her shoe over the ground before she put her food down. The light increased dramatically. Of course! She was the cause of her own blindness. Another step, this one surer, and the daylight poured in. It did not illumine the rear of the cave; that was still smothered in dark a few feet back. But it showed her what she'd come here to find.

She'd never seen a skeleton before, not close up. It took her a few seconds to realize that's what she was looking at. Another few to see more than a heap of bleached bones. When she could discern the shape, she realized that the head was turned away; no grinning death mask peered at her. The body was lying on its side, with what she took to be the arms folded over the chest and the legs curled up, one knee slightly higher than the other. The same fetal position of protection she'd instinctively wanted to adopt. Staring, she tried to clothe the figure with flesh and life, but hadn't the imagination for it. She knew, or thought she knew, who it was, but the knowledge stayed in her brain. It had no power to move, not here like this. She might have been looking at an exhibit in a science museum. Utterly still and laden with the dust of centuries, Urtaya's mortal remains neither spoke to her heart nor celebrated her coming. Perhaps they had no wish to be disturbed after their long, long sleep.

Barbie thought of ancient curses and primeval taboos, and she shuddered and turned her eyes away. Then she saw the other thing. It was lying at her feet. One further step and she'd have stumbled on it. It too was face down, a lump of black volcanic stone like a hundred others she'd seen since she came to Lanzarote. Pick it up, she told herself, you're supposed to pick it up. She couldn't. She just stood there, staring at the thing whose very presence told her the Lady was no dream manufactured by her imagination, afraid to admit all the many truths that single truth confirmed.

"Barbie! For God's sake, Barbie! Where the hell are you?"

Hank's voice. And getting closer. In a moment he'd be beside her and she'd have failed. He'd see what he must not see, and the Lady would be betrayed. Barbie turned her head and leaned over slightly, so her face was close to the shaft of light. "I'm in the cave. Don't try to come in, the opening's not wide enough for you."

She drew back and reached down quickly, with no further speculation. It was surprisingly light, as volcanic stone so often was, and she turned it in her palm and brushed away the crumbs of powdery red soil that clung to it. The jeweled green seam appeared beneath her fingers, and finally the face. One indrawn breath, the lightning flash of delight at the presence, the very existence, of such perfection of beauty, then she plunged the statue into the pocket of her windbreaker and squeezed out the opening into the sunlight.

ROLLES STARED WILDLY IN THE DIRECTION HER WORDS HAD come from. Thin air. There wasn't any goddamn cave. Just this few inches of ledge at the edge of a jagged outcropping, and a sick-making drop beyond and below.

He studied the cliffside. It fell away in a series of angles, as if great bites had been taken from the mountain. Erosion was endemic to the geology of the place, the local curse. So maybe there was a cave, and the ground in front of it had been sliced away by time, and endless wind, and the occasional fierce rain. That had to be it, because while he watched, Barbie materialized. She seemed to ooze out of the mountain like the ectoplasm of an old-fashioned spiritualist. Phony, but effective. But Barbie was real, and she was smiling as she moved serenely toward him. It was a truly animated smile. If he'd known her better, Hank would have said she looked like her old self.

"YOU NEARLY KILLED US BOTH, AND YOU VIOLATED EVERY professional rule I ever learned." Rolles spoke through clenched teeth, a white line of tension and fury along his jaw. He took a long swallow of rough Spanish brandy, waited for it to soothe him, and for Barbie to speak. She hadn't said anything for the past hour, not while they descended the mountain and not while they drove to Teguise and the Jesuit slammed on the brakes and led the way into the bar. She looked dreamy, preoccupied, unaware of his existence. "I think I'm entitled to some explanation," he muttered when he could endure her silence no longer.

"I'm sorry. I didn't mean to upset you. It was just something I had to do."

"Why, goddamn it?"

"I can't explain that. I'll tell you about the cave, though, if you'll stop shouting at me." He gave her a sour look but didn't say anything. "There's a skeleton. A young woman, I think, though I'm just guessing. There's no penis, but maybe it just withers away. I never thought about that. Do skeletons have genitals?" She didn't wait for an answer. "Anyway, I think it's a woman. Maria's Urtaya."

The Jesuit knew his mouth was sagging open. He closed it. "That's nuts. What else beside the skeleton?"

"Nothing I could make out," she lied. "It was dark and I only went a few feet inside. I didn't see anything except the skeleton, but I had an impression of water." She closed her hand around the small thing in the pocket of her jacket, protecting it with her fingers, knowing she'd die before she'd let go.

"Let's get out of here," Hank said gruffly. "I'm taking you home and going back there with my cameras and equipment. If you breathe a word of this to anyone, I'll strangle you with my bare hands. I swear it."

"I have to tell Maria," Barbie said. But he didn't hear, because he was already out the door.

"DON'T LOOK AT ME LIKE THAT," BARBIE SAID. MARIA WAS staring at her as if she'd grown a second head. "It was all in your book, wasn't it? The girl ran away to the mountains because her lover's family wanted to kill her, and she was never heard from again. So she must have died up there. Isn't that the legend?"

"Yes, but that's what it is, a legend. I wrote fiction, Barbie. You aren't supposed to go leaping along the cliffs proving it's true." Maria pressed her hands to her temples. "You're making me dizzy."

"I don't understand you. Joe and Hank and you, you're all supposed to be Catholics. But anything that isn't ordinary and of this world and measurable makes you nervous." She stood up and started to pace.

Maria watched her, thinking that Barbie was a kind of miracle. She was restored to normalcy in less than twenty-four hours. As if the tragedy that stalked her had been sloughed off like a dress she didn't like, didn't choose to wear. That offended somehow. "I wish to hell you'd stop measuring me by whatever you think of as Catholic. I don't know about Joe or Hank, but I'm not scoring very high on the test for believers these days."

"Poor Maria," Barbie whispered. And she wouldn't say more.

THE LITTLE STATUE LIVED IN THE DRESSER DRAWER BENEATH Barbie's underwear. No one but she knew it existed. Once or twice a day she looked at it, but she didn't do so as an act of worship. Only because the thing was so exquisite. Of itself it wasn't the Lady, any more than the heroic-size sculpture of the Madonna of the Universe was the Lady. Symbols of her, that's all. And not really of her, because no one really understood who or what she was.

Barbie had asked her the night of the party when she came to the mezzanine bedroom and was so real, so ordinary, the way she had been those first times in Peabody. "Who are you really?" The question was dredged up from the depths of the despair with which she'd lived of late, from the gray, hurting sadness she was sure would never go away. "Who are you, and why do you come to me? How do I know I'm not just making you up, inventing you?"

"You asked me to come," the Lady said, ignoring the last question. Her smile was something wonderful. Barbie had often tried to recall and describe it to herself, but she never could. Nonetheless, each time it seemed to her the most loving smile in the world. And the Lady's voice was low and also full of love, but all the same an ordinary, human voice.

Barbie looked long at the Lady who was so real when she was present and so obscure in memory. Her eyes filled with tears, and she spoke again from the depths of her pain. "Where's my baby? Why was she taken away?"

The Lady spoke softly, almost sadly. "I cannot tell you such things. Certainty is not for now." The shawl shadowed her face as it always did; only the smile shone forth. "I have something for you to do," the Lady said. And she told Barbie about the cave and more or less where to find it and what she must look for.

So now Barbie fingered the little statue and wondered what she was supposed to do with it. Probably the Lady would come back and tell her. Meanwhile, she could wait. It didn't matter a great deal, because one certitude had come to replace all the doubt and pain. The Lady existed. Life wasn't just what you saw and felt and smelled. And that changed everything.

Even unbearable pain was bearable when she remembered that.

WHEN THE HOT SUN OF JULY MADE THE AFTERNOONS AN inferno, everyone at Casa Capricho took siesta. Soon after four they emerged from their darkened rooms and blinked in the white glare of the terrace and stretched their limbs and drank glasses of brackish mineral water. Tom took to lacing his with a large amount of scotch, but neither Barbie nor Maria drank anything alcoholic until later. Then, differently refreshed, the three would drift apart.

Tom and Maria returned to their typewriters and Barbie went to the place in the shade where she sat with a book on her knees, but with her eyes half closed. Some days one or the other of them might swim, but if they did, it was a silent and individual pursuit. There was nothing sociable in the post-siesta routine of the house. So it was surprising when one afternoon Tom didn't climb up to his tower but waited instead for Barbie to leave, then perched on the corner of Maria's writing table.

"Indalencio brought this with the mail," he said. He held out the pale blue envelope that signified a cable.

Maria's reaction was quick and instinctive. "Who's it from? Bad news?"

"No, I wouldn't say that. It's from Si. He's coming to visit."

It was ten days since she'd written him. Maria saw the knowing way in which Tom was smiling at her, a sad little grin with a hint of hurt in the eyes. She made herself ignore it. "That's nice! I'm surprised. I thought he never took vacations." She knew her voice sounded forced and phony, but it was the best she could do.

"Yeah, sure." Tom leaned forward and chucked her under the chin. "It'll be fun for you, anyway. I hope you'll be the one to entertain him. I can't take much time from my work just now."

Maria felt a spontaneous flash of anger. What about her work? She suppressed the thought as inappropriate to the circumstances. "Of course. When's he coming?"

"Day after tomorrow. You know Si, loves all the old movies. He understands that the cavalry can't take too long coming over the hill."

With that he left her, and Maria stared after him, feeling the sting of tears behind her lids. He was thin and stooped, from the rear he looked like an old man, and she had the distinct feeling she'd attacked the only thing he wanted to preserve. Some kind of dignity and independence. But what else could she do? It was just too damned much responsibility.

She picked up the telegram he'd left beside her typewriter. "TAKING A WEEK OFF AND INVITING MYSELF TO LANZAROTE. ARRIVE FRIDAY SIXTEENTH THREE PM."

FRIDAY WAS A DISASTER. THE HOT *LEVANTÉ* WIND BLEW IN from Africa, desiccating everything in its path. By noon it had become a full-fledged *sirocco,* swirling red Sahara dust into an enveloping shroud that obscured the sun and the sea and anything that wasn't three feet away. Amazingly, the plane landed despite the visibility.

Si was one of the first people to come down the steps. He wore nondescript chino pants and a sportshirt, and carried a tweed jacket slung over one shoulder. His craggy face turned to survey the people meeting the flight, and when he saw Maria he broke into a wide grin. By the time he trudged from the aircraft to the terminal, he was wheezing and choking and rubbing his eyes.

"Tom couldn't come to meet you in this," Maria explained. "It's hard enough for him to breathe in good weather."

"How can anyone breathe in this? What happened to the idyllic climate you boast about?"

"It went west. Literally. C'mon. I've got a taxi waiting."

They talked aimlessly. Maria wanted to prepare him for his brother's appearance, but instead they both avoided the subject of her letter, as if unable to drop the pretense even while alone. Si seemed more concerned with Barbie than with Tom.

"She's great," Maria said. "So much better since coming here. It's amazing, really. The other day an archaeologist friend took her sightseeing and Barbie discovered a cave that's excited him so much we hardly see him anymore." Maria could hear herself chattering nervously.

Apparently Si heard it too. "What about you?" he asked, reaching for her hand.

"Oh, I'm fine. Good old solid Maria, you know me."

He looked at her oddly but didn't say anything. The taxi turned left onto the washboard road that led to Playa Negra, the driver muttering beneath his breath about the damage to his car. Perversely, Maria didn't warn Si what to expect, and when they rounded the last curve she watched his consecutive reactions of despair at the sight of the grubby village and astonishment when the wondrous whimsy house appeared. The *sirocco* made the village look worse, but it couldn't diminish the house. Casa Capricho stood on the end of its improbable spit of land, curtseying to the ocean and looking more than ever a mirage in the swirling red dust storm.

"Listen," she said at the last possible moment. "You haven't seen Tom for four months. Brace yourself; he's lost a lot of weight."

"I've been braced for some time," Si said, walking forward without hesitation.

MARIA HEARD THE SOFT SOUND OF THE BROTHERS' VOICES long into the night. Si's, mostly; Tom didn't have the strength to talk for hours. She wondered if Si was arguing with him, and if he was having any success. And she remembered the expression in Si's eyes when he realized that she and Tom didn't share a bedroom. Reproachful almost. Crazy.

She awoke at five and knew she wouldn't sleep again. The *sirocco* had blown itself out during the night and the sun was a thin pink line on the horizon, but it was still dark enough to require a candle. In its flickering light Maria thought her face drawn and shadowed and prematurely old. Impatiently, she blew out the flame and pulled on the white bikini she'd acquired since coming to Lanzarote.

The finger of land on which the house sat ended by flinging itself into the sea in a tumble of great boulders, but there was a narrow concrete jetty with a guiding rope that led to the deep ocean. Maria hadn't liked it at first; you couldn't walk yourself into the water gradually, as on a sandy beach. Eventually she'd grown accustomed to the demands of the single plunging dive into the sea.

Now the water cushioned her fall and welcomed her to its buoyant saline embrace. For a while she floated, watching the sun climb over the horizon and gild the world. After about ten minutes she struck out in the strong but inelegant crawl she'd learned as a child in Revere. Then she was conscious of being overtaken and paced. She could see Si's broad shoulders breaking the water beside her. Once their eyes met, and he grinned.

Maria led the way. They swam the length of the clutter of houses that made up the pueblo and rounded a corner to a tiny inlet. "Careful," she yelled. "The bottom's very stony."

453

They let the current carry them to a flat outcropping of dark black rock, worn shiny smooth by the endless ebb and flow of the sea. Si scrambled to his feet and pulled Maria up beside him.

"That was some workout," he said breathlessly. "Do you do this every morning?"

"No," she said between gasps. "If I did, I wouldn't be breathing so hard."

"Just showing off, then?"

"Yes, I guess so. You're terribly white."

"We don't do much sunbathing in Spanish Harlem."

"You'll have to be careful or you'll get a bad burn."

She told herself that's why she was studying his body. The wide shoulders tapered to a slim waist and narrow hips, and his chest hair was a lighter shade of gold than she expected. She looked down at herself and thought of how very brief her bikini was, and how white it appeared against her dark tanned skin. Si drew one finger along the halter strap that tied around her neck, but didn't say anything.

The sun was full up now, warming them and drying the droplets of water that pearled their flesh. They were in a miniscule cove, delineated by the mesa of smooth rock on which they stood and by steep walls formed of burnt earth, crusted over and pocked by a few plants of spiny camel thorn. The isolation was absolute. While the tide was in the only approach was by sea. In the distance to their right was the headland known as Punta Gorda. The sun coaxed a spectrum of improbable color from its tawny expanse.

"Sorry if I sound like a hick," Si said softly. "But, Wow! Fantastic! And a few more adjectives I can't think of."

"Better without the *sirocco,* isn't it?"

"Yes, but I suspect that can be beautiful too, in its way."

Maria sat down. The smooth black stone was pleasantly warm against her buttocks and her thighs. Si dropped beside her, and all at once the tension between them was a tangible, physical thing. Her hands started to tremble, and she clasped them together in a futile bid for control. She was conscious of the weight of her heavy breasts straining the scant bikini bra, and that her nipples were swollen and pressing against the thin polyester fabric.

"Look at me," Si said. She did, and his eyes were dark blue, almost black. "I want you very much. I've wanted you for a long time. Unless you get up right now and go back in the water, it's going to happen."

Maria took a deep breath and closed her eyes. Go, she told herself. But she didn't move. The seconds went by, marked by the sound of the sea lapping against the rocks. The sun burned her shoulders and the nape of her neck. When at last she felt Si's fingers untying the straps of the bra, they seemed an extention of the promised heat of the morning. Her breasts came free of the cloth's restraint, and she felt a surge of pure pleasure. Si lifted them in his hands and she was proud of their bigness in some atavistic response she didn't need to analyze.

She opened her eyes, and their glances locked. "I want you," he said again. She nodded. "It's going to be very good," he whispered.

His voice made her spine tingle. The words were feathers dancing along her backbone and lodging finally between her thighs. She could feel her pelvic muscles relax and contract in anticipation. No illusions and no subterfuge, not even the mental sort. She wanted him inside her. That was all, it was the only important thing. Slowly Maria drew her tongue along her lips. Si was still holding her breasts. He didn't let them go when he leaned forward and slipped his tongue into her mouth. It wasn't a demanding or forceful gesture, merely an exploring one. He was tasting her. Maria waited.

He removed his mouth and his hands from her, and rose. The bulge in his swimming trunks was at her eye level and she thought of tasting him, but not now. Such refinements were no part of this particular moment. Si knew it too. He slipped off his suit and she looked for a moment at the great, jutting thrust of him, then he sat beside her once more and put his hands on her shoulders and gently pushed her back so she lay full length. Maria's palms turned upward, fingers splayed; her thighs fell apart. Her body was opening to admit him.

He knelt over her and released the little gold hip clasps that held the bottom of the bikini in place. The fabric bunched beneath her buttocks, and he pulled it free and set it aside. Then with his strong, sure hands he spread apart her flesh and moved forward and entered her. The penetration was slow and purposeful, and their eyes remained locked. For some seconds neither moved. Maria could feel him swelling inside her, filling the hollow depths of herself with his assertion. "Yes," she whispered.

His thrusts were slow and deliberate at first, each one yet deeper than before. She strained to take him completely inside her; her hands gripped his forearms and she rose and fell to

455

the rhythm he dictated. The hard, hot stone slapped her buttocks each time, and when suddenly he increased the tempo of the movements, the pain intensified and became a sharp, delicious counterpoint to the building frenzy concentrated in her loins. Their two pulses seemed to be synchronized, it was as if she could feel his blood coursing through her veins and pumping life into her heart. That they climaxed together was inevitable. A bursting, breaking, tidal release finally closed their eyes, and heightened both the separateness and the unity of their pleasure.

THE TIDE WENT OUT AND BARED THE ROCKY COAST, AND THEY walked back toward the house, picking their way carefully from foothold to foothold, avoiding the cutting barnacles, and stopping occasionally to study iridescent limpids in the rock pools. When the house came into view they could see that the terrace was empty. Neither Barbie nor Tom was awake.

"Is he going home?" Maria asked. No preamble was needed. This conversation had lain in wait for them since they swam together and stole joy from the morning.

"No," Si said. "He's not going home."

"He'll die then."

"Yes, of course. But he'll die anyway. It's only a question of time. And where."

"You can't be sure of that! The right treatment, a modern hospital—"

"Will change nothing," Si interrupted. "I talked with Dr. Ambrose before I left. Tessa ignored the professional ethics and called Tom's doctor, then reported to me. Tom has lung cancer. 'A pervasive, inoperable malignancy,' to quote her words. He's known for five months."

Since before we came here, Maria thought. Aloud she asked, "How long?"

"They can't say for sure. Six months was the outside estimate."

Only a month left if that was true. "Will there be pain?"

"That's not completely predictable either. Perhaps not, but it depends on the nature of the metastases. The worst danger is a spread to the brain. He'll be a vegetable or perhaps insane if that happens."

"Oh, my God." Her voice was a long moan and Maria realized she was terrified for herself as well as for Tom. Si, of course, knew that.

"You don't have to stay on as nurse, you know. He wants to remain, but he'll understand if you don't."

"I can't leave him now. It's a monstrous idea."

"Yes, and I thought you'd say that." They were almost at the house, and he paused and turned to face her. "Maria, don't get yourself into some twisted guilt trip. It's no good your staying if you wind up hating Tom for inflicting his dying on you, and yourself for enduring it."

"That may happen," she admitted. "I can't say if it will, but it may. It doesn't change anything. I can't leave until it's over."

"No," he agreed. "I don't suppose you can." He reached up and traced the line of her cheek with one finger. "Maybe afterwards," he said softly.

Maria felt a band of pain encircle her chest and tighten on her heart. "No," she whispered, and ignored the flash of anguish in his eyes. She felt anguish too, because she had just realized how much she loved him. But each time she looked at him she thought of Spanish Harlem and of filth and ugliness and hatred. Whatever she felt for Si, she knew she couldn't live with that.

"We'd better go in," she said. "I'll make some coffee. Watch for a little blue van. It's the bread man. He comes every morning around this time."

IN THE EVENING HANK ROLLES CAME, THE FIRST TIME THEY'D seen him in days. He was ecstatic about the cave. Definitely pre-conquest. He was sure. Dating from around fourteen hundred, was his educated guess. "The skeleton's a young female, and I'll bet my life she's one of the original population. Madrid's sending a team of experts and we won't know anything definite for a while. But I can feel it."

"Urtaya," Barbie said.

"Don't start that," he admonished, wagging his finger at her. "You almost ruined everything. Spain might have reinstated the Inquisition just for you."

"I thought it was Barbie who found the cave," Si said benignly.

Hank looked chagrined. "True." Then, to Tom, "Was your brother always such a pain in the ass?"

"Always," Tom agreed. "The more you know him the more you'll hate him."

The three men continued their banter. Barbie was quiet and

subdued, but she didn't appear unhappy. To Maria it seemed as if Barbie was contentedly biding her time. Waiting. For what Maria didn't know. Only what she herself was waiting for.

Maria was living in expectation of the moment when everyone would go to their rooms. She was hoping desperately that Si would wait until the house was quiet, then come to her. But if he intended it, he gave no advance warning. He was as warm and friendly as always, and nothing in his glance or occasional, accidental touch betrayed the intimacy of the morning. She fantasized that she'd dreamed the whole thing. But then she let herself feel the warmth that memory generated between her legs, and she knew she hadn't.

Suddenly there was a lull in the conversation, and Barbie spoke into the momentary silence. "I am going to go to a convent," she said.

"I DON'T MEAN I WANT TO BE A NUN," BARBIE'S GLANCE SWEPT round the four astonished faces in the room. "At least I don't know about that yet. But I want to live with some nuns for a while."

Maria found her voice. "Barbie, are you thinking of becoming a Catholic?"

"What's that got to do with it?"

Maria shook her head. Barbie's ingenuousness continued to astonish her, even after so many years. "What do you know about convents anyway? You'd hate it, believe me."

"You're projecting a bit, aren't you, Maria?" Hank said. His tone was slightly harsh and more than slightly supercilious. "Your experience isn't necessarily representative of everyone's."

Maria made a sound of disgust, and Tom, looking from her to the priest, picked a banana off the table and held it to his mouth. "Dong! End of the first round, folks. Looks like a draw." He put down the banana and picked up his perennial cigarette. "If a noninterested nonbeliever can make a serious comment, aren't there different kinds of convents? You've told me so often enough, Maria."

"Sure." Hank spoke quickly. "Maria was in a teaching sisterhood. Maybe what Barbie has in mind is some kind of monastic community. Contemplatives, perhaps. But the first question Maria asked is pretty basic. I know plenty of Catholic convents and a few Protestant ones, but Barbie's got to decide about her religious affiliations first."

As if she didn't realize they were discussing her, Barbie sipped the robust Spanish cognac and surveyed the scene. She wondered if anyone besides her knew that Tom was dying. And wondered if Maria realized that Hank was a little in love with her. And wondered why they all insisted on being so sectarian and narrow-minded. They seemed to think that God could only exist if they gave him a label. Catholic God this way, folks, the Protestant God's in the other room, and nobody's seen the Jewish one for years.

Barbie took another swallow of her brandy and turned to the shadows on the edge of the room. Si had been silent for some time. Now their eyes met and held, and he smiled at her. It was a slow, sweet smile and she thought about the fact that Maria was in love with Si but scared to death by his life-style. Maria didn't talk about it, but Barbie knew.

Si moved his chair closer to the candle glow that lit the center of the group. "Balls," he said softly. Tom, Hank, and Maria were all talking at once, and he had to say it louder. "Balls. That's not what Barbie meant. Don't nuns sometimes have guests? She only said she wanted to live with some nuns for a while."

The rest looked at Si as if he were the sage come down from the mountain with the answer to the meaning of life. "A retreat, you mean?" Hank asked. He turned to Barbie. "Is that what this is all about? You want to go on retreat?"

Barbie had long understood that certain kinds of men always patronized her. It went with her looks. She'd immediately recognized Hank as one of those. It didn't offend her. "I'm not sure about that, either," she answered. "I just want to live in a convent with nuns."

"Permanently or for a visit?" Maria's incredulity made her sound as condescending as the priest. Barbie chose not to answer.

Si reached across the table and poured himself the last of a bottle of wine. "Do you all need to make so much noise about something so simple? Barbie wants to spend some time in a place where people pray. What's the hassle?"

Barbie turned to him with one of her radiant smiles. "That's it exactly. I want to be in a prayed-in place. I think the one I have in mind is in England."

Si saluted her with his glass. "We Jews have to stick together, baby. The *goyim* never did have any brains. *L'chaim.*"

"*L'chaim,*" she said, raising her brandy.

"A prayed-in place," Tom repeated. "That is one hell of a

phrase." He chuckled softly and lifted his glass too. "*L'chaim*. To life, what's left of it." The laughter was without bitterness and took the sting from his words.

"We *goys* have been effectively isolated," Maria told Hank. "Did I ever tell you that some of my best friends—"

"The plural is *goyim*," Si corrected.

Hank wasn't listening. "Do you mean you have a specific convent in mind, Barbie?"

"Oh, yes. Didn't I make that clear? It's on the Isle of Wight. That's England, isn't it?"

"Yes. Just across from Southampton. In the Solent. It's a small island, but I think there are nuns there. Some Benedictines, in fact. They probably take lady retreatants."

"Do they wear white habits and black veils?" Barbie asked.

Maria felt the hairs rise on the back of her neck. She was conscious of both Tom and Si staring at Barbie, and thinking what she herself was thinking. "How do you know so much about the nuns you have in mind?" Maria asked.

"Oh, I don't know," Barbie said airily. "I think I read about them in a magazine. Ages ago. I just remembered, that's all."

"A white habit and a black veil probably means Dominicans," Hank said. He thought for a moment, then added, "Hold on, I do know a convent of Dominican nuns on the Isle of Wight." To Maria he added, "Second order contemplatives. They've got two or three houses in England."

"Are they cloistered?"

"I'm not exactly sure. One of them was doing some research at Cambridge, that's how I heard about them. They seem to have flexible ideas. It would probably be a good choice, if they'd have her."

"Oh, I'm sure they'll have me," Barbie said, giggling softly.

MARIA WAITED FOR HOURS, LYING ON THE BED, RIGID WITH wanting him. A crazy pulse on the inside of her thigh kept jumping. The degree of her desire was frightening and perhaps a little shameful. Particularly since it was apparently not shared. Si did not come that night. Or the next.

The day in between was passed in the usual way, everyone seeming wrapped up in their own affairs until they came together briefly for lunch, and then dinner. In between the two communal meals Si and Tom went for a long ride in the jeep. Afterwards they didn't talk about what they'd seen, much less said. No one mentioned Barbie's intention of going to live with some Dominicans on the Isle of Wight. Hank had promised to write to the convent and explain the situation, so that too was now in limbo. Certainly neither Si nor Maria acknowledged any change in their relationship. Except that each time Tom addressed her with proprietary affection, Maria had to keep herself from flinching.

On Monday the weather changed. Following Friday's *sirocco*, the weekend had been a travel agent's dream. Now the heat increased until a thermometer in the shade showed 46 degrees Centigrade. "That's about one hundred and twenty plus, folks," Tom announced. Maria noted that he was almost pathetically cheerful. For Si's benefit, probably. The heat drove any further analysis from her mind, helped by her frustration and her anger and her sense of being used by both men. Like everyone else, she escaped to her room. Hived off, she thought, that's what we are; separate drones in our separate cells.

Midnight on Thursday. A spangled sky, a sliver of moon, and Maria, sick with all the waiting and the wanting, went to him. Tomorrow he'd be gone, returned to his garbage-infested world and his pitiful attempts to stem a tidal wave of hate. Tonight at least he was here and could be hers.

He slept at the top of one of the house's many wings. Maria climbed the narrow staircase in bare feet, her candle making surreal shadows on the rough plaster walls. Si's door was open. His room had large windows, and it was washed in blue starlight. She could see the still, solid, male outline of him in the narrow stone bed that was built into an upholstered alcove. A fantasy from a Moorish dream. Complete with houri, Maria thought. She blew out her candle and slipped off her robe, letting it fall to the floor. Gently she lifted the sheet and lay naked beside him.

Si wasn't asleep. He turned to her instantly, as hungry as she was. In seconds he was inside her, pounding her flesh, punishing it. "You bastard!" she cursed, as he came so swiftly it seemed to be over before it began.

"That's what we're about, isn't it? Using each other."

Maria was choked with rage and conscious of the silent, sleeping house that prevented her from screaming out her anger. Instead she raked his shoulders with her fingernails, and he made a sound between a groan and a sigh and used the strength of his arms to roll them both over so she was on top, still impaled on his turgid rigidity. "You want it," he hissed, "work for it."

She moved frantically, sheening her skin with sweat, conscious of his hands holding her breasts, fingering the nipples. The starlight illumined his face, and she saw that he was grinning. Maria sobbed deep in her throat and felt tears wet her cheeks. She wanted to stop and run from the room, hide where he'd never see her again. She couldn't, her need was too great. She was too close. So close. Almost there. And he doing nothing to help her, only lying still and staying hard and waiting. Letting her continue to struggle until finally she knew she was going to make it. And she did.

Suddenly there was tenderness. They were lying side by side, he was holding her gently, cradling her in his arms, kissing her cheeks and her eyes and her hair. Eventually she realized that they were both crying, and soon they fell asleep, but only for minutes it seemed. It was still night when she woke to the realization that he was inside her again. Slow this time, the final moment forestalled in a long, loving exploration of ecstasy.

"Don't go," she begged in the balm of afterwards.

"I have no choice."

"Why not?" With urgency, and a touch of returned anger.

"I've got to do my thing, my way. But I love you, Maria."

She couldn't answer that. She loved him too, but she couldn't promise to share his life of squalor and ugliness. Silently she got out of the bed and found her robe and put it on. "Good night," she whispered.

"Good-bye," he said.

Two months later, in New York on a cruelly beautiful autumn day, Simon Shore received the news of his brother's death. It came in the form of a brief telegram, and somewhere between Lanzarote and America the word "sleep" was misspelled. The message read, "TOM DIED PEACEFULLY IN HIS SLIP YESTERDAY." He thought of Tom in a slip, but the laugh came out as a groan and unshed tears made the words blur.

A head poked around the door of his office. A grizzled old man, once a short-order cook, who worked part-time at the hostel. "Hey, Si, you know that case of hot dogs? I just broke into it, and they're all rotten. Covered with mold. You want I should cook 'em anyway? Maybe I can wash 'em off or something."

Shore swallowed the lump in his throat. "No, don't do that. There are six cans of beef stew. They'll do for lunch." He tugged a key off a laden ring. "They're in the cupboard under the stairs. On the right."

The cook nodded and went away. Si took the telegram and went into his tiny bedroom behind the office and closed and locked the door. The hostel was of necessity a place of locked doors. There was no alternative, but it made him feel like a jailer.

Tom's last letter lay on the bed. He'd been reading it this morning, and now he picked it up again. "When it comes, don't make a big deal out of it," Tom had written. "I don't know if there's any me-ness of me that goes to some big writers' conference in the sky, but I'm damned sure that putting my corpse in a hole in the ground, or a crypt as they do here in Lanzarote, has little to do with it. As for Maria, she's got all her Catholic mumbo jumbo to get her through. She says she doesn't believe any of it, but it's in her bones or her genes, or something equally obscure. She'll be okay, at least until later. I think she'll need you then, or you'll need her. But that's not my concern. Except to say, blessings on both your heads, my children."

Si folded the letter and the telegram. He would not have been ashamed to cry, but tears were not part of his arsenal of defense. He'd never had the knack, though he'd often wished he had. Only one thing seemed to him an appropriate response. But he hesitated, remembering Tom's crack about mumbo jumbo. In the end he dismissed the comment and fished in the back of the bookcase for the little prayer book.

It was a thing of yellowed ivory covers and faded blue velvet spine. Printed in Philadelphia in 1890, it was a crazy piece of Victorian kitsch spun from the impoverished reality of turn of the century immigrant Jewry. It had been a *bar mitzvah* gift from Mr. Greenburg, who lived across the hall in Brownsville. Si opened the book to the *Kaddish*, then hesitated again. This time he rummaged around in his underwear drawer and came up with the black skullcap he'd worn at the synagogue in Holyoke. Only after he put it on did he intone the words. Softly, his big body swaying of its own accord to rhythms more ancient than time, passed on to him with his blood and his genes, as Tom had said about Maria. *"Yis-ka-dal v' yis-ka-dash . . ."*

When the prayer was finished he put the book and the yarmulke where they'd be close at hand. He'd find a synagogue and say *Kaddish* for Tom every day for a year, and if his brother was at some huge writers' conference in the sky and had a big laugh, so be it.

He started to return to his office, then remembered another letter. It had come ten days ago from somebody in the Department of Health, Education, and Welfare in Washington. "Dear Professor Shore," it began. The words looked odd; few people addressed him thus these days. This time was because he was being asked to join a Presidential task force to study the role of public schools in the acculturation process of Hispanics. He'd dismissed the idea as another grandiose federal scheme involving talk instead of money. Now, on impulse, he put the letter on top of the prayer book. Just so he could find it again in case he decided to reply.

16

THE CHOIR OF THE DOMINICAN NUNS ON THE ISLE OF
Wight was a long nave leading to a circular apse containing the altar and tabernacle. The walls were white
and bare, the only decoration the carved wooden stalls and the
far crucifix. Barbie kept her eyes fixed on the Jewish God-man
and let the plainsong ebb and flow around her.

"Concede nos Domini ad pupillum oculi," a tremulous single
voice intoned. Keep us Lord as the apple of your eye. The
voices of twenty more women chanted the response. *"Sub
umbra alarum tuarum protege nos."* Shelter us in the shadow of
your wings. The ancient service of Compline continued, last of
the hours of the Divine Office, a prelude to sleep.

"Latin," Sister Imelda had explained, "is a sacred language,
a symbol of the mystery and otherness of God. Some of us
think that's important. But not all of us, so we sometimes
chant in English." She'd laughed, and the sound had as much
music as her Welsh lilted speech.

The nun who was the point of contact between guests and
the monastic community was a woman of fifty-three. She'd
been an Oxford don before she entered the convent at thirty.
She had bright blue eyes and a ready smile, but without the
dignifying influence of the simple white wimple and black veil
she'd probably be homely. And probably not care very much.
Sister Imelda was not ordinary and not likely to fit any mold,
conventual or otherwise. Few religious communities could

have absorbed her independence or her inquiring mind. But this one could and did. In this priory fewer than twenty women had come together to live a life of discovery and of prayer. They saw nothing as very sure and never as rigid. That wasn't their way.

"We're oddities," Sister Imelda admitted to Barbie. "Even among contemplatives, who are accustomed to being out of step with the rest of the world, and often the Church."

Barbie didn't find them odd or out of step. She'd never felt more at home in her life. She wondered if Maria would feel that way too.

The final haunting notes of the Salve Regina, anthem to the Jewish Mother of the Jewish God, died away. The formal ranks of opposing choirs melted into an easy flow of women going their own way. A few nuns found places to kneel or to squat on low wooden prayer stools. Some would spend the night thus. No mention was ever made of it, and because their faces were shadowed by their veils Barbie couldn't identify them. They were unmoving studies in black and white. Two or three followed her out of the chapel and smiled good night as she took up her vigil by the front door. The silent community knew she was waiting for her friend.

"Don't ring the bell," she'd told Maria earlier on the telephone. "Just knock. I'll be waiting. I'll hear you."

"I could get a hotel for the night and come in the morning," Maria had said. "I expected to arrive earlier, but I missed the ferry and now there isn't one for two hours."

"It doesn't matter," Barbie had insisted. "Just be quiet so we won't disturb the grand silence." She'd started to explain that she meant the time between Compline and Morning Prayer, then remembered that of course Maria would know. Now, waiting for her, Barbie wondered how much Maria would remember, and find familiar. And if she'd hate it for that reason.

There was the sound of a car in the driveway. Barbie had the door open before Maria paid off the cab.

Hugs, muffled greetings, and a few seconds of searching each other's face in the dim light of the nineteenth-century psuedo-Gothic building to which electricity had come as a reluctant afterthought. On impulse, Barbie took Maria's hand and tugged her toward the chapel. The choir was lit only by the sanctuary candle. Its steady flame revealed those few silent, huddled figures, rapt in prayer, half hidden in the shadows. Barbie started to move forward. She was still holding Maria's hand, and she felt her stiffen and pull back. Barbie acquiesed, and they left, closing the tall doors behind them, locking out the particular vision of life they guarded.

The two women moved quickly through a maze of corridors to the room designated for Maria. It was next door to the one Barbie had occupied for three months. There was a small fireplace, but it was boarded over, and the large ungainly radiator was ice cold. A two-bar electric heater struggled against the October chill of the evening. Damp—the English curse. Maria shivered. "It smells just the way I remember," she said. "All convents must smell alike."

"No," Barbie said sharply. "Judging from what you've told me, this one's unique. You'll see." She gave up the attempt to explain. Maria would have to form her own opinion. "I made us a thermos of coffee." Barbie poured two cups and produced a plate of sandwiches. "Sister Imelda made these. They're some ghastly English thing called Marmite. It's not edible."

The spread was dark brown, gooey, and salty. Obviously a taste one had to be born with. "Never mind." Maria pushed the sandwiches away. "I'm not hungry."

"You look exhausted," Barbie said. "I put a hot-water bottle in the bed. There are plenty of blankets."

Maria thought of the lavender-and-lace guestroom on East Seventy-second Street, and the welcome Barbie had provided when she'd escaped from another convent. A year and a half that was a lifetime ago. Suddenly she didn't have the strength to speak. Barbie understood and kissed her good night and left.

Maria took off her dress and found her robe on top of the suitcase, and put it on over her bra and pants. When she crawled into the hard, unwelcoming bed, she started to cry. Insane. She wasn't weeping for any reason that made sense. Not because she'd buried Tom a month ago, in Lanzarote, as he'd requested. Not because Si didn't come to the funeral. Not because she didn't know what to do with her life, or why the fact that *A Lasting Fire* was finally published and was now number three on the *New York Times* best-seller list gave her so little pleasure. Only because she felt alone and scared, and trapped in an environment both alien and agonizingly familiar.

THE SAMENESS WAS A VENEER, A LACQUER-THIN ENCRUSTATION on the surface, covering a reality quite different from anything Maria had known as a Servant of Bethlehem. She understood that after a few days. The nature of the difference was not so readily identified. "It's such a peaceful place," Barbie had said. "Come and have a rest, you must need it." She did, of course. But she wouldn't have chosen the Dominican Priory, except that Barbie was there. And as well as feeling somehow responsible for that extraordinary fact, Maria was curious.

"What are you doing here?" she asked the first day, when they sat together in the convent garden, listening to the birds celebrate a golden autumn afternoon.

Barbie smiled. "Nothing much. Mostly I'm just enjoying myself." She stretched luxuriously and tipped her face to the sun. Her hair was longer than it had been in years, a shaggy bronze frame for her perfect features.

Maria noted that Barbie's exquisite feline grace was intact. She'd remembered how the convent in Lynn tried to shape even their physical selves, and half expected Barbie would have become straight-backed and silent moving, her hands clasped at the waist, her eyes modestly cast down. She was nothing like that. Neither were the nuns. Two of them were picking apples in an orchard some fifty yards away. Their black-and-white habits were hitched up around their waists, and jean-clad legs flashed up and down ladders propped against heavy bearing trees. Occasionally their laughter was caught by a breeze and carried across the garden.

"Are you planning to stay here?" Maria asked.

Barbie shrugged. "I'm not sure what I'm planning. Tell me about Tom. How was it at the end?"

"Nothing like as bad as I feared. He just . . . drifted away. I don't know any other way to put it. He finished his book and went to bed and stayed there for a few days. One morning I brought him up a cup of coffee, and found him dead." She didn't tell about standing beside his corpse unable to weep or to pray, feeling that there was something dead inside her, too. But not because of him; something that predated Tom and what they'd been, and not been, to each other.

"The nuns have been praying hard for him since I came. I asked them to. Was Hank there?"

Maria shook her head. "He'd left for England a few days earlier. He's in Cambridge writing up his Lanzarote finds."

"Too bad, Tom might have wanted him there at the end. But I'm so glad it was peaceful."

It was getting late and chilly. Maria buttoned the cardigan she wore. "I can't help wondering why he didn't fight. Maybe he could have lived longer, if he'd wanted to."

"Maybe he knew there was nothing to fear," Barbie said.

Maria wanted to probe that remark, and the knowing expression in Barbie's eyes, but the bell for Vespers sounded. Barbie rose to its summons with as much alacrity as any nun.

For a few days the routine of the priory absorbed them, measured their hours. In this regularity it was like the life Maria had known, but the discipline seemed to have a purpose she'd never found in Lynn or Beverly or Wrentham. Once Sister Imelda sought her out, and they walked together and talked. Figures lifted whole from a medieval tapestry.

"It's a rhythm, that's all," the nun said. "A cadence that prepares for prayer. It's freedom."

Maria nodded, but she didn't pursue the conversation. The nun recognized her reluctance to speak of such things and went away.

Maria intended to go away too. Far away, to London and then to New York where she would deliver to Sam Hill the two manuscripts in her suitcase. She carried Tom's last testament, which she'd not yet found the courage to read, and her new novel, which she couldn't judge. The agent was waiting for both. But almost against her will, Maria lingered on the Isle of Wight.

She slept late each morning, ignoring the convent bells. But on the fifth day she woke to the full-throated summons to Mass that pealed throughout the corridors and over the countryside. She had thus far taken no part in any of the services. She'd heard the plainchant of the Divine Office, sometimes standing outside the chapel doors until it ended, but she'd not entered the choir since that first evening when she'd resisted Barbie's attempt to lead her there. Now she lay awake listening to the bells, and thinking about Barbie, the enigma. It occurred to her that one aspect of that mystery was soluble, and she jumped out of bed and threw on her clothes.

Barbie was at the rear of the choir, her flaming hair a startling contrast to the black veils. One of the nuns stood at the lectern, reading the lesson for the day. It was November 1, Maria realized, the feast of All Saints. She listened to the reader's voice. "Then I saw a great multitude, past all counting, taken from all nations and tribes and peoples and languages. These stood before the throne . . ."

Vision of Apocalypse, the voice of prophecy. Maria turned to Barbie, but there was no answering glance, no smile of welcome. Barbie's eyes were closed, and Maria doubted she was aware of anything happening around her.

The time for communion came and the nuns received the

consecrated host from the priest. The chalice they took from each other, passing it from hand to hand. Barbie did not go forward to join in the rite, and one question was answered. Whatever she might be, Barbie hadn't become a Catholic.

Maria too remained where she was in the rear of the choir. She felt no desire for the sacrament, nothing but anger and unreasoning fear. She looked up and saw not the elegant wrought-iron and wood crucifix of the Dominicans; instead she saw a garish plaster statue of the crucified Jesus, with thirteen gold thorns and thirteen drops of bright red blood. In her head she heard again the words, yes, I will be a nun. She was twenty-eight years old and she'd tried but never kept the promise made when she was thirteen. If there was a God, that must be His fault.

That afternoon it was Maria who looked for Sister Imelda. "I don't understand what Barbie's doing here," she said. "You know her daughter died a short time ago and Barbie came close to having a nervous breakdown. I'm worried that she's hiding from reality in this place."

The nun smiled. "There's a lot of reality in this place. Too much, perhaps. It's not a comfortable place for hiding. I had an Irish grandmother; she would have said that Barbie was 'touched by angels' wings.' It's true, but she's saner than most of us."

Maria didn't argue. "I don't understand your life," she said, getting to the point really on her mind. "I never heard of a contemplative community taking lay women inside the cloister."

"It's our apostolate," Sister Imelda said. "We pray and we share our life. Never more than two or three guests at a time, and only those who ask to come. We don't advertise or make a lot of noise about it. The doors all unlock from the inside, Maria."

THE FERRY DOCKED AT RYDE, A TOWN ON THE NORTHEASTERN side of the island. It lumbered into a slip at the end of a long wooden pier built in the time of Queen Victoria. There was a broad sandy beach, but it was deserted in the gray November noon. There was also a funny little train that covered the distance between the ferry slip and the main road a quarter of a mile away. Philocles Williams chose to walk. The wind and the damp penetrated his suit, and he regretted not having a coat. It had been deceptively sunny when he left London that morning, and he'd forgotten about the infamous British weather.

Like the pier, Ryde was a Victorian town, all gingerbread and curlicues climbing from the shorefront up a series of steep hills. At eye level the boardwalk betrayed the image. It was cheap and tawdry, and reeked of tired frying oil that warred with the smell of the sea.

The British had a genius for beauty, centuries of it, but the coast everywhere was thus desecrated. As if they wanted to hide the inland treasures from pirates, they surrounded the breathtaking interior in an ugly frame. Williams wondered what that said about the national character. That it was inward looking and insular perhaps, but not if you thought about the empire. He thought of it only as long as it took him to reach the road and find a taxi.

Twenty minutes later, the driver announced that they'd arrived. Williams opened his eyes for the first time since the journey began. He'd lost his taste for sightseeing and speculation as soon as he gave the cabbie the address. He glanced at the meter and fished an extra five-pound note from his wallet. "Pick me up here in an hour." He looked at his gold watch, Patek Phillipe and thus reassuring. "At two-fifteen exactly."

The driver nodded. Something about the American kept conversation at bay. A kind of icy formality, and a way of giving orders that allowed for no dissent. But what the hell, five-pound tips didn't grow on trees. Not on the Isle of Wight in November. "Yes, sir," he murmured.

Williams climbed out of the car and waited until it had disappeared down the hill, then he looked at the granite priory across the road. It was a gray stone fortress surrounded by a formidable wall, inspired perhaps by the Norman castle on the other side of the valley. From where he stood he could look from one building to the other, and take in at the same time the rolling hills the guidebook had told him to call downs. The downs were made of chalk and had been separated from the mainland by some ancient geological upheaval. He'd read that too.

There was a small sign by the gate at the foot of the driveway opposite. "Dominican Nuns," it announced. Crazily he searched for something more, some statement that would explain what Barbie was doing inside such a place. The mist rolled up the valley and a gull squawked. Nothing else. He might be alone on the planet.

There was a bench nearby, a reminder of absent civilization. Williams crossed to it and sat down, keeping his eyes on the priory. The damp of the stone seat seeped through his trousers. He wondered if it was warm inside, if Barbie was warm. He wondered too what he was doing here.

He understood what had brought him to England. He'd lived so long with his need and his hunger, he knew it well. But this excursion, which had no purpose other than to see the place where she was, had about it the marks of madness. Once more he toyed with the notion of going up to the front door and ringing the bell. All day long he'd schooled himself to avoid that trap. He knew her too well not to recognize the danger.

Eventually the cabbie returned. Automatically, Williams looked at his watch. Two-fifteen, as ordered. It gave him a good feeling to be obeyed, made some sense of his world. They were back in Ryde in time for him to catch the three o'clock ferry to Portsmouth. There Harris waited for him in a rented Rolls-Royce Silver Ghost. The car was perfectly sprung and took the narrow byways and the new highway with equal ease, but by the time they reached London at five-thirty Williams felt drained. He longed for a soak in a hot tub with a tall drink in hand, but not more than he longed for Barbie.

In the lobby of the Dorchester he took from the inside pocket of his jacket a letter written the night before. It was addressed to the Isle of Wight, and today he'd carried it there and back. Now he was going to mail it. Crazy. Like everything else he'd done this day, it was the behavior of desperation.

AT LUNCH THAT SAME DAY BOTH GUESTS FOUND FOLDED NOTES at their places in the refectory, requesting them to join Sister Imelda in the common room at two. She's probably going to ask us if our intentions are honorable, Maria thought. And if not, will we please get the hell out of here. It turned out to be nothing like that.

"I knew you'd both be interested because it concerns the Canary Islands," the nun said. "There's a priory like this one on Tenerife. We're all autonomous, that's the way St. Dominic arranged it, but we try to help each other when we can. The Spanish nuns are particularly interested in the history of their island and the others in the archipelago. They study the old sites, particularly those that were places of worship before the European conquest. Now they've become involved with a group of women who want to found a house of prayer on Lanzarote. Not nuns, lay people from Barcelona. There's a lot of that kind of thing these days."

Barbie was grinning like a child on Christmas morning. "That's it," she whispered.

Maria heard her, but she didn't know if Sister Imelda had. "What do they need to go ahead with their plan?" she asked.

"Money, of course." The nun made a rueful face. "We haven't very much. The community thinks we can spare a hundred pounds. We'll send it, but it probably won't do much good. Everything's so expensive these days."

Maria started to say that she would have money when her royalty payments began in a few months, but Barbie didn't give her the opportunity. "I can help," she said breathlessly. "It will take a few days to work things out."

They left the common room. Maria felt stifled, oppressed by Barbie's sudden agitation. She glanced out the window. If she hadn't known it was impossible she'd have sworn she saw Phil Williams climbing into a taxi across the road. The notion was too preposterous to mention.

Barbie tugged at her arm. "Come to my room right away. I want to show you something."

MARIA STARED AT THE STATUE IN AWE. "IT'S EXQUISITE. BUT I don't understand; where did you get it?"

"On Lanzarote. The day I discovered the cave. This was lying on the ground next to the skeleton. Just where it was supposed to be."

Maria didn't speak for long seconds, and when she did her voice was a whisper. "The sacred statue that was lost when the *hamagadas* were killed, the one Tisa looked for but never found."

"Yes. Urtaya must have taken it into the mountains with her."

"Does Hank know about this? How come he never said anything?"

Barbie shook her head impatiently. "Hank doesn't know. I found the statue. It could have been any tourist who happened on the cave by chance, but it wasn't, it was me. That's how it was meant to be. The statue is mine now."

"But that's theft! Barbie, you can't just walk out of a country and take their artifacts with you. Something old and beautiful like this, it's outrageous."

Barbie was unmoved. "Forget all that. I did what I was told to do. It will bring a lot of money if it's sold, won't it?"

"Yes, but you can't sell it. It doesn't belong to you. What do you mean, you were told? Who told you?"

"Never mind. Don't you see, the money will allow the House of Prayer to be opened. That's what the Lady wants." She stopped speaking and looked away.

"That's what you mean about being told," Maria said. "Your visions of Our Lady, or whoever she's supposed to be."

Barbie sighed and sat down on the bed. "You don't sound surprised."

"Joe told me years ago. He thought you were hallucinating. He wanted me to talk to you."

"Do you think I'm hallucinating?"

"I don't know. Maybe."

"But you can't be sure, can you? And you have to be careful, 'lest you speak against God.' " She saw Maria stiffen and knew her thrust had gone home.

Maria stared out the window. The view, usually lovely, was obscured by mist. "I'd like to be sure, but I suppose I never will be. That's not my luck, it seems."

Barbie ignored the plea for assurance. Certainty is not for now, that's what the Lady said. Everyone has to find their own way to God. Faith, in whatever form, isn't something one person can give to another. "Listen, you've got to give me your word you won't try and stop me. Please, Maria. I know I'm doing the right thing."

"How can you know?"

"I told you. I have instructions."

Maria shook her head in frustration. "If you want money for these Barcelona women you can probably get it from Phil. Will you try that first?"

"I can't. That's not what I've been told. Don't you see, Maria? There's a pattern, a tapestry. It's complicated and we never see all of it. Just the tiny bit that involves us. If we break the threads other people can be hurt or miss opportunities—" She broke off, unable to explain more.

Maria stared at her for a moment. "All of a sudden it's Barbie the philosopher." Finally she chuckled. "Mr. Marcus wouldn't believe it."

"So I'm not just another pretty face, right?"

More laughter and a few tears, and in the end Maria promised to do nothing Barbie didn't want done. "I'm not sure why, but okay."

"Good. And relax, this time you're on the side of the angels."

THE LETTER FROM PHIL WAS DELIVERED THE FOLLOWING morning. Barbie recognized the handwriting and noted the London postmark. Without opening it she told Sister Imelda, "I'll be leaving in a few days. My time here has been wonderful, but it's over."

"Yes." The nun smiled. "I thought it might be. Will Maria stay on, do you think?"

"I don't know."

"Yes," Maria said when she was asked. "I'd like to, just for a bit. To think some things through."

BARBIE HELD THE RECEIVER TO HER EAR AND WAITED. PHIL answered on the third ring. "It's me."

"Where are you?" Not what he'd intended to say at all. And sounding strangled, the need showing. "I mean, hello."

"Hello yourself. I'm in London. No, wait, don't say anything yet. Hear me out. I've got some things to do. I want to do them alone. My hair, some new clothes . . . you understand. I'll meet you at the Dorchester the day after tomorrow."

A long silence. Then, "I miss you. It's been almost six months."

"Two more days. That's all."

"Promise?"

"Yes, promise, promise, promise." The old formula they'd used with Norma. And she could say it without choking. It even made her happy in a way.

"A three-times promise can't ever be broken," Phil answered. "Okay. Day after tomorrow. Noon, here at the Dorchester. That suit you?"

"That's fine. And Phil." She hesitated. "Leave me alone until then. No spies."

"Promise, promise, promise," he said before he hung up.

Barbie waited until the line was clear, then dialed the number of the Elizabeth Arden Salon. She chose it because it was a name she recognized and because she knew they had a boutique as well as a beauty parlor.

"Cut and blow dry," she told the very grand English accent. "And a facial, a manicure, a leg wax, and a pedicure. This afternoon. Can you do all that?" It was November, nadir of the tourist season; they could do it. Afterwards she checked her wallet and made sure all her credit cards were current. That settled, she called Cambridge and left a message for Father Hank Rolles.

Williams too made a number of phone calls. His were less direct, a matter of opening some lines of inquiry and closing others. It took time and discretion because he was distant from his power base, but for a man of his resources it was not impossible.

Whatever his last words to Barbie, this was one promise he couldn't keep. No matter how solemnized. Once before she'd made him back off and leave her unprotected, the time in New York when she'd been so angry and he'd agreed to stop watching her and Joe DiAnni. That had ended in disaster, caused her pain. He didn't intend to repeat the experience.

"Check all the hairdressers," he told the man. "I don't care how many people you have to put on it." There was a protest about the number of places a woman could get her hair done in London.

"She'll probably choose someplace well known. Don't argue, just do it. Once you pick her up she's to be left strictly alone. But let me know who she sees and where she goes." There was a question, and Phil replied, "Yes, reports of any conversations might be helpful. Just make sure the tail knows his business."

Eventually he was satisfied with the arrangements. Time now to savor the pleasure of anticipation. No, that wasn't strong enough. What he felt wasn't anticipation, it was gratitude, gut level thanksgiving. Because he'd been scared stiff that the gray stone fortress had swallowed her, dragged her across a line even he couldn't erase. He'd cursed himself for being all kinds of a fool to let her leave New York in the first place. Then he'd remembered the shattered thing she'd been, and known he couldn't have done anything else. Now he'd spoken to her and she sounded like herself again. Like his woman, the only truly precious thing in his life.

Careful, he told himself. A long line and a loose hold, that's the only way it will ever work.

THE JESUIT STARED AT THE THING BARBIE HAD UNWRAPPED. IT stood on the table amid the clutter of silver coffee pots and china plates heaped with croissants. They were in Cambridge, in the quiet Garden House Hotel, having what the British called "elevenses." The view was of the River Cam and the placid fens that skirted the city. Neither Rolles nor Barbie looked at it, and their mood was not placid. It could not be, since she had just revealed a stolen piece of unique art.

It was incredible, but Rolles had to credit it on the evidence of his eyes. "You aren't kidding me, are you? You really found this in the cave that first day?"

"Yes, I really did."

He touched it. Professional avarice, outrage, and shock fought for dominance in his head. "Is there any point in asking why you did such a thing? Why didn't you tell me then?" He was speaking through clenched teeth, but not really listening for her answer. He was too busy picking up the little statue, holding it in his palm, studying the exquisitely carved face and trying to fathom its existence. That was a greater mystery than Barbie's erratic behavior.

"No point," she said.

"What?"

"There's no point in trying to explain what I did or why. The only thing that matters is, can you sell it? To some museum, perhaps. Or a private collector."

"You're crazy!" He spat out the accusation with venom. "This goes back to the Spanish government. Now."

"No," Barbie said quietly. "It does not. It's going to bring a large sum of money. It belongs to some nuns who wish to remain anonymous. If you handle it any other way, Hank, I'll say you stole it. I'll wreck your reputation, destroy your credibility as an archaeologist."

He looked at her, intending to say she'd never do such a thing, but her amber eyes told him otherwise. "I'll deny it," he said instead. "Your word against mine."

"Yes. Who do you think is likely to be believed?" She sat very still, conscious of her beauty as she was always conscious of it when she needed it, grateful for the sleekness she'd purchased at Elizabeth Arden. "Besides," she added, "you're a Jesuit. They don't have much of a reputation for honesty, do they? Especially not here in England." It was icing on the cake; she didn't need it, but she could take no chances.

Hank Rolles continued to look into her unwavering eyes. The right words were there, stuck in the back of his throat. He would say that he didn't give a damn what she said or to whom, that his reputation didn't matter, that the statue belonged to the Spanish government and to the people of Lanzarote. Noble words. And unspoken. "I don't know how much I'd get for it. That's a job for a specialist."

"No, a job for you. Get as much as you can." She reached into her handbag. It was new, elegant moroccan leather, one of the world's gorgeous things, like her. Rolles wondered why he'd ever thought her vulnerable. "After you get the money you're to give it to Maria," she said. "She's with the Dominicans on the Isle of Wight. Here's the address."

"Is Maria in this with you?" he asked dully.

"No, not the way you mean. You might say I've black-mailed her, too." Barbie stood up. There was no apology implicit in her voice or her manner. "I want this settled before I leave England. You have two weeks. Unless Maria tells me she has the money by then, I go to the newspapers and report a scandal. I'll say I was ill and now that I'm well again I remember what I saw." At the last second, her voice softened. "It's going to be all right, Hank, trust me."

"Like I'd trust a snake," he murmured.

Then he looked again at the beauty he held in his hand. Merely seeing this incredible thing almost made the rest worthwhile.

THE LOBBY OF THE DORCHESTER HOTEL WAS A MUTED symphony of mahogany and brass and polished mirrors and brocade. It was thoroughly English, a place that bespoke luxury in a quiet, cultivated voice. Standing and waiting for Phil, Barbie was a startling contrast to the surroundings, an exotic among the aspidistras.

She wore a dark brown trouser suit of fine wool with narrow velvet lapels. It was tailored like a gentleman's tuxedo, what the French called *"le smoking."* Her blouse was of apricot silk and had a matching bow tie. Her cap of shining bronze hair was topped by a brown velvet bowler hat, and she carried a furled umbrella. The outfit was outrageous and utterly intoxicating. Dozens of pairs of eyes sneaked discreet glances, but as usual she seemed surrounded by an invisible barrier holding the hunters at bay. In fact she'd debated the choice of clothes a long time. Maybe something softer, more feminine. Only she sensed a yawning chasm, a mutation of reality. The tough-lady look was part of hanging on to the way things had been: Phil the supplicant, her the bestower of favors.

When he approached her, Williams was conscious of surveillance, the jealous gaze of men who envied him. He enjoyed that. When he was close enough to smell her scent, a musky gardenia fragrance only she would have chosen to wear with such clothes, he forgot about the audience.

"Hello, my beauty," he said softly. Her smile was balm for long months of his aching loneliness. He wanted so badly to touch her, his arms cramped. But he dare not touch her here; once he did, he wouldn't be able to stop. He motioned to Harris, and the chauffeur stepped forward and claimed the Vuitton suitcase at Barbie's feet.

"Hello, Harris. I didn't know you were in England."

"Oh yes, Mrs. Gold. Can't let Mr. Williams travel without me, can I?"

Phil listened to her voice, drank it in, and realized she'd not yet spoken directly to him. "Come," he said.

"Aren't we staying here?" The first words, and the most mundane of questions.

"No." There was an irrational sharpness to the reply. He cursed himself, but she didn't seem to notice, only walked beside him to the street.

"Impressive," Barbie said when she saw the Silver Ghost. Harris held the door and she slid gracefully into the plush depths. The upholstery was red brocade and gunmetal leather. There was at least five feet between the backseat and the window separating passengers from the driver. Harris skillfully moved out into the chaotic London traffic.

With sure and deliberate motions Barbie drew the curtains that screened them from the chauffeur. She looked for curtains on the side windows, but there were none.

"One-way glass," Phil said. "We can't be seen." He kept his eyes on her.

She reached up and took off her hat, laying it on the seat beside her. "How long will it take to get where we're going?"

"Depends on the traffic. Ten, maybe fifteen minutes."

"That's time enough."

They'd not yet touched. Now she leaned over and unzipped the front of his trousers. Phil drew in his breath with a low gasp of surprise and pleasure. When she bent down and took him in her mouth, he put his hand on her head; apart from that, he didn't move. A few seconds later he climaxed, suddenly and silently, and she waited until it was over, then leaned back and smiled up at him. "Hello," she said.

"Thank you." His voice was hoarse with emotion.

"It was selfish," she said. "You'll be better for me later. And I'm sorry I stayed away so long. And that's nicer than the usual hello kiss." And I'm still in control. But not for long. A panoply of new emotions were welling up inside her. She still wasn't ready to deal with them. "Where are we going?"

"You'll see." He smiled. "Someplace very special."

Typically, he'd found something infinitely superior to the Dorchester or the Connaught or Claridge's. The hotel was off Birdcage Walk, tucked into a tiny mews between Green Park and the gardens of Buckingham Palace. There was no sign outside to distinguish it from an elegant private townhouse. Inside the decor maintained that impression, and the service was smooth and effortless. They were greeted as the lord and lady of the manor might have been welcomed home.

Their suite was on the top floor in the rear. The only sounds that penetrated were the birds singing in the trees of the park below their balcony. A log fire burned in the sitting-room grate, and another in the bedroom. There were flowers, anemones and freesias arranged by a hand as talented as Barbie's own, and a table laid for lunch with a selection of cold food waiting under silver covers. A bottle of champagne stood in an ice bucket, and one of brandy on the sideboard.

"Do you like it?" Phil asked. "I don't think there are a dozen Americans who know this place exists."

Barbie smiled at the childlike pride in his voice. "I like it very much, but I'll appreciate it more after you make love to me."

Three long strides brought him across the room. For a moment she remained motionless in the protective circle of his arms, then they were tearing at each other's clothes and rolling frantically on the thick carpet. Had she not enacted the scene in the back of the Rolls it would have been over in seconds. As it was, he lay over her for long minutes, thrusting and retreating and thrusting again.

Barbie sobbed with the pent-up hunger of many months and sank her teeth in his shoulder and pounded her fists on his back. She felt tension build in the pit of her stomach, and there were moments she thought it would never be released. Then his hands moved and drew her flesh into closer contact with his, until the long, hard length of him felt as if it were in her belly, and all the places that needed touching were touched. And she cried his name aloud in the lovely room.

They bathed together in an enormous sunken marble tub, then lay on the bed beneath a silk canopy and ate cold roast pheasant with their fingers. Later they slept, and when they woke she murmured, "Fuck me again," and he did, and it was almost as good as the first time on the sitting-room floor. In a way better, because this time she understood that the place inside her she'd always kept separate from him didn't exist anymore. There were no ghosts. This was her man. She'd fought that knowledge for a long time, right up to this morning. She'd known what she was going to do, but not that she'd do it with so much joy.

"I've got something for you," he said into the afterglow.

"You've already given it to me."

He chuckled and crossed the room to his briefcase. She expected some wildly extravagant gift, but he handed her a letter instead. It was sealed, and addressed to her in New York. She recognized Joe's handwriting. "Shall I read it, or will you just tell me what it says?" She smiled despite the accusation.

He started to protest, then looked at her and grinned, only slightly sheepish. "DiAnni's apologizing for the things he said that last day. And telling you he's in some thoroughly isolated monastery in the wilds of Vermont, and is happy as a pig in shit and thinks maybe he'll stay there. He says eventually they may even let him be a priest again."

"Okay." She put the unopened envelope on the bedside table and saw the relief in his eyes because she didn't rush to open it. "That does it," she said. "All the jacks are back in the box." He looked at her quizzically and she added, "Maria's in the Dominican priory and Joe's going to be a priest again. Just the way it was, more or less."

"I see. You think Maria's going back to being a nun?"

"I'm not sure. Maybe. Anyway, I don't want to talk about them. I want to know if you're really such a big-deal mover and shaker this side of the ocean."

Williams wondered what she may have noticed the past two days while she was supposed to be roaming around on her own. He watched her eyes, but they told him nothing. "Try me," he said coolly while he poured two snifters of cognac.

"Can you arrange a wedding without having to wait days and days, and go through a lot of red tape? Tomorrow, for instance?"

He handed her one of the bulbous glasses and fixed her with his silvery glance. "Who's getting married?"

Barbie took the snifter. "Us. I bought a great wedding dress. Beige raw silk. I figure if we get married right away we can spend a couple of weeks honeymooning in England. Then we'd be home for Christmas."

Phil put his untouched brandy on the table and sat down beside her on the bed. She was sipping her drink and studying him over the crystal rim. "You're sure?" he asked. "I can't change, you know that."

"I know. And I'm very sure."

He grabbed her, causing the dark liquor to spill over her naked breasts. "I'll lap that up in a second," he said. "First there's one more thing I'm waiting for."

"I love you."

And she meant it. Oh, God! She really meant it. But maybe it wasn't exactly what he wanted to hear. His mood changed abruptly and he didn't say anything, just traced the shape of her mouth with one finger. Barbie started to pull his head down to hers, but he got up and went into the sitting room. She could hear him doing something with the yet unpacked suitcases, and when he returned he held a slim Gucci notecase. She'd given it to him their first Christmas together.

"I'm not Greek," he said tonelessly. "At least not entirely."

She felt panicky, scared. She'd always been so sure of his love. "I'm sorry. I see that's supposed to be important, but I don't get it. What difference does it make?"

For answer, he passed her a wad of clippings from the notecase. She flicked through them quickly. They were reports of the doings of some society matron in Maryland: Charity Balls, Hunt Breakfasts, the opening of this or that museum or hospital. A few included pictures of the woman. She was in her late fifties, Barbie guessed. Still fashionably thin, and nice-looking in an icy, patrician sort of way. She looked from the clippings to Phil. "So?"

"She's my mother. She'd die before she'd admit it, but she is. I was the result of a foolish schoolgirl affair in Rome. With a Greek drifter the family paid off. I've only seen her once."

She saw him shiver at the memory. "Did she put you up for adoption?"

"No, nothing so clean-cut." He told her how it had been, sitting on the windowseat staring out at the park so only his naked back was turned to her. It was a very hard, very straight back, with nothing of softness about it, like his voice.

When the monologue was ended, Barbie got off the bed and went to him, standing close but not touching his flesh. "I'm not going to make a lot of meaningless sympathetic noises. But thank you for telling me."

He turned round, and his opaque eyes studied her face. "Do you understand?"

She hesitated before answering. When she did, her words came slowly. "Not about growing up as you did or finding out about your mother. How could I? No one could unless they'd been through it. But about why you told me, yes, I think so."

She waited, but he didn't say anything. "You either trust my love or you don't, Phil. I can't convince you of it by talking."

"I need it so much." The words were wrenched from him; the pain of speaking shadowed the lean planes of his face. "You're the only person I ever really needed. Really loved. And Norma, because she was part of you."

She reached out, wanting to touch him, half afraid he'd pull away. He didn't, and she lay her palms on either side of his face. "I know. All this time we've been apart, even though I didn't know the things you've told me today, that's what I was thinking about. How much you need me. It's not the whole reason I love you, but it's part of it." He started to say something, but she shook her head. "Wait, let me finish. It's not pity or sympathy or anything so simple. Need is part of loving. It must be. You need me, and I . . ." She stopped and drew a short, painful breath. "I need you. I once told Maria that loving and being loved came to the same thing. It was truer than I realized. I need to be loved the way you love me. And I love you for that. Until today I didn't know how much."

For a long while he didn't say anything. The sun went down and the room grew chill. Barbie moved to the fire and poked ineffectually at the charred logs. Phil rose and took the brass poker from her hand and did something to the embers that was better than whatever she had done. The flames leaped up and made crackling sounds, and he put on another log, then went and got the jacket of the suit she'd been wearing earlier and put it round her shoulders. "We'd better get someone up here to unpack."

"Are we staying?"

"For a couple of days at least. Until after the ceremony, anyway. If you still want a ceremony, that is."

"I do."

He grinned. "You're jumping your cue. That line comes later."

She started to laugh, and it came out like a little sob.

"Don't cry," he said. "I don't want you ever to cry again."

"That's not possible. Nobody can take all the pain out of life for somebody else."

"No, I suppose not. But you can try pretty hard." He walked to the bed and gathered up the notecase and the wad of clippings and returned to the fire and dropped the papers into the flames and watched them burn.

"Don't throw the case in," Barbie said. "It cost two hundred dollars."

They both giggled, and he put his arms around her and held her close. They remained like that for a long time.

WEAK WINTER SUNSHINE OUTLINED THE BARE BRANCHES OF the linden trees and ruddied the white stucco facades of the fashionable Chelsea houses. The Jesuit thought how benign it all looked. Minus the fog, even the narrow mews where the dealer lived seemed less malevolent. He stared at the enameled black door for a moment. It sported a glittering brass knocker shaped like a woman's boot. Once he'd read of a nineteenth-century Boston whorehouse that announced its business in that same manner. Appropriate. He and the dealer and the avaricious collectors, prostitutes all.

"Good evening, Father; you're prompt. Good of you."

The dealer led Rolles into the room where they'd spoken before. This time the ebony table displayed a delicate vase made of some translucent stuff that refracted even the dim light of late afternoon. The tiny statue was nowhere to be seen. Rolles had the crazy notion that maybe it was hidden in the vase.

The dealer followed his glance. "That's Medici porcelain. Made only in Florence between the years 1575 and 1580. This may be the only piece in existence. Might you—?" He broke off and smiled. "No, I think not. Silly of me, I forget that not everyone shares the affliction. Collecting can be a madness, but a *folie de grandeur,* don't you think?"

"Where's the statue?" The Jesuit's hostility crackled in the rarified air.

The dealer raised his eyebrows and indulged in a small shrug. "Not here any longer. I have this for you instead."

He handed over a cashier's check from Barclay's Bank. It was made out to "bearer" for the sum of fifteen thousand pounds. Rolles studied it for some seconds, then folded it and put it in his wallet. "You were quick, I'll say that for you. Who bought it?"

The Englishman waved a cautionary hand. "Don't ask, Father. It will save us both embarrassment. In this instance I couldn't tell you anyway. A man arrived soon after you left. He offered to purchase the 'little figurine I'd lately acquired.' Quite astonishing. You probably know more about it than I do."

"I don't know a damn thing."

"Not even if I say the man was an American?"

The Jesuit shook his head, and the dealer shrugged again.

"Well, it doesn't matter." He started to move to the door. "Doesn't pay to be too curious in my line of work. You understand, I'm sure. Now, if there's nothing further I can do for you, Father . . ."

There was nothing at all. Hank Rolles left the mews flat. As well as fifteen thousand pounds, he carried a burden of anger and self-disgust that grew heavier with each step.

THE ENGLISH DECEMBER WAS GRAY AND WET, NOTHING LIKE as cold as the East Coast of America, but Maria felt it more. Perhaps because she was never really warm. The priory had something they called central heating, but it operated only a few hours out of each twenty-four, and did little to dispel the chill in the stone cloisters or the high-ceilinged rooms. Every day Maria told herself she should leave and go someplace where at least she'd be physically comfortable, whatever her mental state. Always she put off her departure, held by a force she was afraid to examine.

Mostly she made a blank of her mind. Even the news that Phil and Barbie were married didn't clear the fog in her brain. Less so the announcement that Father Rolles was waiting for her in the room the nuns called the small parlor.

She joined him, and without preamble Rolles pushed a check across the wooden counter that separated them. "I'm told you know all about this," he said.

"Barbie mentioned it, yes."

"Mentioned it. The bitch had it all worked out. It's called blackmail, in case you didn't know."

Maria's dark eyes flashed with something like their old fire. "You can't be blackmailed unless you cooperate." Instantly she was sorry. His look of anguish was eloquent testimony to his guilt. She reached out to touch him, but Rolles drew back and the gesture was stillborn. "Don't worry about it," she said softly. "It's not what it seems on the surface. At least I don't think so."

"Loyal to the end," he said bitterly. "I don't know if you're blind or just stupid. Crazy, maybe. Perhaps we're all crazy, Barbie, you, me, the lot of us taking part in this farce."

"The money's for a good cause." It was a lame explanation and she didn't pursue it. "There's something involved that we don't understand." She stopped. Talking about Barbie's visions and voices would just make it worse.

"Forget it. It's done. I only hope I don't hear about it or her ever again."

He looked around as if noticing for the first time the peculiar half partition between himself and Maria. "What's this thing supposed to be?" He tapped lightly on the counter.

"It's the base of the old grill. You know, the kind of thing cloistered nuns used to sit behind when they had guests. The Dominicans removed the grill a few years ago when they rethought the meaning of enclosure."

"So now they have half a grill instead." He snorted in derision.

"That's not fair. They just can't afford to have a carpenter cut it away. It's a big job."

"Okay, but what are you doing behind it? Another example of rethinking the options?"

Maria hesitated, then shook her head and didn't answer. She could neither think nor talk about that. "Wait here a minute. I'll get us some coffee. Tea, if you prefer."

"No, thanks. I've got to go." He stood up. "I realize I could have mailed the check, but . . ."

"Yes?"

"Nothing. Forget it. I was very sorry to hear about Tom, by the way. And sorry I couldn't get back for the funeral. Was Si there?"

"No, no one but the people from the village. Tom wanted it that way. The last thing he did was write to people at home telling them not to come."

"Can't say I'm surprised. Will I see you in London after you leave here? Or should I say, *if* you leave here?"

"I won't see you in London," she answered. Equivocal, but the best she could do. "Good-bye, Hank. Thank you for everything."

He recognized the finality in her tone and started to comment on it, then changed his mind. "Good-bye, Maria."

Maria gave the check to Sister Imelda, with the explanation that it was Barbie's contribution to the founding of a House of Prayer on Lanzarote.

"I never realized that Barbie was a wealthy woman," the nun said in pleased surprise.

"Her new husband is very rich." Maria let that pass for an explanation.

"I'm sorry Father Rolles couldn't stay for tea."

"He was afraid of missing the last ferry."

And thus ended that drama. Still Maria remained in the priory.

* * *

On December 5, she had a letter from Si. It was full of chat about the hostel and the weather and the fact that Sam Hill had phoned twice asking about Tom's manuscript. Would she please mail it if she wasn't returning to the States just yet. Not a word encouraging her to come home, no hint of anything between them other than friendship.

The sixth was the feast of St. Nicholas. The nuns kept it as a lighthearted holiday to temper the austerity of Advent, the penitential season leading up to Christmas. A feast meant she couldn't work in the library where she was cataloging books, a huge task she'd insisted on taking on. So Maria sat in her room, huddled by the radiator, and stared into space. After an hour of that she took the two manuscripts from her suitcase and laid them on the rickety table that served as a desk. Hers and his. Side by side. Both wrapped in brown paper and string. She carefully undid the parcel containing Tom's book.

Four hours later she turned over the last page and realized she was crying. It wasn't just the poetry of his controlled prose, or the trueness and richness of his characterizations. All that she'd known about before. Thomas Shore was a wordsmith of tremendous talent, that was no surprise. But this book would make the critics search for new superlatives.

It was a shining thing, a story of people battered by the horrors of poverty and the violence of the early days of the labor movement, who nonetheless retained their humanity. What Tom had done was isolate the essentials of that quality. For the first time he'd chosen a subject big enough for his own art. His story pitted hope against despair, and hope won. Not because he wanted to write a book about happily ever after, because it was what his characters truly believed. And so did he. She saw that clearly, knowing the circumstances under which he'd labored to finish the manuscript. Despite everything, Tom had died in hope. Maria had not wept for him before. She did now.

A few days later a Scottish priest came to give the nuns a series of conferences on the effect of the fall of Jerusalem on early Christianity. Typically Dominican and too scholarly to be of interest to her; she was invited but didn't attend his lectures. Instead she began going to some of the services in the priory chapel. Vespers, usually, and Compline. So she got a look at the visitor.

"You should come to his Mass," Sister Imelda urged. "He's a truly holy man and has the gift of discernment. When he says Mass, it shows."

Maria nodded, but she didn't go. She'd only been to Mass that one time when she wanted to discover if Barbie had become a Catholic. A lot of the ghosts that patrolled her psyche had been laid by the catharsis of reading Tom's book, but not all of them. I'm not ready for Mass, she decided. I may never be.

That weekend the quixotic English weather played one of its pleasanter tricks. The temperature rose to the high fifties. Masses of snowdrops bloomed, and even a few roses. The garden was inviting again. Maria was strolling in it, enjoying the warmth of the unexpected sun, when the old Scottish Dominican approached her and smiled.

"We haven't met formally, have we? I'm Gerald MacPhee."

She nodded a greeting. He fell into step beside her, and they walked along the broad paths that crisscrossed the walled grounds. Their talk was of inconsequentials, daily things and small wonders. The improbable color of a blue-violet rose blooming in December, the nesting habits of a pair of magpies fooled into thinking it was spring. Then, when they'd reached the farthest part of the garden, near the cemetery where four generations of nuns were buried, the priest stopped walking and said quietly, "I think you want to go to confession, but you're afraid. You mustn't be afraid of God, Maria."

She stared at him, uncomprehending. Finally, when she was convinced that he'd really said what she thought she'd heard, she whispered, "I can't go to confession. Even if I wanted to. I'm not sorry for my sins."

"What sins?"

She wanted to shock him, so she put it as baldly as she could. "I've slept with two men without being married to either. And I practiced birth control. And given the same circumstances, I'd do it all over again."

There was no shock in his pale, rheumy eyes, only a hint of laughter. "My dear girl, do you really think God cares very much about sex? At my advanced age I've decided He doesn't. He only cares about love."

"I don't believe in God."

"Ah, now, for you that might be a sin if it were true." His Edinburgh brogue was soft and surprisingly clear. It cushioned his words but didn't obscure them. "It doesn't matter in your case, however, for you do indeed believe in God."

"Why do you say that? How can you know?"

"I say it because I've watched you, and I know it because if you didn't believe in Him you wouldn't be running away so hard, and be so desperately unhappy about it."

That stark truth was more than she could tolerate. Tears filled her eyes and overflowed. Soon she was sobbing in the empty garden, with only the magpies and the old priest looking on. When she stopped and wiped her eyes, she saw that he was still there and still waiting.

"God only wants us to try, you know," he said gently. "He doesn't care how many times we fail, if we keep trying."

"Trying what?"

"Trying to love Him and one another. There's really nothing else." He waited until he saw her smile, then he added, "Make a promise to try loving Him, Maria. And don't refuse his forgiveness."

"I can try," she said. It was the merest whisper, but she had said it.

With no further word the priest raised his hand and made the sign of the cross and gave her absolution from all her sins according to the ancient formula, "in so far as she needed and he was able."

Maria didn't analyze the unorthodox theology, or the strange circumstances. She only knew that she felt free of an intolerable burden. She'd been stifled; now she could breathe.

Next morning she went to Mass and received communion. She'd half expected something marvelous, some uplifting experience such as she'd had long ago when she'd been a postulant in Lynn. It didn't come. She felt nothing except the same sense of freedom she'd experienced yesterday. And that coexisted with her doubts. She recalled T. S. Eliot's disturbing line: "The last temptation is the greatest treason: to do the right deed for the wrong reason."

"I'm still not sure if I believe," she told Sister Imelda. "Worse, I'm not sure what I should do about it."

"Being unsure is part of the human condition," the nun said. "Why would we call it faith if it were a certainty?"

"Faith and hope will pass away and only charity remain." Maria was full of quotations today.

"Afterward, yes. But faith and hope, often against all hope, that's what life is this side of the grave. For most of us, at least."

Maria was silent for long moments. "I think," she said at last, "that the thing is, I'm afraid not to try to believe. The emptiness without it is unbearable."

Sister Imelda nodded gravely. "Yes, that's a place to start."

* * *

IN CAMBRIDGE, CHRISTMAS EVE PRODUCED A DUSTING OF
snow. Right on schedule, so everything looked like an illus-
tration for a Dickens novel. The colleges raised frosted spires
to a starry sky, and laughter and carols floated out to the
streets from behind steamy pub windows. Hank Rolles
thought about stopping for a drink, maybe a few drinks, but
the idea held no real appeal. He was too miserable to get pleasantly drunk, the kind of unhappy that liquor only made
worse. Even the picture postcard scenery made it worse.

He walked the streets hunched over, protecting his self-pity
as if it were a fragile something clasped in his arms. Bitterness
accompanied him down Free School Lane on to Bene't Street
and into Market Square. The stalls were deserted, but the
Guildhall on his right was draped in greenery, and lighted
Christmas trees punctuated the night. Sidney Street was better, not festooned with decorations. Sidney Sussex College,
like St. John's farther down the road, did not mar its dignity
with kitsch. So he could forget it was Christmas until he
crossed Magdalen Bridge and eventually turned right up
Honey Hill. Not a hill really, a pretty little cobbled passage accessible only to pedestrians; the England of everyone's
dreams. Tonight it held no charm for Rolles. The sound of
holiday revelry from nearby houses assaulted him.

It wasn't being alone that hurt. He'd not spent a Christmas
with his family since he became a priest. Until this year he'd
always said it was unimportant. Now the Jesuit wasn't so sure.
This Christmas he had only himself and the sense of his
weakness and the acrid taste of guilt. What price virtue, Father? A professional reputation? Yes, as it turned out. Betrayal
didn't require torture or communists or any other bogeymen.
A scandal that would make him *persona non grata* in academia was sufficient.

Haymarket became Mount Pleasant Street. He was at the
edge of the old town, near the twentieth-century fringe of
bungalows with little front gardens and even a few plastic
gnomes. The sounds of Christmas were louder and bawdier
here. Rolles was grateful when the entrance to St. Edmund's
House appeared on his left. Catholic bastion in this city refined by the Reformation and vivified by the exquisite cadences of the Book of Common Prayer, St. Edmund's seemed
to him to smell slightly of its difference and its allegiance to
older, less pure ways.

His room was in the rear. He thought he'd gotten to it unseen until a man stepped out of the gloom of the corridor and blocked his path. "Father Rolles?"

"Yes." It was no one he knew, but someone he immediately recognized as an American. Shit! A visiting fireman the family had told to look him up. On Christmas Eve, no less. "Is there something I can do for you?" He knew his voice was unwelcoming, and he didn't care.

"I have a package for you, Father." The man proferred a small box wrapped in brown paper. It was labeled with his name and address, nothing more. "If you'll just sign this receipt, I'll be on my way."

At least it wasn't a personal visit. For a few seconds relief forestalled curiosity. Rolles signed the receipt, took the parcel, and let himself into his room. That's when he began to wonder what it was all about. He lit the desk lamp and a circle of yellow light shone on the box, but it didn't tell him anything. He thought of a letter bomb. Crazy. He had nothing to do with the IRA or any other terrorists. Hell, he wasn't even Irish. Besides, letter bombs came through the mail, they weren't delivered by messenger.

Nonetheless, his fingers were shaking when he undid the package, as if his subconscious already knew. And when he lifted the top off the box and saw the exquisite face of the tiny lady smiling her inscrutable smile from a nest of tissue paper, he wasn't as surprised as he might have been. A voice in his head said, I always come to those who love me. He looked around, as if the words had been spoken aloud, not in his imagination.

"Incredible," he whispered as he lifted the little statue and cradled it tenderly in his palm. Not just the situation; her, too. The whole thing. "Incredible," he repeated.

There was a note beneath the tissue, creased with the shape of the figurine, as if it had lain there for some time. "You are to return this to the appropriate authorities on Lanzarote," he read. "The utmost discretion is expected, and no mention of the recent history. Your cooperation will be appreciated but unremarked. Any deviation will be dealt with."

The message was typewritten and unsigned. Rolles read it a second time, then sat back and closed his eyes. The threat was unnecessary. He had no desire to accuse Barbie or try to expose her. The only thing he felt was relief. He was curious as to who would go to such lengths to protect her, but not curious enough to want to pursue the matter. His own sordid part in the business was too fresh in his mind.

Briefly he wondered if returning the statue would free him of self-loathing. He'd go back to the island and trump up some plausible story, a new "find," probably. He'd come up smelling like a rose. The thought sickened him anew.

Rolles walked to the window and opened it, pushing his head and shoulders out into the cold night air. He hadn't realized how late it was. The sounds of midnight Mass could be heard from the chapel below. The rector was reading the Lesson. His voice, though reedy and thin with age, carried true and clear.

"Beloved, the kindness of God our Savior dawned on us, his great love for man. He saved us, not thanks to anything we had done for our own justification, but in accordance with his own merciful design . . ."

A Savior who would free his people from their sins. The Jesuit knew that, but he'd forgotten the meaning of the words, allowed himself to believe that his sin was greater than God's mercy. The rector finished speaking, and the choir intoned the first notes of Psalm 117. In Latin; this was Cambridge, after all. *"Deus Dominus, et illuxit nobis . . ."* The Lord is God, He has given us His light. The Jesuit laughed aloud.

He didn't bother to close the window, just turned and headed for the door. Joy bubbled in his veins and pounded in his heart, and it seemed to him the little lady was laughing too. He'd almost swear he heard her. "I'll take you home, little beauty," he promised. "But I can't do it tonight, so if you don't mind, I'm going to do something else."

He'd been invited to concelebrate and refused, now he figured there was just enough time to vest and get himself quietly onto the altar before the consecration.

"Alleluia! Alleluia!," the choir sang as he slipped into the sacristy.

"LISTEN," MARIA SAID HESITANTLY A FEW DAYS BEFORE Christmas. "I've been wondering, that is, it's been on my mind to ask you—"

"No," Sister Imelda interrupted. "I know what you're thinking, and you're wrong. You're not supposed to be a nun, Maria." She reached for the younger woman's hand and held it while she spoke. "You're only drawn to us because you feel guilty about leaving the first convent."

"I promised," Maria whispered. "When I was thirteen years old."

Sister Imelda laughed. "If God held us to childhood promises, He'd be a fool. I don't believe in a God who's a fool."

"I really wanted to do it," Maria said. "And I did try. It was just so . . . sterile and stupid. It never seemed to make any sense. Not like your life here."

The nun was quiet for a while. "I have a theory about the sisterhoods," she said finally. "It's my own idea and I may be mistaken, but I think most of them have outlived their usefulness. They were a kind of interim step between a call to monastic life, which was the only type of religious life the Church knew until the eighteenth century, and the way women can function now. I think the sisterhoods that go on will change radically. The others will fade away. You can't try and mix up traditional monasticism, the point of which is a preparation for contemplative prayer, with a call to direct service of the poor, or work in schools and hospitals. Now that women are free to do the latter when and how they wish, they don't have to. There are lots of valid ways of living Christianity and doing it as a female, but women have to learn to adapt them differently. They no longer have to superimpose one vision, one way of being, on another."

"Why did they, do you suppose?" Maria asked thoughtfully.

Sister Imelda's blue eyes flashed. "Because it suited men, churchmen particularly, to have them contained and never venturing out except in pairs. Yes, Father; no, Father; whatever you say, Father. Women in the Church have been priest-ridden, make no mistake about it."

The words hung in the cold air and mingled with the smell of woodsmoke from the bonfire some of the young nuns had built in the orchard. They were getting rid of the dead wood, preparing for next year's growth. "Will the sisterhoods all disappear?" Maria asked.

"I don't think so, not all of them. But the ones that continue will find new ways of living in community, new ways to bear witness. Please God, the women themselves will design the change."

"There's a novel there, you know," Maria said dreamily. "The storyteller has a function in exposing some facets of some truths. Tom Shore taught me that." Sister Imelda didn't reply, and Maria thought of her ugly, hate-filled manuscript. It was upstairs in her room. Six months' work and she'd have to destroy it. She'd known she must ever since she read Tom's book, but until now she hadn't known what to put in its place. But the work wasn't wasted, it was all grist for the mill, all abetting the crooked lines with which God writes straight.

THE PLANE WAS HALF EMPTY. MOST PEOPLE GOING TO NEW York for Christmas didn't wait until Christmas Eve to travel. Maria had the middle of three seats, and was glad there was no one on either side. She pushed up the armrests and tried to stretch out and sleep, but oblivion wouldn't come. She couldn't turn off her thoughts and hopes, and the lovely feeling that she was going home.

That was a little silly. She had no home. Certainly she couldn't live with Phil and Barbie, though she'd sent a cable announcing her return. She was pretty sure she'd be able to stay with them over the holidays, and after that she'd make a home for herself. Get an apartment, furnish it, it would be fun. She'd need, what? A bedroom and a living room and a room to work in. A kitchen too, of course. She'd learn to cook. Try and remember the things Tom used to do. Not that cooking for one was such a challenge. And that's what it would have to be.

A hostess appeared and handed her a glass of champagne. "Merry Christmas, compliments of Pan American."

"Merry Christmas."

Maria sipped the wine. It wasn't very good, but the thought was warming. Her thoughts were warming too. They were of Si, in spite of herself. Just maybe she wouldn't be cooking for one. A picture of Spanish Harlem invaded her reverie, destroyed its playing-house perfection.

That part wasn't changed. She couldn't live there. So she couldn't have Si. Unless she could convince him that life need not copy the *Ladies' Home Journal.* It was a new age, a new time. There could be different ways of being together, even of being married. A home that would be a neutral space, a place only for them. When his work didn't keep him in the filth and the hate, they could be together. The rest of the time she'd write. Just maybe.

By the time they circled Kennedy, she knew she was kidding herself. Si would never buy it. He'd despise her for being weak, for being unwilling to share his whole life. And she couldn't, so she was back to square one. She couldn't have him. She'd known it all along. That's why she hadn't bothered to let him know she was returning.

Christmas carols assailed her as soon as she landed. In the

passport control area loudspeakers blared holiday music, and the long corridors were festooned with tinsel and plastic greenery. It should have been tacky, but it wasn't. It made her feel good. "Hark, the herald angels sing . . ."

"Merry Christmas, Miss Trapetti," the man said when he stamped her passport. And the customs official just chalked a mark on her bags and said, "Welcome home." It all helped. She'd count her blessings, do something about the frantic requests from Oakes and Randolph's publicity department, see Sam Hill, and get an apartment. Life would be okay. Not great without Si, but okay.

They made you relinquish your wheeled luggage cart as soon as you got through customs. From then on you were at the mercy of the skycaps or your own strength. Maria left her bags in a pile by the door and searched the arrivals terminal for a flash of red hair. Not that she really expected to see Barbie tonight. Friendships could only go so far, even theirs. Harris, perhaps? But there was no sign of the chauffeur. It was Christmas Eve, after all.

Maria's hard-won sense of well-being started to fade. She felt completely alone, despite the carols and the decorations. Because of them, perhaps. Once more she scanned the terminal, this time looking for a skycap. She'd find a hotel for tonight and call Barbie tomorrow or the next day. Then, from the rear, she felt two arms encircle her waist.

"Welcome home," Si's voice said in her ear.

She struggled to turn round, to hug him back. The bulk of the winter coats they both wore nearly prevented the maneuver, and when it was accomplished all she could say was, "How did you know?"

"Barbie phoned me. I made her promise not to come. Are you angry?"

"No, oh no, I'm not a bit angry."

"Well, are you glad?" Hopefully, and a trifle unsure.

For answer she kissed him. Something that started out warm and friendly and glad-to-see-you, and instantly became more.

Si broke away and put his hands on her cheeks and tipped her face back so he could look into her eyes. His were that smoldering navy blue which she knew signaled deep feeling. "Listen," he said, "I've taken a place on Lexington and Eighty-seventh. In Yorkville. It's not that far from the hostel, but a different world. Not great, but it will do for a while. I was hoping that maybe we—"

Maria lay her kid-encased finger over his lips. She could feel the warmth of him despite the glove. "We'll talk about it later," she said. "But I know what you're thinking. I've been thinking something like that too."

Arm in arm they started to walk away, then giggled hysterically when they realized they'd forgotten the suitcases.

"C'mon, baggage," Si said. "Let's get the baggage and go home."

E P I L O G U E

IN ARRECIFE THE JESUIT GAVE THE LITTLE STATUE TO THE authorities and said he'd found it in a cave near the one where he'd discovered the skeleton. Officials and scholars came from Madrid, and there was much discussion and examination of the supposed site of the find and of the statue itself. Eventually there were suggestions that she be taken to mainland Spain, but the Lanzarote bureaucrats dug in their heels and looked grim; and Rolles implied that he'd publish an article that would make Madrid appear grasping and insensitive. And it was decided that the statue would stay on the island.

In the end they put her in a museum of local artifacts, and the day he saw her installed Rolles felt sad and betrayed because the environment was sterile and artificial, and something of such extraordinary beauty deserved better. But the lady smiled from behind her glass case and did not seem to mind.

That same day he went up to Teguise and visited the House of Prayer that had been established there by six women from Barcelona. They were located in an old *finca*, a farmhouse on the outskirts of the town. They told him they'd bought it because it was cheap and available and had done most of the restoration work themselves. "But the local people are beginning to accept us," one of them said. "They've been helping lately."

She pointed through the window to an old man who was

plowing with his camel, singing to the beast in the way his kind did. "That's our field," she explained. "He's getting it ready so we can plant."

The old man turned and saw them looking at him, and motioned for them to come outside. "Look," he said when they joined him. "I've found a portion of an old wall."

It was built in the ancient island fashion, of rough lava stones cleverly fitted together with no need for mortar. "Don't you think it's very old?" the man asked.

"It's hard to tell," the Jesuit said. "Walls like this have always been built here. It may be two thousand years old or it may have been made last year."

"No, it's very old," the man insisted.

The others came to look, and someone suggested they should get rid of the lava stone wall and build a new one of cement. The old man looked sad until the women shook their heads and said no, they liked the rough wall and it would stay.

"You will be happy here," the old man said, apropos of nothing. "This island is a good place to talk to God." And he went back to his plow and his camel.

Rolles watched him for a while, then turned and looked down on Arrecife and spotted the roof of the museum of local crafts and thought of the little lady smiling, and was content.

IT WAS EVERYBODY'S DREAM OF A COUNTRY HOUSE; SHEATHED in weathered gray shingles, low and rambling, seeming one with the earth and the surrounding hills. "And just a forty-minute drive to New Haven," Maria said. "Which is fine, since Si only needs to be on campus three days a week."

Barbie shoved a sofa closer to the fieldstone fireplace that filled one end of the long living room. "That's better, don't you think?"

"Much. What about the blue chair?" Maria started to pull it into position, but Barbie nudged her aside.

"Let me. Pregnant ladies shouldn't move furniture." The chair looked fine on the other side of the fireplace. "You need a big lamp in this corner. I'll see what I can find. How does Si feel about teaching again?"

"He isn't, really. He's part of a think tank examining the ethnic experience in America. They'll be making recommendations and issuing guidelines, influencing the people that make the rules. He feels good about it. At first I worried that it was a compromise made for me. But it's not. It's Tom winning their long-standing argument about Si using his special skills to change the big picture. And Si being ready to move on. What about curtains?"

"Off-white linen maybe, or a small country print. Meet me in town some day this week and we'll look at fabrics."

They went outside, beckoned by the huge maple that was a shaft of ruby splendor in the golden autumn light. "Perfect place for a swing," Barbie said.

"Yes. Si says we bought the tree and luckily the house came with it." She turned and pointed to a small field beside the old barn they'd converted into twin studies. "We're going to have a vegetable garden there. I'll be able to see it from my desk; the swing, too."

"When's the new book going to be finished?"

"About the same time the baby is due. It's a race to see which happens first." Maria reached up and broke off a few sprays of the maple. "Make me an arrangement of these. For the dining room table. Something special because you and Phil are our first dinner guests."

She loaded Barbie's arms with the fiery branches. Then, when she couldn't see her face anymore, "Did I tell you? Norma if it's a girl, Thomas for a boy."

"Very Jewish," Barbie said from behind the leaves. "And thank you."

They began walking back to the house, their footsteps leaving little trails in the grass, making pungent earth smells rise around them. Maria said, "Si's project was funded by an anonymous private donor. His only requirements were that it be based at Yale and they include Greek-Americans in their study."

Barbie smiled and didn't comment.

The kitchen was mellow with two centuries of living. There was a big old range and a scrubbed pine table, and the sun came in through imperfect handblown glass and splintered into shimmering crystals of light. Maria piled the table with food and they worked in silence, moving together in easy woman rhythms hallowed by time, waiting for the sweetness of evening and the coming of their men.

AFTERWORD

There are few certainties about the history of pre-conquest Lanzarote or the origins of the population the European conquerors found in the archipelago. The events described in this story are based on a theory subscribed to by many contemporary archaeologists. The beliefs, customs, ceremonies, and social structure of the indigenous people are factual, and the words quoted from their language are real words. For all this information I am indebted to the people of the Canaries and to many books and their authors, most especially to John Mercer's *The Canary Islanders* (Rex Collings, Ltd., London, 1980).

I have, however, made no attempt to be accurate about the location or description of the Carthusian monastery in Vermont, out of a reluctance to infringe upon the total isolation that is essential to their way of life. Of the nature and spirit of their call, as well as that of the Dominican nuns, I have tried to write truly.

Those knowledgeable about Roman Catholic liturgy will recognize the quotations used in the midnight Mass at Cambridge as being in fact from the dawn Mass of Christmas day. No excuse, except that they suited the purpose. Like God, an author can someti es say *fiat* and it is done.

ABOUT THE AUTHOR

Beverly Byrne was raised in Revere, Massachusetts, and educated at a small women's college in the Midwest. After some time as a freelance journalist in Boston and New York, she sold her first book, a work of nonfiction, in 1967. Soon after leaving the United States for the Isle of Wight in 1978, Ms. Bryne's first novel was published. She's been writing fiction steadily ever since. The author lives at present with her family on Lanzarote, a Spanish island just off the coast of Africa.